TIE-BREAK

TIE-BREAK

A Novel By

Ilie Nastase

W.H. ALLEN · LONDON
1986

Typeset by Phoenix Photosetting, Chatham
Printed and bound in Great Britain by
Mackays of Chatham Ltd, Kent
for the Publishers, W. H. Allen & Co. Plc
44 Hill Street, London W1X 8LB

ISBN 0 491 03573 X

Part I

THE FRENCH OPEN

Field of the Cloth of Green

CHAPTER ONE

He drove with his left hand, pivoting the big car smoothly southwest, through the streets of Paris, while the other wandered languourously over the girl's thigh. The white Rolls Royce 'Silver Streak' progressed almost silently away from the Seine and along the Rue Fontaine. Light drops of late May rain fell sporadically on the windscreen and the wipers smoothed them systematically away. They had just passed the Orphelins and he could see the intersection with Avenue Mozart up ahead.

'You aren't listening to me.' There was a cautious rebuke in the girl's voice.

Isolated behind his sunglasses, the man admitted to himself she was right. He had pulled up the collar of his raincoat and adjusted the felt hat over his forehead to shut himself off more completely from the world of streets and trees, the clamour of Paris – and beautiful women. He had a tough tennis match coming up, a blinding need to concentrate. He felt sorry for the girl, so pretty, so earnest, trying so hard.

'The Rue Fontaine,' she said, learning close, 'is a virtual Guimard museum. There, on the right, you'll find the Castle Beranger, which won first prize for the best façade in the city of Paris in 1900. Guimard is our French Gaudi . . .'

The man smiled to himself. Her mentioning Gaudi, the turn-of-the-century Spanish architect, made him think of Barcelona in early October, a court surface that was too dry, returning balls that came too fast. And this girl with the fiery red hair sitting next to him, her voice hoarser now from his caresses, was trying to repeat the lesson in architecture recently learned at the Camondo School, her alma mater, which specialized in educating young debutantes without specialty.

'That's number eighty-five over there,' she said. 'The house Guimard built for himself.'

She looked at him from the corner of her eye, tracing his angular features, the slightly hawked nose and high cheekbones that revealed his Slavic origins. Despite the seven days' growth of blond beard, the skin stretched over the hard set of his jaw looked almost translucent. She wanted so much to touch it again . . .

'What are you thinking about?' she asked.

He didn't answer. Only his tanned hand stroked the girl's thigh. It was always like that, an hour before a match; looking vaguely pleasant was the best he could do. He was far away and the girl beside him was fading into one of his 'ghosts from the night before'. She was a beauty, not easy to forget, and all he had to do was close his eyes to remember last night, the curves of her body under his hand, her firmness and her softness, her lovely willingness to please. Now, he had to detach himself.

The road to failure was paved with beautiful distractions. He had seen it happen to player after player – Milo Tigrid, Armando Reyes, Mikhail Polak, Will Channer. It would not happen to him.

The girl leaned forward to switch on the radio, and an old Beatles song burst forth, grating on his nerves, jolting him from his half-sleep. He reached forward, and abruptly turned off the music. The girl tried to hide her confusion by re-settling herself on the seat, showing a flash of pretty knees. She had lost him; she didn't know why.

Less happily now, her voice tense with resignation, she went on: 'On the right is one of the few Metro exits designed by Guimard that has managed to survive modernization. Most of the others were destroyed by the city's administrators – those arrogant Philistines. It's a real masterpiece, don't you think? One day the whole thing will be in the Louvre.'

'Porte d'Auteuil,' he said, finally. 'We're nearly there.'

Up ahead, on a billboard, there appeared a giant photo reproduction of the face of Terry Laville, advertising Ryker tennis equipment. Laville wore his famous Indian headband. His teeth looked huge, and his steel-grey eyes seemed faintly crossed. Laville was his opponent today, at Roland-Garros.

'Isn't that the man you fought with? Last night?'

'Yes.'

'Why won't you tell me what it was about?'

'Laville's bigger than I am. He likes to drag our rivalry off the court.'

'You're not taking me seriously!' She pouted.

He smiled sadly to himself, because she was so young.

She tried to keep the conversation light, cheery. 'It must be exciting, to travel to so many places playing tennis. Where do you play next?'

'Only my manager knows.'

'Will you play in Monte Carlo? I was there last summer, for a holiday. I would love to meet the Prince, or the Princess. Did you meet Princess Grace?'

'Yes.'

'What was she like?'

'She was very beautiful. Like you.'

The girl bit her lip. 'Am I going to see you again?'

He turned to face her at last, but his eyes were far away from the pretty girl in the passenger seat. 'I would like that.'

She was thrilled. 'When?'

But the man was watching a Peugeot that was parked at the kerb. He had no answer for her.

Evelyne Dumont was sitting at the wheel of the idling Peugeot 604, an elegant slate-coloured limousine. The coachwork had just been meticulously polished after a brief shower two hours before, over Clignancourt.

In the rearview mirror, she watched the Rolls arriving. Nervously, she swept back a strand of blonde hair from her forehead and bit her lips to make them fuller and redder. Today, the man had to notice her. It was time that she become more to him than the driver who provided him with the same eternally-renewed Peugeot every day. But none of that was in the contract he had signed with the car manufacturers; it specified only that he arrive and leave Stade Roland-Garros at the wheel of their 604. So she would have to amend things a little, write her own contract, to take care of 'the extras'.

Evelyne had plotted and schemed for weeks to get this job, pulling as many strings as she could in the marketing company which had organized the endorsement deal. She had even slept with the manager in charge of the project. When Evelyne confessed her motives, he was stunned. 'You did this so you could drive that sonofabitch around for two weeks?'

What could a man of fifty, with a paunch, two cars, two children and a dog, understand about Evelyne's obsession? At least the manager had not, eventually, been without a sense of humour. He let her keep her job; he gave her what she wanted.

Now she was waiting again for the man in the Rolls to see her. She knew that she was beautiful and men had very willingly proved this to her – with gifts, favours, even money – but she had driven with this man twice a day for over a week and he seemed to be blind to her obvious attractions.

The Rolls pulled up several yards behind the 604. Evelyne had twisted the rearview mirror so that she could follow the approach of the car. She saw him step out and walk towards her. He wore scuffed white tennis shoes, white tennis socks with red stripes, and his legs were bare beneath the Bogart trench coat. As he approached the Peugeot, he took off his soft hat, freeing the striking blonde mane which had become a part of his myth – King Koras, the Samson of the courts. He opened the door, and climbed into the front seat next to her. As he adjusted the wheel, he removed his sunglasses.

'Hello, young lady.'

'Hello.'

'It's turning out to be a nice day, after all.'

'Yes. It's lovely.'

It was always difficult to place his accent exactly. He was fluent in six languages, and could make himself understood in five others. He seemed to change the accent as he pleased.

His name was Pantakoras Belynkas – Koras, for short – as the Rolls heralded on its orange and white number plates: KORAS ONE, NEW YORK CITY. He placed the Ray Bans gently on the tip of his nose, and sighed.

'Now I have to remember how to start this thing.'

He had asked them to give him an automatic transmission – more practical for driving in the city.

Evelyne lounged back in her seat, leaning against the door, watching his clumsy attempts at starting the car. Then the Peugeot glided forward. As they turned into the Avenue de la Porte d'Auteuil, Evelyne had time to notice the silhouette of a young woman leaving the Rolls, walking quickly, holding a white handkerchief to her face as if she were upset, heading towards a taxi stand.

The crowds grew thicker as they approached Roland-Garros. People pointed to the car and its driver. For Evelyne, the ritual of arriving at the stadium was fabulous. For the space of several hundred yards, she would savour the illusion that she had always been there, accompanying someone who embodied the living glory of the grand prix tournaments, one of the gods of professional tennis. No one had to know she was his companion only by contract. She had already had the thrill of seeing photos of herself in *Paris Match,* captioned as 'the mysterious blonde who accompanies Koras to victory'. And as he fought his way up the ladder and towards the finals at the Stade Roland-Garros, an event full of prestige, she had hopes of getting even closer.

They were only about a hundred yards away from the stadium now, and the crowd was almost solid. Koras tooted his horn. When the people on the pavement recognized the impatient driver, the enthusiasts among them greeted him with shouts of encouragement, shouting: 'Koras, you are the greatest! Hey, King Koras!' He smiled at them, safe behind the closed windows. The blonde girl smiled too, letting herself forget that she was merely a gadget that came with the car, courtesy of Peugeot.

Seeing a few photographers among the crowd, Koras slowed to a crawling pace and rolled down his window, to keep the sun from reflecting on their camera lenses. Koras knew this part of the pageant well. He and Evelyne played their part nicely: himself at the wheel, mysterious behind dark sunglasses; and she beside him, looking beautiful and elegant.

He pulled up beside the Suzanne Lenglen gate and parked the car in front of the locker rooms. 'Thank you, Mlle Dumont,' he said, getting out.

'You are welcome, m'sieu.' She got out, too, to stand beside him. 'Good luck today.'

'Thank you.' He seemed very formal, very gentlemanly. 'I'm going to need luck.'

'Your match is against Terry Laville, yes?'

'Correct.' He smiled, but his eyes seemed distant. 'In a week, you have become a tennis specialist.'

Evelyne found herself blushing. 'It is an exciting game.'

He stood looking down at her. 'Each year, the crowds wait.'

'For what?'

'For younger and younger magicians.'

'But you, M. Koras, you're not old.'

That made him smile. He said a formal goodbye, and they made arrangements to meet after the match, again a part of his contract with her company. Standing beside the car, she watched him walk off, looking lonely, his bare legs vulnerable beneath the hem of the coat. He was full of surprises. She'd had no idea he would think himself old.

Koras stepped inside the gate to find Jack Di Rocca waiting. Di Rocca was sturdy and powerful, with a thick chest and burly arms. His black beard was neatly trimmed, to hide a single streak of grey, and his dark hair was cut short. When he didn't dress in tennis clothes, Di Rocca always wore a coat and tie. He owned three warm-up suits, all dark blue, piped in red and white stripes, to display the fact that he was an American star.

Koras, born in New York, felt like a gypsy, a jet-setting citizen of the world. If he was at home anywhere, it was in Paris. Di Rocca, also born in New York, liked to advertise that he was an American. He was thirty-two, two years younger than Koras.

Koras noted the warm-up suit. 'You must have won.'

Di Rocca grinned. 'Yeah. On to the quarters, like they say. If you have a minute, I'd like to talk.'

'What's on your mind, Jack?'

Di Rocca walked a couple of steps with Koras, keeping pace, before answering. 'Sally Vicenti.'

Sally Vicenti was a name from Koras's past, those dangerous immigrant streets, the fabulous fifties, a time of duck's tail haircuts, Saturdays at Yankee Stadium or the Aqueduct, grinning Italian teenagers in their flashy fishtail cars, the beautiful flickering legs of the girls, and himself, a lonely Lithuanian kid with a trick knee, a laughable name that no one could pronounce, and a magical talent at stickball.

'Is Sally out of jail?'

Di Rocca laughed. 'That was a long time ago, Koras. He's out, and he's sitting pretty. Sally wants to make contact with you.'

'What for?'

Di Rocca stepped closer. 'He thought it would be a good way to start. Three New York boys, immigrant kids with something in common, talking a little business.' Koras looked around at a pretty girl passing. She wore a yellow dress, lifted up by the breeze. The girl smiled at him, and Koras smiled back. 'You make it sound poetic, Jackie.'

'Hey.' Di Rocca grinned.

'The last time I saw Sally, it was in front of the Sherry Netherland. He was so fat he couldn't squeeze into a limo. There was a call girl with him.

He was so out of shape, waving at me made him break into a wheeze.'

'He recognized you, didn't he?'

'Sure. He yelled at me and called me Panties, just like the old days.'

'Sally, he never forgets a face. His mind is like a video camera.'

Koras stopped. They were near the locker room. He could hear the murmur of the crowd, out for some sun, an afternoon's diversion. Diversion, that was the story of his career. 'So, what's up?'

'Sally had a heart attack years ago, maybe you heard, so he decided to take up sports, for his health. He wound up on a tennis court, staring up girls' dresses. He wasn't as bad at tennis as he was at golf, so he got himself a membership at the Oyster Bay Club. He met some hackers from Long Island, Saturday morning players from Wall Street, and he was able to exchange favours, place a couple of bets, you know.'

Koras nodded. 'I should have seen it coming, Jackie. Sally's setting up a bucket shop in big time tennis.'

Di Rocca grinned. 'Could be a real money-maker.'

'Don't tell me,' Koras said. 'In the fall, right after the U.S. Open, we'll have Monday night tennis. We'll have bettors in side streets all across America, putting their hard-earned wages on the point spread in the third set between Laville and Dumbo Cooper.'

'It's no joke, Koras. There's big money coming on board. A ton.'

'And Sally wants to get control, is that it?'

'Something like that.'

'What does he want with me?'

'To build an organization. He knew you. From the old days. He likes people he can count on.'

'I used to hit the stickball right through Sally's brother, until he learned not to call my mother names. Is he still around?'

'Joey, he died.'

'He was bound to.' Koras glanced over his shoulder as a security guard passed. 'What do they want?'

'Information. Talk. A trade here and there.'

'What kind?'

'Winners. Losers. Predictions.'

Koras shook his head. Sally Vicenti was a hood, with the morals of a pack rat. He could guess there would be real money in the pool. 'How much?'

'Sal's coming in conservative, right now. Half a million, as a test, merely.'

'What kind of a test?'

'Well, you remember Sally. He hates to lose. He'll play safe, quiet, cards close to the chest. This will be very secure, for everyone connected.'

'I don't have the handle on handicapping. You know that. I picked Armando to win at Monte Carlo. He lost in straight sets.'

'Sally still values your opinion. He knows you need time to think it over, and he wants to have a sit down when you get to New York.'

Koras grinned. 'The money's against him if he waits until the finals.'

'Hey, you understand the game from the inside, King. He trusts you, from the street and all. With you on the team, ranked one, he's got to come in a winner.'

Koras knew what Sally really wanted, which was control of the game, so he could place bets and make sure his people won money. Two years ago, a Miami syndicate had raised a quarter of a million dollars to bet on Wimbledon. As a result, two bookmakers had died, and the newspapers had raised hell. It said a lot about how big tennis had become, if Sally Vicenti was moving in. 'Sally wants me to call the final here, that's what you're saying?'

Di Rocca nodded. 'He's made it worth your while. He's been asking around, the word is that you're a little short of cash, because of the debt service on that fancy real estate.'

Koras felt a momentary twinge of panic, a memory of running through a dirty street, looking back, pale green streetlights, harsh breathing, the boyhood terror of being pursued. 'Tell Sally I think Dumbo Cooper will win. That's free.'

'Come on. Cooper's a hard-court player!'

'He's playing better, and his mother's back in the States.'

'I can't tell Sally that. He'd think I was crazy.'

'Then we'd better not work together.'

Di Rocca grabbed his arm. 'Maybe Laville will get lucky this week and win the French.'

'He'll have to drop something in my beer first.'

Di Rocca gave Koras a shrewd look. He remembered the time in Houston when Laville had dropped something into his beer before the quarters at River Oaks. He was surprised Koras knew about that. He tried to get back on track. 'At the fourth round twenty grand. At the quarters, ten. Cash. To keep the tax guys in the dark.'

'No thanks.' Koras turned away again and started towards the locker room. The time was growing closer for his match, and he needed to focus on how he would play Terry Laville.

'Is that no, for an answer?'

'Yes. It's no, for an answer.'

'Hey, then good luck out there.'

Di Rocca walked away, arms swinging, burly shoulders hunched. Koras opened the heavy door and went inside.

For the thousandth time, Koras immersed himself in the empty sonority, and the disinfected smell common to locker rooms the world over. He thought back to the first time he had played in the French nationals – just out of the army, barely twenty years old, he had not gone any further than the fourth round. In those days, the stadium had still retained some of the faded charm of an old and venerable country club, with all its discomforts. But now everything at Stade Roland-Garros had been remodelled, reorganized, reequipped. The locker room looked like a cross between an Icelandic sauna and an operating room. The scene was functional, but devoid of the anachronistic appeal that had once surrounded the sport.

Across the room, Terry Laville was deep in conversation with his manager, Archer Bell, a round-faced energetic man who owned a basketball team in Chicago. Bell, who had meaty shoulders and a pronounced stomach, exuded success. His picture had been on the cover of two American weekly magazines, once when his team won the National Basketball Association title, and a second time during the huge drug scandal which had swept basketball three years before. In both cover portraits Archer Bell had been smiling. He was a winner, and he had brought Terry Laville up from number seventy-three on the ATP computer to number seven. As Bell always said during press interviews, they weren't finished just yet.

As he passed his opponent, Koras greeted Laville, who answered with a forced smile that barely concealed his anger and frustration.

'Sorry about the mix-up last night,' Koras said.

Laville's face tightened, bringing the high Indian cheekbones into prominence. 'Get lost, and don't try any of this psych-out shit on me, right before a match, okay?'

'Okay.' Koras wanted to ask about Nora, Laville's wife, but now was not the time. The Lavilles' marriage was well-known as a battleground, and Nora Laville was constantly flying home, then reappearing. She drank too much, and the circuit gossips wondered how long the marriage would last.

Koras turned to go, but Laville got up from the bench and took him aside. His eyes were crazy. He spoke in a harsh whisper. 'Isn't my wife a little young for you?'

'I won't dignify that with a reply, Terry. There's nothing between Nora and me.'

'If you say so, pal.' Laville started to walk off. 'But you better watch your step in dark alleys, even with all the Paris cops around.'

Angry now, Koras broke away from a grinning Laville and walked over to his coach, the great Australian player, Will Channer, who was sitting on a bench in front of a TV mounted on wall brackets. Channer was six feet tall, with wavy hair, solid legs, and the wide shoulders of a distance runner. For the last ten years, his craggy Australian face had looked the same.

As Koras came up, Channer flipped the channel changer from the Peter Abraham match. 'I see Terry's in his usual restrained and cheerful mood.'

Koras grinned. Channer had a great sense of humour, and was always pulling Koras back to a stable reality. 'Just a few friendly words between guys who really dislike each other. How's Pete doing?'

'It's the best he's played,' Channer said. 'But he keeps see-sawing.'

Peter Abraham was the president of the Association of Tennis Professionals. He was ranked number twenty on the ATP computer, and he was now winning his match in the last sixteen. There had been a rain delay yesterday, so Abraham was finishing up today, as the quarterfinals got underway. As Channer changed channels, the handsome face of Armando Reyes came into view. Reyes was on the *Cour Centrale*, playing the French hopeful, Ivan Leroy.

'That's Pete's style. When he's on, the see-saw can drive you crazy.'

'It's better to put the ball away,' Channer said.

The two men watched the screen for a moment, before Will pulled out his notebook for a last-minute strategy session.

'How's the knee?'

Koras flexed his right knee, which had been giving him trouble since he was fifteen. 'It's better.'

'Laville looked mad enough to chew nails.'

'Yes.'

'Someday he'll take a run for you in a dark street.'

'Funny. That's what he just said.'

Channer flipped the channel back to the Abraham match. Abraham was toying with his opponent. 'We've got to avoid the Abraham syndrome today.'

'Yes.' Koras nodded.

'It's a sign of age. You think you're losing power, so you hold off. It happened to me.'

'Pete's only twenty-eight.'

'Didn't Tony Roche have his elbow problem about then?'

'Don't think about elbow problems. Or knee problems,' Koras said.

'Okay.'

Koras knew what Channer was talking about. In the late fifties and early sixties, Channer had dominated the men's professional game. Writers compared his power to that of Vines, Budge, and Sedgman. He had been raised in the Australian outback on a sheep station, and had entered the game right after the Hoad-Rosewall heyday. His chief weapons had been a serve that cracked like a whip and a forehand that was flat and punishing. Because of a ready smile for the cameras, tennis fans had taken to the friendly Australian. In his third year as a professional, Channer had won Wimbledon. In his fifth year, he had won the Australian, the British, and the U.S. titles. His loss of the French, to fellow Australian Roy Emerson, had prevented him from taking the Grand Slam.

A nagging shoulder injury had forced Will Channer into three operations. He had come back after the first two, but the third operation had convinced him to retire. He ran a tennis camp for a while, in Texas, then another one in New Hampshire. Four years earlier, Channer had returned to the circuit to coach Koras. They had been perfecting Koras's serve ever since.

Earlier that morning, they had worked out at the Polo, but the sudden showers had cut them off before they had finished. Now, because of that, Channer was exasperated. All winter, they had worked on Koras's serve, which was still erratic under pressure because of some minute changes in the grip, from continental to backhand, then back to continental. One grip gave more control. The other gave more power. Koras wanted to serve like Tilden. Channer thought he should follow the style of Jack Kramer. The ideal, of course, was a controlled serve that was packed with power, a real stinger of a weapon, but so far the two men had not found the right combination. Koras remembered icy days at his home on Long Island, the winter wind howling outside, while he and Will struggled with the serve on Koras's specially-constructed indoor court. Two weeks earlier, Koras had lost to Laville in Rome, at the Foro Italico. Channer thought the loss had been due to the serve, so they had continued to experiment once they got to Paris. Today, as a test, Koras would play Laville in the quarterfinals. Because the French title was the second step for the Grand Slam, both Koras and his coach felt the pressure.

Will flapped the pages in his notebook, going over strategies. 'All right, we'll play our Mr Laville down the middle. Hit deep, and then come to the net behind the shot. Try some lobs when he's facing the sun, and try them early in the match, to jolt his confidence. The same goes for the drop shot. And try coming in on the high balls to his backhand. Laville hates high balls.'

'All right.' Koras had heard the advice before, but he made mental notes. That was what a coach was for – to remind you about the basics.

'Hit the slice deep, with more pace than you used in Rome. It set the ball up there.'

'The Italian clay is slower.'

Channer nodded. 'Okay.' He slapped Koras on the arm, in a comradely way. 'How's your mental health?'

'The lady departed,' Koras said.

Channer smiled. 'Where do you find them?'

'They find me.'

Channer grinned, and turned back to the television. The coaching session was over, and Koras needed some time to himself. As he removed the raincoat and threw it onto a chair, Koras wished that Channer hadn't reminded him he was thirty-four. Was this his last real shot at the Grand Slam?

Koras sat down on a bench and leaned against the wall. Taking some deep breaths, he let his arms and legs dangle. With his eyes closed, he began to concentrate on his breathing, counting slowly from zero to five, inhaling through his nose; then to ten, keeping the air in his lungs; and then to twenty, exhaling through his mouth. He had learned to control his respiration in his way after he had discovered yoga, during the Italian Championships two years before, with an Italian countess whose eyes were as black as a Roman night. After the games, she would take him back to her palace, just off the Via Veneto, and in a sitting room as large as the Foro Italico she had taught him the 'Scorpio in Lotus' position beneath the disapproving stares of her ancestors, from their portraits on her walls.

At first, that scene had amused Koras. But eventually the beautiful black eyes of the countess had become too demandng, and he had been forced to make his exit from her life and the endless distractions it offered. But he had used her techniques ever since to increase his self-control.

The next year, he remembered, he had chosen to play in the Bavarian Championships, which took place at the same time as those in Rome. Bavaria put less strain on him in his preparation for the important internationals which followed – Paris, Wimbledon, New York – but, as usual, material considerations had also weighed. His manager, Frank Fenwick, had been negotiating an important contract with a German construction company, so Koras's presence in Munich had been an important diplomatic move. They had offered him $600,000 over a period of four years, on condition that he abandon his Rolls for some prestigious German auto during his rounds in the States. He had thought of the lovely countess, waiting eagerly for him in her sitting room, and the thought had made him sad. She had read about his Bavarian tournament in the papers and had sent him a telegram that said, simply, 'I wait.'

This year, Koras had returned to Rome, but her gate had been locked and she had not appeared at the tournament. He had asked about the countess, and someone had said she was away, refreshing herself in some mountain fastness of India or Tibet.

Her smile had been maddening, and she possessed a truly wicked body . . .

Koras opened his eyes. Will Channer had stopped twisting the dial and was now engrossed in the match on the first court, where Armando Reyes, nicknamed the Peruvian playboy, was beating the French tennis hopeful, Ivan Leroy. Even though Leroy was a finalist at last year's Roland-Garros, there was little hope for him this year. Injuries were part of the problem. At the beginning of the season he had strained his right shoulder, which had slowed down the pace of his shots. Unwilling to disappoint his public, the popular French player had fought bravely for every ball, plunging for the most desperate ones, only to miss the easiest.

'Leroy is giving it everything,' Channer said.

'He's always had a great heart,' Koras said.

'If he keeps pushing, it means another injury. Then he won't play Wimbledon.'

'He hates the grass, anyway.'

Koras stared at the screen, where Armando Reyes was amassing points with an ease that was staggering. So far, in Paris, Reyes was playing in the

Zone, a nickname borrowed from the TV series, *The Twilight Zone*. Playing in the Zone meant a player was in a no-miss state beyond hypnotism, where his racket could do no wrong. Armando Reyes was a devout Catholic, so he referred to his own personal zone as 'a state of grace'. Now, as Koras watched, Leroy saved a match point, then one more. A television close-up of his face showed he was white with pain. The score was deuce, but the Frenchman's energy was spent. Although his honour was intact, it was clear that he had lost all hope of victory.

Watching Leroy's struggle, Koras rubbed his right knee and remembered how elbow problems had driven Tony Roche, the great Australian, out of professional tennis. He wanted Armando to win. But he felt great sympathy for the Frenchman.

Behind him, a loud voice called: 'Watch out! Today's the day of the Paris freak show!'

Koras saw Milovan Tigrid, the mad Montenegrin, approaching from the showers. Milo was wrapped in one bright red towel and was carrying another, which he used to scrub himself vigorously. Water drops glistened on his hairy back and shoulders. 'Scarlet,' he bellowed, 'to mask my blushing cheeks if a girl were to find her way by chance into the little boys' locker room . . .'

Milovan Tigrid, whom everyone on the circuit called Milo, was an enormous Yugoslavian who had descended from the mountains of Montenegro, had crossed national frontiers, and was now living in less rugged countries off a combination of his immmense charm and his immense strength.

Other globe-trotting Yugoslavs with similar talents had become wrestlers or football players or mercenaries. But Milo, who was quicker of foot and brighter of mind, chose to try his hand at a more elegant, less strenuous sport. Ten years before, he had been the reigning tennis champion for two straight years, and he was still considered to be one of the most brilliant players of all time. Although ranked twenty-eighth in the world, he continued to do the circuit rounds remorselessly, having transformed his will to win and his legendary talent into a one-man tennis show, perfected, or so it seemed, for his amusement alone. When he played, the crowds and officials could always be sure that some extracurricular event would interrupt the placidity of the game. At White City, back in January, Milo had come onto the court accompanied by a tame orangutan, dressed in top hat and tails, and had tried to seat the animal in the umpire's stand.

Milo's fans were overjoyed with his antics. The officials, more often than not, reacted with heavy penalties. So far this year, Milo's fines totalled more than $6,000.

People who had known Milo at his peak were divided about his decision to continue playing professionally. On good days, he demonstrated the flashes of artistry and genius that had made him a member of the Top Ten for almost a decade. On bad days, he resorted to being a clown. And tennis afficionados knew that beneath the agile clown, there lurked a desperate man.

Koras knew Milo felt the madness of the whirlwind of the circuit: endless flights in the dead of the night, finishing a tournament on Sunday and flying a thousand miles to another tournament that started at noon on Monday. It was Australia in January, then Japan, Hawaii, Florida, while all the time one thought of Rome, and the change from American hard courts to slow European clay, and the preparation for Paris. And then Paris rolled around, and while one suffered on the slow clay there were thoughts of Wimbledon, and changing to the erratic grass surface, and then, lurking behind everything, the U.S. Open in New York, the gaudiest and richest tournament of them all. The madness of the circuit pressured you to keep going. It was addictive.

'Well, are you ready for Dumbo?' Koras asked.

'Aha!' Milo took a karate fighter's stance. 'Bring on the stupid one!'

Koras smiled. He knew there was no chance that his old friend could beat Dumbo Cooper, who was ranked number four on the ATP computer. And yet, miracles still happened. 'Well, best of luck.' He shook Milo's hand.

'Tigrid plays for the hearts of the women.'

'That's your big secret, Milo.'

Milo turned to stare at Koras. 'What do you think of our glorious Princess taking up with an Arab?'

Koras knew his friends was talking about Abdul Saadi, the latest conquest of Princess Athena von Heidelberg. Koras had seen Saadi around, but they had not yet been introduced. 'How long has it been now?'

'Weeks. Perhaps even months. They met in Los Angeles, while I was winning my exhibition at Pauley Pavilion. In Honolulu, she was alone, seeking companionship, which I tried to provide. In Rome, she was with Saadi. Her choice cannot be explained with logic.'

Koras grinned. 'Because you were available?'

Milo thumped his chest, and then leaned down closer to Koras's ear. 'A pox on wealthy Arabs. I hear he is doing a capitalist manoeuvre on Sport City, those purveyors of tennis shoes, what you profiteers call a leveraged buyout.'

Koras laughed out loud. Milo's perspective on economics was a mixture of opportunism, Karl Marx, and J. Pierpont Morgan. He paid lip service to communism, but only went back home for special holidays, or when his mother was ill and called for her son. 'What circus treats have you planned for today?'

Milo stood up to stare again in the mirror, grinning. 'They will have to wait and see, until mighty Tigrid takes the court.'

'Keep them in suspense, right?'

'Precisely. As the great Jaroslav Drobny before me.' Drobny was a brilliant player from Prague who had begun his career in 1938 on the slow courts of Roland-Garros, and had finally won Wimbledon in 1954 by beating Ken Rosewall in four sets. Drobny was Milo's hero, who had stood firm against the onslaughts of capitalism. Now he pranced in front of the mirror, flexing and making faces like a Zulu witch doctor. He heard his name on the intercom, calling him out of the courts. Milo winked at Koras, who was watching him in the mirror, and then he secured the towel about his middle and ran screaming from the room.

'Mad,' Will Channer said.

'One of us,' Koras said.

The girl on the closed circuit television screen spent eleven minutes and thirty-one seconds under the shower spray, the time clocked in infinite precision by the solid gold timepiece of Abdul Saadi's grandfather. The watch and its chain had been given to the grandfather, a Bedouin sheik, by Sir Walter Drummond, a petroleum geologist whose skill made the Saadi family rich beyond their wildest dreams. The watch had been passed down from father to son, until it came to rest in the hands of its present owner, Abdul Saadi, now thirty-one and the head of Sahara Sports.

Waiting made Abdul restless. But that was the drawback of watching the closed circuit TV live.

The picture was in colour. The system was Japanese. It had excellent resolution, sound that was crystal clear, and a special tint-control that brought out the magical lustre of a young girl's skin. Saadi was a busy man. Technology helped him get through the day.

In each of his hotels, in the major cities of the world, the same system had been installed.

When the girl came out, dripping, reaching for a thick yellow towel while she pushed back the wet hair from her face, Saadi was reminded of the Botticelli portrait of Venus rising from the waves. Steam rose from the shower; grey clouds, filmy and soft, tinged with silver. Water droplets beaded on the camera lens, slightly distorting the image of the naked girl. Saadi shifted in his swivel chair and licked his lips.

Pressing a control button for a series of close ups, he scanned her naked body. She had trim legs, long for a French girl, swelling subtly into strong thighs, a slim waist and tight buttocks. He relished the flare of rib cage, the tremulous thrust of high breasts with erect nipples, the tufts of hair beneath her arms. She had a smooth throat he longed to kiss. Her severe lips, slightly slanted eyes, gave her a face like a Modigliani.

The face was not beautiful, Saadi thought, as the girl wrapped the towel around her waist, sarong style, and strolled into the bedroom. A better word would be arresting. He felt arrested by those greyish-blue eyes.

Standing at the French doors opening out onto the balcony, looking pensively out at Paris, one hand on the door frame, the girl made Saadi sweat.

Her name was Laure Puget. She was a distant cousin of his current mistress and travelling companion, the Princess Athena von Heidelberg. This was Mademoiselle Puget's third visit. She had her own room in the penthouse of Hotel Paladin, on the Right Bank of the Seine.

She turned away from the window, unwrapping the towel. The simple action made him remember Clothilde, his father's Parisian mistress, now dead. In 1973, at the age of eighteen, Abdul Saadi had seduced Clothilde in her flat on the Rue Bienfaisance, near Gare St Lazare, while his father had been busy, buying up gold in London. Saadi had been in love for the first and only time in his life. Clothilde had been in her mid-twenties, like Laure Puget. Slender, dark, with grey-green eyes and a face that radiated sensuality.

The seduction had been all the more exciting because it had taken place in his father's bed. Saadi had known pure joy because he was replacing his father between her legs.

When Clothilde had died, a motoring accident three years ago in Monaco, Saadi had wanted to commit suicide. His religion kept him from it.

Saadi adjusted the controls. Laure Puget sat naked on the rumpled coverlet, right knee raised, foot on the edge of the bed, toes curled upward as she trimmed her toenails. The position made visible her most secret parts. His mouth was dry. He wet his lips with his tongue and mopped his face with a silk handkerchief.

For two months, an arm of Saadi's vast Sahara conglomerate had been providing financing for the girl's archaeological project, an excavation of the fortress of Alesia in northeastern France, where Caesar's army had vanquished the Gauls under Vercingetorix. The money was a minor sum – three million U.S. dollars so far – and Saadi, who was interested in history, had been waiting for the girl to demonstrate the degree of her gratefulness.

So far, Laure Puget had been polite but distant. Saadi sighed, thinking of Clothilde and her willing sensuality.

The girl turned her back and Saadi turned his mind to business. He was here in Paris to discuss endorsement contracts with tennis players on their way up. He wanted the right names to launch his Sahara line of rackets, shoes, and clothing. The date for the launch was August. The event was the U.S. Open. Already, Saadi had rejected Koras, the number one, because of his past intimacies with the Princess. Saadi was a jealous man, and just hearing the old stories about Koras and Athena made him sick. With Koras eliminated, that left three players on the rise – Dumbo Cooper, Terry Laville, and Mikhail Polak. At the moment, Saadi wanted Polak, the archangel of Gdansk. He was a star from the eastern bloc. He was ranked number two in the world. Best of all, Polak seemed innocent, untouched by the jaded jet set world of the tennis groupies.

Saadi's family owned thirteen hotels in major cities across the world: London, Tokyo, Singapore, Hong Kong, Honolulu, Acapulco, Los Angeles, Dallas, Chicago, New York, Vienna, Berlin, Cairo. The New York Paladin was being refurbished, but delays had been caused by strikes. That summer, he would open Casino Paladin in Atlantic City. It would boast 2,500 rooms, and accommodate 4,100 gamblers at once, on one gigantic floor. A party was already planned. In his mind, Saadi thought of it as the Polak Party.

The girl on the screen began dressing for the matches. Underwear first. Then a bra, a half slip, a pretty dress. What was her price? In Saadi's view, every woman was a whore – only his sister and mother were excluded – and all whores had a price.

A red button winked on the console. The maid. Saadi pressed the button. 'Oui, Suzette?'

The maid told him the Princess had phoned from the Rue St Honore. She was finished with her shopping. They would leave for Stade Roland-Garros within the hour.

Saadi did not like taking orders from the imperious Princess.

'Oui, Suzette.'

On the screen, Laure Puget stood in front of the mirror. She was dressed now. His pleasures were, for the moment, at an end.

Milo's sudden exit had left a strange silence in the dressing room. Koras went back to his deep breathing. Laville talked to Archer Bell while he jogged in place to keep warm. Laville was still angry, from last night, and his eyes registered blank hatred. Before a match, Laville allowed his anger for his opponent to build in an irrational and uncontrolled way; he felt it helped him get pumped up for victory. This kind of behaviour, in Koras's view, was demented. You should save your emotion and feed it into the magic of the match. So far, Laville's anger build-up hadn't worked against Koras, who had twenty matches to seven over Laville. Someday, the anger would wash over the court, drowning the players and the crowd.

Now, Koras's only urge was to be out on the court, into the game, confronting his opponent at last. Koras also knew that, a few feet away, Laville was summoning all his energy to win, to beat him. And his anger was even greater, because of last night . . .

Koras winced as he remembered. The night before, Regine had thrown a party for him at the club. It was still too early for the place to be really crowded, but the dining room had been full, and Koras, tired by the day's training, had been absentmindedly reviewing the unattached women, listening to the talk around him.

'You'll probably want to leave early,' someone said.

'I beg your pardon?'

'You're playing tomorrow, aren't you?'

'Yes.'

Koras didn't know this man with the soft, featureless face. Where had he seen him before? Paris? New York? He hated to be counselled, especially by strangers. Advice always came from bogus sports enthusiasts, the tennis players' equivalent of the Monday morning quarterback, who could tell you where you went wrong in the last match you lost.

Koras turned away just as a lovely strawberry-blonde girl came by, returning from the ladies' room. She wore high heels, which gave her a swaying walk, like an island maiden. Passing Koras's table, the girl gave him a long look and smiled. She wore dark green, to enhance her colouring. She sat down three tables away. Her companions were three men, two in their early thirties, a third who was fifty-five or so. The older man wore a business suit of expensive cut and he was trying to monopolize her. As he spoke, gesturing candlelight winked off a gold ring and a gold watch. The two younger men watched, awaiting their chance for an opening.

Through all this, the girl started right at Koras, with a faint smile of amusement on her face.

With considerable fanfare and nearly a dozen waiters in tuxedoes, the maitre d'hotel brought in the desserts. Koras, bored by the predatory atmosphere and the endless meal, had the urge to be far from this room, maybe alone with the lovely Titianesque girl. Koras had a reputation for leaving social occasions early, especially when he was playing a tournament. His eyes met the girl's clear gaze. She smiled, and he smiled back. 'Tell me,' his neighbour said. 'Are you going to give us the Grand Slam this year?'

'First, I must win the French.'

People were desperate to be familiar with him. Strangely, his fame seemed to work against him, triviliazing his talent, making him feel like a waning star.

'Is that the way one does it, one step at a time?'

'It's the way I do it. One stroke at a time. Otherwise, you forget why you're out there.'

'Why are you out there?'

'To give my best.'

The man smiled at Koras with a shrewd gleam in his eyes. He was about to go on with his interrogation when a terrible clamour came from the bar next door. In the next instant, Nora Laville, Terry's wife, hurried in, looking haggard. She wore no make-up, and her rich brown hair was dishevelled. When she saw Koras, she ran up to him, and threw herself into his arms.

'Nora. What's wrong?'

Waking from her trance, Nora realized people were staring at them. She stared at Koras, her face a mask of anguish. 'Terry. He . . .' She was breathless, her bosom heaving, and two spots of colour showed in her pale cheeks.

'Nora, will you tell me what's happened?'

Koras led Nora to an adjoining room. Trembling, she pressed herself against him, wetting his neck with her tears.

'You must think I'm crazy. I just can't stand it any more. Terry's insane. He –'

She began to cry again.

'It was horrible. We had a fight. He's always bringing up my past. A few harmless photographs in a magazine and he makes me feel like the worst whore. Tonight, he even slapped me.'

Koras looked into her eyes. He knew she had posed in two different women's magazines, for lingerie ads. Her husband had not thought them to be risqué until after the marriage. He smelled alcohol on Nora's breath.

Just then, a murmur rose from the people in the main room, and he heard Terry Laville calling for his wife. 'Nora!'

Someone must have sent the Canadian after them, because in seconds he was standing in the doorway, glowering at Koras and his wife. Involuntarily, Nora huddled close to Koras. Terry wore jeans and a jacket thrown carelessly over his red and white striped pyjama top. His feet were bare inside tennis shoes; his ankles looked huge.

'Koras, you sonofabitch!'

'Terry,' Nora said. 'Go away!'

Agitated faces appeared in the doorway behind Laville, who advanced on Koras and Nora, clenching his huge fists. Koras moved Nora aside just as Laville took a swing. Koras danced away from the blow, which went wild. At the same time, he caught the rank smell of alcohol. It had been a bad night for both Lavilles, and while he felt sorry for them in their marriage, he didn't want to stop one of Laville's roundhouse punches. One hammer blow would put a fit man in hospital for a week.

Nora grabbed Terry's left hand, but he threw her aside. He took another wild and drunken swing, but Koras grabbed his arm and swung him with a thump into the wall. Laville hit his left shoulder, spun around, and crashed into a table. The maitre d' rushed in with three waiters to put a stop to the fight. Nora was sitting on the edge of a chair, crying. The fight solved nothing. Koras would have liked to take her with him, keep her in a safe place until Terry cooled down. But he had to stand there, doing nothing, while Terry marched out with Nora.

Back at his table, Koras thought of going after them. Then the polite table talk started up again, and the foolhardy impulse passed. Koras ordered a beer, which tasted bitter. When Regine came up to talk for a moment, he realized the muscles in his back and shoulders were tight as violin strings. He had a match tomorrow. It was time to go.

'Regine, I'm sorry for the trouble. It was a super party.'

'Well, you see why Terry wasn't invited. The man's an absolute bore. I don't see why she stays with him.'

Koras did not answer. Instead, he kissed Regine on both cheeks, and waved a general goodbye to the other guests. Waiting for the elevator, he stretched, testing those tight muscles. When the elevator door opened, the strawberry blonde stood inside, leaning casually against the back wall. One strand of her brilliant hair had come loose and dangled down the right side of her head. The rich green dress clung to her body. Her eyes were shining and the faint smile still lurked at the corners of her mouth.

'Mademoiselle?' He made way for her to exit.

The girl did not move. 'I'm coming with you.'

His car was waiting in front of the club. As if nothing could be more natural, the pretty girl slipped in beside Koras and curled up on the front seat, facing him . . .

As the loudspeakers announced that the court was free, Koras gave a start and came out of his reverie. Jean Hoffman, the fussy tournament umpire, came to collect the two players in person.

It would begin again, the same motions, the same battle. Koras took the time to pull on his lucky black Lavel warm-up suit. He was thinking about saving it for the final, but something about last night, and the way Laville had acted, made him bring the suit along for the quarters.

He walked out behind Laville who advanced with his slow, bear-like step. Both men stayed silent, and Koras knew Laville was thinking about last night at Regine's. They left the locker room and walked through the labyrinthine passages under the stands, until they came out onto the *Cour Centrale*, flooded in sunlight, and heard the applause of fifteen thousand spectators. For once, the weather forecast had been right – the sky was cloudless.

Koras squinted, raising his eyes to the scoreboard, which still showed the scored from the preceding match. He heard the announcer giving results of other matches: 'Armando Reyes beats Ivan Leroy, 6–2, 6–4, 6–7, 6–1; on the second court, Milovan Tigrid is leading David Cooper 5–4 in the second set. Mr Tigrid took the first set 7–5.'

It was unbelievable. Milo was leading Dumbo. Dumbo Cooper, a young player from New York, was well known for his irascibility on court, never beaten until the last ball. The tenacious power player punctuated each shot with a strange grunted guttural tribute to pagan gods known only to himself. If Milo won today, he would be all smiles and would spend the season buying drinks for everyone.

Koras tore his thoughts away from Dumbo and concentrated on his match against Laville. He sat down in his chair and looked at the stands. Athena von Heidelberg had not yet arrived, and Saadi's private box was empty. Koras brought out three rackets, all Belynkas Autographs, made by his major equipment sponsor, Laval Sportif. He checked the tension on each one, pressing his fingertips against the strings, and then tapping the strings on the edge of a second racket. He chose the middle one to start the match.

The net cord judge flipped a coin. Koras won, and chose to serve. Laville took the side that put his back to the sun. Staring at Laville, Koras felt a flutter of dread. The tournament in Paris would mark the second leg of the Grand Slam. He had won Australia in January. He was thirty-four, and this might be his last chance.

What if he lost here today, to a man as out of control as Terry Laville?

CHAPTER TWO

The loudspeaker made the announcement, and Koras was always surprised to hear his name – it meant the dream had come true. He was really here, about to play for a huge crowd: 'The quarterfinals of the French Internationals. Pantakoras Belynkas, of the United States, versus Terry Laville, of Canada.'

Before walking to the end of the court, Koras put on the forest green headband which held his hair back out of his eyes. He felt especially sensitive to vibrations today, so he took extra care not to step on the white lines as he walked to his end of the court for the warm-up. Once the ball was in flight, his superstition about the lines vanished. He could not explain it, and he seldom spoke to anyone about how he felt. All he knew was that the lines vibrated, as if charged with magnets.

During the warm-up, slamming the ball at Laville, Koras felt his fears subside, to be replaced by the familiar detachment. Now, there was only the ball crossing the net, touching down, the red earth below, the feel of the rubber sphere as it met the sweet spot in the centre of his racket. Above all, there was Laville, his grinning opponent.

Laville, the Calgary woodcutter. Calgary, the railway crossing where he had been born, was an old pioneer town famous for a rodeo and a collection of refineries, with not much else to place it on the map until Terry's ascension in the world of tennis.

At twenty-five, Terry Laville still had the intense aggressiveness that had marked his first appearance on the tennis circuit half a dozen years ago. Indeed, with his height, his incredible power, and his heavy lumbering game, Laville was like some natural force sprung from his native forests of Alberta. The Laville myth, promoted in the media by his clever manager,

Archer Bell, had him training by felling trees by lamplight with his brothers in the darkness and gloom of the Canadian northwest.

There was some truth to the myth. Felling huge trees had taught Laville the secrets of balance, but the real benefit of his life in the woods had been that he had learned to swing an axe with great accuracy. This exercise, which built up the muscles in his shoulders, back, and upper arms, had given him the most powerful serve in tennis. Stop-action photographs of the Laville serve, taken the previous summer at Hilton Head Island, showed the ball in flight being compressed into a fluffy wafer. The caption beneath the photo read: 'How would you like to be a tennis ball served at 148 mph by Terry Laville, the Canadian woodcutter?' Tennis writers compared the power of Laville's serve to Roscoe Tanner's and the easy, deceptive motion to Pancho Gonzales's.

Terry was always complaining to the press that tennis kept him away from his homeland. These days, he spent what little time he had in Canada jogging in the woods around the house he had bought near Vancouver.

Laville's ascent had begun the day he had won the Alberta championships. Given a scholarship by the University of Winnipeg, he had rapidly risen to the summit of the game at home, to become Canada's long-awaited tennis hope. Unfortunately, Laville had come onto the circuit when Koras had been playing his best tennis. Milovan Tigrid had started to fade, and his place at the top had been assumed by Koras. Three years earlier, on the verge of winning at Roland-Garros, Laville was eliminated by Koras in the semifinals. Since then, Koras had kept winning against him.

It was just one more grudge Laville held against Koras.

They finished warming up their serves. From the other end of the court, Koras watched Terry Laville shake his astonishing white hair, his face screwed against the glare. That face, accentuated by its sharp planes, the narrow-lidded eyes, the long aquiline nose, reminded Koras of an Indian warrior preparing for battle. He could sense the violent hatred emanating from Laville like a huge force, vibrating toward him in waves. The referee gave the signal to play. Koras held up the ball in the time-honoured opening gesture, and then he served. The ball kicked high on the soft clay, going to Laville's backhand. Laville hit a short return. Koras intercepted the ball just in front of the service line, hit a forcing volley that pinned Laville to a spot deep in the court, behind the baseline, and won the first point with his knifing second volley. The stands responded with a round of applause.

He won three games in a row before Laville got a point.

At the changeover at 4–1, Koras surveyed the stands, packed to the top of the steep stadium, very full for a Wednesday of quarterfinal play. In the private boxes near the courtside, he recognized all the partially notorious faces, people of the jet set who flocked to premierès and openings to compete with whatever spectacle there was.

These were the stars, the luminaries. They came from the world of film and theatre, from music and art and politics. He saw Gerald Duncan, a best selling writer, and next to him was Charles St Etienne, the movie star. He recognized Harrison Cabot, the wealthy president of the United States Tennis Association. Cabot was not one of Koras's favourite people. The man had never worked in his life, and existed in splendour on an income earned by his great-grandfather, a banker in Connecticut. Cabot had gone to Yale to study English and the classics. He had crewed, of course, had played varsity tennis, and then, back in the forties, had represented the United States in the Davis Cup. Koras was angry that American tennis had been controlled for almost a century by men like Cabot.

In the players' box, Koras spotted Armando Reyes, smiling and making jokes with his latest inamorata, an attractive redhead. The woman wore a fashionable jumpsuit and kept turning away from Reyes to snap pictures of people in the crowd with an expensive-looking camera. He had heard the woman was married, but that had never fazed Armando.

All of wealthy Paris had turned out for the tennis and had set up camp in the main stand, certain in the knowledge they would be a focus of attention of both the public and publicity-seeking cameras.

As Koras watched, Princess Athena von Heidelberg made her entrance. Saadi was not with her, but she had her maid and a chauffeur in livery and a young girl with dark glasses and a large leather shoulder bag. The girl looked familiar, but Koras could not place her.

The Princess's title made him smile. No one could say whether or not she actually had a right to it, but this did not matter to Athena, because in the circles which she frequented, discretion was the keynote for behaviour. Athena was a fountain of gossip, and if any one of her countless acquaintances had dared to question her right to be called 'Princess', she would have fought them with every subtle weapon at her disposal. The Princess was a formidable foe, as Koras had found.

It was almost time. On the other side of the umpire's chair, Terry Laville was mumbling to himself as he re-wrapped the yellow gauze around his racket handle. Was he on the verge of a temper tantrum?

Koras took some water, to rinse his mouth.

Today, Princess Athena was resplendent in a gorgeous tomato-red dress. Two spaghetti-thin straps crossed her tanned shoulders and the soft velour clung to her breasts. Whenever Athena twisted in her seat to wave at someone, people turned to watch. She was a beautiful woman, sensual, wealthy, magnificently regal.

As he stood up, Koras looked again at the pretty young girl. Who was she?

'Mr Belynkas?' said the umpire. 'Shall we resume?'

Laure Puget, wearing a dress of raw silk, eggshell colour, and a cerulean blue jacket, watched with amusement as her cousin Athena told the maid where to put the picnic hamper. The chauffeur followed, carrying a cooler filled with ice, beer, wine, and Dom Perignon champagne.

All across Europe and the major cities of America, Athena was famous for not wearing a brassiere, and not needing to. Her breasts – high, full, and insolent – were legendary. At sporting events, carnivals, the opera, photographers were constantly turning away from their subjects to capture a few pictures of Athena's spectacular figure. Now, at Stade Roland-Garros, spectators craned their necks for a look at the rich aristocrat. The Princess obliged. She was there to be admired, and strangers were always waving, pointing, asking for her autograph. Because her photo appeared in newspapers every week, people felt they knew Athena. Wherever she went, people waited for Athena to lean over, bend, laugh, move.

Everyone loved her.

She had a ready laugh, a saucy walk, a beautiful winning smile. The smile, when combined with her money and impelling confidence, had won her a screen test with a major Hollywood studio. But the Princess refused to get up before dawn to go to work on the movie set. Still, she was the consummate entertainer, bringing light into a dark world.

Athena was the daughter of Helga von Heidelberg, a Belgian beauty who was as spectacularly endowed as her daughter. Helga had married Count Osten of Augsburg before the last world war. Count Osten had been a great hunter and a manufacturer of military weapons. He had made huge sums of money, which he had smuggled into secret accounts in the Zurich banks. But in staking so much on the new rulers of Germany, the Count had been as short-sighted as he was ambitious. In May 1945 he had put a bullet through his head rather than face the humiliation of defeat.

His young and beautiful widow had grieved properly and circumspectly. Her problem was not money, but rather how to find another husband who would allow her the same noble station to which she claimed to belong. True, her reputation was slightly tainted by her late husband's politics, but as national economies blossomed and the world again enjoyed relative peace, Helga was able to survive, and quite nicely. Forced down into the ranks of the plebians, Helga married a wealthy and politically ambitious American army colonel named Riker, who had his eye on a Senate seat in Virginia. He never became a senator, but he did amass millions. When the colonel died, in 1962, Helga became an even richer widow.

Athena was only six when her mother found herself alone again. Helga secured both their livelihoods by placing her massive inheritance with a Wall Street broker who became her financial adviser, and her lover. She and her daugher kept her maiden name, von Heidelberg, which had a more impressive ring than Riker.

Athena had gone to school at Montesano, in Gstaad, where she gained an education equal to her ambitions. At Montesano, she studied French, German, English, mathematics, art, history, and classical literature. She mixed with girls of her own social class, and saw her mother only twice a year, in the Bahamas, at the summer house, and at St Moritz, where they spent a lavish Christmas.

At Montesano, Athena played her first tennis, and proved to have a natural talent for the game. On the court, she was flashy, bold, adventurous. Like many of the players from France, Athena lacked discipline, or she would have become a champion. Instead, she drifted into the role of tennis groupie, and by the age of eighteen had slept with most of the Top Ten. For Athena, that was a good enough ranking.

Athena handed the chauffeur a bottle of champagne. 'Here, Eduard. Be a good boy. Put this between your powerful legs and pop it open.'

Laure laughed as the chauffeur blushed and then opened the champagne. As the champagne cork exploded, a handsome man arrived, wearing a warm-up suit of bright yellow. He had strong legs, a deep tan, and a booming voice that carried in the steep confines of the stadium. Athena introduced him as the player Armando Reyes, from Peru. Reyes, who had won his quarterfinal match, bent over to kiss Laure's hand. 'Ah, Mlle Laure. So nice to have you here. Do you know tennis?'

'Not very well, I'm afraid.'

'Laure is an archaeologist, Armando. She digs in the dirt of France.'

'Amazing,' Reyes said. 'What do you dig for?'

'Artifacts,' she said. 'Connections.'

'Connections leading where?'

'Between past and present.' Laure crossed her tanned legs.

She got another admiring look from Reyes, and Athena noticed. 'Here, Armando. Have some champagne. Take your mind off the tennis.' She handed Reyes a glass.

'Are you here for the tournament, Mlle Laure?' Reyes asked.

'Laure finds tennis decadent,' Athena cut in.

'Let her speak, cheri.' Reyes turned back to Laure.

'Actually, I've been in Mexico, on a dig. I came back to France in early spring, for another dig, down near Dijon.' She said nothing about the financing that came from Saadi's business.

'Ah, how interesting.' The Peruvian leaned closer. Even though he was trying his best to be charming, he wasn't really interested in her work. 'Near Dijon?'

'Um, yes. At Alesia. It's just north. Near Montbard.'

'I know Dijon. In 1978, I had a wine there to curl the toes.'

'Armando, you have a favourite wine everywhere.' Athena spoke to Laure. 'Once, after the tournament finished up here, Armando had his pilot fly us around France. There was a car waiting. We stopped at every vineyard from Bordeaux to Dijon. Truly.'

'That was in the old days,' Reyes said. 'We stayed borracho until Wimbledon.'

'The pilot was mad, a daredevil. Whatever happened to him, Armando?'

'He is in Peru. He works for my brother.'

'Give him my best, will you.'

Reyes spoke to Athena over his shoulder. 'Only you can do that, cheri.'

When Reyes spoke to Athena, he was making love. It was an automatic gesture, and Laure wondered if Saadi was alert enough to notice. Laure did not care for Saadi, and had been surprised when he came through with money to finance her excavation at Alesia. Saadi fancied himself a scholar with an interest in history. Still, Laure felt uneasy around him.

Down on the court, Belynkas won a long point from the huge Canadian.

'Poor Laville,' Reyes said.

'Why do you say that?' Laure asked.

'He plays so hard. Yet he can never win against Koras.'

Athena cut in, with her opinion. 'They say Pantakoras has the "Indian Sign" on Laville.'

'I know what that means,' Laure said. 'An American expression, having to do with a hold on someone.'

'Bravo,' Reyes said, and smiled out at the players. 'I admire Koras immensely, you know?'

'You do? Why?'

'He is always giving his time; for clinics, for charity exhibitions. He calls it paying his dues.'

'To whom?' Laure asked.

'To the world. The world helped him when he was starting out by sending along a man named Al Moscowitz. Now Koras wants to pay it back.'

'I find that awfully abstract,' Athena yawned.

But Reyes went on. 'He even helped Terry Laville, at first.'

'But not any more?'

'No. Not any more.'

Laure understood. She liked helping people. After she had finished her studies, and had turned the material into a substantive little book, she wanted to become a teacher. She was thinking of this when another man, Jean-François Colombier, entered the box. Before introducing him to Laure, Athena gave him a huge hug. The conversation swirled around her – rich people in Dallas, Paris, Singapore. A fur coat Athena had just bought in Rome, a bargain at $97,000.

Laure read for a while, a treatise on Alesia by Wallensborough. When she looked up to watch Koras, she had the feeling he had changed since their tennis lesson, on the shady court at Innsbruck, so many years ago. Through Athena's opera glasses, Laure studied Koras's face; strong, with wide set eyes and an expressive mouth. The man she remembered had been younger, less experienced, more spiritual. This man, playing so surgically, made her edgy.

Beside her, Armando Reyes was acting as tennis tutor.

'That's a cross-court volley. He's too far from the net to do any good. Close in, Señor Koras, close! Excellent.' He looked at Laure, to see if she understood.

She smiled back. 'You like him, don't you?'

'Like him? To me, Koras is next to God and Jack Kramer.'

Laure changed the subject. 'Has he never married?'

'Almost.' Armando glanced towards Athena, who had her back turned as she spoke to someone in the next box. 'A Swedish lady, some artist type he met in Paris.'

'What happened?'

Armando shrugged. 'I don't know. He refuses to talk about it much.'

At that moment, they were joined by a dazzling redhead carrying a camera. She wore a white jumpsuit. Armando introduced her as Muriel Broussard-Gauthier. Shaking the woman's hand, Athena was all smiles, but Laure sensed an electric jealousy.

'Are you photographing for business, madame? Or for pleasure?'

The redhead smiled. 'It began as pleasure.' She glanced at Armando. 'But now I think I shall make a book.'

Armando Reyes stood up to leave the box. 'I shall leave you now. It is time to warm up.'

'Good luck, Armando.'

As Reyes left the box, Athena turned to the redhead, who snapped her photo before turning the camera on Laure.

Koras took the first set of his quarterfinal 6–1, with an ace. Laville seemed to be chasing a phantom ball. Leading 2–1 in the second set, Koras looked at the brunette, who was still reading. Armando's redhead had left the players' box and was chatting away with Athena. Time for some fun, so he tossed the ball very high in the air and put his hands on his hips, watching it come down.

The ball hit him squarely between the eyes. There was laughter from the stands. The girl looked up.

Across the net, Laville thought Koras was making fun of him, and began to play better tennis. He won three games.

Koras realized he was losing his hold on the match. He quickened the pace of the game, sending explosive passing shots that barely touched the ground, devouring the ball with his eyes, taking the ball on the rise with wicked half-volleys. He crunched away the shots at the net. He wanted a lot of applause, to distract the brunette from her damned book. He hoped it was fascinating.

'Mr Belynkas takes the second set, 6–4.'

In the middle of the third set, Terry Laville threw a tantrum over a line call. He spent several moments berating the line judge, a portly man wearing dark glasses and a beret. Then he turned his venom on the umpire. The umpire was forced to call the crowd to order. 'Please serve, Mr Laville.' Laville prepared to serve. The first shot went wild, out of court. The second slapped against the tape of the net.

He threw his racket to the ground in a rage.

The crowd jeered. In the boxes, people turned around disapprovingly. The whistles and cat calls continued. It was more like a football game in the European Cup than a staid tennis match at Stade Roland-Garros. If the Federation did nothing to control this type of behaviour from the spectators, the day might come when they would be throwing firecrackers and smoke-bombs, and perhaps worse, onto the courts.

'Match point.'

The Canadian survived two match points, but succumbed in the third, under the applause of a crowd that would surely have fed him to the lions. Straight sets: a massacre. Koras walked to the net to shake hands, but Laville, in a pique about last night at Regine's, only brushed his fingers against Koras's hand.

Laville was now eliminated from the French Open, but Koras would advance to the semifinals, where he would play the winner of the Polak-Colombier match.

For almost two weeks, the stadium of Roland-Garros is transformed into a 'Field of the Cloth of Green,' where the sovereigns of tennis defy each other on the courts. In the grounds adjacent to the courts, the green and white tents of the commercial enterprises set up a rival spectacle, displaying their famous trademarks like coats of arms.

In this slick world of marketing, almost anything that sells can be made acceptable, and although the law prohibits cigarette manufacturers from advertising in stadiums, they sidestep the problem by becoming sports clothes manufacturers. As MacLaren rolls on, so does Marlboro.

The stands resembled an entrenched camp, Gauls versus Intruders. It is known as the Village, and that afternoon, after the matches were finished, Lavel Sportif held a cocktail party to celebrate the signing of its new contract with Pantakoras Belynkas, and to introduce their new line of sportswear.

At the party, lost in a swirl of faces, Koras found Frank Fenwick, his manager, who had arrived from South Africa only an hour before play began. Fenwick wore his usual costume, twill jacket, twill trousers, Stetson hat, and boots. His pockets bulged with notebooks and slips of paper. Fenwick was due in Hamburg that evening, for dinner. He would return to Paris on Friday for the semifinals. Koras liked Fenwick, but he wondered what the man was chasing. F.F. was worth millions. Athena had wryly said that Fenwick's watch was five minutes too fast, and that he was circling the globe trying to catch that tiny unit of unattainable time.

Once, at Narita airport in Tokyo, Koras and Fenwick had been about to board a flight for California when the porter from the hotel where they had been staying caught up with them, breathlessly. He wanted the room key, no doubt taken by mistake.

'No,' Fenwick said. 'It's not a mistake.' And he'd insisted on keeping the key, and had written out a cheque to pay for the installation of a new lock. Koras had watched the scene, bewildered.

'I collect keys,' F.F. said. 'In New York, I have a entire room full of hotel keys. I have these dreams, that if I keep all the keys to all the rooms I've ever slept in, death will never be able to find me. But if that time does come, I'll be able to choose when and where it happens.'

Fenwick had his quirks, and one of the strongest was that he did not like surprises. Even if he was in Borneo, Fenwick liked to know where Koras was and how he was playing. Fenwick was a superb manager, professional, solid, with a genuine gift for foresight. Koras and Fenwick had no written contract; instead, a strong bond of friendship had underwritten the business they did in big time tennis.

'Great news!' Fenwick boomed, in his Texan accent.

Koras smiled. 'Give a guy a break, F.F. No contract talk just yet. I just finished working.'

Fenwick took Koras by the arm. 'You don't understand. I made two holes in one, in six days.' Fenwick waved his arm, indicating the hubbub at the Village. 'Now, when you have to give all this up, you can play golf with me. Arnie'll give you lessons.'

Despite the veiled reference to his age, Koras smiled as he pictured playing golf with Arnie Palmer as his mentor. This year, he guessed Palmer might make four million dollars. He was probably sitting on fifty million more, and still he continued to teach, making the game accessible to others. Arnold Palmer was a man to admire.

'Koras, I need a favour.'

'What?'

'After Paris, I need you to play Palermo.'

'Why Palermo?' Koras looked around, hoping to catch sight of the brunette who had been with Athena.

'We need the money.' Fenwick's voice was suddenly serious.

'You're kidding.'

Fenwick shook his head. 'It's an easy $125,000. And there's this contract with a fruit juice outfit. They want your beaming face on their label, and they'll pay $75,000 more.'

'If we're making all this money, F.F., why don't I feel rich?'

Fenwick grinned at his number one client. 'You spend it real fast, son. Two new cars this year, and we'll be paying for the refurbishing of Court's Court for the next three years.'

'I thought it was a tax shelter.'

'Yeah. But they cost money, too.' Fenwick dug into his pockets and pulled out a crumpled envelope, covered with numbers. 'This year you'll hit the four million mark.'

'That's why I don't understand about Palermo.'

Fenwick pointed to a column of neatly printed figures. 'See that? Two million of this is the Grand Slam bonus. But you haven't won it yet. *That's* a cash flow problem, to the tune of thirty-nine thousand a month. That's what goes out.'

Koras shook his head. He was playing his heart out, pleasing the fans, taking home trophies, signing cheques. There was a studio apartment in Paris on the Ile St. Louis he'd had his eye on for three years, but Fenwick said they couldn't afford it. Koras didn't like to worry about money. He'd spent his first twenty-five years scrimping pennies. When you became a household name, you shouldn't have to sweat money. 'If I go to Palmero, I'll have to play Jackie Di Rocca in the finals. They throw salami at the outsider.'

Fenwick grinned. Di Rocca had cousins in Sicily, and they would control the atmosphere of the matches with their cat calls. 'Just think of the money.'

'I was counting on a week in Nice.'

'That reminds me we need to unload that villa.'

Koras stared at his manager. 'Are you telling me everything, F.F?'

'Just play Palermo. We'll make it.'

Just then, a marketing vice president from Laval Sportif came up to take Koras away, to meet some important people.

'In a minute,' Fenwick said.

The vice president backed off, chastened. Both men watched him go. At that moment, the Princess Athena entered the tent. Armando Reyes was with her, and also the girl with the book. The girl removed her dark glasses and surveyed the room. She had a long face, with deep set eyes and skin that seemed translucent despite her early summer tan. She was tall, Athena's height, but more slender. As he watched, she turned to Athena and whispered something. Athena laughed, and both women turned to look in Koras's direction. Koras excused himself and started for the girl, but was intercepted by the vice-president.

'You simply have to meet these people.'

While Koras chatted and shook hands with smiling buyers who congratulated him on the brilliance of his passing shots, the girl stood aside from the crowd, by the buffet, drinking champagne. Athena had been joined by Saadi, who wore a white suit and a flaming red tie. Jean-Alain, the reigning French movie star, sidled up to Koras, his eyes narrowed, his eyebrows arched, to make a wild prediction: 'You want to hear something?'

'From the mouths of the oracles?'

Jean-Alain was notorious for his interest in the Tarot, the Ouija board, clairvoyance, and other tools of the occult. He had a long, sad face that women found irresistible. His latest movie had been a French version of the H. Rider Haggard novel, *She*, where the central character gets burnt up in a tongue of living fire.

'They tell me that you will play the Yugoslav, Milovan Tigrid, in the final,' he said.

'Who are "they"?' Koras asked.

The actor smiled, enigmatically, and fluttered his eyes. Perhaps, at this very moment, he was communicating with an unseen spirit world. 'My Guardians, who else?'

'What will the score be?'

The eyes fluttered again. 'They also say someone will die.'

'Can they get more specific?'

'Someone close.' The eyes were really going now, the lids fluttering faster. His face was contorted. 'Someone who . . .' He paused, opening his eyes. 'No. They have gone.'

Koras handed him a glass of champagne. 'Here.'

The actor drank, stared at Koras. 'Well, how are you playing?' He seemed suddenly back to normal reality.

'Judson Garwood called it "surgical".'

'Ah, that one.' The actor moved close again. 'He has the Evil Eye.'

They were still discussing the tennis writer, Garwood, when Princess Athena found him. She wanted to introduce Koras to her cousin.

Walking across the pavilion, the Princess held his arm. 'You played brilliantly today.'

'And you, my love, are as sensual as ever.'

She squeezed his arm. 'Money does seem to agree with me.'

'Tell me you don't make love with him.'

She turned to look at Koras, smiling. 'How well you understand me, Pantakoras.'

The brunette was waiting, and as they were introduced, Koras had time to study her. She did not smile. Her blue-grey eyes were curious, cool, distant. Her look, a sweeping glance at the false gaiety of the Village, seemed disapproving. Perhaps she was a revolutionary.

'Pantakoras, this is my cousin, Laure Puget. Laure, this is Pantakoras Belynkas.'

'Hello.' They shook hands. Her hand was feminine, but rougher than he had expected.

'What is the book?'

A half-smile flickered across her features, then faded. 'Wallensborough. On Roman ruins.'

He didn't recognize the name.

'Laure is an archaeologist,' Athena said.

'You dig things up?'

'Yes.'

The conversation wasn't going well and Koras thought of the pretty girl from last night. She had been willing, and her willingness had allowed him to stay cool and detached. He had fought hard to become famous, and now that he was famous, he was accustomed to gushing admiration from pretty young women, if not outright hero-worship. Nothing like that was coming from this one. Watching Laure Puget, her erect back, the line of her tanned throat, he tried to remember where he had seen her before. Athena stepped away to talk to some people from Dallas.

'Have we met, mademoiselle?'

'Perhaps. I don't remember.'

The smile was gone altogether now. She spoke English with a husky French accent that gave her added sex appeal. As she stood there with her leather bag over her shoulder, the off-white dress making a pleasant contrast to the blue of her jacket, he knew he was taking her distance as a challenge. With her long face and strange eyes, she was not as beautiful as Athena, but she seemed deeper, more mysterious, perhaps more enduring.

'Your English is excellent.'

'Thank you. I studied in the States.'

'Oh? Where?'

'Los Angeles. At UCLA.'

He was about to ask her about Los Angeles when Athena rejoined them. For a moment, he listened to a story about the Dollmers from Dallas. The girl said nothing. Was that a chill he felt coming from her?

'Athena, I really must go,' the girl said. 'I have work to do.'

'Laure thinks we are very decadent, traipsing around the circuit.'

'She's got a point.'

The girl looked at him as she held out her hand. 'Goodbye.'

Athena invited him to a party later in the evening.

If he went, he might see Laure Puget again. 'I'll try.' Koras said goodbye and then watched the two women walk away. Nice hips on the girl, and sweet long legs.

A waiter passed with a tray of drinks and Koras asked him for a beer. Behind the waiter, a security guard carrying a sub-machine gun was surveying the guests.

Times were changing at Roland-Garros.

Someone came up behind him. 'Mr Belynkas. There's someone you have to meet.'

As he turned to shake hands and give a weary smile, Koras thought – well, if she wasn't available, there was always the willing Mlle Dumont, the Lady of the Peugoet.

But he admitted to himself Laure was far more intriguing.

Armando Reyes, ranked number twelve on the ATP computer, was about to fly through the roof. He'd climaxed three times, the last one bringing forth a scream, and was now winding toward a fourth. The woman was tireless. She rolled over on top of him, bringing him with her, still connected. He felt smothered, enveloped, enclosed by her flesh, her royal lust. She was a tall woman, statuesque, solid, regal, with a sweet smell that reminded him of springtime in Peru.

'Aiyee, Princess!'

'What is it?'

'Prepare yourself.'

They spoke in German, her language, or in Spanish, his language, or in English, which they had both learned in private schools in their respective countries. Sometimes, they spoke in French, the language of love.

The Princess laughed, a sound of triumph, a goddess of passion in the garden of love. She rose above him, a pulsing shadow, a pure Valkyrie out of a Wagnerian opera. He closed his eyes, feeling the power surge, the drive, the reach. She was whimpering now, begging, on the verge of release. What *was* in those red pills? He had watched Athena take two, then one more. How many could a person take?

'Ah, ah, Ah.'

'Yes. Holy mother! Si!'

'Ja. Ja. Jaaa!'

They soared together, toward the sun, toward a bright light inside their minds. He was Icarus, heading out, powerful wings pumping, eyes strong against the sun. The pills had brought his youth back. She was Aphrodite, Venus, Helen of Troy, Athena.

She came down before he did, sighing, snuggling into him like a peasant girl, not a princess. Armando loved these moments, so tender, where she seemed vulnerable. Clothes made the woman, but then again . . .

It was well after midnight at the Sofitel Hotel. Outside, traffic whirred through the Paris streets, towards the Seine, the Heliport, The Eiffel Tower. He had beaten Leroy, the French hope. Tomorrow afternoon, he had a semifinal match against Tigrid. Tigrid had beaten him on the slow clay in Rome, so there was reason to worry. If he took another pill, and then added a blue – what his brother's physician back in Peru prescribed for anxiety and stage fright – what would happen? Could he outlast his friend Milo? Could he go all the way to the top? What a surprise for the fans . . . the Sublime Peruvian triumphs in Paris.

'Was it good, my darling?' The Princess stirred.

'Marvelloso.' Reyes squeezed her shoulder. 'What are the contents of those pills?'

'I am not a chemist.'

'And you got them from Saadi?'

'From his desk, as I said.'

'Where did he get them?'

'He uses them when he sees his mistress. Sometimes, with the maid.'

Reyes laughed. He was an educated man, sophisticated, world weary. Life was full of ironies. 'Where can we obtain more?'

'From his desk. I counted over a dozen bottles. But we must be careful.I take three from each bottle.'

'It is too late in my life for being careful.'

'No.' She snuggled closer to him. 'Don't say that.'

Reyes was thirty-six that year, next to Tigrid the oldest player on the circuit. The family fortunes, which had once seemed to provide an endless flow of money, were dwindling. The OPEC ministers were to blame for the falling oil prices. The Americans and the Argentinians and the chicken marketeers of Latin America were to blame for the glut of beef on the market. In April, wholesale beef had fallen 8 cents in America. One could buy a sirloin for $2.55 a pound, prices from twenty years ago. The thought made Reyes ill. For twenty years, he had lived the high life, playing tennis, flying around the world in his private jet, falling in and out of love with women like the Princess. Now, the Reyes jet had been sold. And reports from his brother spoke of belt-tightening in the family business, of trimming the fat.

There was money enough for one more season on the circuit, May through the first week in September. After that, Reyes, would have to return home, to Lima. There would be no more tennis, no more late nights in hotels across the world, no more high life.

'What time is it?'

He checked the travel alarm with the luminous dial. 'Just after one.'

'What time is your match?'

'Two-ish. Unless almighty Clavier chooses to shift the times around. He has a soft heart for the women.'

'You should talk.' The Princess rolled away from him, stood up, and walked to the chair where she had folded her clothes, neatly, like a professional. She began to dress.

'Must you go?'

She spoke without looking at him. 'I must, dearest. Saadi will be returning.'

'I like waking up with you.'

'Yes. That is sweet.'

'When will this business be over with Saadi?'

She continued dressing. 'I am not certain. He gives me what I want.'

'You want to marry the bugger, don't you?'

'Not want to, dearest. Need to.' She walked into the bathroom and turned on the light.

Reyes sat up against the pillows. The dizziness that had plagued him for most of last year had gone away, perhaps because of Saadi's pills. He felt marvellous. It was going to be a magnificent summer season. He wondered what the day would bring. After a few moments, he walked naked to the bathroom, to stand in the doorway, where the Princess was putting the finishing touches to her make-up. She wore the blue cocktail dress from her dinner party. He wondered where she got her awesome energy.

The Princess turned from the mirror, to see that Saadi's pills were working. Armando was ready for love.

'Has Saadi signed Polak yet?' he asked.

'No. They spoke twice today. Saadi was very persuasive.'

'Does anyone else know?'

'No. It is an industry secret.'

Armando stepped into the bathroom and stroked Athena's buttock. 'I heard rumours that Saadi was working with some Albanians. Perhaps that's where the drug came from.'

Athena looked at Reyes in the mirror. 'Saadi is the son of a sheik. He has connections with anyone you want.' She finished, turned her head for a profile check. She was thirty that year, and more beautiful than ever, or so said the tabloid newspapers. Athena's mother, Helga von Heidelberg, had elected to have cosmetic surgery at the age of forty-two, shortly after she married her fifth husband.

Even in this horrid hotel light her rich blonde hair looked magnificent. She was a beautiful woman, with the confidence of a top fashion model. The abundant hair was one of her best features.

'I must go, darling. Do have good luck against Milo.'

'You sound as if you want us both to win.'

'Milo is a dear friend.'

'And I? What am I?'

She kissed him on the mouth, pressing her lips down on his. 'You are my dearest friend.'

'That's what Muriel calls me. Her dearest friend.'

Athena grabbed his arm. 'Be careful of little Muriel.'

Armando smiled. He loved making women jealous. 'Now who's acting possessive?'

'A woman has more reason than a man.'

'Ho. Spoken like a Princess.'

'Is Muriel French?'

'Belgian. From Brussels.'

Athena chucked him under the chin, stepped away. Playtime was over. 'Good luck against Tigrid. Really.'

'Thank you, my dear.' He held out the pills. 'You have given me all the luck I need.'

CHAPTER THREE

The fans arrived early for the first match of the women's semifinals, which had all the appearance of an American national tournament. Three of the players were from the States. Tania Pikeste, the little Rumanian player who had stolen the hearts of spectators in Paris, stood alone against the North Atlantic onslaught. The French newspapers had nicknamed her 'the fairy of the courts' and 'The Comaneci of tennis,' titles which had been unanimously accepted by the international press covering the tournament.

Evelyne Dumont parked the Peugeot 604 in the lot reserved for players and officials. Early that morning, she had picked Koras up at his hotel and had driven him to Bagatelle, where she had watched him training.

For an hour, Koras had warmed up with his coach, Will Channer. They worked the hardest on his serve, pounding ball after ball, aiming at tennis ball cans placed strategically in one corner or the other of the service court, forcing ballboys to replenish the bucket without respite. As their legs pumped tirelessly around the court, Koras never stopped, never hesitated. He served to the right court, then to the left, varying the angles, alternating the spin, shaving the net. He perfected his stroke by replacing the empty cans with a small circle of white pasteboard, five inches in diameter. Evelyne was amazed that the ball made contact with the targets so frequently. The coach, a lean man in a white jogging suit, drove Koras mercilessly. Near the end of the workout, Channer had made his pupil serve blindfolded. As Koras served, Channer would call out where the ball had landed: 'Three inches to the left, two inches behind. That one was five inches to the right, and level with the target.' And then, when Koras adjusted, the coach would grin and say 'Bingo!' And Evelyne would applaud.

After an hour, Koras ripped off the blindfold. 'Finished!' he said. 'And time for breakfast.' He looked up at Evelyne and she nodded.

'You need another ten,' Channer insisted.

'No. I am finished.'

Koras walked off the court, to where his charming chauffeur waited. With the light playing in her blonde hair, she suddenly seemed very attractive. He formalized his invitation for brunch.

Delighted, Evelyne slid behind the wheel, taking advantage of the movement to reveal a lovely expanse of bronze thigh. Bending forward to start the engine, Koras caught a glimpse of her breasts through her gaping shirt, her nipples hardened by the excitement of being seen and allowing herself to be seen. Koras looked at her steadily. She was pretty, but she seemed a little desperate. He flicked on the radio, Evelyne watching him.

He stopped the dial at France Musique, the classical music station. For some reason, the music made him think of Laure Puget.

'A lot of men would envy me,' he said.

'For the ride in the car?'

'For the ride with the chauffeur.'

She liked that. 'Where shall we breakfast?'

'That I leave to the expert.'

She smiled. 'I know just the place.'

The Peugeot slid smoothly along the tree-lined street. Koras sat back against the seat, letting the music fill his ears, to think about his next match, a semifinal against Mikhail Polak.

On the day of the most important semifinal in his long career, Armando Reyes woke at mid-morning, the scent of Athena still with him. He could still sense the shape of her body, the maddening pressures, the sheen of her long blonde hair. Years ago, he had fallen in love with Athena, when she was younger and wilder and on the rebound from Koras. This time, they were both older, and his feelings for her were far more intense, far more real. Why did one have to become older to feel with such depth? It seemed unfair, and last night, with the new strength from the pills, he had been on the verge of asking her to marry him, a sure sign that he was experiencing a new vulnerability. It would have been a wasted question. If she married anyone, she would marry Saadi, who had endless petro-dollars stored away in vaults in London, Zurich, New York, Tokyo, Hong Kong, and Singapore.

What could they do about Saadi?

Armando phoned down for coffee, noting that service the world over seemed slower, the servants more surly, when one ran short of money. Hotel employees had a built-in radar detector that told them who was tipping lavishly and who was not. While he waited for the coffee, Armando took a long hot shower. He would take the pills an hour before his match. He had the mix figured out by now. Four of the reds, for energy. Two of the blues, for stability and a temporary end to stage fright.

He finished his shower. The coffee had not yet arrived. Staring at the small suite, he phoned down again. Oui, monsieur, the coffee was on its way. Compared to last year's huge suite, his present room at the Sofitel seemed confining. He wondered how many people noticed.

Coffee arrived while he was reading the account of yesterday's matches by the London columnist, David Kollmore. Kollmore's writing was typically English, not a spare adjective anywhere. Among the sports writers, Armando preferred the work of Judson Garwood, the American, who called Armando 'the dark horse of Lima.' Now that phrase, *el caballo de Lima*, had a particularly nice ring to it.

The surprise visitor arrived while Armando was drinking his second cup of coffee. There was a knock on the door, and he thought perhaps it was Athena, coming back to console him for leaving last night. Muriel wasn't due until noon. They were driving to Roland-Garros in her BMW Alpina. When he squinted through the security peephole, Armando was surprised to see Jack Di Rocca standing there. Di Rocca, who had lost in the quarters, wore a coat and tie.

Di Rocca was the black sheep of professional tennis. Born in a New York slum, he had grown up hitting balls against the side of a derelict building next to the one he lived in with his mother and two sisters. Di Rocca's father had abandoned the family the year Jack was born and had not been heard from since.

Di Rocca's obsession with the tennis racket had begun the day he stole one from a department store. Di Rocca knew baseball, soccer, basketball. Tennis was mystery turf, a country club world.

While teaching himself the rudiments of tennis on a cracked concrete court with a neighbourhood parish priest, Di Rocca was also a member of the Devil's Rebels, a fearsome Bronx gang noted for hot-wiring late model cars, which they sold to a middleman, who sold them in turn to a strip shop, where they were cannibalized for parts. At sixteen, he had been arrested for armed robbery of a gas station in Brooklyn. The cash drawer had held only twenty-four dollars, but the station attendant had given evidence, in revenge for the beating he had suffered during the holdup. Di Rocca ended up in prison, with a three-year sentence.

When Di Rocca entered prison in January, he took with him all his possessions – two tennis rackets and a sports bag containing odds and ends of tennis gear. He stayed sane by hitting balls against a concrete wall.

He got his chance when a tournament was organized between the prisoners from different penitentiaries. The trophy was to be presented by Walter Tray, the first American black player to reach world class. Tray would play an exhibition against the winner.

Di Rocca.

In the exhibition, Tray managed to win only after three gruelling sets, two hours and twenty-one minutes.

From the stands reserved for relatives and friends, a moon-faced man with narrow Aztec eyes studied Di Rocca's moves. After the match, he introduced himself to Di Rocca as Paco Ortega. Ortega, who had been a circuit player himself, was in the prison visiting a cousin. His business was managing professional tennis players. He liked what he saw in Di Rocca – hunger, ambition, a killer instinct that kept him going – so the next day he obtained a permit to visit. He and Di Rocca talked for a long time.

'In four years, if you work, you'll make the Top Ten.'

'In another month, I'll rot in this hole.'

'Not if you follow my advice.'

'What's that?'

'Keep hitting.' Ortega stood, ready to leave. 'My lawyer will contact you. We'll start working on parole, right now.'

Six months later, Di Rocca was out on parole. Ortega wisely started him out in the minor leagues, playing local tournaments in Texas, Arizona, New Mexico, California, Florida. In four years, he had not yet made the Top Ten, but he was ready for Europe, where he discovered his game was meant for clay. His first big win came at the age of twenty-eight, in Monte Carlo, on a blustery day in November. His best day was the day he handed a cheque for a thousand dollars in damages to the owner of the gas station. That was a triumph. Di Rocca had never been great. This year, he was number nine on the ATP compuer and he had lost in the quarters to Mikhail Polak.

Now he stood in the hotel room of Armando Reyes. Di Rocca had a deal for the Peruvian.

Armando checked the time. Half-past eleven. His match began at two. He knew Di Rocca was aware of the schedule.

Di Rocca walked to the window, stared out, toward the Bois de Boulogne. 'You alone?'

'Si. Would you like coffee?'

Di Rocca sat. 'This won't take long.'

'Too bad you lost in the quarters.'

'I played okay. Polak was in the Zone again.' Di Rocca crossed his legs. 'You're playing tough yourself. You thinking of going all the way?'

'It has been a long time between wins.' Armando poured fresh coffee, added warm milk, two cubes of sugar. 'I need a win. So does my brother.'

Di Rocca leaned closer. 'Armando. I got friends in New York would like to see you lose.'

Armando smiled. 'Really? I have friends in Lima who would like to see me win. The President of Peru, he would like it, for example.'

Di Rocca nodded, but he was not impressed. 'These friends in New York, they're willing to pay you quite a bit. To lose, I mean.'

Armando took another look at Di Rocca, and then used an American expression. 'Get serious.'

Di Rocca nodded. His thick eyebrows made him look like a forest creature. 'I am. And they are.'

'Who are these people?'

'Just . . . friends. Acquaintances. Guys I grew up with, did business with. You wouldn't recognize any names, if I told you.'

Armando set the coffee cup down. He felt the raw edge of fear. 'Why me, Jack?'

Di Rocca shrugged. 'They want Tigrid to get through. He's a long shot, longer than you.'

'What about the final?'

Di Rocca grinned. 'That's our business. What we want from you is to lose today.'

'I might lose anyway, against Tigrid.'

'Call this insurance. Armando. Clay's your surface. You're playing over your head. There's a boatload of money coming in from South America and Mexico. Before your fourth round win, you were 35 to 1. Now you're 6 to 1.'

Armando understood. 'Your people in New York, they bet against Armando?'

'That's right. And for Tigrid.'

Armando set the coffee cup down. It was unbelievable. 'They are willing to pay?'

'Fifty grand, to go under in the fourth set.' Di Rocca's face told Armando they knew he was having money problems. Fifty thousand would keep him on the circuit another three or four months. This life style could continue. If he stretched the money, and made another semifinal or two, he would have another year in bed, with the Princess.

'The fourth set?' Armando's mind was spinning. He was playing the best tennis of his career, and some small-minded criminals from New York City wanted him to throw the match.

'Yeah.'

The room was quiet. Armando stood up, trembling. 'Tell your friends . . .' He stopped, furious. The blood rushing to his face had made his cheeks red beneath the tan. He felt a tiny pain, deep in his chest, disturbing. 'How do I contact them?'

'Through me. They'll want to know before the match begins.'

'I have time?'

'Until ninety minutes before the match starts.'

Armando walked to the door, opened it for Di Rocca. 'They are the same people who bet on the baseball? The football?'

Di Rocca nodded.

'And now, the tennis?'

'This is a trial run, to see how it goes.'

'If they can buy me, you mean?'

'Part of the test.'

'And others?'

'Just let me know, amigo.'

Armando nodded, but said nothing. Di Rocca walked into the corridor. He left without shaking hands.

Armando stood in the doorway, watching him move down the corridor. Fifty thousand dollars would not stretch far enough. They were paupers, coming to him for so little. And why was he standing here, considering the offer? The pain in his chest came again, a tiny pin-prick. He tried to think. What would happen next year? No one knew. If the cattle herds dwindled, beef might soar. OPEC might collapse. He could use the money to buy himself some time. He loved this live, travelling, the women.

But a stinking fifty thousand!

Did he have a real chance at the title? Or was he only shouting in the wind? He had a chance of beating Tigrid, but probably not Koras, in the final.

Of one thing he was certain. He was not afraid of these faceless men in New York, Di Rocca's friends. As he closed the door, his beautiful morning seemed ugly.

Armando walked into his bedroom closet and took down a black leather bag. Inside were seven phials of pills. Two . . . no, three of the blues. Four of the reds. He walked into the bathroom, stared at his face in the mirror. Another chest pain came, sharp, more bothersome than the last. He swallowed a blue pill, for his anxiety. He followed the blue with three calciums, to calm the nerves, and two large Vitamin Cs, for the adrenals, and then a Vitamin E, for oxygen in the blood. Gradually, the chest pain had eased, making him think it was a case of nerves. He knew now why he was thinking of marriage. Where was Athena now that he needed her?

On the sunny terrace above the courts, Princess Athena introduced Koras to Saadi, her lover. Koras wore a green tracksuit, new from Laval Sportif. Saadi, as usual, was dressed in white, with a bright red necktie. Koras had heard of Saadi, but this was the first time they had been introduced. As they shook hands, it was clear from Saadi's demeanour that he was jealous of all Athena's old lovers.

'Mr Belynkas, I still remember your first title, in Rome, back in 1975, wasn't it?'

'Paris, a year earlier.'

'Oh?'

Koras looked directly at the Princess. 'My win in Paris brought me an invitation to Monte Carlo. And that's where I met your beautiful companion.'

'Pantakoras,' she said. 'You love the past far too much.'

Saadi's smile tightened across his dark face. He was tall for an Arab, but he looked soft, out of shape. 'Singles is far more important. No one remembers who won the doubles.'

'You do, dear,' Athena said. 'Abdul is a walking tennis encyclopaedia.'

'Amazing,' Koras said.

The Princess looked away from the men and swept the terrace, to see whom she knew was there. Her dress was white, a creation from Yves St Laurent, with a manageable neckline and long sleeves that called attention to her hands, which were lovely. 'Would you get me a champagne, darling.'

'I think,' Saadi said, 'that it is time to return to the matches. Coming?'

'In a moment, dear.'

Saadi left them and walked hurriedly out of the pavilion. Athena took Koras by the arm. 'Well, what do you think?'

'A jealous man. He's King Farouk. He wants you to become his Rita Hayworth.'

Athena laughed. 'There is small chance of that.'

'I was wondering, just how does all that money smell?'

The Princess put a hand on his arm. Her eyes were slightly sunken today, and a wisp of golden hair had come undone and now trailed down her left ear, toward her mouth. 'Oh, Pantakoras. What good times we had, you and I . . .'

Koras remembered the good times, but he did not think they outweighed the bad. He remembered the first time he had seen her, stepping out of a Mercedes limousine in front of the Casino, all sun-rinsed hair and bronzed skin. He'd stared at her, and she had brushed by him, letting her eyes slide away, like a Princess looking past the stable boy. Koras was a poor kid from Brooklyn, out to carve a name for himself in the world of professional tennis. That goal looked a long way off. But he and Milo had just made $200 apiece, plus expenses, for winning the French National Doubles title. If they won here, at Monte Carlo, they'd make $500 apiece. In those days, tennis was dominated by 'shamateurism,' an outworn philosophy that hurt the players. In shamateurism, if you were lucky, and if you had crowd appeal, you got paid under the table.

How could that compete with the Princess and her diamonds?

She had been unattainable, unreachable. At a cocktail party in the Royal Palace, Koras managed a dance with Athena. She mocked him with her eyes, tantalized him with her smile. Her body next to his trembling hand was sensual, firm yet yielding. He knew some French, but he didn't know how to talk to a Princess. Her hip moved beneath his hand. She wore a low-cut dress, yet he was afraid to look down, for fear that she would vanish in a puff of smoke. She was eighteen, ripe. Koras was twenty-two, and broke.

He had decided to take a chance, follow his instincts, try telling the truth. 'You know what you smell like?'

'No.' Sardonic eyes, smokey and smirky. 'Tell me, Mr Pantakoras.

'You smell like . . . fresh baked bread. In the morning. While they are washing the streets.'

Her sky blue eyes had narrowed. 'Summer or winter?'

'Summer.'

She had laughed, throwing her head back, aristocracy on wanton display. Koras had been surprised. They danced into the shadow of a potted palm, beyond the eyes of the other guests. She moved close, put her mouth up against his ear, and sank her teeth into his earlobe. Her teeth were sharp, and for a mad moment he thought of the chipmunks in the movie, *Cinderella*.

'*Cinderella*,' he said.

'I beg your pardon.' She spoke while still biting his ear.

'Chipmunks. In the movie. I don't remember their names.'

This made her laugh even more, made her body shake. They were reaching out now, touching in more than just a physical sense. He couldn't believe she would be so friendly. That night, she came to his room. 'And you not even in the Top Ten,' she said.

'But I will be.'

'I know.'

Naked, she had slid between the sheets.

They made good copy, the Lithuanian athlete and the Austrian Princess. Athena taught him about sex, art, novels, poetry, Vivaldi, Mozart, the best champagne, how to live in the moment, how to spend money, a life beyond the edge of worry.

He had tried to teach her about honour and pride and tenacity. Athena didn't mind sweating, but she hated to practise. If she couldn't learn it easily, or didn't already know it, she'd drift off, or call to someone to bring her a drink. She'd played tennis at her girls' school in Switzerland and even amazed the fans at the Foro Italico when she was fifteen, by defeating Adrianna Pardona, an Italian champion. When urged, the Princess would sometimes still take the court for a celebrity exhibition.

So Koras and Athena were together for part of a season, an item for the newspapers, and then they drifted apart. The Princess spent money with abandon, while Koras had to pinch pennies. For the next year, he saw her around the circuit, while she travelled with Armando Reyes, a Peruvian who kept cars in every major city on the tennis circuit. Koras decided having lots of cars was an idea with merit.

When Koras won his first major singles title, at Wimbledon, Athena reappeared in Koras's life as if by magic, looking wiser, more beautiful, more mature. She seemed to thrive on love affairs. After Armando, there had been an Italian duke, an Austrian baron, an English country squire named Teddy, and a short-lived marriage to a manufacturer of munitions from Milano.

Athena convinced Koras to buy a villa in Nice. A down-payment of $750,000, cash, payments of $33,000 a month, the deal made with a banker she knew, in Zurich. Today, according to Fenwick, they were still losing money on the villa. Athena had helped him pick out the cars, so he could follow in Armando's footsteps – two Mercedes, two Rolls Royces, one Jaguar, one BMW, one vintage Volvo – stashed in seven different cities across the world. Only two were left now. Koras One: New York, which he kept in Paris. And Koras Two: New York, which he kept in the garage at Westhampton.

'Will you marry this one?' Koras asked.

She smiled. 'What do you care?'

'I am jealous of every man you look at.'

She laughed, throwing her head back to show her lovely throat. 'Pantakoras, you are always a devil.'

He asked her what he really wanted to know. 'Tell me about Laure Puget.'

'Why?' Athena's eyes twinkled.

'I knew you had lots of cousins. I didn't know you had any who could read.'

'Awful man!' She pummelled his chest.

Koras waited, Athena looked around at the Parisian crowd. Mikhail Polak was at the bar with his new wife, the American girl from Chicago. 'First,' she said, 'and this is important, she is young.' The Princess sighed with recollections of her own wild youth. 'That means she can eat whatever she wishes, and does not get fat. She wears sensible clothes. She prefers not to dance, yet she can dance all night. She has one tiny laugh line, here, at the corner of her mouth. Otherwise, her skin is perfection itself. Her greatest expense is books, pencils, papers, subscriptions to dry scholarly journals. She reads, constantly, probing books for the secrets of life. Her greatest desire is a computer, from America.'

'From what I know of the von Heidelbergs, she sounds like a very distant cousin.'

'Mummy adores Laure. She feels Laure will help me contain myself.'

Koras laughed. 'She'll need some magic for that.'

'She studies some magic.'

'Oh?'

'Um. She searches for a connection between the Holy Grail and Vercingetorix.'

'The Hero of Gaul?' Koras had not attended college, but he knew a smattering of this and that about Roman history.

'Um, yes.' Athena swivelled to speak to a French tennis official, Alain Clavier, head of the federation. The white dress swirled about her legs, and Koras watched, enjoying the show. The Princess possessed perfect balance, and he had always regretted that she had not continued playing tournament tennis. It would have given her more reality. Now, flirting was her sport.

'See you later.'

Athena broke off talking with Clavier to pluck Koras by the sleeve. 'Where are you going?'

'I feel restless. Thought I'd do a quick jog, just to stay loose.'

'Where?'

'In the Fleuriste Municipal. The air there is so healthy.'

'You are a fanatic.'

Koras said goodbye to Athena and Clavier and walked out of the pavilion.

When Saadi arrived at his box, followed by a waiter carrying a magnum of iced Chardonnay, Laure was sitting alone, enjoying the sun. The women's semifinal was dead even, a set all, three games apiece. Princess

Athena was nowhere to be seen. Laure was reading when Saadi joined her.

'Ah, Mlle Laure. I was hoping to find you here.'

He sat down, pulled his chair close. Laure adjusted the hem of her dress. 'Where is Athena?'

'I left her in the pavilion, with some admirers. Would you like some wine?'

It was her favourite. 'Yes. Please.'

They concentrated on the match while the waiter opened the wine. When the cork was out, Saadi sampled it, then nodded to the waiter, who filled both glasses. Saadi touched his glass to Laure's. 'To the project.'

'Yes. To the project.'

Saadi was sitting close and Laure could feel the heat from his body. She smelled sweat mixed with expensive cologne. She wondered how Athena felt, making love to him.

'I should like to invite you to our yacht,' he said. 'When the matches are finished.'

'Thank you. But I must go to Dijon. They are expecting me.'

He put a hand on her shoulder. 'I would consider it a special favour if you were to accompany us.' The hand felt like a claw. 'There will be people – your own age, of course. Jean-Francois. The Polaks. Perhaps the young American, Dumbo Cooper.'

'Thank you.' She moved away from his hand, leaning until his arm was straight and he was forced to let go. 'Perhaps another time.'

Saadi moved his chair closer. He was acting strangely. 'Tomorrow I must drive to Le Havre. Perhaps you would like to accompany me.'

'No.'

She felt trapped. Why was he doing this?

'We could make a day of it. A picnic lunch. A walk by the river.'

Laure stood up, quickly. 'Pardon me. I must go.'

He blocked her way. At the same time, spectators higher up hissed at her, whispered for her to sit down.

'They are playing a point,' Saadi scolded. 'You should wait until the changeover between sets.'

Laure sat down. The trapped feeling would not go away. Saadi patted her hand.

'How is the project going?' he asked.

'Fine. They appreciate the money you've provided.'

She felt his fingers close on her hand. 'And do you?'

'I? Of course.'

'You have a strange way of communicating your appreciation.'

His eyes bored into hers. Where was Athena?

'What would you want of me, m'sieu?'

'Have I told you about Clothilde?'

'Clothilde who?'

'Clothilde le Gros. She was my father's mistress. You remind me of her. In the most remarkable way.'

Enough. Laure tore her hand free and jumped up. Her sudden, awkward exit spoiled a point for the spectators. More hisses rained down, but she didn't care. A spectator swore at her; someone told her to sit down. A security guard with a severe look blocked her way. Laure stopped, trembling, to wait until the point was over, then hurried out of the stadium. She was breathing hard. The leather shoulder bag flopped against her hip and she was not aware that she clutched her book in one hand until her fingers began to hurt. She knew that Saadi could stop the flow of money at any time. It would be her fault, and now she started to cry.

Laure waited for a break in the traffic and then she trotted across the street to the cool sanctuary of the Fleuriste Municipal, a timeless green world. Except for a few old gentlemen escaping the exhaust fumes from the streets, the vast public greenhouse was deserted.

Breathing the sweet air, Laure walked to the largest greenhouse. Still trembling, she sat down on an iron chair, grateful to be alone. In here, it felt like a peaceful womb, green and shadowy. She opened her book, but the words blurred. It was time to leave Paris, to get away from Saadi somehow and return to Alesia, where she had her work. If her instincts were right about him, the money would dry up soon enough. It was clear that he had compromised her terribly, and she felt like a fool for not having seen the signals sooner.

What would she tell her colleague, Jean-Luc, at the excavation?

Laure opened her book and forced herself to read. She was deep into a chapter on the speech of Critognatus, a noble Avernian who advised the entrapped Gauls at Alesia to feed on the flesh of the weak and the infirm. Winter was approaching, Critognatus reasoned. If only the Gauls could hold out, snow would drive the Romans away. She had read the speech before, but today the vision of cannibalization brought tears to her eyes. She did not hear the footsteps until they stopped, in front of her.

Laure left her book and looked up. Mr Belynkas stood there. He wore a forest green tracksuit with three white stripes along the sleeves, and matching stripes along the trousers. His blue eyes danced sardonically. His blond hair was wet around the forehead, as if he had been running.

She was surprised to see him. His green suit matched the green of the plants inside the Fleuriste Municipal. 'Ah, Miss Puget.'

His smile, suggestive of vast experience in the world of the jet set, made her uncomfortable. Where was the young man with the innocent face who had given her that tennis lesson so long ago? 'Hello. Where did you come from?'

He sat down, but changed the subject. 'What are you reading?'

'A monograph on Critognatus.'

Koras was studying her face. Had the tears made her eyes red? 'It must be a very moving book.'

She brushed the tears away from her cheeks. 'Yes.'

'Have you been at the matches?'

She thought of Saadi's advances. 'For a while.'

'Who was winning?'

She shook her head. 'I didn't even know who was playing.'

Koras laughed. 'I like that. Come and have a coffee.'

'I cannot.'

'Why?'

'I am leaving Paris.'

'Really? When?'

'Today.'

'It's a little sudden, isn't it?'

'Yes. But it's important that I get back.'

'The lure of the past.'

'Yes.'

His voice was full of playful confidence. She was sure he had used the same argument, the same tone of voice, with many women.

'How can I persuade you to stay? You must watch me play in the semifinals.'

'I watched you play against Terry Laville.'

'What did you think?'

She looked into Koras's blue eyes. 'Does he get angry often?'

'Only when I beat him in front of fifteen thousand fans.'

Laure sensed there was more. 'You seem so confident here. And out there. Don't you ever have bad moments, Mr Belynkas?' 'Oh, yes, many. Before the match, I am nervous about my knee. During the match, I worry whether it will carry me or not. After the match, the knee hurts.'

He was smiling, but the seriousness in his eyes told her he had an enemy within his body. Suddenly, in that moment, he seemed less a golden gladiator, a little more vulnerable. 'You make it sound painful.'

'I'm trying to get your sympathy.'

His offhand comment spoiled the moment. Laure snapped her book closed and stood up. 'Goodbye, Mr Belynkas.'

She started out of the Fleuriste Municipal and Koras walked along with her. 'Let me buy you a drink.'

'Sorry.' She thought of where she would go, of having to explain why there would be no more money for the excavation. For a moment, she thought of going back to Saadi, begging. Or to Athena – but it was too humiliating. So many people depended on that money to continue their work. And it was valuable work, full of promise and meaning. The man walking beside her only reminded her of the frivolity of these idle rich.

'Did I say something wrong?'

'No. Not at all.'

They had reached the sidewalk. A cruising taxi passed. Laure waved at it, then watched it continue on up the street. She looked around for another.

'Something is wrong.' He put a hand on her arm and she looked up, seeing again the sadness in his eyes.

'I'm sorry. It's got nothing to do with you.'

'Let me see you again.'

A taxi had spotted her and was drifting to the curb. A shiver went through her and for some reason she wanted to taunt this famous man. Or test him, perhaps. 'All right. One drink.'

His faced brightened. 'When and where?'

The taxi had stopped, purring impatiently. 'Next week. At our excavation site.'

'Where's that?'

'Alesia. Near Dijon.'

He laughed shortly. 'That's a long way to go for a drink.'

She opened the door and got into the taxi. Her skirt rode up and Mr Belynkas looked at her legs.

'How will I find you?'

'From Dijon, you go north, toward Alise Sainte Reine.'

'You are a complete mystery, Mlle Puget.'

Leaning forward, Laure told the driver to take her to the Hotel Paladin. Koras stepped away from the taxi as it pulled away. He was still standing there on the curb when the taxi turned a corner. She wondered how many women he had known. Perhaps, one day, she would ask Athena.

CHAPTER FOUR

The telephone.

A young man in white trousers and a red Lacoste shirt picked up the receiver and listened calmly. 'I'll get him for you.' Placing his hand over the mouthpiece, he called: 'It's Katignon on the line.'

Alain Clavier, president of the French and also of the International Tennis Federation, tightened the knot of his navy blue tie. It was decorated with many little elephants. When he had been elected for the first time to the presidency, he had declared in his inaugural speech: 'The International Federation is much like a horde of elephants; slow to get going, but once it is started, impossible to stop.' The elephant had become his mascot, the emblem on his tie, and principal decorative symbol in Monsieur le President's office.

His desk was a battlefield. On it, Clavier had lined up a hundred elephants of all shape and sizes. Unavoidably, he had been nicknamed Hannibal, by virtue perhaps of his strategic talents. Clavier was flattered by the analogy. After all, Hannibal was surely the greatest general in history, and in order to win this tennis war, he had to be both soldier and politician.

'Katignon,' repeated the young secretary.

'The Prime Minister?'

'I don't know, sir, they didn't make it clear.'

Clavier smiled. For fifteen days every year during the spring he became one of the most sought-after notables in France. Public officials and people in power hung on his telephone lines, throwing their rank to the winds as they pleaded for seats in the main stand, or for boxes, or for just a modest seat, high up the *Cour Centrale*. Clavier could not please everyone. He was indifferent to political conflict. His only concern was for the protection and perpetuation of the sport. When he gave away a seat at Roland-Garros, he made a pact. He always achieved some bit of influence that would one day serve the game of tennis.

Clavier took the telephone.

'There are other calls coming through –'

'Let them wait.'

Clavier turned his attention to the Minister. 'Clavier here.'

'This is Katignon,' the voice said. 'How are things going at the tennis?' Katignon was the Prime Minister's cabinet secretary, one of the most important posts in France.

'Fine. Everything goes well, thank you.' Clavier waited. There was always this normal show of interest in the sport.

'The Prime Minister asked me to convey his regrets, but he is unable to attend the finals on Sunday.'

'How disappointing.'

'He asked me to inform you, he'll be in London for the summit. His agenda is more crowded than we had thought.'

'I am sorry. But then the interests of the country come first.'

'Naturally, I'm accompanying the Prime Minister.' A pause. The request was about to come. 'My daughter, you know, is mad about tennis. She spends her days in front of the television when she should be preparing for her exams. She has an autograph from the Canadian, Laville. And from Armando Reyes, the South American. And I was thinking, wondering, if perhaps you might see your way clear to . . .'

'Of course,' Clavier said. 'But not in the main stand.'

'Anything. That will be fine.'

'I'll have three tickets sent to you.'

'They'll be delighted, thank you.'

'Yes. I must ring off now. Someone is waiting on the other line.' He hung up. 'Who is next?' he asked his secretary.

It was the Minister of Sport, a friend of Clavier's from the early days at the Ecole. The two men talked for a while, evoking memories of former tournaments, champions long gone. Clavier was promising places for five of the Minister's friends in boxes booked by advertisers, when there was a knock at the door.

Archer Bell, full of furious energy, barged uninvited into the room. Clavier rang off and looked up from his work. Bell managed Terry Laville and Dumbo Cooper. His chief rival was the Texan, Frank Fenwick, who managed Koras, Tigrid, and Polak. Mercenary and impulsive, Bell had been labelled 'green thumb' by the tennis writers, mainly for his cultivation of the most ruthless financial tactics to enrich the careers of his players. 'Alain, I need a minute.'

'All right.' Clavier knew Archer Bell would take more than a minute.

'I'll get to the point, Alain. I think Tigrid should be disqualified, before he screws up another tournament. He's an embarrassment to the whole circuit. At this stage in the competition, you can't keep letting him pull that crap and still play.'

Clavier had heard these arguments before, but he preferred to stay above them, in his Olympian post of command. There were people to handle such matters.

'He was fined,' Clavier said. 'After that he calmed down, so the umpire ruled that the match was in order.'

'You need to intervene personally, Alain. The man's a goddamn menace to the game.'

Clavier knew that Bell wanted to give his own players every advantage. 'I have confidence in my staff, Archer.'

Bell took out a cigar which he lit with a gas lighter shaped like a storage tank, bearing the logo of a petrol company which sponsored his basketball team, the Chicago Crocodiles.

'He still shouldn't be out there, in that semi.'

Clavier stood. 'Aren't you being just a little prejudicial, because your man lost? There is no question that a computerized version would have had Dumbo Cooper beating Tigrid. But the clay beat your man, and Tigrid, like most Europeans, is a past master at clay.'

Bell sighed. 'Jesus. Where's Mama Lorraine when we need her'

Lorraine was Dumbo's mother. She had a habit of travelling with her son around the circuit, and letting her influence be felt. Circuit gossipers said that Lorraine had kept her 24-year-old son at the same age – thirteen and a half – for the last decade.

'I spoke with Mrs Cooper before she left Paris. There is some vast financial scheme in New York, real estate, I think, that demanded her attention,' Clavier said.

'I don't know why I even mentioned her. I never trust a woman with money.'

'Yes. But Dumbo does.'

'Poor Dumbo.'

Bell laughed and Clavier joined in, dissipating the flickers of annoyance between the two tennis impresarios. Clavier poured two glasses of Bordeaux. The two men toasted.

'To the game.'

'Yes. To the lovely, beautiful game.'

Armando Reyes rode to Stade Roland-Garros with Muriel in her red BMW Alpina. Today, she looked very beautiful, in a white dress that displayed her figure to perfection. As she drove, Armando admired her hands, with the long tapering fingers.

Their conversation was friendly without being sexual. Armando was distracted. He could not keep his mind off the visit from Di Rocca.

It was just before one o'clock when Muriel parked the Alpina in the reserved zone, near the Suzanne Lenglen gate. She held Armando's arm as they walked past the security guards into the stadium. Di Rocca, wearing a blue summer suit, was waiting outside the door to the dressing room. Armando introduced Muriel, and then asked to be left alone, so he could speak to Di Rocca for a moment. When she was out of earshot, he turned to Di Rocca. He had a painful headache. This was the worst moment of his life.

'All right,' he said, his voice choked. 'I shall do as you say.'

Di Rocca answered with a knowing smile. 'Hey.' He grabbed Armando's hand. 'You won't be sorry.'

'I am already sorry. Where is the money?'

Di Rocca took his arm and pulled him around a corner, then handed him an envelope, which Armando dropped into his tennis bag. 'Half now. Half when the match is over.'

'You are the incarnation of Satan,' Armando said, and walked off, carrying twenty-five thousand dollars.

As she left the two men, Muriel knew something was terribly wrong. During the ride from the Sofitel to the stadium, Armando's face had been pale and he seemed to be short of breath. He was distracted, and his conversation, usually so witty and brilliant, was dull. When she had commented on it, his reply had been curt. 'I didn't get much sleep.'

Now, at the corner of the stadium, Muriel paused to look back. Di Rocca was talking earnestly to Armando, who seemed to be leaning against the wall for support. Without really thinking about it, Muriel chose the mini camera rather than her Hasselblad. She brought the mini out of her purse and pressed the red release button. The two men stood in grey shadow and she could have used the built-in flash. But something told her this particular shot should be taken discreetly.

The phone kept ringing. As they were calls from important people,

Clavier had to answer. Archer Bell flipped through some copies of *Racket World* while he waited for the matches to start. At two o'clock, Milo Tigrid and Armando Reyes walked onto the *Cour Centrale* for their semifinal. Because Clavier was still on the phone, Bell watched the screen with the volume off.

Reyes came onto the court first, tall, lean, handsome, the perfect example of classical beauty. His features were finely drawn, set off by sculpted lips which betokened his Indian heritage. His deep black eyes explained his enormous success with women.

Bell knew that Armando Reyes was an uneven player, capable of the best and the worst. His greatest success in a Grand Slam tournament had been to reach the final at Wimbledon, four years ago. He lived the life of a jet-setter, on the outer edge of the circuit. At home, the family business interests were managed by Reyes's brother.

The Reyes family owned 50,000 acrs of good land, along the ocean on the coast of Peru. There was oil there, and huge mountain meadows for grazing cattle. The tennis writers thought of Reyes as the last of the gifted amateurs. If open tennis had not come along, he would have whiled away his life at cocktail parties.

Wearing a headband with strings of multi-coloured pearls hanging down, Milo Tigrid walked a few yards behind Reyes. With each step, an enormous sports bag banged against his hip. Applause greeted both players. Tigrid walked with a weary step.

Clavier put the phone down and turned to the screen. On the court, the umpire had called Milo over. Clavier turned up the volume.

'Mr Tigrid, your headband is distracting. I'm afraid it will inconvenience your opponent.'

Milo's face on the screen twisted in mock outrage. 'This? It's a traditional headband from my country.'

The umpire's face betrayed his opinion of such traditions. 'I don't doubt that. I still must ask you to remove it.'

Milo obeyed. Rummaging in his sports bag, he took out a series of objects, which he placed in front of him. A packet of sliced bread, a pot of jam, a thermos flask, a cup and saucer, and a black frame containing a yellowing photograph of an old lady.

The referee was angry. 'Mr Tigrid, this behaviour will not be tolerated.' He was shouting, and he had not thought to turn off the network microphone. All the world heard, via satellite.

'See what I mean, Alain,' Bell said. 'It's not a semifinal. It's a goddamned circus.'

On the screen, Milo was brandishing the bread. 'Are you asking me to hide the face of my mother? Her noble face brings me luck. And where is the regulation which refuses a player the right to eat or drink during short breaks?'

'Please, Mr Tigrid.'

'I prefer hot tea to the cold drinks you provide. They are bad for the heart.' Tigrid thumped his huge barrel chest. 'Ask Armando.'

'Please.' The umpire was livid.

'Furthermore, I'll hand over these to your medical people, so that they can be tested for drugs. Nothing I use is contaminated.'

In Clavier's office, Bell stood. 'I can watch this farce better from the stands. If he does it again, I'm throwing the first tomato.'

Bell walked out. Clavier returned to his desk, to work on the enormous time chart which laid out the tournaments for the season. Clavier's organization was forced to compete with a series of tournaments started several years ago by G.H. Houston, a wealthy Texan who had tried to grab the best players for himself. It was a freebooting tradition that talent-sharks like Bell and Fenwick were still carrying on.

The semifinal match got underway.

At 4–3 in the second set, Armando was sorry he'd taken Di Rocca's offer and he was beginning to wonder what would happen if he just beat the hell out of Tigrid and gave the money back. His game had never been better. He was seeing the ball in slow motion. The power came in long surges, moving him to the ball, giving him time for the set-up before his opponent was back in position.

Then, suddenly, as he prepared to serve out the second set, leading 5–3, 40–15, the pills stopped working and a chest pain competed for his attention. He lost two games in a row before rallying. He won the second set at 7–6. He had to admit Milo was playing beautifully. At the changeover, Armando was grateful for a minute to rest.

In the stands, he saw Muriel sitting between his brother, Leonardo, and Di Rocca in the players' box. She held a camera to her eye and shot his picture. He thought she was smiling and for a moment wondered what it would be like not to play the circuit. Leonardo said, again and again, that this was the last year of tennis. The money had been used up. In a way, it was Leonardo who had forced Armando into taking Di Rocca's offer.

A few rows away, he saw Athena and Saadi in Saadi's private box. And Armando wondered what it would be like to be married to Athena. A quiet life in the suburbs. A pleasant home. Children. The only problem was that Athena was a groupie, married to the eternal round of the circuit. There was no sign of the cousin, Mlle Laure Puget.

Taking a glass of water from the ball boy, Reyes gulped down a vitamin C, two Es, three potassium pills, and a red HBO-10.

Muriel shot him through her camera lens.

He felt the pills lift him immediately. Now, he would show the world what a player he was. Armando stood, walked to the baseline. Applause boosted him. His mind was sharp and clear. He felt wonderful. He would win. A Peruvian could still grasp the concept of honour. Damn Di Rocca and his New York contacts.

In the players' box, Muriel spoke to Di Rocca while she loaded the camera with fresh film. 'Have you known Armando long?'

'Four years. Maybe five. When I came on the circuit, he was one of the big players.'

'He is playing well today, no?'

Di Rocca looked at his watch. 'He's on a tear.'

'An American expression, isn't it? What does it mean?'

Leonardo Reyes grinned at her. He was not as handsome as his younger brother. 'It means he's playing well.'

She finished loading the camera and went back to work, shooting photos of people in the stands.

'You burn up a lot of film.'

'I have decided to make the book. One summer of tennis. Paris, London, New York.' She turned to face Di Rocca with the camera ready and shot his picture. At the changeover, she left Di Rocca and Leonardo and moved down closer to the umpire's chair for her photos.

Milo served, and the ball slid away from Reyes.

'Fault,' shouted the linesman.

'Are you crazy?' Milo stared at the linesman, then walked to the umpire's chair to protest. 'That was an ace, sir. Not a fault. The chalk clearly flew. The man needs a seeing-eye dog.'

The linesman left his chair, bent down, pointed to a spot in the orange clay where the ball had landed. Milo trotted over, showed the linesman another spot, nearer the centre of the line. 'This is it, blind man.' Milo raised his arms, appealing to the crowd. A few people applauded. At last, the umpire got Milo back to his side of the court. Play resumed. With the momentum shifted for the moment, Milo won the next two games, to lead, 3–4.

At the changeover, Milo poured a cup of tea, which he drank like an old maid at the Ritz in London.

Trailing 3–4 in the third set, Armando took two reds, for energy. His anxiety was building and the lines were starting to blur, so he took another blue, the drug for stage fright.

Inside his mind, the ball came slower now, meaning he had control again. He hit a drop shot, sucking the Montenegrin to the net, then lobbed over him for a clean winner.

Applause rained down.

From the sidelines, near the umpire's stand, Muriel shot his picture. He wondered what she was like in bed. The fact that he had not tried to seduce her showed how much he was enamoured of the Princess.

He walked to the baseline, feeling slightly dizzy. As he readied himself to serve, he felt the anxiety leave him, like great dark wings receding into the sun, and he knew he was feeling the pills.

Applause came, faintly, from one of the field courts and for a moment Armando wanted to be there, under the shade of an ancient tree. Those trees had been planted in the twenties, before Armando had been born. He remembered his first sight of them, as a boy of eighteen, on his first visit to Paris. The women had been . . .

He heard the umpire speak to him. 'Monsieur Reyes? And he realized he had been daydreaming. It was his serve. Across the net, a thousand miles away, Milo Tigrid was waiting. Milo was his old friend, the only person besides Athena who knew about the glorious pills. Not even Leonardo knew.

Armando checked the scoreboard, which seemed to waver in the soft afternoon sunlight. The score was 40–30, Armando trailing 3–4. Preparing to serve, he saw the toss clearly, the ball barely rotating against the bright Paris sun, and then his arm cranked, the racket picking up speed as it made the loop and darted forward to make contact with the ball.

He felt himself falling, thought it was his weight driving forward, into the ball.

And crashed into the orange clay of Stade Roland-Garros.

When she saw Reyes falter and fall through her zoom lens, Muriel's finger froze, but only for an instant; then it contracted, taking pictures from reflex. Hearing the buzz of the crowd, she acted professionally, keeping the camera to her face, pressing hard against her eye socket. The tears started as she continued shooting, and when she took the camera away, it gleamed with wetness. 'Oh, no,' Muriel moaned.

At that moment, two men brushed past her, Leonardo and Di Rocca, on their way down to the *Cour Centrale*, where Armando lay face down in the dirt, unmoving.

'Get up, Peruvian!' Milo called. 'They know you're faking.'

Nervous laughter, from the stands.

But the Peruvian lay still.

Muriel watched, horrified, as Leonardo Reyes pressed his mouth to his brother's and began to pump the rib cage with both hands. A security guard stepped up, to stand guard. In a moment, men in blue uniforms trotted out onto the court, carrying a stretcher. A doctor, carrying a black bag, knelt down in the orange dust beside the body and used a stethoscope to listen to Armando's chest. Behind the doctor stood Leonardo Reyes and a stricken Milo Tigrid. Off to the right, Jack Di Rocca stood, watching Reyes's Laval tennis bag for him.

At last, the doctor said something to the uniformed men, who lifted Armando onto the stretcher. They carried him off, followed by Leonardo and Di Rocca, who bought the tennis bag. As they walked off, President

Clavier arrived on the scene. Still crying, Muriel shot the President, hoping to capture his agitation and forget her own.

Running down the stairs from his office, Clavier had tried to reorganize the tournament in his mind. Two days to go, a second semifinal, a women's final, a men's final. The doubles had to be played, men's, women's, the mixed. If the doctors declared Reyes unable to continue today, play would have to begin immediately in the next semifinal. Perhaps there was a chance that Reyes and Tigrid could continue their match tomorrow, before the women's final. If Reyes could not continue at all, that would put Tigrid the clown into the final.

By the time Clavier had reached ground level, the men were loading the stretcher into an ambulance. Clavier had to get to the stands, to make an announcement, so he snapped at the doctor. He needed a prompt diagnosis. He guessed it would be heat prostration. 'Well, how is he, doctor?'

The doctor shook his head. 'The man is dead.'

'What?' Clavier was horrified. 'You can't be sure of that here. Let's get him to hospital.'

'He's dead. It will do no good.'

'Take him to my office.'

'Sorry, M. le President. We must inform the police.'

'The *police*?'

The doctor nodded and turned to watch Reyes's brother get into the ambulance. The men closed the doors behind him. Milo Tigrid stood off to one side, alone, holding a tennis bag. His face was covered in tears, as if he was responsible for his friend's death. Thinking of what he must say to the spectators, Clavier walked out onto the *Cour Centrale*. His legs trembled.

President Clavier took the microphone from the umpire and cleared his throat.

From a phone booth on the Boulevard Murat, two blocks from Stade Roland-Garros, Jack Di Rocca used a special credit card to call long distance from Paris to New York. As he listened to the phone ringing on the other end, his palms grew wet with sweat. Armando Reyes had been dead less than twenty minutes.

'Yeah.'

'This is Di Rocca. Get Sally on the line.'

'It's early, pal.'

'I don't care if he's in his pyjamas. Get Sally.'

He waited three minutes, then four. At last, Sally Vincenti came on the line. 'Hey, Jackie.'

'Reyes died. Right on the court.'

There was a pause while Sally digested the information. Di Rocca imagined he could hear the numbers ticking through Sally's mental computer. 'Tough. What was the score?'

'Reyes was losing in the fourth set.'

'Going to make it a photo finish, was he?'

'Just want we planned.' Di Rocca didn't voice his suspicion that Reyes had changed his mind, had died while trying to win.

'Where's the green?' Sally asked.

'Returned.' The money had been in Reyes' tennis bag, along with two bottles of pills. Di Rocca had handed the bag to Milo.

'Perfect.' Sally made Di Rocca wait while he talked to someone at the other end of the line. When he came back on, his voice sounded happy. 'We stay with Panties Koras for the Paris final. For Wimbledon, let's put the squeeze on this Polak, the commie. The plan is that Laville wins in London.'

Di Rocca didn't like it. Polak was a good sport, right down to his toenails. He had a little weakness for vodka. There were rumours around the circuit that Polak had been a virgin until he married this Gail Hofstedter. A few circuit wags like Laville claimed Polak stayed a virgin after the wedding. 'All right. I'll start watching him.'

Sally chuckled. 'How did Reyes leave us?'

'He was on something, so it looks like an overdose. Maybe heart failure.'

'Are we clean?'

Di Rocca thought of Muriel, walking away as he was about to hand over the money to Reyes. She wouldn't have seen the transfer. 'Yeah. We're clean.' He knew the cops would come sniffing around him first, because of his prison record. You could be the number one in the world, and if you had a sheet, the cops would roust you first.

'How's the weather over there?' Sally asked.

'A beautiful day for tennis. Sunshine. Birds chirping in the trees. A shitty day to die.'

'Well, let me hear from you,' Sally said, and hung up.

On Friday evening, the Médecin Legiste had refused to sign the burial permit after examining the body of Armando Reyes in the morgue. The Procureur de la République had intervened, asking for a speedy autopsy, and on Saturday morning the inquest had been handed over to the police, Criminal Division.

Clavier had been called to the morgue, along with Abraham, Leonardo Reyes, and a man from the Peruvian Embassy. Outside the lab, the waiting room was like a sterile chamber, vacant except for an oppressive atmosphere of formaldehyde and human sorrow. Leonardo Reyes sat slumped in a hard wooden chair, staring blindly at the white floor. Next to the grieving Leonardo, in chairs along the wall, were Clavier, Peter Abraham, president of the Association of Tennis Professionals, and the

Embassy man, a dry, scholarly fellow who displayed all the discomfort of a military officer out of uniform. The scene was depressing, and the men did not talk.

Inside the autopsy room, Louis D'Argent, the lab technician, threw soapy water from his grey bucket onto the thick metal table. The water flooded the surface, mixing with the bloody refuse from the post-mortem. Louis grabbed a huge broom and began pushing it along the messy concrete floor, toward the drain. He was angry. He hated working nights, and if things kept up, he would be here on Sunday, when they were running at Longchamps. Louis was good with a knife. He could cut up corpses as well as his boss and he had good intuition, backed up by years of observation on the job, about what killed people. In this case it was drugs. He had made the mistake of broaching his opinion to the Médecin Legiste, who was late for dinner at the house of the Minister of the Interior. An argument had ensued. The Médecin Legiste had left, ordering Louis to write up the report, and not to mention drugs until he had the go-ahead. The pathologist's rubber gloves and large brown apron were still hanging over the wash basin. To smother the smell of the dead, the Médecin Legiste smoked constantly. Now Louis had the usual post-autopsy headache, and the left-over smoke from the pathologist's pipe was making him sick.

Clavier had made the mistake of wearing a thick gabardine, too heavy for this late in the spring. As he sat there, he was trying to clarify events in his mind. The players had been shocked by the death of Reyes, but even more shocked when his body had been taken to the police morgue for an autopsy. Clavier had hoped an inquest by the office of the Médecin Legiste would clear the allegations that were being made about drugs on the tennis scene. Gossip ran rampant – stories of cyclists dead during their races, the monstrously mutated muscles of eastern bloc athletes. The tennis authorities knew they had to counter-attack to stop the rumours from spreading.

Footsteps approached down the hall. Clavier looked up to see two men. One was lean and spare, and reminded him of his wife's cousin, Jacquimard, who was a schoolmaster in Toulouse. The other man was shorter, and carried more authority. Well over fifty, he was sombrely dressed in a plain grey suit, a white shirt with a starched collar, and a tie which did nothing to enliven his appearance. His hair was grey, untidy, and needed cutting. The short man stopped in front of Clavier, and produced some identification. His name was Inspector Pierre-Aimé Marechal, of the Prefecture.

Marechal turned to his assistant. 'Stay here, Demetz, and get some statements from these good people.' The Inspector stopped halfway through the door, to speak in passable English to the men on the bench. 'Oh, I forgot to tender my regrets, about the dead man.'

And then he swung the door open and vanished into the autopsy room.

Clavier and the others answered routine questions for several moments. The tall officer, Demetz, wrote down their answers in a notebook. After a quarter of an hour, the swinging doors opened and a small man dressed in a high-necked white jacket beckoned toward them. 'If you'll follow me, please?'

He led them into a large room, the walls painted a sickly green, which was divided in two by a thick pane of glass. Behind the glass lay the body of Armando Reyes, resting on a table. Except for his face, Reyes's body was covered by a white sheet.

The small man spoke. 'Our autopsy shows that Armando Reyes died of a drug overdose. His bloodstream and viscera were flooded with two drugs which conflicted in his body. The strain, added to a weak heart, was too much for him. When compounded by vigorous physical exercise, the drugs killed him.' The man turned to Marechal. 'Inspector?'

Marechal stepped forward to address the group. 'We have two distinct possibilities here. On the one hand, Reyes overdosed himself, while trying to improve his performance on the court. On the other, he was deliberately fed the drugs by someone.' Marechal smiled. 'As you might imagine, I and my department prefer the second hypothesis.'

'Murder?' Reyes's brother gasped. 'But who would want to murder Armando?'

'That, Senor Reyes, is the question we hope to answer. Quickly.' He turned to President Clavier. 'A team of my detectives will be working with your organization to discover the activities of all the tennis players. We are hoping you will be cooperative.'

'But the finals at Roland-Garros, they are scheduled for this afternoon and tomorrow! Surely you could wait a few hours. This is a premier tournament, an event of national and international importance.'

Marechal smiled. 'We shall be discreet, M. le President. But we do have our job.'

'This is terrible!' Clavier said to Abraham. 'It could ruin the entire game!'

'We don't need any more disruptions,' Abraham challenged. 'Paris is the start of the summer circuit. We need to finish up and get on to Gstaad and Munich and London.'

Marechal stared at Abraham, then swung to confront Clavier. 'Let me be clear about this. If a crime has been committed, we shall detain anyone connected with the case, by house arrest if necessary. To avert the possibility of terrorism, I have already alerted my counterpart in London. If it becomes clear that a conspiracy is involved, we shall widen this investigation to include everything.' The Inspector paused while he swept the men with his eyes, indicating the breadth of his power, and then intoned. 'We shall investigate here, in Gstaad, in Munich, in London, in all the world.'

Clavier and Abraham said nothing.

Marechal let the words hang there, in the morgue, and then he turned on his heel and stalked out, followed by Demetz.

'Crap,' said Abraham.

Reyes had died on Friday. By Saturday at midday, the rumours were flying about the cause of his death. Early Sunday morning, Sven Skaar, the great Scandinavian player, attempted to discuss the situation in a live interview before a television camera. Before his retirement half-a-dozen years ago, Skaar had had a brilliant career. Three French titles, two Australian, three U.S. Opens. The only title which had eluded him had been the Wimbledon. He was now seen as the conscience of professional tennis. On the screen, Skaar looked shrewd, experienced, wily, the veteran of years on the circuit who had come within a few strokes of winning the Grand Slam. The interviewer, Judson Garwood, was trying to probe into the death of Armando Reyes.

Q: I'd like to talk about the pressures athletes are under these days. Can you describe that?

A: Well, it varies, of course. I used to feel the most pressure about two hours before a match. It would start then, and it would continue until the first point was over. Then it would go away, just like that.

Q: Didn't you make your fortune in tennis?

A: Yes. What's wrong with making money in a job one loves?

Q: What about the players who don't make a lot of money? What kind of pressures are on them?

A: If you are speaking of Armando Reyes, he came from a wealthy family. He didn't need to make lots of money.

Q: What kind of pressure *was* on Reyes?

A: Obviously, the pressure of time. Armando and Tigrid are the oldest on the tour. Armando had to keep in very good shape.

Q: Otherwise, he's not marketable. Is that right?

A: There is a pressure to remain at an optimum level. We try to preserve the best possible form. That's only natural.

Q: A lot of people say that tennis players are like race horses.

A: Absurd. It's not worth discussing.

Q: Are you aware that Armando Reyes is suspected of having used drugs?

A: I knew he took vitamins. Are those the drugs you refer to?

Q: I think the report will tell us he was using something harder.

A: Then I prefer to wait for the report.

Q: Do you know of other players who have used drugs?

A: What sort of drugs? In France, you have sent veal to court for being full of antibiotics. When I have an infection, I use antibiotics.

Q: Let's get specific, Sven. Do tennis players use anabolics?

A: Impossible, especially now that we know that artifically grown muscles are easily ripped.

Q: What about cortisone?
A: No. No. There is too much risk of stomach ulcers.
Q: What about stimulants, for the actual match?
A: Some sportsmen, or sportswomen, might use stimulants if they knew when precisely they would have to run, to jump, to play ball. A tennis player never knows exactly when he's going onto the court. He can sit in a room and wait two hours, three, four, while other matches go on, or while it rains.
Q: All right. What about hard drugs?
A: Such as?
Q: Cocaine.
A: There is some confusion in your mind between a tennis player and a rock star. We are both professionals. We must entertain, from time to time. There, the resemblance ceases.
Q: All right, Sven. When you were winning out there, what did you do to sustain the desire to win?
A: I did two things. First, I thought about the money. Second, I thought about hatred.
Q: You mean you have to hate your opponent?
A: A player who wishes to reach the top can't afford to feel nice. He must want to kill.
Q: Could we have some more on that?
A: It is common knowledge. On the court, we are enemies. As soon as the match has ended, my opponents become my friends again. Personal ties fall back into place.
Q: Are all players like that, Sven?
A: No. Only the ones who win.

Sunday afternoon at Roland-Garros; the men's finals of the French Open. The sky was overcast and gloomy. The fans were restless and there were more security guards evident in the stadium.

Down two sets to one, Koras knew he was going to lose. This was his thirteenth year at Stade Roland-Garros, his seventh time in the final. He'd won here twice. This year, he was seeded number one, but Milo Tigrid, his opponent, was playing out of his mind.

During the changeover, Koras kept looking at Saadi's box, hoping to see Laure Puget, but only Athena sat there, with her entourage. No Saadi. No Laure Puget.

His eyes swept the stands, the faces of the fans. In a box directly ahead of him, a man wearing a straw hat filled delicate balloon glasses with red wine, a metaphor for the good life at Roland-Garros. In the players' box, Jack Di Rocca sat with Terry Laville and the Polaks and Shirley the starlet. If Laville was with a woman, that meant poor Nora was out of town.

On court again, Milo seemed fresher than a man half his age, as if he hadn't run three miles of stop and start across the clay. He was booming the ball, probing Koras's fatigue. Koras narrowed his concentration, tried to slow the pace of the game.

He aimed for the lines, managed to hit a couple of winners, and all the time he kept thinking the crowd hadn't come out today to see tennis. They were here to see someone die.

At 3–4 in the third set, Milo leading, Koras felt his right knee buckle beneath him. He was on his way to a forehand, running wide, and as he pushed off to hit the ball, the knee gave out from under him. The next thing he knew he was in pain, lying on his back smelling the dust of the orange clay while a loud murmur came from the crowd.

Across the net, Milo Tigrid hit the ball long, losing the point. Koras's fall had distracted him. In the next minute, he was at Koras's side.

Milo's face showed fear. 'Pantakoras! Damn you! Get up!'

From where he lay, Koras saw Milo, and beyond him, the figure of a Paris policeman. Koras sat up, shook his head. Milo helped him to his feet. 'What happened?'

'It's the knee again.' Koras rubbed the offending joint. From the edge of the court, officials wearing jackets and ties hurried toward him. The crowd buzzed as a doctor arrived.

Koras took his three minutes and the pain ebbed as he walked slowly around at the baseline. Worried officials asked him if he could continue playing. Finally, he said okay.

He was shaky at the start, but then he found his rhythm. On the first wide forehand he ran slowly, moving to his right with the utmost caution, waiting for the pain. When it came, a sharp knife in his knee, he was ready. He gritted his teeth and made the winning shot. Across the net, Milo applauded.

But the wily Montenegrin kept playing the forehand, hitting to Koras's weakness. Koras bore Milo no grudge. Tennis was a man's sport. And if you stepped onto the court, you came to play.

The injury had made Koras aware of time limits. He stopped thinking about Laure Puget and Armando Reyes and began stroking the ball. He forgot the score, forgot Milo, Athena, the voice of the umpire, the buzz of the crowd. He focused on the ball as it flew through the air, slipping across the net, touching down.

At the changeover between odd games, Koras drank some water and closed his eyes. He did his deep breathing. He played a game in slow motion on the magical court inside his mind. In his trance, he was young again, with two perfectly good knees.

At 5–4 in the fifth and final set, Koras brought loud gasps from the crowd when he fell again as he went into the air for an overhead. This time, he caught himself before he fell, and staggered a couple of steps.

'Are you all right for play, M. Belynkas?'

Koras answered in French. 'Oui. It is okay.'

But it was his serve now, at 40–15, and as he tossed the last ball in the air he knew it would pull Milo off court. The ball went spinning through the air and Milo was already moving. The return came as if shot from a canon, but Koras was there, covering the alley. He volleyed deeply cross-court. Milo answered with a backhand dipper. Koras closed on the net and volleyed again, a scoop shot just over the net. Milo raced for the shot, but he was too late for a winner, and when he lobbed, Koras had anticipated him, and cracked away the last point of the men's final with a booming overhead.

That one, he knew, was for Armando.

'Ahhh!' the girl moaned, writhing. 'Oh, darling!'

The girl in the bed at the Sofitel Hotel was named Shirley Nash-Winters. She was half English and half American. She'd grown up in England, but attended high school in Winnetka. Shirley had been discovered in a Miss Illinois run off by Nicky Fortunato, the Hollywood producer.

Three months ago, her flawless face with its peaches and cream complexion had been on the cover of *Cosmopolitan*. A month before, on the cover of *Mademoiselle*. A month before that, on the cover of *Elan*. Shirley was pretty, but the feature that set her apart was a set of sleepy grey eyes that, in real life, projected a come hither look. On camera, the eyes deepened, making her look intelligent and sophisticated. Inside *Mademoiselle*, Shirley had modelled eight pages of springtime clothes for the readers, suburban girls between the ages of sixteen and twenty-one who envied her the saucy look that had helped make Shirley a starlet.

After the *Mademoiselle* layout, her agent had come up with a deal from Marvon, the giant cosmetics conglomerate. In the autumn Shirley would go on television and tell everyone how terrific Marvon products were.

Lots of money kept rolling in. Money was exciting, but it didn't make her happy, did not fulfill her the way Terry Laville did.

When she wasn't squirming on her knees and elbows in Room 405 in the Sofitel Hotel in Paris, Shirley Nash-Winters lived in Bel Air, California, in an eighteen-room house belonging to Nicky Fortunato, the latest boy-genius who was tearing up the track making silly sexploitation films for teenagers. In eleven months, Shirley had made three of them.

In addition, she had just finished filming a remake, in Morocco, of the Hitchcock classic, *The Man Who Knew Too Much*. The leads in Nicky's remake, originally played by James Stewart and Doris Day, had been Bruce Warner, twenty-four, and herself, aged twenty-two.

On location in North Africa, Shirley had fought with Nicky, the director and executive producer of the film. The fight was about money. Shirley knew what she was worth these days. She had the Marvon deal, three magazine covers. She had three scripts to read, sitting in her suitcase this very minute, amidst the stockings and the expensive underwear. NBC wanted her for a fall special. Agents called her long distance, to ask was she unhappy with Lolo Darling, her present one.

To spite Nicky, to make him a little jumpy about the future of his newest property, she had flown to Rome, where she connected with the man who was making her moan and twist that steamy May evening in Paris. That man was Terry Laville.

He stood six-three, weighed 205 pounds. He had arms like Conan the Barbarian, legs like a linebacker for the Dallas Cowboys. Terry was one eighth Iroquois Indian, one half French-Canadian, and the rest north woods timber wolf. He could lift Shirley by the waist, grin at her, white teeth against his dark face, hold her body high, limp as putty, set her down in any position he chose, and then make her moan for hours, literally.

The Indian part excited Shirley, especially the way his tawniness contrasted with the hair, which was almost white.

With other men, before Terry, Shirley had faked sexual pleasure. In Hollywood she had been faking it simply forever, knowing that's what they expected – men, producers, directors, stars, baseball players, beach hunks on the make, bankers, stockbrokers with houses in Malibu.

They wanted a scene from the camera, and Shirley obliged. They got a scene from the camera.

At an early age, Shirley learnt that a loud moan from her meant her lover was a big man, while a small moan meant disappointment, or worse. For Shirley, volume was no problem.

The faking stopped the minute she met him. He'd been playing a pro-celeb thing at the L.A. Tennis Club, bounding around the court, slamming the ball. One look, and Shirley had started to vibrate, her special way of communicating sexual attraction.

A boy back in Winnetka had called her Shirley the hummer. She'd simply shake, and her lips would tremble, and she'd feel the energy starting all the way down – stomach, pelvis, thighs, knees, toes, toenails even. It hadn't happened since high school, this special feeling. When it did, Shirley tried to act on it. Life was short, and a girl could burn out in Hollywood in a year, maybe less. That's why she'd flown to Rome. That's why she was in Paris, in Terry's bed, because life, ah, was, ah, short.

'Ahhh!' she cried, squirming.

'You like it, don't you, baby? You like it!'

As her knees twisted into the sheets, Shirley remembered their first meeting, the way his eyes lit up when he saw her. She'd been with Nicky and some friends from the studio and Terry had grinned and whispered in her ear that he'd like to lick her all over. From anyone else, it would have been just a bad line.

'Are you –?' she asked, quivering. 'Are you gonna –?'

'Shut up, goddamit. Don't talk.'

Shirley closed her eyes and tried to visualize Terry on the tennis court, rushing to the net for the kill, but all she could see was Terry, naked, in the shower, soaping himself, grinning. One grin made her feel like jelly.

The phone by the bedside rang, pulling her mind away from pleasure and back to the world. Behind her, Terry didn't pause. She started counting after a while. Three rings. Or four. Missed one. Six. Seven. She counted to ten before twisting her neck around.

'Terry. The phone.'

'Did you tell anyone you were here? That's probably your pal, Ivan Leroy. Or that fag of a producer.'

The phone stopped. In her mind, lost in a whirlpool of pleasure, Shirley reconnected, tears in her eyes.

'Ahhh –' she said.

The phone started again. This time, Terry Laville broke rhythm to curse at the caller.

'Sonofabitch! Shut up!'

He had been angry ever since he'd lost to Koras Belynkas in the quarterfinals. He'd quarrelled with his wife and sent her back to the States. It was probably her calling. The only time Terry talked about his wife was when he was drinking. Why didn't he answer? Shirley had a superstition about phones, probably from living in Hollywood where everyone was waiting for a call from their agent about a part. When a phone rang, Shirley felt compelled to answer.

Thirteen rings, she counted. Fourteen. Missed a beat. Sixteen, ah, seventeen. How long would she let a phone ring before forgetting it? Eighteen was too much. Shirley reached for the phone and felt Terry grab her wrist. The phone clattered to the floor.

'Ouch. You're hurting me!'

Terry let her go. She felt him move away and turned her face to watch. Naked, Terry walked around the foot of the bed, grabbed the phone, and ripped it from the wall connection. In Paris, that would probably get someone thrown in jail. One powerful motion, and it was over.

'There!' Terry grunted.

She held her left wrist and pouted. 'You hurt me!'

'Fucking phone.'

He stood there above her, holding the phone in both hands.

Inspector Marechal knew nothing of tennis except that two years ago a French tennis player named Claude Benoit had been caught at a party on the Right Bank using cocaine. Marechal remembered the scene when he and three uniformed officers had broken down the door – the smell of marijuana smoke, a movie projector flashing pornography, the heavy sound of American punk rock, the unmistakable reek of sex, and a man in the corner, using a short straw to sniff cocaine from the surface of a hand mirror. The time had been three o'clock in the morning. Complaints had come rolling in, a dozen calls, unusual for a week night. It had been a slow evening, so Marechal, who was strictly homicide, had gone along as senior officer. The tennis player had been sentenced to a year in prison, and the sentence had been suspended.

Marechal was a conservative man who wore a three-piece suit even in summer. He drank Vichy water for lunch. At dinner, he allowed himself two glasses of red wine, but only if not on duty. He viewed the world as a dark place. He believed innocence was a temporary condition, and that, sooner or later, everyone wanted to kill someone else.

The Inspector thought Armando Reyes had been murdered. Eventually, the coroner would arrive at the same conclusion. Meanwhile, Marechal had been taken off an important case – a lonely and moderately attractive woman from the 14th Arrondissement was being tried for a triple axe murder – and had been asked to investigate the death of a Peruvian playboy.

There were pressures here from the Peruvian embassy, and from the man's brother. On the other side, the people from the lofty tennis establishment, from M. le President Clavier down to the lowliest circuit gypsy, seemed to want to ignore what had happened.

It was Marechal's intention to bring reality to bear on the situation.

Who would profit from the death of Reyes? Tigrid, the mad Yugoslav? Comrade Polak, the dour man with dual residences in Dallas and Gdansk? Pantakoras Belynkas, who would have had to play Reyes in the final? Jack Di Rocca, the Italian-American with the prison record? David Cooper, who seemed to take orders from his mother? One of the managers – Bell? Ortega? Fenwick? Or perhaps the strange man with the albino hair and the temper, Terry Laville.

Now, being driven through the early morning traffic to the Hotel Sofitel, Marechal lit a Gauloise. 'I recognize that name. Terry Laville,' he said to Sergeant Demetz.

'He is the one I bet on. Two thousand francs.'

'His face, it is everywhere.'

'My sister says Laville will be on the cover of *Paris Match* in a week. He is becoming the long lost Frenchman.'

Marechal looked out the window. 'Laville must be French Canadian, no?'

'Yes. I hear he's from Alberta. They say he is part Indian.'

'They have incredible accents, those French Canadians. My cousin Bertholde married one, a bureaucrat from Quebec, and her opinion is that they should all be forced to attend grammar school in Paris, Or, at the least take a course with Berlitz.'

Demetz laughed, and turned a corner. They were at the Sofitel.

The concierge was very tanned, a typical travel industry type who probably spent his lunch hour with his shirt off on the banks of the Seine, staring at the girls. He wore a blue jacket with a soft collar, set off by a striped tie. He irritated the Inspector by spending time examining their credentials. At last he looked up, sardonic smile crinkling the corners of his mouth.

'Well, how may I be of service?'

'We need a list,' Demetz said, 'of every tennis player staying here, along with room numbers.'

'That will take some time.'

'You have a half hour. Is anyone down for breakfast yet?'

'Yes. Mr Di Rocca and his manager. They went in a quarter of an hour ago.

The Inspector knew the name Di Rocca, but he checked the list anyway, part of the routine of doing his job. 'The sergeant here will stay with you, to expedite that list.' Marechal smiled at the concierge and walked into the breakfast room. He was looking forward to ruffling the feathers of M. Di Rocca.

CHAPTER FIVE

Jack Di Rocca was not a tall man. His immense power stemmed from a fund of nervous energy that was always seeking release. On Monday, following the finals at Roland-Garros, he wore his navy blue track suit bearing the name of Ryker, his main sponsor, and the La Rocca brand shoes he wore as part of a contract with Distaff Inc, a shoe firm in California. It had often been rumoured on the circuit that the contract was bogus, a simple cover allowing Di Rocca to be paid for unspecified acts he tendered for unnamed, but powerful, criminal interests.

When possible, Di Rocca left public relations talk to his coach, the moon-faced Paco Ortega. Ortega's answers were as evasive as Di Rocca's silence. Once, he had been interviewed by *Racket World*, by a pretty staff member who had played two years on the Avon circuit. The staffer had a degree in political science from a prominent women's college on the East Coast, and she prided herself on possessing the only conscience in America.

'Is your man Di Rocca the Mafia's man on the circuit?' she'd asked.

'Yeah, that's right,' Ortega answered, 'and I'm their ambassador, which gets me more power than the Secretary of State, the Secretary of Defense, and the President. Jackie and I are also working for the CIA, FBI, DIA, DOD, and three secret groups that I can't name here. If you think about it, it's a wonder we find time for the circuit.'

Di Rocca and Ortega had the same stocky build. Di Rocca had a black beard. Ortega was clean shaven and his face gleamed with sweat. Di Rocca kept in shape, running three miles a day, working out in the gym. Ortega, on the other hand, was fifteen pounds overweight and preferred to limit his athletics to the bedroom.

Ortega had been named in connection with rigged games in hockey and horse racing, and the gossip followed him into tennis, where he managed half a dozen South American players as well as Di Rocca. Nothing had been proven, but neither Ortega nor Di Rocca did anything to dispel the criminal reputation which surrounded each of them.

The speculation made them visible in a sport where personality flourished. It also got them interviews with the police. Often.

At eight-thirty that Monday morning – too close for comfort after Di Rocca's pitch to Armando and their meetings before the semis – they were interviewed by a fussy French cop in plain clothes, who came to their table in the breakfast room, pulled up a chair, and sat down. His identification said his name was Inspector Marechal. He wore an amply cut charcoal wool suit and a subdued blue and grey silk tie. He asked to speak to Di Rocca alone, so Ortega moved to another table.

The inspector was heavy-boned and deliberate. As he asked his questions, he made notes in a small black notebook. His English was careful, with a heavy French accent.

'Where were you on Friday, the day of the semifinals?'

'Before you ask another question,' Di Rocca said. 'I'd like a lawyer.'

Marechal looked up. 'What for?'

'When policemen ask questions, a person is allowed to have a lawyer present.'

Marechal smiled. 'At this stage that is unnecessary. You are in France, not the United States.'

'Still, I'd like a lawyer.'

Marechal widened his smile and shook his head. 'Would you prefer to answer questions here, or at the Prefecture?'

Di Rocca took a sip of coffee. 'Okay. So it won't hurt to answer a few questions.'

'Your whereabouts, m'sieu? For Friday, the day Reyes died?'

'In the morning, I was with a lady.'

'Her name, if you please.'

'Danielle.'

Marechal wrote it down. 'And her surname?'

'Nightingale,' Di Rocca said.

'I beg your pardon?'

'Danielle Nightingale.'

Marechall allowed a small smile to creep across his lips. 'Pretty name. What was her address?'

'We went to a hotel, off the Rue St Denis. I paid cash for a room. I met her Thursday night. We were together Friday morning.'

Marechal knew the section of Paris frequented by young and beautiful prostitutes. 'This is quite an alibi, monsieur.'

'Did I break the law, Inspector?'

'No. I was merely thinking, that with so many pretty women about, it seems strange that a man like you should –' He let the idea sit there.

Di Rocca leaned forward. 'Inspector, do you know the difference between phony and real?'

The Inspector sat back in his chair. He could see that Di Rocca was inverting the ordinary notion about prostitutes.

Di Rocca finished his coffee. The pot was empty, so he signalled for more. 'There are a lot of phonies on the circuit. After a while, they get to you, and you need to get back to reality.'

'Yes.' The Inspector wrote down the word *réalité*. 'This Danielle, would she remember you?'

Di Rocca gave the Inspector a look, man to man. 'If necessary.'

'Very well. How well did you know Armando Reyes?'

'Armando and I saw each other around the circuit. We played pretty much the same tournaments, and we're both over thirty, which segregates you from the younger players. But his real buddy was Milo Tigrid.'

'And what was your opinion of M. Reyes?'

'I thought he was a grade A gigolo.'

'In what way?'

'Reyes operated like a fancy whore. You never saw him without a lady on his arm. Have you seen his wardrobe?'

'Tell me about that.'

Di Rocca grinned. 'Reyes was the first guy on the circuit to have a silk warm-up suit. For a couple of years there, he wore tennis shorts that shimmered, like running shorts. He had them especially made, in Hong Kong.'

Marechal made a note. Fancy dress, the victim. 'Did you see M. Reyes the day he died?'

More coffee arrived, with a cup for Marechal. After the waiter had gone, Di Rocca looked the Inspector in the eye. 'Mind if I ask why you're asking all these questions?'

Marechal shrugged. 'A simple inquiry, m'sieu, brought about by the request of the Peruvian Embassy.'

'Who have you talked to so far?'

'I would prefer to ask the questions, if you don't mind.'

Di Rocca sipped his coffee, then added two cubes of sugar. 'That means I'm the first, doesn't it?'

'Let me repeat my question. Did you see M. Reyes the day he died?'

'Sure.'

'Where was it?'

'I talked to him outside the locker room.'

'What time was this?'

'Around noon. Maybe half-past.'

'And what was the topic of conversation?'

'I wished him luck against Tigrid.'

'Did you mean it?'

'Sure. Tigrid's no friend of mine.'

'How did M. Reyes appear? What was his mood?'

'He seemed high as a kite.'

Marechal had not heard that expression. 'Depressed? Sanguine?'

'He seemed confident as an elephant stepping on an ant bed. His eyes were all lit up. He told me he had a good chance of winning the French Open.'

'You say that as if it surprised you, monsieur.'

'Well, he hadn't won a big title in four years, maybe five. Hell, he partied too much.'

'So, you had a brief meeting, and then you went your separate ways.'

'That's right.'

'And where were you when he died?'

'In the stands.'

'Were you alone?'

'Dumbo Cooper was with me. And Terry Laville. And that movie starlet, Shirley what's her name. Reyes's brother. And a French lady named Muriel.'

The Inspector wrote down the names.

'What do you know about M. Reyes's companion, Madame Broussard-Gauthier?'

'I only met her once before, at a party given by that Arab.'

'Saadi?'

'Yeah.'

Marechal checked back through his notebook. 'Reyes seems to have been quite friendly with Saadi, and also with the Princess von Heidelberg.'

'Yeah. Armando palled around with the quality.'

'You sound envious.'

'I wish I knew his secret for getting along on not much sleep.'

'You are aware that drugs have been found in his bloodstream, are you not?'

'That's the rumour going around.'

'What do you know about that?'

'About drugs?' Di Rocca put up his hands. 'I know nothing.'

'Did you ever use drugs. M. Di Rocca?'

Di Rocca thought back to Houston five years ago, the tournament at River Oaks, when Terry Laville had popped a couple of sleeping pills into his beer the night before a major semifinal. He still owed Laville. 'Not since I was a kid. They screw up your head.'

'Did drugs have anything to do with your incarceration, in New York?'

Di Rocca grinned, took another sip of his coffee. 'Have you been digging into the Interpol files, Inspector?'

'Please answer the question.'

'No. It was armed robbery, pure and simple. I was a dumb kid, scared to death. I paid my dues on that.'

The Inspector paused in his note-taking, made an underline to emphasize a key word. He stood up. 'I must ask you not to leave Paris, monsieur.'

'What?' Di Rocca stood, too, gripping the table.

'An investigation is underway.'

'What are you investigating?'

The Inspector answered with a small smile. 'There are those of us who believe M. Reyes was murdered.'

'That's a crock!'

'I beg you pardon?'

'You're crazy!'

'Perhaps. In any event, do not leave Paris.'

'But I've got a tournament coming up, in Palermo! I'm scheduled to play.'

'I am certain that your manager, M. Ortega, will be able to manipulate something.'

Di Rocca was tight-lipped with fury. 'This means over a hundred thousand dollars, Inspector.'

But Marechal walked away, as if he hadn't heard. Di Rocca knew he should get out of Paris right away, before the police stumbled onto his deal with Armando. He had Sally's money, and he'd given the bag with the pills to Milo. There was more to find out, especially now that he was making deals with Sally Vincenti.

As Ortega came up, Di Rocca was ticking off alternate scenarios. What if Sally had had Reyes killed? What if Muriel hadn't been sleeping with Reyes? What if there was another woman between the sheets with Reyes? What if Reyes had been killed for another reason, something to do with his brother and Peru?

'What did he want?' Ortega asked.

'Just practising his rousting techniques.'

'Can we leave for Palermo?'

'Not just yet, apparently.'

'How long?'

'Until they're finished.'

'I'd better make a call. You're the second seed, behind Koras. They can't start without you.'

'Yeah,' Di Rocca said. 'Remind them my mother was Sicilian.'

'I'll tell Clavier. Maybe he knows somebody who can pull strings.'

'Come in!'

Standing in the corridor, Marechal knocked again, to make sure he had been heard, then opened the door. He found Koras Belynkas, who had beaten Milo Tigrid in the finals the day before, sat on the floor in the middle of the small sitting room of his suite. He wore a bathrobe of white terry cloth. In front of him on a tray was enough food to feed a battalion – ham, cheese, scrambled eggs, white bread, dark bread, croissants, butter, jam and a large pot of coffee – a Scandinavian breakfast.

'Yes?' Koras said.

'Inspector Marechal. We met briefly, yesterday afternoon.'

'I remember, Inspector. Come in. Have some bacon, some eggs. How about a slice of ham?'

'Thank you.' The sight of so much food so early in the morning made Marechall nauseous. 'What a magnificent meal.'

'Yes. I love France. But I cannot abide your petit dejeuner.'

'How did you get them to prepare such an . . . extravaganza?'

'A little persuasion,' Koras said, in French. 'A little silver across the palm.'

'Your French is excellent, M. Belynkas.'

'Thank you. I have lived here, off and on, for years. It is a beautiful country, full of charm, good wine, and beautiful women.'

'Thank you. On behalf of my country, I accept.'

'Sit down, please.'

The Inspector sat. 'Again, congratulations on your victory.'

'Thank you. Perhaps we should not have played, considering the circumstances. Milo was certainly distraught. But we are all entertainers. And the show must go on.'

'In my opinion, the continuation of the tournament helped stabilize the spectators. And the spectators, in turn, helped to stabilize Paris.'

Koras smiled. 'I didn't know tennis had such far-reaching import.'

'The world of sport, Monsieur Belynkas, is a microcosm of civilization. Arenas lie at the very centre of our collective subconscious.'

Koras bit into a piece of dark bread. 'That's a little over my head, Inspector.'

Marechal pulled out a notebook. 'I was wondering if you might be willing to answer a few questions?'

'Of course. What about?'

'About M. Reyes. And the events surrounding his death.'

'I'll try. What do you want to know?'

'How well did you know M. Reyes?'

'Not as well as Milo Tigrid. They were buddies. But we had a drink together. And up until a year ago, Frank Fenwick was Armando's manager.'

'Oh? Why did that end?'

'Armando thought Frank was taking too much of a percentage. They parted company.'

'As friends?'

'Sure. Business is business. Armando hadn't been winning much, and he was always a big spender.'

'Who was his manager after that?'

'He didn't have one. He got business advice from his brother.'

'Did he also obtain pills from his brother?'

'You mean the vitamins?'

Marechal watched him. 'Yes. The vitamins.'

Koras poured a half cup of coffee, then sat with his back against the hotel sofa. 'When I first came on the circuit, back in the mid-seventies, Armando had a chauffeur named Raul whose main job was to seek out the herb shops, so that Armando would have a good source of vitamins.'

'Do you have any idea what he took?'

Koras shook his head. 'No. I know he was a vitamin freak.'

'Were you aware, M. Belynkas, that Armando Reyes was taking aphrodisiacs?'

Koras put down the coffee cup slowly, a look of surprise on his face. 'Aphrodisiacs? Are you kidding?'

'No.' Marechal was leaking the information one piece at a time, sorting out his subject's reactions to each. 'Traces of a cantharis derivative were found in his blood stream, along with another drug.'

'Jesus Christ. Then the rumours are right.'

'What rumours?'

'That Armando died of an overdose.'

'Yes.' Marechal nodded. 'That is correct.'

'There's something else, isn't there?' Koras asked. 'You're asking these questions because –'

At that moment, the door leading to the bedroom opened and a naked young woman appeared. From where she was standing, she could not see Marechal. Except for one strip of white, she was tanned everywhere. She was tall, with long legs and tight firm breasts. She walked unembarrassed into the centre of the room to the breakfast tray.

When she saw the Inspector, she stopped. 'Oh! I am so sorry.' She turned and hurried back into the bedroom. When she came out again, she wore a man's shirt, the buttons left undone. It made her look far more sensual than she had been naked.

She sank down to pick at the breakfast tray.

'This is Inspector Marechal,' Koras said. 'Inspector, may I present Mlle Evelyne Dumont.'

'Enchantée, mademoiselle.'

'How do you do, Inspector.'

'The Inspector is here investigating the death of Armando Reyes.'

Marechal lit a Gauloise, and puffed on it. The girl had a lovely face, skin as smooth as the butter she was spreading on a croissant.

'Did you know M. Reyes, mademoiselle?'

'No. I saw him play a few times.'

'Mlle Dumont is in marketing,' Koras said. 'And public relations.'

'Sorry to interrupt,' the girl said. She had fashioned a sandwich out of ham and cheese and a croissant. Holding the sandwich, she walked back into the bedroom, trim hips obvious behind the hem of a shirt. The door closed. Koras turned to Marechal.

'You think someone murdered Armando, don't you?'

'That is correct.'

Koras stood up, to pace the room. 'Tennis players aren't worth killing. There's nothing to gain.'

Marechal waited before replying. Then he asked. 'What did you think of the Sven Skaar interview? The one that was broadcast around the world via satellite?'

'I only caught part of it. I was working out when it came on.'

'There was a point he made, about hating one's opponent, about using the hate to build momentum for the ultimate victory.'

'Sven's always been full of theories. Most of them are crap.'

'Yet, in this, he seemed altogether serious.'

Koras stopped his pacing.

'My theory,' Marechal went on, 'is that someone got angry enough to kill him. Perhaps the competitive hatred boiled over.'

'Well, you do build up some steam when you're out there. But it blows off when the match is done.'

'A pure anger,' Marechal said. 'An anger for athletes and Olympians?'

Koras grinned. 'You make it sound silly. But yes, that's what it feels like. Pure.'

Marechal smiled. He loved playing cat and mouse, and this man Belynkas was intelligent. 'Do you know the Parsifal legend, Monsieur Belynkas?'

'He was off saving the world from dragons, wasn't he? Hauling maidens out of trouble?'

'Yes. But his mental state reminds me of the way you and Sven Skaar think about tennis.'

Koras smiled. 'Well, don't tell it to the newspapers, Inspector. They'll never leave us any peace.'

'Are you aware of any players on the circuit who use drugs, Monsieur Belynkas?'

Koras waited before replying. 'There was a player named Eddie Trowbridge, from California. He had to drop off the circuit last year. He used uppers and downers to keep himself levelled out. Eventually, it caught up with him.'

'No one else.'

'No.'

'Have you ever used drugs, M. Belynkas?'

'Pencillin, when I was in the service.'

Marechal stood. 'Well, thank you for your time. I must be going.' The two men shook hands, and the Inspector walked to the door. 'Oh, I must ask you not to leave Paris.'

'What?'

'Yes.'

'For how long?'

'A day. Perhaps two. Until we have finished our investigation.'

'But I've got a tournament! In Palermo!'

'My regrets.'

Marechal opened the door and walked out, leaving the American to his breakfast and his pretty young woman.

On Tuesday, President Clavier and Peter Abraham were sitting at a table in the restaurant of the Sofitel Hotel, waiting for Inspector Marechal. Until Reyes's death, which the police were now calling a possible homicide, tennis had been a cloistered world, and the impresarios had been able to clamp down on problems before they became public knowledge. Now the situation called for some delicate liaison work.

Clavier, who seldom allowed anything to keep him from eating a good lunch, had consumed everything. The fish course had been excellent: the wine, superior. Abraham, a moody man, had barely touched his food.

'How long can they keep us here?' Abraham asked.

'Another day. Perhaps two. I spoke with my friend, the Minister. He is working to allow the players to move on.'

Abraham poured more wine. Since the announcement about Reyes being murdered, he had been drinking too much. 'They're talking about another strike, Alain.'

'Mon Dieu! Please ask them not to. It would damage what little unity we have.'

'Sven Skaar called, to tell me he's doing another interview. The public trusts him, and we've been getting some good mail and a lot of phone calls about it.'

'Skaar is a good man.'

'You don't sound convinced.'

'What I am sensing, my dear Peter, is that people want to hurt us. We have such a positive image, and some people will stop at nothing to tarnish us.'

Abraham sighed. 'I keep feeling like this happened behind the Iron Curtain. Cops everywhere, poking around. A grey Renault followed me when I went shopping yesterday.'

'My main worry,' Clavier said, 'is that the problem will spread to the other tournaments and damage the entire season. Archer Bell has been speaking to me about this. So has Saadi.'

'You know, when I was in my twenties, I wouldn't have minded hanging around Paris for another week. I had time to burn. But each year I think, Pete, this season is your last. And that's why I want to get out of here. I've got a tournament to play in Gstaad. Wimbledon's less than a month away, for God's sake!'

'Patience, my dear Peter.' Clavier looked beyond Abraham's shoulder, to see Inspector Marechal making his way through the tables. He came up to their table and shook hands with both men. Clavier invited him to sit down, and a waiter hurried over to take his order. 'Would you like to order something, Inspector?'

'Perhaps, a small aperitif.'

Clavier ordered a cassis. The men made small talk until it arrived.

Marechal sipped his drink, then held it up, between himself and Clavier. 'Well, M. le President, I toast your political connections.'

'What does that mean?'

'I had a call this morning, from the assistant to the Minister. While I do not appreciate the intrusion, it appears that your tennis players will probably be able to depart, to flee to all corners of the universe – if I get cooperation with my remaining interrogations.'

'Ah, very good.' Clavier glanced at Abraham.

'The Minister, you see, has become convinced that the death of Reyes was an accident.'

Clavier had hoped as much.

'But I, on the other hand, differ.'

'It's your job to think he was murdered.'

The Inspector took a healthy sip of his drink and stood up. 'So. I shall keep all players here until tomorrow morning. After that, they should be free to leave Paris.'

'Terrific,' Abraham said.

'However, if the investigation should take a different turn . . .' Clavier listened carefully at the veiled threat. '. . . then I shall have to contact Scotland Yard and pursue the investigation to London.'

'You don't mean you've got the jurisdiction to harass us in England?'

'Police forces cooperate with one another, Mr Abraham. In today's terrorist climate, we must be on twenty-four hour alert.'

'In the middle of the tournament?'

'I'm afraid that our work cannot always fit in with your schedules. I think you are forgetting that this is a criminal case, and that the murderer might very well be among you.'

'Impossible!'

'Or,' Marechal went on, 'among those who follow the circuit.'

The Inspector bowed, a stiff little motion, and walked away from the table, leaving both men with a sense that things had somehow become worse.

'I'm going to pack.'

'Not yet, Peter.' Clavier put a hand on his arm.

'Why not?'

'We still have an internal problem. We need to do something about it.'

Abraham looked at his watch. 'There's a plane for Switzerland at two. I'm going to be on it.' He stood up.

'Give me half an hour,' Clavier said, as he dropped a sheaf of French francs onto the table. 'To call a war council.'

Abraham walked out. Clavier went straight to the office of the concierge, where he used the telephone.

A huge traffic jam extended from the Avenue George V to the Champs Elysees. The taxi containing Archer Bell and Peter Abraham was stuck. They were about ready to get out and walk when the taxi squeaked through an opening. The driver sped to the Rue Quentin Bauchart, turned left at the next corner, and stopped in a swirl of kerbside water. Abraham got out. Bell handed the driver a bank note.

'Keep the change.'

Bell and Abraham walked up Avenue George V until they reached Fourquet's. A fussy maitre d'hotel led them to a private sitting room where the other guests were assembled. It was Clavier's party. Fenwick was there, along with Sven Skaar, Abdul Saadi, Paco Ortega, and Harrison Cabot, the President of the USTA. A worried Sir Francis Malcolm, the chairman of the All England Club and the man who would preside at the Wimbledon Championships, had arrived that morning from London.

These were the men who controlled professional tennis.

A waiter served the champagne. Saadi had Perrier, with a twist of lime. Clavier opened the discussion.

'Gentlemen, we have a problem.'

'I hope we can get on with it, Alain,' Fenwick said, looking at his watch. 'This meeting just cost me half a million. I was due in Geneva three hours ago.'

'And I've got to catch a plane, myself,' Abraham said.

'Gentlemen, we are all making sacrifices.'

'What's the latest from the lab?' Abraham asked. 'On the drugs?'

'There is nothing, I'm afraid. A new drug which acts as a stimulant and a second drug, which is an aphrodisiac.'

Bell cut in, leaning forward in his chair, frowning, using his bulk. 'Drugs are what we've got to worry about. We need to squelch this drug connection, here and now.'

'I agree,' said Ortega. 'We don't want the newspapers to run with this.'

Tension was rising in the room.

'Gentlemen, please.' Clavier held up his hand, palm out. 'We are in accord, but we must keep cool. The French Open is over. We have a winner, and a *grand crise* has been averted. But the season, it is ahead of us.'

'Hear, hear,' said Sir Francis, looking at Harrison Cabot.

Wimbledon was coming up next. Already, the publicity generated about drugs was dirtying the air, and ticket scalpers were going a huge business. What happened at Wimbledon in mid-summer would affect that happened at the end of the summer, at Flushing Meadow, in New York.

Clavier made an attempt to summarize. 'Our problem, as I see it, is that we are being invaded. The police. The press. There has been a queue outside my office for two days, photographers, television people, magazine writers. The phone never stops ringing.'

'What we need,' Archer Bell said, 'is some protection.'

'I don't buy this murder theory of Marechal's,' Abraham said. 'Who would want to kill Armando?'

'I agree with Pete,' Bell said. 'We need to play this as an accident, and not a murder. Everyone knew that Armando was a vitamin freak, and it's not that big a step from vitamins to the hard stuff.'

Abraham turned to Fenwick. 'When you were managing Armando, F.F., how did he seem?'

Fenwick thought a moment before replying. 'He started taking a drug last year, something for his anxiety. Hell, I've got friends back home in their sixties who take the same kind of thing, and they don't collapse.'

'But Reyes was mixing drugs,' Abraham said, 'letting them combine in his bloodstream.'

Fenwick shook his head. 'I didn't know about that. He must have been on the edge, more than I knew.'

'What we must do,' Saadi said, 'is protect the game as a whole. Reyes is dead. Others live on after him.'

The talk swirled through the room. It was a closed meeting, and the waiters had left, so Clavier poured more champagne all round. Archer Bell leaned back in his chair and studied the situation. Bell had a single priority – keeping his own players out of trouble. In the past, Terry Laville had been connected with dropping something into his opponent's food, but so far as Bell knew, that was just a rumour. If it had happened, it had been before Bell and Terry got together as manager and player. But Laville was crazy and highly strung, and when he got desperate, the man was capable of anything. It was too late this year for the Grand Slam – Koras had the momentum there – but Laville could win his first Wimbledon and go on from there to win New York. Laville needed a personal watchdog.

Bell, watching the momentum of the discussion shift and wobble, seized his moment. 'I have a proposal, gentlemen.'

'What?'

'We need information. We don't know anything, and that makes us a hostage to rumour, to speculation, to the investigators leaking exaggerations to the press to make themselves look heroic. If the police do come sneaking in undercover, we want to be informed. If someone's pushing drugs, we want to know which players are involved, before we read it in *Le Figaro*. Am I right?'

Information was a safe topic. For the first time, the men agreed. So Bell laid out his strategy.

'All of you know I own a basketball team. Three years back, we had a similar problem come up – drugs, doped players, threats of a news leak, which would have generated some rotten publicity, not to mention fines, suspensions, and maybe jail terms for some of our people. We hired a private investigator. He nosed around, posing as a writer, found out who was using, who was clean. We had some private talks with our users – there weren't many – and the threatened criminal investigation never went anywhere.'

Clavier nodded. Ortega looked at Bell, suspiciously. Abraham looked around the room. Saadi smiled, an enigmatic smile.

'Who is this man?' Clavier asked.

'Malone's his name. Matt Malone. He's ex-Army, ex-police. Had a year or so of law school. He's tough, and reliable.'

'Is he available?' Saadi asked.

'I can check.' Bell looked at his watch. 'If you gentlemen give me the go-ahead.'

'What will this cost us?' Fenwick asked.

'Money's no object, F.F., if he does the job. When he worked for us, he got four hundred a day, plus expenses.'

'This is ITF money, I presume?'

'I suggest a private fund,' Bell said. 'With everyone at the table contributing. That way we keep the ITF out of it.'

'A sound plan,' Clavier said, glad to be insulated from this business.

'Who will Malone report to?' Abraham asked.

'Let him talk to Mr Bell,' Clavier said. 'And Mr Bell can report to us.'

Abraham stood. 'Three days ago, I would have voted no. But since that insinuating cop Marechal has been breathing down my neck, I think it's a good idea. I vote yes, and if I hurry I can catch that plane.'

'Good luck at Gstaad, Pete.'

'Thanks.'

Abraham walked out, and Archer Bell turned to face the impresarios. 'I have one vote for Malone, gentlemen. What is your pleasure?'

The Advisory Group voted to buy themselves a little discretion.

CHAPTER SIX

It was mid-afternoon and the Avenue de Breteuil was calm, at last. Even so, Sergeant Demetz could not find a parking space. Paris was getting too crowded, even for Parisians.

'Stop in a double lane,' Marechal ordered. 'For heaven's sake, we are the police.'

'Yes.'

Demetz complied, but Marechal knew it was against his principles. Demetz was a man who went by the book. He dressed precisely, and his reports were works of art. Marechal smiled. He could bend the law here and there. But his aide, never.

Inspector Marechal was ten minutes early for this meeting with Muriel Broussard-Gauthier. He had done his homework, and had discovered that her husband was an attorney with close associations in high places in the city. Marechal's task was to impress her with the fact that, without her husband's connections, she would have been taken to the Quai des Orfevres and questioned there.

As he rode the elevator up, Marechal flipped briefly through the file which contained photographs of Reyes with a dozen beautiful women. They were from magazines, and from the files of professional and amateur photographers. One had caught Reyes at the moment of his death, collapsed on the red earth at Roland-Garros. Several photos showed Reyes and Milo Tigrid, who was one of the last players left in Paris. Marechal had an appointment with Tigrid later in the afternoon.

Another series of photos, from a glossy magazine covering a society party, showed Muriel between Reyes and her husband, the powerful attorney. The husband had a long, sad face, typically French. It was clear he did not like being photographed.

In the photo, Muriel was resplendent. She was much younger than her husband. Her hair fell like silk over naked shoulders, and the low cut dress did little to hide the voluptuousness of her breasts. A discreet set of diamonds – a choker with a matching bracelet and a glittering ring – complete the image of wealth and eternal beauty.

Marechal knew that face, from an investigation five years ago, a scandal involving twenty important people from the fashion world, from politics, from the army. Drugs had been involved then, and a call girl network had been uncovered. And in the midst was the beautiful woman named Muriel X. She had not been married then. As he stepped off the elevator, the Inspector wondered how much her husband knew about her past.

If the husband knew nothing, Marechal would have his leverage.

She lived in a sumptuous apartment on the fifth floor. Marechal rang the buzzer, looking around the hall, which had floors and walls made of marble. A maid answered the door. She was dark, and her accent told Marechal she was from the French Antilles. She led him to a sitting room furnished in authentic Louis XV, and left him there. In a moment, Mme Broussard-Gauthier, alias Muriel X, appeared. She wore a viridian dress that brought out the colour of her eyes, and carried a hat in one hand. The hat told Marechal that she was going out.

He stood. The lady greeted him and sat down, carefully, on the edge of a silk brocade settee. She crossed her legs, a movement by a women conscious of her sexual allure.

'Thank you for taking the time to see me, madame.'

'Not at all. I try to cooperate with the police. My husband is an officer of the court.'

'Yes, madame. I know that. I am here to ask a few questions about Armando Reyes.'

'It was terrible. I saw it, from the stands. One moment, he was playing beautifully, looking exceptionally strong, and the next he –'

'Are you aware that the case has been turned over to Homicide?'

'No.' Her pretty features registered shock. 'Why?'

'We think Reyes was murdered.'

She put her hand up to clutch her throat. At the same time, her face grew pale, making her look older and more vulnerable. 'It is not possible! Who would want to *kill* Armando?'

It was just the reaction he wanted. Marechal pulled out his notebook. 'Madame, it is well known that you were seen with Reyes in the days preceding his death. You drove him to the stadium the day he died.'

'Is that a crime?' She recovered her composure by adjusting her position on the settee. She had excellent legs.

'There are rumours that you and the victim were lovers.'

'The rumours are only rumours.'

Marechal brought out the file of photographs. 'How did he appear? That day?'

'He was nervous. It was just before the match.'

'Was this a change in his behaviour?'

'I cannot be certain. We had lunch a few times. We saw one another at parties.'

Marechal tried putting on more pressure. 'I was wondering if your husband might be able to help us dispel these . . .'

Muriel stood up. 'You are threatening me, M. l'Inspector.' Her eyes flashed, and a tremor passed through her body. When angry, she was magnificent. A man might be tempted to treat her badly, just to see her this way. Marechal wondered if that had been Reyes's mistake. 'Now,' she said, 'I must ask you to go.'

Marechal stayed where he was and showed her the picture of herself, between Reyes and her husband. 'I take it your husband was friendly with Reyes.'

'My husband was interested in getting Armando's opinion on some investments in South America.'

'Where is your husband, madame, in case we need to question him?'

'Singapore,' she said. 'Now, Inspector, if there is nothing else?'

She trembled, and the green dress rippled. Marechal suddenly considered that if she was telling the truth about herself and Reyes – they saw one another over lunch and at parties – that meant there was another woman.

'I understand that you are collecting your photos into a book. *Une histoire de tennis?*'

'Yes.'

'I should like to see the photos.'

Muriel walked into another room. When she came back, she carried two albums of photos. As the Inspector leafed through the pages, he kept up his interrogation. 'What can you tell us about Reyes's habits?'

She looked at her watch. 'I can tell you I am late for an appointment.'

'Who else did he see? What did he do when he wasn't playing tennis?'

'He was very debonair. He loved having a good time. His secret ambition was to be a racing driver.'

Marechal noted that. 'Were you aware that he took drugs, madame?'

'I knew that he took vitamins. He was what the Americans call a health nut. Frankly, I thought he drank too much.'

Marechal wrote that down in his notebook, then closed the photo albums and stood up. 'This photo book you are doing, will it take you to other tournaments?'

Her answer was clipped. 'Yes.'

'In that case, I would appreciate it very much if you would keep your ears open.' He handed her a card.

'I am not a police informer, monsieur.'

Marechal gave her his special inspectorial smile. 'Oh, there is one small matter. A scandal five years ago, involving M. Bretton and some members from L'Ecole Militaire.'

The woman blushed, then grew pale. 'What about it?'

'I was just wondering how much your husband knew of that affair?'

'He knows enough.'

Marechal nodded, pointed to his business card, and closed his notebook. 'I bid you good day, madame. And good luck with your publishing venture.'

The Inspector let himself out. Standing at the door of the elevator, waiting, he noticed that Mme Broussard-Gauthier had not yet come out. Perhaps she had forgotten her urgent appointment.

Going down in the elevator, he wondered how many pictures she had held back from him.

Milo Tigrid was sitting at the deserted bar, thinking about the death of his friend, when Inspector Marechal appeared at the door. He waved the policeman over. The Inspector sat down and ordered a half beer on tap.

'We do not have beer on tap,' the barman said.

'An Amstel then.'

The barman opened the beer, and poured half of it into a tall glass. Marechal drank, then turned to Milo.

'M. Tigrid, thank you for granting me this interview.'

'I am here. You are here. What is it that you want?'

'You were good friends with the deceased, were you not?'

'The best. We drank together. I taught him everything he knew about tennis, life, women, having fun.'

'What did he do for you?'

'Years ago, Armando loaned me money, so I could continue playing. I was on a losing streak. I had not won anything in more than a year. He kept me afloat.'

'A good friend, then.'

'The best.'

'What did you think of his vitamins?'

'They were horse shit. But Armando could not function without them.'

The Inspector switched subjects. 'How well do you know Muriel Broussard-Gauthier?'

Milo gave the Inspector a look. 'Not well enough.'

'May I take it that means you and she were not intimate?'

'You put it delicately, Inspector, and my bruised ego thanks you. We were not intimate.'

'And how did that make you feel?'

Milo shrugged. 'You win some, you lose some.'

'Could you be more specific?'

Milo signalled for another beer. 'Women are like buses. If you miss one, another will be along in a quarter of an hour.'

Marechal smiled. 'You are a philosopher, monsieur. Do you think M. Reyes was intimate with her?'

'Who knows? If she could not have Tigrid, she might as well settle for the Peruvian.'

'Does that mean you tried with her?'

'Is the world dark at night? Does a duck swim? Listen. Armando and I had a pact. If he so much looked at a woman, I would try for her. And the same for him, when I looked.'

'It was a game, then?'

'Yes. A small competition, off the courts, to keep us amused on the eternal round.'

'This competition with Reyes, did you keep score?'

'Informally.'

'Who was ahead?'

Tigrid grinned. 'I was. I am older. But Armando was closing in on me.'

The fresh beer came, and the Yugoslav held his glass up. 'To Armando, you handsome bastard, wherever you are.'

'Do you know for a fact that Reyes and Mme Broussard-Gauthier were intimate?'

'I would bet my life on it. Why do you ask?'

Marechal knew someone was lying, so he tried a police ploy. 'There was a woman seen leaving Reyes's room, the night before the murder.'

'Why are you calling it a murder?'

Marechal sipped his Amstel. 'Do you have any idea who that woman might be?'

'Muriel, of course.'

'What if is wasn't Muriel?'

Tigrid brightened, then grinned at Marechal. 'I see it this way.'

'Yes?'

He held his glass up to the light and intoned to the room and the world at large. 'For Armando, women were like buses . . .'

Marechal stopped him. The man was drunk, and a clown. How best to use him? 'What would you do if you could find the person who killed Reyes?'

Instantly, without thinking, Tigrid's eyes blazed and he smashed the empty beer bottle against the bar. 'If I find the sonofabitch who killed him, I swear I'll throttle him with these two hands.'

And they were big enough hands to do the job.

There was a dream girl on the jumbo jet to Paris who kept Matt Malone's attention, all the way from the take off at Chicago to the landing at Charles de Gaulle. She was a college junior from Beloit College, a liberal arts school in Wisconsin, just north of the border with Illinois. Malone, who worked out of Chicago, knew the area. A couple of years back, he had handled a case for a doctor from Rockford, Illinois. The doctor spent seventy hours a week in the emergency room, and he was certain his wife was cheating on him, with a good friend from college days. The lady in question, a stunning blonde who jogged in the snow in pink warm-up suits and who appeared in the society pages in a dazzling sable fur, had led Malone a chase across a landscape that resembled his nightmares about Siberia – Milwaukee, Madison, Chicago, Kenosha, Dubuque, Peoria – wheeling her pale blue Seville down the narrow winter roads like a crazy woman.

The doctor had been right about his wife stepping out on him. But he'd been wrong about the college friend. The lady was seeing three different men, and having one hell of a time doing it. At the end of the case, the doctor had threatened not to pay Malone's travel expenses, and had to be taken to small claims court.

Oh, yes, Matt Malone remembered that winter. He'd drunk many boiler-makers, and the wind chill had often been below fifty degrees.

The honey-skinned girl on the plane, however, washed all the cold memories away. She was sunny and warm. Her name was Deborah Hansen and she was majoring in sociology. She had perfect white teeth, clean hair the colour of an Iowa wheatfield, blue eyes that smiled at you, and a healthy chest that punched her sweater out in front. The sweater was pink and fuzzy, reminding him of how things were back in the fifties, Malone's own heyday.

Ah, sweet memories.

So he chatted with Deborah Hansen. They had a complimentary cocktail, then one more.

And when she excused herself, squeezing past him, brushing him with her knees, letting the touch linger for just that extra split second that made him think she might be coming on to him, Malone told himself to clam down. He was old enough to be her father.

Malone had known a few girls like Deborah Hansen, but mostly from a distance. He'd had his first crush on a distant dream girl when he was a delivery boy at a grocery in Skokie. She was an untouchable teenager on her way to being a pristine clean college girl. She had shining hair and the confident walk that came from having money, as if she owned half the world and was making plans to buy the other half on Saturday. He'd stare at her when she came in to shop, getting out of the car, with a flash of leg, walking into the store with a little knowing smile, standing in the aisles, hips tight and compact inside her tartan skirt, while she studied a label. She dressed casually, but Malone could tell the clothes were expensive. Her name was Sally Atkinson – he found that out after seeing her twice – and she represented money, wealth, power, the never-ending good life. Malone reckoned Sally was about his age, but that only made her more distant, more unreachable. When she went away to college, somewhere back east, he spent September and October waiting for her to come back to the A&P. When she didn't, Malone joined the army.

Sitting there, on the jumbo jet, Malone could still remember Sally Atkinson getting out of her car, swinging those pretty legs, the skirt climbing up, like a class television commercial for women's stockings.

Now, at forty-seven, Malone still marvelled how easy it was to close your eyes and reach back and connect to teenage longing, teenage pain. Here he was, a veteran of the U.S. Army, the Chicago police force, Marshall Field's department store, the United Insurers Ltd of Northern Illinois, Malone's Typing Service at the University of Illinois, and the Niles Center A&P Skokie. And he was still lusting after college girls who smelled faintly of Ivory soap. The weighty emotion made him reflect on longing and hunger and appetite.

He'd enlisted in 1957, for airborne training at Fort Bragg, North Carolina. The army had shipped him to Germany, where a girl named Ilse Hausmeier had fallen in love with him. Ilse was icy blonde, with cold blue eyes and a frigid way of holding her mouth when she spoke. She had money from her father, who turned out to be your friendly neighbourhood black marketeer. Out in the world, Ilse walked stiffly and inspired chills. In private, between the sheets, she was all passionate action – serpentine legs, lips, sweat, moans, warm skin.

That dream girl had lasted four months.

After Germany, he spent some time in France, training French airborne troops to jump out of transport planes. From France, he went to Vietnam, where he was wounded. In 1963, he framed his discharge papers and entered the University of Illinois at Urbana, majoring in political science. After a semester of theory, Malone switched to criminology. He'd always been a jock when he had time, so he tried out for the baseball team and played catcher on the varsity. He was older than the average college boy, so he got elected captain. For a couple of years, the dream girls swarmed, nice clean college girls, none as pretty as his vision of Sally Atkinson – where was she now? – but enough to let him know the world was there for the taking.

He was twenty-seven when he graduated and entered law school at the University of Chicago. He married Gretchen Hill Finch, from Evanston. Gretchen reminded him, from a distance, of sweet Sally Atkinson. After four months of bickering, Malone knew he shouldn't have tried to marry a dream. Gretchen divorced him and took a plane to New York. Her dream was making it big on Broadway.

Depressed, Malone dropped out of law school and became a skip tracer for Marshall Field's department store. He went on from Field's to insurance work, investigating arson cases, tracking insane firebugs who sent whole city blocks up in flames, and then were dumb enough to try to beat the insurance company. Malone enjoyed tracking the types who thought they could get away with it, and he kept meeting all kinds of people, the best and worst his metropolis had to offer.

There was a certain circle of men in Chicago, a few years older than Malone. They dressed in suits from Brooks Brothers. They had seats on the commodities exchange. They arrived at meetings in long black cars, piloted by polite chauffeurs in sharply tailored uniforms. These men lived in Evanston, Grosse Pointe, Kenilworth. Their wives were good clean college girls like Sally Atkinson, now grown into mature society women.

And these men came quietly to Malone, asking him to fix this, or to hide that, or to do a little cover-up. They trusted Malone. They needed him. And that gave him an idea for his own business.

He left United Insurers Ltd, and went into business for himself. Matt Malone, Investigations. And that's how he met Archer Bell . . .

'Hi!' He looked up to see Deborah Hansen starting to slide back into her seat. 'Did you miss me?'

Coming out of his memory, he smiled. 'How about a refill?' Malone rang the buzzer for the flight attendant.

Deborah pointed back down the aisle. 'I met the nicest man, a doctor, from Madison. He works for the Med Center in out-patient care. Would you believe he wanted me to interview for a job?' She showed Malone a card, James G. Belton, MD. The guy wore five hundred dollar shoes and an expensive cashmere jacket. He was the type who would hire Malone to pick up the pieces after he had tooled through the world, hurting people.

'You're picking up the work, flying to France.'

'Isn't it wonderful?' she smiled.

'Yeah. What's the job?'

'Research.' Deborah Hansen's smile was bright enough for a Gleem ad. 'I would interview people in the emergency room. Ask them questions. For a national survey he's putting together.'

'Sounds great.'

She hugged herself, which brought on a pretty shiver. 'This is my day, I guess. Meeting two exciting men. Getting an actual job offer!'

'Yeah.' Malone stretched, yawned. When you were young, you could still stabilize the dream.

Leaving the aircraft, he and Deborah Hansen got separated. He was in one transparent tube, heading down to customs, and she was in another, behind him, off to the right, with the doctor from Madison. One more dream girl, gone.

The customs police at Charles de Gaulle had guns and duck-billed caps and little moustaches. They held out their hands for passports, and their eyes kept flicking over the passengers, and every so often they would pluck someone out of the line and take them through a door.

Customs made you realize you were a foreigner.

Archer Bell was there to meet him, with a driver in a snappy grey uniform who spoke French. Mr Bell had gained a few pounds. He wore a three-piece suit. As they shook hands, Malone felt Bell's eyes, scanning him, measuring.

In minutes, they were heading south in Bell's deluxe Mercedes, away from the airport. Malone could see Paris, the famous skyline. It was after ten in the morning. He'd lost eight hours, flying against the sun. Jet-lag fuzzed his mind. Bell handed him a manila envelope. Inside were photos of the principals of the case, mostly tennis players. They were handsome athletes with showboat smiles, strong faces, and deep-set eyes.

'This is Reyes,' Bell said. 'The man who died. This is Pantakoras Belynkas. This one is Milos Tigrid. Here's Polak with his wife, a Chicago girl. Fenwick manages them. Here's Fenwick.'

'He always dresses like that?'

'F.F.'s a Texan. You know how they are.'

'Who's this?' Malone pointed to a photo of a man with a moustache.

'That's Jack Di Rocca. Our ex-con.'

Malone flipped through the photos until he found the picture of Reyes. 'They played his death up on national TV. Is the official Paris verdict still heart failure?'

'Yes. Brought on by a drug overdose.'

'What were the drugs?'

'One was an aphrodisiac. The second was something to calm his nerves. He was an emotional player, a real party-boy. A hotdog cop named Marechal thinks it's murder.'

'Who would want to kill Reyes?'

'There are several ideas kicking around. I put my money on a French hit

man, hired by the husband of the woman Reyes was cuckolding.'
'Sounds promising.'
Bell handed Malone a piece of note paper containing a name and phone number. 'His wife, Madame Muriel Broussard-Gauthier, is busily putting together a book of tennis photos. You might interview her.'
Malone studied the note, then put it into his pocket. 'Who else?'
Bell looked out the window at the scenery, then shifted his eyes to Malone. 'Your "official" job for the advisory group is to find out who's using drugs before the police do. For the fee we agreed to over the phone. Four hundred a day, plus expenses.'
There was something else, so Malone waited.
'Your unofficial job,' Bell went on, 'is to keep my top players out of trouble.'
'Laville and Cooper, right?'
Bell nodded. 'The rival camp is headed by Fenwick. If any of his players should turn up with drugs. Or if Di Rocca should make a small slip . . . well, you understand.'
Bell handed Malone another manila envelope. Inside Malone found a stack of business cards identifying him as a writer with Andrews Livingston, a publisher with a New York address, and five thousand dollars in French and Swiss francs. Malone understood – this money was from Bell, extra pay for moonlighting.
'So I'm off to Zurich?'
'Gstaad. There's a tournament there.'
'Who do I watch in Gstaad?'
'My players. Also Tigrid and Polak.'
'What about this other guy, Koras?'
'He's going to Palermo.'
Malone tucked the money into his jacket pocket. 'Do the Paris police know about me?'
'Yes. I'll drop you off at the Quai des Orfèvres. To see Marechal.'
'What's he like?'
'A bloodhound.'
Malone sat back against the cushions of the Mercedes. Great way to start your day in Paris, with a visit to the gendarmes.
'Who did Reyes pal around with?'
'Tigrid was his friend. So was Koras. The woman is your best lead.'
'I'm a writer. What if she wants to write a book together?'
Bell looked directly at Malone. 'Do what you have to.'
'I saw Laville on the tube, giving it to the umpire. How's he holding up?'
'Terry is a vast talent. When he's on, a genius. As an artist, he needs protecting. This Reyes business has unnerved everyone. Terry told me, privately, he had a terrible nightmare about Reyes's death.'
Screwballs, Malone thought, as the Mercedes turned a corner, heading

for the Paris police station. Screwballs who paid his fee, and his way to Paris.

The police made Malone wait for nearly an hour. He sat on a wooden bench which had held untold millions of tired, but guilty, derrières, distracting himself by reading an old Perry Mason novel. He was starting chapter seven when they came to fetch him.

'The Inspector will see you now.'

'Thanks.'

Marechal stood on the threshold of his office, a short man with a neatly pressed suit and an expression of watchful disdain. The tidy little man made Malone think about his own clothes, rumpled from eight hours in an airplane seat. He needed a hot bath, some sleep, a drink, and a working girl who spoke ten words of English. Malone was ushered in.

'Do you speak French, M. Malone?'

'A little. I taught some of your élite troops over here how to jump out of an airplane.'

The Inspector smiled. 'We have a background report on you, and on your detective business in Chicago.' He sat down, waving Malone to a chair. 'It seems you also were a policeman?'

'Yes. In Chicago. I worked vice for a while. Then homicide.'

The Inspector nodded as he lit a Gauloise. 'Might I get to the point?'

'Sure.'

'This is a serious crime. I don't welcome foreign investigators who are not licenced here and who have no standing.'

'I won't get in the way,' Malone said.

'Perhaps. But if you do not overstep, perhaps we can cooperate.'

That sounded like a break. 'I'd like to help, Inspector. What can I do?'

'Where do you go when you leave Paris?'

'A place in Switzerland. Gstaad.'

Marechal smiled at Malone's difficulty with pronunciation. 'M. Malone, how would you like to be our man in Gstaad, that is, share your information with me?'

Malone knew a good deal when he heard one. 'What do I get out of it?'

Marechal spread his hands. 'We have a small fund available, for operations of this sort. But I thought perhaps we might be of service to you in other ways. For example, if you required a background report on a certain player, we could get it for you. How does that sound?'

'It's a deal.'

The Inspector smiled, then walked to the window and looked out. He had a fine view of the Quai, a privilege of his senior status, and when he leaned out he could see the Institute's cupola. He watched two *bateaux mouche* sliding down river. 'Is there anything you need from our information system today?'

'Yes. There's a player named Di Rocca. His first name is Jack.'

'Ah, yes. We are aware of M. Di Rocca. There is a file already assembled. It may contain what you want.'

'Terrific,' Malone said.

The Inspector pressed a button, then spoke French into an intercom.

While they waited, Malone asked, 'Have there been any public threats?'

'No. Surprising, isn't it?'

'Yeah. Death brings out the crazies. We had a butcher's strike back home early in the spring, and all kinds of people got into the act, throwing stink bombs in supermarkets, shooting at delivery trucks. This Reyes thing could attract a lot of what we call "tangential activity".'

'We shall be on the alert. And I have alerted Superintendent Weston, my counterpart at Scotland Yard. He is preparing security for Wimbledon.'

The door opened and a man in uniform brought in a file, which he laid on the Inspector's desk. The name on the folder was DI ROCCA, J. USA. Pushing the file across the desk to Malone, the Inspector said, 'You must read it here, in my office.'

'No problem.'

The Inspector left the office and Malone opened the file and began to make notes.

Archer Bell's French secretary made the appointment with Muriel Broussard-Gauthier for seven that evening. Malone was tired, but working on a complex case helped him over the hump, and when the interview was over he planned to get a good night's sleep. He'd made a promising contact with the Paris policeman, Marechal. Moreover, his wallet was full of money, and if he could stay ahead of the intricacies of the case, he could keep working until mid-September, when the tennis season was over. The break so far was the dossier on Jack Di Rocca. Malone had an appointment with Di Rocca tomorrow morning, at Stade Roland-Garros. Malone wanted to meet there, so he could get a feel for what went on in a world-class tennis arena. If he was going to fake writing about tennis, he would have to learn the keys that unlocked the game.

There were always keys.

Malone rode up in the lift, got off on five, and found himself in a ritzy foyer, with shinning black marble walls. He found number 502 and rang the buzzer. An eyeball appeared in the security port.

'M. Malone?'

'Oui, madame. Bonjour.'

The door opened and Malone handed her the business card that said he was a writer. She was attractive, with high heels and a platinum jumpsuit that showed off an excellent figure. She wore a silver bracelet on her right wrist, and her shinning red hair was piled up on her head. The jumpsuit had exaggerated shoulder pads, making her resemble a model from an expensive women's magazine. Her smile was dazzling.

She looked at the card, then stepped aside. 'Won't you come in?' Her English was better than his French.

Malone followed her into a beautifully furnished room, where she invited him to sit down. She poured a glass of wine for both of them, and he tried his pitch about the photographs and the New York publisher. As he talked, she asked occasional questions, and he noted a faint gleam of amusement in her eye.

'Would this be, as you Americans say, a deal of fifty-fifty?'

'I was thinking more of thirty-seventy.'

'Seventy for me?'

Malone smiled. The lady could deal. 'Seventy for me, madame. That is, if my publisher likes your photos, and if you can get more for the rest of the season.'

'I was planning to leave for Gstaad soon. Let me show you the pictures first.'

'All right.'

She left the room, and came back with two photo albums and three white cardboard boxes full of photos. He took his time going through them until he came to the shots that showed Armando Reyes approaching death.

Muriel's photos captured Reyes as he was about to serve. There was the toss of the ball, the racket about to climb toward contact, and then a grainy close-up of his face, beginning to contort, a look of horrified surprise. The next shot showed Reyes dropping the racket, and then Reyes falling, crumpling, his legs giving up the effort to stand. Malone stopped to look at Madame Broussard-Gauthier. She had tears in her eyes. The next photo showed Reyes on his knees, dropping face first into the dust. Then another series of shots of the men carrying the stretcher, and one of a stout man in tennis clothes standing a few feet away.

'This one is Tigrid, right?'

'Yes. A wonderful clown of a man.'

'Tigrid was close to Reyes?'

'They were like brothers.'

Malone was impressed. 'This is superb work. I think we can make an arrangement with my publisher, with no trouble.'

'Thank you. I must tell you, however, I am not satisfied with your seventy and my thirty.'

'No? What would you suggest?'

'Fifty-fifty, monsieur.'

Malone lifted his wine glass. 'We can discuss that. After I talk to New York.'

Muriel sipped her aperitif. 'Are you an *investigative* journalist, Mr Malone?'

Now that was a surprise. 'Why do you ask?'

'You seem so intense. Like a policeman.'

'Have you known many policemen, madame?'

'Once. But that was in another life.'

They smiled at each other.

'It is the way you ask questions. So confident. So questing. So like a . . . *flic*.'

'I used to be a cop, back in Chicago. I didn't know it showed.'

'I suspected as much. And how did you become a writer?'

'I got tired of getting shot at.'

Nervously, she stood, making the platinum material of the jumpsuit shimmer. 'Are you by chance free for dinner?'

'Sure. But I thought . . .'

She put a hand on his arm. 'I know a quiet place, a neighbourhood restaurant where the tourists do not venture. If you would allow me to be your guide . . .'

'Hey. Great. I'd like that.'

They walked through the soft May evening to the restaurant. Two policeman passed, on bicycles, wearing short capes that made Malone think he was in a Humphrey Bogart movie.

'Les hirondelles,' Muriel said. 'With the tails of swallows.'

Over a carafe of red wine in the restaurant, she asked him questions about his life in America. He fudged on the answers. Then Muriel told him some things. 'Armando and I were not lovers. I met him in Rome, three weeks ago. I found him attractive, a charming man. At another time, we might have become intimate. But we did not.'

'How come?'

She shrugged. 'I am particular with my friends. My husband is some years old than I. We have a sensible marriage. He has his other interests, I have mine. But with Armando, I could sense the presence of another woman. It was as if we met . . . for purely social reasons.'

If Reyes was using someone this beautiful as a decoy, it was a sad waste of resources. 'Any idea who the woman was?'

'None.'

'Too bad.'

With the flickering candlelight between them, Malone felt closer to this strange woman. He watched while Muriel refilled their wine glasses.

'Do you like a good mystery, Mr Malone?'

He knew then that she didn't buy his cover, the writer from the States. All the talk about *flics*, the way he asked questions, *les hirondelles*. 'Sure.'

Muriel hesitated for a fraction of a second, then slipped a photo out of her handbag. This one was not of the same quality as the others. It showed Armando Reyes leaning against a wall while he talked to Jack Di Rocca. It was clear to Malone that Di Rocca was putting the arm on Reyes.

'When did you take this?'

'An hour or so before the semifinal.'

'What was going on?'
'All I know is that Armando was under terrible strain. And that he didn't want me to hear what he and Jack Di Rocca were saying.'
'Why did you show it to me?
Muriel shrugged, then looked him directly in the eye. 'I feel something from you, trust – something.'
'Thanks.'
'One day, perhaps, you will trust me enough to tell me who you are, M. Ecrivain.'
Thinking she should have been a cop herself, Malone touched his wine glass to hers. The book idea had been a way to get him inside, for a look at her photos, but now he was thinking he might as well pitch the photo book to New York. He'd done some writing in college and it would be dumb to turn down a co-author as good-looking as Muriel. With her in tow, his cover might hold.
The food came. Malone was no gourmet, but it was excellent. Across from him, Muriel was eating European-style, using her knife to pack a piece of duck on the back of her fork. He enjoyed watching her eat. She had sharp instincts. Maybe fifty-fifty was worth considering.

Abdul Saadi had dinner with four friends from Damascus, then returned to his penthouse suite on the top floor of the Hotel Paladin, on the Right Bank of the Seine. The tournament was over, and he was still engrossed in an elaborate corporate takeover of the tennis equipment firm of Sport City. Things were at a standstill because the stockholders wanted too much per share. There had to be a way to bring the price down.
Entering the penthouse, he went first to Athena's room, but the Princess was not there. If he decided to marry the Princess, he would make certain that she stayed at home, as befits a wife.
Saadi walked through the penthouse, which was vast, to his private study. There were two phone calls from Leonardo Reyes, the brother of the dead man, but when Saadi called Reyes's hotel room, he got no answer. Good.
He sat down at his desk, made two phone calls to Damascus, and then tried clearing his mind of business pressures by writing a few sentences on his monograph. The subject of Saadi's research was an enlightened Arab view of the Crusades, and his mission was to show that race hatred and a lust for plunder had motivated the 'Holy Wars' of the middle ages to a much larger degree than had been conceded by western historians.
The words refused to come.
Saadi pushed away from the desk and thought about Clothilde, then about Laure Puget. Thinking about Laure made him angry, so he shifted his thoughts back to what he was about to achieve for Sahara Sports, the Saadi family's conglomerate.
From a small operation turning over less than a million annually,

Sahara Sports had mushroomed into a huge corporate umbrella for a sporting goods empire which specialized in tennis equipment. Sahara made rackets, balls, nets, shoes, clothes, string, stringing machines, wind screens, sweatbands, energy packs – anything and everything for the game of tennis. Its market share had grown from 1.3% to 35.7%. As a child, Saadi had hoarded coins. Now he hoarded corporations. It was a matter of scale. Saadi liked growth.

The next step was to buy up the competition. Sports City, then Laval Sportif, then Ryker.

Saadi's dream was to turn Sahara into a complete sports equipment system – all the way from production and marketing to distribution and retailing. In the next year, he planned to build the first Sahara Stadium in Dallas, and then build other arenas across the major cities of the world. His tournaments would rival Paris, Wimbledon, New York.

The world wanted entertainment. Saadi was there to provide.

Sitting at his computer console, Saadi leaned back to stare at his books – scientific treatises, business manuals, books on economics, political science, accounting, a complete collection of the works of William Blake. Here, in Paris, there was a special collection of 517 volumes of pornography, in French, Swedish, and English.

His histories of the Crusades had been duplicated for each penthouse study. Several shelves were devoted to his subject, and Saadi had a team of scholars from Harvard who were busy putting all the data from the books into his computer system. The task would take three more years.

Now, Saadi unlocked the top drawer of his desk. A dozen bottles of red pills were there, arranged in a neat row, along with a recent copy of *Racket World*, the premier tennis magazine. He suspected Athena had given some of these pills to Reyes, as he had hoped she might. Saadi smiled at the thought. Nothing ventured, really, yet everything gained. It had been an easy way to rid himself of a nuisance. Only a nouveau riche Peruvian would mix aphrodisiacs with his other medication. The man had a heart condition. He had been a fool. Good riddance.

He set the magazine on his desk, then brought out scissors, a piece of typing paper, a bottle of glue, and a pair of plastic gloves. He put on the gloves and began searching through the magazine for the right words.

Abdul Saadi was going to let the media help him hype tennis to a frenzy. He was an economist and a businessman and he had been the first to notice how the death of Reyes increased ticket sales – and more sales meant more exposure.

This was a way to boost tennis into an even bigger sport. The biggest.

Finding the words he wanted, Saadi went to work.

When Di Rocca entered the stadium, accompanied by Sergeant Demetz, he saw Malone waiting halfway up the stand. Di Rocca climbed up to where Malone sat. Down below, the nets were gone and the net posts had been removed; a crew were working on the orange clay. Today, Roland-Garros seemed ghostly and deserted, like Yankee Stadium after the fans had gone, leaving their hot dog wrappers and beer cans.

Di Rocca wore an expensive business suit, light grey, with a conservative blue tie. Because of the heat, he had removed the jacket. His white shirt was spotless and freshly pressed. By contrast, Malone looked rumpled, and his blue shirt was unbuttoned at the collar. His brown wool tie hung loose.

Fifteen rows below, Detective Sergeant Demetz sat alone, smoking a cigarette.

'All right,' Di Rocca said. 'Your name is Malone. You had the cops bring me here by special escort, for a fireside chat. I have a plane to catch for Palermo.'

'I need something from you, Di Rocca.'

Di Rocca sighed. 'What?'

'Like I said, I've been hired to track down the source of the drugs that killed Reyes, before they kill another one of you people.'

'Why tell me?'

Malone showed Di Rocca the photo of himself talking to Armando. 'So?' He handed it back.

'With this, the Paris cops could put you away.'

Di Rocca sighed, looked at his watch. 'If I'm your idea of a big connection, you're dumber than I thought. What do you want?'

'There's a player I want you to watch for me.'

'Who?'

'The one who wound up winning the French Open after Reyes got killed.' Malone checked his notebook. 'Belynkas. Pantakoras Belynkas.'

Di Rocca grinned. 'Why didn't you say so? What kind of stuff do you want?'

'The little things. If he owes money, who to. If he's seeing a woman, who is it. If he's dealing in drugs, who does he get them from. Just the little things.'

Di Rocca stood, looked around. To the west, a group of clouds gathered. 'What do I get out of it?'

'The police stay off your back, so you can get out of Paris.'

Di Rocca took two steps down, then stopped and eyed Malone. 'You really think you can pass as a writer?'

'I did it before.'

Di Rocca shook his head. 'You move like a cop, talk like a cop. You couldn't fool me.'

'That's why I didn't try.' He handed Di Rocca a business card with a telephone number written on the back. 'Call me in Switzerland.'

'Sure.'

As Di Rocca reached ground level, Malone called. 'How well did you know Armando Reyes?'

'He was lucky with women.'

'Did that tick you off?'

'Not enough to kill him, if that's what you mean.'

Malone watched Di Rocca walk out with Sergeant Demetz, then stood up for a good stretch. A player had lost his life down there, on the court, less than a week ago. Today, a mechanized court roller chugged by, smoothing the sand where the man had died, blotting out every trace. Thinking about Koras, whom he had not met, Malone started down. Koras was getting old, maybe feeling desperate. Reyes had been on a tear. If Koras had felt threatened enough, maybe he had slipped the Peruvian some pills. Here, compadre, these will give you a jolt. Malone sighed. It was great to be working. Maybe Di Roca would find out something useful in Palermo.

Part II

WIMBLEDON

Death In An English Garden

CHAPTER SEVEN

On the grounds at the All England Lawn Tennis and Croquet Club in Church Road in Wimbledon, the head groundsman ordered the careful watering of courts one and two. Already, the grass was yellowing, and the tournament had not yet begun. Such a catastrophe had not occurred for nearly half a century.

The head gardener was also worried. His hortensias were in full bloom, and he feared they might die from lack of water. That week, the ancient ivy climbing over the red brick walls shading the Royal Box had been completely reclipped. There was a plan to sprinkle the ivy at the last minute on opening day in order to revive the lovely green. They were hoping for some cool weather, typical of England in the summer. Why was it so hot?

The head gardener stood on the centre court in the shade thrown by the stands, discussing his problems with the head groundsman.

'Do you see any chance of a break in the heat?'

'No. It hasn't been this bad since right after the War.'

'Twelve days of sun. Is that a record?'

'Almost, but I heard there were drops of rain over Greenwich yesterday.'

'We need more than drops.'

Wimbledon was the cathedral of professional tennis, and since the day the tournament ended the summer before, the groundsmen had been busy getting ready for this year's Wimbledon fortnight. They tilled and raked and re-planted while the head groundsman, an expert in horticulture, went down on his hands and knees, not to pray, but to inspect every blade of grass.

Soon, everything would be ready. The opening ceremony had been rehearsed several times. A band from the Guards would be present because the Prince of Wales was appearing in person. That day would probably be the most important in Wimbledon history, ranking with 1977, when the Queen herself appeared for the tournament's centenary.

Wimbledon had a regal history. Built in 1877, the club was the place for royalty and stars to mingle. Before the First World War, the future King George V had accepted the Presidency of the All England Club, and since then sovereigns had been seen more frequently at the matches. In 1926, the Duke of York had even competed in the doubles. Eliminated easily in the first round, he still remained a stout and stalwart supporter of the tournament. These days, the Duke of Kent presided over the honourable association. Tradition required that Her Majesty's drawing room beneath the Royal Box be decorated with fresh flowers every day, just in case. Unfortunately, the Queen had never used the room, but the flowers were nonetheless changed each day.

This year, however, there was to be significant changes at the All England Club. Security, in the capable hands of Superintendent Leo Weston, was to be tightened, firmed up. And at that very moment. Weston sat in the stands, across the yellowing grass from the Royal Box, while he made a rough sketch of the seating area, the aisles, the exits. Scotland Yard had received reports from Paris, where that Peruvian had died, that there might be attempts at violence, at disrupting the tournament. It might have happened in Paris, but this was England. Nothing like that would happen here.

A few miles away, at the Queen's Club, Matt Malone was walking the grounds with his new friend, Muriel Broussard-Gauthier. They both wore identity cards with the words JOURNALIST AFFILIATED TO WIMBLEDON. This badge was coveted by journalists the world over, and it had taken the Chairman's personal intervention to obtain two extra passes. Muriel was grateful to Malone for it.

For the last three weeks, Malone had researched the sacrosanct world of professional tennis, reading books by all the great players – Tilden, Riggs, Kramer, Budge, Laver, Ashe – and reading back issues of *Racket World, World Tennis* and *Tennis* magazine. He understood now that the most important variable in the game was surface – clay courters had a hard time on grass, hard court players had an impossible mission on clay – and he had come to understand and predict seedings, which is the way the best players are distributed, like seeds at planting time, throughout the draw. A proper seeding meant that the top players would meet in the later rounds of play. Malone could reel off statistics – the longest match in history, the scores of the final in 1977, Tilden's score over Lacoste in the 1925 Davis Cup – and he knew every circuit player by name.

In the stands by the first court, they spotted David Kollmore, the tennis writer with the sports page of the *Financial Times.* Kollmore, who was sitting with Nora Laville, waved him over. Terry Laville was down on the court, working out with Dumbo Cooper. Malone introduced Muriel to Kollmore and to Nora, who was sipping something cool and alcoholic from a tall glass. Down on the court, Laville drilled a ball past Cooper, who grunted as he made a dive for it. Muriel excused herself while she made her way to the far end of the court, to take some action shots of the players.

'Laville's looking good,' Malone said.

'I was just telling Mrs Laville here how good his chances were for winning the tournament,' Kollmore replied.

Nora glanced up at Malone. 'Terry's been very edgy, because of the Reyes business.'

'Yes,' Malone said. 'I've been interviewing players for the book and I've noticed the same thing.'

'I heard an odd story,' Kollmore said. 'This morning, at the Gloucester, Mikhail Polak made a scene by refusing to eat some oatmeal. The manager had to be called.'

'I was there,' Malone said. 'And it was quite a scene.'

Nora shivered slightly, and hugged herself. Today she looked pretty, in a pink tank top and white trousers. Her shoulders were tanned, and they helped to distract attention from the circles under her eyes. Malone knew from circuit gossip that Nora Laville had been in the States and Vancouver for a couple of weeks. Nora had a reputation for sudden departures and unexpected arrivals. She also had a reputation for appearing drunk in public, and everyone said she used to be much prettier, before the drinking started. She had family in Kansas.

Kollmore pulled out a pack of Benson and Hedges, which he offered around. Nora took one.

'Have you been a writer long, Mr Malone?' Nora asked.

'Five years.'

'I had someone check in the library, when I was in Vancouver. They couldn't find anything you had written. Not a single word.'

Malone smiled at Nora. 'I wrote a lot of financial stuff before. They don't give you a byline for that, most of the time.'

'I thought,' Kollmore said, 'that you had done a book on another sport. Basketball? Baseball? Something along those lines?'

'Basketball,' Malone said. 'It was a series of articles. I wrote those under a pseudonym.'

'Really?' Nora asked. 'Why is that?'

'There were mob connections. I didn't want to turn on my car ignition and be blown into fish food.'

'Really?' Nora's hand stopped, holding the smouldering cigarette.

'It was an exposé of the corruption behind the glittering exterior of professional sport.'

Kollmore turned to him. 'Is *that* what your book on tennis will be about? Corruption?'

'I just write about what's there,' Malone answered.

'Isn't it ironic,' Nora said, 'that you happen on the scene just after a man dies on the court in Paris.'

'That did have something to do with the idea,' Malone said. 'Publishers like it when it's hot.'

Nora turned back to concentrate on her husband's workout.

Terry and Dumbo stood near the net, hitting quick volleys with the staccato reflexes of boxers working with a small bag. From the stands, Terry looked far superior to Dumbo. Both men were large, weighing over two hundred pounds each. David Kollmore took a notebook from his jacket pocket and wrote down impressions.

When the workout was over, Terry and Dumbo gathered their extra rackets and came over. Terry's lean features were flushed with excitement and the white hair was wet beneath his Indian headband. He and Dumbo shook hands with Malone and Kollmore. Laville remained standing while Dumbo took a seat next to Kollmore. Malone reminded Laville of their upcoming interview.

'How did I look out there, Mr Malone?' Laville's eyes were blazing.

'You looked great, Terry.'

From the side, Dumbo Copper let out a feigned groan. 'He's trying to get me to kill myself before the championship starts.'

'Dumbo,' Nora scolded. 'That's not funny.'

Muriel shot several photos of the group as they stood talking. Dumbo rubbed his leg and grinned into the camera. 'They'll record this workout in history, and put it right up in the Wimbledon Museum. Dumbo Cooper, speared by Terry Laville in pre-tournament exercise session.'

Everyone laughed.

'I've got a topic for you, Malone. A chapter for that book.'

'What is it?'

'Food poisoning,' Dumbo said. 'At the Wimbledon Championships.'

Malone whipped out a ballpoint and an envelope. 'Tell me about it, Dumbo.'

'Well, my eggs this morning were green, and the bacon tasted like shit.'

'That was the beer you drank last night,' Laville said. 'How can an entire country like warm beer?'

'Seriously,' Dumbo said. 'A lot of the players are jumpy about the food. If something tastes the least bit off, they're sending it back. If there's one case of turista during the next two weeks, the hypochondriacs will come right out of the woodwork.'

Malone and Muriel said goodbye and headed over toward the clubhouse.

'Wait until you see these photos of Laville,' Muriel whispered, when they were out of earshot. 'He looks absolutely to be in a trance. As if he saw nothing except his opponent. When I started taking pictures, he played as if I wasn't there.'

'He's a strange one, all right. Part genius, part timber wolf.'

'The look in his eyes was mad,' she said.

Muriel gripped his arm as they walked along. Up head, a girl stepped out of a phone booth and walked away from them. She had long blonde hair, and she wore high heels and a light blue frock that dramatized her elegant long legs. Malone recognized her as Shirley Nash-Winters, the Hollywood starlet.

'I would like a bite of lunch,' Muriel said.

'Okay. Let's head back to the hotel. I have a little research to do.'

At the Gloucester Hotel, Malone used his lock picks to let himself into Dumbo Cooper's room. The hotel maids were working down the hall, vacuums whining, and that gave Malone about ten minutes for his search. He had timed the maids for two days, learned their names, made a schedule chart of their routines. It took them twelve minutes to do a room, unless the room belonged to Dumbo Cooper. There was dirty laundry everywhere – socks, Ryker shirts, soiled shorts, sweaty jocks, towels slopped over chair backs. When his mother wasn't around, this Cooper was one messy kid. The bed looked like it had been hit by a tornado. In a frame on the bedside table was a photograph of the legendary Lorraine Cooper standing in front of a big house somewhere on the East Coast of America.

The framed picture was the only neat item in the place.

Malone found some Colombian weed in the top drawer, underneath three mis-matched socks. What would mother Lorraine say to that? Surprising he hadn't found any pills. From the way Cooper acted he'd picked the kid as a user-loser.

This was Malone's fourteenth unauthorized room search. So far, he hadn't found pills anywhere, but he had some ideas. His main suspect was the Yugoslav, Milovan Tigrid, mostly because of what Malone knew about the Albanian connection. New drugs were coming out of the Middle East, and the Albanians were starting to compete with the Sicilians for a share of the market. As a Yugoslav, Tigrid might have easy entry into that particular pipeline.

Malone brought out an envelope with some names printed on it, in his square, predictable hand.

Belynkas.

Laville.

Cooper.

Tigrid.

Polak.

Abrahami.

Colombier.

Di Rocca.

Leroy.

Which player would have wanted Armando Reyes dead?

The book Malone was doing with Muriel had developed from a quick idea into partial reality. Malone had called the publisher, Livingston, and had got some interest at that end. He had mailed off two hundred photos, with some hastily written captions, and the publisher was talking about a contract. Now Malone had to decided whether to try to write the chapters himself – he'd done plenty of re-writing of term papers back at the University of Illinois – or to hunt up a writer he knew in Chicago to do the job for him.

One thing was certain, he liked working with Muriel. After Paris, they'd been together for a couple of days at Gstaad, and then again in Munich, and when she'd joined him in London she'd given him a quick kiss on the mouth and one of those lingering looks with a faint measuring smile that told him she had hanky-panky on her mind. Malone was careful not to rush Muriel. She was a lady, and ladies always took their time. With Muriel, the wait was going to be worth it.

Later that afternoon, after a long lunch and some talk about chapters and divisions in the book, Malone spent some time going over his notes on Terry Laville. As he studied the folder, Malone turned the facts around inside his head, thinking about Laville and the woodcutting myth, and how it enhanced his place in the tennis spotlight, and how Malone could help keep that spotlight bright.

Here was the bottom line: Malone had been on the job just over three weeks and so far he'd grossed almost $9,000 for his daily services – he worked every day and got paid for seven days a week – and more than $3,000 for expenses. The $12,000 came from a secret pool filled by the big hitters from professional tennis. No names had been mentioned, but Malone understood that even Harrison Cabot, the President of USTA, had kicked in his share. On top of the twelve grand, Archer Bell had sweetened the pot with three thousand in foreign currency, Swiss, French, British.

The money was good, and Malone wanted to keep the cash flow postive. The way to do that was to study Laville, who was Archer Bell's hope for the future.

The best part of his writer's cover was that every player, even Laville, wanted his name in a book. The players got used to seeing their names in the newspapers and even in the three top tennis magazines. But books were permanent. All Malone had to do was mention he'd like an interview and wave the tape recorder and the players would come hunting for him.

Everyone so far had been easy. Except Pantakoras Belynkas, still the number one player. Belynkas kept to himself and was elusive. He worked through his manager, Fenwick, and stayed out of the range of television cameras.

Walking down the hall to Laville's suite in the Gloucester, Malone thought about tennis. Since the game began, power and control of tennis had been vested in a few men, wealthy gentlemen who had altruistic notions about the beauty of competition and the purity of the game. Today, with tennis more than a hundred years old, the impresarios still paid lip service to the notions of honour and purity.

The noble image of tennis was what made Wimbledon tick along, like a grandfather clock in the hallway of time.

Magazines with slick covers were devoted to its promotion. Every major tournament had blanket TV coverage, the time brought by car companies and stockbrokers. Tennis public relations was a technicolour slow motion film of The Good Life, with happy smiling tennis stars taking a leisurely swim in the Bahamas with their pretty smiling wives, a small blonde child or two in the frame for proper balance. To the American public, tennis was the clean lifestyle, special diets, health, keeping in shape.

But tennis was changing as big money entered the arena. The big corporations wanted to sell the weekend hackers rackets at a minimum of two hundred dollars, shorts at fifty dollars a pair, shoes at seventy-five. They'd lowered the price of tennis balls over the years, to keep the weekend players out there burning up rackets and breaking strings. And in the seventies, the equipment makers had penetrated the market with new products, changing the material with which they made rackets – wood, metal, graphite, boron, krypton, oversize, mid-size, illegal spaghetti string jobs – and they'd tied in the magic myth of the equipment, hooked it right in to winning – an ego trip.

This Cooper Champion, the ads implied, can save your game out there, for only $250. Playing your boss this weekend? Get a demonstration of a Koras Boron. Got a tough match coming up at the Club? Pulverzie the enemy with the new Sport City Polak Autograph.

Malone had hefted several rackets, and they seemed pretty much the same to him, which was why the equipment makers needed the names of tennis players.

Koras. Laville. Polak. Cooper . . .

At the interview, Laville wore a leather jacket, blue jeans that looked new, and hand-tooled cowboy boots. His white hair was slicked back, and the crazy look had receded from this eyes. Malone had learned to interview working with the Chicago police. As he asked his questions, he studied the person giving answers. Several times, Laville's eyes drifted out of focus, as if he were staring at a place hidden somewhere in his memory.

Q: So, Mr Laville. How does it feel to be coasting into your seventh Wimbledon at the ripe old age of twenty-six?

A: Great.

Q: Planning to win?

A: Absolutely.

Q: You're a Canadian, right?

A: Right.

Q: I'm from Chicago. That's right across the lake from me. Where are you from, originally?

A: I was born in Ontario, at a place called Six Nations Reserve, but grew up Calgary. My mother was part Iroquois.

Q: Canada. Is that why they call you the woodcutter?

A: I worked as a logger for three years. They would fly a gang of us up north to the logging camps, a place called La Manique. Using an axe helped me with my service motion, but it also makes these neck muscles tight, right here. When my service starts to go, I drag back the memory of swinging that double-edged axe.

Q: So how did you get started in tennis?

A: I played sports in high school – football, ice hockey, soccer – but there was no money in it. I used to devour the sports pages, and I suppose I hoped sports would help me escape from logging. The summer of my junior year, the logging company went broke, leaving me out of a job. My high school coach helped me find a job in New Hampshire, at a camp for boys. One of my jobs was sweeping the tennis courts. I watched these kids hitting, watched the coach, saw what he was telling them. It looked smooth and kind of beautiful. One day I picked up a racket, hit some serves. The coach saw me, told me I was a natural. I took lessons from him. In two weeks, I was beating him. I liked hitting hard. It gave me – a real thrill. I won my serve 98 per cent of the time. The coach said I had a natural swing, a motion like Pancho Gonzales. I was a Canadian, man, and all I knew about Gonzales was that he had a temper on the court. Back home, I quit the winter sports and concentrated on tennis. When winter came, I hitch-hiked twenty miles to an indoor court. Five bucks an hour, way outside my budget. I read tennis books. After my senior year, I cruised to Florida. For a year, I lived on my tennis, hitting with anyone, working at odd jobs around Miami, scrounging lessons. I played in college for a year, won an open in Florida, decided to turn pro. The first biggie I qualified for was River Oaks, in Houston.

Q: How did you feel?

A: Man, I was scared shitless. All the hoity-toity crowd. Koras was there, sopping up the spotlight. Him and his pals, Mad Milo and Armando the Sword.

Q: Sounds like you had a chip on your shoulder.

A: Those guys owned the world, man. I was hungry for just a tiny piece.

Q: How far did you get? At River Oaks, I mean?

A: Second round. I met Koras, almost had him by the short hairs, but he got lucky. Hell, they wouldn't have let me win, first time out.

Q: Who do you mean by they?

A: The fat cats who ran River Oaks.

Q: You're implying that the tournament was fixed?

A: Not fixed-fixed. But when they're after you, they manage to schedule your singles back to back with your doubles. You have to play at the crappy hours, on a court way the hell away from everything.

Q: What did you do about that?

A: Only one thing to do, and that was get famous.

Q: Are there other fat cats, at other tournaments?

A: Everywhere. They suck the sport dry.

Q: Care to name names?
A: No. I'd better not. This is a secret, okay. I just let it slip.
Q: Okay. You wouldn't regard Archer Bell as a fat cat?'
A: Arch is my manager. He takes a piece of my action. I sweat on the court. Arch does his sweating in the meetings, where he makes deals that keep us going.
Q: Did you have a coach?
A: There was Joe Slater, that summer, in the camp. The college coach was zero help.
Q: There's a story going around that says you were coached by Pantakoras Belynkas. When you first appeared on the circuit.
A: Did he say that?
Q: No. It's just, like I said, one of the myths of the circuit.
A: Koras was the King. He might have given me some tips. But not enough to say I was coached. Man, I learned most of this by myself, the hard way, the only way.
Q: You and Koras are real rivals now, wouldn't you say?
A: He's finished. The guy's thirty-four, he's over the hill.
Q: So you don't think he'll get his Grand Slam?
A: Someone will stop him.
Q: You?
A: Why not? Yeah. I'll stop him.
Q: Mind talking a little bit about the off-court rivalry?
A: Where do these rumours start?
Q: Any truth to some little altercation at Regine's, in Paris?
A: No comment.
Q: What drives you, Terry?
A: I want to be known as the best. I got a late start. Not like these country club fellows.
Q: The fat cats?
A: Okay. Sure, the fat cats.
Q: Are you out for revenge, Terry?
A: Revenge. That's crazy.
Q: Would you say you were getting back at them?
A: Getting back at? I wouldn't even say that.
Q: What about the idea broached by Sven Skaar, in that TV interview after Reyes's death, about having to kill your opponent?
A: Skaar had to retire from the circuit. He's a big quitter, in my book.
Q: It's too late for a Grand Slam this year, but say you win it next year, what happens after that?
A: First, I've got to win it. Some very good players stand in the way.
Q: Like who, for instance?
A: On grass, Dumbo Cooper. He hits harder than I do. When he's on, and the court is burnt out, you can't see his serve. In New York, on the hard surface, it could be Cooper again. He loves New York, and they love

him back. Micky Polak is tough in New York, too, especially since he married a girl from the States. The other players who could win? Maybe Colombier, if he gets it together. Maybe Abraham, who's from Buffalo. Maybe his new kid, Heinz. He's a big hitter. Maybe Ivan Leroy.

Q: I notice you didn't mention Koras.

A: Okay. Koras.

Q: If you do win the Slam, how much do you think it will increase your gross?

A: I'm just the player, Malone. You'll have to ask Arch Bell about numbers.

Q: They're saying a Slam could triple your endorsements.

A: I've heard that.

Q: Mind telling me which companies are after you to sign?

A: That's Arch Bell's area. I just go out there and try to win.

Q: Terry, I was wondering what you thought of all this drug talk.

A: I don't pay much attention to gossip. I took some hits on the weed when I was younger, travelling around, wondering whether or not I'd make it. But now that I'm up there on the ladder I wouldn't touch anything like that.

Q: How do you feel about mandatory blood tests, for all players to clear them to play?

A: I think it's a matter for lawyers. I wouldn't object to a test, personally. But I have a feeling it's a violation of our civil rights.

Q: What did you think of Armando Reyes?

A: I liked Armando. He had a great sense of humour. He was a legend when I came onto the circuit. I thought he was a little off the wall with the vitamins. I guess it's only another step to other pills. I didn't know Armando was a user until it came out in the papers. He was a great guy, but he drank too much, spent a lot of time chasing women. Everyone knew it. That was Armando.

Q: Think anyone would want to kill him?

A: A husband, you mean?

Q: Something like that.

A: I don't think so. Those things happen only in the movies.

Q: You're married, aren't you?

A: Yes.

Q: Any children?

A: No. Not yet.

Q: Does your wife travel with you on the circuit?

A: Most of the time. She likes it back home. We have this great place in Vancouver.

Q: Nice place, Vancouver.

A: Yes. It is.

Q: Well, I've got about enough, Terry. Good luck with Wimbledon.

A: Thanks. What are you going to do with all these interviews?

Q: Put them in a book, with pictures.
A: I'd like a whole chapter.
Q: You've got it, Terry.

The day before the opening of the Wimbledon fortnight, Abdul Saadi held a dinner party at his fashionable Victoria Intercontinental Hotel in London's West End. The Victoria Intercontinental had been built by a German architect named Stoller, then leased to a British hotel firm, which had sold it in the late seventies to the Sahara Corporation, which was owned by the Saadi family. When Saadi was in London, he and his entourage, including his current mistress and half a dozen servants, stayed in the lavish penthouse, with a view of the city and its tableau.

The meal that evening was French, prepared by a chef from the Cordon Bleu school. The guests sat around an oval table, bathed in soft light. Athena was at one end, as hostess, Saadi at the other. The table was lit by candles, supported by some subtle ceiling lights. There was a waiter for each diner. The waiters were monitored by Joshua, a huge Kenyan major domo in a white dinner jacket.

Athena wore conservative black, a dress with a high neck and long sleeves, and a diamond bracelet belonging to her mother, Helga von Heidelberg. The bracelet was rumoured to be worth $1.5 million. Circuit gossip held that Athena had worn it in Los Angeles to attract Saadi, who had a sharp eye for jewels. The dress was new, and attracted comment for the simple reason that it failed to reveal Athena's figure. Archer Bell even remarked to Frank Fenwick that Athena looked like she'd just come back from a funeral in Monte Carlo.

'She did go to Austria for a couple of days,' Fenwick said.

'How do you know?'

'My secret, Arch.'

The conversation that evening was about tennis, how the sport was changing, more crowds, more pressure on the facilities, crowd control, ticket prices and the constant search for new stars, fresh talent.

Filtering through the chitchat was the theme of the death of Armando Reyes, and what it boded for the game. Some athletes had begun to avoid the food at the Gloucester, and even here at Saadi's table, Mikhail Polak, who was the strictest player on the circuit about diet, examined every mouthful of food with suspicion. His pretty wife, the Chicago girl Gail Hofstedter, kept blushing with embarrassment, explaining to Archer Bell and Malone about Polak's diet.

'Micky read this book on high carbohydrate efficiency and he just can't seem to eat enough to keep him filled up. Last night, he got me out of bed at two in the morning, and we drove around until he found an all-night Italian place where he could get some spaghetti.'

Polak looked up from his plate long enough to agree. 'Is called the loading of the carbohydrates,' he said. 'Is recommended for all athletes.'

Malone cut a piece of beef, put it into his mouth, and chewed thoughtfully. 'Sounds like a good theory. What's the name of the book?'

'*The Clean Burn*,' Polak said, between mouthfuls.

'Oh, Micky,' his wife said. 'You are the dearest man.'

Down at the other end of the table, Sir Francis Malcolm addressed himself to a question from Frank Fenwick about security during the Wimbledon fortnight.

'We've been alerted, of course. Scotland Yard is on the job, as usual.'

'I was out at the stadium today,' Fenwick said. 'I didn't see any signs of it.'

Sir Francis smiled. 'That, of course, is the best kind of security.'

Fenwick disagreed. 'The police back in the States work on a different theory. It's called high visibility.'

'I am certain that Scotland Yard will handle things to your liking, Mr Fenwick.'

'I lost a good friend in Armando Reyes. I'd hate to see it happen again.' He looked down the table at Milo Tigrid and Mikhail Polak. Koras had not been invited, because of Saadi's insane jealousy about Athena's past.

It was well known on the tennis circuit that Saadi's favourite dessert was cherries jubilee, which he had discovered in a Paris restaurant during his student days at the Sorbonne. People who were invited to dinner with Saadi either developed a taste for burnt brandy, cold ice cream, and cherries, or they skipped dessert. After a huge dish, Saadi had seconds.

After the meal, Saadi excused himself and went off to have a long business talk with Mikhail Polak and Frank Fenwick, Polak's manager. Mrs Polak was not invited. Terry Laville, who was there with his wife, watched the men leave the dining room and head toward Saadi's study, at the opposite end of the penthouse. Archer Bell, on Laville's left, blew smoke from his cigar into the air.

The three men sat in Saadi's study, a mirror duplicate of his study at Hotel Paladin in Paris, the walls lined with books on French literature, the Crusades, economics, nineteenth-century impressionists, sixteenth-century Dutch landscape, and erotica. Behind the books, on a mechnical platform that worked with the press of a button, was the closed circuit TV system that monitored every room in the penthouse, in technicolour. The TV monitor was hidden until Saadi wanted it visible.

'Well, gentlemen. To business.' Saadi did not smoke, and was obviously grateful to be away from Archer Bell's acrid panatellas.

'A magnificent dinner, Mr Saadi.' Polak pronounced diplomatically.

'Yes,' Fenwick said. 'Great food, Abdul.'

'I have something for you, Mikhail.' Saadi walked to a cabinet, opened it, and came back carrying a handsome wooden box, hand carved. He handed it to Mikhail. The box contained a Colt revolver, .45 calibre, dated 1868. It was a vintage model. Polak's contract with Sport City was about to run out; Saadi was trying to woo him. The gun was magnificent. Polak had seen one like it the year before, at an auction in Dallas. The price had been $25,000.

'For me?'

'Yes. As a token of good will.'

'I am overwhelmed.'

Saadi sat back down. 'Gentlemen, I make no secret of why you are here. Mr Polak's obligation to Sport City terminates next Friday. I am interested in signing him for Sahara. I will offer $500,000, with a proviso that if he should win Wimbledon, the offer will rise to $600,000.'

Fenwick looked at Polak, who was having trouble with his digestion, then at Saadi. 'It's a good offer, Mr Saadi.'

'Well, when may I have your answer?'

Polak took a sip of brandy.

Fenwick pulled a notebook and a pocket calculator out of his jacket. He ran a few numbers, then looked up. 'What did Sahara do last year?'

'Just under eight million.'

Fenwick grinned. 'I heard it was just *over* ten million.'

Saadi spread his hands, a gesture of peace. 'A matter of a few thousand.'

'Tell you what I'm thinking, Mr Saadi. Micky here is about to become a higher ranked player. He's got a good chance of making the semifinals here, and that would boost his ranking to number three, maybe number two. Last year, Tigrid was the best-known player from the eastern bloc. This year, it's Micky.'

'I am well aware of these numbers,' Saadi said, testily.

'Just for starters,' Fenwick said, 'we're going to ask you to raise you ante a little.'

'How much?'

'A million up front, and a percentage of the gross.'

Saadi leaned forward, to study Fenwick. 'A percentage of the gross is unheard of.'

'It's done in Hollywood all the time.'

'In Hollywood, stars take less up front.'

'We think Micky's worth it. He could be the next Koras.'

'Don't mention Koras Belynkas to me.'

'All right.' Fenwick looked at Polak, who nodded.

Saadi sat back, a stricken look on his face. 'You've been talking to someone else.'

Closing his notebook, Fenwick stood. 'Micky and I need to talk over the numbers, Mr Saadi. My daddy always warned me, never make a money decision on a full stomach.'

Saadi's eyes narrowed. He did not appreciate philosophy lessons from someone like Fenwick. When he spoke, his voice was a whisper. 'What percentage?'

'Half of one per cent.'

'Madness.' Saadi swivelled around in his chair, to face the window overlooking London. 'Utter madness.'

Fenwick and Polak got up from their chairs and walked out, leaving Saadi alone.

When they were outside, with the door closed, Polak asked Fenwick what he thought. 'Does the Arab go for the deal?'

Fenwick grinned. 'I think we've got him, Micky. He needs you, and the board back home in Damascus would rather have your name on Sahara's products than anyone else's.'

Polak smiled. It was the first time in his life that his Polish heritage was proving to be profitable.

The sun was hot the day the Wimbledon ball boys were given their mauve and green uniforms, the colours of the All England Club. Ball boys were carefully selected from various local London schools. They all understood the rhythms of the game. They had dreams of one day playing on the sacred grass. These days, they included several black boys and a few girls.

The All England Club was moving with the times.

CHAPTER EIGHT

President Alain Clavier had set up temporary headquarters in the Chairman's office, where he and Sir Francis Malcolm were going over the timetable of matches. Like the tournaments in Paris and New York, the Wimbledon Championships took two weeks to get an army of players through seven rounds of play, and Clavier and Sir Francis were drawing lots for the three early rounds which led to the all-important Round of Sixteen. As they worked, they tried to foresee the worst possible delays. Their ultimate goal was the second Sunday after the opening – the men's final had to be played on that day, starting at two o'clock precisely.

As always, the two men argued, precise French logic against steadfast British tradition. Clavier saw no reason that matches should not start at ten in the morning, or at noon. Sir Francis, known to the press as 'Lord Wimbledon', was horrified at the mere mention of another starting time.

The sacred rule at Wimbledon was that no match would be played before two o'clock. This rule was the backbone of the tradition which set the tempo of studied and classic leisure which made Wimbledon the premier event of international tennis. Yet in their discussion today, Clavier's logic had swung Sir Francis around, and they were already planning a scenario which would have matches in the early rounds starting at mid-morning. Sir Francis shuddered at what the membership would say.

'But not on opening day, understand, Alain. Opening day must begin at two o'clock, on centre court.'

'Yes, yes. I understand.'

Clavier remembered how the same stodgy club members had put up a fuss when coloured shirts and dresses with red piping had been introduced onto the hallowed courts. There had almost been a revolution when the white balls provided for years by Jeffries and Co, of Woolwich, had been replaced by greenish-yellow balls of questionable provenance.

But coloured costumes had arrived shortly after the advent of professional play, which allowed the competitor to use their names to promote certain brand names in sports wear. Coloured tennis clothes had brought more humour to the scene, and Milos Tigrid had been able to expand his range of stunts. Everyone at the club, for example, remembered a doubles match when Milo had been paired with Walter Tray, the black player, and it had been required that both partners wear the same colours.

Tray had come onto the court first, wearing shorts and a matching shirt of sky blue. The spectators waited. When Milo bounded onto the court, he did indeed wear the same costume, but his face was done up with black greasepaint. Once it became clear that Tray was in on the stunt, the referee laughed so hard that he nearly fell out of his chair, and decided to inflict only the minimum fine.

'At least the weather report is optimistic,' said Sir Francis.

'Yes. If it keeps up, Wimbledon will be the focus of the Grand Slam as usual.'

'How good are Koras's chances?'

'I thought he was off his game at Roland-Garros.'

'Before the Reyes death? Or after?'

'In the finals, he seemed to be playing with less zeal, less energy.'

'Hmm. What about our man Laville? Could he win here?'

'He is a brittle player, despite his brute strength. One always feels Laville needs an extra weapon before he can win.'

During his time as president of the federation, Clavier had mastered the art of diplomacy. The thing that tired him the most was the barrage of contradictory interests, and that fact that he had to tend to them all, personally. Each of the Grand Slam tournaments – Australia, Paris, Wimbledon, New York – wanted to see itself as the supreme test for players. The Grand Prix, which took place during the winter, wanted equal time. And now Saadi was broaching plans for his Sahara Circuit, an echo of the World Championship of Tennis, a professional circuit developed several years ago by a wealthy Texan. Clavier, who wanted Roland-Garros to be the ultimate in tennis, had to keep the peace by humouring them all.

'The Palace has confirmed that the Prince of Wales will be opening the tournament.'

'Excellent.' Clavier looked out the window at the solid blue sky, so rare for England in summer.

'Yes, but we have not seen Her Majesty since the Centenary. She is not as enthusiastic about tennis as Queen Mary was.'

Clavier had little patience with British royalty, so he made some notes on a pad, then walked to the map of the stadium which had been unfolded on a table. The matches were shaping up. The draw was completed. 'Have we confirmed the meeting with security?'

Sir Francis consulted his pocket watch, an heirloom. 'Four o'clock, precisely. Security will confer with Special Branch.'

'Is their involvement necessary?'

Sir Francis made a fatalistic face. 'We tighten up a bit when members of the Royal Family come as our guests.'

'I suppose they are keeping track of any known members of the IRA?'

'They always watch the Irish. And the terrorists.'

'What is the police theory?'

'We shall know in a moment.'

'Good.' Clavier was thinking of not so distant times, only a few years past, when tennis tournaments had attracted thousands of well bred and well-dressed afficionados who would not have dared to breathe, much less whistle or utter cat calls, while a player was preparing to serve. Then, tennis had been a religion. Here at Wimbledon some of the religious zeal had been preserved, and there remained fond memories of that transitory period between the wars when women played in long skirts and Suzanne Lenglen had been the rage and all the dandies had dressed like the Great Gatsby.

An intercom buzzed, and the secretary announced that the police had arrived. Clavier prepared himself to see them.

The door opened and the secretary came in, followed by Superintendent Weston. The Superintendent had sandy hair, shrewd blue eyes, and the seasoned look of a gunnery officer at the battle of El Alamein. He was tall and lean, the perfect caricature of an English country gentleman, dressed by Savile Row. His shoes had a high polish. Before taking a seat, he shook hands with Clavier and Sir Francis.

'Well, gentlemen. I've had a look around, and we've developed a plan.'

'Good show,' said Sir Francis.

The Superintendent leaned forward as he spread a chart of the All England Club on the desk. 'We are vulnerable here, in the Royal Box, from these points.' He pointed out a dozen places in the stands. 'These will be covered, as will the roof.'

'What if they are after the players, and not the Royal Family?' Clavier asked.

'Well, sir, for us, the Royal Family must come first. We're increasing our security forces around the courts. As you know, we use off-duty servicemen as ushers. This year, we're arming them.'

'Good show,' Sir Francis said again.

A buzzer rang on his desk. He pressed a button and answered. 'What is it, Gardiner?'

'A letter, sir. It just arrived. I'm afraid it's marked urgent.'

'Very well. Bring it in.'

The Superintendent went on with his explanation of the security measures, which were elaborate, while Sir Francis walked to the door to and get the letter from his secretary. 'Thank you, Gardiner.'

The letter was in a plain envelope, with the address of the All England Club typewritten across the front, and the name of Sir Francis Malcolm in the lower left hand corner. He tore the letter open and a single sheet of paper fell out. It was a Xerox copy of an original, composed of words clipped from a newspaper or magazine. The message read:

REYES WAS ONLY THE FIRST. CANCEL THE WIMBLEDON CHAMPIONSHIP OR A SECOND SEMIFINALIST WILL DIE.

Sir Francis handed the letter over to Clavier, who read it and handed it on to Superintendent Weston. Sir Francis had already begun to tremble.

'A madman!' Clavier exclaimed.

'I shall get right on this,' the Superintendent said. 'I recommend that we keep it between us.'

'We are certainly in no position to cancel the Championships,' Sir Francis said.

'Agreed,' said Clavier. 'You will report back to us, won't you?'

'Of course.' Weston said a hasty goodbye and hurried out, carrying the Xeroxed letter by one corner, using his handkerchief.

Wimbledon, on opening day.

The conductor in his uniform lifted his arms and fixed his eyes on the person who was to indicate the precise moment of the Prince of Wales's entry into the Royal Box. The musicians of the Royal Guards, in full uniform – red jackets, golden epaulets, white leather baldricks, black trousers bearing double stripes – stood sweating in the sun.

At precisely ten minutes to two, the Prince of Wales arrived, in the company of the Duke and Duchess of Kent, an unidentified admiral, three pretty women in coloured frocks, seven attendants, and a full plain clothes security force. Princess Diana had not accompanied her husband, as an added precaution against terrorists. The week before, an IRA terrorist had been convicted and sentenced at the Old Bailey, and there was fear of an act of violence as a reprisal.

The spectators arrived early, to eat picnic lunches on the lawns beneath the lovely summer sun. Fans without tickets had spent the night in Church Road, queuing up for the privilege of buying one of the three hundred tickets put on sale each day for centre court. There was an ironic justice at work here. Some stood in line, or slept outside in foul weather and fair. Some paid hundreds of pounds for tickets. Others were given free seats in the official stands.

One had only to know the right people. Matt Malone sat in Saadi's private box, with Muriel and the Princess Athena. The women looked glorious.

At exactly two o'clock, Koras came onto the court, followed by his opponent, Ramesh Nanda, of Bangalore, India. He was a short man, dark and spare, and this was the high moment of his life, to be playing on centre court, before the Prince of Wales, against the best player in the world. The spectators, to be fair, gave the Indian the same attentive applause as they gave Koras.

Koras began the match by winning his serve, but then his concentration vanished and he lost the first set 2–6. To the spectators, sitting high above, the defending champion seemed to have lost the magic touch that had helped him win last year. Koras rallied in the second set to win 6–4. The third set see-sawed, 2-all, 3-all, ending in a tie-breaker won by Koras, 12–10. The fans were excited now, because first round matches are not noted for their excitement and drama.

In the fourth set, Koras was behind all the way, when his right knee gave way beneath him and he fell to the turf while running down a wide forehand. He was forced to take the three-minute time out, while his opponent paced nervously about near the umpire's chair. Down 5–3, the champion regained his precision at last, climbing back up the scoreboard with a masterful execution of drop shots and well-placed lobs that forced Nanda away from the net. A tentative overhead smash drifted wide on the Indian at 5–all, and Koras moved ahead with three sizzling backhands that left the spectators breathless.

The fourth set ended in a tie-breaker, 11–9, in favour of Koras. As the opponents shook hands, the champion was observed to be pale and shaken.

Koras had almost lost to the Indian.

The spectators were now waiting for Tania Pikeste, already becoming a legend because of her performance at Roland-Garros. Tania was to open the women's tournament, and it was another break in tradition to have the women start on the same day as the men.

Tania, in a white dress with blue trim, came onto the court, followed by her opponent, Beth Brookfield, from Henley-on-Thames, the hope of the British.

The Rumanian would give her no chance.

Back in the dressing room, a weary Koras found his friend Milo Tigrid, dressed in white flannels from another era, a checkered bowtie, and a white cap with a soft bill. The burly Yugoslav was grinning, his face flushed. He had just won his first match on the so-called 'upset court'.

'Ho, Koras. Did you win?'

'Barely. The Indian let me live. And you?'

'Chalk up one dead Australian.' Milos snapped the end of a towel at Koras, who dodged.

'What was your score?'

'6–4, 6–3, 3–6, 7–6. I thank the tennis gods it did not go to five sets.'

'How did they like the Big Bill Tilden costume?'

'It is not Tilden.'

'Okay. Who is it?'

Milo gave Koras a condescending look. 'Have you visited the hallowed Wimbledon Museum? Try something farther back.'

'All right.' Koras unlaced one shoe. 'Major Wingfield?'

Major Walter Clopton Wingfield had invented lawn tennis. He took the net from badminton, the ball from a handball game, Eton Fives; the court from court tennis, an indoor game; the scoring from hard rackets. He named his game 'Sphairistike.' Wingfield got a preliminary patent in February, 1874, in Britain. The British were mad for sport. By the end of the century, they were deeply in love with lawn tennis.

'Too far back. Try the Renshaw era.'

'Willie or Ernest?'

Milo swished the towel at Koras. 'Which Renshaw was more savage, more vengeful, more competitive?'

'Willie. Ernest always lost when things got really tough.'

Milos shook hands with Koras, then struck a pose. 'Announcing, Sir William Renshaw.'

Koras laughed. 'The cap is the *coup de grace*, Milo.'

Milos swept the cap off, bowing to Koras. 'From the races, your highness. How was Palermo?'

'Hot. The women were handsome and proud, with gypsy eyes and breath like wine and garlic. How was Gstaad?'

'Weary. Those bloody Swiss, and their bloody banks.' Milos pulled out a piece of monogrammed stationery and showed it to Koras. It had the name Jessica on it, a phone number.

'What's that?'

'A love note. I tell you, Pantakoras, it's this costume. They see me out there, they see tradition walking. Let me describe her, as she walks in beauty. She is blonde, sturdy but with well-rounded limbs of good English stock, a lady archer riding with Sir Robin Hood. I know she will smell like loam, the good English earth.' He paused. 'I had an instructor once in school who claimed Robin Hood was the first communist.'

Koras grinned and untied his other shoe. His right knee hurt. 'How was the condition of your court?'

'Perfection itself. They say the centre court is already showing wear.

Laville has complained, thinking words can grow fresh grass. So has Polak.'

Koras thought of losing. He had almost lost today. Opening round, and two close tie-breaks. 'Maybe we won't have to worry about that this year.'

'Huh! Speak for yourself, my sagging Lithuanian.'

Koras opened his locker. 'How is Muriel?'

'She has deserted me for a man passing himself off as a writer.'

Malone. 'You're kidding,' Koras said.

Milos nodded, pushed his cheek out with his tongue. 'They are writing a book together. He has contacted his publisher.'

'What does the husband say?'

For an answer, Milo stuck his cheek out with his tongue. 'The husband is French. He has his mistresses. Malone has consoled the lady for the loss of Armando.'

'I have a tough time seeing them together.'

'So do I.'

'No. I meant Muriel and Armando.' Koras turned to look at his friend. 'They just didn't seem to be right for each other.'

'That Peruvian was God's gift to women. Oh, how I miss the bastard.'

'Yes. Me, too.'

'Speaking of Armando, I have something for you.'

'What?'

Milos sat down next to Koras, reached into his tennis bag and brought out an envelope. He passed the envelope to his friend. 'Tell no one. In Montenegrin, they call this magic.' His voice was a whisper.

Koras looked into the envelope, saw a dozen red pills. 'Where did you get these?'

'From Armando's tennis bag. The day he died.'

'How did you get the bag?'

'Di Rocca gave it to me. The pills spilled out.'

'They're what killed him!'

'Because he took too many. I, Tigrid, am a careful man.'

Koras felt a quick flash of anger. One friend dead was enough. 'How do you know there's no residual effect, no build up?'

'Trust me, Pantakoras. I can feel the Montenegrin magic, feel the power coursing through me.' He made a fist of triumph, then shook it in the general direction of the universe. 'Down with Laville, all these pimpled late-comers! You should have seen me, Pantakoras. I tell you, I was superior out there. I was Milovan the magnificent, not Milo the mad.'

Koras handed the pills back, shaking his head. 'Be careful, old friend.'

'Take them. I have more.'

'No, thanks.'

'I have been waiting for this magic for years. I may even take this tournament of the English .'

'They're working now, Milo, making you hallucinate about English blondes with an earthy smell.'

Milo leaned close, his eyes very intense. 'I can tell you, they help one's performance between the sheets of love.'

'Since when did you need help there?'

The door opened and they heard voices, coming their way. Milo tucked the envelope back into his tennis bag as Dumbo Cooper walked in, dressed in street clothes. He was followed by Matt Malone, who carried his writer's notebook.

'Well?' Malone asked Milos.

'Another victory for the geriatrics.'

'Drinks for the victor. I'm buying.' Malone said, shaking Milo's hand, a genuine gesture, then turning to greet Koras. 'Hello, Koras. Good to see you.'

'Hello.' Koras shook hands with Malone, who seemed to be Milo's new pal.

'When can we get in an interview?'

'End of the week.'

'How about tomorrow? I have some time.'

Koras hesitated. 'Phone me at the hotel.'

'Pantakoras is incognito,' Milo said. 'He has his own news blackout.'

'Milo does enough TV interviews for both of us.'

'One of the privileges of being old,' Milo said, 'is that they don't think you are interesting any more.'

'Hell, Milo,' Malone said. 'You'll always be interesting.'

'Any word on the Magnelli contract?' Koras asked.

'They may renew. They may not. One never knows. While they decide, it leaves one free to dress as one pleases.'

'You look like a real fruit, Milo,' Dumbo Cooper said.

'Brat.'

The men laughed.

'Well, I'm buying the drinks,' Malone said. 'There's a bar over by the Gloucester with a waitress who has her eye on Milo.'

Milo spread his hands, a mock gesture of helplessness. 'What can I say? They love Tigrid.'

'The waitress has spike hair,' Malone said. 'Purple to the roots.'

'Only on the right,' Milo countered. 'The left side is green.'

'World's full of fruits,' Dumbo said, then walked around the corner, shaking his head. Koras and Milo laughed with Malone, then headed for the showers.

Malone stayed where he was and listened. He could hear what sounded like Will Channer singing one of his Aussie drinking songs, closing up a locker one aisle over. Malone dropped his notebook onto the bench and started to go through Tigrid's tennis bag. Channer would be coming up this aisle on his way out to see Koras. Malone figured he had about fifteen seconds to find out what was in the envelope he'd seen in Milo's hand.

While Will Channer waited for Koras to come out of the showers, he checked through his notebook for strategy pointers he had gleaned from the match against Ramesh Nanda. Koras had been distracted and his game had not been sharp. Channer was thinking of ways to tell him.

In a few moments, Koras came out, wearing a blue towel wrapped around his waist,and the two men talked strokes and strategies. Channer thought these post-mortem sessions were valuable as a training device, because they helped Koras to get an overview of his own game that was not possible when he was out on the court, stroking and sweating and surviving. Both men agreed Koras had spent too much time in the back-court, and that his topspin forehand needed more shoulder turn. Finally, Channer closed the notebook and handed Koras a shoebox from Laval Sportif.

'They came.'

'Almost too late.' Koras opened the box and brought out a pair of Laval shoes, with leather uppers and hundreds of tiny rubber spikes on the soles. They had been especially designed for him by the people at Laval, strictly for grass play. Koras had been waiting for them for weeks. 'The footing was tricky out there today. It will be worse when it rains.'

Channer nodded. 'If these help you win, Laval will go into mass production.'

'They're only good on grass.'

'I saw Micky Polak earlier. He's trying out a pair from Izanagi.'

Koras knew Micky's contract with Sport City was up at the end of the week. 'Are they after Polak?'

Channer shrugged, then brushed a shock of hair away from his face.'Musical chairs in the endorsement arena. Micky didn't say.'

Koras held up the shoe. 'What this shoe needs is a grass court circuit.'

'The Sahara Grass Court Championships?'

Koras grinned as he leaned down to tie his shoelaces. 'Saadi could mass produce that stuff they used in the Astrodome, for Houston football.' He tossed the shoebox into the rubbish bin and stowed the shoes into his tennis bag.

They heard Milo's voice from around the corner, shouting hello to Frank Fenwick. In a moment, the Texan appeared. He carried a manila folder stuffed with papers for Koras to sign. Koras signed, quickly noting the amounts but not grasping the strategy. A million-three to one account in Boston. Six hundred thousand in a money market fund. A signature card for a new market rate account at a bank in Houston. It was a shell game, and only Fenwick knew where the money was. Koras handed the papers back. He'd been poor half his life, then rich. These days, however, he felt the constant pressure to perform, to hang in there, to keep making money.

'What's up, F.F?'
'You want detail? Or the bottom line?'
'How about the current strategy?'
Fenwick sighed, pointed to the papers with a long finger. 'We owe the contractors a million-two. In a week, we'll pay them seven hundred and sixty-five grand, a number I negotiated. Until then, the money draws top dollar interest. If I can get these finalized, you might stay out of jail until September.'
'Good timing.'
Koras knew he'd spent too much money on the Westhampton house. A million to expand the house. Almost a half million for the two tennis courts, so he could work out year-round.
'One reason we're tight,' Fenwick said, 'the cheque still hasn't come through from Palermo.'
Koras dipped into his tennis bag, brought out a handful of Italian lira. 'Did you talk to Di Rocca? He's got pull down there.'
Fenwick and Channer laughed. Koras stuffed the lira back in this bag and zipped it up.
'I heard Laville outside,' Channer said, 'beefing about the grass.'
'How does Laville seem to you?'
'Edgy. He hasn't killed any linespeople yet.'
Koras hefted his bag and looked at the two men who held his future in their hands. There was a faraway look in his eye. 'Did you see Milo and his lawn tennis rig?'
Channer laughed. 'I like that crazy guy. We played a match at Kooyong back in the sixties, in hundred degree heat. Milo wore cabbage leaves in his hat to keep his head cool and he kept telling me he was Jaroslav Drobny, reincarnated.'
'Milo's a treat.'
'Did they renew his contract with Magnelli?' Koras asked Fenwick.
'Not yet. But it's in the works,' Fenwick said.
The three men walked out together.
'Let's have a beer,' Channer said.
'Sorry,' Koras said. 'Got to hit a bookstore.'
'See you at Queen's Club, eight sharp.'
'I'll call to confirm,' Koras said, and left Channer and Fenwick discussing strategy for the Wimbledon fortnight.

On his way out, Koras ran into Princess Athena. She wore a conservatively cut dress of white muslin which did not have the usual number of revealing vents and startling gaps. She forced a smile and tried to look vivacious, but she seemed subdued, pensive, sad. Koras hadn't seen her smile since Armando had died in Paris.
'Oh, Pantakoras. I watched your match against Ramesh. You seemed so sad.'

He looked at the dark circles under her eyes. 'I was just about to say the same about you. Have you had some bad news?'
'A little.' She gripped his arms in both hands.
'Do you want to talk about it?'
'Perhaps.' The Princess bit her lip. 'Walk with me. I'm meeting Saadi and Nora in the box.'
'Has Saadi decided to lock you in a dungeon and throw away the key?'
'Always perceptive, Pantakoras.' She clung to his arm, a memory of old times.
Koras walked beside her for a moment. 'I need directions to Alesia.'
'Alesia?' Now she smiled. 'What about the matches?'
'I don't play tomorrow. I'll be back for my daily workout.'
'You rascal, Pantakoras.' She told him to fly to Dijon, then rent a car. It was fifty kilometres drive, to the north. 'Are you madly in love, then?'
Her intensity made him wonder if she had sensed his urgent need to see Laure. It was crazy, leaving the tournament, risky. It was a measure of the pull Laure exerted on him.
Instead of answering directly, Koras said, 'Give my regards to Nora.'
Athena squeezed his arm. 'You be good to Laure. She is young. She does not have the benefit of your experience in love.'
'She's a women. That starts her out at five-love, 40–15 in the last set.'
Athena started to protest, but Koras kissed her on the cheek and made his exit.

CHAPTER NINE

The hired Bentley stopped in front of the delapidated building which houses Special Air Travel. It was located behind the air terminal at Gatwick, near the maintenance warehouse. The chauffeur carefully set the handbrake before stepping out of the car to open the door for his passenger.
'Here we are, sir.'
Koras put on his sunglasses and left the car. There were clouds to the east, but the London weathermen had reversed themselves and now no rain was predicted for tomorrow. He wanted one sunny day in France. Picking up his briefcase, he entered the building. The young woman behind the counter recognized him.
'Oh, Mr Belynkas, your pilot is waiting in the lounge. And your aeroplane is getting its final check.'
'Thank you. What is the weather in France?'

'There is light rain, sir, all the way from the Alps to the French Coast. I certainly hope it does not spoil your visit.'

'Thank you. Were you able to arrange for a car at the other end?'

'Yes.' She handed him his papers, asked for his passport and credit card. He handed over an American Express card. After he had signed seven separate forms, the young woman smiled.

'Did you win today?'

Koras thought of this tough match. 'Yes. Thank you. Do you follow tennis?'

'My boyfriend does. He's a player himself.'

'Good. We need all the tennis players we can get.'

Outside again, Koras beckoned to the driver to follow him with the suitcase. Books made it heavy. The plane was a Falcon 10, twin engine, with the insignia of the rental company. A hostess in a sky blue uniform stood at the bottom of the steps. She had a pretty smile. He reminded himself to tip her.

Koras told the driver to come back the following morning. As he was giving his instructions, a taxi pulled up outside the Special Air building. Koras noticed that its light was off, but no one got out. For a moment, he waited, feeling the hairs stand up on the back of his neck, wondering if all the talk of murder was making him jumpy. Then he shrugged if off and handed his driver five pounds. The driver touched his cap in salute.

'Right you are, sir.'

Koras boarded his plane and settled in his seat. He was the only passenger. He asked for a cold beer, which brought another smile from the hostess, and settled down to read a book he had picked up in a secondhand bookshop. The title was *Critical Essay on the de Bello Gallico*, by Sir George Wallensborough. His bag contained a paperback edition of Caesar's *Conquest of Gaul*, a map of Central France, and a guide to rural hotels. When he had the time, Koras was a planner.

When the plane was taxiing out to the end of the runway Malone got out of the cab and walked inside Special Air to inquire about Koras's destination. He left Muriel waiting in the cab. He was back in less than a minute with the news that Koras had chartered a plane to Dijon.

'Where is Dijon?'

'Southeast of Paris.'

'He's going to see the cousin of the Princess, then?'

'If Jack Di Rocca is right.'

'What's the quickest way to get to Dijon?'

'Why not charter a plane ourselves?' Muriel's tone was ironic, playful.

'Bell would kill me.'

Muriel laughed, crossed her legs. 'We can fly to Paris. From there, you can drive to Alesia.'

That meant she would stay in Paris. 'How the hell am I supposed to find him there?'

Muriel smiled at Malone. 'France is a small country. Have you not found men in places much more vast?'

He had sworn her to secrecy and told her he was a private investigator. Every chance she had, she dropped a reference about his tracking abilities.

As Koras's plane roared over their heads, Malone asked the driver to take them to the British Airways terminal.

It was late afternoon when the rented Falcon 10 landed at the airport of Neuilly-Les-Dijon. Rain was still falling, and the air was fresh and clean. Koras came out of the book, closed it, put it back into his case. He stretched, yawned. Wimbledon was behind him. He looked forward to seeing Laure.

Koras made sure the plane would be ready to leave the next morning, sometime before noon, and then said goodbye to the captain and the hostess. He tipped the hostess ten pounds, which brought forth a pretty smile.

He cleared customs in five minutes. A white Renault was waiting in the parking lot. A driver was available, but Koras wanted to drive himself. He produced his international driver's licence, which still had three months to go before expiration. He verified the location of Alesia, which was on a rising piece of ground above the village of Alise Sainte Reine, near Mount Auxois. The man at the car rental desk advised Koras to book a hotel in Dijon for the night. But Koras hoped to stay the night closer to Laure.

Twenty minutes after landing, he was on his way to Alesia.

He drove through the village of Alesia, and took the first turn on his left, in the direction of the small mountain he took to be Mount Auxois. At the foot of if lay the excavation site. Several foreign cars, German makes mostly, along with a Volvo and two Saabs, were parked in a level area with a sign that read STATIONNEMENT. He found a parking spot and slid the Renault in. Behind the car park, a gravel path, slick with rain, led up to a series of terraces, where people in yellow rain slickers moved about. He counted seven tents, their tan canvas sagging and darkened by the rain. The activity reminded him of a movie set.

More people in slickers walked quickly from the tents up to a higher area, where great piles of earth were turning to mud, and wooden scaffolds stood. Below was the village of Alise Sainte Reine, and a grove of trees, a dark green copse, off to the left. Closer lay the road, yellow and white in the rain, winding up from the village.

A man wearing a yellow rain jacket passed, and Koras asked in fluent French about Laure Puget.

'Up there.' The man pointed up the hill, toward the scaffolding. Wearing his rain jacket, Koras rummaged in the boot of the car until he found his collapsible umbrella, black with a carved wooden handle, bought in Vienna five years ago. It was getting old now and he should replace it.

Up here, the rain slanted, driven by the wind. The air, though, smelled fresh and clean. Koras took in a deep breath and realized he was nervous about seeing Laure. It was, after all, her arena, and Koras was more comfortable in the surroundings of the tennis circuit.

He found her working with two men under the shelter of a canvas lean-to. Damp brown hair was plastered around her long face. She wore a blue rain jacket, open to reveal a white safari blouse with two large pockets, and khaki shorts. On her feet, she wore lace-up leather boots. Her knees and bare calves, tanned from long hours in the sun, were stained with splotches of mud. They were excellent legs. Laure looked surprised.

'Well. Mr Belynkas.'

The formality did not surprise him. 'I came to buy you that drink.'

She recovered her composure and introduced him to the two men. One was young, a sharp-faced fellow with wire-rimmed glasses, a white lab coat and a protective intensity about Laure. Laure introduced him as Doctor Jean-Luc Benoit. The other man, Professor Evarts from the Free University of Berlin, had grey hair and a beard. Both men frowned at the interruption, and Koras sensed a certain amount of tension, not so different from what could be felt in the dressing room while a major tournament was being played and there was a lot at stake.

'We are just finishing up, if you don't mind waiting. In a few moments, I can show you around.'

He waited under an overhang in the scaffolding, listening to the voices, Laure's sharp and female in contrast to the two men, who were asking lots of questions. They spoke in German, English, and French, and the topic was money, which they were running short of. She came out after a few moments, her frown changing to a soft smile as she approached. Her blue hood was up, to keep the water off her hair.

Laure led him to a promontory, where she pointed out some of the features of the fortress and the battle where Caesar defeated Vercingetorix. They stood together under Koras's umbrella.

'There were ramparts along there,' Laure said, pointing, 'and a wall two metres high. The Gauls were up here. The Romans had eight camps, laid out at strategic points. These camps were connected by two dozen redoubts. The Roman lines extended nine and a half English miles.'

He had the sense she was avoiding the reason he'd flown over. 'Incredible.'

She turned her face to him. 'I'm surprised you came.'

'I wanted to see you.'

'What about Wimbledon?'

'I won earlier today, a very tough match. I owed myself a visit. I won't play again until Wednesday.'

'How did you get here?'
'I hired a plane. From Dijon, I took a car, a white Renault with French steering.'
'Are you staying the night?'
'Yes. Can you have dinner?'
She shook her head. 'I wish you hadn't come. We are having terrible problems.'
'Money?'
She nodded. 'There are arguments all the time. Everyone is one edge.'
'How much do you need?'
She laughed at that, smirking at him before she turned away to stare down the valley. 'Three million francs might get us through the next month.'
Koras wondered if he could raise even a quarter of that before Fenwick slipped it beneath another tax shelter. 'It's like making a movie, then?'
'Yes,' Laure said, 'only much earthier.'
Koras laughed. She wanted him to know she was excited by the past. As she kept on talking, he began to get the feel for what the Gauls had gone through in their defeat by Caesar. It was getting dark before she finished, so he repeated his invitation for dinner.
Laure hesitated while she thought the matter over. 'All right. I could use a night off from the bickering. Give me a moment.'
Before he could answer, she trotted through the rain to the tent where the two men waited. Koras had the feeling she was breaking some kind of date with the intense Jean-Luc.

At the house where the excavation crew stayed, Koras called the Hotel Metz in Montbard while Laure took a quick shower and changed. He got a room, $27 US dollars for the night, making him realize he was in the provinces, and not in Paris. She came out wearing leather knee boots, a dark shirt, and a red blouse that highlighted her hair. Suddenly she hugged Koras, and he breathed in her fresh, clean smell. Laure Puget was the eternal springtime girl.
In moments, she had worked her magic and had transformed herself from a toiling academic archeologist to a glamorous woman. Over her shoulder was the leather bag, too large for a purse, too small for a suitcase, that Koras remembered from Paris. She stowed the bag in the back seat of the Renault. They drove to the Hotel Caesar in Alesia for the evening meal.
The main course was boeuf bourguignon, red and succulent. For that, that, the waiter recommended a Bourgogne red. By the end of the meal, they were into the third bottle and Laure's cheeks were flushed and conversation had swerved away from Caesar and Alesia to Koras and his life on the tennis circuit.
'I was sorry to miss seeing you in the finals at Paris.'

He heard the words, but her mind seemed to be elsewhere. 'I was sorry, too.'

'You won a lot of money, didn't you?'

Koras was thinking of Armando, dead from an overdose. And also of Fenwick, with his talk of bank loans. 'My manager takes it away.' He reached into his briefcase, produced his copy of Wallensborough. 'I've been reading detective stories.'

Laure was delighted. 'You are always surprising me.'

'I saw you reading. I knew that the way to your heart was through books, mouldy old ones.'

Laure blushed and too another sip of wine.

She stood close to him as he brought out his wallet to pay the bill. When Koras handed the proprietor a credit card, the man shook his head.

'Sorry, monsieur. We cannot accept.'

Koras turned to Laure. 'Damn. I forgot to bring French money.'

Laure rummaged in her leather purse and came out with three hundred francs. She paid the bill. In the car, he handed her some British pounds. She shook her head.

'You owe me a *dinner* now. At a very good restaurant.' Was money one of her interests? She seemed to like having this hold over him.

'I have American money. Lira. Even some German marks, traveller's checks.'

'Sorry, the debt can only be paid in food.'

At the house where Laure stayed, she gave him a quick kiss, soft lips on his cheek. He wanted to ask her to drive to Montbard, to the Hotel Metz, to spend the night. Her good night was firm and he felt suddenly empty.

'Tomorrow?' he asked. 'Breakfast?'

'I must work,' she said, and hurried into the house.

The moon came out as he started north, toward Montbard. Far behind him, Koras picked up the occasional flash from another pair of headlights, but except for them he had the road to himself.

At the hotel in Montbard, they gave him number nine, le numero neuf. As he walked up the stairs, he saw the image of Laure, the shorts, the boots, the tanned legs, her hair wet with rain, and loneliness flooded his heart.

He felt chilly, from the rain and the wet night, so he showered, a long hot one. Dressed in his favourite robe, made of blue terrycloth given to him years ago by Athena, he unpacked. There were Levis and a shirt for tomorrow, socks, fresh underwear. He liked not being at Wimbledon, immersed in the matches, competing, grinding along, clawing up through the draw. Koras had never left a tournament before.

He read for a while, his paperback copy of Caesar's *The Conquest of Gaul*. He read the speech of Critognatus twice, wondering what it would be like to eat roast baby. What could make you hungry enough to eat human flesh?

He was about to turn out the light when there was a soft knock on the door. He opened the door to find Laure Puget standing there, leather bag over her shoulder.

'I came to inspect the room,' she said. 'Le numero neuf.'

She was so beautiful he could not speak. His legs trembled as he held the door open for her.

Laure brushed him coming in, swinging the leather bag with confidence, yet edged with a certain nervousness. She set the bag down on the bed, opened it to bring out a bottle of brandy. 'A local cognac, *très formidable*, or so they say.' She handed him the bottle. One-quarter gone, he noticed. Who were her other drinking partners?

Koras brought glasses from the ancient armoire and poured them both a cognac. As they clinked glasses, he could see her watching him over the rim of her glass, studying him.

They had a drink. Then Laure excused herself to go to the wc. When she came back, her eyes were thoughtful. She poured more cognac and handed Koras his glass. 'Have you recalled the moment when I first saw you?' she asked.

'Of course. At Paris. You were reading while I played my heart out.'

'You don't remember our tennis lesson?'

'What tennis lesson?'

'At Salzburg, at Aunt Helga's. I was fourteen. You were in love with cousin Athena.'

Koras remembered. The skinny kid with the legs and the shy smile. Her forehand had been a natural, but he hadn't taught her to serve. 'I feel stupid.'

She touched his lip with one finger. 'Ah, the great Koras Belynkas, off balance for what must be the only time in his life.'

He sipped his cognac, which burned going down. 'Only fourteen. Are you sure?'

'A very romantic fourteen. I thought you were the handsomest man in the world. And Athena, the luckiest woman.' She took a step close to him. He touched her and she did not move away.

'Laure, I –'

He kissed her then, covering his confusion with instinct, tasting her mouth, pressing the truth of his desire against her. She felt him responding and pushed closer, then broke off the kiss to lick the edge of his mouth, one subtle flick with her tongue. After a long sighing moment, she broke away to put one foot on the edge of a chair.

She unzipped one boot. Laure was a pretty sight with her leg up, her skirt hiked high, long lines of absolute beauty. 'An assist, if you please.'

Koras helped her with the boots. Touching her took him deeper into fantasy.

'Ahh,' she said, as she flopped back on the bed. 'Wonderful night, Wonderful bed.'

As she lay back, he noticed that three buttons on her red blouse were undone, a clear invitation. He saw the mounds of her breasts, gentle slopes, lightly tanned. His breath quickened, and she smiled. He admired her way of controlling the rhythms of love.

When he took her by the wrist and pulled her close, she came willingly. Her movements were supple. Her mouth searched his, probing, her tongue running along his teeth. She put a hand on his leg, caressed him gently. Her neck beneath his lips was total smoothness. She cried out when he bit her ear. 'My skirt,' she whispered. 'Let me take it off.'

They separated. Koras, short of breath, threw off his robe. The lights were still on. Laure noticed his arousal, and smiled, unzipping her skirt, allowing it to fall to the floor. Koras flipped the light switch, throwing the room into semi-darkness. Light pushed into the room, the pale green moon of France. Laure moved to the open window, used the moonlight to finish undressing. Watching, Koras held his breath. It was a beautiful moment, hushed and still. As she bent to remove her stockings, her hair fell down around her face, hiding it. The red blouse, unbuttoned, hung open and she was bathed in moonlight. He caught his breath when she slipped out of her panties, seeing her long legs, bare, sensual. She tossed the blouse away and came to the bed, naked.

His eyes filled with tears. She kissed his face, pausing to nuzzle the blonde moustache.

'You are crying.'

'Because you are so beautiful.'

He licked her toes first, making her writhe as he continued up one leg, then the other. They made love playfully, then seriously, then playfully once more. Twice, he made her cry out. When he was inside her, he felt safe, home at last, all the loneliness from his gypsy life falling away . . .

When they were finished, Laure left the bed to refill their glasses. Her face was soft, but again he sensed distance. Her mind was somewhere else. The brandy warmed him.

'Tell me.'

'Hmm?'

'What are you thinking about?'

For a moment, she didn't answer. 'You won't be hurt? Or angry?'

'I promise.'

'I was thinking about Greece, actually.'

'Why Greece?'

'There is a man in Athens. Professor Colicos, at the University. He sees Alesia as the French Troy. He may help us raise money for the work here.'

'Money again?'

She touched his glass with hers. 'Money, always.'

Koras put a hand on her bare shoulder. Her skin was smooth, flawless. She stared at him a moment in the moonlight, then looked away. Koras got up from the bed.

'Where are you going?' Her voice was sharp.

He flipped the light on. 'Let's make a list.' He returned to the bed with his notebook and a ballpoint pen. 'My coach pumps me full of strategy. I'm supposed to keep notes in here. Writing it down helps.' He flipped past his notes on other players. 'Ready.'

'This is silly.'

'Ready,' he said again.

'I feel foolish, burdening you.'

'Because you hardly know me?'

'No. There is something –'

He poked her lightly with the end of the ballpoint. 'You said three million francs.' He wrote that at the top of the page. 'Let's break it down. Salaries? Dig permits? A fresh white frock for young Dr Benoit?'

Laure kicked him with her bare heel. At the same time, a small smile played at the corners of her mouth. 'All right. Permits for the month, 360,000 francs. Two million francs for salaries. Then we have 46,000 for insurance, 86,000 for our meals, 29,000 to upgrade our X-ray equipment. The diesel generator packed up on Friday and a new one costs at least 70,000. The lab takes 260,000 a week, if we don't bring in experts from Paris and the States.'

Koras made a neat list. The total came to 2,851,000 francs. At the current exchange rate, that was roughly $400,000. He put the pen and notebook aside. There was one sip of brandy left.

'Now, do you feel better?' Laure asked.

'Immensely. You?'

'I'm not sure.'

'When will you go to Greece?'

'Why? Is there a tournament there?'

'In the autumn, perhaps.'

'I must go sooner than that.'

He touched her then and she smiled and turned to him.

'Come to America,' he said. 'I'll introduce you to rich people.'

'The Peabody is in Massachusetts. Are you near there?'

'An hour. Maybe two.'

She set her glass down and rolled on top of him in a movement that seemed innocent, natural, and playful. 'Do you always make lists, monsieur?' Her voice mocked him, gently.

'When it's something important.'

'My excavation at Alesia is important?'

'A noble cause.'

She moved, subtly. In the pale moonlight, he saw the smile on her face. 'Did you really read Wallensborough?'

'I skimmed it.'

She moved again, making him catch his breath. 'Sometime, I would like to read your lists.'

'All right.'

She touched his face. 'I did not expect this.'

'What?'

'The list. Your interest in my work.'

'Neither did I.'

She laughed and that made him laugh and then he was lost in touch and perfume and exploring their mutual desire.

Morning in Montbard, at the Metz Hotel.

Koras woke to find her side of the bed empty. The sight made his heart race. He sat up in bed and saw the note on the dresser. He rolled out of bed and put on his robe. The note said she had to leave early for the excavation. Sun streamed through the window. Koras was disappointed, depressed. One night of love, and then emptiness. He wanted her more than ever.

After doing his knee exercises, he called Will Channer in London, to tell him he would be late for their workout. Will said he was insane to leave London during the fortnight. Then he called the airport to Dijon, to tell them to get ready to leave around noon. He cashed a cheque at the hotel and paid his bill. He spent an hour at breakfast, drinking coffee and ordering more croissants while he read the papers. When breakfast was over, he waited another fifteen minutes for the national bank to open. Then he called his bank in New York, with instructions to wire money to a bank in Dijon. He wanted half a million. All they could advance him, drawing from the construction account, was $400,000.

Malone waited until Koras had settled in with his second pot of coffee and his newspapers. Then he sneaked past the desk of the concierge to room number nine. There was no one on the floor. The locks looked seventy-five years old, not much of a match for a special set of skeleton keys, made up for Malone by J.D. Griswold, an ex-con who lived three houses down in Skokie. Griswold had done time for burglary, breaking and entering. He made the best lock picks and skeleton keys in the business. In the last couple of years, Griswold had built up a reputation for developing a system that could defeat the new electronic hotel locks, the ones that changed combinations with every new customer. A computer punched out a key card and changed the locks, automatically.

Griswold's system was secret. It was also for sale, for ten thousand. Two days ago, Malone had ordered a Griswold system.

Inside the room, he went quickly through Koras's gear. The man travelled light, only one bag for clothes, a custom-made leather job with a strap for the shoulder and wheels for long hauls through airports. A laundry bag. Two pairs of sneakers. The bag was empty. The clothes were stowed in the dresser, an antique from the look of it, and in the armoire against the wall by the window. Koras had a good view from his room, right onto the picturesque street. Not a bad life, being a tennis star. Malone worked fast, finishing his search in less than seven minutes. Not a trace of a recreational drug anywhere. So far, Koras was clean.

Malone was out of the hotel and into his rented car before Koras returned to pack up. As he drove south, toward Dijon, Malone had a choice. He could take a flight from here back to Paris. Or he could wait for Koras to finish up with the girl and try to hitch a ride with him.

Thinking about that, Malone grinned.

In Dijon, Koras picked up the bank draft for 2,851,000 francs, made out to Laure Puget. At the current rate of exchange, that was what his $400,000 would buy on the currency markets. With the draft tucked into his jacket pocket, he made the drive to Alesia. The sun was bright. It was a magnificent day.

With the sun out, activity at the excavation seemed diligent and serious. At least a hundred people were working and today the careful surgery on the earth seemed part of a grand plan. It took him fifteen minutes to find Laure, at the bottom of a deep trench, on her hands and knees in the mud. With her was Dr Jean-Luc Benoit, wearing a mud-spattered lab coat and rubber knee boots. As Koras appeared at the top of the trough, Dr Benoit looked up, sunlight winking off his glasses. Laure was in shadow, examining a shard of pottery. They were excited, but they stopped talking when Koras arrived.

'Oh!' Laure said.

'Good morning.' The cheque was in his pocket. He felt like a Gallic hero, coming to save France.

Laure spoke briefly to Jean-Luc and then climbed a ladder out of the ditch. She was blushing as she approached Koras. A strand of hair fell across one eye and she brushed it away. Was she glad to see him? Or embarrassed? He couldn't tell. She took his arm and walked him away from the trough.

'Did you get my note?'

'Yes.'

'I –' she began, then stopped.

'It was a lovely time,' Koras said.

'Yes. But you have your life. I have mine. Don't we?'

She was in love with the past, all this digging, all these tiny bits of pottery and charcoal. 'I want to see you again.'

'It is not pos –' She stopped, looked around. 'It will not work.'

'I think it will.'

She held out a hand to shake. 'You do owe me a dinner.'

Koras reached into his pocket and handed her the bank draft. She unfolded it, stared at the numbers, looked at him. A blush crept up her throat. From deep in the trough, her name was called, but she did not answer. Her eyelids fluttered as she looked at Koras.

'This is a joke.'

'No joke. It's for-real francs. On a real French bank.'

'But it is so much money! You can't possibly –'

He was feeling better now. 'It's only half what you need to finish the summer. I'll wire the rest.'

'But why?'

He had control now so he smiled at her. 'A noble cause. The French Troy, you said.'

She tried to hand the cheque back, but Koras put up his hand, palm out. 'It's yours.'

'Can you afford it?'

He couldn't. 'Yes.'

Laure's face changed then, from a frown to a smile of ecstatic happiness. She threw her arms around Koras's neck and he felt her lips on his. The kiss lasted for a brief moment. Just then, Dr Benoit appeared on the ladder, his head sticking up over the edge of the excavation. With hopeful promise and yielding finality, Laure pressed herself against Koras before letting him go.

'I have a plane to catch,' he said.

'Goodbye. And thank you.'

'Come to London.'

'I shall try.'

He turned and walked away, toward his rented Renault.

As Koras walked away, Laure felt the fluttering in her heart. He confused her, knocked her off-balance. She was attracted to him and at the same time wary. She had spent her life studying, reading, cloistered by schools and universities. He, on the other hand, was a man of the world, cynical, experienced.

'What is it?' Jean-Luc asked as he came up.

Laure tucked the bank draft into a shirt pocket. 'He came to say goodbye.'

Jean-Luc glanced at Koras, who was almost out of sight. 'Good. Now you can get back to work.'

She almost told him then, almost flashed the cheque in his face. Instead, she ran after Koras, her eyes stinging with tears.

When she reached the parking lot down below the excavation she was out of breath. The white Renault was out of the lot and pulling away. Laure called out, but the Renault kept going. She felt her heart would burst. Waving, she ran behind the car, which was picking up speed. Then, abruptly, it stopped as he saw her in the rearview mirror. She slowed to a walk and Koras put the car into reverse, backed up, and parked on the edge of the road.

'What is it?' He was out of the car, moving toward her. 'Laure, what is it?'

The sun was hot now, burning down. Her face felt flushed and she wondered how she looked. 'There is something,' she began. 'I had to tell you.'

'All right.'

'Let's get in the car. Out of the sun.'

He opened the door for her and she slid into the passenger seat. Her lip trembled. He walked around and got in behind the wheel.

'You know Saadi,' she said.

'Yes.'

'Much of our money was coming from him.'

'From Saadi?'

Laure nodded. She hated talking about this. 'Athena helped us persuade him. Saadi fancies himself as a historian. He came to visit in the winter, after he and Athena –' She left that sentence unfinished. 'He met Professor Evarts and Jean-Luc. He knew quite a bit about stratigraphy and carbon-dating. He wanted a small plaque for his Sahara company. And he started giving us money.'

'But it stopped, right?'

'Yes.' Laure didn't know how to tell Koras the rest. 'In Paris, he invited me to visit his yacht in Juan-les-Pins. I refused. When I arrived here and mentioned it to Jean-Luc, he insisted we go down there to see Saadi. I did not want to go, but at last we did, for a weekend. The yacht is lovely and the area is charming, but Saadi –' Laure paused to wipe her eyes. She was crying now, unable to stop, and the tears felt necessary. 'Saadi made advances to me.'

'This is making my skin crawl.'

'When I refused him, he stopped the money.'

'Does Athena know?'

'She was in Austria. Perhaps she suspects. I don't know.'

'A man like Saadi would count on your being too ashamed to say anything to her.'

Laure wanted to be held then; she came into Koras's arms. Why was life so complicated? Why couldn't powerful emotions come one at a time? Why weren't people's motives admirable and pure?

'Is that why you didn't want to take money from me?' Koras asked.

Laure nodded and another sob escaped. 'We had a lovely night. I hated to spoil it.'

Koras patted her on the shoulder. 'It *was* lovely. And you didn't spoil anything.'

She stayed in his arms a few more minutes. He kissed away her tears. They made tentative plans about seeing one another after Wimbledon, and she wrote down the number for her grandparents in Choisel, in the Chevreuse Valley. Then she gave him a deep searching kiss, and got out of the car and watched him drive away.

* * *

When he turned in his rented Renault at Dijon airport, he made a comment about the loose steering. The man behind the desk said he would have it looked into. Then Koras made his way out of the car rental office. His plane would leave in twenty minutes, something about maintenance, so Koras went into the airport cafe for a beer. He was sitting there, getting ready for Frank Fenwick, when he heard an American voice and looked up to see Matt Malone standing there in a rumpled tweed coat. Malone always looked as if he had slept in his clothes for a week.

'Malone?'

'Mind if I join you?'

'What are you doing here?'

Malone pulled up a chair. 'I need that interview.'

'You followed me to France for an interview?'

Malone nodded. 'Got lost last night, so I hung out here, a rowdy hotel in Dijon. I thought maybe I could hitch a ride back in your private jet, interview you on the way.'

Koras laughed. He knew he could have been angry, but Malone sat there grinning. It was a mad world. He held out a hand and the two men shook. 'It's paid for. Welcome aboard.'

Malone pulled out his notebook, ready to get down to business. 'I know how busy you sports jocks are.' His grin was infectious. 'Have I got time for a beer?'

Koras turned to the waiter to order one.

'How come you speak the language so well?' Malone asked.

The interview had begun.

Koras smiled. 'My only gift, I guess. We spoke Lithuanian at my granddad's house, back in New York. I was a college drop out, but the Army sent me to Monterey, to the language school. I studied Russian, and while I was there I dated a Vietnamese teacher who taught me French. Picked up a lot.'

The beer came. Malone lifted his glass before taking a sip. 'Good way to learn a language.'

'The best.'

'To women, then.'

They clicked glasses, Koras's beer was half gone. Malone finished his in three easy swallows. Then they walked out onto the tarmac and boarded the Falcon. Once they were airborne and heading back for England, Malone continued the interview.

'I've been curious about how it feels, being you. You're the star, the number one. What do you do to keep beating a guy like Laville? He's going strong, steamrolling, driving the crowds wild, while he does everything to distract you except dynamite the umpire's chair. You're not as young as you used to be. This could be your last chance for the Grand Slam. How do you handle the situation?'

'Just lucky, I guess. Judson Garwood says I've got the whammy on Laville.'

Malone chuckled. 'What about Polak?'

'Against Micky, I go to the net all the time. Against Cooper, I lob, to take the pace off the ball. Cooper loves pace.'

'What about the trick knee?'

Koras thought about that. 'It hurts a lot. It went out from under me yesterday, against Nanda. I tried a brace once. Now I try to exercise it every day.'

'How old are you?'

'Thirty-four.'

'What keeps you going?'

'My manager.'

'I hear you owe some money on a house you built.'

'Correction. Rebuilt. And I'd like to keep that confidential.'

'Okay. How long have you known Tigrid?'

'Thirteen years. I won my first major title with Milo, back in the early seventies.'

'What keeps *him* going?'

Koras waited before answering. 'Milo's turned himself into the circuit clown.'

'You think he's on something?'

'Besides women?'

'I was thinking of drugs.'

Koras shook his head. Malone's eyes watched his every move, made him feel trapped. 'Not Milo.'

'What about you?'

Koras grinned. 'I'm not a racehorse, Malone.'

'What about Laville?'

'With Terry, anything is possible.' Koras did a quick shoulder roll. feeling the weight of the universe bearing down on his neck.

'How did you get along with Reyes?'

'Armando was a friend. He was closer to Milo than he was to me.'

'I heard that you and he and the Princess were pretty thick, back in the old days.'

'Yeah. But the circuit back then was even smaller. You knew everyone.'

'I heard she went from you to Reyes and then back to you.'

'In between, there were others. She's a volatile woman.'

'What I'm getting at is Saadi. They say he's got it in for you.'

'When Saadi has a party, I'm not on the guest list.'

'Has he ever interfered with you professionally?'

Koras grinned. 'No. But if he gets control of every company, he can squeeze me on endorsement contracts.'

'How much did you make last year?'

'You'll have to ask Frank Fenwick. He's my numbers guy.'

Malone wrote notes for a moment before going on with the questions. He was very thorough, like a cop, coming back to clarify points. They were over the Channel, starting their descent.

'When did you start playing tennis?'

'I was about twelve, a late start for a player. But I'd honed my hitting eye on stickball in the streets, and a tennis racket seemed easy after that. I used to hang around Central Park, with nothing but a racket and corduroy cutoffs and two paper thin tennis balls, waiting for someone to ask me to hit. Tennis kept me off the street.'

'That's why you stuck with it?'

'Yes. But it felt right, being out there, hitting. It felt, well – beautiful – when you did it just right, the feet and the shoulder swing and the power travelling through your wrist. That sweet spot felt just right. A man named Al Moscowitz coached me after a while. He taught me spin, balance, footwork. He helped me enter some tournaments, where I got whipped pretty badly. My father's business wasn't doing well, so I had to work delivering groceries. When I got better, Al Moscowitz paid for some lessons with a real pro, at the West Side Club.' Koras paused. 'I learned how to dream at the West Side Club. All those gorgeous girls.'

'What happened to Moscowitz?'

'He died, three years ago.

Koras was feeling sad now, remembering Al Moscowitz. Malone switched topics, turning the conversation to drugs.

'Did you know Reyes was on something?'

'Just vitamins.'

'He was mixing two drugs, an aphrodisiac and some anti-anxiety stuff.'

Koras shook his head, but didn't answer. Malone kept probing.

'The aphrodisiac is a Cantharis derivative, right out of the Middle East, through the so-called Albanian connection. It's supposed to turn a simple sexual encounter into a space mission.'

'You've done your research, Malone.'

'When I asked around, it's like those three monkeys. No one knows a thing.'

'Tennis players are supersitious. We protect our turf.'

Malone waited a moment before he started again. 'What if this is a way to sell tickets?'

Koras stared at him, then turned to look out the window. 'Like a ritual sacrifice?'

Malone nodded. 'The arena is right for it. Upper-class audience. Bored. Jaded. Make a good movie.'

'Is this just theory?'

'So far. What do you think?'

Koras was thinking of Laure and her tales of Celtic sacrifice. Maybe civilization hadn't moved so far away from those times, after all. 'Sounds too grim for tennis.'

The plane was descending rapidly now. Koras looked at his watch. The time was 1:15. At Wimbledon, with the new schedule put into effect by Clavier, the matches had been underway for three hours.

Polak was on centre court, sweating in the moist afternoon in a match against Paul Harper, a lanky Californian with a surfer's tan and a smile that he doubtless wore while sleeping.

Micky's forehand was on, but his backhand was off. He'd hit a cross-court and it would sail out by a foot. He tried taking the racket back early, but then he seemed slow getting to the ball. Across the net, Harper saw Micky's problem and kept chipping his approach shot and coming to the net for an easy volley.

The score was 5–3 in the second set and Polak was losing. He'd lost the first set, 6–1, and as he struggled to revive himself on the skittery grass courts of the All England Club, Mikhail Polak, the archangel of Gdansk, came to the conclusion that his wife was to blame for his sagging tennis game. After courting a year, Mikhail and Gail Hofstedter had been married in Rome, just before the Italian Open began at the Foro Italico. Mikhail, the runner-up at the Italian Open from last year, had been seeded number two at the Foro. He was a clay court specialist who had taught himself the game by pounding tennis balls against a grey wall at the soccer stadium in his native Gdansk.

Micky had been discovered by Ferdi Wrezowski, the Polish champion of yesteryear and then the David Cup Coach of a fledgling team. Micky had developed under Wrezowski, had played his first French Open at seventeen, where he had been catapulted into international fame by defeating the reigning champion, a Frenchman by the name of Alphonse Arbintoir, in the fourth round. Two years later, Polak had won the French title, and great things had been expected of him. This year at Rome, the tennis world – and especially his manager and well-wishers back in his native land – had been surprised and disappointed when he lost in the last sixteen to the American, Jack Di Rocca.

Mikhail's wife, Gail, was an American. Her maiden name, Hofstedter, told the financial world she was the daugther of T. Jason Hofstedter, who was a senior partner in the powerful law firm of Hofstedter, Stein, and Barkman, of Chicago. Jason Hofstedter's speciality was corporate takeovers. Gail had grown up in the upscale suburb of Kenilworth, on the North Shore. She was pretty, a blonde debutante whose bland ideas hid completely her extraordinary sexual capacities. She had surprised Micky with her ability to flirt and distract him. To bury the distraction, and to prove himself a man of the world, he had courted her, fallen more deeply under her spell, and then married her. It had been a major error.

As they wheeled around the circuit, it became clear to Micky that his wife was not happy coping with hotels and dirty laundry and his fluctuating moods. On airplanes, Gail babbled constantly of the house they would live in, near her parents, on the North Shore. Micky didn't like it. Chicago was cold, like Poland. It snowed there in November. The ice was miserable. He preferred Dallas, where he owned a house already. There was country near Dallas, and Micky liked to hunt. His idea – they argued constantly about this – was to make their headquarters in Dallas. With Frank Fenwick's help, Micky had purchased some shares in a new shopping mall on Interstate 30, just south of the Dallas–Fort Worth airport. Already, the shares had made money.

Now, inside his mind, Micky was distracted from his best tennis by these endless arguments with his wife. Suddenly, his opponent, the grinning insolent surfer, sent the ball deep to Micky's forehand. Harper was tall, with a huge forehand and a backhand that he hit with two hands. Micky did not like Harper, his beach boy good looks, his manner of speaking in a constant smile. To Micky, Californians were a race of mutants who had mastered two arts – staying tanned all year around and making conversation without unclenching their teeth.

Micky hit the return into the net.

Down love–30 and 5–3 in the second set, Micky decided to send his wife back home. It was too late for Wimbledon, but he might save his focus for New York. He knew there would be a scene. She was a spoiled female, a product of a capitalist economic system plagued by waste and decadence. Still, he would do it.

Now, he was losing in the first round to Paul Harper, and the only thing saving him was a new pair of shoes by Izanagi, a Japanese equipment manufacturer. Through the soles of these shoes, he could actually feel his toes gripping the slippery grass court surface.

Then Harper's service came, the ball flattening out like a thick saucer. Micky got it back, topspin, always topspin. Harper volleyed. Micky retrieved, a high lob, into the grey sky, pushing Harper deep. Micky charged, volleyed away the return.

He won three more points the same way, hammering away the return as he thought of sending his wife off. Just the idea made him feel free. He won the second set 7–5, drawing even with the American. There were other women in the world. Before his marriage, he had received love letters from strange women who had enclosed photos. Most of the photos had been portraits, but a few women had sent along photos of themselves in bikinis. One had even dared to send a nude. Micky wondered where she was now.

Without his whining wife, Micky would be free once more to roam. He was a hunter, and that thought appealed tohim.

He won the next two sets, 6–1, 6–2, to take the match from a surprised Paul Harper. After the match, in the dressing room, Harper came up to him as he was feeling the sole of his right shoe. It was covered with hundreds of square rubber nubs. Micky liked these Izanagi shoes.

'I thought I had you out there, Polak. What happened?'

'I came to some decision,' Micky said.
'You turned into a stroking machine.'
Polak nodded, but said nothing. In the shower, he began singing in Polish.

CHAPTER TEN

At breakfast in the Gloucester Hotel, Matt Malone was back on the late late schedule of the circuit. As he drank his coffee, he realized he had adopted the way of life and the impossible habits of the people in the tennis world. In the afternoons, they played tennis, or waited to play, or watched. After the matches, they stayed up late, to unwind. After unwinding, they slept late, so they would be fresh for the afternoon's matches. Every day, he promised himself he would be up early. Yet every day he arose later, had a good breakfast while he read the *Chicago Tribune*, and looked forward to the day at Wimbledon, or at the Queen's Club out in West Kensington, where the players practised.

Today was Tuesday, the second day of the fourth round. Koras had advanced to the quarterfinals, but everyone was remarking how the defending champion wasn't playing his best. Each time Koras had played, his matches had gone to five sets, and yesterday he had won in an extended fifth set, 10–8, over Ivan Leroy, from France. As a result, the bookmakers had changed the odds on Koras from 2–1 to 4–1.

The two players who were soaking up the media time were Milo Tigrid and Mikhail Polak. Tigrid was playing out of his mind, beating players half his age with shots that were both powerful and accurate. And Polak hadn't lost a set since he'd sent his wife back home.

Malone looked up from his breakfast to see Laville come in, with Shirley Nash-Winters, the pretty starlet, and Mikhail Polak. Laughing and talking like old friends, the three took a table across the room from Malone. Laville waved, but Polak kept his attention fixed on Shirley's valentine face. Today, Shirley wore a soft yellow dress, tight around the hips and thighs, with a deep neckline that threatened to spill her bouncy young breasts. Polak wasn't the only player who had sent his wife back home.

Malone sipped his coffee while he smelled the aroma from the ham and eggs. It was amazing. You cross the Channel in an airplane and you get different food for breakfast. The French liked bread and buttery croissants. In Paris, you had to fight the chef for a boiled egg. The English, on the other hand, liked bacon, toast, and eggs. Malone liked it all. Travelling made him curious about what the Germans ate for breakfast, and the Swiss, and the Dutch, and then the Swedes and the Norwegians and the Finns. Koras was Lithuanian. What did they eat in Lithuania? It was after ten, and the dining room was almost deserted. Milo Tigrid appeared in the doorway; Malone waved him over.

'Ho, you jackal of the press. What news from the world?' Milo sat down.

'This coffee isn't bad.'

A waiter came over to take Milo's order. When he had gone, Milo turned to Malone.

'Have you seen Pantakoras?'

'No,' Malone said. 'Isn't he at Queen's Club, practising?'

'Oh, probably. I think Pantakoras practises too much. His Australian coach is a slave driver.'

'Have you eaten?'

Milo nodded, then leaned close. 'Did you notice the barbarian Laville with Miss Nash-Winters and Comrade Polak?'

'Yeah.'

Across the room, Shirley leaned back and laughed, a tinkling sound, filled with the beauty and promise of youth. The waiter brought Milo's coffee.

'I knew a woman like that once,' Milo said, 'the same grey eyes, the same sleepy intelligence. She was from Montana, land of mountains. Do you know it?'

'I hear it's cold and beautiful.'

'You poet!' Milo slapped Malone on the back.

'What happened to the girl?'

'I taught her the Kama Sutra. She has doubtless gone on to produce a new generation of consumers for your decadent marketplace.'

'Been teaching any Kama Sutra around here?'

Milo grinned as he added sugar to his coffee. 'A woman keeps staring at me, from the member's stand. On Saturday she used binoculars.'

'Have you met her?'

'No. She keeps eluding me.'

'Well, they say you're playing well. The bookmakers have shortened the odds.'

Milo grinned, then pounded his chest. 'Tigrid, the eternal.' He stared at Malone as if he had something important to say, then changed the subject. 'How would you like to accompany me on a shopping spree?'

'Shop? What for?'

Milo sighed. 'I have two sisters who are in love with English wool. In Yugoslavia they pass themselves off as party dignitaries simply by exhibiting the colourful cashmeres I send them.'

'Hey, I could use a little shopping myself.'

'You! Look at you! You are the perfect capitalist journalist. Those crumpled trousers, that jacket with the elbow patches flawed to perfection.'

'I could use some socks, maybe some underwear, and a new shirt.'

'Spoken like a man.' Milo slapped Malone on the back. 'Let us depart.'

'Where to?'

'Burlington Arcade.'

Milo turned out to be an efficient shopper. When they reached Burlington Arcade, he led Malone into the first sweater shop they saw, where he gave the nervous shop assistant precise English sizes. Milo could create a flurry on any stage, and soon they were joined by another shop assistant, older and prettier than the first.

'One of my sisters is about your size, but not as radiant. Are you a Yugoslav, my dear?'

'No, Mr Tigrid. I'm from Hampstead.'

'A beautiful area, Hampstead. I often practise at a club there.'

'Oh? Which one?'

'The Cumberland. Have you been there?'

'Oh, no, sir.'

'Well, then, I must invite you to be among my guests, the next time I am there.'

'Oh, sir. That would be lovely.'

While Milo energized the shop, Malone leaned against a counter to watch the Yugoslav examining sweaters. Forty different varieties were laid out on the counters. Milo went through them, feeling for softness and quality. When he had made his selection, eight sweaters totaling over £650, Milo asked that they be shipped to Yugoslavia, and that meant forms to fill out. The manager had to be called, to help with the intricate paperwork.

They were no sooner out of the clothes shop that Milo spotted a pet shop. He dragged Malone in, looking around with his supercharged energy, and picked up a young bobtailed dog. It was white, with grey hind paws and a long coat of hair which rendered it shapeless. Malone thought the dog was the ugliest one he had ever seen.

'Well, journalist, what do you think?'

'If he has teeth, he'll make a good guard dog.'

'He has teeth, my dear Matthew.'

'Can't see them, under all that hair.'

Milo handed the dog to Malone, then stepped away. 'Consider this dog as a gift. What do you think of it as a gift?'

'Great. Especially if you ship it to Yugoslavia. The paperwork shouldn't take more than a couple of weeks.'

Milo's face lit up. 'I'll take it,' he said to the attendant. 'What is it's name?'

'Swash,' said the attendant.

'A lovely name, as in Swashbuckler.'

'He wants it gift-wrapped,' Malone said.

The dog cost £250, which Milo paid without a blink. There were more papers to fill out. The dog had a pedigree, with a number tatooed on the inside of his left ear. The attendant said the pedigree made the bobtail worth £450, and urged Milo to register the animal at the Kennel Club.

'Hell,' Malone said. 'You've already made a profit, and you haven't even had to feed him yet.'

'I could not sell Swash. What do you take me for?'

Malone laughed.

'Now,' Milo announced. 'I am famished. Let's go to Fortnum's.'

'Hey, I just had breakfast.'

'A man must keep up his strength. And there are beautiful women there.'

Malone thought of Muriel, who would be coming back from Paris tomorrow. 'All right. But then we need to get out to Wimbledon.'

As they crossed Piccadilly, Malone thought he saw Mikhail Polak, driving the other way.

'Did you see him?'

'See who?'

'Polak.'

'With a woman?'

'No. He was alone.'

'I saw him yesterday, with the actress, Shirley. Laville was not around. She was captivating, turning on her charm. You'd think she had just been introduced to Roman Polanski.'

'Maybe she wants Polak for a leading man.'

Milo sighed. 'She is gorgeous, is she not?'

'Too young for you!'

Milo stared at Malone with sardonic laughter in his eye. 'There are few too young for Tigrid, my capitalistic Puritan. And that is because Tigrid has the remedy to remove sadness in the heart of a woman.'

'Okay, what's the remedy for sadness?'

'Tigrid,' he cried, and thumped his chest.

With his wife gone home to America, Mikhail Polak had time to himself once again. He took some time off to pursue his hobby – fine guns.

Mikhail's favourite firearm emporium in the world was Purdey & Sons in London, a temple of gunsmiths. The place exuded tradition and history. The organization dated back to 1763, when the first Purdey had been named official court armourer. Back at his home in Dallas, Mikhail had a superior gun collection. He paid the Polish government a handsome retainer so that he could return to Poland to do some hunting. There was something about hunting – especially the stalking phase – that made him feel alive.

He was well known to the salesmen at Purdey's, which he always visited when in London. Last summer, Mikhail had purchased an antique Franchi Falconet shotgun, twelve-gauge, made by hand at the factory in Brescia, Italy, in 1901. The piece was one of a matched set, and Mikhail had asked the shop to search for its mate. He had been disappointed when they hadn't turned the twin shotgun up.

Two salesmen, dressed in well-cut suits, greeted Mikhail by name. The manager, Mr Jessup, came forward with a smile and a handshake. Mikhail talked with Jessup a few moments. Mr Blade, who usually helped Mikhail, was away from the gunsmiths because of a cold. This morning, Mr Whitlington would look after Mikhail.

Mr Whitlington was thin, with grey eyes and a receding hairline. He knew his weapons, however. In the first five minutes, Mikhail bought a Soviet Margolin sport .22 pistol, which he asked to have shipped to Dallas. While he was looking at shotguns – he had his eye on a Harrington and Richardson over-and-under twelve gauge, dated 1894 – Mr Whitlington vanished for a moment and came back with a Franchi, dated the same year.

'Mr Jessup just informed me, Mr Polak. A customer finds he, ah, cannot acquire this weapon at the moment. It is, if you will permit me, a beautiful piece.'

Mikhail felt the excitement shooting through him even before he hefted the weapon, touched the butt to his shoulder, sighted along the top barrel. Thirty seconds, and Mikhail was in love. He asked about the price, but barely heard the answer. This Franchi was beyond money.

Mikhail told them to add it to his account. He would take the shotgun with him, do some shooting after he'd won Wimbledon. Shooting relaxed him.

With his purchase, Purdey's included a handsome leather case and two boxes of shells. As he rode back to the Gloucester in his taxi, he was already planning a morning at the skeet range in Hertfordshire. There was a better range in Scotland. Perhaps he might go there. He knew a man who knew a man who raised game birds, a private preserve, where one could get in some shooting off season.

When he won Wimbledon, he would deserve a rest. Mikhail smiled, settled back against the seat cushions, watched London glide by. With his wife 7,000 miles away, he felt almost weightless.

When Princess Athena got depressed, she began dressing in darker clothes; high-necked sweaters, blouses that were not see-through, and loose-fitting slacks that her mother would have declared totally lacking in style.

She had never really analyzed her behaviour – the Princess simply acted and left interpretation to the tabloids – but since Armando's death she had felt closed in, caged by gloom. She dressed to fit her mood, buttons buttoned, zippers zipped. She knew people were talking, asking questions, making snide remarks. But Athena, while a darling of the mob, was not of the mob. She lived life as she pleased. And right now, the object of her life was to get away from Saadi. Life in his entourage was oppressive, and in his penthouses – identical quarters in his family-owned hotels no matter what the city – Athena felt both incarcerated and spied upon.

She had taken up with Saadi because she felt she could control him. At first, he had smothered her with presents and allowed her to live her own life. But as they came to be regarded as 'a couple' on the circuit, Saadi had become more possessive, demanding to know where she was going, where she had been, who she had been with. At first, she had found it tiresome, then nerve-wracking.

Her decision to leave had been made in Austria, after the end of the tournament in Paris. Shaken by Armando's death, Athena had slipped away, to Salzburg. Saadi had showed up, landing his private jet nearby, with orders for Athena to join him in Zurich. When she had refused, Saadi had revealed that he had taken over control of some outstanding debts owed by Athena's mother. If Athena did not comply, Saadi would bring pressure to bear.

Making the decision to escape was easy. The hard part was finding a way to neutralize Saadi's power.

On the surface, Abdul Saadi was smooth, a manipulator with a slick smile who shook hands and wore western clothes and made people feel at ease. Down deep, however, he was jealous and vengeful, a man who flew into rages at the least provocation. When the time came to tell him goodbye, she wanted to make certain he understood why, and she was planning to use a particular issue of *Racket World* she'd found in his trash basket as leverage.

She needed a willing accomplice, someone shrewd and tough. She thought first of Pantakoras, her old friend, and then she ran into Jack Di Rocca on the second day of the fourth round. Di Rocca had won his match the day before, putting him into the quarters, and he was dressed in an attractive leather jacket, grey slacks, and a wool tie. Smiling warmly, but without her usual flamboyant charge of sexual electricity, Athena invited Di Rocca to sit with her in Saadi's private box, which was practically next door to the Royal Box. Saadi was the honorary President of his country's tennis league. His private box was one of the many perks of Sahara Sports.

'Nice view,' Di Rocca said.

'Yes. Saadi lives well.'

'Where is Saadi? I haven't seen him around today.'

'When I left the hotel, he was on the phone, making some deal or other. Saadi is frequently on the phone.'

She felt him watching her as she talked, his eyes measuring her. It was not a new feeling. Men had been measuring her since she was a girl. Today, she wore khaki linen slacks, a dark blue blouse, a navy shantung jacket, and a tan scarf around her throat. In her handbag, she carried a blue sweater and an umbrella. The weather was grey, with clouds hanging low over the stands, making the green of the courts even more intense. She could smell the rain about to start, and here and there she could see umbrellas blooming in the stands, then folding up again like flowers in the dark.

A waiter appeared as they were getting settled. She ordered a brandy.

'Make that two, waiter.'

The waiter bowed and went away.

'Congratulations on winning yesterday.'

'I keep getting lucky. The quarters promise to be tough.'

Athena gestured down on the court, where Dumbo Cooper was fighting it out with Jean-François Colombier. 'Who do you pick to win here?'

'Cooper.'

Athena looked at the scoreboard. Dumbo was behind a set, and losing to Colombier in the second. 'I pick Jean-François. At least he is not American.'

'A pound on Cooper,' Di Rocca said.

'Agreed.'

They shook hands and she noticed how strong he was, how firm his grip. The waiter came back with the drinks, and they settled back to watch the match.

'That was a fine party you and Saadi threw the other night.'

'Oh?' She responded to the tone of his voice, which sounded slightly mocking. 'Are you that fond of cherries jubilee?'

Di Rocca laughed. 'Being around Saadi reminds me how the other half lives. He owns fifty percent of tennis and plans to own the rest by September.'

She edged her own reply with matching irony. 'If not September, then by Christmas.'

'Where did you meet Saadi, anyway?'

'In Los Angeles, at the home of mutual friends. Saadi was decorating his house in Bel Air, having the statues painted, Persian rugs in the bath, all that dismal Arab taste. With a few simple suggestions, I dismissed his decorator, who was charging far too much, and dazzled him with my sense of style. His family, of course, does not approve. To them, I am a Teutonic infidel.'

Di Rocca toasted her with the brandy. 'To the price of oil.'

She turned to give Di Rocca an appraising look. 'How old are you, Mr Di Rocca?'

'Thirty-two. And you?'

Instead of answering, Athena shifted in her seat, leaning toward Di Rocca. 'I remember the first time I saw you play, in Gstaad. It was one of your first clay court tournaments, and yet you seemed to have mastered it.'

'I remember seeing you in the stands, and thinking you were the most beautiful woman in the world.'

Athena acknowledged the compliment with a smile. Perhaps this was the kindred spirit she needed to help her with Saadi. 'Why, thank you,' she murmured.

At Fortnum and Mason's, Milo's dog was the object of several wicked glances. Well dressed Londoners kept sticking up their noses. Milo gave them the benefit of his clown face as he handed the leash to Malone and led the way to a table. A waitress appeared and they ordered tea and cakes.

'I don't think they like the dog, Milo.'

'Perhaps it is my beard, or your clothes.'

'No one ever talked straight to me about my "look." Maybe you could help me put together a new wardrobe.'

'I would consider it a duty to society to help you dress like a gentleman.'

Their tea came. Milo sipped, made a face. 'Tea, blah! this is good reason for the British Empire to sink forever into the Sargasso Sea.'

At the next table, two grey-haired ladies turned to glare at Milo.

'It was your idea to come here,' Malone said.

Milo leaned across the table to look Malone in the eye. 'I don't think you are a writer, Malone.'

Malone decided not to work at making denials. 'You're right.'

'So. You admit?'

'Sure.' Malone sipped his tea. 'The Federation hired me, after Reyes died.'

Milo looked offended. 'You are a private eyeball, like Mike the Hammer?'

'That's right.'

'What is your charge, if I might ask?'

'To find out if Reyes killed himself, or if something else did him in. And if so, to find out who.'

'And?'

Malone shook his head. 'I'm working for the Federation, Milo. Not you. And I'd appreciate it if you didn't say anything. I don't want my cover blown.'

'Why should I help you? You are a snake in the house of chickens, as Frank Fenwick likes to say.'

Malone reached into his jacket pocket and brought out an envelope with the logo of the Gloucester Hotel. He upended the envelope and a red capsule fell out onto the table. Milo's face got pale. 'This is why.'

'What is it?'

'It's a red pill, an aphrodiasiac, like the one that killed Reyes.'

'Where did you find it?'

'Your tennis bag.'

Milo looked sick, then his face became angry. 'You search my stuff?' His voice was loud.

'Easy, Milo. Easy.' Malone put a hand on Milo's arm.

'No. You are a –' He finished with something in a language Malone did not understand and hurried out, yanking the dog along roughly.

Malone dropped some money on the table and went after him. Outside, on the pavement, Milo was stalking away. Malone had to run to catch up.

'Goddamnit, Milo. I just got you off the hook with the Paris police.'

Milo turned. 'That scum. How?'

'I told them you were innocent. I sure as hell didn't mention the red pills.'

'You must be on good terms with that fascist, Marechal.'

'We made a deal. I'm nosing around. If I find something useful, I'll let him know.'

'What do you mean, useful?'

Malone shrugged. 'Depends.'

Milo was scowling at Malone. 'Why do I listen to you, after you search my private stuff?'

'Better I found it than someone else. Where'd you get these, anyway?'

Milo sighed. 'From Armando's bag, the day he died. I saw how he played. I knew there was something. They were super-pills.' Milo looked away from Malone and down at the dog. 'Listen, detective. They help Tigrid shove back some years. Okay?' He grabbed Malone by the lapels. 'Do you know where I am? I am in the quarterfinals of Wimbledon for the first time in six years!'

Malone nodded. There were tears in the Yugoslavian's eyes. 'Do you see what I am telling you, Matthew? Do you?'

And before Malone could answer, Milo shoved the dog's leash into his hand and hurried off, running across the street, into the heavy London traffic.

CHAPTER ELEVEN

'Match point,' intoned the umpire from the chair.

Down on the court, Dumbo Cooper was close to being eliminated in the fourth round by Jean-Francois Colombier, a young Frenchman with a ranking of only seventy-two on the ATP computer. The French player had won the first two sets, and was leading 6–5 in the third, 40–15. He was one point away from victory.

And then there was a hint of rain, drops misting down. In the stands, a few coloured umbrellas were already open.

Colombier took the balls from the ball boy. In one minute, he would become a tennis legend. He shut his eyes to the crowd, to his coach's words, to the contracts that would come his way if he eliminated a seeded player. His girlfriend would shower him with love.

He laid the toss up carefully, muscles tense, and came down on the ball with immense force. He wanted an ace to end this match on television. The ball slapped the tape. Fault. He served the second ball with a high kicking spin, but the wet grass kept it low and Dumbo took the point with a screaming backhand, to climb to 40–30.

It was still match point. The sky was a metallic grey, and more rain fell. Colombier was sweating now with the tension. He had to end it now. His serve skimmed the tape for a let call.

'Let,' said the umpire. 'First service.'

The rain came harder now, slanting silver against the dark green of the centre court. Colombier served. Cooper moved in for a damaging return, sent the ball whistling down the line to Colombier's backhand. The passing shot was high. Cooper clipped it off for a sharp cross-court volley.

'Deuce.'

Now the rain drops fell in sheets. On the stands, the umbrellas flourished suddenly, exploding into red, blue, yellow. They played two more points, with Colombier losing his footing and crashing into the net, before the umpire adjourned the match. Before he left the chair, he made certain that the ground crew unrolled the heavy green tarpaulin that covered centre court.

As the rain began to fall in earnest, Athena and Jack Di Rocca left Saadi's box and hurried to the player's tea room, a place of wicker chairs and wicker tables where the atmosphere seethed with deals and deal-makers. The bar here was first-class.

Outside the entrance, a regal blonde hurried up to pluck at Athena's sleeve. She was a friend, Lady Jessica Coatkey, and she whispered to Athena that she was dying for an introduction to the fierce Montenegrin, Milo Tigrid. Always ready to play cupid, Athena brought Lady Jessica in as her guest.

Once inside, she spotted Milo and Koras standing at the bar. Di Rocca went off to speak to someone, which gave Athena her chance. She marched over, leading the blushing Lady Jessica.

'Milo,' Athena said, 'an admirer of yours was outside in the rain.' And as Milo turned to beam at both women, Athena made her introductions.

Milo grasped Lady Jessica's hand. 'A wondrous beauty. How nice to meet you, dear lady. Are you by chance a Yugoslavian?'

'Oh, Mr Tigrid. I so admire your prowess on the court.'

'Did you hear that, Koras? Did you hear that?' Milo beamed.

'It's a real compliment, Lady Coatkey. Milo only passes out a dozen or two Yugoslavian passports per year.' Koras explained.

Watching Jessica and Milo, Athena smiled benevolently. Meeting Di Rocca had given her new hope, and now there was this *tête-à-tête* between two people who were attracted to one another. She gave Koras a quick hug while Milo worked his magic on Lady Jessica. Athena felt alive again, and began to plan a few changes in her wardrobe.

'So,' Athena asked Koras. 'Are you in love at last? Will you admit it to me?'

Koras laughed, but his eyes were serious. 'I've got a long way to fall.'

'Laure is *tres charmant*. So young. So full of possibility.'

'She's a beauty, all right.'

'I remember,' Milo was saying to Lady Jessica. 'You are the vision from opening day.'

'Oh, Mr Tigrid.'

Jessica blushed as Milo took her hand in both of his.

'Please. Call me Milo. My friends all call me Milo.'

Milo did a quick handstand, and coins fell out of his pants pockets. Everyone laughed. When he stood up, his face was red. He led the blonde off, so he could whisper sweet somethings in her ear.

A loudspeaker announced that play was starting again. Athena said goodbye to Koras and walked with Jack Di Rocca back to Saadi's box. She felt better than she had in weeks.

By the time they reached Saadi's box, David Cooper had broken Colombier's serve and was taking over the momentum in the quarterfinal. The sun was out and in the stands people were removing their rain gear. Athena folded her umbrella, took off the shantung blazer and, when Di Rocca wasn't looking, undid the top two buttons on her blouse.

At the changeover between games, she drew closer to Di Rocca. 'Is it true that you were in prison?'

'Yes. I broke into a gas station and took twenty-four bucks.'

'And how long were you in prison?'

'Thirteen months.'

She was shocked. 'That is severe punishment.'

'Ortega got me out. He offered to coach me for a percentage. I would have chewed nails to get out of there.'

'Do you like the game?'

'I like the life!'

'Are you married, Mr Di Rocca?'

He grinned. 'No, ma'am. It ruins the circuit. Talk to Micky Polak. Talk to Laville.'

'Pantakoras says tennis is his wife, his mistress.'

Di Rocca nodded, but said nothing.

'Did you by chance see the film, *Belle de Jour?* With Catherine Deneuve?'

'Nope. Can't say I have.'

'A curious film. The plot is interesting. A woman, a married woman, is persuaded to spend one afternoon a week in a house of prostitution in Paris. Her curiosity grows toward her work. After a time, she enjoys herself, for the power, I think. Her favourite client turns out to be a thief and a murderer.'

Di Rocca stared into her eyes. 'Crazy.'

She smiled at him and drained her glass. 'Can you find the waiter? I seem to need another drink.'

Di Rocca signalled the waiter, three boxes away.

Down on the court, Dumbo Cooper took the third set, 7–6. Athena clapped for both players. She felt warm from the exchange with Di Rocca and the sudden sunshine. Her body hummed its pleasure at being alive. The waiter came with the drinks. When he had gone, Athena continued her conversation about films.

'Would you like to view the film?'

'Anytime.' His dark beard highlighted his ready smile.

'I have it on cassette.'

'Is there popcorn?'

'With butter?' Athena asked. 'Or without?'

'I like it with a beer, maybe two. You eat the popcorn. I'll drink the beer.'

'German beer? Danish beer?'

'Dos Equis. It's Mexican.'

Cooper finished off the fourth set. The Princess took a look at the scoreboard. 'I love Mexico, all that fierce heat. It's so primitive.'

Di Rocca touched his glass to hers. 'Here's to Mexico and old movies.'

'To popcorn,' she said, and felt herself smiling.

On the court, Jean-Francois Colombier wiped his legs with a towel. He had lost his momentum because of the rain delay, and now he had to start again. At this moment, he should have been under the shower singing in ecstasy. Instead, here he was, on the court, with another set to play. The universe was against him. There was a fading headline in his brain: YOUNG FRENCH HOPEFUL DEFEATS DAVID COOPER AT WIMBLEDON. Could he still do it?

He tossed the towel aside and readied himself to receive serve. Cooper served; Colombier shot back a return. Cooper volleyed like a madman, diving, rolling on the grass to make an impossible shot.

Cooper took game after game, the score mounting against Colombier on the scoreboard until the match was over. Final set to Cooper, 6–0. Colombier was finished. He left the centre court in tears.

Within two minutes, Koras came out to play Peter Abraham. The winner would play Mikhail Polak tomorrow.

In Polak's room at the Gloucester, Malone found a tennis bag full of dirty clothes, an electric tea pot and a good collection of herbal teas, an antique Colt cavalryman's revolver in a wooden presentation case, and a shotgun. The shotgun was fancy, an Italian job with the name Franchi of Brescia in Gothic letters on the plate above the trigger guard. There was a date in Roman numerals that Malone could not decipher. The numerals read eighteen-something. He snapped the gun to his shoulder a couple of times, noting the terrific feel. This fellow Polak knew his firearms.

A quick search told Malone there were no pills here either. And that surprised him, because for the first two rounds, Polak had been playing badly, and the bookies had been cranking up the odds. Smart money had it Polak would lose to Tigrid in the quarterfinals, but he'd killed Tigrid in four sets. Now, the bookmakers thought, Polak had an excellent chance of beating Koras in the semis, and they were giving 7–3 he could take either Laville or Cooper in the final.

In Polak's tennis bag, Malone found a photo of his wife, a debutante with a knowing smile and a mean gleam in her eye. Gail Hofstedter Polak looked like daddy's favourite girl. Malone tossed the photograph back. She reminded him of Sally Atkinson, his first dream girl, and that brought up a certain amount of pain he thought he'd escaped. Seeing the girl, all that money, the special cared-for look, reminded Malone that a few lucky people lived, while the rest of the world worked for a living.

He checked his watch, 10:14. As he was leaving the room, the phone rang. Probably Polak's impatient bride, calling from the States. Malone walked out, letting it ring.

He was an eastern bloc player, innocent, puritanical, fastidious about sex, and it was Mikhail Polak's first experience with a real *ménage a trois*. And, he vowed to himself, his last. He felt drunk, guilty, deranged. His head pounded and his desire seemed endless, jagged, decadent. Laville was there, in the bed, and the woman was coiled like a golden snake between the two men.

Earlier in the evening, they'd begun at the Hard Rock Cafe, celebrating their wins in the quarterfinals. From the Hard Rock, they had gone on to a discotheque Laville knew, where Micky had danced with Shirley Nash-Winters. The starlet was sad because she was leaving London to return to Hollywood. Her beautiful face, her larger-than-life grey eyes floated in front of him on the dance floor. Tears glistened on her soft cheeks. 'I'll be back,' she kept saying. 'You'll see.'

Her mood opened Polak up, so he told her about his contract decision. 'I am signing the contract with Izanagi,' he whispered as they were dancing. The drinks had made his mind absolutely clear, allowing him to see around corners. He felt infallible. Tonight, he could do no wrong.

'What's that, hon?' She was soft in his arms, pliable. He was aware of being watched from the darkness.

'I am not signing with Saadi's Sahara Sports. It is a secret. Izanagi has offered me more than a million dollars.'

Shirley smiled at that and gave him a complimentary little push with her thighs. 'Your secret is safe with me, hon. My lips are sealed.' For a while, they danced very close.

They left the discotheque. He was thoroughly drunk and feeling heated by constant contact with the starlet. They had wandered back to the hotel, singing, 'Row, Row, Row Your Boat,' and he remembered Laville sending him with a strange smile into the bedroom where Shirley lay, all warm and lovely and half-undressed, like the seduction scenes in her films, and then his hunger had overcome him, and in the midst of his grand passion with beautiful Shirley the man Laville had joined them and for a while Mikhail had felt as if he and Laville were actually brothers and three people in one huge bed seemed to be the most natural thing in the world.

In his alcoholic daze, he remembered bright lights flashing, a synchronized clicking sound, a keening animal cry, high-pitched and savage. The voice was familiar. He had heard it often, in his dreams. It was his voice.

Now Micky Polak came awake, sitting up in bed with a raging thirst. He stumbled into the bathroom. In the mirror, his face resembled a waxen imitation of a publicity photo in a museum somewhere behind the Iron Curtain. He thought of icy Siberia, the hateful Gulag. Would they send him there someday, when he was old? When he could no longer play? Would he grow cynical, like Koras? He drank, greedily, feeling sick to his stomach when the water hit bottom. Tomorrow, he had a semifinal to play. His watch said 23:43. He felt terrible. There was still time to get some sleep.

Laville was waiting for him as he came out of the bathroom, a camera poised and ready, hiding his grinning face. Laville pressed the button to release the shutter. There was that clicking sound again, and at the same time the blinding light of the built-in flash. Then he knew – Laville had photographed him in his shame, naked, with this woman.

He rushed Laville, with an idea of getting the camera back, but the big man merely laughed and shoved him aside. Micky crashed into the bureau, but caught himself on the wall and pushed off as he was about to slam his eye into the corner of the chest.

Fear made him sweat. 'What do you want?'

'Just having some fun, Micky. Or should I call you Micky Izanagi?'

Micky understood. 'You want Izanagi for yourself.'

Laville answered with a short laugh. 'Forget it.' He aimed the camera and shot another picture. The flash hurt Micky's eyes.

Feeling unsteady, Micky took a hopeless swing a Laville, who danced out of the way. On the bed, Shirley Nash-Winters slept through the drunken fight scene with her mouth open, long golden legs tucked up in the foetal position. Dread closed in around Micky as he stumbled to the living room, dragging his clothes, and began to dress. Laville, wearing a short silk prize-fighter's robe, sauntered out to watch. The camera dangled in one huge hand. His tousled white hair threw his left eye into shadow.

'Why you do this?'

'I was just screwing around. But now I'm wondering what would happen if Saadi knew. About your hot deal. The man has a temper, Micky.'

The woman had told Laville. Micky felt sick. His manager, Frank Fenwick, always warned him. No leaks, he said. 'What are you going to do with the pictures?'

Laville sat down on the sofa with his legs spread. 'Well. They'd go great in the London tabloids . . .'

'You are crazy, like they say.' There was no way Micky could handle this now. There was a gun in his room. He jerked open the door and stalked out, feeling dizzy.

Malone was watching TV with Muriel when Milo rang up, wanting to go pub-crawling.

'Ho, you American eyeball. It is I, Tigrid, calling you and your beautiful lady. The Lady Jessica thinks you are a writer. She wishes to meet you.'

Muriel was about to return to her own room for the night. When Malone told her about the invitation, she was interested.

'Oh, I would like to do that.'

Malone turned back to the telephone. 'Okay, Milo. Shall we bring the dog?'

'We are coming to get you, for creeping the London pubs. Not needing more dogs.'

They rode in Lady Jessica's chauffeured limo to the Dove, where Milo led the crowd in a Montenegrin dance. They went on to the King's Head, where they were joined by a skinny blonde with spiked hair and her black Jamaican boyfriend. The six of them went on to the Cutty Sark, where Milo got into a fight about the beauty of Yugoslavian women, and then from there to the Two Brewers. By then it was closing time, and they had lost the Jamaican, so the five of them drove out to Lady Jessica's house, which turned out to be a castle thirty miles outside London. They were doing Greek dances when the blonde passed out. Lady Jessica went off with Muriel, somewhere upstairs, and Milo turned from the bar, where he had been pouring a drink, to stare at Malone.

'You, detective. You know what you are?'

'The owner of a bobtail dog worth over four hundred pounds if we can figure a way to get him to Sarajevo.'

'Ha! You think you are so smart, police lackey. No, that is not what you are.'

Malone could take abuse from Milo, because he knew that, down deep, Milo was the original softie. 'Okay. You tell me. What am I?'

Milo brought his drink over and sat down on the sofa next to Malone. 'You, my American capitalist dupe, set Tigrid's alibi.'

'Alibi? For what?'

The Yugloslav waved his drink at the stairs in a wide sweep. 'For whatever comes to pass.'

'Do you know something I don't, Milo?'

He leaned close to Malone's face. There was the smell of alcohol, rank, repelling. 'Someone wants me dead, detective. I pay you to figure it out who.' He handed Malone a five pound note.

Malone grinned. 'You've had enough to drink, pal.'

The women came back downstairs. Muriel was smiling. Lady Jessica took Milo by the arm and led him away, back up the stairs. At the top of the stairs, he turned and yelled down at Malone, 'Sleep well, my little alibis.'

Milo and Lady Jessica vanished, and they could hear his voice singing in his own language, and then a door closed. In the lower cabinet of the bar, Malone discovered a half bottle of brandy with the date 1895 on it. He uncapped it, and the smell was wonderful. Muriel agreed. They sat on the huge grey sofa, talking, and then Muriel led Malone up to bed.

He had found his dream girl at last.

CHAPTER TWELVE

Micky Polak slept badly, tossing through the night, and when he woke it was almost ten. His head ached. His stomach swarmed with poisons. If he lost today to Koras, it would be his own fault. Hands shaking, he brewed a pot of strong tea. While the tea was steeping, he worked out a strategy for dealing with the Canadian. He was worried about his sanity, nervous about playing today, and furious at Terry Laville. A cup of tea gave him strength. He dressed in his yellow warm-up, then marched to the closet and pulled out the antique Colt. When he tried tucking it into his waistband, the weight of the pistol was too much for the elastic of the warm-up, so he cinched himself up with a hand-tooled leather belt he'd bought last year in Dallas.

Armed and ready, he took the stairs to Laville's floor. Outside the door to Laville's room, he waited, letting his resolve gather. He had to knock several times before the door was opened by Shirley Nash-Winters. Her face was pale. She wore a floor-length green robe with long sleeves that covered her, made her look ill. Her eyes stared at him as if he were a stranger. The radiant beauty had left her face.

'Terry's not here.'

Micky brandished the Colt at Shirley and walked into the room. Shirley backed away as Micky stomped into the bedroom. The bed was mussed and the room smelled of decadence. Shirley came to the door and leaned against the door frame. He wondered how she felt about last night.

'What is it, Micky? What's going on?'

'He took the pictures. Where is camera?'

'Oh, God, I don't know. I feel awful.'

He pawed through the closets, the drawers in the bedside table.

'You better go. He'll be back any minute.'

'He is mad. Photos will not destroy Polak.'

Shirley laughed at his use of English, which did not improve matters. Micky glared at her and walked to the dresser. He found the camera in the top drawer, with two rolls of exposed film. He had no way of knowing how many rolls Laville had taken. He put the rolls into his pocket, then tried opening the camera. His hands shook.

'I'm warning you, Micky. You'd better not.'

Micky smashed the camera three times on a corner of the dresser. The lens shattered and the back popped open. Micky jerked out of the spool of film. That made three.

When he reached the doorway, Shirley was sitting on the sofa, staring at him. The robe had fallen open to reveal her bare legs. Last night, he had gone to hell for those legs. But now the sight made him sick that he had allowed himself to fall so low. He brandished the Colt at her again.

'You slut! You told him!'

Shirley shook her head and began to cry.

Early on the morning before the semifinals, Koras and Will Channer worked out for an hour at Queen's Club. In the dressing room afterwards, Channer brought out his notebook and went through a series of strategies Koras would use to defeat Polak. The information was not new, but Channer was a conscientious coach, as well as a brilliant one. Like Koras, he left nothing to chance.

'On the approach, keep the ball down the middle, to cut off Polak's angle on the forehand. Off both wings, volley deep and down the line. If you want to drop volley, hit it cross the court, to make him cover the long distance to reach it. Let the topspin lobs go, unless they fall short. He may win a couple of points, but with the wind today the percentages are against him.'

Koras nodded, sipping some water. His knee hurt, and he wanted a beer more than anything. Those were not championship thoughts, and he knew better than to drink beer before a tough match.

'Polak got tougher the minute his wife left town.'

'Yes. The same thing happened to me, back in 1963, when I sent my wife back to Melbourne.'

'That's the Aussie way, right? Leave the wife at home?'

'What's the Koras why? Not to get married?'

'Right.' Koras nodded, thinking of Laure and the money he wanted to send her.

He was aware of Channer studying him carefully, with a frown. 'How's the knee'

'Hurts. I think it will hold out.'

'Pace yourself. You want to stay sharp for Laville.'

'All right. Let's have some breakfast.'

'Bloody good idea.'

Micky had just reached his room and was thinking about ordering breakfast when someone knocked on his door. The antique Colt was still in his belt. He zipped up the yellow jacket and opened the door to see Jack Di Rocca standing there. Di Rocca wore a dark blue suit, a white shirt, and a striped tie. Even with his dark beard newly trimmed, he reminded Micky of a Spanish buccaneer.

'What is it?'

'I just need a minute, Micky. Mind if I come in?'

Micky stepped aside so Di Rocca could come in. Di Rocca had lost his quarterfinal. Probably he had come to wish Micky luck in the semi. He left Di Rocca for a moment while he went back to the closet to put the revolver away. When he came back, Di Rocca was standing at the window, looking out. Micky took a moment to call room service and order breakfast. His headache was fading. He needed to concentrate on beating Koras this afternoon. Di Rocca took a chair. Micky, however remained standing.

'I must get ready, Jack. What is it that you want?'

'Micky, I have a friend in New York who'll pay you a hundred thousand to lose to Koras.'

Polak was astounded. 'What friend?'

Di Rocca repeated his offer. 'A hundred thousand dollars, in cash. Half now. Half after the match. We want you to make it look good by going out in the fifth.'

Micky was stunned. He forced a smile that hurt his face. 'You make the joke.'

Di Rocca nodded. 'It's no joke.'

'What kind of friends?'

Di Rocca shook his head. 'It won't help you to know any more.'

The tennis term for losing intentionally was 'to tank' and he hated the sound of it. Micky was enraged that anyone would even think he would throw a tennis match. Eastern bloc players did not tank.

'You lose your match, so you come to me,' Micky growled.

Di Rocca shook his head. 'That's got nothing to do with it.'

Micky marched to the door and flung it open. 'Get out!'

Di Rocca hesitated, then shrugged. 'I'll be around until noon or so. My room number's 402. If you change your mind –'

'Get *out*, I said.'

Di Rocca stepped into the corridor and Micky slammed the door behind him. Micky stood there, staring at it. His world had suddenly gone mad. He was playing the best tennis of his life. And now Laville had threatened him with lurid photos and some faceless man in New York had offered him money to lose in the semifinal at Wimbledon.

He could deal with the photos now. Micky marched to the tennis bag and dumped the contents onto the bed. Hands trembling, he pried open the first can of film, unrolling it, exposing the frames to the light. He tossed it onto the bed, dug for the second roll, and went through the same process. Cursing in Polish, he probed for the third roll, but with no luck. Quickly, he searched the bag. There was no third roll. Perhaps he had been mistaken? He jammed the two exposed rolls back into his bag and stared outside at the summer sunlight. In two hours he would meet Koras for the match of his life. How could they expect him to play under these pressures?

'Was the gun loaded?'

'Oh, God, Terry. I don't know.'

'How many rolls?'

From the sofa, Shirley shook her head and continued with her bawling. Edgy now, Laville grabbed her shoulders, squeezing hard, and shook her, rattling her teeth, making her blonde hair fly and her breasts shake. It didn't stop her blubbering. Shirley was a wreck. Her face was blotchy with tears and she kept moaning, complaining she was sick. Finally, he threw her roughly onto the sofa and stalked into the bedroom. The camera was on the floor, empty, its lens smashed. At least two rolls of exposed film were missing from the drawer. Laville walked to the bedroom door. Shirley was still on the couch.

'What were you doing while he busted my camera? A stripetease?'

Shirley stared at him. For a moment, the tears stopped. She dabbed at her eyes with a tissue.

'Stupid bitch.' Terry walked back into the bedroom, where he picked up a handful of Shirley's clothes. 'Get out!' he ordered.

'What?'

'I want you gone by the time I get back.'

'Gone? Where would I go?'

'Back to that Hollywood fruitbag, what's his name. Pack up and get out.'

Terry walked out, slamming the door on her tears. One thing he really hated was a wailing female. First Nora. Now Shirley. He moved quickly down the stairs, through the lobby, and onto the street. His mind clicked through an endorsement scenario. He had some hot information. How could he use it to tilt Saadi's cage? Saadi had been counting on Polak. If

Polak was out of the slot, maybe there was a chance for a Sahara contract for Laville. Would Arch Bell be surprised!

Terry walked several blocks, refining his script. Who the hell did Polak think he was, charging into Laville's room with a gun? Passing a telephone call box, Terry fished in his pocket for coins. He had to wait a couple of minutes, while an old bearded fellow finished his conversation. Then Terry stepped into the red booth and dialled Saadi's number at the Victoria Intercontinental. A butler with a French accent answered, and Laville was kept waiting several minutes before he got through.

'Mr Laville, Abdul Saadi here. How are you?'

'Hey, okay. You in the mood for some news?'

'What sort of news?'

'Contracts. Endorsements. What makes the world go around.'

'Get to the point, Mr Laville.'

'You know my contract's running out with Ryker.'

'Is it?' Saadi was playing hard to get. He kept books on the players and knew all the numbers on the contracts of his competitors.

'Yeah. And I was thinking maybe Sahara might want to make me an offer.'

'You are tardy with your idea, sir. Everyone knows we are signing Mikhail Polak.'

Laville grinned as a pretty girl walked by. 'Hey, Abdul. That's what I'm calling about.'

'What's that?' Saadi's voice had lost some of its confidence.

Laville let him sweat for a few seconds. Then he said, 'Yeah. I heard Micky was signing with Izanagi. Loves their shoes, all those rubber spikes.'

There was silence on the other end of the line. Then Saadi said in a cold voice, 'How timely is your information?'

'It just surfaced. The last twenty-four hours.'

'Are you certain?'

'If it's just a rumour, you can check me out.'

'Why are you telling me this?'

'Like I said. I do you a favour, then you return it. I think we'd make a winning team, Mr Saadi. Sahara and Laville. Laville and Sahara.'

'I shall give it some thought, Mr Laville. Goodbye.'

Saadi hung up and the line went dead.

When Laville got back to the hotel, there was no sign of Shirley. Good riddance. A maid who did not speak English was cleaning the rooms with a vacuum so loud he could barely think.

The phone rang. It was Nora, his wife, calling from Heathrow. For a moment, Laville thought he was hallucinating. Nora wasn't due until tomorrow. Her unexpected arrival made Laville sweat.

'Why didn't you call, tell me you were coming?'

'I can barely hear you, darling. Is the maid right on top of the telephone?'

'I could have met your plane, if I'd known.'

'It was a last-minute opening, Terry. I was on three waiting lists, and I wanted to see you play. John Greenwald booked it for me, through the agency. I told John to call and tell you.'

Laville didn't like even hearing Greenwald's name. Also, he didn't want his wife here right now, pressuring him to be nice. He checked his watch. 'Look, Nora. I've been working out, and I need to rest. Why don't we meet at the Members' Enclosure? Say, around one.'

'Oh, I'd hoped we might have brunch.' Nora sounded disappointed, but Laville didn't really care.

Suddenly, the vacuum cleaner stopped, and the maid came to the door holding the broken camera, a question on her face. Laville waved her off. 'We can have a Perrier at one. I was awake most of the night, worrying about the damned grass.'

'Oh, poor Terry.'

Nora always drank on the plane, coming over. By one o'clock she would be drunk. He needed to get rid of Nora. When you were famous, and about to be more famous, the world was full of willing women. Nora's days with him were numbered.

Events had made Micky weary, so he lay down on the bed. No sooner was he down that restlessness came on him. He stripped down to running shorts, shoes, and a T-shirt and went outdoors, for a slow agonizing jog through St James's Park. After a ragged mile or so, listening to the birds, puffing like an old man, he began to loosen up and his mood lifted. He kept up the exercise, feeling the toxins from the night before sweat out of his system. When he got back to the hotel, he felt better and his mind was made up. He would win today. No faceless thugs in New York could force him to lose. Today was his day.

The early spectators for the first men's semifinal at Wimbledon began arriving at Church Road around midday. People in the standing room queue debated whether or not Polak would beat the ageing Koras. The British tennis fans, among the world's most knowledgeable, were well aware that this year was probably Koras's last chance for the Grand Slam. Heated arguments, tempered with logic, helped the time pass. Money changed hands, at three pounds on Koras to two on Polak. The sun was out, there was a breeze, and the grounds of the All England Club were covered with picnickers.

It was a beautiful day for tennis.

Koras went to the dressing room. In a corner, protected from reporters by Will Channer, he examined his rackets, checking the strings, tapping them against the heel of his hand. He could guess the tension in a string job within three ounces. Each of these was strung at forty-seven pounds, a fact which always brought comments from the tennis writers. Koras was a touch player. A power-hitter like Laville would have his rackets strung at seventy pounds.

Koras checked his watch. Almost two hours remained before the match on centre court. He closed his eyes and willed the usual careful emptiness to take hold of his mind.

Nora Laville was sitting on the terraces, getting some sun, when the Princess walked up. Nora was finishing a plate of strawberries with cream, feeling pleasantly loose. A half-empty glass sat next to her. The Princess wore a stunning dress of eggshell white, with rips and tears placed strategically. The dress gave Nora an idea.

'Athena, how would you like to pose for a series?'

The Princess sat down. 'Pose? For what?'

'For *Elan*. I'm just back from New York. I know they'd go for it.'

'So. You are going back to work.'

Nora nodded. 'Yes. On the production side. And you at the centre of the series would be super.'

Athena smiled her willingness. 'It would be a pleasure.'

The two women chatted some more as they waited for the play to get underway. When Athena saw Archer Bell, she left Nora alone, with her thoughts.

Nora was worried about her marriage. Sometimes she even thought of hiring someone to watch Terry, to find out what he really did while she was away. Sitting there in the sun, she thought back to their first meeting, when Terry was playing the Canadian Open . . .

Nora had been in Montreal, working on a layout for *Elan*. The photographer, John Greenwald, was her lover, and they had booked rooms at the Regent, the same hotel used by most of the circuit tennis players. In the lobby, she had been struck by Laville's facial structure, the harsh lines, the wide set eyes that made him seem like a movie star, and she had approached him in the bar where he was sitting alone, nursing a beer. She had never watched more than a few minutes of television tennis, so what she said was a white lie: 'I really like the way you play.'

Over drinks, Laville had questioned her about her work. He had seemed genuinely interested in her modelling career – the intricate lighting procedures, the endless takes, the way she had to get herself 'up' for a session. During a break in his tournament he had joined her for an early morning shoot at Ville de Laval.

'I've never been up this early in my life,' he protested.

'Never?'

'Only in the logging camps. And I left that behind forever.'

Because he was interested in her work, Nora fell in love. He was a big man, with heavy arms, heavy legs, a torso developed by endless exertion, but his smile was sad, disarming. It brought out the mother in Nora. She had expected a womanizer, all those tales about sports stars and their groupies. But Terry had been hesitant with her, distant. When he had stumbled over inviting her to dinner, she knew she had fallen in love.

Her photographer-lover warned her. 'Is this some kind of joke?' he asked.

'No. I met a man. I plan to spend time with him.'

'How much time?'

'A stretch of time.'

'What about us? What about your career?'

'They're not one and the same, John.'

'Who is this guy?'

'A tennis player. A wonderful tennis player. His name is Terry Laville.'

'I've heard of Laville. He uses women like light bulbs. First he screws them. When they burn out, he unscrews them and tosses them away.'

'You don't have to get nasty with your mouth.'

'There's a part coming up, in Hollywood. Burt's casting for the role of Mary Anne in *Dreamer*. You're just right for it.'

'Sorry. I have to go with Terry.'

She had hurt John Greenwald and she was sorry. But she was madly in love with Terry. The 'stretch of time' had lasted over three years. In that time, Nora had discovered fear, and now she was drinking too much and looking older.

Would she ever escape this vicious circle?

Frank Fenwick broke her reverie by sitting down beside her. He said he was just back from Rome, where he had renegotiated a contract with the Magnelli people for Milo Tigrid. Strips of paper protruded from his pockets.

'How nice for Milo,' Nora said.

'Yeah. At his age, it's tough. But the Magnelli people like him, at least for one more year.'

'Don't you get tired of all the running around, Frank?'

'I would if I didn't make money.' Fenwick looked around. 'Is Terry here yet?'

Nora watched at her watch. 'He should be here soon. He's meeting me.'

'How's his mood?'

'Fine.' She knew she was lying. 'Why do you ask?'

'He and Koras haven't said a civil word since Paris. I was thinking of getting them together with a peace pipe.'

'That would be wonderful.'

He looked at her. 'Would you help?'

Nora nodded hopefully, 'Oh, of course.'

Just then Athena came back from her talk with Archer Bell. She said hello to Fenwick and sat down. He studied her with his eyes. It was clear that he was attracted to her.

But what man wouldn't be?'

Walking down the corridor toward the designated room, he noticed that the doors to several rooms stood open for the day's cleaning. Up ahead, he heard the high whine of an industrial vacuum cleaner. When it stopped, suddenly, filling the hallway with silence, he stepped quickly into a room and waited until two uniformed maids had passed, chattering in a language he did not understand.

It was just past midday, and the rooms were deserted. This was a tennis hotel, and everyone had gone out to watch the matches. He started walking again, moving efficiently, his mind alert. He came to the room, 512. The door was ajar. Inside, he heard the shower running. He opened the door. A breakfast cart from room service stood against the wall, next to the windows. A plate with the remains of eggs and bacon. A half-filled coffee cup. The bathroom door was closed and he could hear the Pole humming. The room key lay on the bedside table. He put it into his pocket.

The Pole was singing in the shower, humming, then launching out into words. The tune was familiar. The visitor had been told that Polak was a gun collector. He found a gun – an Italian-made over-and-under shotgun with a hand-etched brass nameplate – in the closet. Two boxes of shells were on the closet shelf.

The visitor loaded both chambers.

Before going into the bathroom, he picked up a big tennis equipment bag which sat on a chair near the bathroom door. He slid the muzzle of the shotgun inside the equipment bag, up against some dirty clothes, and then he zipped the bag up over the barrel. He waited until he heard the vacuum start up again, down the hall, then pushed through the bathroom door. Steam was thick in the bathroom.

At that moment, the man in the shower must have felt the breeze, or the change in temperature from the open door. He poked his head out, rubbed the water from his eyes.

'What do you want?' He saw the gun. 'Give it to me!' As he reached out, grabbing for the gun, he stumbled and at the same time his visitor pulled both triggers.

The tennis bag muffled the blast. The force threw Polak crashing back against the wall. As he fell, he ripped down the shower curtain. Blood spurted onto the white curtain. The second blast, aimed at Polak's face, made him almost unrecognizable.

The murderer was sweating as he backed out of the bathroom. He set the tennis bag on the bed while he replaced the shotgun in the closet. He had worn gloves, so there would be no fingerprints. Now that it was over, he began to tremble.

One end of the tennis bag had burst open. He emptied the soiled clothes – scorched by the blast – onto the bed. Three rolls of exposed film fell out. He put them into his pocket and folded the bag, so that the hole would not show. When he opened the door, there was a vast silence in the hallway. The vacuum had stopped, and that meant the maids might have heard the muffled blast. Down the hall and around a corner, he heard their high-pitched voices, coming closer.

The door to the room across the hall was open. He crossed the hall, into room 513, eased the door shut, locked it, and stood with his back against it, breathing harshly, trying to control the trembling. They were hurrying from room to room, calling to one another. Someone tried the door to room 513. He heard them fumbling with a bunch of keys, and he hoped he would not have to kill anybody else. There was a scream then, as one of the maids found the body, and footsteps rushing clumsily away as they ran for help.

He counted to ten before opening the door. The corridor was empty. Holding the folded sports bag to hide the gaping hole, he walked to the stairs, feeling the excitement start now that it was over. He felt pumped, ready for anything. What a feeling!

Koras was waiting in the men's dressing room for Mikhail Polak to appear, when Frank Fenwick showed up. It was the custom at Wimbledon for the players to walk out together as a symbol of gentlemanly competition, and when one player was late, the other one felt the pressure. The time was 1:45 p.m. and Polak still had not showed.

Fenwick marched up to Koras and Channer with the familiar half-smile that did not hide his anger. 'Give me a minute with Koras, would you, Will?'

Channer moved away and Fenwick sat down on the bench next to Koras. 'I was in Italy when I got word from New York. You withdrew four hundred grand?'

Koras nodded. There was nothing to say.

'That four hundred was earmarked for the construction people.'

Koras started to sweat. 'I'll just have to make some more money.'

'Huh,' Fenwick grunted, as he brought out his notes. 'That ain't the half of it. You *have* to win here. You *have* to win in Ohio, at the ATP. New York is not negotiable.' Fenwick pointed at numbers on the back of an envelope. $100,000, $145,000, $200,000. And then the words GRAND SLAM and LAVAL SPORTIF underlined three times. Koras felt the pressure mounting. He would have to keep playing forever, on knees that buckled when he ran wide.

'I can do it, F.F.'

'You damn well better.' Fenwick stuffed the envelope into his pocket and brought out some legal papers. Koras signed them without reading them, but he knew they prevented him from taking more money out for Laure's dig at Alesia.

He had just signed the last document when a court official approached. 'Mr Belynkas, perhaps you'd like to walk out on the court?'

'Is Polak here?'

'No, sir. But we're told to go ahead.'

Koras gave the man his rackets and Laval tennis bag. Fenwick and Channer wished him luck. And then he followed the man out through the passage between the Royal Box and the west open stand. The head groundsman was there, on a folding chair, ready to rush out and plug up divots raised during the course of the match.

The stands of centre court were packed. As defending champion, Koras received a standing ovation. Where was Polak?

Koras sat down and tried some deep breathing, dropping into that emptiness he achieved through yoga. Just before he closed his eyes, he saw Frank Fenwick join Athena and Nora Laville in Saadi's box. Fenwick had soured his promise to Laure of more money. Yet he knew his manager had been right.

The crowd was growing impatient. This was one of the men's semifinals, traditionally the best matches of the tournament, and many of the fans had placed bets with their bookmakers. Since Polak had been playing so well, the odds had risen in his favour. In the chair, the umpire, Geoffrey Smith, kept talking on his telephone to the head umpire. So far, there was no sign of Polak.

At 2:15, Sir Francis Malcolm himself hurried out from the locker room door to speak to the umpire. Koras came out of his meditations. Something was wrong. Sir Francis whispered to the umpire.

'What's wrong?' Koras stood up.

'Your opponent has been scratched!'

'Scratched? What for? Is he sick?'

Sir Francis hesitated. His face was ashen. 'No. He's not coming. We've had word.'

'What kind of word?'

'In a moment, Mr Belynkas. Please be patient.'

Above his head, Koras heard the announcement that Polak had been defaulted. The umpire was invoking the fifteen minute rule, one more of Wimbledon's hallowed traditions, and awarding the semifinal match to Mr Belynkas.

Koras didn't like it. He was ready to play. The crowd was expectant, eager for the duel that would decide the Sunday finalists. Now, thousands of fans would be disappointed.

To scattered applause from the stunned spectators, Koras walked off the court with Sir Francis.

The atmosphere in the men's dressing room was reminiscent of that bleak day Reyes had collapsed on the *Cour Centrale* at Roland-Garros, only worse. Small groups had formed. There were mutterings about terrorism and death threats. The air crackled with tension, and Koras smelled the stink of fear.

He walked up to Channer and Fenwick.

'We just heard,' Fenwick said. 'Polak is dead.'

'What?'

Fenwick nodded. 'A chambermaid found him dead, in the goddamn bathroom at the Gloucester.'

'What was it?' Koras's first thought was of a drug overdose. 'A heart attack?' He knew that sounded crazy. Polak was only twenty-six.

'We don't know. What we do now is get you the hell out of here. Sir Francis has called a meeting of the war council in the big room. You and Will scoot before the reporters start swarming around.'

The advisory group had met before, at Fouquet's in Paris. The occasion then had been the death of Reyes on court. The men who made the decisions in tennis had convened again: Archer Bell, Frank Fenwick, Paco Ortega, Peter Abraham, Alain Clavier, Sven Skaar, the great Scandinavian player, now retired, and Saadi, who represented his country on the ITF, but who was there mostly because he was rich and powerful.

Sir Francis Malcolm seemed in deep shock. Alain Clavier stared out of the window, at the milling spectators. They did not know what had happened and were waiting restlessly for the next match. Would there *be* a next match?

While they waited for the arrival of Inspector Weston from Scotland Yard, they discussed strategies to keep the tournament going.

'I think we should stop play,' Abraham said, 'While the police carry out an investigation. Send everyone home with a raincheck. Play the damned finals on Tuesday of next week, if it comes to that.'

'It would be awkward,' Sir Francis said. 'The men's final is always on Sunday.'

Paco Ortega, wearing a red tennis shirt from Sport City, swung his massive shoulders as he turned to speak to Archer Bell. 'I thought we hired a detective, to nose around, keep us informed.'

'I'll request a report, on the double.'

Clavier joined the discussion. 'He has been working, but I have seen only one report.'

'You want a report,' Bell said, 'we can have a report.'

'*I'd* like to see a report,' Frank Fenwick said. 'Especially since he seems to be reporting mostly to Arch Bell.'

'Goddamn you, F.F. That was uncalled for.'

'I call 'em like I see 'em.'

Bell sighed. 'If you remember, we hired Malone to check on the death of Armando Reyes because we were concerned about drugs. He's working closely with the Paris police. So far, he hasn't found any drugs. I don't see how we can hold him personally responsible for Polak, or for any player.'

'If there are facts, Arch, we should be getting them,' Fenwick growled.

'Gentlemen, gentlemen,' Sir Francis broke in. 'Let us not bicker amongst ourselves when there are larger issues.'

Bell and Fenwick glared at each other, but stopped talking. Sir Francis went on.

'Here is the problem, as I see it. We have a sell-out crowd, waiting to see a semifinal match. Outside, there are an estimated 9,540 people queuing for tickets. You saw them when you drove in.'

'Took half an hour longer today,' Fenwick said. 'Just getting here from the goddamn hotel.'

'Yes, well. I have been informed that Mr Laville, who was to play the second semifinal, has not yet arrived. We must tell our spectators something. . .' Sir Francis looked around the room bleakly. 'I was thinking perhaps we might assemble a men's doubles?'

'Laville will be here,' Archer Bell said.

'He was supposed to be here already.'

'Terry hangs loose. He knew Koras and Polak would take two hours, perhaps three. He got tied up in traffic and stopped off to phone me.'

'All players should use our limousines.'

'Terry likes driving on the wrong side of the road.'

No one laughed. Sir Francis stiffened.

'Anyway, he'll be here.'

'All right,' Sir Francis said. 'We'll announce the Laville–Cooper match.'

'What will you say about Polak?'

'We'll say he defaulted. We shall hold a formal press conference following the match.'

'I vote for that,' Fenwick said.

Bell leaned toward Fenwick to whisper, 'And your guy gets a day off.'

'Knock if off, Arch.'

Sir Francis buzzed for his secretary, a young man wearing a rumpled blazer. 'Can you find Dumbo Cooper for us, Gerald? Ask him if he would mind terribly playing a bit earlier? There's a good chap.'

The secretary went out.

'This means Koras is in the final?' Ortega asked.

'Yes,' Sir Francis said. 'Unless there is an objection.'

'Polak had been playing well,' Archer Bell said. 'What are the chances Koras could have beaten him?'

'It was fifty-fifty,' Abraham said.

'I disagree,' Fenwick said. 'Koras is on his way to a Grand Slam.'

The men around the table were quiet. At last, the secretary came in, followed by Superintendent Weston. The Superintendent wore a tan suit that fitted perfectly. His lean-jawed face showed signs of strain. His shoes had their usual high polish. Weston elected to stand. Before starting out, he looked fixedly at each man.

Weston removed a notebook from his jacket pocket and put on a pair of half-moon reading glasses.

'Let me bring you up to date on events, gentlemen. This afternoon, at 12:19, a chambermaid named, ah, Mika Franulovich, heard an explosion while hoovering on the fifth floor of the Gloucester Hotel. When she investigated, she discovered a body of a naked man in the bathroom of number 512. The room belonged to a Mr Mikhail Polak, a tennis player and also a citizen of Poland.

'There was another maid, Cosima Branko, who was helping Miss Franulovich do the rooms. Upon seeing the body, both maids ran down the hall, screaming, leaving the door open. Between the time the maids ran down the hall and the hotel security man arrived, at least half a dozen persons, including, I'm sorry to say, at least one freelance photographer, entered the room. Any one of them could have removed the man's wallet, which was missing. The murder weapon, by the way, was an Italian shotgun. This has been corroborated by Dr Sims, our medical examiner. The time of death was approximately noon, which means the murderer could have been close by when the body was discovered.

'As for access, the room is on the fifth floor. One window was open, the others had been latched from the inside. The fire escape is around the corner, and three rooms away, and we are therefore presuming the murderer simply entered through the door from the corridor. Since there was no sign of forced entry, we must presume he had a key. Or he was let in by the victim. We know that the victim purchased the shotgun, a Franchi, from Purdey's three days ago. The victim was a collector of small arms, some for target shooting, some for sport. He has had an account with Purdey's for the past six years. We have begun a background check on Mr Polak, but information is scant so far. We don't expect to get much help from the Polish authorities. He is married, to an American woman in Chicago. I am informed he pays his bills on time, with cheques drawn on a bank in Dallas, Texas. He paid fourteen hundred pounds for this Franchi, made in Brescia, Italy. Records from Purdey's show the shotgun was manufactured in 1894.'

Weston closed the notebook and looked around the table. 'That is all we have at the moment, gentlemen. We are giving this case top priority.'

There was rustling around the table, as the men shifted in their chairs.

Superintendent Weston was an orderly man who hated violence. He was not a tennis player himself, but his brother Clifford had played at university and still managed to get in a game of doubles twice a week. Weston knew that the Wimbledon Championships was the premier event in professional tennis, and that these men would bring pressure to bear to clear this case quickly.

'What I wish to know from you, gentlemen, is who would want this man dead. It's sticky for us, his being a foreign national.'

There was silence in the room as the Superintendent looked from one man to another.

'Well, at least it wasn't drugs,' Paco Ortega said.

There was a general murmur of assent, but the horror of the moment was still overwhelming.

Following the general meeting, Superintendent Weston stayed on for a moment to confer with Clavier and Sir Francis. Clavier asked about the threat note which had been received a day before Wimbledon started – a development that Clavier, Sir Francis and Weston had kept under wraps.

'We worked on it, of course,' Weston said. 'The words themselves could have come from any one of a dozen magazines devoted to tennis. The paper is the type used by copying machines all over the world. Our lab technicians think the photocopier was made in Japan, but that does not narrow it down terribly.'

'But we should have taken it more seriously!' Clavier said.

'Yes.' Sir Francis looked solemn. 'The only thing now is to increase security for the players.'

'That's being done,' Weston said. 'They'll be watched by two-man teams working in shifts until this is over.'

'What about alerting the New York police,' Clavier said, 'in case this madman decides to continue his violence at the U.S. Open?'

'We've already seen to that,' Weston said.

'This is terrible!' Sir Francis said.

'It is like a bad dream.' said Clavier.

'A recurring one, too, I'm afraid,' Weston said.

Coming out of the dressing room, Koras met Terry Laville, dressed in shorts and his bright red warm-up jacket. Laville had a crazy look in his eyes. He stared at Koras for a long moment.

'This story about Polak. It can't be true.'

Koras nodded. 'It's true. A chambermaid found Polak dead, in his bathtub.'

'How did it happen?'

'No one knows yet.'

Laville's eyes darted behind Koras's shoulder. He clutched his rackets to his chest as if about to explode. His face looked haggard. He needed sleep. Was the circuit getting to him already?

'I heard a news flash while I was driving down. I couldn't believe the radio!'

'Stay cool, Terry. There's a reasonable explanation.'

'How the fuck do you know everything?' Terry lashed out. 'As a matter of fact, isn't that some kind of record, Koras?'

'What?'

'You make the finals at the Big W without hitting a single ball in the semis?'

'This isn't the first default in tennis, Terry.'

'It's the first default by a corpse.'

Koras turned away. Laville's behaviour was worse than usual, probably because of the strain of hearing about poor Polak. A crowd of reporters and television people had surrounded them. Koras started walking away, but Laville turned with a forced smile to take advantage of the moment.

'You want a statement? I'll give you a statement. I'm going to beat Dumbo,' he announced. 'And then, even though the odds aren't in my favour, I'm going to kill King Koras.'

A question came from one of the reporters. 'Just what sort of odds are we talking about here, Terry?'

Laville swumg to face the questioner. 'It's simple. Koras didn't have to hit one ball today, so he'll be fresh. I've got to go out there and face the number four player in the world.'

'What do you plan to do about it?'

'Take it up with the boys upstairs,' Laville said. 'As soon as this match is over.'

'But what if you don't win?' asked another reporter.

'Oh, I'll win,' Terry said. 'I've got that part planned.'

A ripple of uneasiness spread through the knot of reporters as Laville brushed by them and vanished into the dressing room.

In the third set of his semifinal against Dumbo Cooper, at one set all and 4–all, Terry Laville saw the ball out. He was running wide on the baseline for a forehand and he saw the ball drop down at least five inches outside the chalk. He played the shot with an open stance, hitting short with topspin, catching Cooper coming in. In the back of his mind, he was listening for the line call that would verify his own judgment, but it never came. Cooper hit a drop volley, soft with backspin, just over the net. Listening for the call had made Laville hesitate, so he was late starting forward for the intercept.

The sun was out, fleecy white clouds slipping across the sky, and Laville could really see the ball, pale against the green grass. It was definitely out, but Cooper still won the point. Feeling the anger pound in his head, Laville marched to the umpire's stand to complain.

'That ball was out. Five inches, at least.'

'The linejudge disagrees, Mr Laville.'

Terry felt the anger building. The legend on the circuit held that when he got hot, he played better.

'He's blind,' Terry said. 'I was right there. I saw it.'

'You are a player, Mr Laville. Players do not call lines.'

'Listen, you moron. That linejudge is incompetent. He's been making mistakes all day. I want the bum replaced.' Terry wanted the crowd to hear. Someone hissed at him from the stands on his right. He turned but couldn't see who it was in the vast sea of faces.

The umpire's face was becoming flushed with anger. 'Play is continuous, Mr Laville. Please play on.'

'Are you telling me that ball was in? Because if you are, you're blind, too.'

'Please Mr Laville. Your time is up. I shall have to issue a warning.'

Furious now, Laville kept on grinning. Up in the stands, the fans buzzed. He was the big name out here, the player they recognized, the one whose fortunes they followed. In Paris, they'd had his face on a billboard, and it was only a matter of time before his face was on billboards everywhere.

'Ahh, have it your way.' He turned his back, and stalked stiffly to the baseline. Down at the other end of the court, Cooper was pacing, gesturing with his elbows, muttering to himself. Laville knew those signs – Dumbo's concentration was shaky, and he was ripe to receive the old *coup de grace*. Laville's tactics had worked; Cooper had won the point, but was about to lose the set.

Cooper weighed 220, a few pounds more than Laville. He was the same height as Terry and he played the big game, hitting big groundstrokes and charging the net to put away the volley.

But Terry had learned to analyze opponents by listening to old Koras, when he first came on the tour. And now, in the fourth set, temperature up, he stroked the ball low, heavy with topspin, and Dumbo would come in and pick up the ball off his shoe tops and Terry would glide in to whistle the shot past him. Three times in the fourth set he hit Dumbo with the ball. Each time, Cooper grinned, like he still thought this was a friendly game.

Terry took the fourth game to surge ahead 3–1. All that stood between him and the Wimbledon title was this awkward player with the boyish smile and the huge feet. And then a nemesis named Belynkas. That thought gave Terry confidence. He made his toss and hit a slice serve, pulling Dumbo wide. He charged to the net to knife away the volley for a clean winner. Laville was almost home free.

Sitting with Archer Bell in Bell's private box, Malone half-watched the men's semifinal while Archer Bell summarized what had gone on in the war council in Sir Francis Malcolm's office. Malone took notes on the way Polak had died.

'They want another report, Malone. What have you got?'

'Nothing on Polak.'

Bell turned to look at Malone. 'What about his room?'

'Nothing there but the teapot, a picture of the wife, and a fancy shotgun.'

'Where was the shotgun?'

'In the closet.'

'Did you touch it?'

Malone nodded. 'I wore gloves.'

'Keep that out of the report, about searching the rooms. We don't want to upset Clavier.'

'Don't worry. I'm not adding myself to Weston's list of suspects. It's between us, Mr Bell.'

'I suppose you had to search rooms?' Bell's pudgy face wore a look of pain.

'It's tough to find recreational drugs without pawing through some dirty underwear.'

'But you haven't *found* any drugs.'

Malone thought of Milo Tigrid and his pills. 'Some marijuana, is all.'

'Where?'

'The two crazy Argentinians. Cooper.'

Bell's eyes narrowed. 'Cooper? Are you certain?'

Malone nodded. 'Bet his mama doesn't suspect, either.'

'Well, keep quiet on that, too.'

'Right.'

'What else are you doing?'

'I'm working on my theory.'

'Oh?' Bell arched his eyebrows. 'What theory is that?'

Malone leaned close. 'I think Reyes was sacrificed for the glory of the game. Polak, too.'

'That's ridiculous, Malone. Who would profit?'

'Whoever sells tickets. Whoever sells equipment.'

Bell's face turned pale. 'Jesus! Are you crazy?'

'Maybe. But the theory fits. Just look at the attendance numbers since Reyes dropped dead. Look what the scalpers are getting out there today.'

'You realize what you're saying?'

Restless, Malone stood up, stuffed his hands in his pockets. Down on the court, Terry Laville was loudly disputing a line call and the umpire was trying to bring the match under control.

'Yeah.'

'Sit down, Malone. You're making me nervous.'

Malone sat down. Terry Laville walked back to the baseline, to receive serve. The crowd grew silent again. Malone knew that his job depended on being able to predict what would happen next.

Dumbo Cooper lobbed over Laville's head. At the last possible moment, when the ball seemed to have drifted out of reach, Laville leaped into the air with the extraordinary trampoline action known as the jungle jump. His face as he stiffened his arm to bring the ball down out of the sky was a mask of harried intensity, an echo of darkness. This was what the fans came for. It didn't matter whom Laville was playing; his desire to win was so intense, so obvious to the spectators, that his victory vibrations reached from the most exclusive private box to the highest seat in the great cathedral, to the fans packed in the standing-room only section. It was, Malone knew, this single quality that had convinced Archer Bell to draw up a contract with Laville in the first place. The other players were wearing out, or getting blown away, and Terry Laville's time of greatness was coming.

'Laville's playing well today, don't you think?'
'He's putting on a real show.'
'This excitement is unreal.'
Death did that to people, but Malone kept this observation to himself. His conspiracy theory was not appealing to Mr Bell. And Mr Bell was paying his way this summer.
Down on the court, Laville crunched away another forehand volley, and Dumbo Cooper went down on his knees in the yellow grass and buried his face in his hands. Malone wondered what were the chances that Laville was on something heavier than Irish coffee. The man was playing like a maniac.

CHAPTER THIRTEEN

From the first, Superintendent Weston was not happy about the arrival of his counterpart from Paris. The French were natural meddlers who draped their investigations in a mixture of logic and innuendo. When Weston took his vacations, he went to Spain or Italy or Scandinavia, but seldom to France.

The body of Mikhail Polak was barely cold when he got word that Inspector Pierre-Aimé Marechal was flying over, for a 'professional' consultation. There was an assumption, unspoken by the French and not yet buttressed by solid evidence from Paris, that the murder of Polak was related in some way to the death of Armando Reyes at Stade Roland-Garros a month earlier.

While he waited at Gatwick for Marechal's plane, Weston remembered a case he handled back in 1979. A top member of the Conservative Party had been caught in a hotel room with the body of a 26-year-old homosexual barman from Manchester. Weston had kept the official lid on, with extreme difficulty, and a scandal had been averted. His circumspection had gained him a promotion. This death of an international celebrity bore the same earmarks as that case. If a man worked, there was always the possibility of advancement.

The flight arrived from Paris and Weston felt a little better when he got a look at Marechal. The Frenchman was short, stocky, with a barrel chest and beady policeman's eyes. Even though it was midsummer, Marechal wore a three-piece suit. His handshake was firm, and he regarded Weston with a no-nonsense gaze.

'Have you had lunch, Inspector?' Weston asked.

'Beer and nuts, on the flight across. It was nothing.'

'I have a place in mind.'

Marechal smiled, warily. 'Excellent. I accept.'

Weston leaned forward, to speak to his driver. 'Let's drive to my club, Jenkins.'

'Yes, Superintendent.'

Weston's club was a sombre building a few minutes' walk from Westminster Abbey. The lobby of the club was dark, and the walls were decorated with dour-looking portraits dating from the glorious days of British colonial power. A grey-haired maître d' led them into the dining room, where a few men nodded as they saw Weston come in with a guest.

Once they were seated, Marechal stared at the menu, which had been hand-written earlier that morning. He ordered sole, but was informed it was off.

'Well,' Weston, turning to the waiter. 'What can you recommend?'

'The curry is quite good, I'm told.'

Marechal made a face, and ordered steak and kidney pie. Weston risked the curry. To smooth things over, he ordered a bottle of white Bordeaux, the best the cellar had. He wasn't accustomed to drinking at lunch time, but several trips to Paris had taught him that he ought to bend a little.

The wine came. After a glass, the two policemen began discussing what they referred to as the tennis murders.

'What sort of gun was it?'

'It hasn't turned up yet. We're assuming it was the Franchi. The two rounds used to kill him were from the boxes of shells he bought to go with it.'

Marechal had finished his wine, so he refilled his own glass. 'Why would the murderer want to take the shotgun?'

'Our theory is that he didn't. Half a dozen people, or more, came into the room immediately after the killing. Any one of them could have taken the weapon. It was worth a good bit of money.'

'The scene wasn't sealed?'

Weston had been expecting the sarcasm. 'It was a public place. It was seven to ten minutes between the time of discovery and the arrival of hotel security.'

'*Merde!*' Marechal drank half a glass of wine. 'This Polak. According to the papers, he was playing well.'

'Yes. Brilliantly. The bookmakers were giving him good odds against Koras in the semifinals, and also against Laville in the finals.'

'It seems quite extreme, doesn't it, for one to murder his next opponent?'

'Perhaps a player has gone mad.'

'Where were these two when it happened?'

'Koras was at Wimbledon, with his coach, in the dressing room. Laville was en route, in a rented car.'

'What about the others? Tigrid? Di Rocca? Cooper?'

'Cooper was at the All England Club, practising. Di Rocca was on the telephone to New York. This man Tigrid swears he was with a lady, but refuses to give her name.'

'Never trust a Yugoslav, is my motto. Could I have another glass of this, please? It's not a bad wine.'

Weston frowned as he poured more wine. If the Frenchman kept this up, they would finish this bottle before the food came and be forced to order another to accompany the meal. They kept on discussing the case. At last, the food came. Weston enjoyed his curry, but he could tell from Marechal's face that the Frenchman was displeased with his pie. The French found it patriotic to dislike English food. Weston gave in and ordered another bottle. When it came, the Frenchman kept on with his questions.

'What time was the murder again?'

'Noon. Perhaps a quarter past.'

'And the maid found the body?'

'Two maids, actually. One of them heard the gunshot. But the other one found the body. We've had to use a translator. All they speak is Serbian.'

'Perhaps you could enlist the services of Tigrid.'

Weston smiled as he chewed his curry. 'Should I get you something else?'

'I am not so hungry as I thought. This wine gets better, however.'

'I was wondering if I might ask you a few questions, Inspector?'

Marechal waved his wine glass. 'By all means.'

'Did you have a chance to interrogate either Di Rocca or this man Malone?'

Marechal looked beyond Weston's shoulder. 'I suppose you know about Di Rocca?'

'The criminal record, yes. Is there something else?'

Marechal shrugged. 'When one speaks with him, there appear to be large portions of the fabric that have holes.'

Weston agreed. 'Di Rocca seems capable of having someone killed. Anyone.'

'Yes. But with what motive?'

'Envy? Perhaps Di Rocca was humiliated on a court somewhere by Comrade Polak.'

'Perhaps. Have you interrogated Malone yet?'

'Later today. Why?'

Marechal poured more wine for himself and his host. 'We have been working together, in a small way. Malone has a theory. Has he told you?'

'What's that?'

'He thinks someone in power is having players killed to enhance the visibility – and thus the profits – of the game.'

'Extraordinary!' Weston covered his shock by drinking more wine. The second bottle was almost gone, so he signalled the waiter for more. Marechal smiled his approval. Both men liked their work and they were warming to the discussion.

'The implications are interesting, wouldn't you say?'

'If there's anything to it, think of who it would implicate.'

'All those at the top.'

Clavier. Sir Francis. Archer Bell. Fenwick. Abdul Saadi. Perhaps even the American, Harrison Cabot. It was quite a list. 'My word,' Weston murmured.

They stopped talking while the waiter opened the wine. Weston tasted it, and nodded at the waiter, who filled both glasses. As the waiter walked away, the two policemen toasted one another.

'This wine has insights,' Weston said, aware that he had slurred his words.

'It accelerates the thinking process.' Marechal pushed the pie around with his fork. 'There is another angle, which could be related.'

Weston was ahead of his guest. 'Gambling, you mean?'

'Precisely.'

'We have a team investigating that, but it is difficult, as you know, to find reliable data where so much cash is involved. What are your thoughts, Inspector?'

'It was discovered, after the tournament at Roland-Garros was over, that major speculation had been taking place.'

'In Paris?'

'Yes. They were using a room out at Longchamps.'

Weston smiled. 'How much money are we talking about?'

'Three hundred million francs. Three times as much as last year.'

'Any idea where it came from?'

'Yes. From Zurich. From South America. And from New York.'

Weston knew that could mean the American Mafia. 'Who was the favourite in Paris?'

'Koras. Who is favoured here?'

Weston hesitated. 'Since Polak died, it is Koras, with Laville closing.'

Marechal finished his last swallow of wine and looked around for the waiter. 'Do you think we could order coffee, Superintendent?'

'Of course. Of course.' Weston caught the waiter's eye. When he had given the order, he said, 'Koras would have had to hire someone to do it. That's not his way.'

'Why not?'

'Koras is an American. Don't they prefer doing things for themselves?'

Athena von Heidelberg's identity and sense of self were directly tied to the men she could attract. She was beautiful,and beauty was a commodity in her world, and as she aged, searching for tell-tale worry lines in her mirror, she remembered how she had looked at eighteen and twenty and even twenty-five. The memory made her feel vulnerable, and now she realized why her mother had chosen to have cosmetic surgery at forty-two. Athena was a dozen years away from that age, but already she was worried. She needed men; their smiles, their admiration, their money, their dynamism. In her lifetime, she had been admired by millions, loved from afar by thousands, courted by hundreds.

Athena had a recurring dream about her first encounter with a man. In the dream, she was a little girl again, wearing a peasant's blue and white dirndl as she danced around the room with a dozen other little girls at a birthday party in a castle at the peak of summer. The voices echoed and there was the sound of music, a harpsichord, the deep throb of a cello, and as the chain of little girls circled around the table where the presents were piled, Athena glanced up into the eyes of Uncle Fritz, a friend of her mother's. Uncle Fritz was smiling. Athena remembered him because he gave her presents – pretty jewellery, a red saddle for her pony, dolls that talk and wet their pants – and at night he stole into her room and sat on her bed and touched her, very lightly, underneath the covers.

From Uncle Fritz, Athena learned what men want from women, always. At thirty, she had no illusions. She had been married twice and in love many times. Men were necessary to her existence. She could handle them. They were her life. And life could be difficult.

She was remembering her dream on the train to Oxford, for a rendezvous in a modest hotel with Jack Di Rocca. Earlier that morning, Saadi had flown to Zurich for a meeting. Later today, the women's final would be played at Wimbledon. Athena regretted missing the final, but this meeting with Di Rocca was important. She needed his help, and she was prepared to entice him with promises, pleas, fantasy, sex.

The room was on the second floor, overlooking a brick courtyard. When she arrived, Di Rocca was already there, watching a replay of the Cooper-Laville match from the day before. As she entered, the announcer made a reference to the death of Mikhail Polak. There was a videocasette player, and two bottles of champagne on ice. Di Rocca opened the first bottle, but was careful to play cool. She drank the champagne and tried to relax. They watched the cassette of the film, *Belle de Jour*, but she could not concentrate. As he poured more champagne for her, Di Rocca asked why they were there.

Athena was offended. 'Would you rather be somewhere else? *With* someone else?' She brushed a strand of hair from her face.

'No. But I know when I'm getting the deep freeze.'

She hadn't expected this. Nervously, she walked over to him, put her hands on his shoulders, and gave him a questioning kiss. When he did not respond, she reached behind herself, to grasp the zipper on the expensive beige dress. She pulled the zipper only halfway down, then turned around so that her back was to Di Rocca. He did not offer to help.

She glanced at him over her shoulder and her lip quivered. Had she lost her power over men? Di Rocca was not a handsome man, and his coarseness made her remember the physical beauty of Armando. Suddenly, she sat down on the edge of the chair and cried. Di Rocca moved to stand beside her. She felt his hand on her hair and she knew that her face would be red and splotchy from the tears. After a moment, she broke away from him and retreated into the bathroom.

She took some time repairing her face. Then she opened her purse and brought out the phial of red pills. As she nervously popped the cap, four pills rolled from the phial into her palm. She was putting them back in when the door opened and Di Rocca stood there. She tried to hide the pills, but it was too late. He entered the bathroom and grabbed her by the wrist. The pills scattered onto the floor.

'Where'd you get them?'

'None of your business.'

He squatted down easily to pick up a pill. Then he turned to her, a hard smile in his eyes. 'You gave them to Armando.'

Feeling faint and sick, she brushed past Di Rocca. He followed her into the bedroom.

'Answer me, goddamnit.'

'Yes. I gave them to Armando. But not before I took them myself.'

'Yeah. But you don't mix them with anti-anxiety pills.' Di Rocca shook his head, then walked to the window and looked out. 'Where'd you get them?'

'From Saadi. From his desk.'

'You stole them?'

'I have a key.'

'Where did you get the key?'

'I had one copied. For my own protection. You don't know what he's like.'

Di Rocca turned to stare at her. 'What if Saadi wanted you to find the pills? What if he knew about you and Armando?'

'Impossible,' she said. But then the idea chilled her and she began to cough.

Di Rocca refilled their champagne glasses. On the screen, the videotape of the movie seem pale, surrealistic. She took the glass from Di Rocca.

'So. You want to tell me why we're here?'

She waited before replying. 'You are a man. You came. I thought you understood.'

'I was curious. And you're a good-looking woman.'

That made her feel better. She crossed her legs and tried to regain her composure. 'You knew my reputation. You wanted to see if the gossip was true.'

'Okay. You turn me on. But I can tell when a woman likes me, or when she needs me for piano-moving up some twisted stairs. This is a baby grand. And the stairs are steep.'

Athena shook her head as she felt the tears starting again. She got up to leave the room. She would find some other way. 'This won't work.' Di Rocca caught her by the arm before she reached the door.

'Tell me about it.'

His face was rugged beneath the beard. He was an ex-convict with rumoured connections in the American underworld. The fierce light in his eyes told her he was attracted to her. She needed his help so she brought out the copy of *Racket World* she had taken from Saadi's study in Paris. As Di Rocca thumbed through it, she explained about the words that had been cut out. And then she showed Di Rocca the list: SEMIFINALIST, WIMBLEDON, CANCEL, REYES, SECOND, ONLY, WILL, FIRST.

Di Rocca frowned as he read through the list. 'A semifinalist will die?'

'And Mikhail Polak was a semifinalist.'

'But there's been nothing in the news.'

She walked back to the chair and sat down. 'Perhaps he waits to send it. Perhaps it has been suppressed by the police.'

'You think Saadi killed Polak for going with Izanagi?'

'I don't know. He was enraged when he heard.'

They finished the first bottle of champagne and Di Rocca opened the second. Athena was feeling better now that she had shared her secret knowledge with someone. They still had no plan.

'Okay. Let's play what-if. What if Saadi knew you were seeing Armando? So he slips you the pills. You slip them to Armando. Armando plays out of his head, takes too many, and dies. Lucky break for Saadi. But does he have that kind of knowledge about the pills?'

'It is possible. He has doctors on the staff at his research facility in California.'

'I read about that. They do research on health drinks?'

'Yes.'

'Okay,' Di Rocca said. 'So that's a possible. Now, what if Saadi was counting on the Polak deal and Polak lets it out that he's signing with Izanagi,and someone tells Saadi and Saadi hires a pro to blow Polak up?'

Athena shivered. 'That is not Saadi's way.'

Di Rocca sipped his champagne. 'Okay, let's talk about the way you lured me here to see a movie about a lady and a thief.'

Athena smiled at his light tone of voice. 'You were right. I do need help.'

'With Saadi?'

'Yes. I want to leave him.'

'Why don't you just walk out?'

'He has a hold on me, through my mother.' She told him about the pressure Saadi had put on her through his Swiss bankers.

'What you need is some leverage.' Di Rocca picked up the issue of *Racket World*.

'Exactly.'
'And what we need is for Saadi to make a dumb move.'
'Something he seldom does,' Athena said.
'Well, maybe we'll get lucky.' He held out his glass to touch Athena's. 'Here's to luck.'
They sipped their champagne. Di Rocca kicked his shoes off and sprawled on the bed with a broad smile, a good sign. 'There's plenty more what-ifs to work on,' he said.
She moved to the edge of the bed and sat beside him. 'And what are you coming up with?'
'Let's say we get lucky. I help you escape the penthouse world of Abdul Saadi. What's in it for me?'
Athena smiled. She liked negotiating. 'Saadi has lots of money. Perhaps you could take it away from him.'
'An annuity,' Dir Rocca mused. 'Payable every quarter.'
'A hundred thousand a quarter?'
'Make it a quarter million a quarter. A million a year. In tax-free bonds.' The figure made him smile. He was enjoying this. 'So. What does Saadi want the most?'
'He wants to control everything in tennis – equipment, clothes, tournaments.'
'Saadi wants to be Mr Tennis.'
Athena nodded.
'So,' Di Rocca said, 'maybe all we have to do is threaten to derail him. Hurt his ambitions just a little.'
'Excellent.' Athena leaned down to give Di Rocca a brief kiss. This time, she felt him respond. When she left the bed to pour the last of the champagne, she kicked off her shoes. She could feel his eyes on her as she returned.
'What we need to do,' Di Rocca said, 'is to pick the perfect time. Saadi's chugging along toward his goal. We take over the switching station.'
Athena smiled then and climbed up onto the bed next to Di Rocca. She felt the flutterings of relief. She smiled and her eyes became watery, a sure sign that she was getting ready to make love. For the first time since Armando had died, she felt the stirring of desire.
'All right, Jack.'

On Saturday afternoon, during the women's singles final, President Clavier called the special meeting to order. Koras was there with Fenwick and Channer. Laville and Cooper were there with Archer Bell. Sir Francis Malcolm sat behind his desk frowning. Outside the door, a policeman was stationed, and was killing time with the security guards who had been following the top players since Polak's murder.
'Let's run Koras around the track, five miles,' Laville said. 'That will assure us an evenly-matched final.'

Archer Bell laughed, but no one else did.

'I'm tired enough, Terry. Have a heart.'

'I'm serious,' Laville said, leaning forward. 'I just played over three hours out there, and because of Polak's murder the number one seed has a whole day of rest on me. How do you call that fair?'

'Please, Mr Laville. Please.' Sir Francis said. 'Today is a rest day for you both.'

'I'm lodging a protest, and I want the world to know, just because a player dies is no reason to screw another player in the match of his lifetime.'

'Is that how you see the final?'

'You're goddamned right, that's how I see it.' Terry's eyes blazed up. He was restrained by Archer Bell, who put a hand on his arm. Laville was not acting like a winner. Everyone in the room could sense it.

Back at the Gloucester Hotel after the abortive meeting, Koras found a message to call Laure Puget. The number was the one she'd given him, at her grandparents' house, in a village in the Chevreuse Valley, outside Paris. While he waited for his call to go through, Koras wondered whether or not he should tell her there would be no more money. Should he tell her now? Or should he wait until after Wimbledon?

Since he had seen her at Alesia, he had thought about her often, the firm, sun-bronzed legs, her face in the rain, her loveliness in the moonlight. She resisted him, resisted his world. That part was hard to grasp. He had worked hard for a foothold in tennis, had fought for stardom and everything that went with it. For a dozen years, women had been attracted to him because he was famous. But Laure seemed, if anything, suspicious of it. Perhaps, if he saw her again, he could sort things out.

'Koras?' Her voice was breathless. 'Are you all right?'

'Yes. I'm fine.'

'On the news they said a tennis player had died at Wimbledon. I was so afraid it was you.'

'No. It was Micky Polak.'

'Was he a friend of yours?'

'I liked Micky. We had the same manager.'

'What will happen now?'

'They've beefed up security. A policeman is with me even in bed.'

She did not laugh. 'They won't cancel the tournament, you mean?'

'No. People are shaken up. But they've sold too many tickets. We have to go on.'

'That sounds just like you.'

He thought of Frank Fenwick, and the money.'How are things going at the dig?'

'Very well.' From her tone of voice, things sounded worse. 'Everyone was impressed with your generosity.'

'Even young Dr Benoit?'

'Of course. He even suggested a commemorative plaque.'

'I feel like a ruin.'

She laughed, but still sounded far away. 'Does the tournament finish on Sunday?'

'Yes. Why?'

She hesitated before saying, 'I am in Paris until Wednesday. Then I go to Greece.'

So Koras's money had run out.

'For Professor what's his name?' he asked.

'Colicos. Yes.'

'Then what you got from me has run out?'

'Please. We must look to the future. Professor Colicos knows people at the Peabody who may be able to help.'

Koras stared at the wall. His first year on the circuit, he'd made $17,000, barely enough for expenses. 'Wednesday, you said?'

'Yes.'

'How is Monday for you? We could meet somewhere. I could pay you back that dinner.'

'I know a lovely restaurant. In Les Halles. The proprietor is an old friend. And you can meet my grandparents.'

Koras was hoping for more, but she sounded so far away that he knew talking about it would not help.

She had to go, so she gave him directions to her grandparents' house in Choisel, and then they hung up. Frustrated, Koras listened to the buzz on the telephone line for a moment, then put the receiver back and lay on his bed. He closed his eyes and tried to think of Mademoiselle Dumont, the lady with the Peugeot in Paris, but images of Laure Puget kept blocking her out.

Was Laure simply playing hard to get? Or was she as uncertain as he was about how she felt? Perhaps, in Paris, he would find out.

CHAPTER FOURTEEN

The Superintendent sat behind his mahogany desk, a seventeenth-century piece, signed by William Kent. Had the desk been an authentic Kent, it would have been worth at least £20,000 at Sotheby's, but it was part of a haul the police had made at an Elizabethan manor house where a group of forgers had installed an operation to bilk the public with the aid of bogus furniture. By the time the criminals were unmasked, they had flooded the London antiques market and had gone into the business of exporting with more success than the Beatles, British Leyland, or Princess Diana.

The Superintendent sat in an executive swivel chair, also part of booty retrieved from thieves. Marechal was at the window, staring out, hands clasped behind his back. A few feet from the desk, Milo Tigrid sat in a hard chair. Instead of his usual outlandish costume. Milo was dressed conservatively in grey flannel trousers, white shirt and tie, and a blazer bearing the badge of the All England Club.

He looked positively elegant.

'If you keep me here more than six hours,' Milo joked, 'my chauffeur has instructions to contact my attorneys. What is it you call them here? Solicitors?'

'I am sure that won't be necessary, Mr Tigrid. Just a few questions, and then you can be on your way,' Weston said evenly.

'You think I killed Polak? You are crazy.'

Marechal turned from the window. 'An odd word, coming from you.'

Milo swung to confront Marechal. 'What's that? What do you say?'

'Crazy is a strange word, coming from the self-appointed clown of the sport.'

Milo folded his arms and glared at both policemen. 'Tigrid is innocent.'

'Yes, well. Would you mind telling us where you were from ten in the morning until one o'clock, yesterday afternoon?'

'I was with a lady.'

Marechal looked at Weston. 'A lady in Paris. A lady in London.'

'Is it against the law?'

'We should like to have her name.'

'She is a lady. You won't get her name from me.'

Weston sighed, then tapped his pipe against the brass ashtray, which was in fact the base of a shell-casing belonging to his predecessor, Superintendent Nigel Curzon, who had served in the Royal Navy during the Second World War. The shell had been fired by HMS *Prince of Wales* during the sea battle which had led to the sinking of the *Bismarck* in 1941. Weston was proud of this symbol of British might and vigour. 'Where you aware that Polak's murderer used clothes stuffed into a Laval tennis bag to muffle the sound of the gun going off?'

'No. I know nothing about murder.'

'The bag is missing. We were wondering whether or not you knew of its whereabouts?'

'Tigrid knows nothing.'

'The bag was a Laval. Isn't that your brand?'

'Laval is everybody's bag. They make the good bags, like nobody.'

Weston smiled cordially. 'Inspector Marechal assures me you were very close to Armando Reyes, the man who died in Paris.'

'We were friends. I did not kill Armando, either.'

'Tell me about this competition with Reyes.'

Milo glared at Marechal. 'It was no secret. If Armando liked a woman, I would do my best to steal her away. It was a game.'

'Who did you compete for in Paris?'

Milo sighed. 'She is with Malone. Her name is Muriel Broussard-Gauthier.'

'Do you compete with this man Malone?'

Milo emitted a snort. 'Do not make me laugh, okay?'

'If I do not have this lady's name, Mr Tigrid, you will very soon become acquainted with our accommodations for recalcitrant foreign nationals.'

Milo reached for the phone. 'I call my embassy now.'

'Later,' Weston said, holding out a hand, palm forward.

Frowning, Milo leaned back and squeezed the arms of the chair. 'Malone knows where I am yesterday. He can tell all.'

'Really? Where was that?'

Milo gave them a trickster's smile. 'We were in bed. Together.'

The two policeman looked at each other, then the Superintendent pressed the button on his intercom. 'Get that detective in here.'

'Very good, sir.'

Malone arrived at Scotland Yard after six, and was kept waiting for forty minutes. When he was admitted to Weston's office, he found himself shaking hands with a smiling man dressed like an ad for *Country Gentleman*. The Superintendent had a ruddy face, as if he spent a lot of time outdoors. He poured Malone a cream sherry.

'This is a tradition in my family, a sherry before dinner. I try to wait until later, but tonight, as you managed to pop round, well . . .' He handed Malone the glass of gold liquid. The drink was too sweet for Malone, but he drank it, in small sips.

'Nice.'

'We're investigating this murder, at the Gloucester. Thought you could help us out.'

'Okay.'

'Mr Tigrid gave us a statement. In it, he implied that you and he were . . . ah . . . shall we say, in the same bed together.'

Malone laughed. 'That goddamn Yugoslav. We were together, all right. But in separate beds. And with different women.'

Weston's face showed vast relief. 'Oh, I say.' He drained his glass and stood up to pour another. 'Could you be a good chap and tell us what happened, and when?'

Malone ran the Superintendent through a travelogue of the pubs they'd visited on Thursday night. As he talked, Weston made notes, nodding as he recognized a name.

'Then when the pubs closed, we went on to Lady Jessica's manor house.'

'Where was it?'
'Outside London, maybe thirty miles west.'
'Does it have a name?'
'Coatkey.'
'*The* Coatkey Manor?' Weston suddenly set his glass down on the desk.
'I suppose. We had a late supper. Lady Jessica took Milo up to bed around two-thirty, maybe three.'
'And when did you see him next?'
'Mid-morning, Friday. We had lunch. Around one, we piled into the Coatkey limo and drove out to Church Road, for the matches.'
'Will you testify to that in court?'
'Sure.' Malone paused. 'Any idea who killed Polak?'
Weston sipped his drink. 'Marechal told me of your theory, if that's what you refer to.'
'What do you think?'
'It has possibilities. But one would want to be extremely certain before one in your position attacked those so high up in the sport.'
'Big guys are easier to bring down than you think, Superintendent.'
'From your expression, it would seem that you relish the thought.'
Malone raised his glass. 'Aim high, Superintendent.'

After leaving the office of Superintendent Weston, Malone walked through St James's Park, to the White Horse Bar. He had a meeting with Jack Di Rocca, and later on he planned to take Muriel to dinner at a fancy Indian restaurant. Malone reached the bar before Di Rocca. He ordered a pint and made a call to Lorimer's, one of the large London bookmakers. The phone rang three times before it was picked up.
'Malone here.'
'You're late. You were supposed to ring earlier.'
'What have you got for me?'
'The day in question, Mr Milo Tigrid was quoted at thirty to one.'
'How heavy were the bets?'
'Someone placed £50,000.'
'Here? In London?'
'No. From Paris.'
'What was the total placed on the men's singles?'
'Just over two million pounds.'
Malone whistled, and did some quick calculations. At the current rate of exchange, two million pounds was close to three and a half million dollars. The basketball games he'd worked on for Archer Bell had sometimes pulled down two million. Tennis was in the big time gambling arena.
'How much was bet on Polak?'
'There was a large pool bet on Mr Polak, in the semifinals. The largest individual amount our office has ever seen.'

'How large is that?'
'Eight hundred thousand pounds.'
'What were the odds on Polak?'
'Seven to one.'
Malone considered. At seven to one, that meant a payoff of over five million pounds. 'How do the finals look?'
'Actually, more money is arriving for the finals. We were forced to put a ceiling on it.'
'Any idea where the money's coming from?'
'The largest amount is from banks in Zurich. The next largest is from New York.'
It was the mob. Malone could smell them a mile away. It would take some proving.
'Thanks. I'll call tomorrow.'
'Yes. You do that.'
Malone went back to his table where he watched the English girls. He was halfway through his pint when Di Rocca showed up, wearing Levis with a sharp crease and a tan flight jacket. Jackie looked relaxed; lazy eyes, a smirky smile. 'Almost didn't recognise you, Jackie. Where's the coat and tie?'
'I'm incognito.' Di Rocca sat down, looked around. 'You like this place?'
'Reminds me of Ireland.'
'You ever been to Ireland?'
Malone grinned. 'Nope. But I'm visiting right after we're finished here.'
Malone went to the bar to get Di Rocca a gin, no ice, slice of lemon. When he returned Jackie asked, 'So. What's up, Malone?'
'I just saved your butt from being tossed in the Tower of London.'
'Gee, thanks. That means I owe you another one, right?'
'I spent a couple of hours with the top cop, in charge of the Polak case. His name is Weston, and he's working with your Paris shadow, Inspector Marechal. Marechal wanted to haul you in for the sweat box treatment.'
Di Rocca sipped his gin before arching his eyebrows. 'Malone, the fixer.'
Malone spread his hands. 'Hey. What are friends for?'
'You want something special, Malone.' Di Rocca readjusted his chair. 'Well, I don't know who wasted Polak.'
'Jackie, there's big money coming into tennis. Something tells me you're leading the charge.'
'Big money, meaning what?'
'Gambling. Endorsements. Ticket sales. Knocking over a player or two whets the public appetite.'
Di Rocca twisted his glass in a pattern on the table. 'You come on so squeaky-clean, Malone. But you don't fool me.'

'Don't change the subject.'
'You're cozying up to Arch Bell like you're Siamese twins.'
'Well, you've got Ortega.'
'Compared to Bell, Ortega is small potatoes.' Di Rocca finished his gin in one swallow, then shoved his chair back and stood up. 'Bell's dirt, Malone. He's scum in a suit from Brooks Brothers. As long as you're with him, expect zero from me.'
Di Rocca walked out, rolling his thick shoulders. Malone looked at his watch. He had thirty minutes before meeting Muriel. Time for another pint, while he gave some thought to the slant on his report to Clavier and Sir Francis for tomorrow.

CHAPTER FIFTEEN

'Are you ready, gentlemen?' said the dressing room attendant. 'May I have your rackets, please?'
The question was part of the timeless ritual of Wimbledon, and it came from the attendant with solemnity enough for the opening of Parliament.
He took three rackets from each player and led the way outside. Two uniformed policemen accompanied the players, and security men in plainclothes were stationed at strategic positions around the centre court.
It was a sunny day, with little breeze, and quite beautiful. Koras had always loved walking out onto the centre court at Wimbledon. The tennis writers called it a cathedral, and that's what it felt like to the players. On finals day, it was hushed, expectant, waiting. The Royal Box was full of royalty. The stands were packed. The grass was in fairly good shape, considering the pounding it had taken over the last two weeks. The blue sky reminded Koras of a final he had played here six years before, against Gustav Romanec, the brilliant Rumanian. The match had lasted three and a half hours. Koras had won, 14–12 in the final set, after being driven mad by topspin lobs.
The crowd stood as they caught sight of the players, and the umpire asked for a moment of silence, in memory of Mikhail Polak, the dead Polish player.
Koras thought back to earlier that morning, in his suite at the Gloucester, when the chambermaid had found him ironing the black warm-up suit he would wear to the match. The maid had tried to do the work for him.
'I always do it,' Koras explained, 'on the day of a final.'
Like most tennis players, Koras was superstitious. This particular suit

was one he had worn for the first leg of the Grand Slam at White City, in Sydney. He clung to this old ritual, pressing his vestment by using a table, a folded blanket, and his compact travel iron.

So far, the ritual of the ironing had worked.

'Gentlemen, if you please.'

The applause rained down. Koras started for his end of the court, and just at that moment Laville fell back into his chair, leaving Koras to walk out alone. Koras looked back at Laville, annoyed. Laville answered with an insane smile, and Koras knew he would have trouble winning today.

Koras kept walking, making certain he did not step on any of the lines until the ball was in motion. That was another ritual.

A plainclothes policeman was directly in his line of sight as he turned the corner and moved a few feet behind the baseline. He took three balls from the ballboy, and stroked a forehand to begin the warm-up. In the stands,a uniformed policeman moved along the aisle, and he found himself thinking about death as he warmed up. Armando had died. Polak had died. Who was next?

He felt stiff today, with occasional sharp twinges from his right knee, and he thought back to those early days on the circuit when he could stay up all night, drinking and dancing and singing, and then come out at ten the next morning and play brilliantly with only three minutes to get loose. These days, he needed at least fifteen minutes. The muscles in his right leg pulled tight, warning him to slow down. He slowed himself down and began counting from five down to zero, calming himself with yogic breathing.

Across the net, Laville had never looked better.

As the players warmed up on centre court, Matt Malone was summarizing his findings to Sir Francis and Alain Clavier. The three men sat in Sir Francis's office, above centre court. Malone could tell from the frowns and the stony looks that he was not getting through with his theory. He had two pages of numbers to accompany his report. When he finished, both Sir Francis and Alain Clavier stared at the wall. Sir Francis was the first to speak, and Malone figured he had just talked himself out of a job. The axe would fall in the next five minutes.

'Are you seriously asking us to believe that there is some sort of . . . conspiracy . . . on the part of the tennis establishment, as you call it, to heighten visibility in this game?' Sir Francis's voice was over-controlled and tight. His eyes were ice-cold.

'The numbers are there, Sir Francis. All I did was try to figure out who would profit from the deaths of two tennis stars.'

'But, my God, man, this is incredible.'

'Look,' Malone focused on Sir Francis, 'players don't have that much to gain by knocking each other off. I mean, the balance at the top see-saws. Koras was a tiger in Australia, but he starts to fade in Paris, and Polak starts to come alive. Now, what if Koras kills Polak?'

'He advances to the finals of Wimbledon,' Clavier said.

'Yeah. But he's taking some kind of risk, just to win one tournament. He's got to plan carefully, and there's not much to gain, because another tournament's coming. He can't kill everybody off, or there won't be anyone to play.'

Sir Francis nodded. 'There was the year of the players' strike,' he said. 'The field was fairly thin.'

Malone went on, building his argument. 'I've spent the last five weeks interviewing, nosing around, talking to the players. They're stand-up guys, juvenile, moody, anxious, irritable. They might kill a lines person over a bad call, but they're not going to kill each other.'

'Even if you were right, how does that leave us with the larger establishment?'

'Look at page two,' Malone said. 'I've condensed the recent trading activity of the major equipment manufacturers. All of them – Sahara, Sport City, Laval, Magnelli, Ryker – are trading like hotcakes on the New York exchange. Their stock prices are up across the board. In sales, I compared some figures from five years ago, when they were small. Now, with the new interest in tennis as a sport with violence attached, these companies are expected to be grossing more, and that means they can act big time.'

Malone had them looking at the figures on the second page of his report. It was now or never.

'We have three areas that gain from the violence, gentlemen. First, the equipment people. Second, gamblers, if they can control things. And third, the arenas themselves.'

Sir Francis lowered the report to the table. 'How dare you?'

Malone waved a hand outside. 'Have you ever felt tension like you've got today?'

'We are not here to assess feelings,' Mr Malone. 'We are here to verify facts.'

'Feelings are what it's all about, Sir Francis. Death, or the promise of it, breeds its own fear and excitement.'

'I am intrigued by your assumptions about gambling,' Clavier said, hurriedly. 'Do you have any facts to support that thesis?'

'The bookmakers here say it's the biggest year ever. And the bets increased dramatically after Polak's death on Friday.'

Clavier looked at Sir Francis, who had walked to the window, and was now staring out, with his back to the room. 'Why should we continue to employ you, Mr Malone, when you bring us reports such as this?'

'Because we'd better get to the bottom of this before the tennis writers do. Anyone can gather these numbers, and good investigative people like Judson Garwood and David Kollmore are nosing around.'

Sir Francis spoke without turning. 'I would love to muzzle that man Garwood.'

Clavier nodded, then swung to face Malone. He was not a large man, but he raised himself up to seem larger as he spoke. 'Mr Malone, I feel that I speak for the Federation when I say your services are terminated, as of this moment. I will confer with Mr Bell about the money still owed to you.'

'Yes,' Sir Francis said. 'And leave your journalist's pass with my secretary.'

'Okay.' Malone was resigned. He'd gambled, and he'd lost. He didn't like losing his golden egg. But he had been fired before, usually when he cut too close to the bone with his view of the truth. He went out of the office without shaking hands.

Malone had just dropped off his journalist's pass with the unsmiling secretary when Superintendent Weston showed up. Today, the Superintendent wore a three-piece suit, grey, with cap-toed shoes like a banker's and a flower in his buttonhole. He carried a manila envelope and his face looked tired.

'Mr Malone. Just the man I wanted to see. Come with me.'

Weston took Malone's arm and guided him back into the office, where Sir Francis still stood at the window, staring out onto the grounds of the All England Club. Alain Clavier was at the bar, pouring himself a glass of sherry.

'I asked Mr Malone to come in with me. I trust you gentlemen don't mind.'

Neither Sir Francis nor Clavier would look at Malone. 'What is it. Superintendent?' Sir Francis asked.

Weston opened the envelope and produced a single sheet of paper. It was a note, addressed to the 'Tennis Owners'. It had been photocopied from an original made by pasting down words cut out of a magazine. The note resembled the one which had arrived in Sir Francis's office just two weeks ago.

AFTER REYES, POLAK HAS PAID FOR IGNORING OUR WARNINGS AND IF THE PLAYERS STILL REFUSE TO PLAY BY OUR RULES, A THIRD SEMIFINALIST WILL DIE IN THE NEXT GRAND SLAM EVENT. BEWARE, NEW YORK.

'Great Scott!' cried Sir Francis.

'Incredible,' said Clavier.

Malone indicated the note. 'Where did this come from?'

'Four London papers received the same message this morning. It had been deposited at a private distribution company which sends urgent mail, seven days a week. Each of the envelopes was contained within a larger one, along with two five pound notes, for the delivery charge.'

'Are they being published?'

'Yes,' Weston said. 'In a matter of hours, the world will know.'

'Do you have the original?'

'No. All were photocopies. No fingerprints.'
'Pretty clever,' Malone said.
'Let's not give them any more credit than is necessary,' Sir Francis said.
The Superintendent spoke to Clavier and Sir Francis. 'Has Mr Malone explained his theory to you gentlemen?'
'Briefly,' Sir Francis said.
'I spent much of the night considering it,' Weston said. 'It seems to have some validity. At least, I am directing our murder investigation along those lines.'
Malone smiled and decided to wait to see what the big hitters said. Sir Francis cleared his throat, preparing to speak. Clavier was faster. 'It is a shock, of course, to think that someone would manipulate an entire sport in this way. But we have retained Mr Malone until the close of the U.S. Open, that is, if he is willing.'
'Well, Malone?' Weston arched his eyebrows. 'It's your theory. My we continue to rely on your absolute discretion?'
Matt Malone grinned. He liked being in the catbird seat. 'Do I get my press pass back?' he asked.

Koras lost the first set 6–4, playing sluggishly, favouring his right knee. Laville exploited every weakness, and it was obvious from the opening point, which Laville won with a booming passing shot down the line, that the Canadian was playing his best tennis of the season, and perhaps of his career.
Laville took the second set 6–2, and the people in the stands tried to rally Koras with solid rounds of applause. For the first time in several years, Koras was the underdog at Wimbledon.
A disputed line call distracted Laville at 3–all in the third set, and he began a protracted argument, forcing the umpire to call the tournament referee, a certain Lord Dunham, who arrived guarded by a policeman.
Koras, who knew all of Laville's tricks, wrapped a towel around his neck and stepped to the sidelines to begin chatting about the weather with a cameraman from the BBC. Behind the cameraman sat a pretty young woman who reminded Koras of Athena, as she had looked twelve years ago.
'Hello,' Koras said.
'Hello.'
'Are you enjoying the match?'
'Oh, yes. Very much.'
By now, the people around Koras were craning their necks to hear the conversation. The cameraman had alerted his director in the control booth, who was focusing on Koras and the spectators. The sky was slightly overcast, but blue patches showed through the grey.
'Are you from around here?' Koras asked the girl.
'Cambridge, actually.'

'Nice town, Cambridge.'

The girl hesitated, then took the plunge. 'Might I ask you a question, Mr Belynkas?'

'Of course.'

The camera focused on the face of Pantakoras Belynkas, veteran of almost two decades of tennis. The girl was about to ask her question. 'Well,' she said, her voice low. 'I want to know, who do you think will be next?'

She wanted to know which tennis star was going to be killed. His smile widened, got tighter, as his face paled. 'No one, I hope.'

'How can you keep on playing, knowing it might happen?'

'It's my job. This is what I do.'

'I think you are very brave, Mr Belynkas.'

'Thanks.' His voice cracked.

'Good luck out there.' Her words carried a terrible double meaning.

In the control booth, an assistant director flipped a switch that sent Koras's conservation with the girl flashing across the world – a legendary tennis star, a pretty young girl, talking about death in the arena.

'Are you getting this?' the director whispered.

'Every word.'

Sweating with the effort, the umpire brought the match back under control by announcing he had awarded the point to Mr Belynkas. The crowd applauded. Terry Laville made an obscene gesture and walked back to serve. For the first time in the final, Laville was momentarily off his game.

Koras won the third set on a tense tie-breaker that went to 12–10. His knee was bothering him, so he asked the referee for a time out. In tennis, that meant three minutes.

'What's going on?' Laville wanted to know. He stood like a white-maned colossus, legs spread, chin upthrust, to accent his question.

'Mr Belnykas is entitled to three minutes.'

'Jesus Christ!' Terry cried.

The official tournament trainer came out to examine Koras's knee. There was talk of a knee brace, and Laville could taste victory. Koras looked tired out, worn down. Taking advantage of the break, Laville jogged over to chat with some people in a private box at the side of the court. When Koras resumed, it was with an elastic knee brace. The veteran was coming apart.

The fourth set was the best set of the tournament. Koras won the first game, Laville won the second. They fought their way to 6–all, and Koras won another extended tie-break, 11–9.

In the fifth set, Laville made a special effort to end the see-sawing struggle, and he took the first three games to lead his opponent 3–0. It was clear the knee was bothering Koras. Twice he fell, accompanied by

groans from the stands. When he got back to his feet, he limped slightly.
Laville kept playing the ball to Koras's forehand. With the bad right knee, Koras could not put much power behind his shot. He lobbed to Laville's backhand. As they passed each other at the changeover, Laville taunted Koras. 'Play like a man, why don't you?'
Koras recovered to make it 4–3 with three brilliant service returns and a wicked topspin lob. At 4–all, Laville started his last argument of the Wimbledon fortnight. The umpire listened patiently, but it was clear that Laville was merely stalling. At last, the umpire ruled that the point be re-played, which did not pacify Laville. He won that point, but his concentration had been shattered. Twelve minutes later, Pantakoras won the men's final at Wimbledon. It was tournament number three for Koras, out of the four needed for a Grand Slam.
Terry Laville's handshake across the net was a sham. His mouth was tight and he glared at Koras with hate in his eye.
As the reigning champion held the trophy high to make a slow symbolic turn around the packed stadium, the fans rose to their feet to shout themselves hoarse with praise. Many of them were crying.
Laville stayed on the court long enough to shake hands with the Duke of Kent. The Duke wore a club blazer and grey flannel slacks.
'Good show out there, Mr Laville. You played well.'
'I'll play better, next year,' Laville growled. 'And I'm going to win in New York.'
The Duke smiled his official smile. 'I'm sure you will.'
Shaking hands with the Duke, Koras felt only the ragged edge of fatigue.
'Congratulations, Mr Belynkas. You always do us proud here at Wimbledon.'
'Thank you, Your Grace.'
Koras had met the Duke before, not just on court, but also when he and Athena had been invited to a small supper party at Kensington Palace. There was more chitchat, about the circuit schedule, before the Duke wished Koras luck in his quest for the Grand Slam and then left the court, surrounded by his security people.
Laville stalked toward the dressing rooms three steps ahead of Koras. Suddenly, when he was a few feet from the door, he stumbled and sank to one knee. An official asked what was wrong.
'I've got a bad pain,' he said. 'Right here.' He pointed to a spot on his left leg, high on the thigh, near the crotch.
'Can you walk?'
'I'll try.'

Koras came out of the baths to find a doctor with a short beard closing up a black medical bag. Terry Laville was spread out in a leather chair against the wall, his left leg propped up on a folded towel on one of the benches.

'I can't find a thing, Mr Laville.'

'Then why does it hurt?' Terry growled.

'It could be psychosomatic, part of the pressures of playing under stress. If you'd like to come to my surgery tomorrow, I'm certain we can do a proper job.' The doctor did not sound sympathetic.

Terry waved him away. 'I'll be there.'

The doctor handed Laville his card and walked out. Laville sat up, with a look of faked pain on his face. Koras opened his locker and began to dress. He knew Laville was up to his old tricks. If the Canadian could talk to some reporters about his alleged injury, it would diminish the victory Koras had just won.

'You played well, Terry.'

'Up yours, Koras. I was beat from playing Dumbo.'

'You didn't seem tired to me.'

'How would you know?' Laville pointed at his leg. 'I pulled a muscle out there, at 3–4, in the fifth. They'll have it on tape.'

'Hope it gets better.'

'You don't believe me, do you? You're not the only guy with injuries.' Laville stood up and moved over to stand close to Koras. His face, huge and hateful, was inches away. 'You think this is your year for the Slam, don't you?'

Koras didn't answer. There was no percentage in talking to a crazy man. He finished dressing. Laville went back to his chair, and sat down heavily, his left leg out in front of him.

Koras turned to him as he prepared to leave. 'See you in New York.'

Without moving from his chair, Terry gave Koras the Italian fuck you sign, a clenched right fist, the left hand tight against his bicep.

'I'll see you in hell, Koras.'

Part III

FLUSHING MEADOW

In The Arena

CHAPTER SIXTEEN

The barrel of the pistol, a shiny chrome-plated .357 Magnum, was less than six inches away from the head resting on the pale yellow cushion of the chaise longue. Koras lay on this stomach, arms by his sides. He was daydreaming, thinking about when he'd seen Laure in Paris, and he had told her about the money. The vision of Laure went away, the sky darkening and Koras sensing danger. He forced himself not to move. There was the clear, metallic click of a hammer being pulled back. Koras turned over. He wanted to see who was going to kill him. Blinded by the glare of the sun, he saw only the huge black hole of the barrel, distorted by his perspective, then the hand holding the weapon, and beyond that a thick forearm covered with black hair. Koras squinted. Beyond the arm, he made out the features of Milo Tigrid, the mad Montenegrin, grinning profusely at the sight of Koras, petrified.

'Are you insane?' Koras cried.

'Only a scenario, my friend.' Milo waved the gun.

'A scenario?' Koras felt sick.

'Yes. I only wanted to prove to the world how easy it would be to kill the great Koras, here, beside the pool at glorious Court's Court.'

Koras was sweating now, and feeling white shocks of relief. 'The gun is real, isn't it?'

'Yes. But there are no bullets.' The Yugoslav removed six bullets from his pocket and showed them to Koras. He counted them off. 'One, two, three . . . six bullets, six famous tennis players, all gone, eliminated from the ATP computer.'

'Milo, you're crazy!'

'Touché, my friend.' He slid the weapon under his belt.

Koras did some deep breathing and tried to stay calm. The two men sat by the side of the swimming pool at Koras's house in Westhampton, on the south shore of Long Island. Koras had bought the house three years before because Frank Fenwick had explained they needed a tax shelter. It was a three-storey house, built in the New England style, with Cape Cod ornamentation, a central cupola, and eight dormer windows across the front. Koras had modified the house, putting in a swimming pool outdoors, and another swimming pool indoors, on the ground floor. There were ten bedrooms, a modern kitchen, and a dining room which could easily seat forty guests. The indoor pool was linked to the outdoor pool by a canal. From above, the pool system resembled a giant tennis racket, with the racket head constituting the outside pool.

There were seven acres of land around the house. The oversize lot sloped off as it neared the coast, and halfway to the beach Koras had built a helicopter landing pad. A hundred yards to the east, forming a triangle with the house and the end and the heli-pad, Koras had built two courts, one above the other. The upper court was where he worked out during the summer. The lower court, with a fifty-five foot ceiling, was enclosed and heated, for the winter months.

'Do you carry it all the time?'

'Since Wimbledon.' Milo plucked the gun out of his belt, and aimed it at an imaginary intruder. 'If a murderer enters Tigrid's room, let him beware. Boom. Boom.'

'What do you do on the court?'

'It is in my tennis bag.'

'What about airports?'

'In my checked luggage, and packed in foil, like a camera.'

'Why don't you find one of those gunsmiths who work for the Mafia and pay him five thousand dollars to build you a two-shot Derringer hidden away in the butt of your racket?'

Milo beamed. 'An excellent idea. Then, when one's opponent got the upper hand, one could aim the butt of the racket at the opponent and strum the strings, and suddenly, no more problem.'

'It's time you retired, Milo. The pace of the circuit is getting to you.'

'I shall save the last bullet for myself.'

'What do you think of this threat? About the semifinals?'

Milo sighed. 'What does an old dog like me care? I haven't reached the semis here in this godforsaken capitalist place since 1976. Remember? I played Armando in the quarters? I bested him.'

'That was at Forest Hills, right?'

'What a lovely place. Why did they do away with it?'

'We needed a showplace. The house that Slew built. Remember?'

'Speak for yourself, my friend. You are a transplanted comrade. I, Tigrid, am not an American. All is not well here, in this land controlled by Mafia dons and Republicans.'

'You always get grumpy in New York, old friend.'

'I need a woman.'

Jack Di Rocca stayed around London for ten days after Wimbledon was over. Saadi was out of town – Zurich, Rome, Damascus – making headlines in the financial papers with big-money deals like the recent takeover of Sport City by his Sahara Corporation, and the Princess Athena had decided to stay in London to irk Saadi and to catch up on some shopping. With Di Rocca's help, her escape plans were taking shape. She had been thinking small. Now, with Di Rocca's support, she was planning to escape Saadi's clutches with an annuity of $1,000,000, perhaps more.

The secret was in the timing. Athena was impulsive. When she felt something, she acted at once. Di Rocca had persuaded her to wait until New York and the U.S. Open. They had three instruments – the pills, the magazine, and the roll of film Di Rocca had picked up in Polak's room.

The Princess didn't know about the roll of film.

She was beautiful, inventive, seductive, and Di Rocca was surprised he and Athena had become intimate. Everywhere she went, men ogled her and it was clear that her sexual attraction gave her power and control. But she seemed to enjoy her afternoons with Di Rocca – three of them so far, plus one languorous night – and as they explored each other with mounting passion he discovered he was jealous of Armando Reyes.

She talked about Saadi, but so far she hadn't said much about Armando. Di Rocca took her reticence as a keep-out sign. He didn't push her for information. But sometimes, his body locked onto hers, Di Rocca had the feeling Armando had joined them in bed.

When he saw her spend money, Di Rocca was glad Saadi was paying the bills. Five hundred pounds for shoes, ten thousand for a designer frock, thirty for a Russian sable. Di Rocca had grown up poor in South Brooklyn. Even though he had money now, he didn't forget what it felt like, being poor. It made you want to steal, to hurt somebody, sometimes even kill.

This was his first experience of the flamboyant decadence of the European aristocracy. And the Princess was a lot of woman; passionate, hot, healthy, with the smoothest skin he had ever touched and the ability to drink through the night, make furious love, and appear bright as a summer morning the next day. She had a good mind. She could recall lines of poetry, the works of many authors, obscure character actors from stage and screen, scores from tennis matches ten years ago. She introduced him to writers and movie people who knew his name from tennis. With Athena, Di Rocca discovered a new world.

Her favourite movie was *Belle de Jour*. His was *Last Year at Marienbad*, a black and white film from the sixties. Lying in bed, sipping champagne, sated, Di Rocca would let the screen roll across his mind.

There was this actor in the Marienbad film who had a face like Saadi – long and sad – long fingers, a deliberate walk and cold eyes that nailed you to the wall.

His wife was a pretty brunette who wore a dress made of white feathers. When the feathers flew, disturbed by the husband's gunfire, the Princess laughed, mostly from remembered shock, and her hands got cold. She had a kinky sense of humour.

There was an Yves St Laurent dress made of white feathers, slit up the back of the skirt, cut low, with a daring decolletage. On the day before Di Rocca flew to New York, for a meeting with Sally Vicenti, the Princess bought it in a fashionable shop for a thousand pounds, charging it to Saadi. 'It might be my last,' she laughed, swirling before the mirror. There were tears in her eyes.

The next day, Di Rocca flew to New York while Athena took a plane to Austria, to visit her mother. After Austria, she would spend a weekend on Saadi's yacht, in Juan-les-Pins, and she would be in New York the week before the U.S. Open. Saadi wanted a party to launch Sahara's latest promotion. It would be Athena's last hostess act and she wanted to depart on a note of gaiety and triumph.

Crossing over, Di Rocca's flight to New York had very little headwind, which made it a six-and-a-half hour trip. At Kennedy, as soon as he got his baggage, he put in a call to Sally Vicenti, to set up a meeting. Di Rocca was an honorary member of the West Side Club in Forest Hills. Sally, who owned stock in the fancy new Racket Club of Oyster Bay, was hungry to be a member at the older club. Sally was a sucker for tradition, and Di Rocca knew he could soften him up with lunch in Forest Hills.

He and Di Rocca had made money, betting on tennis. There was more in the near future. 'I got this terrific plan, Jackie.'

'It will be good to see you, Mr Vicenti.'

'Hey. Call me Sally, okay? See you tomorrow?'

Di Rocca said thanks and hung up, his mind on the Princess. For the first time since he was sixteen and had had a bad crush on Gloria Castelmonte, Di Rocca was hooked. Being hooked made you vulnerable. He needed leverage, an angle, something for his own protection. What kind of leverage would work on Salvatore Vicenti?

Sally Vicenti, the son of immigrants, was a good father, a standard husband, a jolly friend of the world who was nice to kids and dogs and widows, and a man who dearly loved to eat. Eating made Sally feel joyously alive – rigatoni, lasagna, spaghetti with meatballs, veal Parmigiana. His mother, born Angelina Cavalcanti in the old country, was a terrific cook, and Sally always compared the commercial fare he found in the restaurants or in the houses of friends to the food he remembered smelling like Italian heaven, steaming on his mother's table.

Unlike in the television ads, where actors ate Italian from a pink and white checkered paper table-covering, his family ate off a white tablecloth, fresh at every meal.

Sally developed heart trouble early, at the age of thirty-four. He was walking down Broadway in the spring, a week before Easter, thinking of money and Doris Schuler, his current mistress, when the pains came.

He tried to ignore them, but then he saw his brother's grave, which he took as a sign. Joey had died young, so at thirty-four Sally checked into the hospital for open heart surgery. He was on the table twice, for hours a session. The scar was long and reddish-pink and ugly, and it took him six months to recuperate. Sally liked action. Wasting time depressed him.

Lying in bed, hobbling around, he felt weak, not like a man. The doctors told him he'd have to cut back on his food, stop working so hard, get some exercise.

Stop eating, Mr Vicenti, they said. You're killing yourself. He tried diets, raw vegetables, no wine, but he got more depressed.

The only answer was exercise.

When his strength had come back, Sally looked around for a sport, something to keep his mind off food. His father, Nicolo, had played a mean game of checkers. A cousin over in Jersey played an Italian version of that French game, boule. But Sally liked killing, the comforting sound of gunfire, so he took up hunting, and spent some scary times in the woods in Pennsylvania. Because of his weight, he had trouble climbing the hills. When an amateur crazy from the city let a gun go off barely missing Sally and splattering bark and yellow leaves all over, he gave up the woods.

He tried shooting at targets, on the police range, two hands on the pistol grip, wearing ear plugs for the noise, but target shooting bored him, so a friend in the business got him to take up golf. Sally spent two grand on equipment, four grand joining a club in Westchester, five grand on lessons from Ben Bolt, a smooth-stroking pro who'd spent his life playing on the golf circuit.

The only good thing about taking up golf was getting away from home. A side benefit was the scenery – bottoms and brown thighs and young tits under tight sweaters.

When he was forty-two, Sally Vicenti discovered tennis. His daughter, Elena, a junior at Bryn Mawr, brought home her roommate, Julie Edwards, Julie was from California, blonde, outdoorsy, with clear blue eyes and terrific legs.

Julie Edwards had energy to burn. At school, Sally learned, she worked out every day, running laps in the snow, ice skating, doing pushups and situps. Her ambition was to play tennis on the women's circuit. Julie Edwards was a terrific model for Elena, who was already getting beefy, like her dad.

Because of all that tight muscle, so efficient, so nice to watch, Julie's body impressed Sally enough to watch a workout on the courts. Sally had a friend who had a cousin who had a membership at an indoor tennis club, the Tilden Club, right in midtown Manhattan. Outside, it was snowing, the first real weather of the season, making the streets slick. While Julie worked out with the local pro, Sally and Elena watched.

Sally found himself licking his lips as he fell in love with Julie's body. 'How does she stay in that kind of shape?' he asked.

'She works out, Daddy. All the time. Isn't she beautiful?'

'Yeah. But so are you.'

She hugged him. 'Oh, Daddy.'

Sally took his first tennis lesson at the Tilden Club from Julie Edwards, who was a superb teacher. She moved him around, huffing. She stopped when he thought he would die. Sweat streamed off Sally. During the break, Julie told him he had a natural swing on the forehand and a lovely hammer motion on the volley, and all the time he was scheming how to get into her pants without letting his daughter know.

He insisted on paying her for her time. When he handed her two twenties, her eyes lit up and she gave him a quick kiss on the cheek. There was no time to make a move. Julie went back to Bryn Mawr before Sally could execute a safe plan.

He dreamed about her at night, sweaty nightmares, with him racing across the tennis court, huffing, dying for her, his wife asleep and suspicious in a bed that floated next to his in the dream. Julie would hold out her arms, come hither, daddy, with Sally tripping, falling, the floor opening up, a sledge hammer crashing down on his heart, making him wake up sweating, pyjamas soaked, his wife sitting up in her bed, dialling the doctor, her face on red alert.

Money was no object, so Sally found a tennis pro. He took lessons indoors all winter and dropped thirty-five pounds, then fifteen more. Exercise, imagine that, lifted his depression. He could eat more and still maintain the weight. What a deal.

At spring break, Sally played against Julie Edwards, his dreams coming true, a beautiful blonde across the net, the flight of the ball, young legs in short shorts, making his mouth dry. While Sally worked on the court, his daughter Elena sat in the stands, unknowing, innocent, applauding for both players.

After the match, which Sally lost, 1–6, 2–6, he shook hands with Julie, who was amazed at his progress.

'Wow. Have you improved, Mr Vincenti!' Her hand across the net was soft, warm, sexy.

'Meet me for a drink, sometime.'

The cool blue eyes told him she understood, but she played it nonchalantly. 'What?' As if she hadn't quite heard.

'You and me,' he said. 'Mid-week. Anyplace. I'll come to you.'

His daughter was walking over. Not much time.

A cunning look came into Julie's blue eyes. 'All right, Mr Vincenti. But just for a drink.'

Sally smiled. He liked it, her calling him Mr Vincenti. It showed respect.

So in May they met for a drink at a roadhouse in Upper Darby, Pennsylvania, well southeast of Bryn Mawr, far enough away that Elena wouldn't find out. Julie wore black, a diamond bracelet, a gold wedding band for the occasion, and knee boots for the Pennsylvania rain. He had the feeling this wasn't her first time, and that made him jealous. They had one drink in the bar, talking about tennis, the end of school, the summer circuit. They had a second drink in the room, water slicking the windows, sex brimming out around their words.

She talked about her expenses, how much it cost going to school, playing the West Coast circuit. She wanted to hit the European circuit, have summer on the clay courts, Cannes, Milano, Switzerland, but she couldn't begin to afford it.

Sally got the message, took out his billfold and laid two hundred dollars on the table. 'For your trip.'

She left it there, her eyelids fluttering like butterflies. He laid another hundred on the table. She folded the bills into her wallet, put the wallet into her college girl's shoulder bag, and slowly began to undress. She said okay when he asked her to keep the knee boots on. After a beautiful workout, Sally came through, heart banging, without a cardiac arrest.

They met three other times before she took off for Europe. He paid her three hundred a visit, gave her a travel bonus for the trip. 'Watch the European pretty boys,' he said. 'And come back soon.'

Sally tried getting into the West Side Tennis Club, at Forest Hills. It had tradition, stretching all the way to the early twenties, and Sally wanted a club with class. But he had to settle for something less, and that summer, Sally bought his way into the Racket Club of Oyster Bay, on the south shore. He also had membership to a club in Westchester, to please his wife, who saw herself as Lady Astor, and liked to kill time with la-di-da society upper crust mingling.

Getting a membership at the Racket Club of Oyster Bay cost Sally $35,000, what with fees and considerations. He bought $50,000 of their stock, so he would have some respect. The head tennis pro, Johnny Florian, was an Italian-American from Chicago whose biggest win had been the Italian doubles at the Foro Italico. From the pro, Sally learned first-hand how the sport changed with open tennis. Johnny would tell Sally about the bets in the old days, circuit hotdogs playing for ten dollars a set, money under the table.

Johnny set Sally up in a doubles eightsome, four matched teams who met three times a week. Sally met stockbrockers, an entertainment attorney, a computer marketeer, a Broadway producer, and a gambler who played the Aqueduct. Sally had a wicked American twist serve that bounced high to the backhand. And he loved to kill the ball, put it away.

In the summer of his second year at Oyster Bay, the stockbroker came to Sally for money. In the fall, the Broadway producer came to Sally for money. By Christmas, he had lent money to five of his seven tennis pals, and he and his wife were meeting a new class of people.

These were bluenoses with money troubles. Sally's business was mostly cash. He suggested a football pool, and they made twenty-two per cent on their money. He suggested a basketball pool, and they made twenty per cent. That spring, Sally began thinking of a tennis pool.

There was big money coming into tennis, and the scenario reminded him of baseball back in the twenties, when a friend of his grandfather's had fixed the World Series, Sally, who liked conquering virgin territory, wondered what it would be like to make a little pin money betting on some of these big tournaments.

To Sally, the marketplace was like a duck pond. The ducks were the suckers. The businessmen were the hunters. If you got to the pond early, or if you found yourself a new pond at the beginning of a new season, you could do some fancy shooting and leave with a full game bag, before the competition wandered out of the woods.

Tennis was a fresh new pond, swimming with suckers.

One day, watching TV, he saw a name he decided to follow up on. Jack Di Rocca was an Italian-American player from the New York area who'd done some time with one of Sally's soldiers. They were televising an indoor match from Dallas. The announcer was saying how Di Rocca had emerged from nowhere. Sally made some calls. Di Rocca was a survivor, had a clean record since getting out of jail, and seemed to do pretty well for himself playing the horses. Di Rocca had been in the Top Ten for three years.

For their lunch in Forest Hills, Sally wore a Palm Beach suit, cream-coloured, with heavy-soled wing tips. His face and hands were dark, from three hours a day on the courts. He was happy about the money he'd made betting on tennis at Roland-Garros and Wimbledon. The U.S. Open was a week off and more money was filling the pot.

The trick now was to lock in a winner with long odds.

They had just shaken hands and were being seated when Drury and Margaret Matthews, the twins, walked by, their pleated tennis dresses curling around their tanned thighs.

'Nice scenery.'

Di Rocca opened the menu. 'Nice place.'

Sally grinned, leaned close. 'I tried getting in here. They got a waiting list.'

'I could speak to the chairman, Mal Whitwood.'

Sally nodded. 'I'd consider it a favour. I like it out at the Oyster Bay facility, but it's nothing like this. I'm someone who appreciates tradition.'

'Consider it done.'

Di Rocca ordered a roast beef sandwich, rare. Sally ordered salmon, broiled. They decided together on a Valpolicella, 1979. When the waiter had gone, Di Rocca turned to Sally.

'Are we going ahead on schedule at the Open?' Di Rocca asked.

'Those notes in the paper. Whoever sent them didn't have such a bad idea. Guys on the street who never heard of tennis are following Koras and Laville like they played ball for the Knicks.'

'I heard Koras was still two to one.'

'Panties Koras,' Sally said, and sipped his wine. 'We need to talk to him.'

'I'll set something up.'

'Don't let him know I'll be there. A lunch, say, between the two of you.'

'Where?'

Sally looked around. 'I like it here. This is a good place.'

Di Rocca grinned. The waiter arrived with their food. Both men were hungry, so for a few moments they were silent as they ate.

'The pool's up past four million,' Sally said, 'and growing. We need to bet it before opening day.'

'What about this kid Heinz? He's hot enough.'

'Nineteen to one. I like those odds. But I was thinking of another winner.'

'Who?'

Sally chewed thoughtfully, making Di Rocca wait. 'Jackie, how'd you like to be the next U.S. Open champ?'

Di Rocca started to laugh, but the look on Sally's face stopped him. 'You serious?'

Sally nodded. 'Seven to one. We could pick up a bundle.'

'I play Koras in the semis. If I get that far.'

'That's where he loses.'

'He's going to love hearing that.'

'He's in hock to the construction people. I bought some of his paper. About quarter of a million. He gets cocky, I'll buy some more.'

Di Rocca refilled the wine glasses, then held up his hand to signal the waiter for another bottle.

'Where'd you stash the cash you were going to give Reyes?'

'In the Zurich bank. Fifty grand from Paris, and Polak's hundred grand from London.'

Sally dug into his coat pocket, and came up with an envelope which he shoved across the table to Di Rocca. 'Hundred more in there. The money in Zurich, keep it.'

Di Rocca had earned it, with sweat. 'Thanks, Sally.'

'Nothing too good for the next champ of the U.S. Open.' Sally toasted Di Rocca. Jackie knew that if Sally could afford to pay him $250,000, Sally's own take had to be ten times that. Maybe more. Di Rocca could sense control shifting to his paisano here. The price of his win would be steep and he didn't want to be locked in with Sally Vicenti for the rest of his life. Di Rocca started to think about ways to protect himself.

'What about Laville?'

'Something will turn up.'

Di Rocca reached into his pocket and pulled three photos out of an envelope. He handed them to Sally. 'Maybe it already has.' He owed Laville, for that trick he'd played in Houston. Time to get even.

Sally looked at the photos, which showed Micky Polak without any clothes on in a bedroom scene with a very pretty girl. 'Who's the doll?'

'Shirley Nash-Winters. She was with Laville, in Paris, again in London. The guy is Polak. My guess is Laville took the pictures.'

Sally's smile widened. 'Where'd you get them?'

'Out of Laville's tennis bag, the day Polak was murdered.'
'Laville would blackmail Polak?'
'With Laville, anything is possible.'
'Can we tie them to Laville?'
'I got some blow-ups. There's a wristwatch, and a headband on the bedside table.'
Sally banged the table. 'The important thing, Laville will know we know.'
'Yes.'
Sally handed back the photos. 'Nice work, Jackie. You got talent.'
'I'll try to set something up with Koras for the end of the week.'
'Surprise him if you can. How do you think the player vote will go?'
'You heard about that?'
Sally gestured with one pudgy hand. 'The mayor. The cops. The tennis bigwigs. I got people inside City Hall.'
Sally's smile, coupled with the hard-eyed look, clinched it for Di Rocca: he needed protection. 'I think they'll vote to play.'
'God, I love a democracy.'
'You don't miss much, do you, Sally?'
Sally tapped his chest, above his heart. 'When this almost went, I made a decision. Sally, I said to myself, don't rush around so much. Sit back. Check things out. Since I made that decision, I got rich. It's the key, Jackie.'

CHAPTER SEVENTEEN

It was midafternoon. Out of the windows of the mayor's office, Deputy Mayor John McKenzie could distinguish the high towers of the Brooklyn Bridge emerging through the haze of heat and smog. McKenzie, sweating with the task delegated to him by the mayor, had just turned away from the window. 'Gentlemen, let's get to the point. Will there be a Flushing Meadow or not?'
A dozen men sat around the black conference table. The war council from Fouquet's was growing.
Ross O'Brien, the Chief of Detectives of the New York Police Department, sat on McKenzie's right. He was an enormous man, solid, as though carved from a timeless block of granite out of the Irish past.
Next to O'Brien was Harrison Cabot, President of the United States Tennis Association. Frank Fenwick, his pockets bulging with paper, sat on Cabot's left. Next to him was Archer Bell, then Peter Abraham. On

Abraham's left was Paco Ortega, Di Rocca's manager. Ortega had recently picked up three players from South America, eager young men who grinned into the camera and hit big topspin loopers and partied a lot. Their English was monosyllabic, the syntax of heroes. 'I Patricio. Today, I win.' Ortega spoke their language.

Next to Ortega was Alain Clavier. Next to Clavier was Abdul Saadi, owner of Sahara Sports, which had just taken over Sport City. Next to Saadi was Sir Francis Malcolm.

The only man without a coat and tie was Peter Abraham.

For more than an hour, the deputy mayor and the others had listened to President Clavier's summary of the problems they were having in professional tennis.

Clavier looked down at his notes. The meeting was the second one in twenty-four hours, and no solution was in sight. In less than a week the tournament was scheduled to begin. Ticket sales had already outstripped last year, and there was little doubt that it was because of the threat note published in the London papers. The entire circuit was smothered in a climate of tension, which grew worse each day.

After Wimbledon, the players had dispersed to less important tournaments, hoping a win would bolster their confidence for the upcoming struggle in New York's major arena. The horror of Polak's death had come to the surface again here in New York, with the newspapers reprinting the grisly pictures of his body slammed up against the bath tub, and below the photos a facsimile of the threat note that had turned up on finals day in London. The *New York Post's* headline was WHO'S NEXT?

Now, there was talk of letting the players vote on whether or not to hold the U.S. Open. As a player, Peter Abraham wanted the chance to vote. The other men in the room felt the situation was getting out of hand. Archer Bell had already put forth analogies with big business and labour. 'It's like letting United Steel Workers call the shots at U.S. Steel,' Bell said.

'Bad comparison, Arch,' Frank Fenwick said. 'This is entertainment and that's the rust belt.'

'It's a power struggle, F. F. You'll see it when your balance sheet comes in for the season.'

Fenwick pointed to his head. 'I carry my balance sheet here, Arch. Right here. So it's handy.'

'Gentlemen, please,' said Clavier. 'We have two issues before us. There is the matter of the player vote, which seems to be the only solution. Second is the matter of player security, and here we need the help of the city.'

Sir Francis broke in. 'The last player vote was to boycott Wimbledon in the seventies. I hesitate to raise ghosts, but there it is.'

'We don't want a goddamn boycott,' Archer Bell said. 'What is this, the United Farm Workers?'

'Let's say we vote to play,' Abraham said, 'what about security?'

'That,' Clavier said, 'is in the hands of the city of New York.'

The deputy mayor smiled. 'We'll do our best. But you've got one hundred twenty-eight men and sixty-four women to watch over. If we start at the – what's it called right before the quarters?'

'The fourth round.'

'Yes. If we start there, and try to cover the sixteen, on both the men's and the women's, we might have some success.'

Peter Abraham broke in. 'We need a player referendum. It's easy enough to sit up here in air-conditioned safety and talk, but the players have to go out there on the court and face the possibility of getting killed.'

Archer Bell turned to Abraham. 'Polak was killed in his hotel room, remember?'

Abraham flared up. 'If we walk out, Arch, there won't be a tournament. Remember Wimbledon, the year the pros struck? You people barely *had* a tournament.'

'Mr Abraham is talking about cancelling the tournament?' the deputy mayor asked.

'Absolutely.'

'You're crazy, Pete,' Archer Bell said.

'A lot of people would lose a lot of money, Pete,' Frank Fenwick said.

'Better to lose some money than to have one more player killed.'

The deputy mayor walked back to the window. When the time came for him to make a crucial decision, he had to be standing. It was an old habit, one that hung on from his days as a trial lawyer. New York had protected the Pope, the Shah, even Yasser Arafat. If he allowed the U.S. Open to be aborted because of a lack of confidence in his police force, he could kiss the tournament goodbye, permanently, along with his job. McKenzie looked out at the teeming city without speaking, then returned to his chair. He turned to Harrison Cabot. 'Will your people cooperate with our security measures?'

'We'll do our best, certainly.'

The deputy mayor turned to his chief of detectives. 'Can you do it, Ross?'

'It won't be perfect,' O'Brien said. 'Let me bring in my chief security officer. He can brief us.' O'Brien walked to the door and opened it.

'We're ready, lieutenant.'

Lieutenant John Lucchesi was five foot ten, slightly built, with expensive taste in clothes and the trim look of a long-distance runner. His chief saw him as a man for the long haul. Although Lucchesi had not been home during the last forty-eight hours, his face, shadowy with fatigue, was freshly shaved. In fact, Lucchesi spent a lot of twenty-hour days on the job, not sleeping, or catching cat naps on a cot at one of his precinct houses. From his eyes, you might take him for a musician, or a college professor. But when he spoke, showing that little glint of a smile that marked the professional policeman, Lucchesi was all business.

'Gentlemen, I can make this brief. We've talked to our counterparts in London, and in Paris. We've checked with Interpol, Scotland Yard, the FBI. No one has a line on the killer – or killers. There are theories around, mostly terrorist talk. The IRA could be in it, but they don't operate in this sphere unless they get locked out of England. We've got a full task force working around the clock, even though no crime has been committed here. Anyone who has any information should get it to us. I'm leaving business cards on the table, and I'm planning to sleep at the National Tennis Center until after the finals. My people are setting up a command post now, in an RV near the entrance gate. If you know something, or even think you know something, give me a call.'

'The lieutenant will take questions,' the chief said.

Archer Bell spoke up. 'There's talk of a player vote, lieutenant. If that goes through, and our players vote to have this tournament, how quickly could your people set up security?'

'Are we talking individual security here?'

'Yes.' It was clear Bell was thinking of his players, Dumbo Cooper and Terry Laville.

'So far, what we plan is to cover the top twenty-five men and the top twenty-five women. As we get closer to the semifinals, we'll blanket the players still left in the tournament.'

'Oh, terrific,' Peter Abraham said. 'If a player doesn't get killed, *then* he gets protection.'

'We're looking for ideas, doing everything we can. The people at the Tennis Center are being asked to beef up their security.'

'Metal detectors?'

'If we have to. There are so many ways to fool them, they're not considered effective.'

While Lucchesi answered questions, Fenwick leaned back in his chair and thought about the way things were going. Saadi had just bought up Sport City, adding it to his Sahara corporation, and there was talk he was looking at Laval Sportif for his next takeover. Laval held Koras's endorsement, and Fenwick knew Saadi would make things rough on Koras. Now, there was a rumour going around that Saadi was about to sign Terry Laville, to replace the dead Micky Polak. On that, Archer Bell wasn't talking. The news would be leaked tomorrow night, at a party Saadi was giving, at his new casino in Atlantic City. Koras wasn't invited, but everyone else in tennis who counted would be there.

The lieutenant finished talking and left the room. Fenwick walked out with Harrison Cabot, who was on his way to an interview with the garrulous journalist, Judson Garwood.

'Garwood smells something,' Fenwick said.

'Don't worry. I can handle him.'

'What do you think of the overall situation, Harry?'

'Tickets sales are astronomical. Profits will double from last year. One is tempted to go on the black market.'

'You don't have the temperament for a scalper, Harry.' Fenwick said.

'Yes. Quite right.'

Cabot's black limousine slid to a stop at the kerb. The door opened and Cabot got in. The day was typical for New York in late summer; hot and humid and getting more so. Fenwick stood on the kerb, watching the limo pull away into the New York traffic. Fenwick hoped Cabot could handle Garwood.

'The history of the largest and richest tennis tournament in the world is a recent one,' wrote Judson Garwood in the *New York Daily News*. 'Flushing Meadow began in 1977, after a disagreement between the USTA and the directors of the West Side Tennis Club, at Forest Hills. Since 1924, the U.S. national championships had been played at the West Side Club. But the tournament grew beyond the bounds of the club, and a new site had to be found.

'They called it the house that Slew built.

'Slew Hester, a businessman from Jackson, Mississippi, was the first USTA president to come from the deep South. During the Second World War, Hester worked with the U.S. Army to develop a transportation system for France. Since then, he has served in several large conglomorates at the corporate level, gaining the experience in leadership which would aid him in developing the new stadium at Flushing Meadow Park. Hester, an inveterate entrepreneur, left the corporate world to become an independent oil producer.

'The legend of the Tennis Center goes this way: Hester was flying in from Dallas to La Guardia when he spotted the site from the air. It was the Singer Bowl, site of the 1964–65 World's Fair, which had been renamed the Louis Armstrong Stadium in 1973. The new site had sixteen acres, and the plan was to save the original structure and to build on or around it, with a huge stadium court as the centre, a grandstand court off to the side, emulating Wimbledon, and the two connected by a walkway, to accommodate spectators wishing to see what was going on next door. The National Tennis Center, as it was to be called, would have twenty-seven outdoor courts and nine indoor courts, all air conditioned.

'It was a glorious dream – a symbolic site for the greatness of American tennis – but the obstacles were immense. To begin with, the plans had to be approved by nine municipal agencies. Then the winter before the opening was hard, causing many delays. And as the warmer months came, and everyone looked forward to completion, the contracts the builders had with various unions ran out – this was in June – and seven different unions went out on strike. Things were brought under control by Hester and his Number One, Hy Zausner, who had founded the Port Washington Tennis Academy.

'It took just under a year to build, and Flushing Meadow became the most extravagant tennis tournament ever seen. The new national tennis arena is situated on the axis of the main landing strip at La Guardia. Planes taking off pass over the stadium every two minutes, making the players feel they are in the crater of a volcano always on the verge of erupting. The crowds sit in moist and heavy heat while the huge structure actually shakes. "It is," remarked three-times champion Pantakoras Belynkas, "the only tournament where one cannot hear the balls rebound, where the roar of the crowd is outdone by the roar of angry jets."

'Players and spectators alike adapted themselves to Flushing Meadow, and it became the hardest, the most testing, the most ferocious tournament in the Grand Slam. Here, defeat is most bitter, success most triumphant. Part of it is shock. After the refined rustlings of Wimbledon, the players are plunged despite themselves into a game of killers, taking place in a climate of noise and furore, of heat and pungent odours, of thunderous tantrums and sudden despair. Here, Jack Di Rocca, a product of the Bronx streets, rediscovers the rough rules of his adolescence. In the U.S. Open's merciless struggle, Di Rocca's rage to win finds its proper expression. Here, at Flushing Meadow in Queens, New York, tennis becomes the sport of the toughest, and Di Rocca the idol of the rough and ready New York fans who flock to the stadium to applaud their hero.

'A player like Dumbo Cooper, on the other hand, has never been able to conquer, arouse, or placate the spectators. Cooper more often than not plays under jeers which punctuate and exacerbate his faults, driving him further and further into a solitude close to martyrdom.

'Here, in New York, the ambiance of the Roman circus has been revived, and the spectators, swigging beer from paper cups, devouring hot dogs and steak sandwiches, reject the losing gladiator, thumbs down. New Yorkers are winners. They will root for the underdog, but they reserve their cheers only for the hot victory of the winner.

'But the tenor of the game has been altered by the spectacle of murder. Peruvian Armando Reyes died of a drug overdose on the orange clay in Paris. The police are still pressing a homicide investigation. And Mikhail Polak was gunned to death in his hotel room in London. The deaths were tennis-related: Reyes collapsed during a semifinal; Polak was two hours away from a semifinal. And the threat note to the London papers specifically mentioned semifinalists as targets.

'So what does this mean for tennis at Flushing Meadow? The police are on the job. Spectators at the massive Tennis Center will be met with metal detectors and the occasional security frisk. Players will be guarded, especially as they approach the semifinals. But as the machinery locks into position for play and for protection, one wonders what is going on in the minds of the person – or persons – responsible.

'The police theory is secret. Terrorism is a possibility. But if you are a tennis fan you love the game for its pure arc, its flowing line, and the last thing you want to think about during a tennis match is a madman stalking the semis.

'And you have the feeling that's just what this madman wants, wherever he is.'

Ross O'Brien, chief of detectives, put down the copy of the *Daily News* and lit a black cigarillo. The situation seemed increasingly tense, and he was worried that the threats against the tennis players would become epidemic, would spread until the sports world beyond tennis would be endangered. That was the way strings of assassinations got going.

The deputy mayor was standing at the window, looking out at his city.

'Okay, Ross. Let's bump lists. Who do you see for the murder in France? Then the murder in London? Then the crazy notes. Let's hit them one by one, see what we've got.'

O'Brien shifted in his chair as he brought out his notebook. 'We've got four possibilities. My number one is the Cavalcanti family. Tennis is ripe for those monkeys. My number two is the players. In no particular order, I've got Tigrid, this Heinz kid, Di Rocca, Cooper, and Laville.'

'I've got Koras on my list.'

'Maybe.' O'Brien looked at his notebook. 'Koras seems cool and above it all.'

'Maybe he lets it build until it explodes in his face.'

'Maybe. My number three is a lone crazy, a fan or a groupie. My number four is the big hitters club: Clavier, Malcolm, Cabot. For my money, those guys couldn't deliver an order for lunch at Sardi's much less a contract to a hit man.'

'I've got them at number three,' the deputy mayor said, sitting down again. 'What's new with Lucchesi?'

'Security is tight. And there's money piling up, all right. A bundle is being bet in Canada, where we can't touch it. Another bundle in Switzerland.'

'Maybe we should haul in that private cop. What's his name?'

'Malone. He's checked in with Lucchesi. Seems like your everyday ex-cop.'

The deputy mayor swung his feet up on his desk. It was summer, and he had counted on Flushing Meadow to provide a distraction. Now, it was one more problem to cope with. 'We need a clear motive. What about this idea? Maybe Reyes and Polak messed with Laville's wife.'

O'Brien laughed, curtly, then furrowed his brow as he looked at McKenzie. 'Anyone ever tell you you've got a dirty mind?'

'Anyone remind you the tournament's five days off?'

CHAPTER EIGHTEEN

It was late afternoon when he sat up in bed, covered with sweat and unable to catch his breath. His temples were pounding relentlessly. In the glaring bright light of the bedroom, the objects around him assumed awesome and unfamiliar shapes. It was August, late summer, humid, and he had forgotten to shut the curtains that would close him off from the rest of the world.

He turned to stare at the numbers on the electric clock, flashing in time with the alarming beating of his heart, his thumping temples. Sleep had not refreshed him. He felt worse now than he had before. But when he closed his eyes, he kept seeing the ghostly face of Mikhail Polak. It stared at him from out of the newspaper, alive, from a tennis court in the past.

He felt remorse for Polak, with a pretty wife, a great career ahead of him. He rolled over now and tried to think about the party tonight, at Saadi's new casino in Atlantic City, and the money Saadi would pay him if he overcame the hex and won here in New York.

He clenched his sweating hand on the pillow. He could win. He had to.

'Terry?' Nora's voice floated in from the front room. She was back from her shopping. Hoping she would leave him alone, he didn't answer. He heard a door close, then footsteps approaching. The bedroom door opened and Nora looked in. 'There you are. Did you have a good rest?'

'No.'

'Oh, you're sweating. Are you all right?'

'Yes.' He hated answering her questions. They made him feel like a child.

'Can I get you something?'

Nora sat down on the bed, reached out to feel his forehead. There were times when Laville didn't like being touched. He grabbed his wife's wrist.

'Oh, you're hurting me.'

He let her go, then rolled off his side of the bed and stomped into the bathroom, to wash away Polak's face.

Just before six, one of Saadi's limousines picked Laville and Nora up to take them to the heliport at South Street Seaport. In the limo, Nora had a highball while Laville looked at the story in *Racket World* about his recent victory over Koras in Ohio, in the ATP Championships.

His photo was there, a colour shot showing him hitting a winning forehand. A caption under the photo asked: 'Can lumberjack Laville stop Belynkas's quest for the Grand Slam?'

He began studying the story, hoping to find the answer to the question. Laville was sensitive to what the press said about him. He assembled the adjectives that the writer used to describe his playing style. 'Masterful' was a word he liked. 'Artistry', that was good. 'Black magic' and 'magician', however, made him vaguely uncomfortable.

Laville tossed the magazine aside, yawning, stretching out his muscles. He was glad to be out of the claustrophobic apartment. Two years ago, Nora had nagged him until he bought it, and they stayed there when they were in New York. It was small and dingy and reminded Laville of his poor-boy childhood in Montreal. What he wanted in New York wa a posh suite at the Meridien, for now, and then a classy estate on Long Island, like Koras had. Someday, he would own this city. He was looking forward to the evening, to Saadi's party, and to the big announcement about Laville and Sahara Sports.

He heard the steady throb of the helicopter as they pulled into the heliport. The chauffeur parked the car and got out to open the door. The sound was deafening, a heavy blast that threw Laville back against the seat cushions. Nora didn't seem to notice. She was out of the car, waiting for him. A hand reached in for him and a face appeared. The face was Micky Polak's and he was grinning.

'Ready, Mr Laville?'

'Don't touch me!' Laville backed away on the seat until he was up against the other door. Micky Polak leaned aside, his hand still out. He was saying something now but his words were drowned out by the blast of the shotgun inside Laville's head. Laville grabbed for the door handle, missed, grabbed again. The door opened and Laville scrambled out. Micky was coming around the rear of the limo now. Nora stood on the other side of the car. Laville sprinted for the helicopter. A flight attendant held out a hand. Laville brushed that aside. He didn't want any ghosts touching him.

Nora joined him in the cabin.

'Terry?' Nora asked. 'Terry, what is it?'

Laville was sweating. He looked out of the window for Micky, but saw only the chauffeur in his uniform and peaked cap.

'It's nothing.' He turned to the flight attendant. 'When does this thing get going?'

'There are a few more in the party, sir. It will be a few moments.'

'Terry, what is it?' She touched him and he took his arm away.

'I thought I saw Micky Polak,' he whispered.

'Where?'

'Back there, in the limo.'

'It's those awful pictures,' she said, 'in the papers. Poor Terry.'

He was still sweating, but his breathing was under control. He was aware that Nora was watching him strangely. He didn't care. What the hell did she know? He was the one who had to go out there and risk everything.

* * *

On the helicopter ride down to Saadi's Atlantic City casino, Laville felt the morbid sensation lift, and he bounced himself into a better mood. He told stories about the early days on the circuit. As long as he talked, he could forget about the immense pressures of being a tennis superstar.

There were seven people riding down with them. Malone and Muriel, and behind them Di Rocca and his manager, Paco Ortega. Also in the helicopter was Judson Garwood, the nosiest man in tennis, and Mr and Mrs Harrison Cabot. Mrs Cabot wore an expensive necklace containing enough diamonds to finance Laville for the rest of his days.

'Oh, look!' Nora cried. 'What's that?'

'Asbury Park, coming up,' Malone said. 'Behind us is Long Branch.'

'It's gorgeous!'

'Right south of there is Port Pleasant.'

'Terry, don't you think it's simply gorgeous?'

'It's the greatest.'

The helicopter landed on the casino roof, setting down in the centre of a big white circle with a cross painted on it. Laville felt shaky when he entered the penthouse and saw Polak again, walking towards him. But then the light changed and he saw it was Saadi, wearing a white dinner jacket and a red bow tie. Behind Saadi there was a poster of Laville, the old woodcutter, twelve feet high and ten feet across. He stood at the net in Ohio, holding up the trophy for the ATP Championships.

'Hey!' Lanville said, walking up to it. 'Great!' The colours were good, bringing out the white hair, and also the red and the black in his headband.

'It is a good likeness,' Saadi said.

Across the room, Nora chatted with her pal, Princess Athena, and Jack Di Rocca. After a month or so of dressing conservatively, the Princess was back in her old style, in a sequined black suit worn over a sheer black blouse through which her breasts could be glimpsed. Against his wishes, Nora was going back to work. The Princess was donating her time to help Nora get started.

'May I offer you something?' Saadi said.

'Yeah. An escalator.'

Saadi chuckled. 'We have escalators downstairs.'

'I was thinking of one worth about half a million.'

Saadi's eyes hardened. 'That's an expensive escalator.'

'My idea,' Laville continued, 'is a new clause in my Sahara contract. If I win at Flushing Meadow, I get half a million. If I win the Australian, I get a million.'

'That was not our original deal.'

Laville looked at his right hand, then at Saadi. 'And I haven't signed yet.'

'Does Archer Bell know?'

'This is between you and me.'

'It's absurd.' Saadi started to walk away, but Laville stepped smoothly to block him.

'How would it be if the people in this room knew you were the first to know about Polak's deal with Izanagi?'

Saadi stared at Laville. 'You are mad,' he said, and walked away to give instructions to the servants.

Laville picked up a drink from a tray and strolled to the window, a huge curved wall of glass that gave the penthouse at Casino Paladin a view of the brightest sections of Atlantic City. Nora came up to take Laville's arm. She was excited about the the Princess's outfit. Her cheeks were flushed and he knew she'd had a couple of drinks already.

'It's from Metamorphis. The blouse is from Norma Kamali. She wouldn't tell me how much the whole thing cost, but I'd say four thousand five, easily. Everything was custom-tailored. The choker is from Brandwynne of Los Angeles. Saadi just bought it for her.'

'Just can't wait to get back to work, can you?'

'Oh, Terry. It's only part-time. Athena's being wonderful. And the circuit drives me crazy.'

'What it drives you to is the nearest bar.' He glared at her before walking away.

The second wave of guests arrived, including Archer Bell and Clavier, the President of the ITF, and right behind them Milos Tigrid, accompanied by an attractive brunette in a blue dress, and Hammer Heinz, the hot young player who was the tennis writers' hope for the future. Laville sipped his Scotch. He thought Heinz was too cocky, too full of himself, but he had to admit the young player could hit when he was on. Milos shook hands with people, introducing his companion as B.J. Where did Milo meet these women? Di Rocca, wearing a dark blue suit that made him look like a corporate executive, came up to stand next to Laville.

'I just talked to my bookie. They've got you at seven to one for the finals.'

'So?'

'So I wondered if you were voting to play.'

Laville laughed, a derisive bark. 'Get set to lose, Jack. I'm playing.'

Di Rocca waved his drink at the room, indicating the symbolic poster, then regarded Laville with a thin smile. 'Remember that time in Houston when we were supposed to play in the quarters?'

'No. I don't remember we ever played in Houston.'

'Come on. We went out drinking after we'd won in the last sixteen. When I went to the men's room, you slipped something in my beer.'

Laville didn't like Di Rocca's smile. 'Get lost. Jack. You're making things up.'

'As you go for the top, kid, remember Houston.'

Laville brushed past Di Rocca.

Dinner for sixty was at a long table under a million lights. The table was black and shiny, darker than ebony, and when you looked down you could see your hands moving, the glitter of silverware and jewellery, the reflection of your face. Giant candelabra were positioned about every six feet along the centre of the table.

The Princess sat at one end, Saadi at the other. Laville, sitting on the Princess's right hand, wondered how much money you'd need to live like this, above the dirt, never breaking sweat, buying up buildings, companies, people, anything you wanted. Down the table, in the bubbles of conversation, he heard his name, Terry Laville, the woodcutter, Terry this, Terry that, the magician, wizard Laville. Already, there was talk of a new racket, a Laville Autograph. Saadi wanted to call it The Brave, to highlight Laville's Iroquois heritage. Archer Bell said that had an exploitive, crude ring to it, and it was too obvious. Laville, on the other hand, thought The Brave was a good symbol for the standup image he wanted to project to the fans. Archer Bell wanted to call the racket Black Magic. That name made Laville jumpy.

The Princess was talking across him to Nora, about the layout for *Elan*, and Lanville remembered that time in Los Angeles, when he'd spent a night with her. He'd just come on the tour, and was struggling to stay afloat. The Princess had been on the rebound from another affair. On a smoggy day in September, Laville had clawed his way to the semifinals, where he'd been beaten by Koras, the surgeon. After losing, he'd had a drink with the Princess in her hotel room on the Pacific Coast Highway in Malibu. She was younger then, honey-skinned, reckless. She'd made Laville dress up in an Indian costume, rented from a costume rental place in Hollywood. He felt stupid, but the Princess gave him a pill to loosen him up, and he dressed in the buckskin, pants with no back and no front. The Princess had worn a heavy white nightgown, which she wanted torn off her, in strips. Laville had obliged . . .

'I'm so glad for you, Terry.'

He came out of his reverie. 'Hey. Thanks.'

'If you're careful, you can go a long way with Saadi.'

Laville looked around the room. This room with the rich people and the ebony table was a long way from the dirty snow of his Canadian childhood. Behind the candle's reflection in the black table, he saw the face of Mikhail Polak. It made him sweat.

'Careful. What's that supposed to mean?'

Instead of answering, the Princess looked away, at a string of servants, wheeling in carts covered with white cloths. 'Oh, here's dessert, everyone.'

Dessert was cherries, ice cream and burning brandy.

'Saadi's favourite,' the Princess was smirking.

'Crazy.'

'I detest it,' she said.

'Where do the cherries come from?'

'He has them flown in, all year around, to wherever he happens to be. These are from Michigan. Last week, he fired someone when his precious cherries didn't arrive on time.'

Laville dug into the burnt brandy-soaked-fruit.

At the other end of the table, Saadi rose to make a toast to the new contract Sahara Sports was about to sign with Laville. Everyone stood except Terry, who smiled bravely into the glitter.

'I'm sure you tennis illustrious have guessed why we are here tonight,' Saadi said. 'Which is to congratulate the next number one player in the world. What you might not know is that Terry Laville and his manager, Mr Archer Bell, have negotiated a contract with Sahara for $1.5 million dollars, the highest single amount ever paid to a tennis player by a sports equipment firm.'

There were appreciative gasps from the dinner guests. Saadi paused before going on. His face was pale and he seemed to be having difficulty with his words.

'To underscore our confidence in Mr Laville, Sahara has included a contingency clause which will pay him another half million the moment he wins here at Flushing Meadow.' Saadi paused to let his guests gasp. Was Saadi offering hazard pay to get his players to compete in the most dangerous tournament in the world? 'And if he can win the Grand Slam in the next two years – and this seems a certainty – he will earn five million dollars, making Mr Laville the highest paid tennis star, a luminary, if you will, in the history of our beautiful sport.'

Saadi coughed and then stepped away from the table.

'I'm glad Koras isn't here,' Malone whispered to Muriel.

Applause swept down on Terry. He stood, red-faced, grinning, trying to look larger than life so he could fulfill his star potential, to say thank you, and to tell the people how he was going to win the Grand Slam.

At that moment, gasps exploded from people at the other end of the room, and Laville looked around to see four men in blue coveralls rolling a car into the room. At the far end, a section of the wall had swung aside, automatically.

The car was hidden beneath a tarp. Murmurs came from the guests as a flashgun went off, then several more. Carrying a cordless microphone, Saadi walked to the car. 'Terry, a token of our esteem. And our faith.'

At his signal, the four men began lifting the tarp off the car. Ohs and ahs came from the crowd. The car was a custom Porsche 911, sleek, low to the ground, bright red and gleaming.

Saadi beckoned Laville forward to hand him the keys.

'Hey. You outdid yourself. This is the greatest night of my life.'

The keys were hot in his hand. Saadi stood near him as the applause swelled. Laville opened the door of the Porsche and sat behind the wheel.

Saadi got in the passenger seat. 'Enjoy it while you can,' he said.

'What's that supposed to mean?'

'This odd idea you have about my having anything to do with Polak. I think the authorities would be interested in how *you* came by your information.'

Laville gripped the wheel. 'Should I mention that on ABC's *Wide World of Sports*? Maybe while I'm wearing equipment by Sahara?'

Saadi opened the door and started to get out. 'I shall have the contracts delivered to Mr Bell.'

'Great.'

'There's just one thing.'

'What's that?'

'If you're going to be a household word, do something about your wife's drinking. It blurs your public image.'

'I'll handle my wife. And thanks for the car.'

Saadi got out of the car. Archer Bell, holding a brandy snifter in his right hand, stuck his head in. 'Hey, you negotiating your own deals without me?'

'He needs us, Arch. No sweat.'

Bell shook his head. 'Nice going, kid.' Before walking off, he toasted Laville with his brandy.

Laville was alone with his new toy.

CHAPTER NINETEEN

It was a large house, six miles from the Verrazano Narrows Bridge which links Brooklyn to Staten Island.

Dumbo Cooper had established his New York headquarters in this huge villa for the season, leasing first, then buying. Some people in the area thought the purchase price had been too high.

Dumbo's family was installed there – his mother, Lorraine, his wife, Nancy, Jody and Jane, his two children, and two cousins who worked for him, developing investment deals for his corporation, David Cooper Enterprises, Inc.

Lorraine Cooper was a widow in her early fifties. She was blonde, attractive, with a very good figure which she kept in shape by jogging three miles every morning before breakfast. Buying the villa had been Lorraine Cooper's plan. It was like living in the country, calm, peaceful, but Lorraine had inside information that the area was ripe for development, and already her investment had paid off. The villa had cost $1.7 million, and she had already received an offer of $2 million for it.

Lorraine was in the study with Sean Hilary, the lawyer who ran David's affairs. Hilary had the mottled complexion of the perpetual heavy drinker. It was just after eleven in the morning, and he was on his second glass of whisky. He drank it straight.

'Are we ready for David?' Lorraine asked.

'Yes. I think so. Will he go along with this?'

For an answer, Lorraine looked at the lawyer with disdain. She got up from her chair behind the desk and walked to the French doors. Outside, in the pool, David was splashing water with Jody and Jane. Nancy Cooper, looking soft and pliable, sat in a chaise longue reading the latest copy of the *Journal*. Lorraine and Nancy got along, mostly because Nancy seldom put up an argument.

'David! We're ready for you.'

'Coming, mother.'

Dumbo heaved himself onto the edge of the pool and pulled himself out of the water. He grabbed a towel from the white metal chair, kissed his wife on the nose, and walked inside. He didn't like money discussions, and he hoped Hilary would be brief.

'So. What's the verdict?'

Hilary indicated a map of the area, spread out on the huge walnut desk. 'Seventeen parcels, David. We can pick the whole thing up for just under three million.'

Dumbo whistled. Last year, he had made almost two million. His mother kept track of it for him. 'Have we got that kind of money lying around?'

'We'll need to sell some stock. That will make us more liquid than we are now. The chemicals are down anyway, and we can unload some of that Silicon Valley stuff.'

'What do you think, mother?'

'I think we should buy the land, dear.'

Dumbo nodded, and pretended to be thinking. He stared out the window, and saw Peter Abraham talking with Nancy. He knew Peter was here to find out how he was voting. With this new burden. Dumbo had to play the Open. 'How much can we make on this?'

'Our money should double in three years.'

The lawyer handed him a pen. As Dumbo bent over to sign, his mother smiled over her son's head at Hilary.

Back at poolside, Dumbo got together with Peter Abraham. The two men were close friends. They walked out of earshot of Nancy, who smiled warmly. Abraham's face was serious.

'Most of the votes are in, Davey, Everyone's voting to play.'

Dumbo took a moment to look at his wife, sitting there on the chaise longue, and at his children, frolicking in the pool. Then he nodded. 'I'll play.'

'You're seeded three. There's a good chance you'll get to the semifinals.'

'I said I'd play.'

'Okay. It's your decision.'

'You're playing, aren't you, Pete?'

'Yes. But I don't think I'll make the semis. And that's where the heat is.'

Koras had a lunch date with Frank Fenwick, at the West Side Tennis Club. But before he left his house, he tried calling Laure at the number in Choisel. Laure was not there. Koras spoke to her grandmother briefly, then hung up and headed west in his Mercedes on the Sunrise Expressway, towards Queens.

The U.S. Open would begin in a couple of days and things were already tense. A team of police had examined the house, and had decided it was undefendable. Once the matches got underway, security guards would appear at his gate and he would be escorted to and from the Tennis Center. Meanwhile, a Lieutenant Lucchesi had advised Koras to move into town, to the Meridien, where most of the players were staying. But Koras had refused. Better to die at home, if you had to die at all.

The call to France had brought back memories of Laure in Paris, that Monday after he'd won Wimbledon. He kept thinking about her, the charming grandparents, the tiny village of Choisel, the quaint restaurant in Paris . . .

The garden at Choisel had been hidden beside an overgrown park, just outside the small village. He had stopped three times to ask for directions before finding the low stone wall, the dry fountain, the impudent water sprites left over from another age. The driveway had been narrow and thick with summer growth, and he had parked close to Laure's car.

'Don't run over my pumpkin!' she had yelled, running to meet him. Her smile had been warm and she had kissed him on the cheek. The grandparents obviously cared for Laure immensely. Emile Puget was a retired cavalry officer, a hero of the Liberation, and he still wore his civilian clothes with military precision and elegance. His wife, Vivianne, was animated and beautiful, with a musical voice that put Koras at ease immediately. Both had treated Koras as Laure's suitor, framing him in a role he was not quite ready for.

They had an aperitif, an orange wine with a curious bittersweet taste that the old man called 'the elixir of life'. Koras tried to imagine how many of Laure's men friends had sat here in this same garden, sipping orange wine.

'This is the recipe of Laure's mother,' the old man said.

'It's very good.' Actually, the wine was too sweet for Koras.

'She was very beautiful,' the old man said.

'Yes. I can believe that.' Koras toasted them all with his raised glass. Opposite him, Laure smiled shyly.

'What sort of name is that, Belynkas?'

'Lithuanian, sir.'

'Wasn't there another Lithuanian? Also a tennis player?'

'Yes. Gerulaitas.'

'Another curious name.' The old man paused. 'What do you intend, with my lovely Laure?'

'Sir?'

'Grandfather, please!' Laure cried. 'Mr Belynkas is just here for a visit!'

The old man sat back, unabashed but smiling now, and turned to Laure. 'I may be an old man, but I know love when I see it.'

Laure stood up, her orange wine unfinished. 'We have to be going.' She was blushing.

'To Paris, I suppose.'

'Yes. Just for the evening.'

'Well, be careful driving. The roads are insane.'

'We're taking the train.'

'Be careful, those fools strike every week these days. Not like it was when I was your age. Today, chaos is everywhere.'

They had left the charming grandparents and then had boarded the train into the city. Laure took Koras to a pleasant restaurant in Les Halles where she knew the proprietor. It wa a warm evening, and they sat out on the pavement where a small table was laid with white cloths and inexpensive wine glasses. Laure's eyes were shining, and Koras had never been so happy. After a leisurely dinner of trout and cabbage salad and a flan for dessert, they took coffee and strolled around the city. Koras wanted her badly, but she seemed distant.

Laure had been in a walking mood. They walked west, up the rue St, Honoré to the Faubourg, where Laure pointed out a scarf shop where she had worked while a student in Paris. Holding hands, they came to Avenue Friedland, where they turned left toward the Place d'Etoile. For a long silent moment, they stood gazing upward at the Arc de Triomphe.

'God,' Koras said. 'I love this city.'

It was summer and Paris was alive with tourists. A group of students passed, laughing, and one of the young men whistled and made wolf eyes at Laure, who moved closer to Koras and squeezed his hand.

From the Arc de Triomphe, they walked south to the Trocadero. They passed a small hotel where Koras had spent time with Athena during their fiery courtship. It had been twenty-five francs for a room back then, and he had to borrow money from Athena for coffee and hard rolls. Laure seemed to sense what he was about to ask and withdrew again, into herself, making it clear she was not in the mood for love.

Koras was frustrated. On the train riding back to Choisel, Laure's mood changed again and she rested her head on his shoulder.

At the door to her grandparents' house, she turned, suddenly, to throw her arms around his neck for a passionate kiss. She arched her body into his with surprising urgency. He held her.

'Laure. What is it?'

She said nothing but shook her head fiercely. She led him into the shadows and they continued to hold each other. 'Laure, I have to break a promise.'

'Oh?' She stiffened slightly.

'The money. What I promised you, back at Alesia. I can't come up with it.'

She kissed him lightly and he tasted salty tears on her cheeks. 'You have done too much.'

'I wanted to do more.'

'I could not accept more.'

Perhaps that was the problem. 'Why not?'

He could feel her hesitate before she whispered. 'It costs so much. Things are so expensive. I knew, yet I did not know.'

'What do you mean?'

Her voice was husky, filled with emotion. 'The cheque, it was in my name. And when I signed it over I felt strange, all those thousands of dollars you worked for. And then, poof, it was gone.'

'Did you get a new diesel generator?'

She nodded, her head against his chest. 'Yes.'

'That's what counts.'

She was trembling now. 'I am sorry about – tonight. Walking around Paris, all those tiny hotels. They did beckon, didn't they?'

He grinned in the darkness. 'They were probably full anyway.'

'Please wait for me, Pantakoras.' She was gripping his arms.

'All right.'

'I know there are other women around. Wait for me anyway.'

'While you go to Greece?'

'No. It is not Greece. It is something . . .'

But she never finished her sentence. Suddenly, she kissed him quickly, her final goodbye, and in seconds she was out of his arms and inside the safety of her house.

And he was outside, heart pounding, confused . . .

So now Laure was in Greece with Jean-Luc Benoit, talking to Professor Calicos, and Koras was on his way to talk to Fenwick about the never-ending subject of money.

He continued west on the expressway until he reached the traffic buildup outside JFK airport, then turned on Rockaway Boulevard, which took him northwest to 678, and then onto Queens Boulevard. From about there, you could start to smell the old money around Forest Hills.

In a few moments, he was down off the Boulevard, onto the streets. The houses here were large, sedate in the sunlight of a waning summer. Even though it was hot, he could sense autumn on the air. Forest Hills had made him weak with envy as a boy – not too far from Brooklyn, as the crow flies. But worlds away if you were a poor kid fighting for survival on the streets.

Over to his right, he saw Station Square, the Long Island Railroad, the one way streets. He remembered the crowds packing these same streets in the seventies, when Forest Hills was the site of the U.S. Nationals. Koras had won here, three times. His career had really started here, and that made him feel old.

He passed the vine covered front of the old Forest Hills Inn, memories floating in his head. He remembered Billy Walters, from Texas, his doubles partner, killed in a plane crash. He remembered Jocelyn White Hodges, a debutante with rich parents, a yacht, a sassy rich girl walk, and a terrific forehand, saying no and laughing – a mocking sound he would never forget – when he asked her to marry him. They'd made hectic, goodbye love all night. The next day, Koras went out to win a semifinal against Armando Reyes, wealthy, handsome, the playboy from Peru. Jocelyn and her partner had lost in the doubles against an Australian pair, and Koras had not seen her since.

Memories.

He turned the Mercedes over to the parking valet and walked toward the clubhouse. He liked the building, the English Tudor facade, the steep gabled roofs. In Koras's book, Forest Hills would always be the site of the real American championships. The Tennis Center at Flushing Meadow was garish, a carnival for the crowds.

Frank Fenwick was ahead of him, seated at a window table. The Texan had his calculator out and was punching numbers into it. He looked up and smiled as Koras arrived. The two men shook hands. Fenwick got right to business.

'Hell of a figure, what Saadi's paying Laville.'

'Like selling your soul to the devil.'

'At least the price is good. I ordered roast beef.'

The waiter came up and Koras ordered a salad and a beer.

'How's the vote going?'

'I just talked to Pete Abraham. Dumbo Cooper's in.'

'Any numbers on the betting?'

'There are different numbers,' Fenwick said. 'Anywhere from fifteen million to fifty.'

'Did you read the paper? Jud Garwood's "Scenario for the fourth round"?'

'Garwood's a crock.' Fenwick pulled a thick brown envelope out of his pocket, and took some papers out, which he spread in front of Koras. 'Here.'

'What are they?'

Fenwick handed Koras a pen. 'Deal with a new bank, to extend your loan and give us some cash to operate with.'

Koras was waiting for Fenwick to mention the $800,000. He handed back the pen to Fenwick. 'How much will I make this year?'

'When you add the win here, tie in the promotional stuff I've got sitting with the endorsers, the gross will be just over the four million.'

'Why do I feel poor?'

Fenwick continued. 'We pay off the construction people. And you keep the lid on expenses. You stay out of jail and hope that Saadi doesn't do a leveraged buyout of Laval.'

'Should I sell the house?' Koras was joking.

Fenwick folded the papers and struck them into his pocket. 'Not unless you lose here.'

'Is it that serious?'

Their food came. Fenwick busied himself with rare roast beef. 'I wouldn't use that word, serious.'

'What word would you use?'

'Tight. I would use the word, tight.'

'Terrific.'

Fenwick finished first, gulped a quick cup of coffee, and left Koras alone at the table. He was due back in the city at three, for more discussions. Koras ordered a third beer. He was sitting there thinking about money and pressure and dying in the semifinals when Jack Di Rocca came up with Sally Vicenti.

Jack wore a nifty seersucker suit with a striped tie. Sally was dark from the sun and he wore cream-coloured tennis shorts, a matching shirt, matching socks, and new leather shoes, Sport City, that retailed for a hundred dollars.

'Can we join you?' Di Rocca asked.

Koras knew what they wanted. 'Sure.' A waiter in a white coat and black pants came to clear the table. Sally ordered a bottle of Valpolicella.

Koras crossed his legs. He was having trouble getting comfortable and wanted to be out of here, in the fresh air, driving the Mercedes.

'You're looking good, Panties. A little grey in the blonde hair, there. Moustache needs a trim. But fit and tight. This life, it agrees.'

'Thanks, Sally. You look tough yourself.'

'I got eight years on you, maybe nine.' With a blunt finger, Sally tapped his thick chest. 'Heart troubles almost did me in, but surgery brought me back. And tennis. I love this game. Wish I'd discovered it years ago.'

'Jack mentioned your heart trouble. When was it, again?'

'Ten years ago. Or is it eleven? Yeah, there I was, on that fucking table with the lights, listening to myself breathing, and I said to myself, Sally Vincenti, it's time for a new leaf. If I get out of this, I'm changing. So I took up tennis.'

'Back in Paris, Jack said you wanted something.'

'I have this friend, at the Oyster Bay Club, who did some work for your house. Says you owe him some money.'

'And?'

'He sold the paper to me.'

The beer was almost gone. Koras was thinking of the new bank papers he had signed for Frank Fenwick. Jesus, did Sally have his dirty hands in that? Or, rather, the clean hands of one of his money-laundering fronts? Koras looked at Di Rocca. 'How much paper?'

'Quarter of a million.'

'So now I owe you?'

'Yeah.' Sally sipped his wine. 'Did I tell you what I see in the finals of the U.S. Open?'

'No. But you will.'

'I see crazy Terry Laville versus Jack Di Rocca. Laville loses. Di Rocca wins.'

'His first big win on a fast surface,' Koras said.

Sally ignored the sarcasm. 'What this means is that you lose to Jackie in the semis. We tear up your note. You keep the fancy house.'

Koras leaned forward. $250,000, to lose. His head was hurting. 'What about Laville? He's crazy to win here.'

'Laville's going to be very reasonable. Just like you are.'

Koras leaned back, drained the beer. It had a decidedly bitter taste. Two-hundred and fifty thousand was more than he would make winning the tournament. If he didn't take Sally's deal and then lost, he would make even less. This was easy money, after a decade of trying for the fans. The pounding in his head was worse. He stood up. 'No.'

'Hey, don't go away mad.'

Koras walked away from the table. He was out of the door, heading for the Mercedes, when Di Rocca caught up with him. 'You pissed Sally off, Koras.'

'You're good enough to take the Open, Jack. Play it straight.'

Di Rocca shook his head. 'I'm in too deep. Anyway, this is guaranteed.'

'You tried the same shit, didn't you, with Armando?'

Di Rocca didn't answer, but just good there, looking stolid.

'And with Micky Polak, right?'

Again, Di Rocca refused to answer.

'I thought I knew you better, Jack.' Koras kept moving.

Di Rocca grabbed his arm. 'Sally's got a lot at stake here, Koras. If your end is two-fifty, you can imagine what his will be.'

'Yeah,' Koras said, and kept walking. He did not look back at Di Rocca in his pale summer suit.

'He'll protect himself,' Di Rocca called. 'He's a tough one. He expects you to change your mind.'

Koras hit the starter several times before the Mercedes came to life. The sun had made the interior steam hot and he was sweating as he swung the car out of the parking lot. His hands shook and he felt sick. Only he knew just how close he had come to thinking seriously about Sally Vicenti's offer.

Milo's taxi stopped in front of the long red and gold canopy. The building was a perfect example of late nineteenth-century New York architecture, the era of the Astors and the Rockefellers.

Milo handed the driver his fare, along with a handsome tip, and stepped out. It was a little past seven o'clock. The porter, resplendent in his uniform plastered with gold braid, opened the wrought iron gates that led into the lobby. Milo addressed himself to the concierge, who announced him on a handsome brass interphone, and then led him to the elevator.

'You are expected, Mr Tigrid. Twelfth floor.'

'Which suite number?'

The concierge smiled. 'Mrs Jameson has the whole floor, sir.'

Milo was impressed. The elevator opened on twelve, and he saw black marble, a curving staircase, fruit trees, expensively dressed people chatting, and beyond them, an actual indoor garden. A butler took Milo in. The attractive brunette, B.J., who'd been at Saadi's party with Milo, came forward to greet him.

'Your flowers were magnificent,' she said, 'Let me introduce you around.'

Her hands were warm, and she looked terribly beautiful. Twelve storeys above the New York streets, he met financiers and their wives, a mogul from CBS, the publisher of a newspaper, two stockbrokers from Wall Street, and a conductor of the New York Philharmonic. The publisher asked him about the tennis tournament, and Milo said he was playing.

'Only one player has opted not to play,' Milo said, 'and he was a Frenchman.'

Everyone laughed.

They dined in the roof garden, at a table beneath the stars. Milo sat on his hostess's right.

The last guests left at one o'clock. Milo and B.J. stayed on the terrace awhile, contemplating the dark expanse of Central Park, dotted here and there with street lamps.

'Those were nice people,' Milo said.

B.J. drew his face close, for a kiss. He smelled her perfume and her lips were terribly soft. Suddenly, he broke free.

'Where are you going?'

'To the w.c.'

In the bathroom, Milo removed a silver pillbox from his jacket pocket. Six pills remained, Armando's legacy. Without hesitating, Milo flushed them down the toilet.

In the tiny private hideaway he had rented near Greenwich Village, Terry Laville poured himself a stiff drink, a Chivas, neat, then settled down with the phone to make some calls to Canada. It was after one in the morning, and Nora was asleep in the Central West apartment after drinking too much wine. He phoned his Montreal connection, Wally Dolan, who had taught Laville how to shave points in high school soccer. It took seven calls to locate Dolan. Laville got right to the point. He wanted a name in New York.

'Don't tell me you need a bodyguard, Laville.'

'Yeah,' Laville said. 'Somebody's killing off tennis players. I don't want to be next.'

Dolan gave him the name Torelli. 'You get around, Laville. London. New York.'

'How's the weather up there?'

'Drizzle. Haven't seen the sun for a week.'

'I remember,' Laville said, and hung up. He waited a moment, sweating with the thought of what he was about to do. Then he called Torelli to set up a meeting.

The man who answered the phone had a flat voice, emotionless. Laville gave his own name as 'Dick' and said he wanted to talk, but when he dropped Dolan's name, Torelli wasn't impressed. He wanted a thousand dollars, just to meet. Laville agreed and they set a time thirty minutes away. They would meet in Brooklyn, at the Cherry Hotel.

Laville put on gloves, a dark windbreaker, and a small-brimmed hat. From his money cache, the only way he felt safe travelling the jet stream, he took ten thousand dollars in crisp hundred-dollar bills.

He was calm as he let himself out of the building. He wanted this settled tonight. As soon as the tournament began, security people would blanket the players, himself included. He took the stairs down to the ground floor. The new Porsche was parked in the garage, underneath the building.

Laville loved driving it, feeling the road when he cornered, cruising easily at 120 mph; but now, heading toward Brooklyn, Laville kept to the speed limit. There was no use getting pulled over for speeding on a night like this. When he reached the Cherry Hotel, he parked down the street, locking the car and making certain the alarm system was set. In a neighbourhood like this, anything could happen.

The Cherry Hotel was miserable, with a façade so dilapidated and windows so worn it looked abandoned. Inside, the neon lights from the street drifted into the room through torn curtains. A fat mountain of a man sat behind the reception desk, as though imprisoned there by his own bulk. Two prostitutes, each with a nervous client in tow, asked for keys, and the fat man took his time handing them over. He liked watching johns perspire.

One of the hookers was a mulatto, sexy, with honey-caramel skin and wide, innocent eyes. She smiled at Laville, and then led her trick upstairs, hips moving nicely under the thin blue dress.

Laville paid $50 for a room. 'When a guy comes in, tell him Dick is in number thirty-two.'

The fat porter watched him climbing the dark staircase. Gays, probably, he thought, who like to do it in a whore's hotel. Real kinks, because they had money and didn't need to come to a hole like this.

In the room, Laville made certain the lights were down. The knock came on the door in less than five minutes. By then, Laville was sweating.

'Come in.'

The door opened, and he was face to face with an automatic pistol. Torelli was tall, with a hard and emaciated face. He was built like an athlete, lean and muscular. His blonde hair was short, his eyes clear and unmoving as though permanently fixed on some distant horizon. He wore tight-fitting jeans, a pale blue shirt, and a black leather flying jacket. On his hands were Ranger driving gloves, also black, with holes in the back for ventilation. He put the gun away.

Laville stayed seated while he told Torelli what he wanted. 'If he wins, hit him. If I win, you got paid to do nothing.'

Torelli listened without expression. When Laville had finished, he grinned, showing a broken tooth. 'You think like God.' He moved to the window, stared out at the brick wall next door. 'It's a tricky hit,' he said. 'I have to be there, make a decision. Fifty grand.'

'Forty,' Laville said trying to bargain.

'Fifty. If you want a cut-rate job, get yourself another mechanic.' Torelli started to leave.

'Wait.' Laville brought out the money. 'Here's ten. I'll pay you fifteen more tomorrow. You get the other half if you do the hit.'

'I don't like it this complicated.' Torelli took the money, counted it. He told Laville he wanted to meet on Monday, at the Tennis Center.

'Why?'

'To get a feel for things. And to pick up the fifteen.'

They arranged to meet at the Steak Place, a sandwich pavilion.

Laville was curious. 'How will you do it?'

'It's better you don't know. That way, you just see the result.'

Without another word, Torelli walked out of the room.

Laville waited, his heart pounding. He took off the windbreaker, which was making him sweat. When Torelli had been gone five minutes, Laville left the room.

He was moving quickly, jerking the door closed, eager to get the Porsche started. As he whirled, he bumped into someone, smelled cheap perfume. His cap fell off and he caught it in mid-air.

'Jesus. Watch it!'

He saw a pretty face, a creamy shoulder, a swatch of blue dress and swirling black wig. He remembered the same dress, heading up the stairs. Laville pulled away from her, tugged the cap back down to hide his hair, and hurried on down the stairs.

He took the stairs three at a time. The Cherry Hotel reminded him of his childhood, the same smells, the same dead faces, and he wanted out.

Malone sat in his rented Plymouth outside the Cherry Hotel. The second 'R' was missing from the blue neon sign, and the 'O' in hotel kept popping on and off. Malone was tired. He'd followed Laville on a hunch, from the apartment on Central Park West to a place in the Village, and now here.

At 2:42, a black man in a white three-piece suit and white shoes sauntered down the steps, taking his time. He looked up and down the street, then turned right, heading uptown. Under his left armpit, Malone spotted the bulge of a shoulder holster. Malone shot three frames of infra-red film with the automatic camera. At 2:44, a man with a week's growth of beard hurried out, carrying a battered black suitcase. As he left the hotel, the man turned and stared up at the façade. He shook his head, then turned left and hurried away. Malone shot his picture, too.

At 2:48, a guy in a leather flying jacket came out. He was tall, rangy, blonde. He wore new jeans, boots, dark gloves. Malone aimed the camera and took a couple of pictures.

The guy in the flight jacket climbed into a Ford pickup and drove away. Malone used the long range lens to shoot two photos of the licence plate.

His watch said 2:53. Laville had been in there twenty minutes. Was he seeing a hooker, or what? The Porsche was parked five cars away. At 2:58, Laville came out, walking like a jock, easy, with a ton of confidence. As he got into the Porsche and headed back toward Manhattan, Malone snapped his picture, with the neon Cherry Hotel sign in the back.

Malone put the rented Plymouth in gear and followed Laville back to his apartment. He was getting closer to something, but had no idea what it was.

CHAPTER TWENTY

Three days before the start of the U.S. Open, Chief of Detectives Ross O'Brien sat in his office getting a report from Lieutenant Lucchesi. As usual, Lucchesi wore a seven-hundred dollar suit he'd been given at wholesale. He looked like a movie cop on the way to the top.

'I love this.' O'Brien stared at the numbers on the report. 'I've got forty-one detectives on overtime, trying to tag one of these players as a murderer. And I've got your security force *protecting* the same guys.'

'We've had a couple of snags, Chief. On moving the players.'

'Like who?'

'Koras, for one. We're working with the county people to set up security at his place.'

'I see him as a prima donna,' O'Brien said. 'Who else?'

'Di Rocca. He doesn't trust the police, and would rather rely on his own security force.'

'Bikers with leather heads, I'll bet.'

'Yes.' Lucchesi nodded. 'Di Rocca's old gang, the Rebels. And a coalition of blacks calling themselves the Royal Bloods.'

O'Brien sighed and swung away from Lucchesi to stare out of the window. 'Keep working on Di Rocca. Have we got everyone else at the Meridien?'

'We're working on this kid, Dumbo Cooper. He's with his mother and family, out on Staten Island. They live in this unbelievable house, and I heard on the grapevine they spend all their time buying up investment property.'

O'Brien turned back to his desk, so he could make a list of the three names. 'Who does that leave?'

'Laville. Tigrid. Abraham. Colombier. Leroy. This Swiss kid Heinz. We've convinced Laville to move. He and his wife have an apartment over by Central Park West. The other top players are already there, at the hotel. We'll work a three-team rotation, around the clock, eight hours per team. We'll chauffeur the players from the hotel to the Tennis Center, using police vehicles. If that's not possible, we'll make sure we have escorts to the Center.' The lieutenant flipped a page in his notebook before going on. 'Security wasn't visible enough in Paris and London, so we're using uniforms at the Center, with conspicuous firearms. We'll have a command post set up in a van, located near the entrance, and we'll monitor the crowds with a dozen TV cameras. We'll do stop-and-search at random, but without a couple of hundred extra people we can't handle the crowds with metal detectors.'

Lucchesi closed his notebook. O'Brien sat in his chair, thinking. 'What does the gambling look like on this show?'

'I have three reports. One says three million. Another says seven. Another, fifteen.'

'There have to be connections. Are you watching the families?'

'Around the clock.'

Milo sat up and blinked several times, feeling disorientated by his surroundings. The walls were hung with white silk; the ceiling above the bed was canopied with deep blue curtains, held back by golden girdles. The carpeting was white, deep, and the furniture was modern, with low, straight lines.

He smelled coffee, and then B.J. walked into the room carrying a tray with a pot and two cups. She wore a pale yellow robe, tied loosely around the waist. The robe displayed the breasts that had given Milo such pleasure the night before. He watched her legs as she came forward, and the bottom of the robe parted.

'Welcome back, champion.'

'What time is it?' he growled.

She set the tray down and kissed him. 'It is morning. Why?'

'I have to meet Laville for a workout. If I don't he will be grumpy for weeks.'

'What do you care?'

He reached over to turn the clock around so he could see it. It was 11:01. 'My God! I have slept the day away!'

B.J. laughed as she poured steaming coffee. It smelled delicious. 'Have a cup of coffee before you go.'

Milo sat on the bed while he dialled the Tilden Club in midtown Manhattan and asked to speak to Laville. B.J. sat next to him, her bare legs crossed. Milo had trouble keeping his eyes off her. The yellow robe had come open all the way to her thighs, and she was happy to distract him. He could hear them paging Laville, the voices echoing over the loud-speaker. After a while, the man came on, saying that Laville was not there. Milo felt relieved as he set down the phone.

'Not there,' he said.

'Good. Then you can have lunch with me.' She patted his thigh, then moved her hand slowly along his leg.

'You are inexhaustible, woman.'

'I have champagne, salmon, a bite of egg salad.'

The hand went away as B.J. leaned across Milo to open a drawer in the bedside table. Inside the drawer was Milo's chrome-plated .357 Magnum. B.J. did not take the gun in her hands. She looked at the gun, then at Milo. 'Why are you carrying that?'

'For protection, what else?'

'My God!' she said, with alarm in her voice.

He put down his coffee cup and took her into his arms. She was stiff at first, but then she gave way and collapsed onto him. 'Hold me,' she murmured. 'Hold me.'

The man with the pock-marked face wore green overalls with big letters in yellow plastic stuck on his back. He was carrying equipment for cleaning windows – a plastic pail, sponges, assorted rags, a squeegee with an extension, a bottle of spray cleaner – as he walked slowly down the corridor reading numbers off office doors.

A policeman passed, the seventh one he had seen inside the Tennis Center. There were cops everywhere, but he had his ID badge and they were leaving the hordes of workmen alone.

On the lawns dividing the field courts, enormous yellow and white striped tents had been erected. Refreshment stands were being put up and there was hope of outdoing the previous years' records: 115,000 hot dogs, 200,000 hamburgers, four tons of steak, 18,240 helpings of straw-berries and cream, 43,200 ice creams, 6,000 cases of beer, 40,000 coffees, 115,000 sodas – all this not including whatever treats the spectators brought for themselves, loaded in picnic hampers. Huge trucks were parked in rows outside the buildings from which food was being unloaded and then carried to the freezers.

The man in the green coveralls had studied the layout of the labyrinthine stadium. He had stopped in the locker room to stow a narrow suitcase, and he now stood outside the door of the office of Harrison Cabot, President of the USTA.

He knocked three times, and then opened the door without hesitating. A young man wearing a bow tie was bending over a huge desk. He turned around, his steel-rimmed glasses giving him the aspect of a clergyman. He was Cabot's right hand man, Darrell Whisner. In one corner of the big room was a locked wooden cabinet.

'Well, it's about time.'

'I was backed up down the hall,' the window washer said. 'I'll be out of here in a quarter of an hour.' He walked to the window, opened it, leaned out, and began daubing the panes with cleaning solution, which he then wiped away with the squeegee. While he worked, he watched Whisner from the corner of his eye. The young man sat down at another smaller desk, working his way studiously through a file, taking notes in a careful hand.

The outside of the window was finished. He closed it, then walked casually to the trophies that lined one wall of the office.

At the desk. Whisner looked up from the file. 'They're beautiful, aren't they?'

'Yes, especially the big one.' The window washer moved closer, to examine the plaque on the trophy. It was time for the telephone call. 'But there's no name.'

'No. Not yet.'

'This is the winner's trophy, then? For the whole tournament?'

'Yes. Half the players in the world would kill to have their name on that plaque.'

'Only half?'

The telephone rang, half a minute early. He watched Whisner pick it up, then went back to his work and waited. Whisner got up, took the file that he had been working on, and started for the door. 'I'll be right back.'

The window washer nodded.

When the door was closed, the window washer put down the squeegee, and crossed the room to the locked wooden cabinet. The lock was cheap and it needed oil. He had it open in less than twenty seconds. Inside he found a ledger and a box of official USTA entry passes that would get them inside the stadium once the tournament had started. The ledger had several names repeated. Forsyte, Alcock, Castelmonte, O'Ryan, Smythe. He used one repeated name for each pass, numbers 702, 803, and 904. By the time Whisner came back, whistling, the cabinet was closed and the man was finishing up the last window.

'There,' he said, gathering up his equipment to leave. 'Now you'll be able to see what's going on around you.'

Whisner nodded. He was already back at work on his reports.

The restaurant was called the Catania, located at the end of a blind alley just off Charlton Street. The sign on the door indicated that service would not begin until seven o'clock.

Lieutenant Lucchesi walked to the door and knocked on the pane. The curtain rustled and he recognized the face of his cousin Marco. The door opened and the two cousins embraced.

'Johnny. Papa's waiting for you.'

'God, it smells great in here.'

They crossed the main body of the restaurant. The walls were tiled white and decorated with florid photographs representing scenes of Vesuvius, scenes from operas like *Aida* and *I Puritani*. On the tables were fishing buoys which had been transformed into lamps. They could have been in any restaurant in Little Italy. Varied salamis and sausages hung from the walls, filling the room with their splendid scents.

Uncle Beppo sat at a corner table in the back room. He was a patriarch, dark and stocky, with a muscular body that was very unwillingly turning to fat. In his youth, Beppo had been a boxer, but he had realized after losing badly that it was never the boxers themselves who reaped the benefits from their combat. Now, he owned boxing centres in upstate New York where he trained champions. When he saw Lucchesi, he smiled.

'*Buona sera*, Uncle Beppo.'

'Sit, Johnny. Sit.' Beppo turned to his son and pointed to a bottle of chilled Mammertino in the ice bucket. 'Marco, serve Johnny some wine.'

Marco poured the wine and handed glasses all around.

'How's your father?' Beppo asked.

'Fine.'

'And the hardware store?'

'It's going well.'

'And your beautiful wife? And the children?'

'More beautiful, with each day.'

Uncle Beppo smiled. 'One Sunday very soon, you bring them all to my house. The children can run in the garden. The tomatoes are ripening. It will be good for them.'

'I'll talk to papa. We'll set a day.'

Beppo and his older brother had not spoken to each other for twenty years. It had started with an argument over who got their mother's silver crucifix after the old lady had gone to live with Beppo during the last days of her life.

The two men ate with good appetite. In the middle of the meal, Beppo brought up the subject.

'I have asked around, about this business with the tennis. So far, there is nothing.'

'There's a lot of money coming in to the bookies. Someone's controlling it.'

'The families stay out of that. It's too new.'

Lucchesi looked at his uncle. He knew about the draconian methods used by the Mafia to keep conversations like this from going anywhere. Tonight, he had the feeling that his uncle was not being completely sincere. He himself was a policeman; his uncle was a very well connected criminal. He speared a piece of meatball and washed it down with a swallow of red wine. Maybe Uncle Beppo was out of touch.

'Could this be something you don't know about?'

The old man filled the squat glasses. 'Which Sunday do you bring the children? Next week?'

The U.S. Open began the next day. 'Sorry. I have to work the tennis.'

'The Sunday after?'

Lucchesi shook his head. The old man was stalling. 'Maybe in three weeks.'

'Such a business. A man should save Sunday for his family. Even your father doesn't work on Sunday.'

'Weren't the Cavalcantis into football pools?'

Uncle Beppo paused in his eating. 'This is not our style, notes in newspapers, that sort of thing. That's the style of a crazy man. Maybe a terrorist.'

Lucchesi continued eating. The food was excellent. It was all Lucchesi was going to get out of Uncle Beppo.

On Monday, the first day of the U.S. Open, traffic was heavy going east into the Tennis Center. The guards recognized Laville and waved the red Porsche through. The escort vehicle which had followed Laville from the Meridien turned around. Inside the Center, he would still be watched, but from a distance.

Laville was discovering that he relished the sense of danger.

He swung into a parking slot reserved for players. He had half an hour before his meeting with Torelli, and he wanted to walk around while he got the feel of the stadium. He strolled by the tent occupied by the Steak Place, an outdoor pavilion in the Food Village with a striped awning and waiters in cutaways. He found a seat next to a table where three pretty girls were sitting and ordered a Coke. They were giggling, and finally one of them became brave enough to ask for his autograph. He signed it, 'With love, Lumberjack Laville.'' He was finishing the Coke when Jack Di Rocca, in tennis clothes, sat down at his table.

'Terry, there's a man in the stands who wants to talk to you.'

Laville made a show of checking his watch. 'Sorry. Got a date.'

Di Rocca pulled a 3 × 5 photo out of his warm-up pocket and shoved it across the table to Laville. It was a shot, taken at a crazy angle, of Polak making it with Shirley that night in London. The flash illuminated Polak's face, made it look ghostly. Laville turned pale. 'What's this?'

'Souvenir. From Wimbledon.'

Laville crumpled the photo.

'Your girl. Your stuff on the bedside table. It won't take much police work to put you behind the camera.'

Laville was sweating now. He looked around the pavilion, where the light had suddenly become too bright. 'You want something. What is it?'

'Like I said, a man wants to talk to you.'

Laville looked at his watch.

Di Rocca leaned close, with a strange gleam in his eye. 'Torelli won't be coming . . . Dick.'

Laville was feeling sick now. Gripping the table edge, he felt his future start to crumble. 'So what they say is true?'

Di Rocca stood up. 'Coming, Terry?'

Laville was frantic now. 'My match. It's in an hour. I need to hit, loosen up –'

'Just take a minute.'

Laville's legs were unsteady as he walked with Di Rocca into the noisy stadium. Policemen were all over the place, here to protect him! At the entrance to the stadium, he and Di Rocca flashed players' passes, which were scrutinized carefully by guards with walkie-talkies. There were gun-butts peeking out everywhere. Di Rocca led him to a box right down on the court. Out on the court in a first round match, Koras was playing Paul Harper, from California. According to the scoreboard, Koras wasn't having any trouble winning. The box, which was the same size as the one Saadi owned, sat twelve people. The man he would talk to was swarthy and Mediterranean looking, his age somewhere in the late forties. He wore a tennis shirt with a crocodile logo. Two more men, wearing business suits, sat in the rear of the box. Bodyguards. One of them listened through earphones to a pocket radio.

As Laville came into the box, the swarthy man stood up smiling, and extended his hand. 'Mr Laville. I'm Sally Vicenti. Have some wine.' He spoke with a low, raspy whisper. As he poured wine into a stubby glass, he kept chatting.

Laville refused the wine. 'Let's get on with it.'

'I understand. Take a seat, please.' Sally pointed down onto center court. 'I was just watching your friend Mr Belynkas give a lesson to the youngster from California.'

Laville sat down, his edginess combining with a terrible curiosity.

'Mr Laville, I'll get right to it. Our Mr Torelli told us of a plan you have. To eliminate a competitor.'

'I don't know what you're talking about.'

'Mr Torelli works for us.'

Laville felt a cold chill on the back of his neck. 'So? Call the cops, Mr Vicenti.'

Vicenti spread his hands in a gesture of helplessness. 'Call me Sally. Everyone does.'

'Okay. Call the cops . . . Sally.'

Vincenti grinned, showing white teeth, but the eyes stayed cold. 'I like your style, Mr Laville. You are a man who goes for what he wants. Think you can win here this year?'

Laville watched Koras knifing the ball down the line, coming to the net behind it, putting away the volley. It was only the first round, but the stands were packed. 'Yes. I can win.'

'Would you be willing to bet on it?'

'I already have. I put down five thousand on me, to win the final.'

'We know about that. I was thinking of betting on something more valuable. Like your life.'

'I don't have to listen to this.'

'Mr Laville, we have a big pool of money, put up by friends of mine, from across the country. We bet on Mr Di Rocca here, to win the tournament.'

Laville grinned. 'At seven to one, right?'

'You're astute, Mr Laville.' He turned to Di Rocca. 'Didn't I tell you, Jackie, this Mr Laville is astute.'

Di Rocca nodded, but said nothing.

'Di Rocca has to reach the final first,' Laville said. 'That means he has to get by Koras.'

'We're handling that part. If he reaches the final, we want to know we can depend on you.'

'You want me to tank?'

'Yes. In four sets.'

Laville barked out a short laugh. 'Jack showed me the photos. They're yours, not mine. There's nothing to connect me with them.'

'Show him the blow-up, Jackie.'

Di Rocca handed Laville a manila envelope. Inside was a blow-up showing Polak with Shirley. On the bedside table was his travel alarm with the date and time, and a tennis headband. The room number was clearly visible on the telephone. There had been three rolls, after all. Laville did some heavy thinking. Maybe there was money in this somewhere . . .

'You want Koras out of the way,' Sally said. 'So we might work together.'

'Not a chance.'

'The way you might lose, is to develop a symptom of your famous hex. The one that gets to you here in New York.'

Laville leaned forward. 'What's it worth to you?'

Sally Vincenti smiled. 'How many good years are left for you in this game?'

'Half a dozen. Maybe more. I want the Slam.'

'Your wife is a drunk. The Arab, Saadi, is pressuring you to straighten up, clean up the image for public relations. You have a hex hanging over you. Until Ohio, you hadn't beaten Koras in the last six meetings. Surely you don't want the tennis public – not to mention the eager beaver police out there – to become aware of the photos you took of Mr Polak, so shortly before he died. With the photos, they might even believe your plans for Mr Belynkas. The rivalry between you two is famous. A couple of photos could terminate your career.'

Laville's jaw was tight. 'So you keep me clean if I tank to Di Rocca in the finals?'

'Yes.'

'What about Torelli?'

'Your deal with him was for the finals, in case you lost to Belynkas.'

'Right.'

Sally Vincenti took a sip of wine. 'If a Laville-Belynkas final occurs, Torelli keeps going.'

'Who pays him?'

'We'll take care of him.'

Laville let out a sigh. 'Okay. But if Di Rocca wins this one, I get to win a Grand Slam. Next year.'

'Sounds good. What do you say, Jack?'

'Why not?'

They shook hands and Sally Vincenti studied Laville as he sipped his wine. 'It is nice doing business with you, Mr Laville.'

Laville was dismissed. He left the box in a hurry to warm up for his match. Watching him go, Sally turned to Di Rocca. 'I always like personal vendettas. They got so much energy.'

'What did that mean, a Laville-Belynkas final?' Di Rocca asked. 'I thought I was supposed to win.'

'We're covering all the bases, Jackie. All the bases.'

CHAPTER TWENTY-ONE

The stadium was filled to capacity when Milo Tigrid walked onto the court for his quarterfinal match with Di Rocca. Twenty thousand people were shouting and waving their arms in the air like so many banners. The cries of the crowd competed with the deafening transit of a Boeing 747 on its way out of La Guardia.

At the bottom of the crater, the humid heat seemed to have been concentrated like the focus of a solar oven. The clamour of the crowd cascaded down the stands like a waterfall of noise. The great American tennis fair had been in motion over a week now. So far, there had been no incidents. In the excitement of the spectacle, the tennis fans had talked less of the threats that had been made and gossiped instead about the tennis. After a few days of pure tennis, the media set aside the violence theme and concentrated more on games, sets, matches, personalities – and contracts.

To enhance the public relations aspects of the matches, Dumbo Cooper had practised with a giant racket bearing the logo of Ryker Equipment, his main sponsor. Pentakoras Belynkas had held a clinic on the grandstand court for a group of fifty young black players selected by the Harlem Methodist Church. Milo Tigrid had played the opening five minutes in a soccer game with the New York Cosmos. There was a photograph of Milo shaking hands with the famous Pele, who was wearing shoes made by Magnelli, Milo's main sponsor. In the fourth round, Terry Laville had come onto the court carrying a large cardboard tree trunk with a facsimile of a woodcutter's double-edged axe. On the tree was written 'Laville's Forest Country', which was the newest development by a group of Canadian chalet builders.

Even the diminutive Tania Pikeste had succumbed to the mirages of advertising by dancing with the pom pom girls of the baseball team which had its headquarters in the field adjacent to the Tennis Center. For this U.S. Open, the spectators had been offered all the circus tricks that Madison Avenue could dream of.

Nothing about the tournament appeared to have changed, but a close look might reveal many more plainclothes policemen patrolling the stands, talking on hand-held radios, watching for suspicious behaviour. And in several instances, cartons destined for the refreshment stands were opened, and their contents checked. None of this was overt enough to disconcert the crowds. In the skies above the stadium, two police helicopters hovered, competing with the din of passing aeroplanes.

Di Rocca had not appeared yet. Milo walked to the referee's stand, pointing up at the 747 which was taking off, a roiling trail of grey exhaust pouring from its engines.

'I see you still haven't managed to keep the birds quiet.'

'We haven't given up hope. Mr Cabot is talking about buying up La Guardia.'

As the aeroplane passed, the stands shook, as if from an earthquake. Most of the crowd was standing, waiting for the entrance of Di Rocca. In the top rows, hundreds of youths in black leather were killing time drinking beer, silent for the moment. They had arrived in hordes, leaving their motorcycles in a parking area especially cleared for them. The security people had been worried about the invasion, but the chief of detectives said he had no basis to exclude them.

'They'll make a moving wall around Di Rocca,' said O'Brien, putting the best face on it he could. Indeed, with their black helmets pulled down over Ray Ban glasses, their lips dark from the sun, they were an impressive counter-threat.

Now, in the upper stands, people grew restless and began to throw beer cans. There were some outcries and a few minor injuries until policemen broke up the skirmishes and took the culprits away.

Milo checked the clock on the scoreboard, noting that Di Rocca was already five minutes late. A wave of panic seized the Yugoslav, as he remembered the death of Armando Reyes. He wondered if Koras had felt this way at Wimbledon, when Polak had failed to show up. Milo sat in his chair, his face buried in a white towel. Before the match, he had prepared a farce for the crowd, something to keep things moving, but now he knew he would not use his jokes today. Today, he wanted to win.

As he sat there, he thought of B.J., his new lover. Sitting on her terrace, she had asked him to handle the sports service of a television station she ran in Chicago.

'I know nothing of television,' he had protested.

'But you know sports, Milo. And you are lovely with people. You would be behind the scenes, organizing, smoothing rifts, giving counsel.'

Inside his mind, he saw his face on a television set. It wasn't a bad idea, and certainly easier than sweating your heart out on a hot tennis court. 'Let me consider it . . .'

Milo was jolted by a thunderous round of applause as Di Rocca came onto the court. Milo grinned. He had never been so happy before to see an opponent. The two men walked to opposite ends of the court and began to warm up.

When Nora Laville came into the players' cafeteria at the Tennis Center, Athena von Heidelberg was dreamily stirring a wilted straw in the remains of her strawberry ice cream soda. It was almost eight in the evening and the Princess wore a man's silk shirt with three buttons undone and a pair of designer jeans. Nora was dressed in black, with a pearl necklace. Athena waved at Nora, who came over, trying to smile.

'How is the apartment?'

'It's . . . pleasant.' A waiter came up to take her drink order. Nora's eyes were sunken, and she wore too much make-up.

'Terry wants a divorce,' Nora said, as the waiter walked away.

'That brute. When did he tell you?'

'He came by this morning, looking terrible. I had a feeling he was with his little Hollywood tart, Shirley What's-her-name. I got angry, and he –' She paused. 'He hit me.'

'The bastard.'

Nora nodded.

'Leave him.' Athena said. 'A judge would give you a nice settlement.

And there are thousands of men around who would take good care of you.'

'Yes. I should have married my photographer when I had the chance.'

The waiter arrived with Nora's drink. She signed for it and took a long swallow.

At 5–all in the fourth set of the quarterfinal between Koras and Peter Abraham, play was halted because of a commotion in the stands, near the broadcast booth. Half a dozen plainclothes security men ran onto the court to surround Koras and his opponent. The crowd buzzed, and one could hear the sharp crackle of the walkie talkies.

The closest security man wore an ID badge. His name was Rivera.

'What's up?' Koras asked.

Rivera surveyed the crowd with field glasses. 'Guy with a rifle. Up there.'

'Have they got him?'

'Yeah.'

'Thanks.'

Koras felt a sense of relief, like a too taut rubber band going back to normal. Rivera was dark, well-dressed, with even teeth and the poise of an anchor man on the evening news. He shook Koras's hand. 'Tell you a secret, Mr Belynkas?'

'Sure.'

'I got a hundred on you, to win.'

'Today?'

'No. Sunday. The final.'

'You're a gambler. I'm not there yet.'

'You'll get there. I seen you play before.'

'Hope you don't lose your life savings.'

Rivera grinned. 'You can hurt Laville, or whoever. I'm betting on it.'

'Thanks.'

'Know what I think? That Laville's a bum.'

The stands were buzzing as uniformed police brought down a man wearing a grey jacket and Levis. He was handcuffed. He was normal looking, someone you would never glance twice at on the street.

It took ten minutes for the crowd to settle down. People returned to their seats. Rivera and his security force retired to the seats near the court. The umpire, voice shaking, called for play to resume.

As they started up again, Koras felt luck on his side. Abraham hit two shots out, one into the stands, showing the delay had hurt his confidence. Sensing weakness, Koras strung the younger man out with drop shots and slices, pulling him wide of the forehand, dinking the ball across the net, forcing Abraham to sprint for the next shot. Abraham was fast. He got to everything. But the sting had left his spectacular returns.

Koras won the fourth set 7–6 in the tie breaker, which put him into the semi-finals. The crowd chanted 'King! King Koras!' echoing the old days. As he walked off the court with Abraham, he thought about people like Rivera, the security man, guys who probably made only three hundred a week and who had bet a third of that on him. To win.

Malone had to call Archer Bell, who had a contact in the NYPD, to find out the gun wasn't loaded – the man hadn't bought the right size ammunition. The gun was a Colt Commando, army issue, telescopic sight, so the police could hold the guy on that. Army weapons were illegal. His name was Alva G. Wreston, from the Chicago area. A computer check showed that he had a record for car theft, B & E (mostly upscale homes in Kenilworth and Evanston), and two convictions for pushing dope in high school.

'According to the police report, the man's a klutz when it comes to weapons,' Bell told him.

'The crazies are out as we approach the semis.'

'Yes. Four players, three New Yorkers. The fans will be badgering us for a larger stadium if things go on.' Bell was still at the Tennis Center, on Harrison Cabot's private line. Malone was at the hotel. Laville had won his quarterfinal against Colombier, but the match had not held the tension of the Koras-Abraham duel. 'You've done a good job, Matt.'

'Thanks, Mr Bell.'

'After this is over, let's sit down for a heart-to-heart. When Terry wins here, he'll start training for the Grand Slam. I have plans for making this a historic move. I'll need your help.'

'I'd like that, Mr Bell.'

But after he'd hung up, Malone wondered. Did he really want to work for Archer Bell? The guy was prissy, rich, fussy as an old maid eating warm jelly.

And Malone still had a hunch about Laville.

Alain Clavier met Frank Fenwick at the entrance to the locker rooms, while Laville was playing Colombier in the quarterfinal. Fenwick was studying a memo card containing numbers in well ordered rows.

'F.F, there is a rumour you are planning to sign Di Rocca, to bring him into your stable.'

The Texan grinned. 'The surprise of New York. A clay courter doing this well on deco turf. That's made him worth more money.'

'Sometimes, my dear Frank, you are disgusting.'

'Heck, Alain, I just know where the money is.'

Fenwick put away his card and rubbed his face, to churn away the fatigue. The players had been great so far, but Fenwick, as an old hand at tennis, knew there hadn't been a really great match out there. He had personally been in on two meetings in the offices of sponsors where all the talk had been of death at the semifinals. More tickets had been sold, and the profits of the sponsors were soaring. Now, if Koras could just win this Grand Slam, a cut of that money would be his.

As Fenwick and Clavier continued to talk, Milo Tigrid came in from his match with Di Rocca.

'Well, Milo. What happened?'

Milo grinned. 'I have lost the match, but I have saved my miserable life.' He began to undress.

'What was the score?'

'It was 12–10 in the tie break, fifth set. I was planning to win. In fact, I could taste the sweet meat of victory. And then one of your damnable aeroplanes flew over, and I was momentarily disconcerted. That is the word, I hope. And my service lost its sting, and Di Rocca closed me out.' Milo sighed. 'I assure you, I tried my best, despite this threat of death we are under.'

'I speak,' said Clavier, 'for the entire tennis community when I offer my thanks.'

Milo waved a hand. 'Now I shake these security guards. They follow one into a lady's very boudoir.'

The men laughed. Milo kept on undressing. His voice was light, easy, full of mirth; but his face was serious. Perhaps the reason was that he felt this was his last professional tournament.

And now he was out of it, for good.

Malone's room was on the same floor as Laville's at the Meridien, so he could move about without attracting a lot of attention. During the late afternoon, when the floor was deserted, Malone had used the electronic lock-picking system from Griswold to open the door of Laville's suite. It was late afternoon on the day of the men's quarterfinals. The maids had been here. The beds were made.

The suite was good-sized. The living room had a big sofa, three easy chairs, a bar, and a wall-sized TV. There was a bedroom off to the left, with a king-size bed, and private bath. There was a small kitchen, and a smaller bedroom off to the right, with a second king size bed, and a smaller bath. Laville's clothes were in the bigger of the two bedrooms, still in suitcases. Apparently, Laville hadn't had time to unpack when they had moved him here for security reasons.

Malone walked through the living room to search the bigger bedroom. He systematically worked the clothes, the pockets, the toes of the shoes. He went through three suitcases without finding anything. There was a separate tennis bag containing nothing but shoes. In the tip of a pair of Magnelli running shoes, he found a slip of paper with a phone number on it, and the name 'Torelli'. He jotted the number down on the back of an envelope, along with the name.

As he tidied the suite back the way he'd found it, Malone thought about his work during the summer.

This had been the best summer of his life as a private detective. He'd worked eighty-seven days straight, making $400 a day from the ITF, which came to almost thirty-five grand. He'd been paid twenty thousand dollars already, with the rest to come after the U.S. Open was over. He'd used some of the money to buy the Griswold system. And if he kept Laville out of trouble, Malone would hook in another ten grand from Archer Bell.

When Malone got back to his room, Muriel was sitting in front of the dressing table, combing her rich red hair. On the small desk was a stack of photographs Muriel had taken at Flushing Meadow.

'There is something interesting, you might want to see it.'

She walked over to the table and picked up three photographs she had taken of someone in the stands. Malone recognized Laville because he was so huge. The big Canadian was in a private box down near courtside, talking to a heavy-set man in a tennis shirt. The man had a glass of wine in his hand. Behind them sat Jackie Di Rocca. Behind Jackie, a man listening to a radio through headphones.

Malone looked more carefully. 'Can we get a blow up of this? All the faces?'

'I think so. Does it mean something?'

'Maybe. How soon can we have it?'

'As soon as I can find a lab, if any are open.'

'Great.' Taking the envelope out of his pocket, Malone walked to the phone and dialled the number. After three rings, a mechanical voice came on the line to tell him the number was no longer in service and there was no forwarding number listed.

Chief of Detectives Ross O'Brien had eaten dinner with a U.S. senator at the Four Seasons. There was a lot of talk about Flushing Meadow, which had taken over the headlines of major newspapers all across the country. O'Brien assured the senator that things were under control.

He got back to his office around ten, where he sat down to do some paperwork. He took an hour to read through the daily report from Lieutenant Lucchesi, on the security at Flushing Meadow. Everything had gone well, and the four semifinalists were known at last. David Cooper would play Terry Laville. Pantakoras Belynkas would play Jack Di Rocca. It was magnificent for the fans – three New York players among the four best tennis players in the world. That flattered O'Brien's civic pride.

But now these four men had to be protected as though the very future of America depended on their wellbeing.

Lucchesi arrived at a quarter past midnight. 'Chief, I think we've got something.'

'What?'

'There's word out on the street, about a hit being set up. It's not much. But there's a bomber who goes by the code name TNT.'

O'Brien leaned forward. 'What about it?'

'No one knows who's going to be hit, or how. But this guy, TNT, is supposed to have learned his explosives with the military.'

'What's his real name?'

'My people are checking army records, but so far we haven't turned anything up.'

'Well, keep going. How many men have you put on this thing?'

'Counting the plainclothes people, three hundred and change.'

'An army.' O'Brien puffed on his cigarillo. 'Anything from your sources?'

Lucchesi shook his head. 'Nothing yet. I've got my lines out.'

'Do some rousting. I need results now. Tomorrow is too late.'

'Right, chief.'

As Lucchesi walked out, O'Brien wondered if his right hand man was telling him everything he knew.

CHAPTER TWENTY-TWO

Will Channer found his player in the downstairs kitchen at Court's Court. Koras was supposed to be concentrating on the semifinal match he would be playing in a few hours' time. Channer suspected he was waiting for a call from Laure Puget.

From the fanlight in the basement, Channer could see the legs of the police security force, patrolling the grounds. There were also policemen in cars, securing the estate and the roads around it. For an hour this morning, a helicopter had circled Court's Court, until Channer had called to complain.

'So you got through the militia,' Koras said.

'Finally. They have a chain of command that would make the ITF look small by comparison.'

'What will happen after the semis? Will they scale down the security?'

'Hell, no, mate. They'll scale it *up*.'

Koras sat down at the table. 'Tell you a secret, Will?'

'Sure.'

'Now that we're almost finished here, I'm having second thoughts about having voted to play.'

'Are you crazy? With the Grand Slam only two matches away?'

'I don't give a shit about the Grand Slam.'

'What?'

'We're ruining the game, Will. We play for the love of it. That's why they used to come out to watch us hit. Now they come out to see who's going to die.'

Will walked to the sink and ran water into a glass. 'Listen to you, for Christ sake. This is the first time since I've known you that a woman has interfered with your tennis.'

'Is it that obvious?'

'I knew it when you ducked out on Wimbledon to see her.'

'I remember when I first came on the circuit. I wasn't winning. No one knew me. I'd be out there getting killed, wondering how to hang on for another week. Then I met Athena, and everything changed. And after Athena, there were lots of girls, a whole world full. And now there's just one.'

'Put her out of your head. Or you can kiss the Grand Slam goodbye.'

Koras said nothing for a moment. Then he stared at Will. 'You're right. I'll try to stop thinking about it.'

Koras was upstairs when the phone rang. 'Laure!' Koras was excited. 'Where are you?'

'I am here,' she said, and burst out laughing.

'Here?' He felt momentarily confused. 'Where?'

'In New York. At John F. Kennedy. You invited me, and here I am!'

'When did you get here? *How* did you get here?'

'I took a charter flight, from Luxembourg. We landed an hour ago, but there was the *douane*. How far away are you?'

'Don't worry. Not far.' He was frantic with haste now. 'I'll come and get you. With the police –'

'The police? But why, Pantakoras?'

'Security,' he yelled. 'For the tournament. Tell me where you will be, which airline. Give me a landmark.'

They made plans to meet at the TWA reservation desk. Koras hung up and ran out of the house. He fumbled in his pocket for the keys to the Mercedes, but discovered they were not there. A security man with a submachine gun asked if something was wrong.

'Kennedy,' Koras said. 'We've got to get to JFK.'

'Why?'

'To meet someone,' Koras said, and ran back into the house, where he encountered Will Channer.

'So she's here.'

'Yes. Can you bring my gear to the Tennis Center? I'm going to pick her up – I'll meet you there.'

'All right.' Channer was smiling. It was not usual for Koras the surgeon to be so emotional. 'You go on ahead.'

Koras found the car keys. His hands were shaking. Followed by two escort vehicles, his Mercedes headed west, toward JFK.

The policemen posted at the players' entrance to the stadium could not believe their eyes. The convoy escorting Di Rocca was straight out of Walter Hill's *Streets of Fire*.

The lime yellow Buick convertible, with its chromed rear wings looking like sharks' fins, advanced slowly, flanked by a motorcycle escort; fifty huge bikes, ridden by gang members wearing black leather. Silver studs glistening on their wrist bands. Between the bikes, they carried banners bearing slogans glorifying Di Rocca.

'Holy shit,' exclaimed a cop. 'Would you like to beat this guy in tennis? Or would you rather lose?'

'Maybe they'll riot, right on the court.'

The vintage Buick passed the cordon of policemen and drove inside, to the parking lot. A group of inspectors in plain clothes met Di Rocca as he got out of the car. Ortega was behind the wheel.

'Have a good night, Jack?' asked one of the security men.

'Terrific. You?'

'We buttoned this place up. Between police and the regular ushers, we've got six hundred men in the stands, six hundred more watching the entrances.'

'What about a kamikaze attack?' Ortega asked, as he came up.

To answer, the security man pointed up, where a helicopter circled lazily.

The policemen surrounded Di Rocca, who looked at his coach and laughed.

At JFK, Koras left the Mercedes in the no parking zone and hurried inside to find Laure, followed by a red-faced plainclothes security man. His heart was pounding. He didn't really have this kind of time; he was due at the Tennis Center in an hour. Then he saw Laure standing at the TWA counter. In a moment, they were in each other's arms. Her cheek was warm against his. Her face was wet with tears.

'How was Greece?'

'Very warm. And full of tourists.'

He was watching the time so he steered her toward the exit. 'I can't believe you're here.'

'There is a man following us.' She indicated the security guard.

'Oh, that's Johnny Holmes. Frank Fenwick hired him to protect me.'

Laure stiffened. 'It is my fault.'

'I play in an hour. What's your fault?'

'Monsieur Fenwick made the call, about the money. You are in trouble because of it, and because of me.'

Koras looked at her and grinned. 'And that's why you're here?'

She nodded. Her face was serious. 'One of the reasons.'
'What's the other?'
'You know, Pantakoras,' she said, quietly. He could feel his heart beating wildly, telling him he was in love with the right woman.

Headquarters for the security force was in a large tan RV parked near the main entrance to the Tennis Center. Inside, police personnel wearing headphones were monitoring a bank of TV screens that lined one entire wall. At one end of the room, Chief Ross O'Brien was talking to Lieutenant Lucchesi while he kept an eye on the television monitors. A dozen cameras routinely swept the entrances and the spectators in the stands. On the desk in front of the two men was a file. The name on the file was SABRINA.

'You know anything about this?'
'There was a hooker working the area a year ago, using the name Sabrina. They change names like Di Rocca changes socks.'
'We need to check it out.'
'I'll send someone over.'
'Hanrahan should be in midtown.'
'This is dated four days ago, chief. She could be long gone by now.'
'We still need to check it.'
O'Brien sat down in a swivel chair and began absorbing the visual information from the television monitors. It was the day of the semifinals and everything was on alert. Lucchesi put in a call to 'Red' Hanrahan.

At the changeover, Koras drank some water, then closed his eyes to concentrate on the deep breathing that would keep him in control. The score was 4–3, in the fourth set, and he was about to draw even after losing the first two sets to Di Rocca. Koras had started off slowly, feeling out his opponent, but Di Rocca had come on with a new ferocity, hitting winners and taking chances. The first set had gone to Di Rocca, 6–2; the second, to Di Rocca, 7–5.

Now Koras was ahead and he could feel the momentum starting to build. He was playing steadily and he could sense Di Rocca's indecision. In the private boxes at the courtside, he kept looking at Sally Vincenti, who had offered him $250,000 to lose. And three boxes away, Laure sat with Athena, Colombier and Saadi.

He could feel the twin pressures pushing at his conscienceness, trying to distract him. On the one hand, there was his honour as a player and a sportsman. Honour had brought him out here today, to play for twenty-thousand spectators. It had kept him going when he got tired, when he felt sick, when he wanted to lose, go home, take a shower, drink a beer.

He thought about Sally and his threat. He thought about Laure and her envelope of money. Koras did not want to die, and he did not think of himself as a hero. But in the end, he knew there would be no reason to keep on tomorrow if he did not do his best today.

As he passed Jack Di Rocca at the umpire's chair, he smiled in a friendly way and said: 'You're out, Jack. Kiss the finals goodbye.'

And Di Rocca answererd: 'And you're dead, King.'

At the Cherry Hotel in Brooklyn, Sergeant 'Red' Hanrahan took some time to examine the decayed façade before crossing the street. Two youths leaned against a wall, jiving to a ghetto blaster. Down the block, three young girls in bright mini-skirts exposed their wares to the passers-by.

Hanrahan went inside. The lobby was filthy and smelled of vomit and forgetfulness. Behind the desk sat a porter who must have weighed four hundred pounds. He was digging into a greasy bag of popcorn as he watched a soap opera on television. The man wore a fluorescent shirt and a soft brown wig.

Hanrahan took a look at the grease-covered counter and decided not to lean on it. He showed his badge. The porter looked over, then swung his eyes back to the television.

'Sabrina,' Hanrahan said.

'Who?'

Hanrahan walked around the desk, grabbed the back of the swivel chair, and dumped the porter out of it. The fat man yelled, clawing the air for balance. It was no use. He wound up in a heap on the floor, his feet tangled in the voluminousness of his pants.

'Sabrina. She's a working girl. You want this flea trap to stay in business? Or how about I put in a call to City Health?'

The fat man struggled to his knees. He picked up a phone and pressed three buttons. 'There's a cop here, wants to see you. Yeah, I know.' Pause. 'Tough.' He put down the phone and turned to Hanrahan with a pale face that did not mask his anger. 'She'll be right down.'

'Thanks.'

While he waited, Hanrahan leafed briefly through a soiled pornographic magazine that had been left on the counter, and then walked to a dilapidated chair at the furthest corner of the room. Before sitting down, he wiped the seat of the chair with his handkerchief, which he did not put back into his pocket.

Sabrina was a magnificent mulatto who could not have been more than twenty years old. Despite the years of drugs and prostitution, she looked fresh, young, almost innocent. Her skin was a soft creamy chocolate. She had a pretty smile that made Hanrahan wonder how she had found her way to this hell hole.

He asked her if she'd heard anything suspicious.

'Oh, sure. There were these two guys – I thought maybe they were gay because they come here a lot – in the next room. I'd just finished a trick and was lying there feeling a little sick. Anyway, I overhear this one guy say he wants someone taken out, a hit, like. And the other guy says it will cost fifty grand. And then they talk it over, only I can't hear that much, except I hear this one word, *flush*, two or three times, and another word, *player*.'

'What were their names?'

'I only heard one name. Dick.'

'Did you get a look at them?'

'I bumped into one. He was coming out. So was I.'

'What did he look like?'

'Big, like a football player. He moved like a young guy. And I think he had blond hair. It's hard to tell in here, it's so dark. His hat fell off.'

'What kind of hat?'

'It looked, I don't know, too small for his head.'

Hanrahan wrote it all down, double-checked everything, and told Sabrina he would be in touch.

'I like cops,' the girl said, touching his sleeve. 'Any time you feel like a party, give me a call.'

'Thanks.'

After Sabrina had left, Hanrahan questioned that fat porter. It took him thirty minutes to pinpoint the night, more than a week ago. The porter had a bad memory and was used to forgetting his clients. With careful prompting, and a promise he could answer the same questions downtown, he did remember a few details.

'Okay, this guy Dick. He was big, with a face that looked carved, like a statue, if you know what I mean.'

'Anything else?'

'He wore a hat. Had crazy eyes.'

'What colour was his hair?'

'Light blond, I guess.'

'What about the other one?'

'Him, I've seen around. Goes by the name of Mike.'

'What's his line of work?'

'How should I know?'

'What was he wearing, this guy Mike?'

'Leather flying jacket. I think. Sharp. He had on jeans that looked new, and gloves, the kind racing drivers wear.'

'And they were here how many times?'

'Once.'

'Who paid for the room?'

'Dick paid. In cash.'

Hanrahan kept the questions going, but didn't get much more information. He told the porter he would send around an artist from the department with an identikit. Then he called Lucchesi at the Tennis Center. Let him figure it out.

After beating Di Rocca in five sets, Koras showered, then put on his lucky warm-up suit and went to look for Laure. A group of six security men went with him, keeping in touch on their walkie-talkies. Laura was sitting with his coach and Fenwick in the cafeteria. Laure hugged Koras, and he introduced her to the swarm of photographers and journalists who were there for the post-match interview. There were questions about the match and about the Grand Slam. Near the end of the interview, Judson Garwood asked: 'What will your strategy be tomorrow against the winner of the Cooper-Laville match?'

'I'll play them the same. Both have big forehands, so I'll play that side first, hoping to open up the backhand for a putaway. I'll go to the net behind everything. And I hope I don't get tired.'

Eleanor Stark asked, 'How much credence do you put on this hex that Laville has when he plays New York?'

'I haven't seen any evidence of it so far. It looks like Terry's beaten his hex at last.'

There was one last question, about money. Frank Fenwick took it.

'When Koras wins the Grand Slam on Sunday, he'll pass the four million mark. Also, I'm negotiating a contract with a company whose name I cannot divulge for a two million endorsement. As you know, that will top Terry Laville's recent contract with Sahara Sports.'

There was a clamour to know the name of the company, but Fenwick wouldn't say another word. In the corridor, walking out, Koras took Fenwick aside to ask for more information.

'I didn't know about this new deal, F.F. What's up?'

'Let me handle the deals. Koras. You just get your butt out there and play tomorrow.'

'Will it fix my bank loans?'

Fenwick smiled at Laure as he answered. 'It will fix everything.'

The Laville-Cooper match had begun five minutes after Koras had finished beating Di Rocca. In the centre of the stadium the noise had risen to an unbearable pitch. The tension had mounted during the previous match, and now that Laville was playing and no one had been killed, fans were starting to let off steam by whooping and throwing beer bottles. Three times police flying squads charged into the stands to remove troublemakers. And at the base of the crater, the blows between the players became harder and harder. Cooper pounded a forehand. Laville pounded one back.

At 3–4 in the fourth set, with Cooper leading, Laville threw a tantrum over a line call. He swore at the lines person, a pretty woman in a blue blazer and official khaki skirt, and then he demanded she be removed. The tournament referee had to be called, and Harrison Cabot himself came down to the court to calm the players.

Dumbo Cooper, who wanted the point badly, appealed to the stands by grabbing, a clipboard and walking around taking votes from the fans in the boxes at the courtside.

At last, the umpire brought the match back under control. He removed the lines person and awarded the point to Dumbo. Laville's fury seemed to make him play better.

Dumbo lost the semifinal 7–6 in the tie breaker in the last set.

Terry Laville was watching a replay of his match against Cooper when the phone rang in his suite at the Meridien. Laville answered. It was Jack Di Rocca.

'Don't talk. Just listen.'

'Okay.'

'Things have changed. They want you to win tomorrow.'

'Terrific. Just like that?'

'Yeah. Forget the hex. Forget the other stuff. Just go out there and win.'

'That's an order?'

'From the top,' Di Rocca said, and hung up.

Laville tried watching TV again, but kept getting distracted. If he went out, about eleven cops would follow him. He was bored with Nora. He wished Shirley were here. Something kept bothering him and made him try and check with Di Rocca, but when he dialled Di Rocca's house, he could only get the answering service.

CHAPTER TWENTY-THREE

On Sunday, the day of the men's final at Flushing Meadow, Lieutenant Lucchesi and Chief Ross O'Brien left the Mayor's office feeling optimistic. The semifinals were over, and no one had died.

In a brief ceremony, played out with a medium-priced California sherry and some key people from the newspapers, the Mayor had congratulated his police force for their management of the Flushing Meadow affair.

When the lieutenant and the chief were comfortably installed in the back seat of O'Brien's command car, O'Brien blew out his breath, a sure sign of anxiety, and asked for an update.

'The Brooklyn hooker, Sabrina. What have you developed on the guy she described?'

'Our only connection was with a rumour floating around,' Lucchesi said, 'about a contract hit. They were bringing in a shooter from the Coast. We've had men on the airports, and not a single pro has arrived since we heard.'

'He could have already been here.'

'Yes. But they like to operate from a base, the same way we do.'

'Don't lecture me on the criminal intelligence, okay?' O'Brien snapped.

'Sorry chief.' Lucchesi laid out three dossiers on the back seat. 'We've narrowed it down this far.'

O'Brien flipped open the first dossier. Edmund Schell, a small-time killer wanted in Miami, with two prison terms and a stint in an institution for the criminally insane in Delaware. The photo showed a sweet-faced smiling youth with dreamy eyes. 'Pretty boy,' he grunted.

The second dossier was fat. Its subject was Rinaldo J. Florentino, who specialized in ice-pick murders. Florentino had been employed by various families in Las Vegas and Pueblo, Arizona. His photo showed a round-faced man with shadowy cheeks. He had relatives in Hoboken.

O'Brien glanced at Lucchesi.

'We've got round-the-clock surveillance on the relatives.'

The third dossier was Henry Corelli, alias Michael Mancini, alias Frederick H. Smith, alias Frank Torelli. Corelli/Mancini/Smith/Torelli had served in the Army in Vietnam. He was an expert with pistols and automatic weapons. At the age of twenty-eight, he had competed for a place on the Army's Modern Pentathlon team. The photo showed a blonde man with hard eyes and a lean-jowled pock-marked face. Adjectives in the dossier caught O'Brien's attention: 'shrewd', 'resourceful', 'imaginative in the field', 'a survivor', 'master of disguise'.

O'Brien sighed, closed the dossier. 'Let's watch for this guy.'

Lucchesi answered with a grin. 'We're circulating copies of his mug shot.'

O'Brien swore. His cigarillo was out. 'Let's get out there, where the action is. Maybe we'll get lucky.'

'I heard it would be ninety-two this afternoon.'

'I'm afraid so.'

Leaning over the table, lighting a cigarette from a candle, the Princess smiled seductively at the camera. For this set of pictures, she wore a white skirt and matching jacket with a filmy red blouse. The skirt had a modest slit up one side, perhaps ten inches in length. For the occasion, she wore a brassiere. Every brand name would be documented in classy type near the relevant photo. The *Elan* layout would be eight full pages, in colour. Nora had worked hard, to take her mind off Terry. She was the editor in charge. She would make seven thousand dollars. The Princess would make ten thousand.

'That's it!' the photographer said. 'Thank you, ladies.'

'Thank you, John.'

Nora kissed John Greenwald on the cheek. Until this summer, she hadn't realized how much she'd missed the old life. When he had packed up his equipment and gone out with his assistants, Nora and Athena sat down to lunch.

Nora was excited. Doubles was filled with the most beautiful, the most powerful, and the most expensive women in New York. In the daytime, there were no men, and Doubles was the exclusive province of women. And Nora had selected this upscale women's domain as part of the background for her fashion layout on Athena. With the session over, the two women could concentrate on their food. Nora wanted to talk to her friend about Terry, but now that the photographer was gone, Athena seemed distraught. She kept looking over Nora's shoulder.

'Are you all right?' Nora asked.

'I'm expecting a phone call.'

'Who from? Saadi?'

'No.' Athena paused. 'Someone else.'

'A secret?'

'Yes.' Athena speared a lettuce leaf. 'How do you think the session went?'

'Just great.' Nora was pleased. 'I'm a big name at *Elan* now. I owe you.'

'I am glad I could help you.' She looked past Nora again, distractedly.

'If it's a man, you'll have to wait awhile,' Nora said.

'Hmmm.' Athena turned back to Nora. 'How are things with Terry?'

'Worse. He still wants a divorce. He came back this morning, to get a racket and couple of headbands. There were policemen, so he couldn't hit me. I hated looking at his eyes.' Nora paused. 'They were so . . .'

'Terry's under a lot of strain.'

'Yes. John Greenwald says I might even get back into modelling. They're using older women these days, searching for new markets.' Nora bit her lip. 'I'm not even thirty, and that hurt!'

Athena patted her hand. 'Thirty is a remarkable age. Take it from me. You'll do very well.'

A waitress came up to tell Athena there was a phone call for her. Athena excused herself and went to answer. Nora watched the Princess walk off, such a strong woman, so self possessed. Could she ever be half as strong as the Princess?

When Athena came back, she was smiling.

'Good news, I hope.'

'Yes.' Athena touched Nora's shoulder. 'I'm going away after the tournament. So we won't see each other for a while.'

'Going away? Where?'

'I can't tell you right now. But I'll keep in touch.'

'Where can I reach you?'

Athena smiled mysteriously. 'I shall have to reach you.'

'What about Saadi?'

'Saadi is about to receive a huge surprise. Perhaps the biggest one of his life.'

The man in Sahara tennis clothes identified himself at the gate as Arthur

Smythe. The number on his official USTA pass was 702, and he moved through the security with minimum hassle. Smythe was a lean man in his early forties with short blond hair and a pock-marked face. He moved with the precision of the trained athlete. In his right hand was a tennis bag made by Laval Sportif.

Smythe made his way to the USTA locker room, where he opened a padlock on a locker and retrieved a narrow leather suitcase. There were players in here, suiting up, which made it impossible for him to change, so he left the locker room and made his way to the executive offices, where he located a men's room with a large stall designed to accommodate a wheelchair.

Behind the locked stall door. Smythe changed into the uniform of a police officer of the city of New York. When he emerged, he wore shooting glasses and carried a high-powered rifle fitted with a telescopic sight. His name tag said Estevez. In his right ear was an earplug connected to a radio attached to his belt. With the radio, he could communicate with Sally Vincenti.

By noon on Sunday, Sally Vincenti was tired of calling Jack Di Rocca's house and getting no answer. He told Enrico to find Jackie. Enrico relayed the instructions to Carmine. Then Sally and Enrico took the Mercedes out to Flushing Meadow. In the trunk of the Mercedes was a picnic basket containing three bottles of Valpolicella, salami sandwiches, Italian cheese, olives from Tuscany, and a compact black Sony shortwave radio rebuilt to copy police tactical frequencies.

Wearing the headphones, Enrico listened to the police talking to each other on the walkies. It took him five minutes to find the band Torelli was using. He talked to Torelli through a tiny boutonniere mike clipped to the lapel of his windbreaker. Enrico was good. He made it look like he was talking to the boss.

'I got him. Torelli.'

'Tell him to stand by.' Sally liked the ring of that, stand by.

'Stand by, Torelli.'

Sally checked his watch. The men's final was supposed to begin at two, sharp. It was ten minutes after, and no players had yet come on court. Sally needed this day to be a good one. He had lost $750,000 when Koras had beaten Di Rocca in the semifinal. The problem was, it wasn't all his money. He owed some people. He also needed to make back the $750,000. That's why he had bet on Koras, to win.

After that, he would let Torelli kill him.

At 2:17, there was still no sign of the players, and Sally could feel the nerves at the side of his head pounding, the sure sign of a headache coming on. Then he saw Terry Laville walk onto the court, with Panties Koras right after him. Laville walked with his usual cocky confidence. Koras looked the same; cool, easy. Di Rocca had said the Lithuanian did some crazy kind of exercise to chill out before a match. Applause rained down from the packed stadium, a few shouts of 'King! King Koras!' Sally smiled. It was a beautiful day, sunshine, pretty girls, a good breeze. Made you feel alive.

He told Enrico to open the first bottle of wine.

Muriel was late returning to the hotel, and then she took extra time dressing, so Malone watched the warm-up and the first couple of games on the television in the room. There had been a fifteen minute delay, with no explanation. Now that the players were hitting, Koras looked sharp, but Laville looked like murder on wheels. They were into the fourth game, tied 2-all, when Malone and Muriel got ready to leave their hotel room for the Tennis Center. Malone was just closing the door when the phone rang. He went back in to answer. It was Di Rocca.

'I been trying to get you, Jackie.'

In the background, Malone could hear jets taking off, which meant Di Rocca was at an airport. 'I got something for you, Malone.'

'What?'

'Information.'

'What kind of information?'

'Can't say, over the phone. I'm at JFK.'

Di Rocca was on the move. 'Christ,' Malone said.

'Let me meet you, outside Pan Am, twenty minutes. Sooner, if you can make it. If you can't, it's tough.'

'Twenty minutes! Give me a hint, Jackie. It's about you and Laville and the paisan in the tennis shirt?'

'See you at JFK,' Di Rocca said, and hung up.

'What is it?' Muriel asked.

'I have a feeling it's my bonus, from Archer Bell.'

'Bonus?'

'Yeah. It's about to go out the window.'

Sunday traffic made the trip to JFK an agony of delay for Malone and Muriel. It took almost an hour to get there from the Meridien, and then when their taxi pulled up in front of Pan Am, there was no sign of Di Rocca. Malone told the driver to wait, meter running, and gave him a twenty.

He and Muriel got out and hurried along the sidewalk. Still no Di Rocca, so Malone headed inside, to the ticket counter, while Muriel stayed to watch the sidewalk. The doors were automatic. As Malone stepped through, a soldier in the dress green uniform of an army captain grabbed his arm. It took Malone a very long moment to realize it was Di Rocca, complete with a short military hair cut, dark glasses, and no beard.

'Over here. My flight's about to leave.'

Malone walked with the heavy set tennis player to the security gate. As they walked, Di Rocca fished into his green flight bag and pulled out a micro cassette, which he handed to Malone.

'What's on it?'

'Laville and a Mafia capo named Sally Vicenti. They plan to waste Koras.'

'Jesus! How?'

'Hit man, named Torelli, one of Sally's. My guess is a rifle, right after the finals.'

'How long you have you had this?'

Di Rocca handed Malone a diagram, drawn in pencil, of the seating area in the stadium. 'Sally's box is here, at courtside.'

Malone's mind raced through scenarios as he studied the diagram. 'Not much time, Jackie.'

'Listen, I know what you're thinking, but I had my own ass to cover. I thought Koras would play ball with Sally. When he didn't, I had to make some decisions.' He indicated the uniform, ran his hand over his bare face.

Malone stared at the time. 'What does the hit guy look like?'

'Never saw him.'

'What am I supposed to do?'

Di Rocca jabbed a finger at his rough diagram. 'Throw a monkey wrench into Sally's plan.' Di Rocca shifted uncomfortably. 'Look, you work for Arch Bell, and his boy Laville. I wasn't going to help any of you. But Koras is okay. I'd hate to see him buy it. See what you can do.'

'I ace Sally,' Malone said, touching the material of the uniform, 'and you get back on the circuit?'

Di Rocca grinned. 'I did have that thought.'

Malone checked the clock over Di Rocca's right shoulder. It was almost three. The match had been underway forty-five minutes. Hold out, Koras.

Di Rocca tossed his flight bag onto the security conveyor. As he passed through the metal detector, he pushed the dark glasses down on his nose and winked at Malone.

Before Di Rocca was out of sight, Malone went to the nearest pay phone and dialled the hotline number Lieutenant Lucchesi had given out. But all Malone got was a busy signal. Sweating now, he tried three more times. Muriel ran up and he told her briefly what was happening. Using another pay phone, she tried calling. The time ticked away. The lines must be overloaded; they could not get through to the main Tennis Center number, either.

Malone dialled 911. After four rings, a dispatcher answered.

'This is an emergency.'

'Go ahead, please.'

'I've got information on an attempted hit at the Tennis Center. I need you to alert Lieutenant –'

The dispatcher cut him off. 'An attempted hit? Did you say "hit"?'

'That's right, officer. It's a Mafia hit, a guy with a rifle. He's about six-one, blonde, with a pock-marked face . . .'

There was a disinterested, procedural drone to the dispatcher's voice as he interrupted again. 'Where are you calling from, sir?'

'Me? I'm at JFK.'

'And your name?'

'Malone. Matt Malone. Listen, I'm not kidding. This is –'

'Yes sir, excuse me a moment. There's a call coming through on another line. Your call will be handled in turn.'

Malone heard a crackle and he was standing there sweating, holding the receiver. The dispatcher thought he was a crank. Malone hung up and grabbed Muriel. 'Come on.'

They ran back outside. The taxi was still waiting, the meter up past $40. Malone told the driver to head for the Tennis Center. The time was 3:40. The match was an hour and a half old.

At 4-all in the fourth set, Lavill threw his third temper tantrum of the afternoon, arguing with the umpire, trying to muddy Koras's timing.

Waiting for the tantrum to subside, Koras walked to the players' box, looked up at Laure, her face a sad smile. She passed a note down. The note said, *'Je t'aime'*.

Koras folded it, put it in his pocket, and blew Laure a kiss.

Beside her, Milos started chanting, 'King! King Koras! King! King Koras!'

The crowd took up the chant. Watching Laville, Koras felt his spirits lift. Across the court, Sally Vincenti sat with his number one, who was still plugged in to his baseball game.

Laville, still arguing with the umpire, put his hands on his hips and looked up. He could hear the umpire's voice, low and controlled, but now the man's face had become Mikhail Polak's. Micky sat in the umpire's chair, his back to the sun, staring down at Laville. The sun threw his figure into silhouette, but Laville could sense the lean features, with those sad eyes, staring down at him in judgment. 'Hey?' Laville said, and moved to the side, so he could see better.

'The ball was out, Mr Laville.'

Laville wiped the sweat out of his eyes and looked past the umpire, into the stands, where Nora sat in Saadi's box. The Princess was with her, looking terrific, her blonde hair blowing a little in the breeze. Saadi was behind the Princess. As Laville watched, Saadi's chauffeur came up to whisper in Saadi's ear. The Arab left the box.

'Let's play, Mr Laville.' It wasn't Micky's voice.

'Yes, sir.'

Laville walked back to receive serve from Koras. As he hunkered down in the ready position, he thought of all the photographs taken of himself as the woodcutter, lumberjack Laville, awaiting serve, eyes straight ahead, sun glinting off the brass brads in his headband, elbows out.

The ball came, a fluffy floater, making Laville grin at how slow it was. He knew all the shots Koras had. He was cranking his arm now, winding up for the big kill, sending across a winner for sure.

He was surprised when Koras volleyed it back, deep. Out of position, Laville lobbed. Koras angled his overhead, sucking Laville off court, right into the box where Sally Vicenti sat. Laville slapped at the shot, kept going, climbed the wall of the box, and grinned at the wop, who had stood up to get out of the way.

'Sorry, partner.'

The crowd applauded. Laville's shot was wild. The point had gone to Koras. Laville fought back, hearing a soft buzz in his ears, the sure sound of failure. A tear came to his eyes when Koras won the game, to lead him for the first time in the match, 5–4.

Then Laville understood. The buzzing was applause. He felt tired now. As he walked to the chair for the changeover, he had a satisfying thought – if he lost, Koras was dead.

In the broadcast booth, tennis commentator Judson Garwood was hoarse with emotion. The final of the men's singles in the U.S. Open was a classic, youth versus age, the young wizard against the mature master.

'A cross-court from Koras, dipping, short, pulling Laville wide. Laville hits it down the line, barely in, and now he charges the net. Koras holds the ball on the strings – he's famous for that – until the last minute. We don't know whether it's a lob or a passing shot. It's a lob! Laville goes back, looking tired now himself, all that high living perhaps catching up, with him, Jim . . . and he slams an overhead down the sideline. The ball hooks; Koras barely catches it. He's in the forecourt . . . and cagily dumps a drop volley over the net. Laville charges up, but not in time. Not up.'

'Love-30,' said umpire.

'Laville starts to protest, then remembers he's got two penalty points, one warning, one point taken away. The next penalty point awards an entire game to Koras. And that could end the match. So, Terry Laville backs off.'

At 5–6 in the fifth set, Laville leading, Koras didn't care whether he won or lost. He was too tired. His right knee ached. He wanted to be off the court in a therapy bath. He wanted a beer, some sleep, Laure by his side. But he could tell from the crowd noise – the oohs and aahs on the lobs, the quick machine gun applause on the put-away volleys, the tightrope tension during the longer exchanges – he could tell that they were enjoying it.

You tried to forget. The world reminded you.

And that was why he and Laville were here – for the crowd, for anonymous tennis fans all over the world, watching on television. They were here for the kids growing up, playing tennis outdoors, under the sun. He wasn't here for himself, for fame and money and applause. Maybe Laville was.

But only because Laville kidded himself.

He and Laville weren't here for Saadi, or for Archer Bell. Or even for Frank Fenwick. No. They were here for the spectators who had paid their hard-earned money to see this match.

That was all. And that was everything in the world. To play your best, no matter what.

'The score in the final set is 6–5,' intoned the umpire. 'Mr Laville leads.'

On the walkway between the stadium and the grandstand court, Saadi passed three uniformed policemen, hard-faced men with glinty eyes. The chauffeur was three paces behind him. 'Wait here,' he said. The chauffeur, an Englishman named Bryce, touched his cap with two fingers. On the stadium court they were playing the finals of the mixed doubles. The western bleachers were in shadow and spectators were scattered about. Everyone with a stadium seat was next door, watching the men's final. A man came up to Saadi. It was Leonardo, the brother of Armando Reyes. He was three inches shorter than Armando, with a flat Indian face and dark eyes. He wore a red warm-up jacket and tennis shorts.

Saadi started to offer his hand, but Reyes moved toward him menacingly. His eyes looked overheated. 'Señor Reyes. What is it?'

On the rim of the court, two policemen stood, watching the match. Reyes came close. 'Do not lie to me.'

'Lie. About what?'

'You and your man, Laville. I read in the papers you are paying him millions. To you, he is important.'

'So?'

'Even in Peru, a man protects his investment.'

Reyes's face had a tortured expression. Saadi circled to his left, for a better view of the Peruvian's face. 'What is it you want from me?'

'Someone gives the drugs to kill my brother. This someone I am here to determine. Like the tennis, I am conducting my own eliminations.'

The man was insane. Saadi's mind raced through several possibilities. 'You are mistaken.'

'No. I see your woman with Armando. With her, he is El Señor Amor. Also, I hear *historias* of this Laville, King of the Sleeping Pill.'

Saadi was sweating now. 'Those stories are untrue.'

A policeman came into view behind Reyes and Saadi weighed his chances of calling out. At the same time, Reyes opened his hand to reveal a knife with a yellow handle. 'Why, is my question? Why does someone give my brother these things?'

'It wasn't Laville.'

'You lie. I see it in your eye.'

Saadi allowed his gaze to slide away, with Reyes watching every move. 'He had no reason, you see.'

Reyes stepped closer and Saadi smelled sweat and foul breath. 'You are a bad liar, señor. He has the reason.'

'What?'

'Armando thrashes him in Palm Springs, Atlanta, Tokyo, Hawaii. He flirts with Laville's wife.'

Saadi frowned for effect. 'I wasn't aware of –'

But before he finished, Reyes snorted derisively, then turned away from Saadi with a look of triumph and hurried back along the passageway, toward the stadium court. Saadi sat down for a moment to wipe his face with a silk handkerchief. From the stadium he could hear applause and the roar of the crowd. There were twenty thousand spectators packed inside and every one was a potential customer of Sahara Sports.

When Saadi reached his box, his legs still trembled from the encounter with Leonardo Reyes. Nora Laville had left the Princess alone. The score was 6-all, and the umpire was announcing the sudden death tie-break.

Traffic held Malone and Muriel up. What should have been a thirty minute ride took more than an hour. Malone was perspiring. Maybe he should have stuck with the telephone. Muriel watched the traffic, her eyes filled with dread.

Before the taxi pulled to a complete stop in front of the security van at the Tennis Center, Malone shoved a hundred at the driver. He and Muriel were out of the cab before it stopped rolling, heading for the gate, where they were searched. Once inside, Malone headed for the security van. He flashed his writer's pass and asked for Lieutenant Lucchesi. Instead, a smooth-faced cop in uniform stepped down out of the van and started asking questions. Lucchesi couldn't be contacted.

Malone knew he was getting the run-around. 'What's the score in the final?'

'Almost finished. They're in the middle of a tie-breaker.'

'Come on.' Malone grabbed Muriel's hand and they started into the stadium.

On the court, Laville won the point, drawing ahead 5–4 in the tie-break, and as the crowd jumped to its feet to applaud, Athena decided it was time. She leaned close, smiling radiantly, and told Saadi she was leaving him. 'I'd like an annuity. Let's say a million a year, paid quarterly, for the next ten years.'

The Arab started to laugh, but then his face grew pale as he turned away from the tennis to stare at Athena. Despite his European education, his years at an English public school and later at the Sorbonne, Saadi was a suspicious Bedouin at heart. He curled his lip as he snarled at the Princess. 'Does this mean you are refusing my offer of marriage?'

'Your mother would never have permitted it. They think me an infidel.'

'You don't dare. I took care of your mother's creditors.' He grabbed her wrist, but she reached into her bag with her free hand, pulled out a Xerox copy of a page from *Racket World*, which she handed to Saadi. The rectangular holes which had once been words showed up clear and black.

'I think you will still take care of them.'

'What's this?'

'From your desk.'

He stared at it before crumpling it up and thrusting it into his jacket pocket. Today, Saadi wore a white suit from Palm Beach with white shoes and a brilliant red tie. Did he remember carefully slicing the words out of the page, pasting them down on the piece of paper? 'What makes you think –'

Athena leaned forward, and locked her eyes on Saadi's. 'I am not working alone. My partner knows the ins and outs of this. We have your fingerprints on the cover. It was found in your wastepaper basket, in Paris. The subscription was in your name. We have photographs, photocopies.'

Saadi looked as if he might faint. 'The police will never believe you.'

Athena shook her head. 'We don't need the police. All we do is leak it to the papers, and to the directors of your companies, and then to the Securities and Exchange Commission. The tennis writers will ruin you. You'll be hooted out of the game.'

'What do you want?'

Athena was preparing to leave the box, gathering her possessions. 'Koras is about to win. You should have signed him.'

The score was 8–7, Koras leading.

Saadi laughed, a dry, mechanical sound. 'A half million.'

'No. Ten million, paid as indicated. And the loan papers that concerned my mother.'

Saadi grasped his chair.

To thunderous applause, Laville pulled even. There was dead silence on the next point. After a brilliant exchange, with Laville manoeuvring Koras all about the court, Laville won the point, to make it 9–8.

It was now match point. With one ace, Laville could become the American champion. He could prove the hex did not exist. He could stop Koras in his march towards the Grand Slam.

Laville arched his back for the serve. The ball seemed to hang in the air for an interminable moment. He leaped off the ground for maximum leverage as he cracked the ball with a resounding echo which was even louder in the rapt silence of the stadium.

Koras made a courageous dive for it, but it was too late.

Terry Laville was the new U.S. Open champion.

Athena stood with everyone else to applaud the winner, but her tears were for the defeated champion.

'I shall be in touch, Saadi.' Feeling terrified but free, Athena left the box, walking proudly.

People were already leaving the stadium as Malone and Muriel started in. He grabbed a man's arm.

'Who won?'

'Laville, the Canadian.'

Malone glanced at Muriel and they kept hurrying forward. The jogging made Malone breathe hard, reminding him he wasn't in shape. It was time to give up beer, steak, eggs, Mexican food. People coming out early got in their way. The stadium court was just up ahead.

They shoved past two couples in their mid-thirties. The women were handsome and well-groomed. The men had corporate haircuts.

'Hey!' one of the men said.

'Sorry! What's going on?'

'Just the presentation.'

Malone charged on, through the door, leaving Muriel behind. Down on the court, the presentation was being made. Microphones had been set up. An official was about to hand the trophy over to Terry Laville. Malone could see Archer Bell in his box, and across the court, in his box, was Sally Vincenti. Muriel ran up, red-faced and panting. 'There!' he pointed the don out to Muriel.

Sally Vicenti was having stomach pains, indigestion, pangs shooting up to the centre of his chest. He took a heart pill, washing it down with red wine.

Enrico leaned close. 'You all right, Sally?'

Sally nodded, coughed. The dizzies came, whirling his head around, and then he saw the flapping of a black window curtain, his mother's house in Borough Park, near the cemetary, the night his father had died. Sally knew he was going to die. Soft dark curtains closed around his face and eyes.

Then, like magic, the pill worked, a miracle, and Sally opened his eyes to see the crowd. Laville was on the court, holding the trophy, Panties Koras standing off to the side, talking to a girl with brown hair, tall and lean, like a college girl. Laville had just made a big mistake and cost Sally a lot of money, winning when he should have lost. And Sally was in trouble.

Two days before, he'd taken a real hammering betting on Di Rocca to win the semis. Then he'd been up all night, shifting the pool of $32 million over to Koras to win. Now Laville had won his first U.S. Open and there was egg on Sally's face. Losing the money was bad enough. Being out of control was worse. Control was Sally's business, where every act was measured in terms of order and discipline, keeping the ducks in line.

And now in Maimi and Chicago and Vegas and Palermo, the capos from the rival families would know Sally had lost his grip. They could take a loss in the millions. They would not take a faulty judgment revealing one of their own out of his depth. There was only one way out – assassinate Koras, right here, as a sign. Use the television to send a message. As he made up his mind and turned to Enrico, Sally had a sickening vision of Koras in front of a hundred microphones, camera whirring away at the post-match press conference, confessing to the world about the deal Sally had made him.

Laville could be quietly taken care of afterwards, after Sally found out why Laville had double-crossed him but Panties Koras was a household word, a big rangy Lithuanian jerk with an honest face. People would believe him. The whole world would believe him.

'Execute it,' Sally wheezed.

'Right.' Enrico pressed the Talk button on the short wave, to signal Torelli to proceed.

Police patrolman Estevez was standing up, like the other twenty thousand spectators, but he was in the shadows at the top of the stadium, right beneath the press box. Everyone else was facing down. He followed the ceremony, and this was what mattered. Terry Laville, the winner, carried the trophy forward. Estevez heard the beep and Enrico telling him to go ahead. He raised the rifle and adjusted the scope until Belynkas appeared in the cross-hairs. At that moment, Terry Laville cut in front, filling the scope. The rifleman swore and more sweat came out on his forehead.

Holding the trophy, Terry Laville walked forward. He was slowly coming out of his trance to hear the ovation from the stadium, underscoring his win over Koras in the finals.

Laville beamed his best smile for the cameras. Now that he had won, Koras would live to fight another day. Playing today, beating Koras, Laville had also beaten the hex. A new day was dawning for Terry Laville. He had won the U.S. Open, fair and square. He had his revenge – he hadn't needed the hit man, after all. By winning, he had actually saved Koras's live. The irony appealed to him. He lifted the cup above his head, offering it symbolically to the public that now shouted his name.

'Laville. Laville. Terry Laville!'

The trophy glinted in the afternoon sun as Laville began a slow circle around the court. The chanting continued. He was halfway around when he spotted Micky Polak coming purposefully toward him. This time Micky wore a shiny red warm-up jacket and seemed to float like a ghost.

Laville wanted to run, but his legs wouldn't work. No one else seemed to notice Micky. No, of course they wouldn't – he was a familiar face, with a player's pass. He was closer now, five feet, three feet. He was smiling and speaking Laville's name. Laville. Laville. Or maybe that was the crowd . . .

Laville saw the blade flash in the sun. Funny, because Micky was a gun freak. Everyone knew that. Laville swung the trophy at Micky, who dodged. The knife went in. Then Micky became Armando Reyes; the knife went in again. Laville felt life draining out of him. Armando the Sword. He kicked, landing a good one. Cops were running toward him, jerking guns out. Oh God, if the knife didn't get him, the cops were going to, for using the shotgun in London. As he staggered, Armando stood over him, but it wasn't Armando any more. It was his brother, the short Peruvian, Leonardo, his face a fallen monument to despair and vengeance.

Laville reached out for the knife which glittered in the sun. He felt a cool breeze, but hardly any pain. The knife flashed again, in slow motion. He heard screams then, and saw the green court coming up to him, and then he was down.

Estevez was about to squeeze off a clean shot into the chest of Pantakoras Belynkas when pandemonium broke out. Officials crowded onto the court as police and paramedics surrounded Laville. Ballboys and ball-girls broke ranks and headed for the entrance. Fans at the courtside, unable to move into the aisles, spilled out onto the green deco turf. Two alert-looking security people came up to stand by Koras as a group of four huddled around Laville.

'What's going on?'

'Let's get you to the security area, Mr Belynkas.'

Koras didn't know either of these men. Where had they come from? Where was Rivera? He saw Laure; she had left the box and was racing toward him, with Milo Tigrid behind her.

'Pantakoras!'

'Let her through,' Koras said.

Then Laure was in his arms.

Laure went with Pantakoras and the two security men towards the exit leading to the main gate. Spectators jostled them and she could hear Pantakoras talking to Milo. As she glanced up into the stands, she saw a man aiming down with a rifle. She screamed just as the man fired. In front of them, one of the bodyguards fell to the ground, clutching his arm. The second security man dropped down by the first, with his gun held in both hands.

'Up there!' she cried, and pointed. There was no one there. Several uniformed officers, their weapons drawn, were working their way towards the spot from where the shot had come .

Milo shoved Pantakoras ahead and grabbed Laure. They headed for the exit, shoving through the crowd.

'Laure! What did he look like?'

'He wore a uniform. Like a flic! Oh, Koras, the police are shooting at you!'

Koras steered them in the opposite direction. 'We've got to get out of here.' There seemed to be no one they could trust.

Behind them, Milo reached into his equipment bag and brought out a lead-foil wrapper for getting film through a metal detector. Inside was his chrome-plated pistol.

Running through the labyrinth beneath the stadium, Malone knew two things. Number one, Di Rocca had waited too long. Number two, against an experienced mob hitman the only weapon he had was a ball point pen. Beside him, Muriel was exhausted. 'Who are we looking for?'

'The guy Sally hired, the one named Torelli. He's going to kill Koras!'

'But Koras lost.'

'Maybe he was supposed to win.'

Then, through the crowd, Malone spotted Koras and Tigrid and the French girl, Laure Puget. They were fifty yards ahead, moving towards the Marquee Entrance. A cop in an NYPD uniform was behind them, covering their retreat and trying to stay with them.

Koras, Laure and Milo were passing The Food Village when a vendor with a hand truck loaded with empty Coke bottles lost control of his cart. The bottles reeled off it shattering as they hit the concrete. Koras pulled Laure out of the way, but the hand truck slammed into Milo.

Milo swore.

'Are you all right?'

Milo stood with difficulty. 'You go ahead. I guard your behind.'

Koras looked at Laure. 'All right. Thanks.'

Glass was everywhere. A man with a push broom appeared, to start sweeping it up. The Coke vendor got two policemen to detour the crowd around the mess.

Milo looked to be in some pain. He put a hand on his hip, and then took up a position in a vacant hotdog stand, where he could watch Koras's back.

When he reached ground level, Estevez saw two uniformed men coming towards him. Neither one had a rifle, and he knew he would look conspicuous if he kept his. It was a nice weapon. Too bad. He ditched the rifle.

'Who's in charge?' he asked one of the policemen.

'Lucchesi. We're headed for the Marquee.'

Estevez trotted along with them, his right hand on his holstered pistol.

As Malone and Muriel passed the Food Village a voice called out. 'Ho, you, Malone.' Milo stepped away from the shadow.

'Milo, where's Koras?'

The Yugoslav pulled his coat aside to show the butt of his revolver. 'I cover their retreat.'

Malone moved to him and pointed at the gun. 'Can you use that thing?'

'I am trained, I tell you. In the army.'

'How long ago?'

'A mere nineteen years.'

Malone held out his hand. 'Give me the gun, Milo.'

With a sheepish look, the Yugoslav handed it over.

Koras and Laure reached the Marquee Entrance to find a police barrier, sawhorses strung with yellow banners labelled 'NYPD' in black letters. The crowd had backed up, waiting to be checked by police.

'Damn!' Koras said. They were struck there.

They shuffled forward with the crowd. Fear was in the air. People kept shoving and pushing, and an officer with a bull horn was calling for calm.

'Be patient, folks. Just be patient.'

When they arrived at the checkpoint, Koras recognized the officer in charge, Lieutenant Lucchesi. Lucchesi looked cool and in control in his three-piece suit. A walkie-talkie crackled in his hand as he beckoned to Koras and Laure.

'When can we get out of here?'

'We're securing the area, Mr Belynkas. You'll have to wait over there for a minute until we can get a police vehicle in here for you.'

Koras began arguing with Lucchesi, who broke off to answer his walkie-talkie. At the same time, he motioned to four uniformed officers, who formed up around Koras and Laure.

Koras was fuming. He wanted out *now*.

Before they had taken ten steps, Muriel had to stop and rest. Malone was red in the face and breathing hard, Milo grimaced with pain. 'Go on,' he said. 'Go on.'

As they stood there at the edge of the Food Village, trying to catch their breath, three policemen jogged easily by. One of them, a lean man with a pock-marked face, looked familiar. Where had Malone seen him before?

'How are you feeling?' he asked Muriel.

She nodded but was too winded to speak. Up ahead, people had simply stopped moving.

'What's up there, Milo?'

'The Marquee Entrance.'

Just then, one of the policemen doubled back through the Food Village and headed back toward the stadium. There was something familiar about that one, the way he moved, the efficiency. Malone pulled Milo's chrome-plated pistol from his belt and checked the cylinder to make sure the gun had six bullets.

'Stay with Muriel,' he said to Milo.

'Why? What are you –'

Malone was gambling.

Estevez climbed the stairs two at a time. When he reached the rim of the stadium that looked across the tents of the Food Village right onto the Marquee Entrance, he was breathing deep and easy. Down below, he saw the yellow banners of the police barrier rippling in the breeze, nervous fans backed up a hundred deep and six across at the checkpoint, cops everywhere, a police cruiser stuck in the crowd, nobody able to move. Estevez smiled. He liked panic. By the car, off to the right, he saw his target wearing tennis shorts and a black warm-up jacket. A girl was with him. They were surrounded by four uniforms. One of the uniforms had a rifle. Take him out first. He checked his watch.

Estevez had done shots like this before. He settled into a comfortable shooting position, resting the revolver on the ledge. He took off his cap and aimed.

The last spectators were leaving the stadium as Malone came in. He saw the cop in the uniform high above him, facing out away from the court and towards the parking lot. The sun was hot and Malone was sweating. Sunlight flashed off metal as Malone ran awkwardly up towards the killer atop the wall. His feet felt heavy on the hard concrete steps.

The first bullet hit the policeman with the rifle, the second one slammed into Koras, hitting him in the left arm and shoving him back against the door of the police car. Laure screamed. Koras grabbed her and pulled her to safety behind the car. At the same time, Lucchesi ran over to take command and directed the fire of the policemen to the top of the stadium.

'Okay, now. Keep the shooting steady. No spraying lead.'

Two policemen were dragging their downed comrade to safety.

Above them, the shooter fired three fast rounds. Lucchesi swore. It was chaos; the crowd shoved against the police barrier and stampeded through the checkpoint. A woman screamed: 'Michael!' There were hoarse shouts from the men.

Lucchesi grabbed three officers and pointed up. 'Get a squad into the stadium!'

The policemen trotted off, pistols out, muzzles pointed up.

Estevez fired once more, but when they opened up on him from down below, he dropped down behind the concrete wall. They hadn't seen anything but his bare head, without the cap, so he figured the uniform might get him out. His gun was still in his hand. Once down below the line of sight from the parking lot, he put the policeman's cap back on. Random firing continued but passed harmlessly over his head. He hadn't taken two steps before he saw the man coming up the steps of the stadium.

The man was in his middle-forties, with a paunch and a rumpled brown jacket. His face was red from running. His tie was askew. He stood in the shooter's stance, both hands holding a chrome-plated pistol. It was aimed right at him. Estevez knew guns. The piece was a .357 and the man handled himself like he knew a little. Estevez stopped moving, stood there with the police revolver at his side. He only needed a split second. If the man blinked or looked around, he was dead.

Swaying in the hot sun, Malone knew he had never seen eyes colder than these. This was a killer, a reptile. 'Put down the piece,' he ordered. His voice was harsh from the exhausting chase through the stadium, the climb.

He knew it wouldn't to any good to talk. His man squatted down, at the same time raising his gun. Malone dropped to one knee and fired the '357. His first slug took Torelli in the chest, ramming him backwards. Torelli's gun went off, so Malone still kneeling, fired again.

The killer dropped the gun, sagged to the metal seats of the bleachers. For a moment, he hung there, the dark wet stain spreading on his chest, and then he toppled over and rolled down three steps onto his back.

For a moment, Malone stood above the killer, with the muzzle of the gun pointed down. He heard shouts below. When he turned, he saw uniformed police entering the stadium. Guns were pointed up at him. Someone on a bullhorn ordered him to throw down his weapon. Malone tossed the gun aside. He was starting to tremble now.

If he had shot the right cop, the tennis killings were over.

CHAPTER TWENTY-FOUR

Milo Tigrid looked at the man in the wheelchair one last time. The wheelchair faced out, towards the window which looked out on the world beyond the hospital. Beyond the double panes, the lawns stretched away to the distance in a smooth and silent sheet of immaculate snow, dotted here and there with frozen trees.

Milo left the room.

Behind him, in the wheelchair, the patient barely stirred when the door closed. He remembered talking to the journalist about a match he had played on a court somewhere in the past. And then he had gone on to describe, in detail, the match at Flushing Meadow in the waning summer afternoon. The match was over, or was it? He kept meeting his opponent every day, in match after mirrored match, beating him again and again, only to see him rise up, renewed, ready for battle. And he, a champion, drunk with the crowd's ovations, soared above the stadium.

He shut his eyes, allowing himself to slide into a half sleep before the next ordeal of a match, only a few hours away. He felt sure of himself, sure of his game, sure of the mastery over his opponent. He knew, in his mind, that he would beat Koras once again.

Milo found Matt Malone talking to a young doctor dressed in pea green hospital clothes. His name badge read Dr W. Shoung; his face was unsmiling.

'It doesn't sound good,' Malone said.

Milo thought of the tight bandages around Laville's hands. 'What about his hands, doctor?'

'His hands, yes. He used them to shield himself from the knife. Major tendons were severed. In the right hand, he will have partial use. We are hoping for ninety per cent in the left.'

'And his eyesight?'

'The knife missed his eye while slicing away part of the cheek, so we must assume his eyesight problems are psychologically based. Dr Shapiro from psychiatry feels that the patient wishes to construct a world of his own design, and has used this temporary blindness towards these ends.'

'He didn't recognize me,' Milo said. 'He thought I was a journalist.'

'He thinks everyone is a journalist,' the doctor said, 'coming to interview him after his biggest win.'

'Jesus,' Malone said.

'You mean he'll never recognize anyone again?' Milo asked.

'That is a distinct possibility. His world was evidently distorted before, or he could not have committed those crimes. Now, with the organic brain damage, it may be distorted permanently.'

Milo and Malone drove slowly through the park. Malone waited awhile, then said: 'Muriel sends regards.'

'How is she?'

'Beautiful as ever. She's coming over next week.'

Both men were glad to be away from the hospital. 'I need a drink, detective.'

'So do I. Point me the way to the nearest watering hole.'

They drove through the streets of the small town until they found a sign that said DRINKS, EATS. Malone parked the car and the two men went inside. It was warm, cozy, and almost empty at this time of day. Malone ordered whisky. Milo ordered a martini.

'Did you hear about Di Rocca?' Milo said.

'No. What about Di Rocca?'

'He is in Mexico, they say, with the Princess.'

'An unlikely pair.'

The drinks came. Malone raised his glass. 'To Swash, then, a noble animal.'

'I shall one day teach him to play tennis,' Milo said.

Malone laughed. 'Did they ever figure out who sent that threat note?'

Milo shook his head. 'I wouldn't know. I think Laville sent it, to throw off the cops, after he killed Polak.'

'I put my money on Saadi, to goose the numbers for Sahara.'

Milo sipped his drink, making an appreciative face. 'And you. Did you ever extract your money from Mr Bell?'

'I got the last payment just before I headed out for Paris. He threatened to take me to court, until I told him what was on that tape and showed him the photos of his boy Laville talking to Sally Vicenti.'

'I always wanted to be a policeman,' Milo confessed, 'in order to wield vast power with a just hand. As a boy, I was a fan of Sherlock Holmes, you know.'

'You could go into partnership with me. Milo and Malone, intercontinental investigations.'

Milo nodded, then looked away. 'They say that your American underworld is filled with hordes of beautiful women, waiting to be rescued. Alas, I have this television station to run.'

Outside, it was snowing again. They looked through the window as the cars ploughed down the street.

'What's your next tournament?' Matt asked.

'The Masters, in New York. But that one, I fear, is my last.'

'You said that about the Open. I saw them quote you on TV.'

Milo sighed, signalling for two more drinks. 'B.J. keeps after me to quit, so that we can snuggle together in her Lear Jet. I think that now I play mostly doubles, with some young tiger who can run down the lobs.'

'How is B.J?'

'Ferocious. She wishes to invite you for dinner.'

'Done. If we get back to New York.'

Milo settled into the booth. The fresh round of drinks came. 'There is no need to leave when the blizzards rage. Once, in the mountains outside Sarajevo, I was snowed in for a week. My only companion was a girl of twenty, an American student named Drusilla. It was a lovely time.'

The two men touched glasses. It was good to be inside, safe from the cold, with a friend.

Mrs Pantakoras Belynkas was working on her thesis about the Celtic connections with the Grail legend in the huge library at Court's Court in Westhampton, when the phone rang. It was Athena, who was in Puerto Vallarta, with 'a friend'. Athena was calling to find out the news. As the exiled queen of the tennis groupies, she missed the circuit gossip.

What about Laure and Koras. Athena wanted to know. How was marriage? Where had they been? Where were they going?

'We are just back from Brussels,' Laure said. 'Koras won the European Champions' Championship. He beat Dumbo Cooper in four sets.'

'His arm must be better.'

'He groans at night, to get my sympathy. But the doctor says he is fit again.'

'A stubborn man heals more quickly, they say. How goes the archaeology?'

'My thesis is almost finished. Koras has a friend at a university press who is interested in seeing it, perhaps for publication.'

'You have it all, my dear. Brains. Beauty. A good man.'

'And what about you? What are you up to, with your mysterious lover?'

'We are investing in a hotel in Puerto Vallarta.'

'Is it Jack Di Rocca? Everyone thinks so.'

'An amazing man,' Athena said. 'He touches things, they turn to money.'

'Oh, Athena, it's you with the Midas touch.'

'I try, my dear. Is there news of Saadi?'

'The last we heard, he was in Damascus.'

'I wish nothing but the best for his mother. Her prejudice saved me from a grisly life in a harem.' Athena paused. 'When are you inviting me to your house?'

'Oh, please come. Whenever you get to New York.'

'Christmas, I spend in Austria. January, in Mexico. April, I think, for New York.'

'I'd love to see you.'

'You should consult Pantakoras, make certain I won't be intruding, like the witch of the west. Where is he, anyway?'

'Oh, on the inner court, working out with Will Channer.'

'The ageless champion.'

'How is the weather in Mexico?' Laure asked.

'It is raining, always raining. And then the sun comes out, there is dust, and one swelters. Ah, well, give my love to Pantakoras.'

'I shall. Goodbye, Athena.'

'Goodbye, cousin.'

Before going back to her writing, Laure poured herself a fresh cup of coffee. She worked another hour. The old Lithuanian cook could be heard in the kitchen, preparing lunch. Pantakoras was punctual and liked to eat at one, sharp.

Outside, the security patrol drove by. They had been hired by Frank Fenwick, and had been on duty ever since the shooting at the U.S. Open.

The police had arrested a gangster named Sally Vicenti. He was still awaiting trial, as was Leonardo Reyes, for his distraught knife attack on Terry Laville. Everyone on the circuit now knew that it was Terry who had killed poor Mikhail Polak.

There were guests for lunch: Will Channer, looking pink-faced from his workout; Frank Fenwick, who had driven out from his New York office with a new endorsement contract for Pantakoras; Milo Tigrid, who was in town for the Masters; Muriel Broussard-Gauthier, who had flown over from Paris to confer with her publisher, and Matt Malone, the 'writer' whom everyone preferred to think of as the investigator who had saved Koras's life, and hers. He would always be welcome in her house.

Most of the talk around the table was of a rising young player named Henrik Heinz, from Switzerland, nicknamed The Hammer after the powerful way he hit the ball. Frank Fenwick wanted to form a corporation to finance him. He wanted Milo and Pantakoras to invest, but he spoke mostly to Laure, who was handling the financial figures for her husband more and more.

Laure had to admire Fenwick's financial acumen. He had had the foresight to insure Pantakoras with Lloyds of London against any 'unforeseen' incident that might hamper his playing career. When the sniper had wounded Koras in the arm, Fenwick had made claims and they had been awarded $750,000 in damages. And the day following the incident, Fenwick had negotiated a book contract for Pantakoras. The advance had been two million dollars, as much as Pantakoras would have made winning his Grand Slam. Finally, Fenwick's lawyer had stymied any claims for repayment notes held by Sally Vicenti, who had been pressuring her husband about some outstanding construction loans. Thinking back to the money Koras had given her for the Alesia excavations, Laure could only shake her head at the way he handled money.

'We can't lose, folks. It's an investment in the future.'

'Bah, F.F., here we sit, surrounded by two beautiful women who have to be Montenegrin, and you talk only of money.' Milo patted Laure on the hand and winked at Muriel. 'Where is your romance, my good man?'

'I am not a Montenegrin, Milo,' Laure said.

'Nor am I,' said Muriel.

'All beautiful women have some Yugoslavian blood, whether they know it or not. If you have the misfortune not to be born in Yugoslavia, we can make you honorary citizens. I, Tigrid, will arrange.'

There was laughter around the table.

'What percentages are we speaking of, F.F?' Laure asked. She was a shopkeeper's daughter, with a sharp eye for numbers and investments. Already, she had studied the stock market and had nudged Pantakoras into two different stock buys that had appreciated in value. With the profits, she had bought herself a personal computer – she had wanted one for years to facilitate her work – and used it to keep track of the investments of Koras, Inc., the new company he had formed.

'See,' Fenwick said to Koras. 'Laure understands what I'm talking about here.'

'In my wife's veins runs the blood of many generations of Celtic accountants.'

Laure kissed her husband on the cheek. Later, when lunch was over, she would quietly get together with F.F. and go over the details of the new venture. Pantakoras was an artist, temperamental, creative. He preferred to spend money and let someone else keep tabs on what he had spent. He had not time for planning. In this family, Laure had the head for business.

'Pass me the chicken,' Milo roared. 'This money talk makes me hungry.'

Laure passed the *poulet sauté à la Bercy* to Milo. Over the steaming platter, she saw the eyes of her husband, gazing at her. He smiled, and she smiled back, and as she did so she thought of the new life she carried within herself. Pentakoras winked at her and looked at her with love, making Laure blush. She knew that look. It meant he wanted her. And this afternoon, after they had made love, she would tell him about their child that would soon stir in her womb, the one they had made together.

And for a while, life would be truly beautiful.

T… OK OF

MYTHS AND LEGENDS

THE GIANT BOOK OF
MYTHS AND LEGENDS

Edited by Mike Ashley

MAGPIE BOOKS
London

This edition first published by Magpie Books Ltd in 1995,
a division of Robinson Publishing

Magpie Books Ltd
7 Kensington Church Court
London W8 4SP

ISBN 1 85487 603 1

A copy of the British Library Cataloguing in Publication Data is available from the British Library.

Typeset by Hewer Text Composition Services, Edinburgh
Printed by Griffin Paperbacks, South Australia

CONTENTS

INTRODUCTION

Mike Ashley

MYTHS HAVE FASCINATED me ever since I was about ten and was introduced to the tale of the Trojan War. I had heard of some of the characters before, particularly Achilles and Odysseus, but they hadn't been much more than names. But on that quiet autumn day, when my English teacher began to unravel the story of the Trojan War, reading, I think, from *The Greek Myths* by Robert Graves, I rapidly became hooked. In the years following I have explored and delighted in the world of myths and legends.

I suppose we all start with the Greek legends, the world of Classical mythology. Many of the heroes and their deeds have passed into our language. We talk of the strength of Hercules, an Oedipus complex, the music of Orpheus, the song of the Sirens, an Achilles heel. And we are almost as well acquainted with their Roman equivalents, when we refer to Mercury, as the messenger of the Gods, or the legend of Romulus and Remus, or even swear the oath 'By Jove!'

We may not be quite so aware that we are also fairly well acquainted with much non-Classical mythology. After all, the British Isles were, for some five centuries, dominated by the Saxons, and their own Nordic mythology passed into our language. Most of the days of the week are named after gods: Tuesday is named after Tiw or Tyr, the Teutonic god of war. (This was the Roman equivalent of Mars, so it is no coincidence that the French for Tuesday is *mardi*, after Mars.) Wednesday is named after Woden, the father of the Gods; Thursday after Thor, the god of thunder; and Friday after Freya, the wife of Woden. We are also well acquainted with such terms as Valhalla, the home of the Gods, and Ragnarok, the Nordic Armageddon. And probably because of the operas of Richard Wagner, we will be acquainted with the adventures of Siegfried which are fundamental to Norse mythology.

And then there are the many Turkish, Persian and Indian legends that found their way into the *Arabian Nights*. We remember them more today as fairy tales, or maybe just as material for Christmas pantomimes, and forget that these are every bit a part of distant myths and legends as any of the Greek and Nordic tales.

Britain, of course, has its own myths and legends. One has only to think of King Arthur or Robin Hood to consider two of the most popular characters in folklore. Folklore is only another term for legends although, for some reason, probably due to the influence of the Brothers Grimm, folklore has come to be more associated with fairy-tales, and thus with stories for children. But myths and folktales should not be reserved solely for children. In my own mind there is no difference between traditional fairy-tales, folklore, myths or legends. Indeed, the key word is 'tradition'. These are stories that captured the imagination and have been passed from generation to generation. Embellished and finely honed by the story teller's craft, such legends have, in fact, become some of our very best and most popular stories, and can and should be enjoyed by readers of all ages.

Legends don't have to be that old, and can frequently be replenished. We have only to think of our own legends of the Loch Ness monster or Jack the Ripper to know how events of fairly recent vintage can pass into the myth of the nation. Anything that captures the public imagination will do that. During the First World War Arthur Machen wrote a story called 'The Bowmen' which overnight created the legend of the Angel of Mons and this has been perpetuated ever since. A legend, quite clearly, is any story which strikes a chord with the public, regardless of whether it is based on fact.

And that is true of every nation. There is not a culture on earth that does not have its own traditional stories of far-off days and wonders. Stories which help explain the world about us and which bring with them keys which enable us to unlock the experience of others.

This volume gathers together a selection of those myths, legends and folk-tales. I have cast the net wide to include as many countries and cultures as I could, although far fewer than I would have liked. I have also sought to select a mixture of stories, some of which will be familiar and thus serve as home territory, so to speak, and many that you will probably not previously have encountered and yet will seem familiar – because that is the very magic of myth.

I have also tried to keep the selection varied in theme. It would be easy to have filled the anthology purely with stories of adventurous quests or heroic battles, but I wanted to show that myths cover the whole range of human experience.

For that reason I have set the stories in a sequence which parallels life. We start with birth or creation. Every culture has its own creation myths and some of the most colourful come from the tales of the native American Indians, a selection of which I have included here along with the Celtic legend of 'The Ever-Living Ones'.

We then enter our childhood, with our own struggles for self-discovery and identity. As we mature we set out on wider voyages of discovery and here I have included a range of stories of inner and outer quests from ancient Greece, Japan, Persia and India.

Our struggle for identity and our quests for discovery may make us into mighty heroes or heroines, and no book of myths would be complete without a few of their adventures. I have selected these from various nations of Europe, including some of the most famous Greek myths.

Warriors will naturally venture into battle, and I have included several stories of war and conquest from Europe and North America. But there is one thing that will conquer all heroes – love. And to show how universal that is I have included a wide range of stories about love, revenge and self-sacrifice from cultures the world over.

With maturity comes wisdom and with wisdom may come an exploration of more mystical or magical worlds. In this section I have included a variety of stories about magic, faith, monsters, and the mysteries of the world about us including the wonder of nature and the animal world.

The mysteries of life will lead us to consider the mysteries of death, and the anthology closes with a series of stories which seek to explore fate, death and the world beyond.

These divisions are there to provide some structure and cohesion to the volume and hopefully add to the enjoyment. They are, though, fairly arbitrary, as many myths include one or more of these themes and in the final analysis I have sorted stories into which I felt was the most satisfactory sequence.

Many of the stories are selected from the writings of Victorian explorers and antiquarians who were able to convey the thrill of their discoveries and were the first to begin the still unfinished task of identifying and cataloguing the world's myths and legends. Some of these stories I have edited to exclude any excesses of Victorian moralism, but most were compiled by master story-tellers and are left as written.

I have also been helped by Jessica Amanda Salmonson and Peter Tremayne. Jessica is an American writer and anthologist who has long been fascinated with legends, especially those from the Orient and from her native soil. Peter Tremayne, under his real persona of Peter Berresford Ellis, is an established authority on Celtic myth, history and culture, and he has provided several stories using a variety of Celtic backgrounds.

In total there are over fifty stories of ancient wonder. I hope this anthology serves as a key to open the door to the magic of the past, and to open the mind to the wonders of the world about us, and perhaps even to open the heart to the romance of legend. It stole my heart years ago, and it is a love that has never failed.

Mike Ashley,
Walderslade,
December 1994

PART I:

THE DAWN OF TIME

Irish

THE EVER-LIVING ONES

Peter Tremayne

IT WAS THE time of primal chaos; a time when the Earth was new and undefined. Arid deserts and black bubbling volcanoes, covered by swirling clouds of gases, scarred the grim visage of the newborn world. It was, as yet, the time of the great void.

Then into that oblivion, from the dull, dark heavens, there came a trickle of water. First one drop, then another and another, until finally there gushed a mighty torrent down upon the earth. The divine waters from heaven flooded downwards and soaked into the arid dirt, cooled the volcanoes which turned into grey, granite mountains, and life began to spring forth across the Earth. The dark, redden skies, grew light and blue.

From the darkened soil there grew a tree, tall and strong. Danu, the divine waters from heaven, nurtured and cherished this great tree which became the sacred oak named Bíle. Of the conjugation of Danu and Bíle there dropped two giant acorns. The first acorn was male. From it sprang The Dagda, 'The Good God'. The second seed was female. From it there emerged Brigantu, or Brigid, 'The Exalted One'. And The Dagda and Brigid gazed upon one another in wonder for it was their task to wrest order from the primal chaos and to people the Earth with the Children of Danu, the Mother Goddess, whose divine waters had given them life.

So there, by the divine waters of Danu, from where those waters rose and flooded through the now fertile green valleys of the Earth, eastwards towards a distant sea, The Dagda and Brigid settled. And they called the great course of eastward rushing water after the Mother Goddess, which is Danuvius, whose children still know it as the mighty Danube. And four great, bright cities they built there on its broad banks in which the Children of Danu would live and thrive.

The four cities were Falias, Gorias, Finias and Murias.

The Dagda became their father, thus humankind call him 'The Father of the Gods'. And Brigid became the wise-one, exalted in learning and much did she imbibe from the mighty Danu and from Bíle, the sacred oak. She was hailed as the mother of healing, of craftsmanship and of poetry; indeed, she excelled in all-knowledge. She showed her children that true wisdom was only to be garnered from the feet of Danu, the Mother Goddess, and so only to be found at the water's edge. Those who gathered such knowledge, also paid deference to Bíle, the sacred oak. Because they were not allowed to speak his holy name, they called the oak *draoi* and those learned in such knowledge were said to possess oak (*dru*) knowledge (*vid*) and thus were known as Druids.

The knowledge of the Children of Danu grew and each of their four great cities prospered. In Falias they held a sacred stone called the Lia Fáil or Stone of Destiny, which, when a righteous ruler set foot on it, would shout with joy; in Gorias, where Urias of the Noble Nature dwelt, they held a mighty sword called the 'Retaliator', fashioned before the time of the gods themselves, and which Urias presented to Lugh Lámhfada, who became the greatest warrior among the gods; in Finias, they held a magic spear, called 'The Red Javelin', which, once cast, would find its enemy no matter where he hid; and in Murias they held the 'Cauldron of Plenty' from which The Dagda could feed entire nations and it still would not be emptied.

For many aeons, the Children of Danu grew and prospered in their beautiful cities.

Then, one day, The Dagda, Father of the Gods, and Brigid, the Exalted One, called their children to them.

'You have tarried here long enough. The Earth needs to be peopled and needs your wisdom to advise and direct them so that they may live lives of virtue and merit. Our Mother, Danu, has directed you to move towards the place where the bright Sun vanishes each evening.'

'Why should we go there?' demanded Nuada, the favourite son of The Dagda.

'Because it is your destiny,' replied Brigid.

'And you, Nuada, shall lead your brothers and sisters, and their children, and the land that you shall come to will be called Inisfáil, the Island of Destiny. There shall you abide until your destiny is fulfilled.'

'If it is our destiny,' said another of The Dagda's sons, named Ogma, 'then we shall accept it.'

Ogma was the most handsome of the Children of Danu. From his long curly hair, the rays of the sun shone and he was called Ogma *grian-aineacg*, of the Sunny Countenance. To him fell the gift of honeyed words, of poetry and of languages, and he, it was, who devised how man could write in a form of calligraphy which was named after him as Ogham.

Brigid smiled at her eager children.

'I am allowed to give you one word of warning. When you reach Inisfáil you will find another people who will claim the Island of Destiny as their own. This people are the Children of Domnu, who is the sister of our mother Danu. But beware, for Domnu is not as Danu. For each sister is the inverse of the other, as winter is to summer.'

'Then,' Nuada said, 'should we not take something to defend ourselves with, less the Children of Domnu fight us for the possession of Inisfáil?'

The Dagda gazed at them kindly and replied: 'You may take the four great treasures of the cities of Falias, Gorias, Finias and Murias.'

And the Children of Danu took the treasures and they went to the mountains overlooking the headwaters of the Danuvius, the divine waters from heaven, and ascended in a great cloud which bore them westward to Inisfáil, the Island of Destiny. And among them were three beautiful young sisters who were the wives of the sons of Ogma. Their names were Banba, Fótla and Éire and each sister nurtured an ambition that this new land of Inisfáil would one day be named after her.

* * *

Night wrapped her darkened mantle over Magh Tuireadh, which is called the Plain of Towers, which lay in the west of the land of Inisfáil. On each side of the great plain, separated by the River Unius, myriads of small campfires glowed in the gloom. Two armies had gathered for combat.

Seven years had passed since the Children of Danu had landed in their cloud on the shores of the Island of Destiny. They had fought initially with a strange race of people called the Firbolg who challenged their right to rule in the Island of Destiny. These they had met at the Pass of Balgatan and the conflict went on for four days. And in that conflict there came forth a champion of the Firbolg named Sreng who challenged Nuada, the leader of the Children of Danu, to single combat. So strong and mighty was Sreng that, with one sweep of his great sword, he cut off Nuada's right hand.

But the Firbolg and their king, Eochaidh, were defeated and dispersed.

Dian Cécht, the god of all physicians, came to Nuada after the battle and fashioned him an artificial hand of silver, so strong and supple, that it was little different from the real hand. Thus did Nuada receive his full name Nuada Argetlámh, of the Silver Hand. Because he was maimed, the other Children of Danu had to choose another of their number to lead them, for they had been told by Brigid that no one with a blemish must rule them. In choosing a new leader, they made a disastrous choice. As an act of conciliation between themselves and the Children of Domnu, they chose Bres, son of Elatha, king of the Children of Domnu who were also known as the Fomorii, or those who dwelt beneath the sea. And to further consolidate the alliance, Dian Cécht married Ethne, the daughter of the foremost Fomorii warrior named Balor of the One Eye. And the condition was that if Bres did anything which displeased the Children of Danu then he would abdicate and depart in peace.

Those years marked a period of strife. Bres, being a Fomorii, refused to keep his word and began to lay heavy burdens on the Children of Danu. For a while Bres and the Children of Domnu, the children of darkness and evil, dominated the land, and the Children of Danu, the children of light and goodness, were helpless and as slaves.

Then finally, Miach, the son of Dian Cécht, aided by his sister, the beautiful Airmid, fashioned a new hand of flesh and bone for Nuada. His hand replaced Dian Cécht's silver one and now, without blemish, Nuada reclaimed the leadership of the Children of Danu. So jealous was Dian Cécht of his son's achievement that he slew Miach. But that is another story.

Nuada chased Bres back to the land of the Fomorii where Bres demanded that Elatha, his father, provide him with an army to punish the Children of Danu.

Thus, on the plain where ancient megaliths stood, thrusting their dark granite skywards, Magh Tuireadh, the Plain of Towers, on the evening of the Feast of Samhain (31 October), the Children of Danu faced the Children of Domnu in battle.

At dawn the battle commenced. Combats broke out all along the line as Nuada led his warriors, both male and female, against the warriors of Bres and his Fomorii. Across the battlefield, the Mórrígán, Great Queen of Battles, with her sisters, Badh the Crow, Nemain the Venomous and Fea the Hateful, rushed hither and thither with their wailing cries which drove mortals to despair and death.

As time passed, Indech, a Fomorii warrior, approached Bres, and pointed out that whenever the Children of Danu were slain, or their weapons broken and destroyed, they would be carried from the field and, shortly after, would appear alive and well again with their weapons intact. Bres summoned his son, Ruadan, to his side and ordered him to discover the cause of the endless supply of weapons. And he summoned the son of Indech, a warrior named Octriallach, to discover how the Children of Danu, once slain, could come alive again.

Disguising himself as one of the Children of Danu, Ruadan went behind the lines of warriors and came across Goibhniu, god of smiths, who had set up a forge to one side of the Plain of Towers. With Goibhniu were Luchtainé, god of carpenters, and Credné, god of bronze workers. As each broken weapon was handed to Goibhniu, the smith-god gave it three blows of his hammer, which forged the head. Luchtainé gave the wood three blows of his axe and the shaft was fashioned. Then Credné fixed the shaft and head together with his bronze nails so swiftly that they needed no hammering.

Ruadan went back to his father and told him what he had seen. In a rage, Bres ordered his son to kill Goibhniu.

In the meantime, Octriallach had found a mystic spring on the other side of the Plain of Towers at which stood Dian Cécht, the god of medicine, with his daughter Airmid at his side. Whenever one of the Children of Danu were slain, they were brought to the spring and Dian Cécht and his daughter plunged the body into the spring and they reemerged alive again. In a rage, Bres ordered Octriallach to destroy the healing spring.

Ruadan returned to the forge and asked for a javelin from Goibhniu who gave it without suspicion, thinking Ruadan was one of the Children of Danu. No sooner was the weapon in his hand, than Ruadan turned and cast it at Goibhniu. It went clean through the smith-god's body. Mortally wounded as he was, Goibhniu picked up the spear and threw it back, wounding Ruadan who crawled away back to his father and died at his feet. The Fomorii set up a great *caoine*, or keening, which was the first ever heard in the Island of Destiny.

Goibhniu also crawled away and came to the spring where Dian Cécht and Airmid plunged him in and he emerged healthy and healed.

That night, however, Octriallach, son of Indech, and several of his companions, came to the spring and each took a large stone from the bed of a nearby river and dropped them into the spring until they had filled it. So the healing waters were dispersed.

Bres, satisfied the Children of Danu were now mortal, and angered by the death of his son, determined that a pitched battle should be fought. The next morning, spears and lances and swords smote against buckler and shield. The whistle of darts and rattle of arrows and shouting of warriors made it seem as if a great thunder was rolling over the Plain of Towers. The River of Unius, which cut through the plain, was stopped up, so filled was it with dead bodies. The plain was red with blood, so cruel was the battle.

Indech of the Fomorii fell by the hand of Ogma. And Indech was not the first nor last of the leaders of the Fomorii to feel the steel of the Children of Danu.

Neither did the Children of Danu go away from the battle unscathed.

To the field of slaughter came Balor of the Evil Eye, son of Buarainench, the most formidable of the Fomorii champions. He had one great eye whose gaze was so malevolent that it destroyed whosoever looked upon it. So large and awesome was this eye that it took nine attendants, using hooks, to lift the mighty lid to open it for Balor. It happened on that fateful day of the battle that Balor came upon Nuada of the Silver Hand the leader of the Children of Danu, and hard and fierce was the contest. Yet in the end, after shield was shattered, after spear was bent and sword was broken into pieces, it was the blood of Nuada that gushed in a never-ending stream into the earth of the Island of Destiny. And not content in this slaughter, but Balor turned upon one of Nuada's beautiful wives, Macha the Personification of Battles, goddess of warriors, and slew her also. Nor did Dian Cécht have the means to restore life to them.

At the death of their leader, the Children of Danu wavered and became fearful.

It was then that Lugh Lámhfada, Lugh of the Long Arm, approached the battlefield. Now Lugh was the son of Cian, which means 'Enduring One', who was in turn son of Cainte, the god of speech. Now the council of the Children of Danu had forbidden him to come to the battle, for Lugh was all-wise and all-knowledgeable and it was thought that his life was too valuable to risk in battle for his was the wisdom needed to serve humankind. Indeed, so wise was Lugh, that Nuada had let him become ruler of the Children of Danu for thirteen days in order that they might receive his wisdom. Therefore the Children of Danu had him imprisoned for his own safety during the battle with nine warriors to guard him. But on hearing Nuada was slain, Lugh escaped his prison and his guards and, leaping into his chariot, he hurried to join his brothers and sisters on the Plain of Towers.

Bres was standing triumphantly with his Fomorii warriors when he saw a great light in the west.

'I wonder that the sun is rising in the west today,' he muttered, scratching his head.

One of the Fomorii shamans approached Bres trembling.

'It is not the sun, mighty Bres. The light stems from the countenance of Lugh Lámhfada! It is his radiance.'

Lugh, with his weapons sheathed, drove his chariot out from the lines of the Children of Danu; straight he drove up to the tightly packed lines of Fomorii champions.

'Where is Balor?' he cried. 'Let him who thinks himself a great warrior come forward and be taught the truth!'

The lines of Fomorii parted and the great figure of Balor was seen, seated on a gigantic chair. His one mighty eye was closed.

Lugh's challenge rang out again.

This time Balor heard it and said to his attendants: 'Lift up my eyelid that I may gaze upon this prattling little man.'

The attendants began to lift Balor's eye with a hook. They stood well out of range. For anyone on whom that eye fell upon would perish immediately.

Lugh was ready with a sling and in it set a *tathlum*, a slingshot made of blood mixed with the sand of the swift Armorian sea. As the lid was lifted, Lugh hurled his shot into the eye. It struck it, went through the brain and out the back of Balor's head. The great Fomorii champion's eye was knocked out and fell on the ground. In its dying glint, thrice nine companies of Fomorii warriors were destroyed for they saw its malignant gaze.

Balor fell screaming to the ground in blindness.

A great anxiety fell on the Fomorii.

Lugh now raised his sword, and the Mórrígán set up a paean of victory: 'Kings arise to the battle . . . .!' And so, the Children of Danu took heart, and echoing the song they began to move forward. Great was the slaughter now as they pressed back on the Children of Domnu. It is said that more Fomorii were killed on the Plain of Towers than there were stars in the sky or grains of sand on the seashore, or snowflakes in winter.

And Lugh came upon Bres, who was fleeing for his life from the battlefield.

'Spare my life, Lugh, great conqueror,' cried the son of Elatha, sinking to his knees, for he no longer had the strength nor spirit to fight. 'Spare it, and I will pay whatever ransom you require.'

'What ransom?' demanded Lugh, his sword held at the throat of the Fomorii leader.

'I will guarantee that there will be no shortage of milk from the cows of this land,' offered Bres.

Lugh then called the Children of Danu to him.

'What good is that if Bres cannot lengthen the lives of the cows?' they demanded.

Bres could not grant longer lives so he offered: 'If my life is spared, every wheat harvest in Inisfáil will be a good one.'

'We already have enough good harvests. We need no other guarantees.'

Finally, Bres agreed to instruct the Children of Danu as to the best times to plough, sow and reap and for this knowledge, which they had not, they spared his life.

And when the battle was over, when the Fomorii were pursued back into their undersea fortresses, and they accepted the right of the Children of Danu to live in peace on the Island of Destiny and rule over it as gods and goddesses of goodness and of light, the Mórrígán went to all the summits of the highest mountains of the island and on each summit she proclaimed the victory of the gods and goddesses of light and goodness. And she sang in triumphant voice a paean to the Mother Goddess, Danu.

> Peace mounts to the heavens
> The divine waters descend to earth
> And fructify our lives
> Earth lies under the heavens
> We are of the Earth now
> And everyone is strong . . .

And while Danu smiled on the victory of her children, her sister Domnu scowled from the depths of the earth and she chose the goddess Badh the Crow as her mouth to utter a prophecy to Danu and her children.

'All life is transitory. Even your Children are not immortal, my sister. The time will come when they will be defeated. The time will come when no one will want gods and goddesses to nurture them, when they will be driven into the darkness like my Children have been this day.

'The time approaches when the summers of Inisfáil will be flowerless, when the cows shall be without milk, and the men will be weak and the women shall be shameless; the seas will be without fish, the trees without fruit and old men will give false judgements; the judges will make unjust laws and honour will count for little and warriors will betray each other and resort to thievery. There will come a time when there will be no more virtue left in this world.'

* * *

Indeed, there came that time when the Children of Míl flooded into the Island of Destiny and when the Children of Danu were driven underground into the hills, which were called *sídhe*, which is pronounced *shee*, and in those mounds they dwelt, the once mighty gods and goddesses, deserted by the very people who they had sought to nourish. The descendants of Míl, who live in the Island of Destiny to this day, called the Children of Danu, the *aes sídhe*, the people of the hills, and when even the religion of Míl was forgotten, when the religion of the Cross replaced that of the Circle, the people simply called the *aes sídhe* by the name of fairies.

Of the greatest of the gods, the victor of the battle on the Plain of Towers, Lugh Lámhfada, god of all-knowledge, patron of all arts and crafts, his name is still known today. But as memory of the mighty warrior, the invincible god, has faded, he is known only as *Lugh-chromain*, little stooping Lugh of the *sídhe*, relegated to the role of a fairy craftsman. And, as even the language in which he was venerated has disappeared, all that is left of the supreme god of the Children of Danu is the distorted form of that name *Lugh-chromain* . . . leprechaun.

THE STAR MAIDS

Jessica Amanda Salmonson

THE STARMAIDS AND THE FLEA MAN

FIVE MAIDENS LIVED happily in the sky. They played together every night. Flea Man decided to marry all of them, so he hopped upward to catch them.

The star maids saw him coming and flew toward the East. They were swift, but Flea Man was persistent.

'That awful Flea Man is still coming,' said Moki-girl.

Moki was formerly a robin. She was the sister of that bad trickster Coyote. When she had to marry Salamander against her will, she fooled him into jumping into a hot spring so that he boiled to death.

'We should run faster!' said Kipi-girl.

Kipi was the famous girl who cut out Coyote's tongue to cook it, and it took him a very long time to grow another.

'If we make love to old scratchy,' said Tewe-girl, 'we'll go bald.'

Tewe's daughter was the well known Rabbit Huntress, who was strong like her mother.

'He's not strong enough to catch us,' said Pahalali.

Pahalali was the daughter of Frog-maid. Frog-maid was a warrior who battled the moon-devouring lizard. Every month, when the moon was nearly eaten by the lizard, Pahalali's mother ran forth with weapons to chase away the lizard and restore the moon.

'We'll go this way,' said Tukwishhemish. 'When Flea Man goes to sleep, we'll surely lose him.'

Tukwishhemish was the leader of the star maids. She was

a very clever girl and always decided their course across the night sky.

Flea Man went to sleep in the morning. When he woke up the next night, the star maids were way over by the horizon. 'Oh! My wives!' he shouted, and streaked eagerly across heaven.

'Here he comes again,' said Moki-girl.

'Let's get running,' said Kipi-girl.

'Is he close?' asked Tewe-girl.

'He's gaining,' said Pahalali.

'Let's go under the sea,' said Tukwishhemish, and led her companions downward.

The five star maids vanished under the sea. When they came back out, Flea Man still hopped after them, scratching and loping the whole way.

'Well, it's no use running,' said Moki.

'He'll never give up,' said Kipi.

'We'll have to try something desperate,' said Tewe.

'Let's kill him,' said Pahalali.

The star maids stopped running and turned around to face Flea Man.

'Come any closer,' Tukwishhemish warned, 'and we'll tear you to pieces.'

They stood their ground and Flea Man was afraid to come any closer. To this day, the five women are close together in the sky. Flea Man is that little speck of a star a little to one side.

THE STAR MAIDENS' LAUGHTER

Moki, Kipi, Tewe and Pahalali were happy star maids and always laughing. But Tukwishhemish never laughed. Moki and Kipi slept side by side in the daytime, just as Tewe and Pahalali slept side by side. At night, they woke up to play and laugh.

But Tukwishhemish had no partner. She was the prettiest of the five and the others courted her, but she rebuffed their intimacy. In the daytime she slept alone.

One day, Tukwishhemish's companions leapt on her and held her down, tickling her all over her body. This made her open up her mouth and laugh. The others saw that she had two rows of teeth in her mouth! They laughed so hard that Tukwishhemish left them to live on the earth.

The star maids were sad without her. They came down from the sky to find her. They met Old-Mother-With-Dogs. She said, 'Tukwishhemish was adopted by Thunder Woman. The Thunder's daughter lures men and women to their deaths in the mountains. It is too late ever to reclaim her, so you girls had better fly back up to the sky.'

But the star maids would not stop looking. They sought Tukwishhemish despite the warning of Old-Mother-With-Dogs.

They spied Tukwishhemish high on a mountain carrying a basket of ice balls and arrows on her back. These she threw down at the star maids, but they dodged the ice balls and arrows. Then Tukwishhemish went down from the mountain through thorn bushes that opened in front of her and closed behind her. The star maids were scratched and bloodied, but would not give up the chase.

Tukwishhemish led them into the Valley of Rattlesnakes, while Thunder Mother shouted in the sky, waking up the serpents. So the star maids put on thick moccasins that went up to their knees and kept after Tukwishhemish.

But when they came to the Valley of Old Age, a thousand years went by in a second. The star maids became whitehaired and slow.

'We'll never catch her now,' said Moki-hag.

'I'm so tired,' said Kipi-hag.

'Let's stop here and rest,' said Tewe-hag.

'But if we delay,' said Pahalali, 'we'll continue to get older and then we'll die.'

They talked it over and all agreed they would rather die than live without Tukwishhemish. Therefore they sat down in the Valley of Old Age and waited. Tukwishhemish sent a magic bird which plucked out four of its feathers. These the star hags put in their hair and were made young and strong. They followed the magic bird through the air and came to the Sweat Lodge of Thunder Mother. Steam was pouring out of the mountain peak of the Sweat Lodge. The star maids went into the lodge and sat at the feet of Tukwishhemish and Thunder Mother.

'Come back with us to our home in the sky,' said Pahalali.

'We have missed you so much,' said the rest.

And Tukwishhemish opened her mouth wide and laughed for joy.

BEARSKIN WOMAN AND GRIZZLY WOMAN

Jessica Amanda Salmonson

BEARSKIN WOMAN DREAMED of the spirit called Double Moon Woman, who only *kwame*[1] dream about. Thereby she knew where her future lay. She went into the forest and met a grizzly bear. They got along so well that Bearskin Woman went to live with Grizzly Woman in a cave.

When her father and brothers learned of it, they were furious. They gathered together some braves and surrounded the bear cave, intending to slay Grizzly Woman. But Bearskin Woman had also become a bear, due to an amulet that she had made. The two bears rushed out to confront Bearskin Woman's brothers, father, and the many braves that had accompanied them. The she-bears killed many who had set their faces against the bears. Only when Bearskin Woman's sister Sinopa stood before her did the two bears stop slaughtering.

The survivors had run off, so Bearskin Woman took her former shape and told her sister, 'Return to the tribe and tell them I have dreamed of Double Moon Woman and I am happy with Grizzly Woman in our cave together. We are holy women and cannot be destroyed. We will bring good luck to everyone, and cause the land to be green and fruitful, unless they trouble us again.'

The tribe was satisfied by this explanation, and were even glad to have holy women living in the forest with promises of good luck. But the six brothers felt insulted that their own sister and her bear-lover had defeated them and killed many of their

[1]lesbians

friends. They weren't about to let the women get away with it. So they gathered together a large number of prickly pear cacti. They slipped up to the cave in the deep of night and strew the prickly pears at the entrance. Then they made war-hollers and woke up Grizzly Woman and Bearskin Woman, who came running out, fierce and growling.

They got prickly pears in their paws, and roared with pain and anger. Even so, they came across the barrier so swiftly that the six brothers knew they would be defeated a second time.

Their younger sister Sinopa appeared from behind a bush. She had a bow and arrows. She didn't want any of her family killed, so she shot an arrow over the heads of her brothers, and it flew a great distance. As it was a magic arrow, her six brothers found themselves suddenly a surprising distance away, where the arrow had landed.

The two she-bears pursued. They were gaining on the brothers who were running across the prairie. Wherever the blood of the two bears' cactus-pierced feet touched the ground, trees sprang up. Wherever they angrily dug their claws into the earth, lakes appeared.

The six brothers were caught and scattered about the prairie like sticks. They got to their feet and ran to the biggest tree that had grown from the bloody footprints of the she-bears. Grizzly Woman and Bearskin Woman sat down underneath the tree and licked their paws. The six brothers knew that if they fell asleep, they would tumble out of the tree and be eaten.

Their little sister Sinopa appeared unexpectedly at the very top of the tree. She drew forth one of her arrows and fired it into heaven. One of her brothers vanished from the tree and became a star. She shot another arrow, and another, until all six brothers became stars. Then she rode upon the bow, which was the Moon, and joined her brothers, so that she was queen of six princes of heaven, and the seven stars are visible to this day.

Bearskin Woman and Grizzly Woman lived happily for many years. When they died, they became the Two Bears of Heaven, and still chase the six princes around and around the sky.

PART II:

YOUTH AND SELF-DISCOVERY

THE QUEST FOR DISCOVERY

Andrew Lang

In olden times a young woman called Aethra bore a son. This was her only comfort, and she thought that she saw in him a likeness to his father, whose true name she did not know. Certainly he was a very beautiful baby, well formed and strong, and, as soon as he could walk he was apt to quarrel with other children of his own age, and fight with them in a harmless way. He never was an amiable child, though he was always gentle to his mother. From the first he was afraid of nothing, and when he was about four or five he used to frighten his mother by wandering from home, with his little bow and arrows, and staying by himself in the woods. However, he always found his own way back again, sometimes with a bird or a snake that he had shot, and once dragging the body of a fawn that was nearly as heavy as himself. Thus his mother, from his early boyhood, had many fears for him, that he might be killed by some fierce wild boar in the woods, for he would certainly shoot at whatever beast he met; or that he might kill some other boy in a quarrel, when he would be obliged to leave the country. The other boys, however, soon learned not to quarrel with Theseus (so Aethra had named her son), for he was quick of temper, and heavy of hand, and, as for the wild beasts, he was cool as well as eager, and seemed to have an untaught knowledge of how to deal with them.

Aethra was therefore very proud of her son, and began to hope that when he was older he would be able to roll away the great stone in the glen. She told him nothing about it when he was little, but, in her walks with him in the woods or on the sea shore, she would ask him to try his force in lifting large stones. When he succeeded she kissed and praised him, and told him stories of the famous strong man, Heracles, whose name was well known through all Greece. Theseus could not bear to be beaten at lifting any weight, and, if he failed, he would rise early and try again in the morning, for many men, as soon as they rise from bed, can lift weights which are too heavy for them later in the day.

When Theseus was seven years old, Aethra found for him a tutor, named Connidas, who taught him the arts of netting beasts and hunting, and how to manage the dogs, and how to drive a chariot, and wield sword and shield, and to throw the spear. Other things Connidas taught him which were known to few men in Greece, for Connidas came from the great rich island of Crete. He had killed a man there in a quarrel, and fled to Troezene to escape the revenge of the man's brothers and cousins. In Crete many people could read and write, which in Greece, perhaps none could do, and Connidas taught Theseus this learning.

When he was fifteen years old, Theseus went, as was the custom of young princes, to the temple of Delphi, not to ask questions, but to cut his long hair, and sacrifice it to the god, Apollo. He cut the forelock of his hair, so that no enemy, in battle, might take hold of it, for Theseus intended to fight at close quarters, hand to hand, in war, not to shoot arrows and throw spears from a distance. By this time he thought himself a man, and was always asking where his father was, while Aethra told him how her husband had left her soon after their marriage, and that she had never heard of him since, but that some day Theseus might find out all about him for himself, which no other person would ever be able to do.

Aethra did not wish to tell Theseus too soon the secret of the great stone, which hid she knew not what. She saw that he would leave her and go to seek his father, if he was able to raise the stone and find out the secret, and she could not bear to lose him, now that day by day he grew more like his father, her lost lover. Besides, she wanted him not to try to raise the stone till he came to his strength. But when he was in his nineteenth year, he told her that he would now go all over Greece and the whole world seeking for his father. She saw that he meant what he said, and one day she led him alone to the glen where the great stone lay, and sat down with him there, now talking, and now silent as if she were listening to the pleasant song of the burn that fell from a height into a clear deep pool. Really she was listening to make sure that no hunter and no lovers were near them in the wood, but she only heard the songs of the water and the birds, no voices, or cry of hounds, or fallen twig crackling under a footstep.

At last, when she was quite certain that nobody was near, she whispered, and told Theseus how her husband, before he disappeared, had taken her to this place, and shown her the great moss-grown boulder, and said that, when his son could lift that stone away, he would find certain tokens, and that he must then do what the gods put into his heart. Theseus listened eagerly, and said, 'If my father lifted that stone, and placed under it certain tokens, I also can lift it, perhaps not yet, but some day I shall be as strong a man as my father.' Then he set himself to move the stone, gradually putting out all his force, but it seemed rooted in the earth, though he tried it now on one side and now on another. At last he flung himself at his mother's feet, with his head in the grass, and lay without speaking. His breath came hard and quick, and his hands were bleeding. Aethra laid her hand on his long hair, and was silent. 'I shall not lose my boy this year,' she thought.

They were long in that lonely place, but at last Theseus rose, and kissed his mother, and stretched his arms. 'Not today!' he said, but his mother thought in her heart, 'Not for many a day, I hope!' Then they walked home to the house of Pittheus, saying little, and when they had taken supper, Theseus said that he would go to bed and dream of better fortune. So he arose, and went to his own chamber, which was built apart in the court of the palace, and soon Aethra too went to sleep, not unhappy, for her boy, she thought, would not leave her for a long time.

But in the night Theseus arose, and put on his shoes, and his smock, and a great double mantle. He girt on his sword of bronze, and went into the housekeeper's chamber, where he took a small skin of wine, and some food. These he placed in a wallet which he slung round his neck by a cord, and, lastly he stole out of the court, and walked to the lonely glen, and to the pool in the burn near which the great stone lay. Here he folded his purple mantle of fine wool round him, and lay down to sleep in the grass, with his sword lying near his hand.

When he awoke the clear blue morning light was round him, and all the birds were singing their song to the dawn. Theseus arose, threw off his mantle and smock, and plunged into the cold pool of the burn, and then he drank a little of the wine, and ate of the bread and cold meat, and set himself to move the stone. At the first effort, into which he put all his strength, the stone stirred. With the second he felt it rise a little way from the ground, and then he lifted with all the might in his heart and body, and rolled the stone clean over.

Beneath it there was nothing but the fresh turned soil, but in a hollow of the foot of the rock, which now lay uppermost, there was a wrapping of purple woollen cloth, that covered something. Theseus tore out the packet, unwrapped the cloth, and found within it a wrapping of white linen. This wrapping was in many folds, which he undid, and at last he found a pair of shoon, such as kings wear, adorned with gold, and also the most beautiful sword that he had ever seen. The handle was of clear rock crystal, and through the crystal you could see gold, inlaid with pictures of a lion hunt done in different shades of gold and silver. The sheath was of leather, with patterns in gold nails, and the blade was of bronze, a beautiful pattern ran down the centre to the point, the blade was straight, and double edged, supple, sharp, and strong. Never had Theseus seen so beautiful a sword, nor one so well balanced in his hand.

He saw that this was a king's sword; and he thought that it had not been wrought in Greece, for in Greece was no sword-smith that could do such work. Examining it very carefully he found characters engraved beneath the hilt, not letters such as the Greeks used in later times, but such Cretan signs as Connidas had taught him to read, for many a weary hour, when he would like to have been following the deer in the forest.

Theseus pored over these signs till he read: 'Icmalius me made. Of Aegeus of Athens am I.'

Now he knew the secret. His father was Aegeus, the king of Athens. Theseus had heard of him and knew that he yet lived, a sad life full of trouble. For Aegeus had no child by his Athenian wife, and the fifty sons of his brother, Pallas (who were called the Pallantidae) despised him, and feasted all day in his hall, recklessly and fiercely, robbing the people, and Aegeus had no power in his own kingdom.

'Methinks that my father has need of me!' said Theseus to himself. Then he wrapped up the sword and shoon in the linen and the cloth of wool, and walked home in the early morning to the palace of Pittheus.

When Theseus came to the palace, he went straight to the upper chamber of his mother, where she was spinning wool with a distaff of ivory. When he laid before her the sword and the shoon, the distaff fell from her hand, and she hid her head in a fold of her robe. Theseus kissed her hands and comforted her, and she dried her eyes, and praised him for his strength. 'These are the sword and the shoon of your father,' she said, 'but truly the gods have taken away his strength and courage. For all men say that Aegeus of Athens is not master in his own house; his brother's sons rule him, and with them Medea, the witch woman, that once was the wife of Jason.'

'The more he needs his son!' said Theseus. 'Mother, I must go to help him, and be the heir of his kingdom, where you shall be with me always, and rule the people of Cecrops that fasten the locks of their hair with grasshoppers of gold.'

'So may it be, my child,' said Aethra, 'if the gods go with you to protect you. But you will sail to Athens in a ship with fifty oarsmen, for the ways by land are long, and steep, and dangerous, beset by cruel giants and monstrous men.'

'Nay, mother,' said Theseus, 'by land must I go, for I would not be known in Athens, till I see how matters fall out: and I would destroy these giants and robbers, and give peace to the people, and win glory among men. This very night I shall set forth.'

He had a sore and sad parting from his mother, but under cloud of night he went on his way, girt with the sword of Aegeus, his father, and carrying in his wallet the shoon with ornaments of gold.

* * *

Theseus walked through the night, and slept for most of the next day at a shepherd's hut. The shepherd was kind to him, and bade him beware of one called the Maceman, who guarded a narrow path with a sheer cliff above, and a sheer precipice below. 'No man born may deal with the Maceman,' said the shepherd, 'for his great club is of iron, that cannot be broken, and his strength is as the strength of ten men, though his legs have no force to bear his body. Men say that he is the son of the lame god, Hephaestus, who forged his iron mace; there is not the like of it in the world.'

'Shall I fear a lame man?' said Theseus, 'and is it not easy, even if he be so terrible a fighter, for me to pass him in the darkness, for I walk by night?'

The shepherd shook his head. 'Few men have passed Periphetes the Maceman,' said he, 'and wiser are they who trust to swift ships than to the upland path.'

'You speak kindly, father,' said Theseus, 'but I am minded to make the upland paths safe for all men.'

So they parted, and Theseus walked through the sunset and the dusk, always on a rising path, and the further he went the harder it was to see the way, for the path was overgrown with grass, and the shadows were deepening. Night fell, and Theseus hardly dared to go further, for on his left hand was a wall of rock, and on his right hand a cliff sinking sheer and steep to the sea. But now he saw a light in front of him, a red light flickering, as from a great fire, and he could not be content till he knew why that fire was lighted. So he went on, slowly and warily, till he came in full view of the fire which covered the whole of a little platform of rock; on one side the blaze shone up the wall of cliff on his left hand, on the other was the steep fall to the sea. In front of this fire was a great black bulk; Theseus knew not what it might be. He walked forward till he saw that the black bulk was that of a monstrous man, who sat with his back to the fire. The man nodded his heavy head, thick with red unshorn hair, and Theseus went up close to him.

'Ho, sir,' he cried, 'this is my road, and on my road I must pass!'

The seated man opened his eyes sleepily.

'Not without my leave,' he said, 'for I keep this way, I and my club of iron.'

'Get up and begone!' said Theseus.

'That were hard for me to do,' said the monstrous man, 'for my legs will not bear the weight of my body, but my arms are strong enough.'

'That is to be seen!' said Theseus, and he drew his sword,

and leaped within the guard of the iron club that the monster, seated as he was, swung lightly to this side and that, covering the whole width of the path. The Maceman swung the club at Theseus, but Theseus sprang aside, and in a moment, before the monster could recover his stroke, drove through his throat the sword of Aegeus, and he fell back dead.

'He shall have his rights of fire, that his shadow may not wander outside the House of Hades,' said Theseus to himself, and he toppled the body of the Maceman into his own great fire. Then he went back some way, and wrapping himself in his mantle, he slept till the sun was high in heaven, while the fire had sunk into its embers, and Theseus lightly sprang over them, carrying with him the Maceman's iron club. The path now led downwards, and a burn that ran through a green forest kept him company on the way, and brought him to pleasant farms and houses of men.

They marvelled to see him, a young man, carrying the club of the Maceman. 'Did you find him asleep?' they asked, and Theseus smiled and said, 'No, I found him awake. But now he sleeps an iron sleep, from which he will never waken, and his body had due burning in his own watchfire.' Then the men and women praised Theseus, and wove for him a crown of leaves and flowers, and sacrificed sheep to the gods in heaven, and on the meat they dined, rejoicing that now they could go to Troezene by the hill path, for they did not love ships and the sea.

When they had eaten and drunk, and poured out the last cup of wine on the ground, in honour of Hermes, the God of Luck, the country people asked Theseus where he was going? He said that he was going to walk to Athens, and at this the people looked sad. 'No man may walk across the neck of land where Ephyre is built,' they said, 'because above it Sinis the Pine-Bender has his castle, and watches the way.'

'And who is Sinis, and why does he bend pine trees?' asked Theseus.

'He is the strongest of men, and when he catches a traveller, he binds him hand and foot, and sets him between two pine trees. Then he bends them down till they meet, and fastens the traveller to the boughs of each tree, and lets them spring apart, so that the man is riven asunder.'

'Two can play at that game,' said Theseus, smiling, and he

bade farewell to the kind country people, shouldered the iron club of Periphetes, and went singing on his way. The path led him over moors, and past farm-houses, and at last rose towards the crest of the hill whence he would see the place where two seas would have met, had they not been sundered by the neck of land which is now called the Isthmus of Corinth. Here the path was very narrow, with thick forests of pine trees on each hand, and 'here,' thought Theseus to himself, 'I am likely to meet the Pine-Bender.'

Soon he knew that he was right, for he saw the ghastly remains of dead men that the pine trees bore like horrible fruit, and presently the air was darkened overhead by the waving of vultures and ravens that prey upon the dead. 'I shall fight the better in the shade,' said Theseus, and he loosened the blade of the sword in its sheath, and raised the club of Periphetes aloft in his hand.

Well it was for him that he raised the iron club, for, just as he lifted it, there flew out from the thicket something long, and slim, and black, that fluttered above his head for a moment, and then a loop at the end of it fell round the head of Theseus, and was drawn tight with a sudden jerk. But the loop fell also above and round the club, which Theseus held firm, pushing away the loop, and so pushed it off that it did not grip his neck. Drawing with his left hand his bronze dagger, he cut through the leather lasso with one stroke, and bounded into the bushes from which it had flown. Here he found a huge man, clad in the skin of a lion, with its head fitting to his own like a mask. The man lifted a club made of the trunk of a young pine tree, with a sharp-edged stone fastened into the head of it like an axe-head. But, as the monster raised his long weapon it struck on a strong branch of a tree above him, and was entangled in the boughs, so that Theseus had time to thrust the head of the iron club full in his face, with all his force, and the savage fell with a crash like a falling oak among the bracken. He was one of the last of an ancient race of savage men, who dwelt in Greece before the Greeks, and he fought as they had fought, with weapons of wood and stone.

Theseus dropped with his knees on the breast of the Pine-Bender, and grasped his hairy throat with both his hands, not to strangle him, but to hold him sure and firm till he came to himself again. When at last the monster opened his eyes, Theseus gripped his throat the harder, and spoke, 'Pine-Bender, for thee shall pines be bent. But I am a man and not a monster, and thou shalt die a clean death before thy body is torn in twain to be the last feast of thy vultures.' Then, squeezing the throat of the wretch with his left hand, he drew the sword of Aegeus, and drove it into the heart of Sinis the Pine-Bender, and he gave a cry like a bull's, and his soul fled from him. Then Theseus bound the body of the savage with his own leather cord, and, bending down the tops of two pine trees, he did to the corpse as Sinis had been wont to do to living men.

Lastly he cleaned the sword-blade carefully, wiping it with grass and bracken, and thrusting it to the hilt through the soft fresh ground under the trees, and so went on his way till he came to a little stream that ran towards the sea from the crest of the hill above the town of Ephyre, which is now called Corinth. But as he cleansed himself in the clear water, he heard a rustle in the boughs of the wood, and running with sword drawn to the place whence the sound seemed to come, he heard the whisper of a woman. Then he saw a strange sight. A tall and very beautiful girl was kneeling in the thicket, in a patch of asparagus thorn, and was weeping, and praying, in a low voice, and in a childlike innocent manner, to the thorns, begging them to shelter and defend her.

Theseus wondered at her, and, sheathing his sword, came softly up to her, and bade her have no fear. Then she threw her arms about his knees, and raised her face, all wet with tears, and bade him take pity upon her, for she had done no harm.

'Who are you, maiden? You are safe with me,' said Theseus. 'Do you dread the Pine-Bender?'

'Alas, sir,' answered the girl, 'I am his daughter, Perigyne, and his blood is on your hands.'

'Yet I do not war with women,' said Theseus, 'though that has been done which was decreed by the gods. If you follow with me, you shall be kindly used, and marry, if you will, a man of a good house, being so beautiful as you are.'

When she heard this, the maiden rose to her feet, and would have put her hand in his. 'Not yet,' said Theseus, kindly, 'till water has clean washed away that which is between thee and me. But wherefore, maiden, being in fear as you were, did you not call to the gods in heaven to keep you, but to the asparagus thorns that cannot hear or help?'

'My father, sir,' she said, 'knew no gods, but he came of the race of the asparagus thorns, and to them I cried in my need.'

Theseus marvelled at these words, and said, 'From this day you shall pray to Zeus, the Lord of Thunder, and to the other gods.' Then he went forth from the wood, with the maiden following, and wholly cleansed himself in the brook that ran by the way.

So they passed down to the rich city of Ephyre, where the king received him gladly, when he heard of the slaying of the Maceman, Periphetes, and of Sinis the Pine-Bender. The Queen, too, had pity on Perigyne, so beautiful she was, and kept her in her own palace. Afterwards Perigyne married a prince, Deiones, son of Eurytus, King of Oechalia, whom the strong man Heracles slew for the sake of his bow, the very bow with which Ulysses, many years afterwards, destroyed the Wooers in his halls. The sons of Perigyne and Deiones later crossed the seas to Asia, and settled in a land called Caria, and they never burned or harmed the asparagus thorn to which Perigyne had prayed in the thicket.

Greece was so lawless in these days that all the road from Troezene northward to Athens was beset by violent and lawless men. They loved cruelty even more than robbery, and each of them had carefully thought out his particular style of being cruel. The cities were small, and at war with each other, or at war among themselves, one family fighting against another for the crown. Thus there was no chance of collecting an army to destroy the monstrous men of the roads, which it would have been easy enough for a small body of archers to have done. Later Theseus brought all into great order, but now, being but one man, he went seeking adventures.

On the border of a small country called Megara, whose people were much despised in Greece, he found a chance of advancing himself, and gaining glory. He was walking in the middle of the day along a narrow path at the crest of a cliff above the sea, when he saw the flickering of a great fire in the blue air, and steam going up from a bronze cauldron of water that was set on the fire. On one side of the fire was a foot-bath of glittering bronze. Hard by was built a bower of green branches, very cool on that hot day, and from the door of the bower stretched a great thick hairy pair of naked legs.

Theseus guessed, from what he had been told, that the owner of the legs was Sciron the Kicker. He was a fierce outlaw who was called the Kicker because he made all travellers wash his feet, and, as they were doing so, kicked them over the cliff. Some say that at the foot of the cliff dwelt an enormous tortoise, which ate the dead and dying when they fell near his lair, but as tortoises do not eat flesh, generally, this may be a mistake. Theseus was determined not to take any insolence from Sciron, so he shouted—

'Slave, take those dirty legs of yours out of the way of a Prince.'

'Prince!' answered Sciron, 'if my legs are dirty, the gods are kind who have sent you to wash them for me.'

Then he got up, lazily, laughing and showing his ugly teeth, and stood in front of his bath with his heavy wooden club in his hand. He whirled it round his head insultingly, but Theseus was quicker than he, and again, as when he slew the Pine-Bender, he did not strike, for striking is slow compared to thrusting, but like a flash he lunged forward and drove the thick end of his iron club into the breast of Sciron. He staggered, and, as he reeled, Theseus dealt him a blow across the thigh, and he fell. Theseus seized the club which dropped from the hand of Sciron, and threw it over the cliff; it seemed long before the sound came up from the rocks on which it struck. 'A deep drop into a stony way, Sciron,' said Theseus, 'now wash my feet! Stand up, and turn your back to me, and be ready when I tell you.' Sciron rose, slowly and sulkily, and stood as Theseus bade him do.

Now Theseus was not wearing light shoes or sandals, like the golden sandals of Aegeus, which he carried in his wallet. He was wearing thick boots, with bronze nails in the soles, and the upper leathers were laced high up his legs, for the Greeks wore such boots when they took long walks on mountain roads. As soon as Theseus had trained Sciron to stand in the proper position, he bade him stoop to undo the lacings of his boots. As Sciron stooped, Theseus gave him one tremendous kick, that lifted him over the edge of the cliff, and there was an end of Sciron.

Theseus left the marches of Megara, and walked singing on his way, above the sea, for his heart was light, and he was finding adventures to his heart's desire. Being so young and well trained, his foot and hand, in a combat, moved as swift as lightning, and his enemies were older than he, and, though very strong, were heavy with full feeding, and slow to move. Now it is speed that wins in a fight, whether between armies or single men, if strength and courage go with it.

At last the road led Theseus down from the heights to a great fertile plain, called the Thriasian plain, not far from Athens. There, near the sea, stands the famous old city of Eleusis. When Hades, the God of the Dead, carried away beautiful Persephone, the daughter of Demeter, the Goddess of corn and all manner of grain, to his dark palace beside the stream of Ocean, it was to Eleusis that Demeter wandered. She was clad in mourning robes, and she sat down on a stone by the way, like a weary old woman. Now the three daughters of the king who then reigned in Eleusis came by, on the way to the well, to fetch water, and when they saw the old woman they set down their vessels and came round her, asking what they could do for her, who was so tired and poor. They said that they had a baby brother at home, who was the favourite of them all, and that he needed a nurse. Demeter was pleased with their kindness, and they left their vessels for water beside her, and ran home to their mother. Their long golden hair danced on their shoulders as they ran, and they came, out of breath, to their mother the Queen, and asked her to take the old woman to be their brother's nurse. The Queen was kind, too, and the old woman lived in their house, till Zeus, the chief God, made the God of the Dead send back Persephone, to be with her mother through spring, and summer, and early autumn, but in winter she must live with her husband in the dark palace beside the river of Ocean.

Then Demeter was glad, and she caused the grain to grow abundantly for the people of Eleusis, and taught them ceremonies, and a kind of play in which all the story of her sorrows and joy was acted. It was also taught that the souls of men do not die with the death of their bodies, any more than the seed of corn dies when it is buried in the dark earth, but that they live again in a world more happy and beautiful than ours. These ceremonies were called the Mysteries of Eleusis, and were famous in all the world.

Theseus might have expected to find Eleusis a holy city, peaceful and quiet. But he had heard, as he travelled, that in Eleusis was a strong bully, named Cercyon; he was one of the rough Highlanders of Arcadia, who lived in the hills of the centre of Southern Greece, which is called Peloponnesus. He is said to have taken the kingship, and driven out the descendants of the king whose daughters were kind to Demeter. The strong man used to force all strangers to wrestle with him, and, when he threw them, for he had never been thrown, he broke their backs.

Knowing this, and being himself fond of wrestling, Theseus walked straight to the door of the king's house, though the men in the town warned him, and the women looked at him with sad eyes. He found the gate of the courtyard open, with the altar of Zeus the high God smoking in the middle of it, and at the threshold two servants welcomed him, and took him to the polished bath, and women washed him, and anointed him with oil, and clothed him in fresh raiment, as was the manner in kings' houses. Then they led him into the hall, and he walked straight up to the high seats between the four pillars beside the hearth, in the middle of the hall.

There Cercyon sat, eating and drinking, surrounded by a score of his clan, great, broad, red-haired men, but he himself was the broadest and the most brawny. He welcomed Theseus, and caused a table to be brought, with meat, and bread, and wine, and when Theseus had put away his hunger, began to ask him who he was and whence he came. Theseus told him that he had walked from Troezene, and was on his way to the court of King Peleus (the father of Achilles), in the north, for he did not want the news of his coming to go before him to Athens.

'You walked from Troezene?' said Cercyon. 'Did you meet or hear of the man who killed the Maceman and slew the Pine-Benders, and kicked Sciron into the sea?'

'I walk fast, but news flies faster,' said Theseus.

'The news came through my second-sighted man,' said Cercyon, 'there he is, in the corner,' and Cercyon threw the leg bone of an ox at his prophet, who just managed to leap out of the way. 'He seems to have foreseen that the bone was coming at him,' said Cercyon, and all his frends laughed loud. 'He told us this morning that a stranger was coming, he who had killed the three watchers of the way. From your legs and shoulders, and the iron club that you carry, methinks you are that stranger?'

Theseus smiled, and moulded upwards, which the Greeks did when they meant 'Yes!'

'Praise be to all the gods!' said Cercyon. 'It is long since a good man came my way. Do they practise wrestling at Troezene?'

'Now and then,' said Theseus.

'Then you will try a fall with me? There is a smooth space strewn with sand in the courtyard.'

Theseus answered that he had come hoping that the kind would graciously honour him by trying a fall. Then all the wild guests shouted, and out they all went and made a circle round the wrestling-place, while Theseus and Cercyon threw down their clothes and were anointed with oil over their bodies. To it they went, each straining forward and feeling for a grip, till they were locked, and then they swayed this way and that, their stamping the ground; and now one would yield a little, now the other, while the rough guests shouted, encouraging each of them. At last they rested and breathed, and now the men began to bet; seven oxen to three was laid on Cercyon, and taken in several places. Back to the wrestle they went, and Theseus found this by far the hardest of his adventures, for Cercyon was heavier than he, and as strong, but not so active. So Theseus for long did little but resist the awful strain of the arms of Cercyon, till, at last, for a moment Cercyon weakened. Then Theseus slipped his hip under the hip of Cercyon, and heaved him across and up, and threw him on the ground. He lighted in such a way that his neck broke, and there he lay dead.

'Was it fairly done?' said Theseus.

'It was fairly done!' cried the Highlanders of Arcadia; and then they raised such a wail for the dead that Theseus deemed it wise to put on his clothes and walk out of the court; and, leaping into a chariot that stod empty by the gate, for the servant in the chariot feared the club of iron, he drove away at full speed.

Though Cercyon was a cruel man and wild, Theseus was sorry for him in his heart.

The groom in the chariot tried to leap out, but Theseus gripped him tight. 'Do no hurry, my friend,' said Theseus, 'for I have need of you. I am not stealing the chariot and horses, and you shall drive them back after we reach Athens.'

'But, my lord,' said the groom, 'you will never reach Athens.'

'Why not?' asked Theseus.

'Because of the man Procrustes, who dwells in a strong castle among the hills on the way. He is the maimer of all mortals, and has at his command a company of archers and spearmen, pirates from the islands. He meets every traveller, and speaks to him courteously, praying him to be his guest, and if any refuses the archers leap out of ambush and seize and bind him. With them no man can contend. He has a bed which he says is a thing magical, for it is of the same length as the tallest or the shortest man who sleeps in it, so that all are fitted. Now the manner of it is this – there is an engine with ropes at the head of the bed, and a saw is fitted at the bed foot. If a man is too short, the ropes are fastened to his hands, and are strained till he is drawn to the full length of the bed. If he is too long the saw shortens him. Such a monster is Procrustes.

'Verily, my lord, King Cercyon was tomorrow to lead an army against him, and the King had a new device, as you may see, by which two great shields are slung along the side of this chariot, to ward off the arrows of the men of Procrustes.'

'Then you and I will wear the shields when we come near the place where Procrustes meets travellers by the way, and I think that tonight his own bed will be too long for him,' said Theseus.

To this the groom made no answer, but his body trembled.

Theseus drove swiftly on till the road began to climb the lowest spur of Mount Parnes, and then he drew rein, and put on one of the great shields that covered all his body and legs, and he bade the groom do the like. Then he drove slowly, watching the bushes and underwood beside the way. Soon he saw the smoke going up from the roof of a great castle high in the woods beside the road; and on the road there was a man waiting. Theseus, as he drove towards him, saw the glitter of armour in the underwood, and the setting sun shone red on a spear-point above the leaves. 'Here is our man,' he said to the groom, and pulled up his horses beside the stranger. He loosened his sword in the sheath, and leaped out of the chariot, holding the reins in his left hand, and bowed courteously to the man, who was tall, weak-looking, and old, with grey hair and a clean-shaven face, the colour of ivory. He was clad like a king, in garments of dark silk, with gold bracelets, and gold rings that clasped the leather gaiters on his legs, and he smiled and smiled, and rubbed his hands, while he looked to right and left, and not at Theseus.

'I am fortunate, fair sir,' said he to Theseus, 'for I love to entertain strangers, with whom goes the favour and protection of Zeus. Surely strangers are dear to all men, and holy! You, too, are not unlucky, for the night is falling, and the ways will be dark and dangerous. You will sup and sleep with me, and tonight I can give you a bed that is well spoken of, for its nature is such that it fits all men, the short and the tall, and you are of the tallest.'

'Tonight, fair sir,' quoth Theseus, 'your own bed will be full long for you.' And, drawing the sword of Aegeus, he cut sheer through the neck of Procrustes at one blow, and the head of the man flew one way, and his body fell another way.

Then with a swing of his hand Theseus turned his shield from his front to his back, and leaped into the chariot. He lashed the horses forward with a cry, while the groom also turned his own shield from front to back; and the arrows of the bowmen of Procrustes rattled on the bronze shields as the chariot flew along, or struck the sides and the seat of it. One arrow grazed the flank of a horse, and the pair broke into a wild gallop, while the yells of the bowmen grew faint in the distance. At last the horses slackened in their pace as they climbed a hill, and from the crest of it Theseus saw the lights in the city of Aphidnae.

'Now, my friend,' he said to the groom, 'the way is clear to Athens, and on your homeward road with the horses and the chariot you shall travel well guarded. By the splendour of Lady Athene's brow, I will burn that raven's nest of Procrustes!'

So they slept that night on safe beds at the house of the sons of Phytalus, who bore rule in Aphidnae. Here they were kindly welcomed, and the sons of Phytalus rejoiced when they heard how Theseus had made safe the ways, and slain the beasts that guarded them. 'We are your men,' they said, 'we and all our people, and our spears will encircle you when you make yourself King of Athens, and of all the cities in the Attic land.'

* * *

Next day Theseus said farewell to the sons of Phytalus, and drove slowly through the pleasant green woods that overhung the clear river Cephisus. He halted to rest his horses in a glen, and saw a very beautiful young man walking in a meadow on the other side of the river. In his hand he bore a white flower, and the root of it was black; in the other hand he carried a golden wand, and his upper lip was just beginning to darken, he was of the age when youth is most gracious. He came towards Theseus, and crossed the stream where it broke deep, and swift, and white, above a long pool, and it seemed to Theseus that his golden shoon did not touch the water.

'Come, speak with me apart,' the young man said; and Theseus threw the reins to the groom, and went aside with the youth, watching him narrowly, for he knew not what strange dangers might beset him on the way.

'Whither art thou going, unhappy one,' said the youth, 'thou that knowest not the land? Behold, the sons of Pallas rule in Athens, fiercely and disorderly. Thy father is of no force, and in the house with him is a fair witch woman from a far country. Her name is Medea, the daughter of Aeetes, the brother of Circe the Sorceress. She wedded the famous Jason, and won for him the Fleece of Gold, and slew her own brother Absyrtus. Other evils she wrought, and now she dwells with Aegeus, who fears and loves her greatly. Take thou this herb of grace, and if Medea offers you a cup of wine, drop this herb in the cup, and so you shall escape death. Behold, I am Hermes of the golden wand.'

Then he gave to Theseus the flower, and passed into the wood, and Theseus saw him no more; so then Theseus knelt down, and prayed, and thanked the gods. The flower he placed in the breast of his garment, and, returning to his chariot, he took the reins, and drove to Athens, and up the steep narrow way to the crest of the rock where the temple of Athene stood and the palace of King Aegeus.

Theseus drove through to the courtyard, and left his chariot at the gate. In the court young men were throwing spears at a mark, while others sat at the house door, playing draughts, and shouting and betting. They were heavy, lumpish, red-faced young men, all rather like each other. They looked up and stared, but said nothing. Theseus knew that they were his cousins, the sons of Pallas, but as they said nothing to him he walked through them, iron club on shoulder, as if he did not see them, and as one tall fellow stood in his way, the tall fellow spun round from a thrust of his shoulder. At the hall door Theseus stopped and shouted, and at his cry two or three servants came to him.

'Look to my horses and man,' said Theseus; 'I come to see your master.' And in he went, straight up to the high chairs beside the fire in the centre. The room was empty, but in a high seat sat, fallen forward and half-asleep, a man in whose grey hair was a circlet of gold and a golden grasshopper. Theseus knew that it was his father, grey and still, like the fallen fire on the hearth. As the king did not look up, Theseus touched his shoulder, and then knelt down, and put his arms round the knees of the king. The king aroused himself with a start. 'Who? What want you?' he said, and rubbed his red, bloodshot eyes.

'A suppliant from Troezene am I, who come to your knees, oh king, and bring you gifts.'

'From Troezene!' said the king sleepily, as if he were trying to remember something.

'From Aethra, your wife, your son brings your sword and your shoon,' said Theseus; and he laid the sword and the shoon at his father's feet.

The king rose to his feet with a great cry. 'You have come at last,' he cried, 'and the gods have forgiven me and heard my prayers. But gird on the sword, and hide the shoon, and speak not the name of "wife", for there is one that hears.'

'One that has heard,' said a silvery voice, and from behind a pillar came a woman, dark and pale, but very beautiful, clothed in a rich Eastern robe that shone and shifted from colour to colour. Lightly she threw her white arms round the neck of Theseus, lightly she kissed his cheeks, and a strange sweet fragrance hung about her. Then, holding him apart, with her hands on his shoulders, she laughed, and half-turning to Aegeus, who had fallen back into his chair, she said: 'My lord, did you think that you could hide anything from me?' Then she fixed her great eyes on the eyes of Theseus. 'We are friends?' she said, in her silvery voice.

'Lady, I love you even as you love my father, King Aegeus,' said Theseus.

'Even so much?' said the lady Medea. 'Then we must both drink to him in wine.' She glided to the great golden mixing-cup of wine that stood on a table behind Aegeus, and with her back to Theseus she ladled wine into a cup of strange coloured glass. 'Pledge me and the king,' she said, bringing the cup to Theseus. He took it, and from his breast he drew the flower of black root and white blossom that Hermes had given him, and laid it in the wine. Then the wine bubbled and hissed, and the cup burst and broke, and the wine fell on the floor, staining it as with blood.

Medea laughed lightly. 'Now we are friends indeed, for the gods befriend you,' she said, 'and I swear by the Water of Styx that your friends are my friends, and your foes are my foes, always, to the end. The gods are with you; and by the great oath of the gods I swear, which cannot be broken; for I come of the kin of the gods who live for ever.'

Now the father of the father of Medea was the Sun God.

Theseus took both her hands. 'I also swear,' he said, 'by the splendour of Zeus, that your friends shall be my friends, and that your foes shall be my foes, always, to the end.'

Then Medea sat by the feet of Aegeus, and drew down his head to her shoulder, while Theseus took hold of his hand, and the king wept for joy. For the son he loved, and the woman whom he loved and feared, were friends, and they two were stronger than the sons of Pallas.

While they sat thus, one of the sons of Pallas – the Pallantidae they were called – slouched into the hall to see if dinner was ready. He stared, and slouched out again, and said to his brothers: 'The old man is sitting in the embraces of the foreign woman, and of the big stranger with the iron club!' Then they all came together, and growled out their threats and fears, kicking at the stones in the courtyard, and quarrelling as to what it was best for them to do.

Meanwhile, in the hall, the servants began to spread the tables with meat and drink, and Theseus was taken to the bath, and clothed in new raiment.

While Theseus was at the bath Medea told Aegeus what he ought to do. So when Theseus came back into the hall, where the sons of Pallas were eating and drinking noisily, Aegeus stood up, and called to Theseus to sit down at his right hand. He added, in a loud voice, looking all round the hall: 'This is my son, Theseus, the slayer of monsters, and his is the power in the house!'

The sons of Pallas grew pale with fear and anger, but not one dared to make an insolent answer. They knew that they were hated by the people of Athens, except some young men of their own sort, and they did not dare to do anything against the man who had slain Periphetes and Sinis, and Cercyon, and Sciron, and, in the midst of his paid soldiers, had struck off the head of Procrustes. Silent all through dinner sat the sons of Pallas, and, when they had eaten, they walked out silently, and went to a lonely place, where they could make their plans without being overheard.

Theseus went with Medea into her fragrant chamber, and they spake a few words together. Then Medea took a silver bowl, filled it with water, and, drawing her dark silken mantle over her head, she sat gazing into the bowl. When she had gazed silently for a long time she said: 'Some of them are going towards Sphettus, where their father dwells, to summon his men at arms, and some are going to Gargettus on the other side of the city, to lie in ambush, and cut us off when they of Sphettus assail us. They will attack the palace just before the dawn. Now I will go through the town, and secretly call the trusty men to arm and come to defend the palace, telling them that the son of Aegeus, the man who cleared the ways, is with us. And do you take your chariot, and drive speedily to the sons of Phytalus, and bring all their spears, chariot men and foot men, and place them in ambush around the village of Gargettus, where one band of the Pallantidae will lie tonight till dawn. The rest you know.'

Theseus nodded and smiled. He drove at full speed to Aphidnae, where the sons of Phytalus armed their men, and by midnight they lay hidden in the woods round the village of Gargettus. When the stars had gone onward, and the second of the three watches of the night was nearly past, they set bands of men to guard every way from the little town, and Theseus with another band rushed in, and slew the men of the sons of Pallas around their fires, some of them awake, but most of them asleep. Those who escaped were taken by the bands who watched the ways, and when the sky was now clear at the earliest dawn, Theseus led his companions to the palace of Aegeus, where they fell furiously upon the rear of the men from Sphettus, who were besieging the palace of Aegeus.

The Sphettus company had broken in the gate of the court, and were trying to burn the house, while arrows flew thick from the bows of the trusty men of Athens on the palace roof. The Pallantids had set no sentinels, for they thought to take Theseus in the palace, and there to burn him, and win the kingdom for themselves. Then silently and suddenly the friends of Theseus stole into the courtyard, and, leaving some to guard the gate, they drew up in line, and charged the confused crowd of the Pallantids. Their spears flew thick among the enemy, and then they charged with the sword, while the crowd, in terror, ran this way and that way, being cut down at the gate, and dragged from the walls, when they tried to climb them. The daylight found the Pallantidae and their men lying dead in the courtyard.

Then Theseus with the sons of Phytalus and their company marched through the town, proclaiming that the rightful prince was come, and that the robbers and oppressors were fallen, and all honest men rejoiced. They burned the dead, and buried their ashes and bones, and for the rest of that day they feasted in the hall of Aegeus. Next day Theseus led his friends back to Aphidnae, and on the next day they attacked and stormed the castle of Procrustes, and slew the pirates, and Theseus divided all the rich plunder among the sons of Phytalus and their company, but the evil bed they burned to ashes.

THE STRANGE TALE OF CARIBOU AND MOOSE

Cyrus Macmillan

TWO WIDOWS LIVED side by side in the forest. Their husbands had long been dead. Each widow had a little boy. One boy was called Caribou; the other was called Moose. One springtime the widows were gathering maple sap to make sugar. The two boys played at home. They talked of the great forest, and decided to travel, to see the big woods, and the mountains far away. In the morning they set out on their journey. They walked all day, and in the evening they came to a camp far away in the woods. The camp was that of the Porcupines. The Porcupines were kind to the boys, and gave them food. In the morning they gave them new moccasins, and told them the road to follow. The road, they said, had many giants.

The boys travelled all day without mishap. At last they came to the edge of the wood where the giants lived. Here they met a woman. She was half Indian, for her mother was an Indian woman who had been carried off by a giant. Her mother had long been dead. The woman they met knew that the boys were of her mother's people, and she treated them kindly. She told them that ahead of them were three great giants they would have to overcome before they could pass on their way. She gave them a box containing two dogs. The box was very small; it could be hidden in one hand. The dogs were no bigger than a fly, but when they were rubbed with the hand they grew very large and very cross; and the more they were rubbed, the larger and crosser they became. The dogs were to be used, she said, to defeat the first giant. Then the woman told them of the second giant. She said he was very terrible, and that his head was covered with great toads, the poison of which would kill anyone who touched them. She told them that the giant would ask them to kill a toad because it hurt his head, hoping thereby to poison them. She warned them not to touch it, and she gave them some cranberries, and told them to crush the cranberries in their hands when the giant made his request and the noise would make the giant think they were crushing the poisonous toad. Then she told them of the third giant; and she gave them a knife with which to overcome him. It was a very wonderful knife that could not be turned aside from anything it attacked.

Then the boys went on their way. Soon they saw the first giant standing by the side of the path. He rushed at them as if to kill them; but they opened their magic box and took out the dogs. They rubbed them until they grew very large and cross, and when the giant came near they let them loose. The dogs soon killed the giant, and the boys went on their way, leaving the dogs to go back to the woman who gave them. Soon they came to the second giant. He was very ugly and terrible, and he had long hair covered with toads. He met the boys kindly, hoping to deceive them. Then, just as the woman had told them, he said, 'Something hurts my head. Do you see what it is?' And they said, 'Yes, it is a great toad.' 'Kill it,' said the giant. Then the boys put their hands close to his head and crushed the cranberries the woman had given them, and the giant thought the noise was that of the crushing of the toad. The boys then went on their way. The giant was well pleased, for he thought they would drop dead very soon because of the poison, and that next day he would find them and have a good meal. Soon the boys came to the third giant. He was very terrible, and he attacked them at once. But one of the boys drew the magic knife and plunged it into the giant's breast. The giant could not turn it aside; it pierced his heart, and he fell dead. Then the boys knew that they were safe.

The next morning the boys decided to separate, and to go each his own way. Moose went north, and Caribou went south. By and by Moose came to a tent where dwelt a woman with one daughter. The daughter wished to be married, but her mother was jealous of her daughter's charms, and she killed every suitor who wooed her daughter. Her mother had the power of a witch, which she had received from the Evil Spirit of the forest. The daughter loved Moose when she saw him. She warned him that her mother would try to kill him. Moose asked the mother if he might have the daughter as his wife, and the mother said, 'Yes; but first you must do whatever I bid you.' To this Moose agreed. When he went to bed, the daughter warned him to be on his guard. The mother put a thick skin over him for a blanket, covering him all up. Then she went to get another, saying that it was a cold night. Moose knew he would soon smother without air under the thick skins when she piled them over him, and while she was gone he cut a hole through the skin with his magic knife so that his nose would go through it. The woman came back with other skins, and covered him with a great many, but in each skin Moose cut a hole over his nose so that he might get air. The woman left him, believing that he would smother in the night, for she did not want her daughter to wed; but Moose breathed freely and slept soundly.

The next morning the woman uncovered him, thinking that he was dead; but Moose said he had slept well. The woman wondered greatly, and resolved upon another plan to kill him. A great tree grew near the tent. It was hemlock, and bigger than a haystack at the bottom. It had thick bark which was loose at the top. The woman gave Moose a long pole and told him to knock down the bark. Moose took the pole and knocked a piece off, but as it fell he jumped from under it, for he could jump far. The heavy bark fell with a great crash. Then he knocked off all the bark until the tree was stripped, but he was unharmed. The woman wondered greatly. She resolved upon another plan to kill him. The next day she took Moose to an island far off the coast. There were no trees on the island. They left their canoe on the beach and walked inland. The woman said, 'Wait here awhile; I will come back soon.' Then she went back to the beach. She took the canoe and paddled home, leaving Moose behind. 'Now,' she said, 'he will starve, for he cannot get off the island, and there is nothing there to eat.' When Moose came back to the beach, after waiting a long while, he saw the canoe a mere speck on the water far away. He was much troubled, for he thought that now he would surely die, and he cried loudly. But the seagulls flying above the beach heard his cries, and two large gulls came down to him. They told him not to cry, for they would save him. One went to each side of him and told him to take hold and hang on. So he put an arm around each gull's neck, and they rose into the air with him and flew over the sea. Moose was very frightened when he looked down at the water. But the gulls took him home safely. He sat a long time on the beach, and then the woman came paddling her canoe from the island. When she reached the land, Moose said, 'What kept you so long? I have been waiting for you a long time.' But he did not tell her how he had come home. The woman was so surprised she did not know what to say. But she resolved upon another plan to kill him.

The next day she invited Moose to a wrestling match on a high hill. The hill was full of stones. Moose decided that to save his own life he must kill the woman, because he had had enough of her treachery. They wrestled, and Moose let the woman throw him down, but because he was agile he saved himself from a great fall. He let her throw him a second time, but again he was unharmed, to her great surprise. The contest was three falls. The woman was sure she could kill him the third time. But the third time, Moose threw her down so hard that her back was broken on the stones. Then he tossed her high in the air, and she fell so hard that she was broken in pieces. Moose was then free from danger. He married the woman's daughter; but he was not very happy. The daughter was like her mother and caused him trouble, for she was often very wicked. She was a great fisher, and went often to the streams to fish. She could go under the water and stay a long time and bring up fish in her hands. One night in winter she went down through a hole in the ice to fish. It was very cold, and while she was down, the hole froze over and she could not get out. She called to Moose to break the ice, but Moose was glad to be rid of her and he would not let her out. So she was drowned in the stream.

Moose never married again and ever afterwards he lived a lonely life. He did not like company any more. That is why he is usually seen by himself, and why he usually travels alone in the forest. But Caribou, on the other hand, likes company, and that is why he is usually seen with five or six others of his kind, and why he seldom travels alone.

THE HERO MAKÓMA

Kingsley Fairbridge

At the town of Senna on the banks of the Zambesi, was born a child. He was not like other children, for he was very tall and strong; over his shoulder he carried a big sack, and in his hand an iron hammer. He could also speak like a grown man, but usually he was very silent.

One day his mother said to him: 'My child, by what name shall we know you?'

And he answered: 'Call all the head men of Senna here to the river's bank.' And his mother called the head men of the town, and when they had come he led them down to a deep black pool in the river where all the fierce crocodiles lived.

'O great men!' he said, while they all listened, 'which of you will leap into the pool and overcome the crocodiles?' But no one would come forward. So he turned and sprang into the water and disappeared.

The people held their breath, for they thought: 'Surely the boy is bewitched and throws away his life, for the crocodiles will eat him!' Then suddenly the ground trembled, and the pool, heaving and swirling, became red with blood, and presently the boy rising to the surface swam on shore.

But he was no longer just a boy! He was stronger than any man and very tall and handsome, so that the people shouted with gladness when they saw him.

'Now, O my people!' he cried waving his hand, 'you know my name – I am Makóma, "the Greater"; for have I not slain the crocodiles in the pool where none would venture?'

Then he said to his mother: 'Rest gently, my mother, for I go to make a home for myself and become a hero.' Then, entering his hut he took Nu-éndo, his iron hammer, and throwing the sack over his shoulder, he went away.

Makóma crossed the Zambesi, and for many moons he wandered towards the north and west until he came to a very hilly country where, one day, he met a huge giant making mountains.

'Greeting,' shouted Makóma, 'who are you?'

'I am Chi-éswa-mapíri, who makes the mountains,' answered the giant; 'and who are you?'

'I am Makóma, which signifies "greater,"' answered he.

'Greater than who?' asked the giant.

'Greater than you!' answered Makóma.

The giant gave a roar and rushed upon him. Makóma said nothing, but swinging his great hammer, Nu-éndo, he struck the giant upon the head.

He struck him so hard a blow that the giant shrank into quite a little man, who fell upon his knees saying: 'You are indeed greater than I, O Makóma; take me with you to be your slave!' So Makóma picked him up and dropped him into the sack that he carried upon his back.

He was greater than ever now, for all the giant's strength had gone into him; and he resumed his journey, carrying his burden with as little difficulty as an eagle might carry a hare.

Before long he came to a country broken up with huge stones and immense clods of earth. Looking over one of the heaps he saw a giant wrapped in dust dragging out the very earth and hurling it in handfuls on either side of him.

'Who are you,' cried Makóma, 'that pulls up the earth in this way?'

'I am Chi-dúbula-táka,' said he, 'and I am making the river-beds.'

'Do you know who I am?' said Makóma. 'I am he that is called "greater"!'

'Greater than who?' thundered the giant.

'Greater than you!' answered Makóma.

With a shout, Chi-dúbula-táka seized a great clod of earth and launched it at Makóma. But the hero had his sack held over his left arm and the stones and earth fell harmlessly upon it, and, tightly gripping his iron hammer, he rushed in and struck the giant to the ground. Chi-dúbula-táka grovelled before him, all the while growing smaller and smaller; and when he had become a convenient size Makóma picked him up and put him into the sack beside Chi-éswa-mapíri.

He went on his way even greater than before, as all the river-maker's power had become his; and at last he came to a forest of bao-babs and thorn trees. He was astonished at their size, for every one was full grown and larger than any trees he had ever seen, and close by he saw Chi-gwísa-míti, the giant who was painting the forest.

Chi-gwísa-miti was taller than either of his brothers, but Makóma was not afraid, and called out to him: 'Who are you, O Big One?'

'I,' said the giant, 'am Chi-gwísa-míti, and I am planting these bao-babs and thorns as food for my children the elephants.'

'Leave off!' shouted the hero, 'for I am Makóma, and would like to exchange a blow with thee!'

The giant, plucking up a monster bao-bab by the roots, struck heavily at Makóma; but the hero sprang aside, and as the weapon sank deep into the soft earth, whirled Nu-éndo the hammer round his head and felled the giant with one blow.

So terrible was the stroke that Chi-gwísa-míti shrivelled up as the other giants had done; and when he had got back his breath he begged Makóma to take him as his servant. 'For,' said he, 'it is honourable to serve a man so great as thou.'

Makóma, after placing him in his sack, proceeded upon his journey, and travelling for many days he at last reached a country so barren and rocky that not a single living thing grew upon it – everywhere reigned grim desolation. And in the midst of this dead region he found a man eating fire.

'What are you doing? demanded Makóma.

'I am eating fire,' answered the man, laughing; 'and my name is Chi-ídea-móto, for I am the flame-spirit, and can waste and destroy what I like.'

'You are wrong,' said Makóma; 'for I am Makóma, who is "greater" than you – and you cannot destroy me!'

The fire-eater laughed again, and blew a flame at Makóma. But the hero sprang behind a rock – just in time, for the ground upon which he had been standing was turned to molten glass, like an overbaked pot, by the heat of the flame-spirit's breath.

Then the hero flung his iron hammer at Chi-ídea-móto, and, striking him, it knocked him helpless; so Makóma placed him in the sack, Woro-nówu, with the other great men that he had overcome.

And now, truly, Makóma was a very great hero; for he had the strength to make hills, the industry to lead rivers over dry wastes, foresight and wisdom in planting trees, and the power of producing fire when he wished.

Wandering on he arrived one day at a great plain, well watered and full of game; and in the very middle of it, close to a large river, was a grassy spot, very pleasant to make a home upon.

Makóma was so delighted with the little meadow that he sat down under a large tree, and removing the sack from his shoulder, took out all the giants and set them before him. 'My friends,' said he, 'I have travelled far and am weary. Is not this such a place as would suit a hero for his home? Let us then go, tomorrow, to bring in timber to make a kraal.'

So the next day Makóma and the giants set out to get poles to build the kraal, leaving only Chi-éswa-mapíri to look after the place and cook some venison which they had killed. In the evening, when they returned, they found the giant helpless and tied to a tree by one enormous hair!

'How is it,' said Makóma, astonished, 'that we find you thus bound and helpless?'

'O Chief,' answered Chi-éswa-mapíri, 'at mid-day a man came out of the river; he was of immense stature, and his grey moustaches were of such length that I could not see where they ended! He demanded of me "Who is thy master?" And I answered: "Makóma, the greatest of heroes." Then the man seized me, and pulling a hair from his moustache, tied me to this tree – even as you see me.'

Makóma was very wroth, but he said nothing, and drawing his finger-nail across the hair (which was as thick and strong as palm rope) cut it, and set free the mountain-maker.

The three following days exactly the same thing happened, only each time with a different one of the party; and on the fourth day Makóma stayed in camp when the others went to cut poles, saying that he would see for himself what sort of man this was that lived in the river and whose moustaches were so long that they extended beyond men's sight.

So when the giants had gone he swept and tidied the camp and put some venison on the fire to roast. At midday, when the sun was right overhead, he heard a rumbling noise from the river, and looking up he saw the head and shoulders of an enormous man emerging from it. And behold! right down the river-bed and up the river-bed, till they faded into the blue distance, stretched the giant's grey moustaches!

'Who are you?' bellowed the giant, as soon as he was out of the water.

'I am he that is called Makóma,' answered the hero; 'and, before I slay thee, tell me also what is thy name and what thou doest in the river?'

'My name is Chin-débou Máu-giri,' said the giant. 'My home is in the river, for my moustache is the grey fever-mist that hangs above the water, and with which I bind all those that come unto me so that they die.'

'You cannot bind me!' shouted Makóma, rushing upon him and striking with his hammer. But the river giant was so slimy that the blow slid harmlessly off his green chest, and as Makóma stumbled and tried to regain his balance, the giant swung one of his long hairs around him and tripped him up.

For a moment Makóma was helpless, but remembering the power of the flame-spirit which had entered into him, he breathed a fiery breath upon the giant's hair and cut himself free.

As Chin-débou Máu-giri leaned forward to seize him the hero flung his sack Woronówu over the giant's slippery head, and gripping his iron hammer, struck him again; this time the blow alighted upon the dry sack and Chin-débou Máu-giri fell dead.

When the four giants returned at sunset with the poles they rejoiced to find that Makóma had overcome the fever-spirit, and they feasted on the roast venison till far into the night; but in the morning, when they awoke, Makóma was already warming his hands at the fire, and his face was gloomy.

'In the darkness of the night, O my friends,' he said presently, 'the white spirits of my fathers came unto me and spoke, saying: "Get thee hence, Makóma, for thou shalt have no rest until thou hast found and fought with Sákatirína, who has five heads, and is very great and strong; so take leave of thy friends, for thou must go alone."'

Then the giants were very sad, and bewailed the loss of their hero; but Makóma comforted them, and gave back to each the gifts he had taken from them. Then bidding them 'Farewell,' he went on his way.

Makóma travelled far towards the west; over rough mountains and waterlogged morasses, fording deep rivers, and tramping for days across dry deserts where most men would have died, until at length he arrived at a hut standing near some large peaks, and inside the hut were two beautiful women.

'Greeting!' said the hero. 'Is this the country of Sákatirína of five heads, whom I am seeking?'

'We greet you, O Great One!' answered the women. 'We are the wives of Sákatirína; your search is at an end, for there stands he whom you seek!' And they pointed to what Makóma had thought were two tall mountain peaks. 'Those are his legs,' they said; 'his body you cannot see, for it is hidden in the clouds.'

Makóma was astonished when he beheld how tall was the giant; but, nothing daunted, he went forward until he reached one of Sákatirína's legs, which he struck heavily with Nu-éndo. Nothing happened, so he hit again and then again until, presently, he heard a tired, far-away voice saying: 'Who is it that scratches my feet?'

And Makóma shouted as loud as he could, answering: 'It is I, Makóma, who is called "Greater"!' And he listened, but there was no answer.

Then Makóma collected all the dead brushwood and trees that he could find, and making an enormous pile round the giant's legs, set a light to it.

This time the giant spoke; his voice was very terrible, for it was the rumble of thunder in the clouds. 'Who is it,' he said, 'making that fire smoulder around my feet?'

'It is I, Makóma!' shouted the hero. 'And I have come from far away to see thee, O Sákatirína, for the spirits of my fathers bade me go seek and fight with thee, lest I should grow fat, and weary of myself.'

There was silence for a while, and then the giant spoke softly: 'It is good, O Makóma!' he said. 'For I too have grown weary.

There is no man so great as I, therefore I am all alone. Guard thyself!' And bending suddenly he seized the hero in his hands and dashed him upon the ground. And lo! instead of death, Makóma had found life, for he sprang to his feet mightier in strength and stature than before, and rushing in he gripped the giant by the waist and wrestled with him.

Hour by hour they fought, and mountains rolled beneath their feet like pebbles in a flood; now Makóma would break away, and summoning up his strength, strike the giant with Nu-éndo his iron hammer, and Sákatirína would pluck up the mountains and hurl them upon the hero, but neither one could slay the other. At last, upon the second day, they grappled so strongly that they could not break away; but their strength was failing, and, just as the sun was sinking, they fell together to the ground, insensible.

In the morning when they awoke, Mulimo the Great Spirit was standing by them; and he said: 'O Makóma and Sákatirína! Ye are heroes so great that no man may come against you. Therefore ye will leave the world and take up your home with me in the clouds.' And as he spake the heroes became invisible to the people of the Earth, and were no more seen among them.

PRINCE YAMATO TAKE

Theodora Ozaki

MANY, MANY YEARS ago, there was born a son to the Emperor Keiko, the twelfth in descent from the great Jimmu, the founder of the Japanese dynasty. This Prince was the second son of the Emperor Keiko, and he was named Yamato. From his childhood he proved himself to be of remarkable strength, wisdom and courage, and his father noticed with pride that he gave promise of great things, and he loved him even more than he did his elder son.

Now when Prince Yamato had grown to manhood (in the olden days of Japanese history, a boy was considered to have reached man's estate at the early age of sixteen) the realm was much troubled by a band of outlaws whose chiefs were two brothers, Kumaso and Takeru. These rebels seemed to delight in rebelling against the King, in breaking the laws and defying all authority.

At last King Keiko ordered his younger son Prince Yamato to subdue the brigands and, if possible, to rid the land of their evil lives. Prince Yamato was only sixteen years of age, he had but reached his manhood according to the law, yet though he was such a youth in years he possessed the dauntless spirit of a warrior of fuller age and knew not what fear was. Even then there was no man who could rival him for courage and bold deeds, and he received his father's command with great joy.

He at once made ready to start, and great was the stir in the precincts of the Palace as he and his trusty followers gathered together and prepared for the expedition, and polished up their armor and donned it. Before he left his father's Court he went to pray at the shrine of Ise and to take leave of his aunt the Princess Yamato, for his heart was somewhat heavy at the thought of the dangers he had to face, and he felt that he needed the protection of his ancestress, Amaterasu, the Sun Goddess. The Princess his aunt came out to give him glad welcome, and congratulated him on being trusted with so great a mission by his father the King. She then gave him one of her gorgeous robes as a keepsake to go with him and to bring him good luck, saying that it would surely be of service to him on this adventure. She then wished him all success in his undertaking and bade him good speed.

The young Prince bowed low before his aunt, and received her gracious gift with much pleasure and many respectful bows.

'I will now set out,' said the Prince, and returning to the Palace he put himself at the head of his troops. Thus cheered by his aunt's blessing, he felt ready for all that might befall, and marching through the land he went down to the Southern Island of Kiushiu, the home of the brigands.

Before many days had passed he reached the Southern Island, and then slowly but surely made his way to the headquarters of the chiefs Kumaso and Takeru. He now met with great difficulties, for he found the country exceedingly wild and rough. The mountains were high and steep, the valleys dark and deep, and huge trees and boulders of rock blocked up the road and stopped the progress of his army. It was all but impossible to go on.

Though the Prince was but a youth he had the wisdom of years, and, seeing that it was vain to try and lead his men further, he said to himself:

'To attempt to fight a battle in this impassable country unknown to my men only makes my task harder. We cannot clear the roads and fight as well. It is wiser for me to resort to stratagem and come upon my enemies unawares. In that way I may be able to kill them without much exertion.'

So he now bade his army halt by the way. His wife, the Princess Ototachibana, had accompanied him, and he bade her bring him the robe his aunt the priestess of Ise had given him, and to help him attire himself as a woman. With her help he put on the robe, and let his hair down till it flowed over his shoulders. Ototachibana then brought him her comb, which he put in his black tresses, and then adorned himself with strings of strange jewels just as you see in the picture. When he had finished his unusual toilet, Ototachibana brought him her mirror. He smiled as he gazed at himself – the disguise was so perfect.

He hardly knew himself, so changed was he. All traces of the warrior had disappeared, and in the shining surface only a beautiful lady looked back at him.

Thus completely disguised, he set out for the enemy's camp alone. In the folds of his silk gown, next his strong heart, was hidden a sharp dagger.

The two chiefs Kumaso and Takeru were sitting in their tent, resting in the cool of the evening, when the Prince approached. They were talking of the news which had recently been carried to them, that the King's son had entered their country with a large army determined to exterminate their band. They had both heard of the young warrior's renown, and for the first time in their wicked lives they felt afraid. In a pause in their talk they happened to look up, and saw through the door of the tent a beautiful woman robed in sumptuous garments coming towards them. Like an apparition of loveliness she appeared in the soft twilight. Little did they dream that it was their enemy whose coming they so dreaded who now stood before them in this disguise.

'What a beautiful woman! Where has she come from?' said the astonished Kumaso, forgetting war and council and everything as he looked at the gentle intruder.

He beckoned to the disguised Prince and bade him sit down and serve them with wine. Yamato Take felt his heart swell with a fierce glee for he now knew that his plan would succeed. However, he dissembled cleverly, and putting on a sweet air of shyness he approached the rebel chief with slow steps and eyes glancing like a frightened deer. Charmed to distraction by the girl's loveliness Kumaso drank cup after cup of wine for the pleasure of seeing her pour it out for him, till at last he was quite overcome with the quantity he had drunk.

This was the moment for which the brave Prince had been waiting. Flinging down the wine jar, he seized the tipsy and astonished Kumaso and quickly stabbed him to death with the dagger which he had secretly carried hidden in his breast.

Takeru, the brigand's brother, was terror-struck as soon as he saw what was happening and tried to escape, but Prince Yamato was too quick for him. Ere he could reach the tent door the Prince was at his heel, his garments were clutched by a hand of iron, and a dagger flashed before his eyes and he lay stabbed on the earth, dying but not yet dead.

'Wait one moment!' gasped the brigand painfully, and he seized the Prince's hand.

Yamato relaxed his hold somewhat and said:

'Why should I pause, thou villain?'

The brigand raised himself fearfully and said:

'Tell me from whence you come, and whom I have the honor of addressing? Hitherto I believed that my dead brother and I were the strongest men in the land, and that there was no one who could overcome us. Alone you have ventured into our stronghold, alone you have attacked and killed us! Surely you are more than mortal?'

Then the young Prince answered with a proud smile: 'I am the son of the King and my name is Yamato, and I have been sent by my father as the avenger of evil to bring death to all rebels! No longer shall robbery and murder hold my people in terror!' and he held the dagger dripping red above the rebel's head.

'Ah,' gasped the dying man with a great effort, 'I have often heard of you. You are indeed a strong man to have so easily overcome us. Allow me to give you a new name. From henceforth you shall be known as Yamato *Take*. Our title I bequeath to you as the bravest man in Yamato.'

And with these noble words, Takeru fell back and died.

The Prince having thus successfully put an end to his father's enemies in the West, now prepared to return to the capital. On the way back he passed through the province of Idzumo. Here he met with another outlaw named Idzumo Takeru who he knew had done much harm in the land. He again resorted to stratagem, and feigned friendship with the rebel under an assumed name. Having done this he made a sword of wood and jammed it tightly in the sheath of his own steel sword. This he purposely buckled to his side and wore on every occasion when he expected to meet the third robber Takeru.

He now invited Takeru to the bank of the River Hinokawa, and persuaded him to try a swim with him in the cool refreshing waters of the river.

As it was a hot summer's day, the rebel was nothing loath to take a plunge in the river. While his enemy was still swimming down the stream the Prince turned back and landed with all possible haste. Unperceived, he managed to change swords, putting his wooden one in place of the keen steel sword of Takeru.

Knowing nothing of this, the brigand came up to the bank shortly. As soon as he had landed and donned his clothes, the Prince came forward and asked him to cross swords with him to prove his skill, saying:

'Let us two prove which is the better swordsman of the two!'

The robber agreed with delight, feeling certain of victory, for he was famous as a fencer in his province and he did not know who his adversary was. He seized quickly what he thought was his sword and stood on guard to defend himself. Alas! for the rebel, the sword was the wooden one of the young Prince, and in vain Takeru tried to unsheathe it – it was jammed fast, not all his exerted strength could move it. Even if his efforts had been successful the sword would have been of no use to him for it was of wood. Yamato Take saw that his enemy was in his power, and swinging high the sword he had taken from Takeru he brought it down with great might and dexterity and cut off the robber's head.

In this way, sometimes by using his wisdom and sometimes by using his bodily strength, and at other times by resorting to craftiness, which was as much esteemed in those days as it is despised in these, he prevailed against all the King's foes one by one, and brought peace and rest to the land and the people.

When he returned to the capital the King praised him for his brave deeds, and held a feast in the Palace in honor of his safe coming home and presented him with many rare gifts. From this time forth the King loved him more than ever and would not let Yamato Take go from his side, for he said that his son was now as precious to him as one of his arms.

But the Prince was not allowed to live an idle life long. When he was about thirty years old, news was brought that the Ainu race, the aborigines of the islands of Japan, who had been conquered and pushed northwards by the Japanese, had rebelled in the Eastern provinces, and leaving the vicinity which had been allotted to them were causing great trouble in the land. The King decided that it was necessary to send an army to do battle with them and bring them to reason. But who was to lead the men?

Prince Yamato Take at once offered to go and bring the newly-arisen rebels into subjection. Now as the King loved the Prince dearly, and could not bear to have him go out of his sight even for the length of one day, he was of course very loath to send him on his dangerous expedition. But in the whole army there was no warrior so strong or so brave as the Prince his son, so that His Majesty, unable to do otherwise, reluctantly complied with Yamato's wish.

When the time came for the Prince to start, the King gave him a spear called the Eight-Arms-Length-Spear of the Holly Tree (the handle was probably made from the wood of the holly tree), and ordered him to set out to subjugate the Eastern Barbarians as the Ainu were then called.

The Eight-Arms-Length-Spear of the Holly Tree of those old days, was prized by warriors just as much as the Standard or Banner is valued by a regiment in these modern days, when given by the King to his soldiers on the occasion of setting out for war.

The Prince respectfully and with great reverence received the King's spear, and leaving the capital, marched with his army to the East. On his way he visited first of all the temples of Ise for worship, and his aunt the Princess of Yamato and High Priestess came out to greet him. She it was who had given him her robe which had proved such a boon to him before in helping him to overcome and slay the brigands of the West.

He told her all that had happened to him, and of the great part her keepsake had played in the success of his previous undertaking, and thanked her very heartily. When she heard that he was starting out once again to do battle with his father's enemies, she went into the temple, and reappeared bearing a sword and a beautiful bag which she had made herself, and which was full of flints, which in those times people used instead of matches for making fire. These she presented to him as a parting gift.

The sword was the sword of Murakumo, one of the three sacred treasures which comprise the insignia of the Imperial House of Japan. No more auspicious talisman of luck and success could she have given her nephew, and she bade him use it in the hour of his greatest need.

Yamato Take now bade farewell to his aunt, and once more placing himself at the head of his men he marched to the farthest East through the province of Owari, and then he reached the province of Suruga. Here the governor welcomed the Prince right heartily and entertained him royally with many feasts. When these were over, the governor told his guest that his country was famous for its fine deer, and proposed a deer hunt for the Prince's amusement. The Prince was utterly deceived by the cordiality of his host, which was all feigned, and gladly consented to joint in the hunt.

The governor then led the Prince to a wild and extensive plain where the grass grew high and in great abundance. Quite ignorant that the governor had laid a trap for him with the desire to compass his death, the Prince began to ride hard and hunt down the deer, when all of a sudden to his amazement he saw flames and smoke bursting out from the bush in front of him. Realizing his danger he tried to retreat, but no sooner did he turn his horse in the opposite direction than he saw that even there the prairie was on fire. At the same time the grass on his left and right burst into flames, and these began to spread swiftly towards him on all sides. He looked round for a chance of escape. There was none. He was surrounded by fire.

'This deer hunt was then only a cunning trick of the enemy!' said the Prince, looking round on the flames and the smoke that crackled and rolled in towards him on every side. 'What a fool I was to be lured into this trap like a wild beast!' and he ground his teeth with rage as he thought of the governor's smiling treachery.

Dangerous as was his situation now, the Prince was not in the least confounded. In his dire extremity he remembered the gifts his aunt had given him when they parted, and it seemed to him as if she must, with prophetic foresight, have divined this hour of need. He coolly opened the flint-bag that his aunt had given him and set fire to the grass near him. Then drawing the sword of Murakumo from its sheath he set to work to cut down the grass on either side of him with all speed. He determined to die, if that were necessary, fighting for his life and not standing still waiting for death to come to him.

Strange to say the wind began to change and to blow from the opposite direction, and the fiercest portion of the burning bush which had hitherto threatened to come upon him was now blown right away from him, and the Prince, without even a scratch on his body or a single hair burned, lived to tell the tale of his wonderful escape, while the wind rising to a gale overtook the governor, and he was burned to death in the flames he had set alight to kill Yamato Take.

Now the Prince ascribed his escape entirely to the virtue of the sword of Murakumo, and to the protection of Amaterasu, the Sun Goddess of Ise, who controls the wind and all the elements and ensures the safety of all who pray to her in the hour of danger. Lifting the precious sword he raised it above his head many times in token of his great respect, and as he did this he renamed it *Kusanagi-no-Tsurugi* or the Grass-Cleaving Sword, and the place where he set fire to the grass round him and escaped from death in the burning prairie, he called *Yaidzu.* To this day there is a spot along the great Tokaido railway named Yaidzu, which is said to be the very place where this thrilling event took place.

Thus did the brave Prince Yamato Take escape out of the snare laid for him by his enemy. He was full of resource and courage, and finally outwitted and subdued all his foes. Leaving Yaidzu he marched eastward, and came to the shore at Idzu from whence he wished to cross to Kadzusa.

In these dangers and adventures he had been followed by his faithful loving wife the Princess Ototachibana. For his sake she counted the weariness of the long journeys and the dangers of war as nothing, and her love for her warrior husband was so great that she felt well repaid for all her wanderings if she could but hand him his sword when he sallied forth to battle, or minister to his wants when he returned weary to the camp.

But the heart of the Prince was full of war and conquest and he cared little for the faithful Ototachibana. From long exposure in travelling, and from care and grief at her lord's coldness to her, her beauty had faded, and her ivory skin was burnt brown by the sun, and the Prince told her one day that her place was in the Palace behind her screens at home and not with him upon the warpath. But in spite of rebuffs and indifference on her husband's part, Ototachibana could not find it in her heart to leave him. But perhaps it would have been better for her if she had done so, for on the way to Idzu, when they came to Owari, her heart was well-nigh broken.

Here dwelt in a Palace shaded by pine-trees and approached by imposing gates, the Princess Miyadzu, beautiful as the cherry blossom in the blushing dawn of a spring morning. Her garments were dainty and bright, and her skin was white as snow, for she had never known what it was to be weary along the path of duty or to walk in the heat of a summer's sun. And the Prince was ashamed of his sunburnt wife in her travel-stained garments, and bade her remain behind while he went to visit the Princess Miyadzu. Day after day he spent hours in the gardens and the Palace of his new friend, thinking only of his pleasure, and caring little for his poor wife who remained behind to weep in the tent at the misery which had come into her life. Yet she was so faithful a wife, and her character so patient, that she never allowed a reproach to escape her lips, or a frown to mar the sweet sadness of her face, and she was ever ready with a smile to welcome her husband back or usher him forth wherever he went.

At last the day came when the Prince Yamato Take must depart for Idzu and cross over the sea to Kadzusa, and he bade his wife follow in his retinue as an attendant while he went to take a ceremonious farewell of the Princess Miyadzu. She came out to greet him dressed in gorgeous robes, and she seemed more beautiful than ever, and when Yamato Take saw her he forgot his wife, his duty, and everything except the joy of the idle present, and swore that he would return to Owari and marry her when the war was over. And as he looked up when he had said these words he met the large almond eyes of Ototachibana fixed full upon him in unspeakable sadness and wonder, and he knew that he had done wrong, but he hardened his heart and rode on, caring little for the pain he had caused her.

When they reached the seashore at Idzu his men sought for boats in which to cross the straits to Kadzusa, but it was difficult to find boats enough to allow all the soldiers to embark. Then the Prince stood on the beach, and in the pride of his strength he scoffed and said:

'This is not the sea! This is only a brook! Why do you men want so many boats? I could jump this if I would.'

When at last they had all embarked and were fairly on their way across the straits, the sky suddenly clouded and a great storm arose. The waves rose mountains high, the wind howled, the lightning flashed and the thunder rolled, and the boat which held Ototachibana and the Prince and his men was tossed from crest to crest of the rolling waves, till it seemed that every moment must be their last and that they must all be swallowed up in the angry sea. For Rin Jin, the Dragon King of the Sea, had heard Yamato Take jeer, and had raised this terrible storm in anger, to show the scoffing Prince how awful the sea could be though it did but look like a brook.

The terrified crew lowered the sails and looked after the rudder, and worked for their dear lives' sake, but all in vain – the storm only seemed to increase in violence, and all gave themselves up for lost. Then the faithful Ototachibana rose, and forgetting all the grief that her husband had caused her, forgetting even that he had wearied of her, in the one great desire of her love to save him, she determined to sacrifice her life to rescue him from death if it were possible.

While the waves dashed over the ship and the wind whirled round them in fury she stood up and said:

'Surely all this has come because the Prince has angered Rin Jin, the God of the Sea, by his jesting. If so, I, Ototachibana, will appease the wrath of the Sea God who desires nothing less than my husband's life!'

Then addressing the sea she said:

'I will take the place of His Augustness, Yamato Take. I will now cast myself into your outraged depths, giving my life for his. Therefore hear me and bring him safely to the shore of Kadzusa.'

With these words she leaped quickly into the boisterous sea, and the waves soon whirled her away and she was lost to sight. Strange to say, the storm ceased at once, and the sea became as calm and smooth as the matting on which the astonished onlookers were sitting. The gods of the sea were now appeased, and the weather cleared and the sun shone as on a summer's day.

Yamato Take soon reached the opposite shore and landed safely, even as his wife Ototachibana had prayed. His prowess in war was marvelous, and he succeeded after some time in conquering the Eastern Barbarians, the Ainu.

He ascribed his safe landing wholly to the faithfulness of his wife, who had so willingly and lovingly sacrificed herself in the hour of his utmost peril. His heart was softened at the remembrance of her, and he never allowed her to pass from his thoughts even for a moment. Too late had he learned to esteem the goodness of her heart and the greatness of her love for him.

As he was returning on his homeward way he came to the high pass of the Usui Toge, and here he stood and gazed at the wonderful prospect beneath him. The country, from this great elevation, all lay open to his sight, a vast panorama of mountain and plain and forest, with rivers winding like silver ribbons through the land; then far off he saw the distant sea, which shimmered like a luminous mist in the great distance, where Ototachibana had given her life for him, and as he turned towards it he stretched out his arms, and thinking of her love which he had scorned and his faithlessness to her, his heart burst out into a sorrowful and bitter cry:

'Azuma, Azuma, Ya!' (Oh! my wife, my wife!) And to this day there is a district in Tokio called Azuma, which commemorates the words of Prince Yamato Take, and the place where his faithful wife leapt into the sea to save him is still pointed out. So, though in life the Princess Ototachibana was unhappy, history keeps her memory green, and the story of her unselfishness and heroic death will never pass away.

Yamato Take had now fulfilled all his father's orders, he had subdued all rebels, and rid the land of all robbers and enemies to the peace, and his renown was great, for in the whole land there was no one who could stand up against him, he was so strong in battle and wise in council.

He was about to return straight for home by the way he had come, when the thought struck him that he would find it more interesting to take another route, so he passed through the province of Owari and came to the province of Omi.

When the Prince reached Omi he found the people in a state of great excitement and fear. In many houses as he passed along he saw the signs of mourning and heard loud lamentations. On inquiring the cause of this he was told that a terrible monster had appeared in the mountains, who daily came down from thence and made raids on the villages, devouring whoever he could seize. Many homes had been made desolate and the men were afraid to go out to their daily work in the fields, or the women to go to the rivers to wash their rice.

When Yamato Take heard this his wrath was kindled, and he said fiercely:

'From the western end of Kiushiu to the eastern corner of Yezo I have subdued all the King's enemies – there is no one who dares to break the laws or to rebel against the King. It is indeed a matter for wonder that here in this place, so near the capital, a wicked monster has dared to take up his abode and be the terror of the King's subjects. Not long shall it find pleasure in devouring innocent folk. I will start out and kill it at once.'

With these words he set out for the Ibuki Mountain, where the monster was said to live. He climbed up a good distance, when all of a sudden, at a winding in the path, a monster serpent appeared before him and stopped the way.

'This must be the monster,' said the Prince; 'I do not need my sword for a serpent. I can kill him with my hands.'

He thereupon sprang upon the serpent and tried to strangle it to death with his bare arms. It was not long before his prodigious strength gained the mastery and the serpent lay dead at his feet. Now a sudden darkness came over the mountain and rain began to fall, so that for the gloom and the rain the Prince could hardly see which way to take. In a short time, however, while he was groping his way down the pass, the weather cleared, and our brave hero was able to make his way quickly down the mountain.

When he got back he began to feel ill and to have burning pains in his feet, so he knew that the serpent had poisoned him. So great was his suffering that he could hardly move, much less walk, so he had himself carried to a place in the mountains famous for its hot mineral springs, which rose bubbling out of the earth, and almost boiling from the volcanic fires beneath.

Yamato Take bathed daily in these waters, and gradually he felt his strength come again, and the pains left him, till at last one day he found with great joy that he was quite recovered. He now hastened to the temples of Ise, where you will remember that he prayed before undertaking this long expedition. His aunt, priestess of the shrine, who had blessed him on his setting out, now came to welcome him back. He told her of the many dangers he had encountered and of how marvelously his life had been preserved through all – and she praised his courage and his warrior's prowess, and then putting on her most magnificent robes she returned thanks to their ancestress the Sun Goddess Amaterasu, to whose protection they both ascribed the Prince's wonderful preservation.

PART III:

QUESTS OF FORTUNE

THE LAD WITH ONE SANDAL

Winifred Hutchinson

I

THERE WAS A king in the olden time, whose name was Pelias, and he dwelt in the fair harbour-town of Iolcos, ruling a folk that were famous seafarers from the beginning. A bold man was he, and a crafty, but he went ever in fear of his life, for he had an ill deed on his conscience, and his sleep of nights was broken by dreams which boded a bitter reckoning for the same. Many and many a time he awoke with a shriek, as a dagger seemed to touch his throat, but the dream-shape that brandished it was dim and wavering, and he could never descry the countenance of that phantom foe. At last he sent a trusty messenger to the holy place of Delphi, where Apollo reveals hidden things to mortals by the mouth of his priestess, to ask the interpretation of the vision. For he thought, 'If I can but learn what man it is whose wraith appears to me, I shall make short work with him, and rid myself of this dread in which I live.' The messenger returned, and brought this answer from the god: 'Let Pelias know that the doom he dreams of will come from the hand of a near kinsman. I bid him beware, above all else, of the man who comes to him wearing one sandal, whether he be a stranger, or born and bred in Iolcos.'

When King Pelias heard this message, his blood froze with fear; it was indeed death, then, that the dreams foreboded. Yet it was some comfort that now at least he had a sign whereby to know when the danger drew near, and he still hoped that he might forestall it if he kept good watch. So he set guards day and night about his palace, and watchmen at all the city gates, and gave strict charge to them all to bring him instant warning, if ever they should see a man with one sandal. And as time went on, his heart grew somewhat lightened of its dread, for there was no such comer seen, and the evil dreams ceased to visit him.

But he that was foretold came in his destined hour to Iolcos, out of the mountains to the northward, and stood in the market-place, while it was yet morning, and the throng of folk was greatest. The watchmen at the gate had seen him pass, but they paid no heed to one who seemed a mere lad, and by his dress a hunter from the hill-country.

This youth carried two hunting-spears, and instead of a cloak a leopard skin hung from his shoulders, above a close-fitting tunic; his head was uncovered, and his long curls flamed golden-red in the sunlight. It was easy to guess, from the shy and wondering glances he cast about him, that he was new to the sights of a city, yet he bore himself with the noble grace of a king's son, and as he stood there silent, many eyes were drawn to the beauty of his face, and his stature, lofty as a god's. Men began to whisper to one another, asking who the stranger was, and when none could answer, a murmur went to and fro among the crowd that one of the Immortals was come among them.

'So might Apollo look,' they muttered, 'or the mailed warrior Ares, fair and terrible. Surely this is some god, or the son of a god.'

'Nay, friends,' said some of the old men, 'the gods come not thus in the sight of multitudes. Rather should we guess this mighty youth to be of that old race of the Earth-born Giants, but they all have perished long since, and only their huge graves are left for a witness to our days.'

Now, while the folks talked thus under their breaths, and durst not, for reverence, question the godlike stranger, a man of the King's household gazed with the rest, and marked on a sudden that he wore but the one sandal. For it chanced, as the youth crossed the ford of a mountain stream on his way to the city, that its fellow slipped from his foot and was carried away by the torrent. Quickly did that henchman bring word to the palace, and at his tidings, King Pelias came in hot haste to the market-place, urging the swift mules of his ivory car to their utmost speed. 'Way there for the King,' cried the slaves who ran beside him, and he drew rein in a cleared space, whence all the people had drawn back for his coming, save the stranger lad only. Pelias scanned him eagerly, and his soul sickened with affright as he saw the dreaded token of the single sandal on his right foot. But he cloaked the fear within him with haughty words, and said, eyeing the lad disdainfully, 'Stranger, what country do you call home? What grey-haired carline of low degree mothered such a dainty pet? Come, speak out your parentage, and disgrace it not with detested lying.'

Then the youth, undaunted, yet with gentlest courtesy, made reply –

'It is mine, rather, to render such answer as shall not disgrace the great Chiron, my teacher. For my home has been in his mountain-cave, and I had my rearing from the virtuous wife and mother of that wise Centaur. Twenty years have I numbered in the care of these foster-parents, and never yet done dishonour to their upbringing by deceitful act or word. But now I am come again to my own native land, to claim the ancient rights that were my father's, which Pelias, as I hear, holds in unlawful possession, even this kingdom of Iolcos.'

'Do you call yourself, then, the son of Aeson,' cried the King, 'who ruled this land until a better than he took it from him? Who knows not that his only child died at its birth?'

'Not so, for I am that child,' answered the stranger; 'but when Pelias, moved by reckless desires, had overthrown his kinsman King Aeson with force and fraud, then for fear of that violent oppressor, my parents feigned that their newborn son was dead, and made great mourning, with all their household. Then, at dead of night, they sent me privily out of the city, a babe wrapped in swaddling-bands of royal crimson, and at their bidding faithful friends conveyed me to Chiron's cave, where I might be reared in safety. And Jason was the name by which that twi-natured Being was wont to call me. Such in brief is my story, and now, good townsmen, since you know me for your countryman, come back to his own city, which of you will show me the ancient house of my fathers, that I know not, though I was born there?'

Before Jason made an end of speaking, King Pelias turned his mules and drove at a furious pace back to the palace; he knew that the folk held him in secret hate because he had dethroned Aeson, that gentle king, and he feared lest they should rise against him then and there, when they heard the lad with one sandal declare himself their rightful prince. But Jason also hurried from the market-place, eagerly following a band of willing guides. One thing he had not found courage to ask of a company of strangers, and would wait to learn within the doors of his home – was his father yet alive? Chiron had told him nothing of the old man's fate, only had bidden him go to Iolcos and claim his heritage from the usurper. Now when he was come to the house, and entered through its pillared porch, he crossed a wide courtyard, empty and silent, where grass was springing from the cracked pavement of marble, and in the hall beyond it he saw no one but an aged man, wrapped in a faded mantle, sitting in a low chair beside the embers of the hearth. The once lordly chamber was bare of furnishing; dust lay thick upon the floor, and cobwebs, where rich hangings should have been, drooped curtainwise from lintel and cornice. The home the youth had come to seemed a house of the dead, deserted save for that motionless figure cowering over the dying fire. But as he moved towards it, the snow-white head turned slowly, the dim eyes looked him in the face, and a trembling voice rang through the silence, 'My son, my son!' Jason sprang to the old king, for he indeed it was, and clasped him to his breast, while tears of joy fell fast from those withered eyelids. It was long before Aeson could find words, in the rapture of beholding his son, come back to him the fairest and goodliest of men, but he told at last how Pelias had stripped him little by little of all he possessed, on this pretext or that, till neither broad lands, nor flocks and herds, nor the rich treasures of his house were left, and he himself, with a few old slaves that tended him for love, lived on the secret doles of his well-wishers among the citizens.

'How comes it, my father,' asked Jason, 'that your two brethren have suffered you to be so evilly entreated of this tyrant, seeing that each of them is a king in his own country, if indeed they yet live?'

'They live and prosper,' answered his father, 'but it is far from hence to where they dwell, and they begrudge to waste blood and treasure in the cause of a feeble old man that cannot have long to live. But word will quickly reach them that you are home again, and when they hear what manner of young man their brother's son is become, I am much mistaken or they will think his cause worth battling for. Be you patient till we have news of them, for it comes in my mind that we shall shortly see either themselves, or the princes, your cousins.'

The old king was a true prophet, and before many days, so swiftly spread the rumour of Jason's return, those two brethren and their sons came to greet him at Iolcos. The name of one was Pheres, and his son was called Admetus; these two were men of gracious and winning presence, speaking words of pleasantness, but their souls within them were little and mean. Amythaon, the other brother, was king in the far south-west; he had a name for wisdom, but the son he brought with him had yet a greater in the after time. For he was that Melampus of whom you may read in the tale of 'The Prince who was a Seer.'

Jason and his father made these kinsmen right welcome, although their hearts misgave them for the bareness of their ancient dwelling and for the wherewithal to feast the princes and their following. But at the first word that Aeson's kinsmen were come to visit him, the townsfolk rejoiced openly because at last strong helpers had appeared for the oppressed king, and they feared not to make their gladness and goodwill manifest by bringing him gifts in abundance of everything needful to entertain his guests. Such store of sheep and oxen, of corn and wine and oil, of tables, couches, vessels of every sort, and all manner of household stuffs, as was gathered that day in Aeson's courtyard, had not been seen within its gates for many a long year. Moreover, the wealthier citizens sent their housethralls both men and maids, by the score, to grind the corn, to bake, and dress meat for the banquet, and to serve the king and his kinsfolk in the hall. So that night there was feasting and good cheer, torchlight and merry stir, in the house that had so long been silent and deserted.

Now Jason had the charge of all, and gave command as master, because of his father's great age and infirmity, and carried himself as a princely host should do, overlooking no point of courtesy, so that it was a marvel to his guests how he had come by these manners in the cave of a Centaur. For they knew not noble Chiron, who in the after time reared Prince Peleus in the like gracious ways, and compassed for him his marriage with the Sea-King's daughter, as I have told already.

Then, to do his kinsmen all honour, Jason feasted them with the best for five days and five nights, saying no word of the matter he had at heart, but tasting in their company the delicious joy of life at its sweetest.

But on the sixth day he began to speak of graver things, and when he had opened all his mind to them, they gave full consent to that which he declared it his purpose now to do, and rising all together from the banquet, they followed him forthwith to the house of Pelias. At the sound of their voices in his hall, King Pelias came hastily from the inner chambers to meet them, and then, with fair-flowing speech of gentle tone, Jason spoke thus: 'Son of a mighty sire, over quick are mortals to barter justice for the ways of iniquity, forgetting that the hour of reckoning must overtake them soon or late. But it well beseems both you and me to rule our hearts aright, and take thought what shall bring us good in days to come. Call to remembrance, I pray you, that your fathers and mine were of one blood, and that the divine Dispensers of weal and woe to men turn their faces from the sight of feuds between kindred. Let there be neither strife nor drawing of swords between us two, to make division of the great inheritance of our forefathers; for if you will follow my counsel, it shall not need. See now, I freely yield the rich lands, and all the goodly flocks and herds, of which you have despoiled the old man, my father; little care I for the wealth these bring into your house, only do you on your part restore me the sceptre that was Aeson's, and the kingly seat where he gave judgment to his people. These, I say, yield up and grudge me not, lest a worse thing come of it.'

Now Pelias was no ways minded to give up the kingship, even though he might keep all the fatness of the land for his own, and besides, he was utterly purposed to destroy the lad with the one sandal, because of the oracle he had heard concerning him. While Jason was yet speaking, his swift and cunning mind devised a plan for his undoing, and he answered with a show of mildness, in these words: 'Behold, I will deal according to your pleasure in all things, but I am now stricken in years, and you are in the flower of your youth, therefore it is for you to undertake a certain task that else were mine. Hear now what it is, since you seek to be head over all our kindred, for the matter touches him most nearly who is chief of our house. There was a prince of our blood, Athamas by name, whose wife died and left him with two young children, and in no long time he wedded another. Now this second bride proved a cruel stepdame, and when sons were born to her, she plotted death for Phrixus, the eldest born of the first wife, that her own children might inherit the kingdom. She caused all the seed sown in the land to be secretly poisoned, and when many that ate the corn sickened and died, she brought her husband to believe that the gods had sent a pestilence on the people, which must be stayed by some great sacrifice. Then did she bribe a wicked seer to declare that the wrath of the gods could be turned away by no other victim than the King's first-born son. But when the boy Phrixus was laid on the altarstone, and the knife upraised to slay him, the gods delivered him out of her hands in wondrous wise. For a ram with curly fleece of gold stood suddenly on the altar, and while all shrank back amazed, the boy threw himself upon its back, and it rose with him into the air. Over land and sea it flew till it brought him to the country of the Colchians in the unknown regions far northward, and there, by divine bidding, he sacrificed it to Ares, god of the land, and hung its golden fleece on a tree of his sacred grove. But that fleece of gold was the bane of the hapless youth not long after, for the king of the Colchians put him to death only to possess the marvellous thing. And now, O Jason, I would have you go to yonder land, and take the Golden Fleece from the keeping of that savage king, since I am given to know that our murdered kinsman's spirit cannot rest till this be done. Yes, such is the message his unquiet ghost has sent me in a dream, and when I sought counsel of the god at Delphi, answer came from the place of prophecy, that I should straightway launch a ship to sail on the hallowed quest. This quest, then, do you pledge yourself to follow in my stead, and I will swear a solemn oath, making Zeus my witness, to yield you the kingdom.'

Now all the tale Pelias told concerning Phrixus was true, but as for the dream and the message from Delphi, they were falsehoods cunningly devised to send Jason on a quest wherein he should surely perish. But the youth neither knew guile in his own heart, nor looked for it in another, so he made the covenant that Pelias asked, and took leave of him, filled with eagerness to achieve so strange an adventure. Then forthwith he sent out heralds to proclaim everywhere that he was bound on a perilous voyage, and would make all welcome to sail along with him who loved danger and renown better than to dwell at home in ignoble safety. At those tidings, high-hearted sons of kings gathered to Iolcos from far and near, for Queen Hera filled their hearts with keen desire to be Jason's shipmates, because she favoured him above all mortals from the day he came to the city to his life's end. And this was the reason: when he came to the ford where he lost his sandal, he saw an old beggar-woman sitting on the bank, crying and bewailing herself because she could not cross the rain-swollen stream. Jason spoke kindly to her, and, though she was both ragged and dirty, he took her up in his arms and carried her over. No sooner had he set her down again than her bent and shrunken form was changed into that of a fair woman in her prime, and her rags into shining raiment, and she said to him, 'For this good deed, count me your friend for ever.' Thereupon she vanished from his sight, and he went on his way with gladness, knowing that one of the Immortals had appeared to him in this shape. Now the beggar-woman was Hera, who was wandering that day on earth, to see what kindness mortals would show to one so feeble and wretched.

So the flower of all the heroes who then lived came to the house of Aeson, making offer to sail with Jason on the quest. The first who came were two noble youths in armour of gleaming silver; so like they were that none might know one from the other, and their silver chariot was drawn by horses white as snow. These were the twin brothers, Castor and Polydeuces, who for the great love they bore each other were never parted their lives long, nor did even death sunder them at the last. The next comer had neither chariot nor shining armour, but trudged on foot, bearing a great bow and quiver, with a tawny lion-skin girt about his sinewy, sun-browned limbs. He was a man in the prime of life, of gallant bearing, though without height or comeliness of person, and he passed unremarked through the crowd that were drawn to Jason's door to gaze on those glorious Twins.

But they, when they saw him stand within the hall, rose up in deepest reverence as at the coming of a god, and Jason also, for he knew by the lion-skin and bow that this was Heracles himself. Much had he heard from Chiron of that great helper of men, and he gazed with awe and wonder on him who had done such mighty deeds by land and sea. But now came into the hall a young minstrel clad in flowing robe of white, with a chaplet of ivy on his fair hair. 'I also, Jason,' he said, 'would fain be of your crew, though I have no weapon but this harp of mine. I am Orpheus of Thrace, come hither at Apollo's bidding, that your brave company may not lack for the minstrelsy warriors love so well.' Right gladly did the princes there assembled welcome that sweet singer, whose fame was gone out into all lands; of him it was told that beasts and birds, nay, the trees and rocks of the Thracian mountains, would follow the sound of his enchanting lyre.

It were long to tell what other heroes of ancient story mustered in Jason's hall that day, but none were so wondrous to behold as the last comers, Zetes and Calaïs, sons of the North Wind, who had bright feathered wings waving from their shoulders.

Meanwhile, the best-skilled craftsmen of Iolcos had wrought busily under Jason's watchful eye at the building of his ship; the tallest pines on Mount Pelion, whose woody top overhung the cave of Chiron, had been felled for her masts and timbers, and her fifty stout oars were hewn from giant ash-trees. When all was finished, and the good ship lay ready for launching, her young captain summoned his new comrades to the harbour, and said to them, 'Here, noble friends, is the bark that shall carry us to the far Colchian land, well found with all we need for the long voyage.' Then all the heroes clapped their hands at sight of the ship, and they called her Argo, that is to say, the Swift. And now Jason called upon Mopsos the seer, that dwelt in Iolcos, to offer sacrifice to Zeus, and entreat him for favourable signs at their setting forth, which the god granted both by the omens of the altar and by the lucky fall of lots that the seer cast to tell their fortunes. So that wise soothsayer bade them embark with all speed, for the hour was propitious to their sailing. But a greater sign followed, for when all were come aboard, and the anchors were raised on either side the prow, Jason stood up beside the helm, holding a golden cup in his hands, and poured wine therefrom into the sea, calling aloud on Zeus, lord of the lightning, on winds and waves, and nights of sea-faring, to be gracious to their outgoing and their homecoming. Immediately a peal of thunder gave answer from the clouds above, and lightning-flashes were seen to the right of the ship, cheering the hearts of all with happiest augury. At that, the seer bade the princely comrades betake them to their oars, and their mighty strokes bore the Argo swiftly out to sea. All that day, and many a day after, they rowed on untiringly, sped along by the strong south breeze that filled their sails. Fifty all told were those sailors, sons of gods and of kings, but none of Jason's kindred was among them, except only the brave Acastus, son of Pelias, who, for all his father could say, would not be turned from the quest of the Golden Fleece. So they fared ever northward, keeping in view the bays and promontories of the western mainland, till they had need of fresh water, and put in to a wooded cove, where a stream ran sparkling to the sea. And here misfortune befell them, for they lost Heracles, the best of their crew. There had followed him to Iolcos a fair lad called Hylas, who served him as cup-bearer. This boy, for his dauntless spirit, and the love Heracles had to him, was made one of Argo's crew, and he disembarked in this place with the rest. But while they drew water from the stream, he wandered along its banks into the woods, till he came to its source in a deep, clear pool. As he bent over its cool depths, the Water Fairies who abode therein fell in love with his beauty, and before he was aware they threw their white arms about him and drew him under. Hylas gave one cry for help as the water closed over him, and Heracles, who heard and knew the well-loved voice, rushed to find him, but in vain; nor, though the hero and his comrades searched the woods the livelong day, could they see or hear aught of the vanished lad. Then when morning dawned again, Heracles bade the others delay no longer from their journey. 'But I,' said he, 'must tarry, for I will never leave this place till I know what has become of Hylas.' Sadly Jason and the rest took farewell of their great companion; their hearts were sore for his grief, but they might not linger, and so once more they stood out to sea with oar and sail.

Now, after that, they came to a long strait of the sea, and on the shore of it there was an old blind man sitting at a table, who seemed to be weeping. 'Let us draw in to land,' said Jason, 'and ask that old man what he does in this solitary place, and what may be his sorrow.' So they brought Argo close in to the shelving shore, and called to him, asking who he was. The old man turned his sightless eyes upon them, and answered, 'I am Phineus, the seer, of all men most miserable. Apollo, in my youth, bestowed on me the power of prophecy, whereby I came to great honour, and my house was filled with rich gifts from the folk who sought to me for soothsay. But I offended the holy gods by greed of gain, therefore in mine age they sent blindness upon me, and a strange evil, the like of which came never on mortal man. For whenever I sat at meat, two monstrous birds, with heads of women, darted screeching upon my food, and snatched it away before I could taste one morsel, leaving but fragments dropped from their foul talons. They were in sight like vultures that prey on carcases, and the deadly carrion smell of them polluted all they touched, and all the air of the house, so that none could endure to abide therein. And at last the men of my city thrust me forth, because of those noisome guests, but that they might still resort to me for prophecies, they builded me a hut on this lonely shore, and daily bring me offerings of choice dainties, such as I love. But woe's me! those fell winged creatures cease not to haunt me, as you will shortly see.'

'Old man,' said Jason, 'our hearts are moved with pity for your wretched lot. Tell us now, by your divine foresight, shall none rid you of this strange pest?'

'Concerning that,' said Phineus, 'only this much is revealed to me; my deliverers are even now aboard this your ship, O son of Aeson, and bound for the far Colchian land. I know you, prince, and your errand, and who your comrades are, but which of them shall rescue me, and in what hour, is hidden from my ken.'

While they talked thus, certain men came thither from the city, bearing baskets of rich viands which they spread on the old man's table, and he put forth his hands to take of them. Instantly, with hideous screams, two vulture-shapes, woman-headed, swooped down from upper air, seized upon the food and soared away swifter than an arrow's flight. And the air was filled with a poisonous savour of decay, so that Jason and his comrades were fain to push off their ship from that tainted shore. But Phineus cried to them with tears not to abandon him in his helpless plight, and they talked with him from Argo's deck, and Jason asked him how the dire monsters were called. 'By mortals,' he answered, 'they are called the Harpies, that is the Snatchers, but the gods name them the Hounds of Zeus. You have seen their swiftness, how it is such that neither javelin nor arrow may overtake them; alas, what could Heracles himself avail me, were he yet with you!'

Then said Jason, 'I know a way,' and he filled a trencher with food, and bade the two Sons of the North Wind carry it ashore and set it before Phineus. They no sooner did so than the Harpies were seen darting upon the table; but swifter still, Zetes and Calaïs rushed between and drove them back with the flapping of their bright wings. The Harpies fled shrieking, pursued by those winged brethren over hill and dale, and the North Wind blew a fierce gale to speed his sons along, till on a desolate mountain they overtook the monsters, and drew their swords to slay them. But Zeus sent Iris, his messenger who rides upon the rainbow, to forbid them, because the Harpies were ministers of his vengeance upon sinners, and she commanded Zetes and Calaïs to put up their swords, and take an oath from them never more to come near Phineus. So the women-headed creatures swore it with human voice, by the great oath that binds the Immortal Gods, even by the Water of Styx, that icy stream which flows from Earth into the Nether World. And the sons of the North Wind flew back to the Argo.

Now when they had bidden Phineus farewell, the heroes sailed along the strait to its opening into another sea, stormy and cold, where never ship had sailed before. For at the mouth of the strait two steep cliffs made a gateway, and they were alive, and whatever passed between them they crushed to pieces, clashing suddenly together upon it. But the comrades were forewarned by Phineus of this dreadful place, and having cast anchor before it, they went ashore and built an altar of stones and sacrificed a bull to Poseidon, god of mariners, with prayers for aid. And Hera, in her love to Jason, prevailed with Poseidon to grant them safe passage through those gates that he had set up to keep mortals from the Northern Sea, and she came herself to the ship in the likeness of a damsel, carrying a white dove. 'Hail, Jason!' she said: 'A friend sends you this bird, even she whom you met by the ford of the stream, and bids you let it loose from Argo's prow. Then, when you see it pass between the Clashing Cliffs, let your comrades row forward at their utmost speed.' With that, she vanished, and Jason, glad at heart, bade his comrades bend to their oars, and let go the dove. Straight through the pass she flew, and the cliffs closed upon her with a roar like thunder, but by Hera's grace she sped between so swiftly that only her tail feathers were caught. Then, as the rocks rolled back with a grinding noise, Argo's crew rowed onward for their lives, and brought the good ship through by a hair's-breadth. The Clashing Cliffs met again that same instant, but too late, and that was the end of them, for their doom was, if ever they missed their prey, to dash each other to powder.

Poseidon, at Hera's entreaty, calmed the northern deep for those first voyagers, and with a fair wind ever behind them they came at last in sight of the low misty shores of an unknown land. It was towards evening when they drew near and saw at hand the mouth of a broad river that flowed between dark woods of beech and pine, and there in a creek of the spreading stream they moored their ship for the night.

II

WITH THE FIRST light of day Jason and two of his comrades set forth inland, that they might find some inhabited place, and learn if this was the country to which they were bound. Presently they spied smoke curling up through the trees of the forest, and they went towards it, and came to a great house of timber, standing in an open glade, with byres and barns around it. As they drew near, a lad met them, driving cows to pasture, and they asked him the name of the land, and who dwelt in that house. 'Strangers,' said he, 'this is the country of the Colchians, and yonder house is the palace of Aeetes, their king.' Then Jason, and the two comrades with him, who were Castor and Polydeuces, were glad, because they were at their journey's end; and they went into the palace and found the King sitting in the hall among his chieftains, dark-skinned men of fierce countenance, clad in golden armour of strange fashion. Aeetes looked grimly upon the strangers, but he bade them sit down and feast with him, and his slaves set food before them in plenty, and dark, sweet drink, brewed of herbs and honey. When they had eaten and drunk, the King asked them whence they came, and where they had left the ship that brought them, for he knew that they must have come by sea to his country, since by land it was walled about with trackless forests. And Jason answered discreetly, not making known his errand, but saying they were come from a land far south, and had moored their ship in the river not far away. 'It is well,' said the King. 'Let your two comrades now go and bring the rest of your crew hither, that I may feast them all. Today we will make merry, and you shall try your mettle in sword-play with my warriors, and tomorrow you shall tell me your errand.'

So the Twin Brethren went forth to fetch their comrades, but the King, under show of courtesy, kept Jason from returning to the ship lest the strangers should put to sea, and escape out of his hands. For this Aeetes was a cruel prince and a cunning, and he thought to make easy prey of these young men and their companions, and seize their fair-wrought arms, and any treasure they might have with them. But meantime he covered his evil purpose with friendly speech, bidding Jason refresh himself after his voyaging, and caused him to be led to a chamber where a bath was made ready. As the youth entered it he saw an ancient serving-woman pouring water into the bath out of a steaming cauldron, and she said to him, 'Prince Jason, when you leave this chamber the King's daughter will meet you, and offer you a posset in a silver cup. Beware you taste it not, for it is deadly, but pour it on the ground, and say, "For Those Below." Then give this to the King's daughter.' So saying, the old woman took a shining thing from her bosom, and gave it to Jason, and went quickly forth. But as she went out the fashion of her changed, and she shone with a beauty not earthly, so that he perceived some goddess had spoken to him. Now the shining thing was in the form of a four-spoked wheel, and it was golden, and the figure of a speckled bird, moulded in clay, was bound upon the spokes by the outspread wings and by the feet. Jason viewed it with wonder, and he bathed himself quickly, eager to see what should next betide. Then, when he was arrayed again, and come out of that chamber, there greeted him a dark maiden, robed in scarlet, and she offered him drink in a silver cup. But he took it from her hand, smiling, and poured the drink upon the ground, and said, 'For Those Below.' The King's daughter looked at the youth in silence, and her olive cheeks turned pale.

'Princess of the Colchians,' said he, 'let it not displease you that I deal thus with your gift, but take a gift in return.' And he laid the golden wheel in her hand, and left her standing mute. Now the daughter of Aeetes was a great enchantress, one that could draw the moon out of the sky by her incantations, and knew all spells that can be wrought with strange drugs and herbs of might. At her father's bidding she had mingled a potion for the stranger prince that would have destroyed him in three days, withering his veins with consuming fire. But, by his offering it to the Dead, she understood that he knew death was in the cup, and great fear of him took hold of her, for she deemed he had that knowledge by art magical, and that his gift was some potent charm. This in truth it was, as shall presently be told.

So soon as Argo's crew were come to the palace, King Aeetes made them cheer with a feast of good things, and after the banquet he had them forth into a meadow, and desired them to show him what skill they had with their weapons. And he set ten chosen warriors to sword-play with Jason and nine of his comrades, while he sat to watch on a grassy knoll, and his daughter beside him. Then, under colour of sport, the Colchian warriors aimed deadly strokes at the strangers, for so had the King given secret command, trusting to see his champions slay those youthful guests right speedily. But the ten comrades fought like young lions with their fierce adversaries, and when they saw the battle was for life or death, they spared not to smite them till all were slain upon the place. Sore wearied, but unwounded in that deadly fray, the heroes sheathed their resistless swords at last, and Jason cried to the King, 'We are guiltless, Aeetes, of the deaths of these men. In an evil hour have we come to such a host as this, who would make it his pastime to see guests slaughtered before his face.'

Aeetes rose up with a laugh, and answered, 'They that fare to strange lands must meet with strange customs. But since you like our Colchian manner of sport so little, I will henceforth deal with you in earnest.' With that he took them back to the palace, but because it was now late, he sent them to the guest-chambers, saying he would hear their errand in the morning.

That night the witch-princess could not sleep for thinking on the bright-haired stranger, and the meaning of the gift he had given her. She was afraid to keep it, and afraid to leave it, and she had it hidden in the folds above her girdle while she watched him fighting for his life with her father's best swordsman; nor for all her skill in enchantments did she know that the spell of it was at work upon her even then. At last she slept, and dreamed that a queen crowned with roses stood at her bedside, and asked her what thoughts those were that troubled her; but, when she essayed to answer, she could find no words, and fell to weeping.

Then said the rose-crowned queen, 'I am Aphrodite, known among gods and men for an enchantress of power, and to pleasure great Hera, I have put a charm upon you mightier than all your spells. For, as the bird is bound upon the wheel I bade Prince Jason give you, so your heart is bound with cords of desire to the giver, by the virtue of that charm. Rise now, and follow me to his chamber; the thoughts that you could not speak I know, and the struggle of your soul, but stronger than all is the thought that he must not die.'

The King's daughter awoke, and behold, she was no longer in her own chamber, but stood beside the sleeping stranger. Moonlight fell upon his face, and hair of ruddy gold, and the drawn sword by his side, and she looked at him long before she aroused him with a touch of her hand, calling him by name.

'Who calls me?' said Jason, springing to his feet and grasping his sword.

'It is I, Medea,' said the King's daughter; 'I am come to bid you fly from this house while it is yet night, for tomorrow Aeetes purposes to slay you and your comrades. Come, awaken the others, and I will unbar the gates meanwhile; the guards shall not hear us, for I have power to keep them slumbering soundly.'

'Noble Medea,' answered the prince, 'I have seen strange things on my way hither, but here is the strangest of all, that you, who would have destroyed me with your potion, are now fain to save my life. I thank whatever god has changed your heart towards me, and praise your kindly thought, but as for flight, neither I nor my true comrades will quit this place without the prize we are come in quest of.' And thereupon he took Medea by the hand, and seated her beside him on the couch, and told her all the tale from the beginning, of the task Pelias laid upon him, and the Argo's perilous voyage. Now, while he spoke of the dangers he had passed, and pleaded with her in sweet persuasive words for help to win the Golden Fleece, pity and love overflowed the heart of the witch-princess, and she forgot all the world but him only, and promised at last to aid him to the uttermost against her father. 'For your sake, prince'; she said, 'I will brave the wrath of Aeetes, though he kill me when he finds his treasure gone, and ask but this for reward, that you think sometimes of Medea when you dwell happily in that far southern home you tell me of.'

Then Jason vowed a solemn vow that he would not leave her to suffer her father's vengeance, but take her home to be his wife, and queen of fair Iolcos, and they plighted troth together in that same hour. Medea then fetched from her own chamber an ivory box of ointment, and bade him anoint himself therewith in the morning, and told him all else that he must do to outwit the crafty King. Thus did Queen Hera, with help of Aphrodite, accomplish victory for Jason over the enchantress, who else would have proved a foe too strong for him and all his crew.

No sooner had the King and his guests broken fast on the morrow, than he said to them, 'Let him that is captain among you now declare the cause of your coming hither'; and Jason made himself known to him, and in courteous words desired him to restore the Golden Fleece to the rightful heirs of Phrixus. Aeetes heard him in silence to the end; then he arose and beckoned Argo's crew to follow him, and they went after him, wondering, to a fallow field hard by the palace. There they saw a huge plough of bronze lying, and two dun oxen stood near it, wondrous to behold; they had horns and hoofs of bronze, and breathed forth smoke and flame from their nostrils. The King marked with his staff a furlong on the ground, took up the heavy brazen plough-yoke, and yoked those great beasts therewith, heedless of their scorching breath, that burnt black the grass around them, and the furious tossing of their terrible horns. Then, taking in hand a sharp-pointed goad of iron, he drove the oxen to the mark, and turned them, and so back again, cleaving the fallow soil with furrows deep and straight. And his guests watched with speechless amaze so great a marvel, till he unyoked his team beside them, and said, 'If your chief can do as you have seen me do, the Golden Fleece shall be his. But I am sworn to give it to no man who cannot yoke my oxen and plough with my plough.' Straightway Jason stripped off his saffron vesture and stepped boldly to the task, putting his trust in divine aid. Even as Aeetes had done, so did he; he took up the yoke as it were a feather's weight, laid it on the necks of the oxen, despite their plungings hither and thither, and goaded them forward with the one hand, while with the other he bore hard upon the plough-stilts, driving a true furrow alongside the King's. Aeetes looked to see him scorched to a cinder when he approached the fire-breathing bulls, but the flames had no power on his flesh by reason of Medea's enchanted ointment, and a wordless cry broke from the King, beholding him unscathed, and the god-like strength that was in him. But all Jason's comrades shouted with a great shout when the task was done, and crowded about him to clasp his hands with praises and glad greetings, and they crowned him with a garland of flowering grasses. In silent rage the King now led the way to the grove of Ares, where hung the Golden Fleece, yet he still had hopes that Jason, for all his prowess, would not be able to achieve the task that there awaited him. For the Fleece had a guardian stranger and more terrible than the oxen whose breath was flame. The grove of Ares was a gloomy wood of ancient oaks, that stooped their gnarled boughs low over dense undergrowths of brambles and juniper. A stone altar stood before it, stained with dark blood, and far within, the green gloom was broken by a spot of radiance like the clear shining of a lamp. No voice of bird sounded in that drear wood, for all winged creatures shunned it except the woodpeckers, whose tapping was heard ever and anon in the deathly stillness. 'Yonder light,' said Aeetes, 'is the glitter of the Golden Fleece, and you, bold prince, will need no other guide to lead you thereto.'

'King,' said Jason, who was forewarned by Medea's counselling, 'I fear to lay hands upon the sacred thing till I have offered sacrifice upon this altar, and besought mighty Ares not to be wroth at the taking away of the treasure which Phrixus dedicated here. Suffer us therefore to return to our ship for the night, and tomorrow we will bring offerings to the god of such things as we have.' Aeetes gave them leave willingly, for now he feared Jason exceedingly, and was well content that he should either depart at once from the land, if such were his secret purpose, or meet his doom on the morrow from the guardian of the Fleece. And one of these things he trusted would most surely befall, for that guardian was a dragon of baleful glaring eye, whose dappled coils were in length and thickness not less than Argo's hull that had fifty oars. So the King returned to his house, and Jason and his comrades went towards the river where their ship lay. But when they had gone a little way, Jason told the others what had chanced in the night, and how the King's daughter had wrought him deliverance from the bulls, and shown him means to overcome a yet greater peril. When they heard of the dragon in the grove, they were full eager to fight the monster, and prayed their captain by no means to encounter him alone, but Jason said, 'That task must be mine only, and with Medea to aid, I shall not fail, if the gods so will. Do you, my comrades, hasten to our ship, and make all ready to sail whenever I shall come to you.'

With that, he turned back and went alone to the dark grove, and at the setting of the sun, Medea came to him there.

But his comrades went on board the Argo, and looked well to all her gear, and set her sails, and when they had taken their supper, they sat each man at his oar, waiting in silence through the first watch of the night, while the autumn moon rose golden up the sky. And at midnight, they were aware of two stately forms coming swiftly through the shadows of the wood, who seemed to carry between them a huge, glittering shield. Then the voice of Jason softly hailed them, and they saw that it was he and the witch-princess who drew near, bearing a spear athwart their shoulders, whereon hung the Fleece of Gold, shining like a sun. Without word spoken, those two laid their burden on Argo's deck, and Jason, with finger on lip, took his own place, and made sign to his crew to give way. Silently they bent to their oars, and the good ship stole out into the stream, and forth to the open sea. The helmsman turned her prow southward, but at that, Medea cried, 'Princes, steer not homeward on the course by which you came, for that way will Aeetes send to pursue you with a great host, and his ships sail fleeter than the wind through his enchantments. Long must be your voyage, even half the circuit of the world, but if you will trust to me for piloting, I will guide you safe home at last.' The comrades hearkened gladly to those wise words, and turned Argo northward again at her command, and sailed for many days over a desolate sea where no man had come since the making of the world. At last, where that sea narrowed into a gulf between hills of ice and snow, they came forth upon the boundless Ocean stream, that girdles the round world, and now, by Medea's guidance they steered eastward and southward, till the cold of the frozen north was left behind, and the sun's heat gladdened them again. Three moons had risen and set, while Argo bore them along the Ocean stream, before they saw on their right hand the red cliffs of a coast, and a wide channel of waters between.

'Through yonder strait lies our way,' said Medea, and they steered northward once again along that firth of ruddy shores. Now at the head of it, they found no passage for their ship, for dunes of yellow sand stretched before them, far as eye could see, and their hearts were discouraged. But Medea bade them draw Argo ashore, and said, 'Beyond this sandy waste lies the Midland sea, whose waters wash the shores of your own dear land. Be not downcast, brave comrades, for in twelve days Argo shall ride on that sea once more, if with stout hearts you endure the toil of bearing her thither.' So when they had rested there that night, she who had been their pilot over a thousand leagues of ocean, guided the crew across the pathless desert, and they, by main strength hoisting the ship to their shoulders, marched onward thus laden under a burning sun. Never in their long seafaring had they known a labour like this, but the spirit of the heroes and the might of their young limbs did not fail nor falter in all that toilsome journey. On the twelfth day, the glittering of water was seen among the sandhills, and they pressed onward joyfully, till they came to the margin of a vast and shallow mere. Now when they would have drunk of its water, they could not, for it was brackish, but Medea cast a certain herb therein, and forthwith it was sweetened. Then she said to them, 'This water is bitter with brine of the sea that neighbours it. Launch Argo now upon the mere, and let us seek a channel among the shallows that may bring us to the open main.'

So they pushed off from the reedy bank, and rowed slowly, steering warily through the shallows of that great lagoon, till the helmsman saw blue water sparkling ahead, and cried, 'The sea, the sea!' Then the glad heroes plied their oars with fresh vigour, and ere nightfall Argo was anchored in a bay of the Midland deep.

At early dawn, when they had hoisted sail and were drawing up the anchors, a voice hailed them from the shore, and they turned in wonder to see who might call them in that lonely place. There, at the waves' edge stood a man, stately and tall, and greeted them with kindly words, and desired them to tarry awhile, and be his guests that day. But Jason and the rest made courteous excuse, pleading their haste to be at home. 'Friends,' said the stranger, 'I will not seek to delay you, but at least take a guest-gift from my hands, for I would fain show you hospitality. I am the king of this desert land, and I know who you are, and the quest you sailed on. Be pleased to take this boon, the only one I have at hand.' So saying, he stooped down and took up a clod of earth of the shore, and held it forth to them. Now Argo's prow was nearest to the land, for thereby she had been moored, as the manner was, and it was not yet turned seaward, and he that stood nearest her curved beak was a young prince named Euphemos. He, springing to the bulwark, leapt lightly ashore, and clasped hands with the stranger, and took the clod, and knew not what gift that was, nor who gave it. But as he sprang on board again, and turned to speak thanks and farewell, the stranger vanished where he stood, and awe came on all the comrades, understanding that they had seen the god of that wilderness. Nevertheless, they set forth again rejoicing, because he had shown them favour and blessed them with a gift. Euphemos showed the clod to Medea and asked her what it might betoken, and she answered that the time was not yet come for him to know, but he must look well to the keeping of it, because there was a magic in it.

But when they had sailed three days, a gale blew from the south-west at twilight, and the waves rose high round the ship, and the enchanted clod was washed from the deck, where it was laid, by the driving spray. Then Euphemos called aloud to Medea, 'Alas, wise Lady, what shall I do? The precious thing is lost, carried overboard by a dashing wave, and it is sunk into the depths of the sea.'

'Nay,' said Medea, 'it has not sunk, for there is a magic in it, but is drifting even now to the shore of yonder island on our lee. Listen, heroes all, and I will tell you what power is in the clod, and what will come of it. It is fated that wherever it is laid upon the ground, the lord of that land shall be lord also of the soil whence it was taken. And if Euphemos had brought it to the fields of his own fair domain, and planted it there, then in the day when his children's children will seek new lordship over seas, they would have sailed to the land where we saw the solitary god, and made it their kingdom. But now, because the clod is flung by the salt waves on the strand of yonder isle, that is yet uninhabited, seventeen generations of men must pass away before the god's gift bears fruit. For the descendants of Euphemos will make their new home in that island, which then shall be called Thera, and long after, they will voyage thence to the land of the clod, and reign there as kings of many cities.' The comrades listened in silence to Medea's prophecy, and pondered it in their hearts, and Euphemos ever after kept it in memory, teaching it to his sons, and they to theirs. And in the seventeenth generation the words were fulfilled.

But now the gale freshened to a tempest, and Argo was driven before it out of her true course, and her crew were fain to run her for shelter under the white cliffs of another island, far to northward. There they found a fair haven where they anchored, and forthwith, an armed host came out to them from the city nigh at hand. Argo's men stared at these warriors with amaze, for they were women, and their leader, a tall, black-haired girl, clad in rich armour. She came to the harbour-side and greeted the strangers, asking who they were, and if they came peaceably.

'Peaceably, in truth, O Queen,' answered Jason. 'We are men of Iolcos, homeward bound from a long seafaring, and we do but seek shelter here till the storm is overpast. Tell me, I pray you, what land this is, and wherefore its warriors are women.' 'Stranger,' said the armed maiden 'This island is Lemnos, and my father was king of it. He and all our men-folk went forth to war against certain pirates of the mainland, and while they were abroad, Aphrodite took displeasure at us women, because we slighted her worship, and she caused us to become utterly hateful to our fathers and husbands when they returned. Therefore they thrust us away from bed and board, and would have taken them wives of the captives they brought home, but we, thus wronged, banded together for revenge, and slew them while they slept, with their own swords. Not one did we spare, except my father, but him, though I had sworn to show no mercy, I hid in a great chest, and had it thrown into the sea, that, if the gods so willed, he might drift to some other shore. Since then, I, Hypsipyle, am Queen, and none but women dwell in Lemnos. Arms we have, as you see, and have learnt the skill of them, to defend ourselves against all comers, but you, if you are what you say, we will welcome as guests.'

Jason had little will to enter that city of dark deeds, and consort with those women of fierce nature, but Medea said, 'Our ship was blown hither not without divine purpose. Let us go ashore, and lodge with the Queen, as she would have us.' So they sojourned seven days in Lemnos, for all that time the wind blew rough and contrary. Queen Hypsipyle entertained the comrades royally, and held games in their honour, setting forth prizes of golden goblets and broidered mantles for running and wrestling and throwing the spear. For these the warrior-women contended with the heroes, and overcame not a few of them, for they were cunning wrestlers, and marvellous fleet-footed. But in feats of strength they could not match Jason and his men, nor in the race for which the Queen gave the richest prize of all, a silver shield, embossed with wild bulls, and hunters driving them into the toils. That race was run by seven of the heroes in full armour, carrying their heavy shields, and there was laughter among the women when the seventh, whose name was Erginos, stepped to the starting-place, because he, though yet young, was grey-haired. Yet he outstripped the rest, and came foremost to the goal, and the mockers were ashamed when he took the silver shield, and the victor's garland from the Queen's hands. After this, the strangers found great favour with the island maidens, who would fain have had them for their wedded lords, and Hypsipyle made offer to Jason of her hand and kingdom, if he would abide in Lemnos. Now she was more beautiful than the Colchian enchantress, and Jason's heart was drawn to her, but false to his word he could not be, and that was given to Medea. But some of his comrades took them brides among the Lemnian damsels, and of these was Euphemos; and Medea, at his wedding, prophesied good fortune to the marriage, moreover, the gods, she said, had willed him to find a wife in that island, for which very cause they had driven Argo to its coast. And the truth of her saying was quickly made manifest, for that very day the wind blew fair again for Iolcos, so that the heroes longed to set sail for home without delay. They listened not to any pleading, but made Argo ready for sea, and put their island brides on board, and went their way. This was the last of their seafaring; the kindly breeze never failed till they dropped anchor once again in the haven where their good ship first floated.

Here ends the story of Jason's quest for the Golden Fleece, for it needs not to tell the joy of his father and of all Iolcos at his homecoming, nor how the brave comrades took farewell, when they had seen him receive the kingdom from Pelias, who durst not draw back from his oath to yield it. Jason and Medea were wedded with splendour and rejoicings, and thereafter they had such happiness as seemed good to the gods. But as for Pelias, although Jason did him no violence, he did not escape the death that was to be dealt him by his own kindred. For his daughters heard that Medea had made old Aeson young again by her spells, and entreated her to do the like for their father. Then the enchantress killed an old ram before them, and cut it in pieces, and threw the pieces with magic herbs into a boiling cauldron, and when she had said certain words over it, forthwith she drew out a lamb, alive and unhurt. And she gave a handful of herbs to the daughters of Pelias, saying, 'Do to your father as you have seen me do to this sheep, which has become a lamb again.' The princesses did so, but Medea had given them common herbs, and they had not bethought them to ask what those words were which she said over the cauldron, therefore they could not bring their slain father to life again. Thus perished Pelias, even as the oracle had forewarned him, by a doom that had its beginning in the coming to Iolcos of the lad with one sandal.

THE SONS OF TUIRENN

Peter Tremayne

No one knew the reason of the feud between the sons of Cainte and the sons of Tuirenn. Perhaps it had its roots in a sharp word, some affront to honour, but the result was that the three sons of Cainte and the three sons of Tuirenn had sworn to shed each other's blood should they ever met with one another.

So it came about that the eldest son of Cainte, Cian, whose name means 'the enduring one', was crossing the great plain of Muirthemne, on his way to join the Children of Danu at Magh Tuireadh, for the news was that a great battle was being fought against the Fomorii. Cian was alone for his two brothers, Cú and Céthan, had gone on before him.

It was as he was on the open plain, some way from any shelter, that he saw three warriors heading towards him. Standing tall in his chariot, Cian narrowed his eyes to examine them. There was no mistaking the grim visage of Brían, whose name means 'exalted one', and his brothers Iuchar and Iucharba. Now Cian realised, because he was outnumbered, that discretion was the better part of valour. But there was no cover on the plain except for a herd of pigs feeding. Being one of the Children of Danu, Cian took a Druid wand and changed his shape into that of a pig, also causing his chariot and horses to be likewise transformed.

Brían, son of Tuirenn, chieftain of Ben Eadair, paused and stared across the plain.

'Brothers,' he said, turning to Iuchar and Iucharba, 'wasn't there a proud warrior crossing the plain a moment ago?'

They affirmed that their brother was right.

Brían saw the herd of pigs and he realised that the warrior

must have shape-changed. If this were so, then the warrior was no friend to the sons of Tuirenn. Now Brían realised that the herd of pigs belonged to Nuada himself and if he and his brothers harmed them, then Nuada would punish them. So he took his own Druidical wand and touched his brothers lightly. Iuchar and Iucharba were changed into two great hounds and straightaway, baying eagerly, they made for the herd, keen noses to the ground.

Cian realised that the hounds would sniff him out and so, still in the shape of a pig, he made a break from the herd. But Brían was standing ready and cast his spear through the pig shape. Cian screamed in agony.

'I am Cian, son of Cainte, and I plead for quarter,' cried the pig.

Brían, now joined by his brothers in their true shapes, stood before the bleeding pig.

'No quarter!' snapped Brían. 'We have all sworn an oath that none would survive our encounters should the sons of Cainte and the sons of Tuirenn meet.'

'Then grant me a last request,' cried Cian in resignation. 'Let me resume my human form before you kill me.'

This Brían granted.

Cian smiled triumphantly at him. 'You may kill me now but remember this, sons of Tuirenn; had you killed me as a pig, your punishment would have only been the *eric* fine paid on the unlawful slaughter of a pig. Since you now kill me as a man, then you will have to pay the *eric* fine of a man. Moreover, as I am Cian, the enduring, the son of Cainte, and the father of Lugh of the Long Hand, the punishment that shall be exacted will be great. Even the weapons which you kill me with shall cry out in horror at this deed.'

Brían thought for a while, for it was true that Cian was one of the Children of Danu. Then he smiled sneeringly at Cian.

'Then it shall not be with weapons you will be killed but with stones of the earth.'

So saying, he threw aside his weapons and picked up some stones and hurled them in hate at Cian. He was joined by his brothers and stone after stone flew until Cian was a disfigured and unrecognisable mess of a man. Then the brothers dug a grave and buried the battered body. But six times the earth refused to cover the corpse before, at the seventh time of burying, the earth accepted the body.

Yet as Brían and his brothers rode away they heard a voice calling from beneath the earth: 'The blood is on your hands, sons of Tuirenn, and there it will remain until we meet again.'

* * *

The sons of Tuirenn distinguished themselves in the great Battle of the Plain of Towers in which Bres and the Fomorii were defeated. But everyone remarked that Cian was absent from the battle which was strange as it was Cian's own son who had taken over the leadership of the Children of Danu when Nuada had been killed by the Fomorii Balor of the Evil Eye. So, after a fruitless search, Lugh Lámhfada finally came to the Plain of Muirthemne and as he was travelling across it the stones of the earth started to speak:

'Here lies the body of your father Cian! Killed by the sons of Tuirenn. Blood on their hands until they meet with Cian again!'

And Lugh had his father's body disinterred and he called his companions together that they might see how the deed was done. And Lugh swore vengeance. Lugh sang a lament over the body:

> Cian's death, death of a great champion,
> Has left me as a walking corpse
> Without a soul,
> Without strength, without power,
> Without a feeling for life.
> The Sons of Tuirenn have killed him
> Now my hatred will come against them
> And follow them to the ends of the world.

And Lugh buried his father's body with all pomp and ceremony and went back to the great hall of Tara where he summoned all the people. Even the sons of Tuirenn were among them but Lugh kept his counsel. Instead he asked those among the gods what they would do to take vengeance on those who had with malice slaughtered their fathers.

Each of the gods suggested ways, increasingly more horrible and more bloody, as a means of punishment. And when the last of them had spoken, the assembly roared its approval. Lugh saw that the sons of Tuirenn, not wishing to be conspicuous in the throng, were also applauding. Then Lugh, with a scowl on his usually sunny countenance, spoke up.

'The murderers of Cian have condemned themselves for they have joined in the agreement of you all as to their punishment. But I am merciful. I will not spill blood in Tara. I claim the right to put an *eric* fine on the murderers. If they refuse to accept it then they must meet me, one after the other, in bloody single combat at the door of Tara's Hall.'

All the while he spoke he was looking at the sons of Tuirenn.

Then Brían moved forward.

'It is known there was enmity between us and your father and his brothers Cú and Céthan. Your words seem addressed to us but Cian was not killed by any weapons of the sons of Tuirenn. Nevertheless, to show that we are honourable, each one of us will accept your *eric* fine.'

Lugh smiled grimly.

'You will not find it difficult. I wish for three apples, the skin of a pig, a spear, two horses and a chariot, seven swine, a hound-pup, a cooking spit and three shouts to be delivered on a hill.'

Not only the sons of Tuirenn stood amazed but the entire assembly could not believe their ears at the little Lugh demanded in compensation for his father's death. The sons of Tuirenn were visibly relieved and clamoured to accept the fine.

'If you think it is too heavy,' Lugh added, 'I will not press the fine.'

'We do not consider it heavy,' replied Brían. 'In fact it seems so light that I suspect some trickery. Are you intending to increase the sum . . .?'

'I swear by our mother, Danu, the divine waters, that the fine will not be increased. And in return for this oath, do you swear you will faithfully complete the *eric* fine?'

They did so with mighty acclaim.

'Very well,' Lugh chuckled grimly, after they had sworn. 'The three apples must come from the Garden of Hesperides in the east. They are of gold in colour and have immense power and virtue. They are as big as the head of a month-old child and never grow less no matter how much is eaten from them. They have the taste of honey and a bite will cure a sick or wounded man. A warrior can perform any feat with one and should he for once cast it from his hand it will return to him.'

The sons of Tuirenn looked thunderstruck.

'The skin of the pig is that owned by Tuis, king of Greece. In whatever stream that pig walked, the water turned to wine, and the wounded and sick became well when they drank of it. These magical properties are enshrouded in that skin.'

The sons of Tuirenn began to look grim.

'The spear is that which belongs to Pisear of Persia and it is called "slaughterer". It has to be kept in a cauldron of blood to prevent it killing for only blood cools its angry blade.'

Lugh paused but the sons of Tuirenn now stood expressionless as they realised the trap that he had set for them.

'The steeds and chariot which I require are those belonging to Dobhar of Siogair. If one of the horses is killed it will come to life again if its bones are brought together in the same place.

'The seven swine are those of Easal, king of the Golden Pillars, which, though killed each day for the feast, are found alive the following morning. The hound pup is Failinis, owned by the king of Ioruiadh. The wild beasts are helpless before her. The cooking spit I want is that from the island of Fianchuibhne which is protected by mighty women warriors. And the hill on which you must give three shouts is that of Miodchaoin in Lochlainn which is constantly guarded by Miodchaoin and his three fierce sons, Aedh, Corca and Conn. Their task is solely to prevent any person from raising their voices on the hill.

'This, sons of Tuirenn, is the *eric* fine I ask of you.'

* * *

When Tuirenn heard of what had befallen his sons, he was upset but he went to them and gave them advice.

'No one can set out on this voyage without the magical ship of the god of the oceans Manánnan Mac Lir. But Lugh owns this ship, the Wave-sweeper, which can navigate itself across the seas. But listen to me, Lugh is under a *geis*, a sacred proscription never to refuse a second request. So go to him and ask for a loan of Manánnan's fabulous horse, Aonbharr, which can gallop over land and water. He will refuse. Then ask for the Wave-sweeper and that he cannot refuse.'

And this they did and it happened as Tuirenn had said. Lugh was forced to give them the loan of Manánnan's boat. And Tuirenn and his daughter Eithne went to see them off from the harbour at Ben Eadair. Their sister Eithne sung a lament of farewell for as much as she loved them, she knew that they had done an evil thing and therefore only evil would come of it.

The three warriors climbed into the Wave-sweeper and Brían commanded it to cross to the Garden of Hesperides. The boat leapt forward at his command and ploughed through the white crested waves more swiftly than if the winds of Spring were blowing into its sail. So fast did it travel that within the wink of an eye it came safely to the harbour of Hesperides on the extreme western edge of the ocean.

The three brothers climbed out. They learnt that the apple orchards of Hesperides were so well guarded that they had no chance of entering without discovery. Then Brían drew up his Druid's wand and changed his brothers and himself into hawks. On his instructions they rose into the air and circled high above the orchard and then they swooped down, travelling so fast that the arrows and spears of the guards could not hit them. Each in turn, they seized one of the golden apples and rose again into the air and raced back to the harbour where they had left their boat.

Now the king of Hesperides had three daughters who were sorceresses and when they heard the news they transformed themselves into three griffins and pursued the hawks, breathing great tongues of fire after them. So fierce were the flames that the hawks were burnt and blinded and could bear the heat no longer. Then Brían used his Druid's lore and changed them into swans who were able to glide down to the sea. The griffins confused flew off still looking for the hawks and the sons of Tuirenn made their way back to the Wave-sweeper.

Next they commanded the boat to take them to Greece and entered the harbour close to the palace of Tuis.

Brían's brothers wanted him to disguise them as animals but

he told them that poets from Inisfáil were well respected in Greece and they would go up to the king's palace and present themselves as such. Indeed, this was truly thought out for the guards allowed the three 'poets' into the king's palace. Tuis himself greeted them and invited them to a great feast. At the end of the feast, the king's poets rose and recited their poems. Then the sons of Tuirenn were invited to recite.

Brían stood up and intoned these verses.

> I conceal not your fame, O Tuis
> Great as an oak among kings,
> A pigskin is a reward without meanness,
> And this I claim in return for this poem.
>
> A war may come when warriors clash
> A war may be averted by a gift
> And he who gives without fear,
> Shall lose nothing.
>
> A stormy army and tempestuous sea
> Are weapons that no one would oppose,
> But a pigskin, a reward freely given
> Is that which we claim.

'It sounds an excellent poem,' mused Tuis, 'yet I do not understand it.'

'I will interpret it,' smiled Brían. 'It means that as an oak excels above other trees, so do you in kingship. We claim the pigskin you have as a reward for our poem, but if it is refused it means that there will be a war between us.'

Tuis stared in surprise.

'I would like your poem if you had not mentioned my magical pigskin. You seem a foolish man, poet, to ask for it. I would even refuse the kings and warriors of your land had they demanded it. So now I refuse you. Yet your poem is good and I will reward you with gold. And three times in gold what that pigskin will hold will be your fee.'

'Generous as you are, king,' Brían laughed, 'let us watch while the gold is measured in the skin.'

The king agreed and the sons of Tuirenn were brought to the treasure house and the skin was brought from its special place.

And when the skinfuls of gold were weighed, Brían suddenly grabbed the skin, drawing his sword and cutting the arm of the man who held the skin clean off. He wrapped the skin about himself and the three brothers fought their way from the palace. In rage and fury Tuis and his court attacked them but not one noble, nor champion of Greece, was able to halt them. Tuis himself fell before the slashing sword of Brían.

They fought their way back to the Wave-sweeper and straightaway they called on it to take them to Persia. It was agreed that the disguise of poets worked well for them and so they presented themselves to the court of Pisear in the same manner. Once more they were asked to recite a poem and Brían did so.

Small esteem of any spear with Pisear
His enemies are already broken
Pisear has little cause for worry
Since it is others who receive wounds.

The yew is the finest tree in the forest
The yew is king without opposition
May the great spear shafts drive on
Through the wounds of those they slay.

When Pisear asked Brían to spell out the meaning of the poem, Brían told him that he wanted his magic spear in payment for the poem.

When Pisear threatened to kill him and his brothers for audacity, Brían remembered that he had one of the apples of Hesperides with him. He took it from his bag and threw it at Pisear, so hard, it knocked the king's head off and returned safely to his hand. Then Brían and his brothers drew their swords and fought their way to the room where the blazing spear was kept in its great cauldron of blood, hissing and bubbling. They took it and went back to the Wave-sweeper.

On they went to Dobhar's kingdom of Siogair. Here they appeared before his court as three champions of Inisfáil seeking hospitality. When asked what they wanted they told Dobhar the king that they would serve him for payment. They spent a long time in Siogair because they were unable to find the steeds and the chariot which were faster than the winds of Spring. Finally, Brían tricked the king into ordering that the chariot be brought to the court, harnessed and ready.

And when the sons of Tuirenn turned and demanded the prancing horses and the beautiful chariot as the price for their service, Dobhar flew into a rage and ordered his guards to kill them.

Brían sprang into the chariot, hurling the charioteer to the ground. He took the reins in his hands and unloosed the spear of Pisear so that the guards of Dobhar were slain and those who were not simply fled. And with Iuchar and Iucharba behind him, Brían drove the chariot back to the waiting Wave-sweeper.

Next the magic boat of Manánnan Mac Lir brought them to the land of the Golden Pillars, the entrance of the Middle Sea, where Easal ruled. And when they came to the shore they saw great armies gathered for now the fame of the deeds of the sons of Tuirenn had travelled before them and news of their banishment from Inisfáil and the nature of their tasks had proceeded them.

Easal the king came down to the harbour to meet them and he demanded to know if it was true that they had come for his swine. They told him it was. Now Easal was a peaceful man and he went and sat in council with his chieftains. Eventually they decided that they would hand the swine to the sons of Tuirenn to avoid the slaughter of the innocent. That night Easal invited the brothers to a feasting where the seven pigs were handed to them. Brían sang a paean in praise of Easal's wisdom and generosity.

When Easal learnt that the sons of Tuirenn were going next to the country of Ioruiadh, the king asked that he be allowed to accompany them for his daughter was the wife of the king of Ioruaidh. Easal promised, in return, to do his best to secure the hound-pup from the king, his son-in-law, without bloodshed.

The king of Ioruiadh would have none of Easal's advice. 'You may be weak, old man, but the gods have not given strength or luck enough to any warrior to take my hound-pup by force.'

Easal was saddened for he knew what bloodshed and mayhem would follow.

A great and bloody battle began. And Brían cleaved through the warriors of Ioruaidh, throwing them back by the nine times one hundred until he reached the spot where the king of Ioruaidh stood. And he bodily picked up the king and fought his way back until he threw the craven man at Easal's feet.

'There is your daughter's husband, o king. It would have been easier to kill him than to return with him alive.'

The warriors of Ioruiadh, seeing their king defeated, threw down their arms. And the king of Ioruiadh now heeded the peaceful tones of Easal and handed over the hound-pup and the sons of Tuirenn took their leave in friendship.

Now only two tasks remained to be filled.

They were to find the cooking spit of Fianchuibhne and give three shouts on the Hill of Miodchaoin.

But so excited were they at their successes that they forgot about the last two tasks. Some have it that Lugh Lámhfada had prevailed upon his Druid to send a cloud of forgetfulness to seep into the brothers' minds after they had left Ioruaidh.

Whatever the cause, the Wave-sweeper returned to Inisfáil. Lugh heard of their coming and was suddenly troubled for he had followed the successes of the sons of Tuirenn with mixed feelings. He was happy that these gifts that they had secured were for him but apprehensive that they might be turned against him. He was also bitter because the brothers were fulfilling the conditions of the *eric* fine which he had devised to cause their deaths.

So when the Wave-sweeper entered the mouth of the Boyne river, Lugh went to the fort of Cathair Crofinn and armed himself with the magical armour of the Ocean god, Manánnan, who was his foster father. He also put on the cloak of invisibility of Fea the Hateful, one of the goddesses of war. For Lugh also feared their coming, thinking the three brothers might mean him harm now that they possessed such wonderful weapons. And when they sent word to Lugh, asking him to come and take his *eric* fine, Lugh sent back asking that they hand over the spoils to the Bodb Dearg, son of The Dagda, who had now succeeded Lugh as ruler of the Children of Danu. Only when the Bodb Dearg reported that he had control of the wondrous gifts did Lugh emerge and come to examine them.

'But where is the cooking spit?' demanded Lugh, 'And I did not hear the three shouts on the Hill of Miodchaoin.'

The sons of Tuirenn then remembered and they were sorely

grieved. So they left and spent a night with their father, Tuirenn, and sister Eithne, at their fortress at Ben Eadair. Now they did not have the benefit of the magical ship the Wave-sweeper for they had foolishly surrendered it to Lugh. So they set sail in an ordinary ship in search of Fianchuibhne. However, the task was a long one. For three months they searched, visiting many islands and asking many travellers if they knew of such a place. No one knew.

Finally, they met an old man; toothless and without eyes for there were so many wrinkles and folds of flesh on his walnut coloured face, that they were hidden. He told them that the island of Fianchuibhne did not lie on the surface of the sea but deep down in its depths.

Brían, telling Iuchar and Iucharba to wait for him, leapt over the side of their ship and sank down into the waves. For two periods of nine days he walked the ocean bed in his search and found many houses, and great palaces. Then he entered a house with its doors open where one hundred and fifty beautiful women were engaged in needlework and embroidery. In the middle of them lay a cooking spit.

Brían saw that the women neither moved nor spoke as he entered. So, without more ado, he walked to the spit, seized it, turned and walked out. At that point the women all burst out laughing. They rose and surrounded Brían who saw they had a formidable assortment of weapons.

'Brave man are you Brían son of Tuirenn. There are one hundred and fifty of us here, every one a warrior, and each one of us able to slay you. But you are brave and courageous to make this attempt knowing the dangers. You shall be rewarded. Take the spit for this is one of many which we have.'

And Brían thanked them and swam upwards to the ship in which his brothers were anxiously waiting. They were overjoyed.

They turned the ship northward now to the great fjords of Lochlainn, for that is what the name means, the place of lochs and fjords. They saw the great hill of Miodchaoin rising upwards and, leaving their ship, they walked to the bottom of it. But there, on the massive slopes, stood Miodchaoin, who was a mighty warrior.

Miodchaoin saw Brían and unsheathed his great sword.

'Killer of my friend and foster-brother Cian! Now you have come to shout upon this hill. You will do that deed only when I am dead.'

Brían flew at Miodchaoin and the two great warriors set about one another. So fierce was their onslaught that the ringing of the swords upon their shields could be heard in every corner of the world. No quarter was asked nor given until Miodchaoin fell dead with Brían's sword thrust through his giant heart.

Then the three sons of Miodchaoin, Aedh, Corca and Conn, having heard the noise of battle, came racing up and fell on the three sons of Tuirenn. The sky reddened and blackened, blood flowed from that mountain slope like the gushing waters of a mountain spring, and the earth trembled from the stamping of their feet even as far to the east as Hesperides.

For three days and three nights the great combat shook the mountains of Lochlainn. Then the sons of Miodchaoin managed to find the flesh of the sons of Tuirenn with their spear points. Each one of the sons of Tuirenn, Brían, Iuchar and Iuchara, were pierced and wounded. Yet the sons of Tuirenn would not give in for they thrust their spears into the bodies of Aedh, Corca and Conn and the three sons of Miodchaoin fell dead.

The sons of Tuirenn fell on the blood-stained grass and it seemed that a heavy veil of darkness was being drawn before their eyes. It was Brían, coughing blood, who called faintly: 'Brothers, how is it with you?' 'Dead are we,' they gasped, 'or as near it as makes no difference.'

'We must climb the hill and give three shouts before death claims us,' replied Brían. 'Only then may we rest in peace.'

With Brían supporting his two brothers on his mighty arms, the three went forward up the steep slopes, stumbling and moving as in a dream until they reached the summit. Then they paused and gave three shouts, weak as they were, they were shouts nevertheless.

Brían, still supporting his brothers, then guided them to the ship and they turned her prow for Inisfáil.

In a delirium they drifted and drifted towards the distant island. Suddenly Brían raised his head:

'I see Ben Eadair and the fort of our father, Tuirenn.'

His brothers raised their heads so that they might see the green hills of their home before they died. The ship gently nudged ashore and Tuirenn came down with Eithne to greet his sons.

'Father, take the spit to Lugh,' instructed Brían, 'and tell him that the three shouts on the Hill of Miodchaoin have been given.'

And Tuirenn mounted his chariot and rode to Tara with the news. And he pleaded with Lugh to loan him the magic pigskin of Tuis which would heal the sick and wounded or one of the apples of Hesperides but Lugh refused him coldly. And Tuirenn returned to his dying sons and lamented:

If all the jewels of the world
Were given to Lugh to ease his anger
It would not be enough to save you
From a gloomy grave.

MY LORD BAG OF RICE

Theodora Ozaki

LONG AGO THERE lived in Japan a brave warrior known to all as Tawara Toda, or 'My Lord Bag of Rice.' His true name was Fujiwara Hidesato, and this is the story of how he came to change his name.

One day he sallied forth in search of adventures, for he had the nature of a warrior and could not bear to be idle. So he buckled on his two swords, took his huge bow, much taller than himself, in his hand, and slinging his quiver on his back started out. He had not gone far when he came to the bridge of Seta-no-Karashi spanning one end of the beautiful Lake Biwa. No sooner had he set foot on the bridge than he saw lying right across his patch a huge serpent-dragon. Its body was so big that it looked like the trunk of a large pine tree and it took up the whole width of the bridge. One of its huge claws rested on the parapet of one side of the bridge, while its tail lay right against the other. The monster seemed to be asleep, and as it breathed, fire and smoke came out of its nostrils.

At first Hidesato could not help feeling alarmed at the sight of this horrible reptile lying in his path, for he must either turn back or walk right over its body. He was a brave man, however, and putting aside all fear went forward dauntlessly. Crunch, crunch! he stepped now on the dragon's body, now between its coils, and without even one glance backward he went on his way.

He had only gone a few steps when he heard someone calling him from behind. On turning back he was much surprised to see that the monster dragon had entirely disappeared and in its place was a strange-looking man, who was bowing most ceremoniously to the ground. His red hair streamed over his shoulders and was surmounted by a crown in the shape of a dragon's head, and his sea-green dress was patterned with shells. Hidesato knew at once that this was no ordinary mortal and he wondered much at the strange occurrence. Where had the dragon gone in such a short space of time? Or had it transformed itself into this man, and what did the whole thing mean? While these thoughts passed through his mind he had come up to the man on the bridge and now addressed him:

'Was it you that called me just now?'

'Yes, it was I,' answered the man: 'I have an earnest request to make to you. Do you think you can grant it to me?'

'If it is in my power to do so I will,' answered Hidesato, 'but first tell me who you are?'

'I am the Dragon King of the Lake, and my home is in these waters just under this bridge.'

'And what is it you have to ask of me!' said Hidesato.

'I want you to kill my mortal enemy the centipede, who lives on the mountain beyond,' and the Dragon King pointed to a high peak on the opposite shore of the lake.

'I have lived now for many years in this lake and I have a large family of children and grandchildren. For some time past we have lived in terror, for a monster centipede has discovered our home, and night after night it comes and carries off one of my family. I am powerless to save them. If it goes on much longer like this, not only shall I lose all my children, but I myself must fall a victim to the monster. I am, therefore, very unhappy, and in my extremity I determined to ask the help of a human being. For many days with this intention I have waited on the bridge in the shape of the horrible serpent-dragon that you saw, in the hope that some strong brave man would come along. But all who came this way, as soon as they saw me were terrified and ran away as fast as they could. You are the first man I have found able to look at me without fear, so I knew at once that you were a man of great courage. I beg you to have pity upon me. Will you not help me and kill my enemy the centipede?'

Hidesato felt very sorry for the Dragon King on hearing his story, and readily promised to do what he could to help him. The warrior asked where the centipede lived, so that he might attack the creature at once. The Dragon King replied that its home was on the mountain Mikami, but that as it came every night at a certain hour to the palace of the lake, it would be better to wait till then. So Hidesato was conducted to the palace of the Dragon King, under the bridge. Strange to say, as he followed his host downwards the waters parted to let them pass, and his clothes did not even feel damp as he passed through the flood. Never had Hidesato seen anything so beautiful as this palace built of white marble beneath the lake. He had often heard of the Sea King's palace at the bottom of the sea, where all the servants and retainers were salt-water fishes, but here was a magnificent building in the heart of Lake Biwa. The dainty goldfishes, red carp, and silvery trout, waited upon the Dragon King and his guest.

Hidesato was astonished at the feast that was spread for him. The dishes were crystallized lotus leaves and flowers, and the chopsticks were of the rarest ebony. As soon as they sat down, the sliding doors opened and ten lovely goldfish dancers came out, and behind them followed ten red-carp musicians with the koto and the samisen. Thus the hours flew by till midnight, and the beautiful music and dancing had banished all thoughts of the centipede. The Dragon King was about to pledge the warrior in a fresh cup of wine when the palace was suddenly shaken by a tramp, tramp! as if a mighty army had begun to march not far away.

Hidesato and his host both rose to their feet and rushed to the balcony, and the warrior saw on the opposite mountain two great balls of glowing fire coming nearer and nearer. The Dragon King stood by the warrior's side trembling with fear.

'The centipede! The centipede! Those two balls of fire are its eyes. It is coming for its prey! Now is the time to kill it.'

Hidesato looked where his host pointed, and, in the dim light of the starlit evening, behind the two balls of fire he saw the long body of an enormous centipede winding round the mountains, and the light in its hundred feet glowed like so many distant lanterns moving slowly towards the shore.

Hidesato showed not the least sign of fear. He tried to calm the Dragon King.

'Don't be afraid. I shall surely kill the centipede. Just bring me my bow and arrows.'

The Dragon King did as he was bid, and the warrior noticed that he had only three arrows left in his quiver. He took the bow, and fitting an arrow to the notch, took careful aim and let fly.

The arrow hit the centipede right in the middle of its head, but instead of penetrating, it glanced off harmless and fell to the ground.

Nothing daunted, Hidesato took another arrow, fitted it to the notch of the bow and let fly. Again the arrow hit the mark, it struck the centipede right in the middle of its head, only to glance off and fall to the ground. The centipede was invulnerable to weapons! When the Dragon King saw that even this brave warrior's arrows were powerless to kill the centipede, he lost heart and began to tremble with fear.

The warrior saw that he had now only one arrow left in his quiver, and if this one failed he could not kill the centipede. He looked across the waters. The huge reptile had wound its horrid body seven times round the mountain and would soon come down to the lake. Nearer and nearer gleamed fireballs of eyes, and the light of its hundred feet began to throw reflections in the still waters of the lake.

Then suddenly the warrior remembered that he had heard that human saliva was deadly to centipedes. But this was no ordinary centipede. This was so monstrous that even to think of such a creature made one creep with horror. Hidesato determined to try his last chance. So taking his last arrow and first putting the end of it in his mouth, he fitted the notch to his bow, took careful aim once more and let fly.

This time the arrow again hit the centipede right in the middle of its head, but instead of glancing off harmlessly as before, it struck home to the creature's brain. Then with a convulsive shudder the serpentine body stopped moving, and the fiery light of its great eyes and hundred feet darkened to a dull glare like the sunset of a stormy day, and then went out in blackness. A great darkness now overspread the heavens, the thunder rolled and the lightning flashed, and the wind roared in fury, and it seemed as if the world were coming to an end. The Dragon King and his children and retainers all crouched in different parts of the palace, frightened to death, for the building was shaken to its foundation. At last the dreadful night was over. Day dawned beautiful and clear. The centipede was gone from the mountain.

Then Hidesato called to the Dragon King to come out with him on the balcony, for the centipede was dead and he had nothing more to fear.

Then all the inhabitants of the palace came out with joy, and Hidesato pointed to the lake. There lay the body of the dead centipede floating on the water, which was dyed red with its blood.

The gratitude of the Dragon King knew no bounds. The whole family came and bowed down before the warrior, calling him their preserver and the bravest warrior in all Japan.

Another feast was prepared, more sumptuous than the first. All kinds of fish, prepared in every imaginable way, raw, stewed, boiled and roasted, served on coral trays and crystal dishes, were put before him, and the wine was the best that Hidesato had ever tasted in his life. To add to the beauty of everything the sun shone brightly, the lake glittered like a liquid diamond, and the palace was a thousand times more beautiful by day than by night.

His host tried to persuade the warrior to stay a few days, but Hidesato insisted on going home, saying that he had now finished what he had come to do, and must return. The Dragon King and his family were all very sorry to have him leave so soon, but since he would go they begged him to accept a few small presents (so they said) in token of their gratitude to him for delivering them forever from their horrible enemy the centipede.

As the warrior stood in the porch taking leave, a train of fish was suddenly transformed into a retinue of men, all wearing ceremonial robes and dragon's crowns on their heads to show that they were servants of the great Dragon King. The presents that they carried were as follows:

First, a large bronze bell.
Second, a bag of rice.
Third, a roll of silk.
Fourth, a cooking pot.

Hidesato did not want to accept all these presents, but as the Dragon King insisted, he could not well refuse.

The Dragon King himself accompanied the warrior as far as

the bridge, and then took leave of him with many bows and good wishes, leaving the procession of servants to accompany Hidesato to his house with the presents.

The warrior's household and servants had been very much concerned when they found that he did not return the night before, but they finally concluded that he had been kept by the violent storm and had taken shelter somewhere. When the servants on the watch for his return caught sight of him they called to everyone that he was approaching, and the whole household turned out to meet him, wondering much what the retinue of men, bearing presents and banners, that followed him, could mean.

As soon as the Dragon King's retainers had put down the presents they vanished, and Hidesato told all that had happened to him.

The presents which he had received from the grateful Dragon King were found to be of magic power. The bell only was ordinary, and as Hidesato had no use for it he presented it to the temple near by, where it was hung up, to boom out the hour of day over the surrounding neighbourhood.

The single bag of rice, however much was taken from it day after day for the meals of the knight and his whole family, never grew less – the supply in the bag was inexhaustible.

The roll of silk, too, never grew shorter, though time after time long pieces were cut off to make the warrior a new suit of clothes to go to Court in at the New Year.

The cooking pot was wonderful, too. No matter what was put into it, it cooked deliciously whatever was wanted without any firing – truly a very economical saucepan.

The fame of Hidesato's fortune spread far and wide, and as there was no need for him to spend money on rice or silk or firing, he became very rich and prosperous, and was henceforth known as *My Lord Bag of Rice*.

PRINCE SEYF EL MULOUK

François Pétis de la Croix

I HAVE ALREADY had the honour of telling your majesty that I am the son of the late Sultan of Egypt, Asem Ben Sefouan, and brother of the prince who succeeded him. One day, being in my sixteenth year I found the door of my father's treasury open. I entered, and I began to scrutinise with much attention the things which seemed rarest to me. I lingered particularly over a little box of red sandalwood, strewn with pearls, diamonds, emeralds, and topazes. It opened with a little gold key, which was in the lock. I opened it, and perceived within a ring of marvellous beauty, with a gold box which contained the portrait of a woman.

The features were so regular, the eyes so fine, her appearance so charming, that I thought at first it was a fancy portrait. 'The works of nature are not so perfect,' I said. What honour to the brush which produced it does this do!' I admired the imagination of the painter who had been capable of forming so beautiful an idea to himself.

My eyes could not detach themselves from this painting, and, what is most surprising, it inspired me with love. I thought it was perhaps the portrait of some living princess, and the more amorous I became the more I persuaded myself of it. I closed the box and put it in my pocket with the ring; then I left the treasury.

I had a confidant named Saed. He was the son of a great lord of Cairo. I loved him, and he was a few years older than me. I related my adventure to him; he asked me for the portrait and I gave it him. He took it out of the box to see whether there were not some writing at the back which could tell us what I longed passionately to know – that is to say, the name of the person portrayed.

We perceived round the box inside these words in Arabic characters: 'Bedy-Aljemal, daughter of the King Achahbal.'

This discovery charmed me; I was enchanted to learn that I was not in love with an imaginary person. I bade my confidant discover where King Achahbal reigned.

Saed asked it of the best informed people of Cairo, but no one could tell him, so that I resolved to travel, to scour the world if necessary, and not to return to Egypt until I had seen Bedy-Aljemal. I begged the sultan, my father, to permit me to go to Baghdad to see the court of the caliph and the marvels of that town of which I had heard so much. He granted me this permission. As I wished to travel incognito, I did not make a pompous exit from Cairo; my suite consisted only of Saed and some slaves whose zeal was known to me. I soon put on my finger the beautiful ring which I had taken from my father's treasury, and the whole way I talked with my confidant only of the Princess Bedy-Aljemal, whose portrait I had always in my hands. When I arrived at Baghdad and had seen all that was curious there, I asked of some wise men if they could not tell me in what part of the world were situated the States of the King Achahbal. They replied in the negative; but if I wished very much to know I had only to take the trouble to go to Bassora and find an old man aged a hundred and seventy, named Padmanaba. This person knew everything, and would doubtless satisfy my curiosity.

I left Baghdad immediately, flew to Bassora, and inquired for the old man. His dwelling was pointed out to me. I went to him. I saw a venerable man still full of vigour, although nearly two centuries had passed over him.

'My son,' he said to me, with a laughing air, 'what can I do for you?'

'My father,' I said to him, 'I would like to know where the King Achahbal reigns. It is of the utmost importance for me to know. Some wise men of Baghdad whom I have consulted, and who have not been able to throw any light upon it, have assured me that you would tell me the name of and the road to the Kingdom of Achahbal.'

'My son,' replied the old man, 'the wise men who have sent you to me think me less ignorant than I am. I do not know exactly where the States of Achahbal are, I only remember to have heard some traveller speak of them. This king reigns, I believe, in a neighbouring island to that of Serendib, but it is only a conjecture, and I am perhaps in error.'

I thanked Padmanaba for having at least indicated a spot where I might hope to be informed of what I wished to know. I formed the resolution to go to the island of Serendib. I embarked with Saed and my slaves on the Gulf of Bassora in a merchant vessel which was going to Surat. From Surat we went to Goa, where we learnt on arrival that a vessel was going to sail in a few days and take the direction of the island of Serendib. We profited by the occasion.

We left Goa with a favourable wind, which took us far on our way the first day; but the second day the wind changed, and towards evening so violent a tempest arose that the sailors, seeing our destruction to be inevitable, abandoned the vessel to the mercy of the wind and sea. Sometimes the waves, opening as if to engulf us, presented frightful abysses to our frightened eyes, and sometimes rising they lifted us to the clouds. The vessel soon filling, we took to the boats. I threw myself into one with Saed. Hardly had we left the vessel than it foundered with a terrible sound, and we lost sight of our companions.

Having drifted all night, we saw at daybreak a little island. We landed on it. Trees, laden with very fine fruit hanging to the ground, first met our view, which rejoiced us all the more that we began to feel very hungry. We picked and ate of them, and found them excellent. When we had taken a little refreshment, we fastened our boat and advanced further into the island. I have never seen a more delightful spot: sandal and aloe woods grew there; there were springs of fresh water, and all sorts of fruits, as well as the most beautiful flowers.

What surprised us most was that this island, although so pleasant to look upon, seemed to be deserted.

'Whence comes it,' I said to Saed, 'that this island is not inhabited? We are not the first to visit it; others before us have doubtless discovered it. Why is it abandoned?'

'My prince,' replied my confidant, 'since no one lives here, it is a sure proof that no one can live here; there is something about it which renders it uninhabitable.' Alas! when the unfortunate Saed spoke thus, he little knew with what truth he was speaking.

We spent the day in rejoicing, and when night fell we stretched ourselves on the grass, which was sprinkled with a thousand sweet-smelling flowers. We slept deliciously; but on awaking I was very astonished to find myself alone. I called Saed repeatedly. As he did not reply I rose to seek him, and, after having searched a part of the island, I returned to the same place where I had spent the night, thinking he might perhaps be there. I awaited him in vain the whole day and even the following night; then, despairing of seeing him again, I made the air resound with cries and groans. 'Ah! my dear Saed,' I cried every minute, 'what has become of you? Whilst you were with me you helped me to bear the burden of my misfortune; you relieved my troubles in sharing them; by what misfortune or by what enchantment have you been carried off from me? What barbarous power has separated us? It would have been sweeter to die with you than to live quite alone.'

I could not console myself for the loss of my confidant; and what troubled me was that I could not think what could have happened to him. I was in despair and resolved to perish also on that island. I said to myself, 'I will scour it thoroughly; I will find either Saed or death.' I walked towards a wood that I saw, and when I had arrived there, I discovered in the middle a very well-built castle, surrounded by a large moat full of water, the drawbridge of which was let down. I entered a large courtyard paved with white marble, and advanced towards the door of a fine block of buildings. It was made of aloe-wood; several figures of birds were represented in relief upon it, and a great padlock of steel, made in the form of a lion, kept it closed. The key was in the padlock; I took hold of it to turn it; the padlock broke like a piece of glass, and the door opened more of itself than from the effort I made to open it, which caused me extreme surprise. I found a staircase of black marble. I ascended, and first entered a great hall ornamented with a gold and silken tapestry with sofas of brocade. From there I entered a room richly furnished, but what I looked at with most attention was a perfectly beautiful young lady. She was reclining on a large sofa, her head resting on a cushion, richly dressed, and beside her was a little jasper table. As her eyes were closed, and I had reason to doubt her being alive, I approached her gently and perceived that she breathed.

I remained for some moments in contemplation of her. She seemed charming to me, and I should have become enamoured of her had I not been so absorbed in Bedy-Aljemal. I was extremely desirous of knowing why I found in a deserted island a young lady alone in a castle where I saw no one. I sincerely hoped she would wake, but she slept so soundly I did not dare disturb her rest. I left the castle, resolved to return some hours later. I walked about the island, and saw with alarm a great number of animals as large as tigers, and formed something like ants. I should have taken them for cruel and ferocious beasts had they not fled at sight of me. I saw other wild animals who seemed to fear me, although they had an alarmingly ferocious appearance. After having eaten several fruits whose beauty charmed me, and having walked for some time, I returned to the castle, where the lady was still asleep. I could no longer resist the desire I had to speak to her. I made a noise in the room and coughed to awake her. As she did not awake, I approached her and touched her arm, but without effect. 'There is some enchantment here,' I then said to myself; 'some talisman keeps this lady asleep, and if this is the case it is not possible to awake her from this slumber.' I despaired of succeeding, when I perceived on the jasper table of which I have spoken several graven characters; I thought this graving might hold the secret. I was about to study the table, but I had hardly touched it when the lady gave a deep sigh and awoke.

If I had been surprised to find so beautiful a person in this castle, she was not less astonished to see me. 'Ah! young man,' she said to me, 'how did you get in here? What have you done to surmount all the obstacles which should have prevented your entering this castle, and which are beyond the reach of human power? I cannot believe you to be a man. You are doubtless the prophet Elias?'

'No, madam,' I said to her, 'I am only a simple man, and I can assure you I have come here without any difficulty. The door of this castle opened as soon as I had touched the key. I mounted to this apartment without any power resisting me. I have not awakened you with ease; that is what I found most difficult.'

'I cannot believe what you tell me,' replied the lady. 'I am so persuaded that it is impossible to men to do what you have done, that I do not believe, whatever you may say, that you are merely a man.'

'Madam,' I said, 'I am perhaps something more than an ordinary man. A sovereign is the author of my being, but I am only a man for all that. I have much more reason to think that you are a superior being to myself.'

'No,' she replied, 'I am, like you, of the race of Adam. But tell me why you have left your father's court, and how you came to this island.'

I then satisfied her curiosity. I ingenuously admitted that I had become enamoured of Bedy-Aljemal, daughter of the king Achahbal, on seeing her portrait, which I showed her. The lady took the portrait, looked at it very attentively, and said; 'I have heard speak of the King Achahbal. He reigns in a neighbouring island to Serendib. If his daughter is as beautiful as her portrait, she indeed deserves that you should love her ardently, but one must not trust in the portraits which are taken of princesses; they are usually painted beautiful. Finish telling me your history,' she added; 'after that I will relate mine to you.'

I gave her a long and detailed account of all my adventures, and then I begged her to relate hers to me. She began thus:

'I am the only daughter of the King of Serendib. One day as I was with my women in a castle of my father's near the town of Serendib, the fancy took me to bathe in a white marble basin which was in the garden. I was undressed, and entered the basin with my favourite slave. We had hardly entered the water than a wind arose. A whirlwind of dust formed in the air above us, and from the midst of this whirlwind there suddenly flew a great bird who pounced on me, took me in his claws, carried me off and brought me to this castle, where, immediately changing its shape, it appeared before me in the form of a young genie. "Princess," he said to me, "I am one of the most considerable genii in the world. As I was passing the island of Serendib today, I saw you in your bath. You charmed me. 'There is a beautiful princess,' I said to myself, 'it would be a pity she should make the happiness of a son of Adam; she deserves the attachment of a genie. I must carry her off and transport her to a desert island.' So, princess, forget the king, your father, and think only of responding to my love. You shall want for nothing in this castle. I will take care to provide you with everything you need."

'Whilst the genie was speaking thus to me, I only wept and lamented. "Unfortunate Malika," I said to myself, "is this the fate which was reserved for you? Has the king, my father, brought me up with so much care only to have the sorrow to lose me so miserably? Alas! he does not know what has become of me, and I fear my loss will be fatal to him." "No, no," said the genie to me, "your father will not succumb to his grief; and as for you, my princess, I trust you will yield to the evidences of affection which I propose to give you." "Do not flatter yourself," I said, "with this false hope. I shall have all my life a mortal aversion to the man who has carried me off." "You will change your sentiment," he replied; "you will accustom yourself to me; time will produce this effect." "It will not work this miracle," I interrupted with bitterness, "it will rather increase the hatred that I feel for you." The genie, instead of appearing offended, smiled, and, persuaded that I should accustom myself by degrees to listen to him, he spared nothing to please me. He went, I know not where, to get magnificent clothes which he brought me. He did his best to inspire in me an inclination for him; but, perceiving that far from making any progress in my heart, he became daily more odious to me, he finally lost patience, and resolved to revenge himself for my contempt. He threw me into a magic sleep; he stretched me on the sofa in the attitude in which you have found me, and put beside me this marble table on which he had traced talismanic characters to keep me in a deep sleep through the centuries. He also made two other talismans; one to make this castle invisible, the other to prevent the door being opened. Then he left me in this apartment and quitted the castle. He returns hither from time to time. He wakes me up and asks me whether I wish at last to become sensible to his passion, and as I persist in refusing him, he plunges me anew in the unconsciousness which he has invented for my punishment.

'Nevertheless, my lord,' continued the daughter of the King of Serendib, 'you have awakened me, you have opened the door of this castle which has not remained invisible to you. Have I not reason to doubt your being a man? I will even tell you that it is surprising that you still live; for I have heard the genie say that the wild beasts devour all those who wish to stop in this island, and that it is on that account deserted.'

Whilst the princess Malika was speaking thus, we heard a great noise in the castle. She ceased speaking in order to hear better, and soon terrible cries met our ears.

'Great Heaven!' then said the princess, 'we are lost. It is the genie; I recognise him by his voice. You will perish; nothing can save you from his fury. Ah! unhappy prince; what fatality has brought you to this castle?'

I thought my death inevitable. The genie entered looking furious. He had a steel club in his hand; his body was enormous. He shuddered at the sight of me; but instead of giving me a blow on the head, or adopting a threatening tone, he approached me trembling, threw himself at my feet, and spoke thus:

'Oh! prince, son of a king, you have only to command me as you please; I am prepared to obey you.'

This speech surprised me. I could not understand why this genie was so grovelling to me, and spoke as a slave. But my surprise vanished when, continuing to speak to me, he said:

'The ring which you have on your finger is the seal of Solomon; whoever possesses it cannot perish from accident. He can cross the most stormy seas in a simple skiff without fearing that the waves will swallow him up. The most ferocious beasts cannot hurt him, and he has a sovereign power over genii. Talismans and all charms yield to his marvellous seal.'

'It is then by virtue of this ring that I still live,' I said to the genie.

'Yes, my lord,' he replied, 'it is that ring which has saved you from the beasts which are on this island.'

'Tell me,' I said to him, 'if you know what has become of the companion I had on arriving?'

'I know the present and the past,' replied the genie, 'and I will tell you that your comrade has been eaten by the ants, who devoured him at night at your side. Those sort of ants are in great numbers and make this island uninhabitable. They do not prevent, however, the neighbouring peoples, and above all the inhabitants of the Maldives, coming here every year to cut sandalwood; but they do not carry it away without difficulty; they come here during the summer; they have on board their vessels very swift horses, which they disembark, and on which they mount; they gallop in whatever direction they see sandalwood, and as soon as they see the ants approaching they throw them great pieces of meat with which they are provided for the purpose. Whilst the ants are occupied in eating these pieces of meat, the men mark the trees they wish to cut, after which they return. They come back in the winter and cut the trees without fear of the ants, who do not show themselves at this season.'

I could not hear the strange fate of Saed without feeling grieved. Then I asked the genie where the dominion of the king Achahbal was and if the princess Bedy-Aljemal his daughter still lived.

'My lord,' he replied, 'there is in these seas an island where there reigns a king named Achahbal, but he has no daughter. The princess Bedy-Aljemal of whom you speak, was indeed the daughter of a king called Achahbal, who lived in the time of Solomon.'

'What!' I replied, 'Bedy-Aljemal lives no longer?'

'No,' he replied, 'she was a wife of the great Prophet.'

I was very mortified to hear that I loved someone whose life was long over. 'Oh! madman that I am!' I cried, 'why did I not ask the sultan, my father, whose portrait it was I found in his treasury? He would have told me what I have just heard. What trouble and anxiety I should have spared myself! I should have nipped my love in the bud. It would perhaps not have gained such control over me. I should not have left Cairo; Saed would be still living. Must his death be then the sole outcome of my chimerical sentiments? All that consoles me, beautiful princess,' I continued, turning to Malika, 'is having been able to be useful to you: thanks to my ring, I am in the position to give you back to the king your father.' At the same time I addressed the genie: 'Since I am happy enough,' I said, 'to be the possessor of the seal of Solomon, since I have the right to command genii, obey me. I order you to transport me immediately with the princess Malika, to the kingdom of Serendib, to the gates of the capital.'

'I am going to obey you, my lord,' replied the genie, 'however unhappy the loss of the princess may make me.'

'It is very fortunate for you,' I replied, 'that I content myself with only exacting from you that you should bear us both to the island of Serendib; you deserve, for having carried off Malika, that I should punish you to the full extent of the power which the seal of the Prophet gives me over rebel genii.'

The genie replied nothing; he prepared immediately to do what I had ordered him: he took us in his arms, the princess and myself, and bore us to the gates of Serendib. 'Is that all,' then said the genie to me, 'that you wish me to do? Have you nothing further to command me?' I replied in the negative, and he immediately disappeared.

We went to lodge at the first caravanserai on entering the town, and there we deliberated whether we would write to the court or whether I should go myself to inform the king of the arrival of the princess. We decided on the latter course. I betook myself to the palace, which seemed to me a singular structure. It was built on a thousand columns of marble, and the ascent to it was by a staircase of three hundred steps of beautiful stone. I passed a guard in the first hall; an officer approached me, asked me whether I had any business at the court, or whether curiosity alone brought me thither. I replied that I wished to speak to the king on an important matter. The officer led me to the grand vizir, who presented me to the king, his master.

'Young man,' said the monarch to me, 'of what country are you, and what do you come to Serendib for?'

'Sire,' I replied, 'Egypt was my birth-place. I have been long absent from my father, and I have experienced all sorts of misfortunes.' Hardly had I said these words than the king, who was a kind old man, began to weep.

'Alas!' he said to me, 'I am no happier than you. I have lost my only daughter, in a manner which increases my grief at not seeing her again.'

'My lord,' I replied, 'I have come to this palace only to give you news of this princess.'

'Ah! what news,' he cried, 'can you give me of her? You have come to announce her death to me? You have doubtless been the witness of her sad end?'

'No, no,' I replied, 'she still lives, and you will see her today.'

'Ah! where have you found her?' said the king; 'where was she hidden?'

Then I related all my adventures to him. I dilated particularly on that of the castle and the genie, which he listened to with all the more attention that he was himself interested in it. As soon as I had finished he embraced me.

'Prince,' he said to me, for I had discovered my birth to him in relating my history, 'what do I not owe to you? I love my daughter dearly: I did not hope to see her again. You have been the cause of my finding her. How can I acquit myself towards you? Let us go together,' he continued; 'let us go to the caravanserai where you have left her, I am burning with impatience to embrace my dear Malika.'

Saying these words, he gave the order to his vizir to have a litter prepared, which was promptly executed.

The king then made me enter the litter with him, and followed by several officers on horseback we went to the caravanserai where Malika awaited me impatiently. No words can express the mutual joy which the King of Serendib and the princess his daughter felt on seeing each other again. After their first transport the monarch wished Malika herself to give a detailed account of her being carried off and her rescue, which she did in a way that gave him much satisfaction. He thought how happily she had preserved her life from the power of the genie, and declared that he could not carry his gratitude to her liberator too far. He seemed charmed with my bearing and my courage.

We all returned to the palace, where the king gave me a magnificent apartment. He ordered public prayers to return thanks to Heaven for the return of the princess. The inhabitants celebrated it with endless rejoicing. There was a magnificent feast at the court; all the nobility of the island were invited.

The King of Serendib showed me every attention; he took me hunting with him: I joined in all his pleasure parties. He evinced such friendship for me that he said to me one day: 'O my son, it is time to reveal to you a plan I have formed. You have brought me back my daughter. You have consoled an afflicted father. I wish to acquit myself towards you. Be my son-in-law and the inheritor of my crown.'

I thanked the king for his kindness, and begged him not to take it ill if I refused the honour he wished to do me. I told him the reasons which had compelled me to leave Cairo. I confessed to him that I could not detach myself from the image of Bedy-Aljemal, nor cease to nourish a futile passion. 'Would you,' I added, 'give your daughter to a man whose heart she cannot possess? Ah! my lord, the Princess Malika deserves a happier fate.'

'How can I,' replied the king, 'recognise the service you have done me?'

'Sire,' I replied, 'I am sufficiently rewarded for it. The reception your majesty has given me – the pleasure alone of having delivered the Princess of Serendib from the hands of the genie who had carried her off, is a sufficient reward for me. All that I ask of your gratitude is a vessel to take me to Bassora.'

The king did as I wished; he ordered a vessel to be filled with provisions and to be held ready to depart when I thought convenient. He kept me, however, some time at his court, and he told me every day that he was sorry that I did not wish to remain at Serendib. Finally the day of my departure arrived. I took leave of the king and the princess, who overwhelmed me with civilities, and I embarked.

We experienced several storms on the way, severe enough to have caused our shipwreck, but the virtue of my ring prevented our being submerged. So, after a long voyage, I arrived happily at Bassora, whence I went to grand Cairo with a caravan of Egyptian merchants.

I found many changes had taken place at the court: my father lived no more, and my brother was on the throne. The new sultan received me at first as a man sensible to the bonds which united us; he assured me he was glad to see me again; he told me that a few days after my departure, my father, being in his treasury, had opened by chance the little coffer which contained the seal of Solomon and the portrait of Bedy-Aljemal; that not seeing them he had suspected me of having taken them. I confessed everything to my brother, and placed the ring in his hands.

He seemed touched at my misfortune, and marvelled at the strangeness of my adventures; he pitied me, and I felt that his sympathy relieved my trouble. All the sensibility that he evinced was, however, only perfidy. The very day of my arrival he had me enclosed in a tower, where he sent at night an officer who had orders to take my life; but this officer had pity on me, and said: 'Prince, the sultan, your brother, has ordered me to assassinate you; he fears lest a desire to reign may possess you and incite you to make trouble in the state; he thinks your death necessary to his safety. Happily for you he has addressed himself to me, he imagines that I shall execute his barbarous order and he expects to see me return covered with your blood. Ah! rather may my hand shed my own! Escape, prince; the door of your prison is open to you, profit by the darkness of the night; leave Cairo, fly, and do not stop till you are in safety.'

After having thanked this generous officer as he deserved, I took flight, and abandoning myself to Providence, I hastened to leave my brother's states. I had the good fortune to arrive in yours, my lord, and to find a safe refuge at your court.

THE JOURNEY TO CONSTANTINOPLE

Hans Shück

THE EMPEROR KARL the Great was sitting under an olive tree. The queen sat by his side, and round about him stood his twelve paladins. These were the bravest and wisest men to be found in the length and breadth of the land, and they always accompanied the emperor on all his journeys and campaigns. These paladins were Archbishop Turpin, the old Duke Nemes, the emperor's nephew Roland, who was looked upon as the finest knight in France, the valiant Ogier the Dane, about whom our folk-songs still have so much to tell, his companion-in-arms the courtly Oliver, and, besides these, Bernard, Villifer, Bering, Ernald, Eimer, Bertram, and Gerin.

The emperor was blithe of heart, and said jestingly to his spouse:

'Do you know any king in the wide world who wears his crown as well as I, or one whom armour equally becomes?'

Without further thought on the matter she answered heedlessly:

'No man should so vaunt himself; for I know a king who wears a higher crown than you and who cuts a more stalwart figure in his armour.'

She had hardly uttered these words before the emperor's good humour vanished, and wrath mounted to his brow.

'Have a care,' said he, 'what you are saying, or it may cost you your life.'

'There is no cause for you to be angry. The king I mean is certainly mightier than you, and richer in lands and gold, but he is not so good a knight, nor yet so brave, as you.'

But seeing that the emperor's wrath was not yet appeased, despite her excuse, she fell upon her knees before him and besought him thus:

'Forgive me, for God's pity's sake, for you know indeed that I am your wife, and would do everything to gratify you.'

'Only tell me the name of him you meant.'

'Ah, my emperor and lord, there is no such king in the whole world. It was but my foolish tongue that wagged and ran away from my wits.'

'Do not attempt evasion. Tell me his name at once, or you will repent it.'

'Well, then, as you refuse to give me peace on any other condition, the king I mean is King Hugo of Constantinople, and no one is so rich and strong and majestic as he, save you alone.'

'Good,' answered the king. 'That we must put to the test, and if you have uttered an untruth it will cost you dear.'

Then he turned to his paladins and addressed them thus:

'You know I have long desired to fare to Jerusalem to behold the places where our Saviour lived and taught. This journey we must now undertake, and, on our way back, we shall visit King Hugo of Constantinople to see if the queen has spoken the truth. Prepare yourselves, therefore, for the journey, which I trow will be long indeed, and, as we are to appear before so illustrious a king, it behoves us to be well equipped, that we may not appear before him like beggars. Let us, therefore, take with us seven hundred camels loaded with gold and silver, but until we have left Jerusalem we must be clad as becomes humble pilgrims, bearing staves and wearing weeds.'

They repaired to the church dedicated to St Dionysius, the patron saint of all the land of France, and, in front of the high altar, solemnly assumed the Cross, whereupon Archbishop Turpin said Mass for them. When all the preparations for the journey were accomplished they mounted their steeds, and rode forth accompanied by their attendants. They took ship at Marseilles, and at length reached Jerusalem, where they found quarters.

On the morrow after their arrival they all went to the church that is called Pater Noster, wherein the Saviour Himself and His apostles had celebrated the holy rites. The church, however, was reckoned so holy that none had a right to enter it without special permission from the Patriarch of Jerusalem. Now the latter, when he heard that some had dared to disregard his orders, hastened at once to the church. The emperor, on seeing him, arose and greeted him reverently. Then the patriarch asked him who he was, adding: 'You are the first who has dared to enter this holy room without my leave.'

'I am Karl the Great, emperor of that land which is called France, and these are my paladins. We have come hither to visit the Holy Sepulchre; we knew nothing about your prohibition, and it was not our intention to show you any discourtesy.'

'Nor do I believe it either, now that I know who you are. I have long heard talk about the mighty emperor Karl the Great, for the fame of his valour and that of his paladins is spread throughout the whole world. Welcome to Jerusalem and the Holy Sepulchre, which has no nobler protector than yourself, before whose sword the Infidels have so long trembled.'

The patriarch then brought out the most precious relics that were to be found, and presented them as a gift to the emperor, who accepted them with thanks and had them preserved in a magnificent gold shrine which he handed over to the care of Archbishop Turpin, and, directly they had performed their devotions once more in the church of Pater Noster, they started for Constantinople, accompanied by the patriarch's good wishes.

When they got within three miles of the town their path led through a splendid garden full of all sorts of wonderful trees and flowers, the like of which they had never beheld before. They saw in the garden thousands of knights clad in purple and ermine, and also as many damsels, each fairer than the other, disporting together, some playing chess and draughts, others amusing themselves with round dances, holding one another all the time by the hand. Now when Karl saw all this magnificence and all that crowd of courtiers, surpassing everything to which he had been accustomed, he had at once a feeling that his queen had not perhaps been altogether wrong when she described this court as the finest in the world; but if he could not rival the mighty King Hugo in riches, still he thought he might, nevertheless, do so in other respects. He, therefore, turned to a knight and asked him where the latter's king was to be found.

'Our king,' answered he, 'you will find down there where they are carrying the purple canopy that you see.'

Karl the Great immediately went there, and saw beneath the costly canopy a man sitting in a golden chariot, holding in his hand a rod likewise of gold, wherewith he goaded the oxen that drew his chariot, and to this chariot was attached a golden plough wherewith he ploughed. The emperor saluted him courteously, but at first he only got a careless nod in return. When the king, however, saw that the stranger was a man of birth he stopped and asked him who he was.

'I am Karl the Great, king of France and emperor of Rome. I have just been to Jerusalem and visited the Holy Sepulchre, and I have now come hither to meet you.'

'Welcome. For many years past I have heard talk of you and praise of your valour; so it is, therefore, a great honour to me that you desired to pay me a visit, and I hope you will be in no haste to leave me. I will unyoke my oxen, and, that done, follow you to the castle, where I trust you will take up your quarters and treat it as if it were your own.'

'But is not someone going to take charge of that costly plough?' asked Karl. 'I am afraid it will be stolen if you leave it behind in that way.'

'It appears,' said King Hugo, with a smile, 'that customs are different in our country. Thank God, justice is so well administered in my land that were I to leave this golden plough lying on the highway for seven years not a soul would dream of venturing to steal it; and even if that did happen, I should, fortunately, be able to bear the loss.'

Karl, whose pride had, for the second time, received a certain humiliation, accompanied King Hugo to the castle, which the latter pointed out to him as his abode in Constantinople. Immediately on their arrival twelve hundred knights approached, took their horses, and followed the guests into the huge banqueting-hall, which occupied the middle of the building. This hall, which was the most spacious Karl had ever seen, was perfectly round; and a lofty dome, adorned with paintings of exceeding splendour, was thrown across it. This dome was supported by a massive pillar, which shot up from the centre of the hall, and around it rose a forest of smaller pillars, which did not serve the purpose of props, but merely supported magnificent statues of gold, silver, bronze and marble. These statues, which represented children at play, stretching out their hands to one another, were so well executed that they looked like living creatures, and all of them had horns at their mouths, whereon they were blowing. The emperor marvelled exceedingly at all this, and began to realise more vividly that the queen was right in what she had said. Soon he had further reason to be still more astounded.

The pillars were hollow, and the wind from outside played into them and came out of the horns borne by the statues, and these gave forth musical notes which sounded like the loveliest minstrelsy. The wind, however, rose and increased to a storm, and then it began to make such a din in the hall that the noise was as the noise of a mill, and with the increasing violence of the wind, the floor likewise began to whirl round like the wheel of a mill, and the gusts grew so violent at last that the Franks had some difficulty in keeping on their feet. They thought that their last hour had come, and tried in vain to open the door in order to rush out of this perilous abode; but at that moment King Hugo entered and smilingly requested them not to be alarmed at such a thing, which was really a matter of no importance to men so brave as they.

'The storm,' said he, 'will most likely subside towards evening,' and he had hardly uttered these words before it grew calm and still once more. The Franks were therefore ashamed of their terror, and no longer looked as if they wished to leave the quarters the king had assigned them.

On a signal from the king a table was now brought in groaning beneath the weight of the most toothsome dishes – venison, wild boars, geese, peacocks, and all sorts of game; and between the baked meats there stood drinking-horns filled with mead, bastard, red wine, and other good drinks. Minstrels entered and played at the same time, and bassoons, fiddles, harps, and other stringed instruments made music while the guests took their seats at table. King Hugo sat in the seat of honour, on his right hand the emperor Karl the Great, and on his left his queen and her daughter, the fairest damsel you could see, with a complexion of roses and lilies.

Many were the glances which the knights in the emperor's retinue cast across the table at the young princess; but she seemed used to such homage on the part of men, and paid no heed to the admiration she excited.

At last the emperor Karl the Great turned to the king and exclaimed: 'How comes it that your daughter, who has already reached the age for marriage, has not chosen herself a husband? With us young maids tarry not so long, and your daughter's beauty makes me believe that she has not lacked suitors.'

'I have never sought to constrain her, but have left her free choice. I have perhaps done wrong, for she has now made up her mind only to accept the prince whose wisdom is on a par with his valour. To every suitor who has come to woo, she has, with this purpose, proposed three riddles which he must resolve if he would win her hand. Besides this, as he must set his head for wager, you can understand that not many have had the courage to make the attempt, and those who were brave enough to do so have paid with their lives the penalty of their rashness. I am sorry, for her sake and for theirs, that it should be so, but as I have given my word, the thing cannot be altered.'

'If such be the state of affairs, then I do not think my paladins can cherish any hopes, for Archbishop Turpin, as a priest, may not marry, Duke Nemes is too old to think of love, and the rest of them have during their lives devoted themselves rather to wielding their swords than to guessing riddles. They would assuredly be worsted at the outset in a task like that, and so we must not indulge in the hope of ever seeing the princess in our fair France. The night, however, is far spent, and we have abused your hospitality too long.'

On a sign from the king the tables were removed, and then he took the emperor by the hand, and led him and his paladins into another hall that was to serve as their bedchamber. This hall was also vaulted, and on the top of the dome there gleamed a carbuncle which blazed as brightly by night as by day. Twelve costly beds of bronze stood in the hall, but the thirteenth, which was in the middle, was wrought of gold. When King Hugo had bidden them take their rest after the fatigues of their journey, he wished them good-night and then withdrew.

Now, in the centre of this hall there was a cunning pillar of stone that supported the dome. This pillar was likewise hollow, and in it King Hugo had concealed a spy who was afterwards to relate to him the conversation of the strangers when they were by themselves. The emperor and his friends, however, went to bed, but as the mirth engendered of the banquet had not yet departed, they found it hard to go to sleep at once, but began instead to talk to each other. They talked about all the marvellous things they had seen, and how far these had surpassed what they had dreamt of in France. When they had got more and more awake through talking, the emperor proposed that they should begin a game which was a great favourite with Frankish knights – to wit, every one was to mention by way of jest some remarkable feat he meant to perform, the object being to hit upon the most improbable and astonishing deed there could be. The emperor himself began.

'Let King Hugo,' said he, 'pit against me the doughtiest knight he has, and clothe him with two coats of steel. Let him, moreover, place four helmets on his head, and give him his strongest horse, which may, if he choose, have a triple covering of mail; yet I will give this knight such a blow that both he and his horse shall be cloven into two equal parts, and my sword shall penetrate a spear's length into the ground.'

Then Roland said: 'Let the king give me his horn Oliphant, and I will go some way off from the castle, and blow so deep a blast on the horn that all the doors of the castle shall fly off their hinges, and if the king himself shall venture to look out, I will blow his hair and beard and clothes off him.'

Then it came to Villifer's turn.

'You have seen,' said he, 'a ball lying out in the courtyard, which is wrought of gold and silver. It is so heavy and big that thirty men are not strong enough to move it from its place. Tomorrow I shall take this ball, lift it with one hand, and hurl it against the castle so that 500 feet of wall at the very least shall crack and tumble down.'

'Well,' said Ogier the Dane, 'I shall do far more injury to King Hugo's castle. You remember the great pillar that stood in the middle of the banqueting-hall. Early tomorrow I shall seize it with my arms and shake it till the whole house comes rattling down.'

'That is mere child's play to what I think of doing,' said the old Duke Nemes. 'Let King Hugo give me four coats of ring-armour, the heaviest to be found in his kingdom. I will put these on and then jump 500 feet higher than the highest towers of the castle, and, when I come down to the ground again, I shall shake myself and all the rings in the armour shall jump out one after the other, and fall to the ground like burnt straw.'

'That should be a very pleasant sight to see,' rejoined Bering, 'but the feat I intend performing is harder still. I shall ask King Hugo to collect all the swords there are here, and stick them in the courtyard with their points upwards and their hilts buried in the ground. When the whole courtyard has been covered in this manner with sword points, I shall walk up to the highest tower and throw myself down, so that the sword-points shall be broken and the blades snap asunder, yet I myself shall be unscathed.'

After this came the turn of Archbishop Turpin, who spoke thus:

'Tomorrow I shall go to the river that flows some way out of the town, divert it from its course, and make it pour all over Constantinople till every house is filled with water. The king himself shall be so frightened that he will flee to his highest tower, and will not venture to come down until I let him.'

'Now, listen,' said Ernald, 'to what I mean to do. I think of asking King Hugo for four loads of lead. When this has been boiled till it melts I shall pour it into a cauldron, and I myself shall go down and sit in it till the lead gets hard again. I shall next shake myself till the lead falls off me and not a single drop remains on my body. Now, beat this who can.'

'I consider myself capable of a more difficult feat even than that,' said Eimer. 'I have a hat, and when I put it on my head I am invisible to everyone. I shall put that on tomorrow when King Hugo has sat down to table. I shall go up to him, eat up his meat and drink up his wine without his perceiving who it is that is playing him that trick. Finally, I shall go behind him and give him a push that will send him falling head foremost on the table. As he will not see who has given him the blow, I shall act in such a manner that he and his knights shall come to blows with one another, and tear and rend each other's beards.'

'As for me,' said Bertram, 'I shall go into the forest tomorrow, and shriek so loud that it shall be heard a hundred miles off. Yes, I shall roar in such a way that the beasts in the forest shall be terrified and flee away, and the fishes in the river jump out of the water in their fright.'

'Now,' said Gerin, 'it is my turn to tell what I intend to do. If the king will give me a spear that weighs a man's weight and the point of which is an ell long, and will then place a couple of small coins, one on the top of the other, on the summit of the tower, I will go three miles hence, hurl the spear and hit one of the coins so that it falls pierced to the ground without the other being displaced in the least. And I shall run back so fast that I shall catch the spear before it has come through the air to the ground.'

'That is something like fleetness,' said Bernard, 'but I fancy I am as quick and nimble as yourself. Tomorrow, if the king will take three of the fastest horses he owns and will drive them in the wildest way, I will run up to them, jump over the first two, and stand on the third; and, in quicker time than it takes to make a single step, I shall take up four apples from the ground, and if I miss a single one of them may the king take my head.'

Now Oliver was the only one who had said nothing as yet of the marvellous things he meant to accomplish, and, when at length he was asked how he thought of rivalling the rest, he answered:

'You have all promised to perform marvels of bodily strength and agility, but we have trained ourselves to such exercises and are to some extent accustomed to them. I shall, on the other hand, attempt something new, and therefore mean to try tomorrow to solve the princess's three riddles. She will either be mine or King Hugo may take my head.'

After he had said this, they began to talk and dispute as to which of them had composed the most extraordinary story; but sleep at last claimed its rights, and they went to sleep. As soon as the hall was hushed to silence, the terrified spy crept back to King Hugo and told him what appalling promises the strangers had made.

'I have never heard the like in impudence,' said he, 'and they have spent the whole night in scoffing and mocking at you.'

King Hugo was exceedingly wroth when he had heard the spy's account of their conversation, and said to him:

'I acted like a madman when I received the emperor with so

many marks of respect, and sneers and ridicule have been my sole reward; but I shall punish these braggarts as they deserve, and if they cannot perform all the labours they have said they would do it shall cost them their lives.'

Then the king had ten thousand knights summoned in haste, and these presented themselves at the castle on the following day to succour their lord in case of need. Meanwhile the emperor Karl the Great and his paladins awoke, got out of their beds, and went to Mass without any presentiment of evil, or further thought of the jesting of the previous night. As they came out of church King Hugo met them, and addressed them in severe language.

'I am aware,' said he, 'that you have spent your night in mocking me, and have repaid with insults the hospitality I showed you; but now it is my turn to speak and tell you of the wonderful things I intend doing. If there is one of you who cannot perform what he asserted he could last night, I mean to have his head, and however intrepid you may say you are, you will hardly, I fancy, be strong enough to withstand the ten thousand knights I have gathered around me.'

When the emperor heard these words he became utterly shamefaced, and for a long time did not know what reply to make. At last he exclaimed:

'When we went to bed last night we were joyous and mirthful, thanks to the wine you gave us in such abundance, and, perhaps in consequence of that, we chattered nonsense; but we did not think of insulting you. You must know that it is customary with us Frankish knights, before going to sleep after a banquet, to vie with one another in such extravagances; and we never thought of engaging in such impossible undertakings as those we were talking about, or of intending by such talk to offend you. But you did not act aright in spying on us when we were alone. I do not say this as a reproach: the one rebuke may outweigh the other, and, on these grounds, I beseech you to let these trifles be forgotten.'

'You cannot smooth over your sneers at me so easily,' replied King Hugo, 'and it shall be as I have said – either you perform the exploits you promised or else I shall cut off your heads. In the course of an hour we shall meet again, and then you are to begin your experiments.'

With these words he left Karl and his paladins. For a long time they stood silent without daring to raise their eyes from the ground, so ashamed were they of their boasting. As brave men I do not suppose they feared death, but they blushed at being compelled to forfeit their lives for such a paltry reason. At last the emperor said:

'We have been foolish, and we must now pay the penalty of our foolishness. I have vaunted myself over others and did not deem that any one could be my peer, and it is, therefore, no more than just that the Lord should now humiliate me and punish my pride. Let us, then, bear our fate without cowardly shrinking, and show that we can at least die like men, even if we have lived like fools. An hour yet remains to us before our heads must fall by the sword. Let us use this time to pray in church for forgiveness of our sins.'

With these words he went back to the church he had just left, and his paladins followed him solemnly and silently. After Archbishop Turpin had celebrated Mass, and each of them had confessed his sins and prayed for forgiveness of them, they arose from their knees, fully resolved on meeting their approaching fate with courage. But at that very instant an angel appeared to them and said:

'The Lord has heard your prayer and will succour you. You have been mad and rash in having trusted to your own strength, and forgotten that you have merely been instruments of the Lord's will. Let the humiliation which has now befallen you serve as a lesson, and do not vaunt yourselves hereafter over your peers. If you will do this, then the Lord will be satisfied, and will not exact the uttermost penalty. So meet King Hugo without apprehension, and I will stand at your side and perform for you all the exploits you have promised to do. Go, therefore, and henceforward sin no more.'

When they heard these comforting words their sorrow vanished straightway. With joyous mien they walked up to King Hugo again and said:

'Once more we beseech you to be assured that we were only jesting and did not in the least degree intend to flout you, for whose hospitality we are deeply indebted; but, since you insist on claiming the fulfilment of the promises we made in jest, we are now prepared, with God's help, to perform the exploits we spoke of; but you yourself must name the person who is to begin.'

'Good,' replied the king; 'we shall begin with the least dangerous, so let Oliver come forward and resolve the riddles my daughter shall propose to him.'

Oliver drew near the throne on which the princess had taken her seat. All the court was assembled around the throne, and the princess began:

'Tell me what the name of that tree is under which race after race sprouts up and withers away. It dies perpetually, but perpetually grows anew. One side turns itself towards the light, but the other is as black as night, and is not touched by the sun's rays. As it grows it plants new rings, and by these rings one can mark the flight of time.'

'The riddle, noble princess,' replied Oliver, 'is easy to guess. The tree is *the year*.'

'Correctly guessed,' said the princess, slightly changing colour. 'My next riddle will therefore be harder. Tell me, now, what kind of picture it is which continually grows and gives fresh images. Its frame is the smallest, yet this picture embraces more than any other. It is more precious than any stone of price; it gives light of itself, yet does not burn. All the great and beautiful world is depicted in it, but the image is often more lovely than the reality.'

'I can solve even that riddle. The picture you mean is *the human eye*, and when I gaze into your eyes methinks the image of the object therein reflected is fairer than the thing itself.'

'Well, solve me the last riddle, then. Name me the implement that is most often despised, but which, nevertheless, becomes even an emperor. It is made to wound, and though it inflicts wounds by thousands, blood does not flow from them. It impoverishes no one, but enriches many a man; it has laid the foundation of the highest sovereignty on earth, and yet has never been employed in war.'

'That implement I should certainly have found difficulty in naming if it had not been the first thing I beheld when I came hither to your father's kingdom, and I saw him with my own eyes ploughing with a golden plough; the implement you mean is *the plough*, is it not so, princess?'

'It is so, and you have saved your head. But do not rejoice

prematurely, for there remain twelve other feats for you to accomplish, and those ought to be harder than this.'

'We have once expressed our willingness to do what we promised,' said the emperor. 'Oliver has kept his promise, and not only saved his own life, but even won the hand of the princess. We will not, however, base any claim on that reward for him, so name only one of us whose strength you wish to test.'

'Well, then,' replied King Hugo, 'let Villifer take the golden ball which lies in this courtyard, and if he is not able to lift it and throw it as he boasted last night, his life and the lives of his companions will be forfeited.'

But Villifer only smiled, being certain that the angel would help him as it had already helped his friend Oliver, whereupon he went up to the huge globe and lifted it with one hand as if it had been a glove, and hurled it against the castle wall, so that the whole edifice tottered, and a rent ten times larger than that which he had promised appeared.

When King Hugo saw this exhibition of strength he was not, as you can well understand, happy in his mind. His beautiful castle was ruined, and he began to fear that these strangers could do more than he had imagined they could. He would not, however, yield yet, but summoned Archbishop Turpin, and called on him to carry out what he had promised.

'As you please,' answered the archbishop. 'With God's help I think the river will rise.'

Then he went down to the shore, fell upon his knees, and besought help from heaven; then he arose, stretched forth his hand, and blessed the water. Then a great miracle took place, for the river began to bubble, and gradually rose out of its channel, making its way over fields and meadows, and rushed at a mighty speed towards the chief city, and there it soon filled all the streets and houses, to the intense alarm of all the inhabitants. King Hugo himself quite lost his presence of mind, and fled for safety to the loftiest tower in his castle. On looking down he saw Karl and his paladins standing under an olive tree which the water had not yet reached, and he called on them piteously to help him.

'Is it your intention,' he cried to Karl the Great, 'to drown me utterly in this flood? If you will save me I promise henceforward to be your vassal and pay you tribute, and you may demand what treasures you will if you will but remove this plague from me.'

'Yes,' answered the emperor, 'I like to show mercy to all who ask it, and I will willingly do what I can for you.'

At the prayer of Karl and Turpin the water withdrew from the town and subsided, after a time, into its old channel. When the ground became dry King Hugo came down from his tower and went up to the tree under which Karl the Great was standing, and said:

'I have now discovered that you are dear to God, and that He is with you in all things. I do not blush, therefore, to do you homage, as my emperor and overlord, in the presence of your knights and mine. I am your vassal, and my kingdom is yours.'

'But,' said Karl with a smile, 'there still remain no less than ten feats for us to accomplish.'

'For God's sake,' exclaimed King Hugo, 'say no more about them. I have had quite enough, and have no wish to make further proof of your strength. If you were to keep on in the same way as you have begun, before night-time I should have lost both my crown and my life.'

'Just so,' answered Karl; 'neither should I like our promises that were made in jest to have grave consequences. Let all be forgotten, and suffer us to go to church instead, to thank God, who has taken compassion on our foolishness, and directed all for the best. In one respect only do I wish to take advantage of the victory we have won, and that is on behalf of my poor Oliver. He has honourably obtained your daughter's hand, and it seems to me that it would not be fair to withhold it any longer. You will have no cause to regret this choice, for a braver and more honourable knight does not live.'

'Let it be done according to your wish.'

Then they all assembled and went to church in a solemn procession, at the head of which walked Karl the Great, and after him, among his other vassals, followed King Hugo. Karl was quite a head taller than King Hugo, and, moreover, wore his crown more majestically. The Franks in the church whispered among themselves: 'Our queen was wrong when she thought there was any king in the whole world to be compared with our emperor, and we never shall come to a country where we shall see his like.'

When they reached church Archbishop Turpin said Mass, thanked God for His goodness, and ended by placing the hand of the princess in Oliver's, after which he pronounced a blessing over them both, and made them man and wife.

A lordly marriage feast awaited them as they came out of church. The cakes offered were of the very rarest, and wine flowed in torrents. During the banquet King Hugo arose and said:

'Let every Frank take of my treasures what he wishes, and carry it to his own land.'

But Karl replied:

'Not a farthing will we take of you, who have shown us right royal hospitality, which we are loth to abuse. We thank you for all the kindness you have shown us, and will withdraw to our own land once more.'

On saying this, Karl and his paladins arose from table, took their leave, and prepared for their journey. And when Karl was about to mount his horse, the king of Constantinople bowed, and held the stirrups for the Frankish emperor.

Whereupon they made their way back to France.

HUON'S QUEST

A. R. Hope-Moncrieff

I

A Christian knight had lost his way in the glades of a Syrian forest. For three days he wandered at a venture without meeting any man, and finding no food but berries and wild honey. On the third day the blows of an axe guided him to a clearing, where he saw a tall figure, half-naked, but almost covered with grizzled hair. So uncouth seemed he, and so sturdily he swung his axe, that the knight's first thought was to rein in his steed and lay hand to his sword. For a time they looked hard upon each other; then suddenly the wild man flung down his axe, and rushed forward to throw himself on his knees, exclaiming:

'Sir Huon of Bordeaux, my good lord!'

'Who art thou?' cried the knight, amazed to hear himself called by name, and his native tongue in this paynim land.

'Who but Geraume, brother of the Mayor of Bordeaux!'

'The most faithful vassal of my father's house! But how comes a Christian here?'

'Years ago, fighting by your good father's side, I was made slave to the Saracens, who in vain sought to turn me from the true faith, till after many sufferings at their hands I broke my chains and escaped to the wilderness. Here I have since lived as a hermit, little hoping ever again to see a kindly face. But say, my lord, what brings a knight of France so far from home?'

'That were a long tale for a hungry mouth,' said Huon; whereon Geraume led him to his hut hard by, and set before him such poor fare as he had to offer.

When refreshed, the knight told at length how he had fallen

under the displeasure of Charlemagne, his sovereign lord. In defence of his own brother he had slain Charlot, the king's spiteful son. In vain he knelt at the father's knees, imploring pardon for a chance blow in a quarrel forced upon him. When Charlot's body was brought in, Charlemagne grew so furious that he would have slain Huon forthwith, had not the twelve peers joined to denounce his injustice. In the end the angry king was moved to spare his life, but only on condition of his undertaking a desperate enterprise. He must go alone to the city of Babylon, where reigned the Emir Gaudisse, from whom Charlemagne had already demanded homage by fifteen messengers, one after another, but not one of them had come back. There, sword in hand, he must haughtily call on the emir to pay tribute, and, as proof of obedience, take from him certain tokens, without which Huon durst not return to France.

'You are sending him to his death!' the peers had cried with one voice; and Charlot's wrathful father did not say them nay.

Learning thus on what a perilous errand the knight was bound, Geraume asked no better than to accompany him as guide and squire; and Huon gladly consented, since the country was as strange to him as its speech. Two ways led to Babylon, the old man told him: the one, safe and easy, making a year's journey; the other much shorter, but full of perils. The bold knight did not hesitate to choose the latter, though Geraume warned him that it led at once through an enchanted forest, haunt of Oberon, the fairy king, who had power to turn them both into monstrous beasts.

'His enchantments have no power over me,' quoth Huon, 'for I come newly from Rome, armed with the blessing of the Holy Father.'

They set out, then, and at nightfall found the forest growing thicker and darker about them, where strange shapes of beasts and birds flitted across their way. A storm of wind and thunder broke out, roaring through the fearsome shades, lit up by flashes of lightning. All at once Huon's horse started aside, rearing in terror, as there glided forth an unearthly figure, a young child in stature, but wrinkled and grey with age, magnificently attired in a jewelled robe that shone like daylight, and round his neck was hung an ivory horn.

'The saints defend us! 'Tis Oberon!' whispered Geraume, and seized his master's bridle to drag him back; but Huon, making the sign of the cross, looked steadfastly on the fairy prince.

'Nay, Sir Huon of Bordeaux, fear me not,' spoke the dwarf in mild and benevolent tones, as if reading his thoughts.

'Thou knowest me, then?'

'And wish thee well! In me see one that, unknown to thee, has watched over thy welfare from the cradle. Now am I here to aid thee in the perilous enterprise on which thou art bound. Trust me; dismount; and my goodwill shall be proved.'

For a moment the knight hesitated; then he leaped from his steed. Oberon waved his wand. Instantly the darkness became dazzling light, and with the sound of entrancing music there sprang up around them, like vapour, such a magnificent palace as no king in Christendom could boast. One moment Sir Huon stood on the ground damp with rain, where the storm wind roared above his head among dripping branches, the next he found himself in a lofty hall, where the walls were of glittering crystal and the pillars of gold, and the roof was starred with gems of every hue. On a carpet of blooming flowers stood a table loaded with sumptuous dishes, at the head of which Oberon sat on a golden throne. The knight's horse was led away, as if by spirits of the air; unseen hands held before him a jewelled basin of perfumed water; the same invisible attendants relieved him of his armour, throwing around him a robe of embroidered silk. Then, before he had fully recovered from his amazement, the enchanter motioned him to a seat by his side, and the invisible hands served them with meat and drink. The guest at that banquet had only to form a wish, then it seemed that a spirit stood beside him who knew and obeyed his slightest thought. Oberon did not eat, but while Huon satisfied his appetite, he pledged him in a cup of wine, and spoke thus:

'I have vowed friendship and protection to thy house; nothing that concerns them is hid from me. I know the purpose of this journey and the charge laid upon thee. For slaying the king's son in a chance fray, a good knight is doomed to do penance after strange fashion. He must ride alone to the palace of Gaudisse, the Emir of Babylon, and present himself in the hall while that miscreant shall be sitting at meat among his vassals and friends. Before speaking a word, he must cut off the head of whomever he finds sitting at the emir's right hand, must then kiss his fair daughter Esclarmonde thrice, and must take from Gaudisse a handful of his beard and four of his great teeth. Having further made the emir swear to be tributary to the crown of France, he is to return with these trophies, or expect no welcome but a shameful death. Say I not truly, and art not thou this luckless knight?'

'Marvellous sage, it is even as thou hast said!' replied Huon. 'All this am I bound to do, who would liefer die by Saracen swords than on the gallows!'

'Fear not, Huon, thou shalt not die, if thou art a worthy son of my friend thy father, and wilt but accept my aid and obey my directions.'

'Noble Oberon, I will obey thee in all things,' vowed Huon, as with a benignant smile the enchanter placed in his hands a crystal goblet and an ivory horn.

'Take these gifts, and learn their value. The goblet will, at the wish of any good man, fill with meat or drink; while in the hands of the treacherous and base it remains for ever empty. When assailed by numbers, let this horn be thy defence. Sound it softly if the danger be slight, and watch what befalls; but in utmost need blow loudly, and I myself will appear with all the host of fairyland. Yet, remember, these charms serve only him whose heart is true and his honour pure; no summons from the coward or the liar will reach my ear.'

'May I never prove unworthy of thy protection!'

'Beware, also, of rashness. I foresee too surely that the hot blood of youth will carry thee into perils where my aid may be of no avail. Above all, take heed to shun the tower of Angoulafre, the ruthless giant of whom all these countries are in dread. His enchantments are even stronger than mine, and he can be slain only by him who wears a coat of magic mail stolen from me years ago.'

'Show me the way to that tower!' was Huon's eager reply.

'Said I not well? Thy imprudence is too strong for good counsel.'

'Nay, friendly enchanter, the imprudence is thine, to let me know this danger that may be sought and overcome. If I am destined to leave my bones in the tower of Angoulafre, so be it; but it shall never be said that Huon heard of a perilous achievement and passed it by.'

'Thy task is already a full hard one,' said Oberon, and sighed to think of the misfortunes that might yet lie before this gallant knight.

But now the morning began to break, when at the first beam of the rising sun the enchanted palace vanished away like a dream, and Huon found himself again in the heart of the forest. The fairy prince conducted him to the verge of it, and gave directions as to the way he must now follow. Then, earnestly repeating his injunctions, he took leave of him with all good wishes.

II

FOR SEVERAL DAYS the bold knight and his squire travelled over a barren desert, where they might have starved but for the magic goblet that never failed to fill in Huon's hands, furnishing them with whatever meat or drink they desired; while they met no enemy on whom to test the virtue of Oberon's horn.

At last they came upon a richer country, where the road led them to a Saracen city named Tormont. At the gate, Geraume begged his master not to enter it; and when the knight laughed his fear to scorn, he added:

'Know that the lord of this paynim stronghold is no other than thine own uncle.'

'My uncle – lord among the unbelievers!' exclaimed Huon in astonishment.

'Even so, to the shame and sorrow of all his kin. Carried away captive by pirates, Sir Eudes, thy father's brother, was sold to the Emir of Babylon; then to save his life, he denied the Cross and turned infidel. Thus he gained that master's favour, who married him to his own niece and made him ruler of this city. Now he hates the Christians, so that he hangs or imprisons all who fall into his hands.'

'It is my duty to visit so heartless a renegade!' declared Huon. 'Before one of his own blood he cannot but blush for the cowardice that made him deny his father's faith.'

'Alas! you know him not. Hardened by debauchery and power, he is past repentance, and will answer such reproaches by a cruel death.'

But Huon was not to be moved from his purpose. He entered the city and took lodging at an inn, where he called together all the poor to entertain them by meat and drink out of his magic cup. The news of such liberality soon came to the ears of Eudes, and he sent to summon the knight to his palace.

That renegade's surprise was not less than his displeasure to find in this stranger his own nephew. Yet he feigned to meet him with joy, while secretly plotting to rid himself of so unwelcome a visitor. Huon, for his part, burned with indignation to see Eudes wearing a green turban crowned by a crescent of gems. It was all he could do to bridle his tongue, awaiting a favourable moment for denouncing the uncle's apostasy. But he, as if divining the nephew's mind, cunningly avoided being alone with him. The whole morning they spent among the train of courtiers and attendants in examining the palace and its gardens, till the hour of dinner sounded and the sultan gave Huon his hand to lead to the hall. Now the young man could no longer restrain his impatience.

'Oh, my uncle!' he whispered in his ear; 'oh, prince, brother of my father, in what a hateful disguise have I the grief and shame to find thee!'

Eudes secretly gnashed his teeth; but he pretended to be moved by this reproach; he gently pressed his kinsman's hand, and replied in the same tone:

'Silence for the present, dear nephew! Tomorrow morning I will explain all.'

Huon, deceived by his uncle's air, calmed himself and sat down by his side with a lighter heart. The muftis, the cadis, and the other officers of the court took their places; there were also some dervishes present, upon whom, like a good Catholic, our knight looked with the greatest contempt and abhorrence. As for Geraume, he remained without, and kept a watchful eye on what was doing in the palace. He began to suspect treachery, and his suspicions were increased when he saw armed men mustering about the hall. But before he could warn his master, what he dreaded had already come about.

At first Huon addressed himself to do honour to the feast, eating with the appetite of youth and a good conscience. All kinds of rich meats were served to him, but, according to the law of the Prophet, no wine appeared on the table. So, after a time, he drew from his bosom the magic goblet, which, at his wish, was at once filled with red and sparkling wine. At this sight the Saracens frowned and stroked their beards, but, feigning not to observe these signs of displeasure, he courteously handed the cup to Eudes, saying:

'Dear uncle, pledge me in this goblet. It is excellent wine of your own native province, and will remind you of your mother's milk.'

Eudes often drank the juice of the grape in secret, though before others he made pretence of abhorring it. Not for long had he tasted the good wine for which his birthplace was famed; the very name of it made his mouth water; surely for once he might transgress the law: so, forgetting what watchful eyes were upon him, he stretched out his hand towards the crystal goblet in which the liquor glowed like a heap of rubies. He felt a thrill of delight as he already thought to taste the delicious flavour, when lo! the cup was empty at his lips, the contents disappearing as if by enchantment. Huon could not restrain a laugh at his confusion and disappointment, yet he drew back from the uncle whose falsity was thus revealed.

'Insolent!' cried Eudes, as soon as surprise allowed him to speak. 'Do you dare to mock me in the midst of my court? Ho! without there!'

And he hurled the goblet at Huon, who, catching it in his hand, replied by tearing the sultan's jewelled turban from his head, and trampling it on the floor. The cadis, agas, dervishes, and muftis rose from the table, uttering cries of horror at this insult. At the same moment the doors of the hall were flung open on every side, and a crowd of soldiers and eunuchs, armed to the teeth, rushed in, running upon the young knight in such haste that the foremost of them tripped and fell in a struggling heap before him.

This gave Huon a moment's respite. He stepped back while his assailants were picking themselves up, and did not even take the trouble to draw his sword, but brought out the ivory horn of Oberon, on which he began to blow gently. Immediately the effects were seen. At the first soft and melodious notes every Saracen stood upright, then fell a-trembling in all his limbs, and, as the sound continued, had, willy-nilly, to break into a dance. The music of the horn was heard over all the palace, and each note thrilled through every limb. The dervishes whirled themselves into the middle of the hall; the eunuchs gambolled like kids; their weapons dropped from the hands of the soldiers, staggering as if they were drunk; the grave muftis and cadis flung their turbans on the floor, and spun round among the crowd; even their lord himself, after stamping and wriggling in a vain effort to keep his dignity, was forced to caper with the rest; and soon all the assembly was one wild reel.

Standing at the head of the hall, Huon blew faster and faster, and the dancers were hurried round and round with more and more vehemence. Howling, leaping, tumbling, tottering, skipping, tripping over their long garments, panting, perspiring, frantically clinging to chairs and tables, and even to each other's beards, dashing their heads against the walls, kicking their slippers up to the ceiling, raging, crying, entreating, struggling, they whirled on, and kept up the dance till they could neither stand nor speak, but still their limbs must jerk, like a child's toy, of which the enchanter did not cease to pull the string. At last Huon had pity on this wretched rout. He suddenly took the horn from his lips, then in one moment every Saracen fell flat on the ground, breathless and exhausted.

Seeing that they were no longer able to do him harm, the knight made his way through the piles of helpless bodies, and sought out the inn, where his prudent squire was already saddling their horses for immediate departure.

III

Before one of the Saracens had recovered strength to move hand or foot, Huon and Geraume left the city and took the road to Babylon. Again they journeyed on without meeting any hindrance, till they arrived upon a plain in the midst of which a huge tower reared itself, losing its battlements in the clouds.

'It is the tower of Angoulafre!' cried Huon.

'Do not approach it!' begged Geraume, not so eager for adventures as his master. 'Call to mind the warnings of Oberon. Back, if you love your life!'

But the knight feigned not to hear his squire's advice. He was determined at any cost to visit this appallingly mysterious tower.

As they drew nearer, they perceived that the wall was pierced here and there with deep windows that resembled human eyes, but through which no human being could be seen. All without and within was dark, silent, and threatening. Round the whole pile ran a wide, deep ditch, crossed by a drawbridge but three feet wide, leading to a gate even narrower. The gate was defended by two tall brazen statues, that whirled round long flails of the same metal, like the arms of a windmill; so broad were these flails and so rapid was their motion, that not even a bird could pass between them without being crushed to pieces.

The more he saw of this fearsome place, the more Geraume urged his master to hold back from it. But Huon was only tempted on by these desperate obstacles. At a little distance from the tower he dismounted, bade his companion remain with the horses, and advanced alone and on foot towards the entrance, where hung a great basin of brass, as large as a shield. He struck it with the hilt of his sword, and the brass gave forth a deep, dreadful clang, echoed throughout the tower.

'Now we shall see who lives here,' said Huon to himself; and a sorrowful cry made him turn his eyes upwards to the loophole above the gate, through which he caught a glimpse of the face of a young and beautiful lady. Before a minute had passed, the whirling arms of the statues suddenly ceased their motion, and the lady appeared at the wicket.

'Rash man, what do you here?' she cried, all pale and shuddering, as Huon ran lightly across the drawbridge. 'You are but hastening upon your death.'

'Nay; what harm can await me in the abode of such a fair one?' said Huon gallantly.

'Alas,' replied she, casting looks of compassion upon him, 'it is not me ye have to fear, but the cruel tyrant that holds me as his prisoner!'

'The giant Angoulafre?'

'No other. At this moment, happily for you, he sleeps. Had he awakened, you were surely lost! When I heard the noise you made, I gave you up for lost; then, perceiving the cross which adorns your shield, I judged that you must be a Christian knight, and would save your life if I could. Now you are warned; oh, fly while there is yet time!'

'Noble and beautiful damsel, I have not come here to fly. And now that I have seen you, and know you to be the captive of this monster, I am more than ever eager to combat him for your deliverance. But tell me, lady, before I seek the giant, who are you, and how came you into his power?'

'Ah! the tale of my misfortunes is soon told. My name is Sibille. I came with my noble father, Guerin of Guienne, on a pilgrimage to the Holy Land; then, returning, would have sailed to France, where a good knight, nephew of Ogier the Dane, waited to make me his wife. But a furious tempest threw us upon this hateful coast; Angoulafre discovered and attacked us; my father and all his knights were slain, and I became his prisoner. For three years have I pined in this house of horror, and now for the first time I hear my native tongue and see the face of a countryman.'

'Nay, fair Sibille, of a kinsman! Know that I am Huon of Bordeaux, the eldest son of your father's brother, and therefore your cousin, and doubly bound to deliver you from this wicked giant. Lead me to him forthwith, and let me deal with the robber of ladies!'

'But ah! he is strong and fierce and — '

'Say no more. Am I not one of the peers of France?'

Sibille, scarcely able to suppress her exclamations of joy, no longer delayed to admit this welcome kinsman; and, walking on tiptoe, led the way to the chamber from which the monster's snoring could be heard all over the tower.

There he lay on his back, a hideous form, seventeen feet long, with such a fierce countenance as even in sleep would have made most men shudder. Huon stood over him and raised his sword; his first impulse was to bury it to the hilt in the giant's throat. But he bethought him that he was a knight, and must in no case attack an enemy who could not defend himself. Moreover, he fortunately remembered that this monster could not be slain except by the man wearing that enchanted coat of mail of which Oberon had spoken; and, while Angoulafre still slept heavily, the knight and his cousin searched for it throughout the tower. It was soon discovered in a cedar coffer that stood in one of the next apartments. Huon seized it, put it on, and was rejoiced to find that it fitted him marvellously well.

'Now, fair cousin,' he said gaily, 'excuse me if I leave you here for a little. I am going to awake Angoulafre, and put him to the death he deserves.'

But it was no easy task to rouse the giant from his nap. Not till Huon had shaken him, and struck him, and shouted in his ear, and pulled his beard, and tweaked his nose, did he begin to move, and slowly raised his head, gaping and rubbing his bloodshot eyes. Then, as he caught sight of this unexpected visitor, he stared wildly, with a bellow that shook all the walls, and sent Sibille, anxiously watching without, to her knees.

'Puny creature, what madness has brought you here to your death? Miserable wretch, tell me your name before I crush you with one blow, and you be never more heard of on earth!'

'Odious monster, my name is Huon of Bordeaux, and I am come to punish you for all your evil deeds. Arm, and prepare for the combat.'

Angoulafre might well be astonished at this bold language. He regarded the knight with attention, and was still more astonished to see him encased in the magic coat of mail.

'By Mahomet,' he said, 'it was generous of you not to have slain me in my sleep, as you might well have done. Come, I pardon you; it would cost me too much trouble to take your life. Only give up that armour, and on this condition I will let you go free and unharmed.'

'Nay, give you up this tower, and the princess whom you hold captive in it; and, moreover, consent to renounce Mahomet, and to follow me to the court of the Emir of Babylon, where I have a certain errand to do; on these conditions will I spare your life.'

The giant laughed loudly, making a gesture of scorn.

'Fool, if I let you go, you could not come at the Emir of Babylon without my aid. He is my vassal, and this golden ring betokens the respect due to me by him and all his. Four gates guard his palace, each of which will fly open at the sight of my ring. Without it you cannot hope to pass. At the first gate they would cut off your right hand, at the second your left, at the third one of your feet, at the fourth another, and when thus you reached the hall it would be but a moment before your head were shorn from your shoulders. Be wise, then; take this ring, and return my armour.'

'Ring, and armour, and all that you have is already mine,'

quoth the bold Huon. 'We but waste our time; arm, and let me slay thee without more to-do.'

Seeing that he could by no persuasion win back from Huon the enchanted mail, Angoulafre withdrew to prepare for the combat. In a short time he returned, covered from head to foot with massive armour, and wielding a huge scythe in both his brawny hands.

'I am ready to fight if you are ready to die!' he roared, brandishing this terrific weapon over Huon's head.

'Look to thyself, pagan,' replied Huon, deftly escaping the blow.

The scythe, swung with all the giant's strength, struck against a pillar, and sank into it to the depth of three feet. Angoulafre made desperate efforts to draw it out; but before he could succeed, Huon rushed forward and cut off both his hands at the wrists. The giant, uttering a hideous howl of pain, turned to fly. He hurled himself into the chamber where the pale Sibille was trembling for the result of this combat, but, missing his footing, fell headlong, and his huge bulk rolled at her feet. She screamed out; but Huon was close at his heels; one good blow of the keen sword ended the cruel monster's life, and the cousins threw themselves into each other's arms.

When Huon had drawn the giant's ring from his finger, they hastened to leave this gloomy abode, and Geraume rejoiced to see his master come back safe. To him the knight confided the care of Sibille, directing him to take her to the nearest seaport and put her on board a ship bound for France, while he himself was achieving his enterprise. So they parted with all good wishes, and Huon pursued his journey alone with the ring of Angoulafre, the enchanted coat of mail, the wonderful goblet and horn, and his own good sword to be his guide.

IV

A FEW DAYS more brought Huon in sight of the rich and beautiful city of Babylon, where upon a high hill rose the marble palace of Gaudisse, the emir, or admiral of that country. Glad to arrive at the end of this long journey, Huon left his horse at the foot of the hill, to climb impatiently up its steep side, wondering whether Gaudisse would easily comply with the requests he had to make, and if his daughter Esclarmonde were indeed of such surpassing beauty as fame reported her.

As a loud flourish of trumpets announced that the emir and his guests were sitting down to dinner, Huon presented himself at the outermost gate of the palace, and demanded admission. That same hour Oberon was dining in fairyland, when suddenly he rose and uttered a cry of pain.

'Alas!' cried the enchanter; 'the brave knight whom I loved so well is at this moment perjuring himself basely, and thus deprives me of both the power and the will to succour him.'

It was too true. Huon had just been asked by the guard whether he belonged to their religion, this day being a high festival among the Saracens, in which none might take part who were not faithful followers of the Prophet. The knight had thoughtlessly answered 'Yea', and was at once allowed to enter without further question. But he no sooner found himself within the precincts of the palace, than his conscience began to smite him for having thus spoken a falsehood and denied his faith. He would have given much to be able to recall the words, but it was now too late. He could only determine not again to be guilty of the like weakness. And when he had advanced as far as the second gate, which was closed and guarded like the first, he drew his sword and called out at the height of his voice:

'Infidel dogs! I command ye to open to a Christian knight!'

The guards sprang to their arms. The barrier bristled with spears and sword-points, and in another moment a cloud of darts would have been hurled upon this rash intruder. But the captain of the guard caught sight of the giant's ring upon the stranger's hand, and called out:

'Forbear! Know ye not the ring of Angoulafre, to whom our lord owes tribute and homage?'

Instantly the weapons were lowered, the gate was flung open, and as the knight passed through, looking sternly around him, the guards fell upon their knees, and the captain, bowing low, conducted him across a courtyard to the third barrier that must be passed.

Here Huon bethought him of again trying the effect of the giant's ring.

'Behold,' he cried, 'the sign before which you must tremble and fall at my feet!'

Again the effect was magical. At this gate, as also at the fourth, he was received with every mark of profound respect. Then, crossing the last court, Huon made his way into the great hall where the banquet was being served, and found himself face to face with the personages upon whom he was to perform his strange mission.

At the head of the board sat the turbaned emir in all his pomp. On his right was the King of Hircania, a cruel tyrant, of whom all the neighbouring lands stood in dread. On the left of Gaudisse was his daughter Esclarmonde, the most beautiful princess of the East, her fair face pale and her bright eyes red with weeping. Sore against her will she had just been betrothed to this hateful king, and in honour of the betrothal was gathered a brilliant assembly of warriors and chiefs, both of Babylon and Hircania, who filled the hall, placed according to their rank. The King of Hircania was rising to kiss his destined bride at the moment when Huon entered; but now every eye turned upon the knight, as, with open visor and naked sword, he marched up the hall amid such a silence of amazement that no sound could be heard but the trampling of his mailed feet and the clattering of his scabbard.

The attendants shrank right and left out of his way, and, thus unopposed, Huon reached the emir's seat. Then, before a word was spoken, he swung his sword, with one mighty blow to hew off the head of the King of Hircania, and it rolled at the emir's feet. Esclarmonde uttered a cry. The feasters sprang up in confusion. Gaudisse, all bespattered by the blood of his guest, and speechless from surprise, gazed openmouthed upon the audacious stranger. What was his amazement to see him calmly walk up to the princess, who, half-terrified, half-rejoiced at the fate of her unwelcome suitor, stood as if spellbound and did not shrink while the handsome knight stooped and saluted her coral lips once, twice, thrice, before all the bewildered beholders! With the last kiss her father found words to express his feelings.

'Madman! Who are you, and in the name of the Prophet, what would you here?'

Huon did not concern himself to reply till he had courteously bowed to the blushing lady. Then he turned to the emir, and said in a clear voice that could be heard in the farthest corner of the hall:

'My name is Huon of Bordeaux, and I am sent hither by Charles, the great king, to do as I have done; and, furthermore, to have from thee a handful of that grizzled beard and four of thy strongest teeth, as tokens of the tribute owed him. Be pleased to do me this favour without delay.'

'This to my face!' bellowed Gaudisse, stamping, and choking, and glowing like a live coal. 'My friend! My beard! My daughter! My teeth! Am I alive to hear such things! Impossible! Outrageous! Irreverence! Audacity! Madness! Never! Ho, my guards, my slaves, my vassals — '

Suddenly the emir checked himself as Huon raised his hand, and displayed the ring of Angoulafre.

'The ring of my sovereign lord, to whom I owe homage and tribute! Stranger, I am bound to hear the man that bears this token. But, speak the truth, how came you by it, and where last saw you the mighty Angoulafre?'

The knight had too well repented of one falsehood to tell another.

'Pagan, thy sovereign lord is no longer to be feared even by such as thou! This arm has ended his wicked life. Think no more of him, but prepare to obey the commands of my king.'

'Angoulafre dead!' exclaimed the emir, and now cared not to restrain his wrath. 'Then, robber and murderer and insolent fool, prepare to meet thy death. My beard and teeth, forsooth! What next? Cowards, how long will ye suffer him to insult your prince. Seize him! Bind him! Off with his head! Tear him in pieces!'

At the first word out leaped the scimitars of the Saracens, and a score of warriors rushed furiously upon the dauntless knight. He stepped back quickly and loudly blew his horn, looking round in confident expectation. But, alas! the charm was broken. The offended enchanter did not regard the summons, and the knight must defend himself alone. The hall rang with the clash of weapons, and above all rose the furious voice of Gaudisse, bidding his men take the intruder dead or alive. The fair Esclarmonde clasped her hands and wept to see the fray. The indignation she should have felt against her father's enemy was lost in regard for this daring youth; and despite of filial duty she could not but wish for his escape.

But wishes were in vain, when one stood against so many. Huon's shield was covered with darts; his sword was forced from his hand; the Saracens rushed in and threw themselves upon him. He was seized, dragged away, loaded with chains, and hurled into the emir's darkest and deepest dungeon, with the assurance that he might expect no better fate than to be flayed alive.

Exhausted from loss of blood, he lay insensible on the cold stones; and when at last he came to himself his condition was most pitiable. He could scarcely move for pain; the emir's dreadful threats rang in his ears; in all that country he had no friend to speak a word or shed a tear for him; and, worst of all, it was by his own fault that he had come into such misfortune. Bitterly he reproached himself for the falsehood by which he had forfeited the favour of Oberon, but for which he might now have been reigning a victor where he pined in fetters, and might have sought the hand of that beautiful princess whose charms had at first sight made such an impression on his heart.

All night long he was tormented by these sad reflections, and the day brought no ray of light to his gloomy prison. He began to feel the want of food; his magic goblet as well as his horn had been torn from him in the struggle, and no one had come near him since he entered the dungeon. Was it the intention of his enemies to reduce his strength by starvation before bringing him to the torture, that they might have the satisfaction of seeing a Christian knight die with unmanly weakness? A burning thirst also distressed him. Thus he passed that day in anguish of mind and body, thinking sorrowfully of fair France and the gallant comrades in arms he should never see more. The death of Charlot was indeed avenged, and his unjust king might well be satisfied.

At last, towards evening, he heard footsteps without. The bolts were drawn back; the key grated in the door of the dungeon. The knight summoned all his fortitude, and prepared to meet his executioners. The door opened softly to let pass a veiled figure bearing in one hand a lamp and in the other a basket. Huon strove to rise, but could not for the weight of his fetters. The figure advanced slowly towards him; the veil was drawn back, the lamp raised, and he saw the pitiful face of Esclarmonde.

V

When some weeks had gone by, a stranger arrived at the court of Babylon, who spoke the language of the country well, and made believe to be heir of one of the great sultans of the East. Such a guest the emir received with open arms, hoping to find in him a husband for his daughter to take the place of the King of Hircania. A great feast was held in his honour, and, as they sat at dinner, the stranger spoke of the death of Angoulafre, with which all the country rang, and asked for news of the Christian knight who had slain him.

'That knight will do no more murders,' said Gaudisse grimly. 'Long ere this he has starved in my dungeons.'

'Dead!' exclaimed the stranger in such tones that Esclarmonde eagerly fixed her eyes upon him and caught a meaning in his words that her father perceived not.

'Aye, dead, and too soon to get all his deserts,' said the emir. 'Know you not how that madman came here, and how he fared?'

The stranger was not unaware of Esclarmonde's glances, and as her father told his tale at full length, he, as if thoughtlessly, drew aside his robe and let her see a rosary that hung beneath this disguise. At the sight of it she started and blushed, and he knew he had not been deceived.

When the emir had ended his story and gone to sleep, the stranger sought private speech of the princess, then, as soon as they were alone, he fell on his knees, crying: 'Lady, tell me the truth, for you can and will. I am come to seek out my dear master, Sir Huon of Bordeaux.'

'You are his faithful squire, Geraume, of whom he has so often spoken to me?'

'I am no other, But say, does he live? Is he in health? Where may I see him?'

'Follow me,' replied the princess, and led the way to a dungeon below the palace. She drew back the bolts, and in another moment the knight and his squire were embracing each other with mutual joy.

Soon now Huon's tale was told, while Esclarmonde stood by, the darkness hiding how her cheeks glowed as she heard him speak of her part in his deliverance. His courage, as well as his misfortunes, had so moved her heart that she could not rest for thinking of his unhappy lot. Overcoming all scruples, she persuaded his jailer to let her visit the prisoner and supply him with food. The more she saw of this knight, the more she was grateful to have been delivered from the hateful King of Hircania. Deserted by the enchanter, Huon now found himself succoured by the powerful magic of love. She secretly restored to him his goblet and ivory horn; and when her father ordered the captive to be led forth to the most cruel death that could be devised, she bribed the jailer to say that he was already dead of hunger, and in proof to exhibit the emaciated body of a prisoner who had really died that very day.

The emir, wrathful to see his vengeance thus escape him, had the jailer executed forthwith, and tried to gratify his hatred by inflicting all imaginable tortures on the senseless corpse believed to be that of his enemy. Esclarmonde shuddered at the horrors from which she had preserved Huon, who became dearer to her day by day. She was easily persuaded of the errors of her faith; she consented to be baptized as soon as possible, and asked nothing better than to be allowed to fly with her lover to his native land, abandoning gladly for his sake her friends, her rank, and her religion.

With the aid of Geraume, they now began to concert measures for escape. It soon seemed that there was need of haste, for the approach was announced of the giant Agrapard, King of Nubia and brother of Angoulafre, who, the emir understood, was coming to seek his daughter's hand. Esclarmonde grew pale at the thought, but Gaudisse exulted in the prospect of such a match, and forthwith began to look coldly on Geraume. He, without exciting suspicion, took his leave and hurried to the seacoast, where it was agreed that he should have a vessel in readiness, while Huon and Esclarmonde watched for the first favourable moment of escape.

But as Agrapard drew nearer the city it appeared that he had come intent on far other thoughts than those of love. He sent a herald before him to reproach Gaudisse with having lost a single day in avenging his brother's death, and to defy him to mortal combat, or to demand a tribute which would exhaust his revenues.

The emir was in despair; vainly through all his host he sought a warrior bold enough to accept the challenge of this terrible giant; and, when there seemed to be no hope for him but in submission, he cursed his gods and shed tears of rage before his daughter, who seized the moment to make him regret the loss of the vanquisher of Angoulafre.

'Ah,' cried the emir, 'I let him starve to death, and now it repents me to have lost such a champion! He alone could save me from this monster. Willingly would I give half my state to bring him to life.'

'Learn,' said Esclarmonde joyfully, 'that he of whom you speak is not dead.'

'Not dead? But no – I saw his corpse! Do you mock me, child?'

'It was the corpse of another. The brave knight, Huon, is still alive, and, if you are willing, will maintain your cause against the giant.'

Gaudisse was astonished, but this was not a time to ask questions. He desired that Huon should be sent for, and was surprised to find him as stout and vigorous as the day on which he was thrown into chains. This must be explained when the present danger was overpast; in the meantime he welcomed the knight and declared what was required of him.

'The brother of the giant whom you slew so doughtily is under our walls, full of threats and fury. As you conquered Angoulafre, so must you conquer Agrapard. Go forth, brave youth, and if you rid me of this foe I promise to give you my daughter and to obey the wishes of your king.'

Huon replied by demanding his armour. It was brought forth to him all rusty and battered, and his sword notched with many a blow. Right glad was he to find himself again harnessed like a warrior. They brought him the best horse in the emir's stables, and after taking a tender leave of Esclarmonde, and assuring her father that there need now be no fear of the giant, he mounted and rode forth to defy Agrapard without the walls.

The combat was long and desperate. For hours Esclarmonde's heart was torn with anxiety, and the emir remained trembling in the middle of his army, till a great shouting announced the victory of their champion, and soon Huon appeared leading the humbled giant bound to his saddle and covered with blood. He brought him thus to the feet of the emir, sitting on the terrace of the palace, and after he had lovingly embraced his lady he turned to her father and said, while Agrapard was being dragged to the dungeon he himself had lately quitted:

'Behold, I have kept my promise. Now it is for thee to perform thine.'

'My promise?' answered the wily Saracen. 'What promise? Thou art still alive: what ask ye more?'

'Emir, the commands of my king are still unfulfilled. Make haste to give me your teeth and beard; and, moreover, you must renounce the law of your false prophet that has taught you thus to lie.'

'Dog of a Christian, I would perish a thousand times rather than consent to such insolent demands. Now will I load thee with ten times heavier chains, from which this time none shall set thee free.'

Esclarmonde screamed and clung to her father's knees, begging for mercy, till she swooned away from terror. Huon ran to support her with the cry:

'Ungrateful miscreant, as well threaten the winds! I grant you one moment to obey me, or else fear my wrath.'

'Seize him! Slay him! Away with them both to the dungeon!' replied Gaudisse, waving his scimitar and shouting to his men; but he held back, not caring to measure himself with the knight that came from proving his strength upon Agrapard.

The guards rushed forward. Huon smiled and drew forth his horn. Rightly he judged that now the enchanter must be appeased by his repentance and his sufferings. He gave one blast so loud that all the walls of the palace quivered, and lo! in a moment Oberon was by his side, and the ground shook with the trampling of invisible horses and the tread of marching men.

The emir's soldiers could not stand against such a foe. As they paused and looked round, to ask each other whence came these martial sounds with which the air was filled, the host of fairyland fell upon them. The dwarf waved his enchanting wand and their arms were struck from their hands; their leaders were seized and dragged away before their eyes; horses and men rolled in the dust; the blood flowed from the wounds of phantom steel; whole troops were laid low, as trees by a hurricane; destruction swept through the ranks like a thunderbolt, and the terror-stricken Saracens turned to fly in wild confusion, without being able to see a single one of their assailants.

Gaudisse beheld this rout of his army with dismay; but what were his feelings when he found himself in the grasp of invisible hands, and loaded with the very chains he had ordered for Huon! Before he could beg for mercy, the irresistible hands had plucked the beard from his chin; he opened his mouth to roar in agony, and four of his largest teeth were torn from his jaws.

'Be this the fate of all cruel and unbelieving princes!' said Oberon, and gave the beard and the teeth to Huon. 'Take now these tokens; return to the King of France; salute him from me, and say that, through my aid and thine own stout heart, thou hast performed the task, and mayst well be forgiven. Take, too, this fair lady to be thy bride, and, so long as ye are loving and true, Oberon the Enchanter will be your friend.'

Thus made master of Babylon, Huon bestowed it as a reward upon his faithful squire. Gaudisse and Agrapard he sent to be kept in prison in the tower of Angoulafre. He loaded the emir's treasures upon camels, and set forth homewards, not forgetting to take with him the most precious treasure of all, the fair Esclarmonde. Arriving at the seacoast, they embarked in the ship which Geraume had provided, and, after many more perilous adventures, reached the city of Rome. There Esclarmonde was christened by the Pope and married to Huon; after which they repaired to France, and the knight, presenting the tokens of his success, was in due time restored to the king's favour.

PART IV:

HEROES AND MONSTERS

PERSEUS AND THE GORGON

Charles Kingsley

WHEN HE WAS FIFTEEN years old Perseus had grown to be a tall lad and a sailor, and went many voyages after merchandise to the islands around. All the people in Seriphos said that he was not the son of mortal man, and called him the son of Zeus, the king of the Immortals. For though he was but fifteen, he was taller by a head than any man in the island; and he was the most skilful of all in running and wrestling and boxing, and in throwing the quoit and the javelin, and in rowing with the oar, and in playing on the harp, and in all which befits a man. And he was brave and truthful, gentle and courteous; for good old Dictys had trained him well – and well it was for Perseus that he had done so. For now Danaë and her son fell into great danger, and Perseus had need of all his wit to defend his mother and himself.

Dictys' brother was Polydectes, king of the island. He was not a righteous man, like Dictys, but greedy and cunning and cruel. And when he saw fair Danaë, he wanted to marry her. But she would not; for she did not love him, and cared for no one but her boy and her boy's father, whom she never hoped to see again. At last Polydectes became furious, and while Perseus was away at sea he took poor Danaë away from Dictys, saying: 'If you will not be my wife, you shall be my slave.' So Danaë was made a slave, and had to fetch water from the well, and grind in the mill, and perhaps was beaten, and made to wear a heavy chain, because she would not marry that cruel king. But Perseus was far away over the seas in the isle of Samos, little thinking how his mother was languishing in grief.

Now one day at Samos while the ship was loading, Perseus wandered into a pleasant wood to get out of the sun, and sat down on the turf and fell asleep. And as he slept a strange dream came to him – the strangest dream which he had ever had in his life.

There came a lady to him through the wood, taller than he or any mortal man, but beautiful exceedingly, with great grey eyes, clear and piercing, but strangely soft and mild. On her head was a helmet and in her hand a spear. And over her shoulder above her long blue robes hung a goatskin, which bore up a mighty shield of brass, polished like a mirror. She stood and looked at him with her clear grey eyes; and Perseus saw that her eyelids never moved, nor her eyeballs, but looked straight through and through him, and into his very heart, as if she could see all the secrets of his soul, and knew all that he had ever thought or longed for since the day that he was born. And Perseus dropped his eyes, trembling and blushing, as the wonderful lady spoke.

'Perseus, you must do an errand for me.'

'Who are you, lady? And how do you know my name?'

'I am Pallas Athené; and I know the thoughts of all men's hearts, and discern their manhood or their baseness. And from the souls of clay I turn away, and they are blest, but not by me. They fatten at ease, like sheep in the pasture, and eat what they did not sow, like oxen in the stall. They grow and spread, like the gourd along the ground; but like the gourd they give no shade to the traveller, and when they are ripe, death gathers them, and they go down unloved into hell, and their name vanishes out of the land.

'But to the souls of fire I give more fire, and to those who are manly I give a might more than man's. These are the heroes, the sons of the Immortals, who are blest, but not like the souls of clay. For I drive them forth by strange paths, Perseus, that they may fight the Titans and the monsters, the enemies of gods and men. Through doubt and need, danger and battle, I drive them; and some of them are slain in the flower of youth, no man knows when or where; and some of them win noble names, and a fair and green old age. But what will be their latter end I know not, and none, save Zeus, the father of gods and men. Tell me now, Perseus which of these two sorts of men seem to you more blest?'

Then Perseus answered boldly: 'Better to die in the flower

of youth on the chance of winning a noble name, than to live at ease like the sheep, and die unloved and unrenowned.'

Then that strange lady laughed, and held up her brazen shield, and cried: 'See here, Perseus; dare you face such a monster as this and slay it, that I may place its head upon this shield?'

And in the mirror of the shield there appeared a face, and as Perseus looked on it his blood ran cold. It was the face of a beautiful woman, but her cheeks were pale as death and her brows were knit with everlasting pain and her lips were thin and bitter like a snake's; and instead of hair, vipers wreathed about her temples and shot out their forked tongues, while round her head were folded wings like an eagle's, and upon her bosom claws of brass.

And Perseus looked awhile, and then said: 'If there is anything so fierce and foul on earth, it were a noble deed to kill it. Where can I find the monster?'

Then the strange lady smiled again, and said: 'Not yet; you are too young and too unskilled; for this is Medusa the Gorgon, the mother of a monstrous brood. Return to your home and do the work which waits there for you. You must play the man in that before I can think you worthy to go in search of the Gorgon.'

Then Perseus would have spoken, but the strange lady vanished and he awoke; and behold, it was a dream. But day and night Perseus saw before him the face of that dreadful woman, with the vipers writhing round her head.

So he returned home; and when he came to Seriphos, the first thing which he heard was that his mother was a slave in the house of Polydectes.

Grinding his teeth with rage, he went out and away to the king's palace and through the men's rooms and the women's rooms, and so through all the house (for no one dared stop him, so terrible and fair was he) till he found his mother sitting on the floor, turning the stone hand-mill, and weeping as she turned it. And he lifted her up and kissed her and bade her follow him forth. But before they could pass out of the room Polydectes came in, raging. And when Perseus saw him, he flew upon him as the mastiff flies on the boar. 'Villain and tyrant!' he cried. 'Is this your respect for the gods, and your mercy to strangers and widows? You shall die!' And because he had no sword he caught up the stone hand-mill and lifted it to dash out Polydectes' brains.

But his mother clung to him, shrieking: 'Oh, my son, we are strangers and helpless in the land; and if you kill the king, all the people will fall on us, and we shall both die.'

Good Dictys too who had come in, entreated him: 'Remember that he is my brother. Remember how I have brought you up and trained you as my own son, and spare him for my sake.'

Then Perseus lowered his hand; and Polydectes, who had been trembling all this while like a coward because he knew that he was in the wrong, let Perseus and his mother pass.

Perseus took his mother to the temple of Athené, and there the priestess made her one of the temple-sweepers; for there they knew she would be safe, and not even Polydectes would dare to drag her away from the altar. And there Perseus and the good Dictys and his wife came to visit her every day, while Polydectes, not being able to get what he wanted by force, cast about in his wicked heart how he might get it by cunning.

Now he was sure that he could never get back Danaë as long as Perseus was in the island; so he made a plot to rid himself of him. And first he pretended to have forgiven Perseus and to have forgotten Danaë, so that for a while all went as smoothly as ever.

Next he proclaimed a great feast, and invited to it all the chiefs and landowners and the young men of the island, and among them Perseus, that they might all do him homage as their king and eat of his banquet in his hall.

On the appointed day they all came; and as the custom was then, each guest brought his present with him to the king: one a horse, another a shawl or a ring or a sword; and those who had nothing better brought a basket of grapes or of game. But Perseus brought nothing, for he had nothing to bring, being but a poor sailor-lad.

He was ashamed, however, to go into the king's presence without his gift, and he was too proud to ask Dictys to lend him one. So he stood at the door sorrowfully, watching the rich men go in; and his face grew very red as they pointed at him and smiled and whispered: 'What has that foundling to give?'

Now this was what Polydectes wanted; and as soon as he heard that Perseus stood without, he bade them bring him in, and asked him scornfully before them all: 'Am I not your king, Perseus, and have I not invited you to my feast? Where is your present then?'

Perseus blushed and stammered, while all the proud men round laughed, and some of them began jeering him openly. 'This fellow was thrown ashore here like a piece of weed or driftwood, and yet he is too proud to bring a gift to the king.'

'And though he does not know who his father is, he is vain enough to let the old women call him the son of Zeus.'

And so forth, till poor Perseus grew mad with shame, and hardly knowing what he said, cried out: 'A present! Who are you who talk of presents? See if I do not bring a nobler one than all of yours together!'

So he said boasting; and yet he felt in his heart that he was braver than all those scoffers, and more able to do some glorious deed.

'Hear him! Hear the boaster! What is it to be?' cried they all, laughing louder than ever.

Then his dream at Samos came into his mind, and he cried aloud: 'The head of the Gorgon.'

He was half afraid after he had said the words; for all laughed louder than ever, and Polydectes loudest of all.

'You have promised to bring me the Gorgon's head? Then never appear again in this island without it. Go!'

Perseus ground his teeth with rage, for he saw that he had fallen into a trap; but his promise lay upon him, and he went out without a word.

Down to the cliffs he went, and looked across the broad blue sea; and he wondered if his dream were true, and prayed in the bitterness of his soul:

'Pallas Athené, was my dream true? And shall I slay the Gorgon? If thou didst really show me her face, let me not come to shame as a liar and boastful. Rashly and angrily I promised; but cunningly and patiently will I perform.'

But there was no answer, nor sign; neither thunder nor any appearance; not even a cloud in the sky.

And three times Perseus called weeping, 'Rashly and angrily I promised; but cunningly and patiently will I perform.'

Then he saw afar off above the sea a small white cloud, as

bright as silver. And it came on, nearer and nearer, till its brightness dazzled his eyes.

Perseus wondered at that strange cloud, for there was no other cloud all round the sky; and he trembled as it touched the cliff below. And as it touched it broke and parted, and within it appeared Pallas Athené, as he had seen her at Samos in his dream, and beside her a young man more light-limbed than the stag, whose eyes were like sparks of fire. By his side was a sword of diamond, all of one clear precious stone, and on his feet were golden sandals, from the heels of which grew living wings.

They looked upon Perseus keenly, and yet they never moved their eyes; and they came up the cliffs towards him more swiftly than the seagull, and yet they never moved their feet, nor did the breeze stir the robes about their limbs; only the wings of the youth's sandals quivered, like a hawk's when he hangs above the cliff. And Perseus fell down and worshipped, for he knew that they were more than man.

But Athené stood before him and spoke grimly, and bid him have no fear. Then:

'Perseus,' she said, 'he who overcomes in one trial merits thereby a sharper trial still. You have braved Polydectes, and done manfully. Dare you brave Medusa the Gorgon?'

And Perseus said: 'Try me; for since you spoke to me in Samos a new soul has come into my breast, and I should be ashamed not to dare anything which I can do. Show me then how I can do this!'

'Perseus,' said Athené, 'think well before you attempt; for this deed requires a seven years' journey in which you cannot repent or turn back nor escape; but if your heart fails you, you must die in the Unshapen Land, where no man will ever find your bones.'

'Better so than live here useless and despised,' said Perseus. 'Tell me then, oh tell me, fair and wise goddess, of your great kindness and condescension, how I can do but this one thing, and then, if need be, die!'

Then Athené smiled and said:

'Be patient and listen; for if you forget my words, you will indeed die. You must go northward to the country of the Hyperboreans, who live beyond the pole, at the sources of the cold north wind, till you find the three Grey Sisters, who have but one eye and one tooth between them. You must ask them the way to the nymphs, the daughters of the Evening Star, who dance about the golden tree in the Atlantic island of the west. They will tell you the way to the Gorgon, that you may slay her, my enemy, the mother of monstrous beasts. Once she was a maiden as beautiful as morn, till in her pride she sinned a sin at which the sun hid his face. And from that day her hair was turned to vipers, and her hands to eagle's claws, and her heart was filled with shame and rage, and her lips with bitter venom; and her eyes became so terrible that whosoever looks on them is turned to stone; and her children are the winged horse and the giant of the golden sword; and her grandchildren are Echidna the witch-adder and Geryon the three-headed tyrant, who feeds his herds beside the herds of hell. So she became the sister of the Gorgons, Stheino and Euryte the abhorred, the daughters of the Queen of the Sea. Touch them not, for they are immortal; but bring me only Medusa's head.'

'And I will bring it!' said Perseus. 'But how am I to escape her eyes? Will she not freeze me too into stone?'

'You shall take this polished shield,' said Athené, 'and when you come near her look not at her herself, but at her image in the brass; so you may strike her safely. And when you have struck off her head, wrap it, with your face turned away, in the folds of the goatskin on which the shield hangs, the hide of Amaltheié, the nurse of the Aegisholder. So you will bring it safely back to me and win to yourself renown and a place among the heroes who feast with the Immortals upon the peak where no winds blow.'

Then Perseus said: 'I will go, though I die in going. But how shall I cross the seas without a ship? And who will show me my way? And when I find her, how shall I slay her, if her scales be iron and brass?'

Then the young man spoke: 'These sandals of mine will bear you across the seas, and over hill and dale like a bird, as they bear me all day long; for I am Hermes, the far-famed Argus-slayer, the messenger of the Immortals who dwell on Olympus.'

Then Perseus fell down and worshipped, while the young man spoke again:

'The sandals themselves will guide you on the road, for they are divine and cannot stray; and this sword itself, the Argus-slayer, will kill her, for it is divine and needs no second stroke. Arise and gird them on and go forth.'

So Perseus arose, and girded on the sandals and the sword.

And Athené cried: 'Now leap from the cliff and be gone.'

But Perseus lingered.

'May I not bid farewell to my mother and to Dictys? And may I not offer burnt-offerings to you, and to Hermes the far-famed Argus-slayer, and to Father Zeus above?'

'You shall not bid farewell to your mother, lest your heart relent at her weeping. I will comfort her and Dictys until you return in peace. Nor shall you offer burnt-offerings to the Olympians; for your offering shall be Medusa's head. Leap, and trust in the armour of the Immortals.'

Then Perseus looked down the cliff and shuddered; but he was ashamed to show his dread. Then he thought of Medusa and the renown before him, and he leapt into the empty air.

And behold, instead of falling he floated and stood and ran along the sky. He looked back, but Athené had vanished, and Hermes; and the sandals led him on northward ever, like a crane who follows the spring toward the Ister fens. So Perseus started on his journey, going dry-shod over land and sea; and his heart was high and joyful, for the winged sandals bore him each day a seven days' journey.

And he went by Cythnus and by Ceos and the pleasant Cyclades to Attica, and past Athens and Thebes and the Copaic lake and up the vale of Cephissus and past the peaks of Oeta and Pindus and over the rich Thessalian plains, till the sunny hills of Greece were behind him and before him were the wilds of the north. Then he passed the Thracian mountains and many a barbarous tribe, Paeons and Dardans and Triballi, till he came to the Ister stream, and the dreary Scythian plains. And he walked across the Ister dry-shod, and away through the moors and fens day and night, toward the bleak north-west, turning neither to the right hand nor the left, till he came to the Unshapen Land, and the place which has no name.

And seven days he walked through it, on a path which few can tell; for those who have trodden it like least to speak of it, and those who go there again in dreams are glad enough when they awake; till he came to the edge of the everlasting night, where the air was full of feathers and the soil was hard with ice, and there at last he found the three Grey Sisters, by the shore of the freezing sea, nodding upon a white log of driftwood, beneath the cold white winter moon; and they chanted a low song together: 'Why the old times were better than the new.'

There was no living thing around them, not a fly, not a moss upon the rocks. Neither seal nor seagull dare come near, lest the ice should clutch them in its claws. The surge broke up in foam, but it fell again in flakes of snow, and it frosted the hair of the three Grey Sisters and the bones in the ice-cliff above their heads. They passed the eye from one to the other, but for all that they could not see; and they passed the tooth from one to the other, but for all that they could not eat; and they sat in the full glare of the moon, but they were none the warmer for her beams. And Perseus pitied the three Grey Sisters, but they did not pity themselves.

So he said: 'Oh, venerable mothers, wisdom is the daughter of old age. You therefore should know many things. Tell me, if you can, the path to the Gorgon.'

Then one cried: 'Who is this who reproaches us with old age?' And another: 'This is the voice of one of the children of men.'

And he: 'I do not reproach, but honour your old age, and I am one of the sons of men and of the heroes. The rulers of Olympus have sent me to you to ask the way to the Gorgon.'

Then one: 'There are new rulers in Olympus, and all new things are bad.' And another: 'We hate your rulers and the heroes and all the children of men. We are the kindred of the Titans and the Giants and the Gorgons and the ancient monsters of the deep.' And another: 'Who is this rash and insolent man who pushes unbidden into our world?' And the first: 'There never was such a world as ours, nor will be: if we let him see it, he will spoil it all.'

Then one cried: 'Give me the eye, that I may see him'; and another: 'Give me the tooth, that I may bite him.' But Perseus, when he saw that they were foolish and proud, and did not love the children of men, left off pitying them and said to himself: 'Hungry men must needs be hasty; if I stay making many words here, I shall be starved.' Then he stepped close to them and watched till they passed the eye from hand to hand. And as they groped about between themselves, he held out his own hand gently, till one of them put the eye into it, fancying that it was the hand of her sister. Then he sprang back, and laughed, and cried:

'Cruel and proud old women, I have your eye; and I will throw it into the sea, unless you tell me the path to the Gorgon, and swear to me that you tell me right.'

Then they wept and chattered and scolded; but in vain. They were forced to tell the truth, though when they told it Perseus could hardly make out the road.

'You must go,' they said, 'foolish boy, to the southward into the ugly glare of the sun, till you come to Atlas the giant who holds the heavens and the earth apart. And you must ask his daughters, the Hesperides, who are young and foolish like yourself. And now give us back our eye, for we have forgotten all the rest.'

So Perseus gave them back their eye; but instead of using it, they nodded and fell fast asleep and were turned into blocks of ice, till the tide came up and washed them all away. And now they float up and down like icebergs for ever, weeping whenever they meet the sunshine and the fruitful summer and the warm south wind which fill young hearts with joy.

But Perseus leapt away to the southward, leaving the snow and ice behind, past the isle of the Hyperboreans and the tin isles and the long Iberian shore, while the sun rose higher day by day upon a bright blue summer sea. And the terns and the seagulls swept laughing round his head and called to him to stop and play, and the dolphins gambolled up as he passed and offered to carry him on their backs. And all night long the sea-nymphs sang sweetly, and the Tritons blew upon their conchs as they played round Galataea their queen in her car of pearled shells. Day by day the sun rose higher and leapt more swiftly into the sea at night and more swiftly out of the sea at dawn, while Perseus skimmed over the billows like a seagull, and his feet were never wetted; and leapt on from wave to wave, and his limbs were never weary, till he saw far away a mighty mountain, all rose-red in the setting sun. Its feet were wrapped in forests, and its head in wreaths of cloud; and Perseus knew that it was Atlas, who holds the heavens and the earth apart.

He came to the mountain and leapt on shore and wandered upward among pleasant valleys and waterfalls and tall trees and strange ferns and flowers; but there was no smoke rising from any glen, nor house, nor sign of man.

At last he heard sweet voices singing; and he guessed that he was come to the garden of the nymphs, the daughters of the Evening Star.

They sang like nightingales among the thickets, and Perseus stopped to hear their song; but the words which they spoke he could not understand – no, nor no man after him for many a hundred years. So he stepped forward and saw them dancing, hand in hand, around the charmed tree which bent under its golden fruit; and round the tree-foot was coiled the dragon, old Ladon the sleepless snake, who lies there for ever, listening to the song of the maidens, blinking and watching with dry bright eyes.

Then Perseus stopped, not because he feared the dragon, but because he was bashful before those fair maids; but when they saw him, they too stopped, and called to him with trembling voices:

'Who are you? Are you Heracles the mighty, who will come to rob our garden, and carry off our golden fruit?' And he answered:

'I am not Heracles the mighty, and I want none of your golden fruit. Tell me, fair nymphs, the way which leads to the Gorgon, that I may go on my way and slay her.'

'Not yet, not yet, fair boy; come dance with us around the tree in the garden which knows no winter, the home of the south wind and the sun. Come hither and play with us awhile; we have danced alone here for a thousand years, and our hearts are weary with longing for a playfellow. So come, come, come!'

'I cannot dance with you, fair maidens; for I must do the errand of the Immortals. So tell me the way to the Gorgon lest I wander and perish in the waves.'

Then they sighed and wept, and answered:

'The Gorgon! She will freeze you into stone.'

'It is better to die like a hero than to live like an ox in a stall. The Immortals have lent me weapons, and they will give me wit to use them.'

Then they sighed again and answered: 'Fair boy, if you are

bent on your own ruin, be it so. We know not the way to the Gorgon; but we will ask the giant Atlas, above upon the mountain peak, the brother of our father, the silver Evening Star. He sits aloft and sees across the ocean, and far away into the Unshapen Land.'

So they went up the mountain to Atlas their uncle, and Perseus went up with them. And they found the giant kneeling, as he held the heavens and the earth apart.

They asked him, and he answered mildly, pointing to the seaboard with his mighty hand: 'I can see the Gorgons lying on an island far away, but this youth can never come near them, unless he has the hat of darkness, which whosoever wears cannot be seen.'

Then cried Perseus: 'Where is that hat, that I may find it?'

But the giant smiled. 'No living mortal can find that hat, for it lies in the depths of Hades in the regions of the dead. But my nieces are immortal, and they shall fetch it for you if you will promise me one thing and keep your faith.'

Then Perseus promised; and the giant said: 'When you come back with the head of Medusa, you shall show me the beautiful horror, that I may lose my feeling and my breathing, and become a stone for ever; for it is weary labour for me to hold the heavens and the earth apart.'

Then Perseus promised; and the eldest of the nymphs went down and into a dark cavern among the cliffs out of which came smoke and thunder, for it was one of the mouths of Hell.

And Perseus and the nymphs sat down seven days and waited trembling, till the nymph came up again; and her face was pale and her eyes dazzled with the light, for she had been long in the dreary darkness, but in her hand was the magic hat.

Then all the nymphs kissed Perseus, and wept over him a long while, but he was only impatient to be gone. And at last they put the hat upon his head, and he vanished out of their sight.

But Perseus went on boldly, past many an ugly sight, far away into the heart of the Unshapen Land, beyond the streams of Ocean, to the isles where no ship cruises, where is neither night nor day, where nothing is in its right place and nothing has a name, till he heard the rustle of the Gorgons' wings and saw the glitter of their brazen talons; and then he knew that it was time to halt, lest Medusa should freeze him into stone.

He thought awhile with himself, and remembered Athené's words. He rose aloft into the air and held the mirror of the shield above his head and looked up into it that he might see all that was below him.

And he saw the three Gorgons sleeping, as huge as elephants. He knew that they could not see him because the hat of darkness hid him; and yet he trembled as he sank down near them, so terrible were those brazen claws.

Two of the Gorgons were foul as swine, and lay sleeping heavily as swine sleep, with their mighty wings outspread; but Medusa tossed to and fro restlessly, and as she tossed Perseus pitied her, she looked so fair and said. Her plumage was like the rainbow, and her face was like the face of a nymph; only her eyebrows were knit and her lips clenched, with everlasting care and pain, and her long neck gleamed so white in the mirror that Perseus had not the heart to strike, and said: 'Ah, that it had been either of her sisters!'

But as he looked, from among her tresses the vipers' heads awoke and peeped up with their bright dry eyes and showed their fangs and hissed. And Medusa, as she tossed, threw back her wings and showed her brazen claws; and Perseus saw that, for all her beauty, she was as foul and venomous as the rest.

Then he came down and stepped to her boldly, and looked steadfastly on his mirror, and struck with Herpé stoutly once. And he did not need to strike again.

Then he wrapped the head in the goatskin, turning away his eyes, and sprang into the air aloft, faster than he ever sprang before.

For Medusa's wings and talons rattled as she sank dead upon the rocks, and her two foul sisters woke and saw her lying dead.

Into the air they sprang yelling and looked for him who had done the deed. Thrice they swung round and round, like hawks who beat for a partridge; and thrice they snuffed round and round, like hounds who draw upon a deer. At last they struck upon the scent of the blood, and they checked for a moment to make sure; and then on they rushed with a fearful howl, while the wind rattled hoarse in their wings.

On they rushed, sweeping and flapping like eagles after a hare; and Perseus' blood ran cold, for all his courage, as he saw them come howling on his track; and he cried: 'Bear me well now, brave sandals, for the hounds of Death are at my heels!'

And well the brave sandals bore him, aloft through cloud and sunshine, across the shoreless sea; and fast followed the hounds of Death, as the roar of their wings came down the wind. But the roar came down fainter and fainter, and the howl of their voices died away; for the sandals were too swift, even for Gorgons, and by nightfall they were far behind, two black specks in the southern sky, till the sun sank and he saw them no more.

Then he came again to Atlas and the garden of the nymphs; and when the giant heard him coming, he groaned and said: 'Fulfil thy promise to me.' Then Perseus held up to him the Gorgon's head, and he had rest from all his toil, for he became a crag of stone, which sleeps for ever far above the clouds.

Then he thanked the nymphs, and asked them. 'By what road shall I go homeward again, for I wandered far round in coming hither?'

And they wept and cried: 'Go home no more, but stay and play with us, the lonely maidens, who dwell for ever far away from gods and men.'

But he refused, and they told him his road, and said: 'Take with you this magic fruit, which, if you eat once, you will not hunger for seven days. For you must go eastward and eastward ever, over the doleful Libyan shore, which Poseidon gave to Father Zeus, when he burst open the Bosphorus and the Hellespont, and drowned the fair Lectonian land. And Zeus took that land in exchange – a fair bargain, much bad ground for a little good – and to this day it lies waste and desert, with shingle and rock and sand.'

Then they kissed Perseus and wept over him, and he leapt down the mountain and went on, lessening and lessening like a seagull, away and out to sea.

So Perseus flitted onward to the north-east, over many a league of sea, till he came to the rolling sand-hills and the dreary Libyan shore.

And he flitted on across the desert: over rock ledges and banks of shingle and level wastes of sand, and shell-drifts bleaching in the sunshine and the skeletons of great seamonsters and dead bones of ancient giants, strewn up and down upon the old sea-floor. And as he went the blood drops fell to the earth from the Gorgon's head, and became poisonous asps and adders, which breed in the desert to this day.

Over the sands he went – he never knew how far or how long – feeding on the fruit which the nymphs had given him, till he saw the hills of the Psylli, and the dwarfs who fought with cranes. Their spears were of reeds and rushes, and their houses of the egg-shells of the cranes; and Perseus laughed, and went his way to the north-east, hoping all day long to see the blue Mediterranean sparkling, that he might fly across it to his home.

But now came down a mighty wind, and swept him back southward toward the desert. All day long he strove against it; but even the winged sandals could not prevail. So he was forced to float down the wind all night; and when the morning dawned there was nothing to be seen, save the same old hateful waste of sand.

And out of the north the sandstorms rushed upon him, blood-red pillars and wreaths, blotting out the noonday sun; and Perseus fled before them, lest he should be choked by the burning dust. At last the gale fell calm, and he tried to go northward again; but again came down the sandstorms, and swept him back into the waste, and then all was calm and cloudless as before. Seven days he strove against the storms, and seven days he was driven back, till he was spent with thirst and hunger, and his tongue clove to the roof of his mouth. Here and there he fancied that he saw a fair lake, and the sunbeams shining on the water; but when he came to it it vanished at his feet, and there was nought but burning sand. And if he had not been of the race of the Immortals, he would have perished in the waste; but his life was strong within him, because it was more than man's.

Then he cried to Athené, and said:

'Oh, fair and pure, if thou hearest me, wilt thou leave me here to die of drought? I have brought thee the Gorgon's head at thy bidding, and hitherto thou hast prospered my journey; dost thou desert me at the last? Else why will not these immortal sandals prevail, even against the desert storms? Shall I never see my mother more, and the blue ripple round Seriphos, and the sunny hills of Hellas?'

So he prayed; and after he had prayed there was a great silence.

The heaven was still above his head and the sand was still beneath his feet, and Perseus looked up, but there was nothing but the blinding sun in the blinding blue, and round him nothing but the blinding sand.

And Perseus stood still awhile, and waited, and said: 'Surely I am not here without the will of the Immortals, for Athené will not lie. Were not these sandals to lead me in the right road? Then the road in which I have tried to go must be a wrong road.'

Then suddenly his ears were opened, and he heard the sound of running water.

And at that his heart was lifted up, though he scarcely dare believe his ears; and weary as he was he hurried forward, though he could scarcely stand upright; and within a bowshot of him was a glen in the sand and marble rocks and date trees and a lawn of gay green grass. And through the lawn a streamlet sparkled and wandered out beyond the trees, and vanished in the sand.

The water trickled among the rocks, and a pleasant breeze rustled in the dry date branches; and Perseus laughed for joy and leapt down the cliff and drank of the cool water and ate of the dates and slept upon the turf and leapt up and went forward again, but not toward the north this time. For he said: 'Surely Athené hath sent me hither, and will not have me go homeward yet. What if there be another noble deed to be done before I see the sunny hills of Hellas?'

So he went east, and east for ever, by fresh oases and fountains, date palms and lawns of grass, till he saw before him a mighty mountain wall, all rose-red in the setting sun.

Then he towered in the air like an eagle, for his limbs were strong again; and he flew all night across the mountain till the day began to dawn and rosy-fingered Eos came blushing up the sky. And then, behold, beneath him was the long green garden of Egypt and the shining stream of Nile.

And he saw cities walled up to heaven, and temples and obelisks and pyramids and giant gods of stone. And he came down amid fields of barley and flax and millet and clambering gourds, and saw the people coming out of the gates of a great city and setting to work, each in his place, among the watercourses, parting the streams among the plants cunningly with their feet, according to the wisdom of the Egyptians. But when they saw him they all stopped their work and gathered round him and cried:

'Who art thou, fair youth? And what bearest thou beneath thy goatskin there? Surely thou art one of the Immortals, for thy skin is white like ivory and ours is red like clay. Thy hair is like threads of gold and ours is black and curled. Surely thou art one of the Immortals!' And they would have worshipped him then and there, but Perseus said:

'I am not one of the Immortals, but I am a hero of the Hellenes. And I have slain the Gorgon in the wilderness, and bear her head with me. Give me food therefore that I may go forward and finish my work.'

Then they gave him food and fruit and wine, but they would not let him go. And when the news came into the city that the Gorgon was slain, the priests came out to meet him, and the maidens, with songs and dances and timbrels and harps; and they would have brought him to their temple and to their king, but Perseus put on the hat of darkness, and vanished away out of their sight.

Therefore the Egyptians looked long for his return, but in vain, and worshipped him as a hero, and made a statue of him in Chemmis, which stood for many a hundred years. And they said that he appeared to them at times, with sandals a cubit long, and that whenever he appeared the season was fruitful and the Nile rose high that year.

Then Perseus went to the eastward, along the Red Sea shore; and then, because he was afraid to go into the Arabian deserts, he turned northward once more, and this time no storm hindered him.

He went past the Isthmus and Mount Casius and the vast Serbonian bog and up the shore of Palestine, where the dark-faced Aethiops dwelt.

He flew on past pleasant hills and valleys, like Argos itself, or Lacedaemon, or the fair vale of Tempe. But the lowlands were all drowned by floods, and the highlands blasted by fire, and the hills heaved like a bubbling cauldron before the wrath of King Poseidon, the shaker of the earth.

And Perseus feared to go inland, but flew along the shore above the sea. And he went on all the day, and the sky was black with smoke; and he went on all the night, and the sky was red with flame.

And at the dawn of day he looked toward the cliffs, and at the water's edge, under a black rock, he saw a white image stand.

'This', thought he, 'must surely be the statue of some seagod; I will go near and see what kind of gods these barbarians worship.'

So he came near; but when he came it was no statue, but a maiden of flesh and blood, for he could see her tresses streaming in the breeze. And as he came closer still he could see how she shrank and shivered when the waves sprinkled her with cold salt spray. Her arms were spread above her head, and fastened to the rock with chains of brass; and her head drooped on her bosom, either with sleep or weariness or grief. But now and then she looked up and wailed and called her mother; yet she did not see Perseus, for the cap of darkness was on his head.

Full of pity and indignation, Perseus drew near and looked upon the maid. Her cheeks were darker than his were, and her hair was blue-black like a hyacinth; but Perseus thought: 'I have never seen so beautiful a maiden, no, not in all our isles. Surely she is a king's daughter. Do barbarians treat their king's daughters thus? She is too fair at least to have done any wrong. I will speak to her.'

And lifting the hat from his head he flashed into her sight.

She shrieked with terror and tried to hide her face with her hair, for she could not with her hands; but Perseus cried:

'Do not fear me, fair one; I am a Hellene, and no barbarian. What cruel men have bound you? But first I will set you free.'

And he tore at the fetters, but they were too strong for him, while the maiden cried:

'Touch me not; I am accursed, devoted as a victim to the sea-gods. They will slay you if you dare to set me free.'

'Let them try,' said Perseus, and drawing Herpé from his thigh, he cut through the brass as if it had been flax.

'Now', he said, 'you belong to me and not to these sea-gods, whosoever they may be!' But she only called the more on her mother.

'Why call on your mother? She can be no mother to have left you here. If a bird is dropped out of the nest, it belongs to the man who picks it up. If a jewel is cast by the wayside, it is his who dare win it and wear it as I will win you and will wear you. I know now why Pallas Athené sent me hither. She sent me to gain a prize worth all my toil and more.'

And he clasped her in his arms and cried: 'Where are these sea-gods, cruel and unjust, who doom fair maids to death? I carry the weapons of Immortals. Let them measure their strength against mine! But tell me, maiden, who you are and what dark fate brought you here.'

And she answered, weeping:

'I am the daughter of Cepheus, King of Iopa, and my mother is Cassiopoeia of the beautiful tresses, and they called me Andromeda, as long as life was mine. And I stand bound here, hapless that I am, for the sea-monster's food, to atone for my mother's sin. For she boasted of me once that I was fairer than Atergatis, Queen of the Fishes; so she in her wrath sent the sea-floods. And her brother the Fire King sent the earthquakes, and wasted all the land, and after the floods a monster bred of the slime, who devours all living things. And now he must devour me, guiltless though I am – me, who never harmed a living thing, nor saw a fish upon the shore but I gave it life and threw it back into the sea, for in our land we eat no fish for fear of Atergatis their queen. Yet the priests say that nothing but my blood can atone for a sin which I never committed.'

But Perseus laughed, and said: 'A sea-monster? I have fought with worse than him: I would have faced Immortals for your sake; how much more a beast of the sea?'

Then Andromeda looked up at him, and new hope was kindled in her breast, so proud and fair did he stand, with one hand round her, and in the other the glittering sword. But she only sighed and wept the more and cried:

'Why will you die, young as you are? Is there not death and sorrow enough in the world already? It is noble for me to die, that I may save the lives of a whole people; but you, better than them all, why should I slay you too? Go you your way; I must go mine.'

But Perseus cried: 'Not so; for the lords of Olympus, whom I serve, are the friends of the heroes and help them on to noble deeds. Led by them I slew the Gorgon, the beautiful horror, and not without them do I come hither, to slay this monster with that same Gorgon's head. Yet hide your eyes when I leave you, lest the sight of it freeze you too to stone.'

But the maiden answered nothing, for she could not believe his words. And then, suddenly looking up, she pointed to the sea, and shrieked:

'There he comes, with the sunrise, as they promised. I must die now. How shall I endure it? Oh, go! Is it not dreadful enough to be torn piecemeal, without having you to look on?' And she tried to thrust him away.

But he said: 'I go; yet promise me one thing ere I go: that if I slay this beast you will be my wife, and come back with me to my kingdom in fruitful Argos, for I am a king's heir. Promise me, and seal it with a kiss.'

Then she lifted up her face and kissed him, and Perseus laughed for joy and flew upward, while Andromeda crouched trembling on the rock, waiting for what might befall.

On came the great sea-monster, coasting along like a huge black galley, lazily breasting the ripple and stopping at times by creek or headland to watch for the laughter of girls at their bleaching, or cattle pawing on the sandhills, or boys bathing on the beach. His great sides were fringed with clustering shells and seaweeds, and the water gurgled in and out of his wide jaws as he rolled along, dripping and glistening in the beams of the morning sun.

At last he saw Andromeda, and shot forward to take his prey, while the waves foamed white behind him, and before him the fish fled leaping.

Then down from the height of the air fell Perseus like a shooting star – down to the crests of the waves, while Andromeda hid her face as he shouted. And then there was silence for a while.

At last she looked up trembling and saw Perseus springing toward her, and instead of the monster a long black rock, with the sea rippling quietly round it.

Who then so proud as Perseus, as he leapt back to the rock, lifted his fair Andromeda in his arms and flew with her to the cliff-top, as a falcon carries a dove?

Who so proud as Perseus, and who so joyful as all the Aethiop people? For they had stood watching the monster from the cliffs, wailing for the maiden's fate. And already a messenger had gone to Cepheus and Cassiopoeia, where they sat in sackcloth and ashes on the ground in the innermost palace chambers, awaiting their daughter's end. And they came, and all the city with them, to see the wonder, with songs and with dances, with cymbals and harps, and received their daughter back again, as one alive from the dead.

Then Cepheus said: 'Hero of the Hellenes, stay here with me and be my son-in-law, and I will give you the half of my kingdom.'

'I will be your son-in-law,' said Perseus, 'but of your kingdom I will have none, for I long after the pleasant land of Greece, and my mother who waits for me at home.'

Then Cepheus said: 'You must not take my daughter away at once, for she is to us like one alive from the dead. Stay with us here a year, and after that you shall return with honour.' And Perseus consented; but before he went to the palace he bade the people bring stones and wood, and built three altars – one to Athené, one to Hermes and one to Father Zeus – and offered bullocks and rams.

And some said: 'This is a pious man.' Yet the priests said: 'The Sea Queen will be yet more fierce against us, because her monster is slain.' But they were afraid to speak aloud, for they feared the Gorgon's head. So they went up to the palace; and when they came in there stood in the hall Phineus, the brother of Cepheus, chafing like a bear robbed of her whelps, and with him his sons and his servants and many an armed man; and he cried to Cepheus:

'You shall not marry your daughter to this stranger, of whom no one knows even the name. Was not Andromeda betrothed to my son? And now she is safe again, has he not a right to claim her?'

But Perseus laughed and answered: 'If your son is in want of a bride, let him save a maiden for himself. As yet he seems but a helpless bridegroom. He left this one to die, and dead she is to him. I saved her alive, and alive she is to me, but to no one else. Ungrateful man! Have I not saved your land and the lives of your sons and daughters, and will you requite me thus? Go, or it will be worse for you!' But all the men-at-arms drew their swords and rushed on him like wild beasts.

Then he unveiled the Gorgon's head, and said: 'This has

delivered my bride from one wild beast: it shall deliver her from many.' And as he spoke Phineus and all his men-at-arms stopped short, and each man stiffened as he stood; and before Perseus had drawn the goatskin over the face again, they were all turned into stone.

Then Perseus bade the people bring levers and roll them out. And what was done with them after that I cannot tell.

So they made a great wedding-feast, which lasted seven whole days, and who so happy as Perseus and Andromeda?

But on the eighth night Perseus dreamed a dream, and he saw standing beside him Pallas Athené, as he had seen her in Seriphos, seven long years before. And she stood and called him by name, and said:

'Perseus, you have played the man, and see, you have your reward. Know now that the gods are just, and help him who helps himself. Now give me here Herpé the sword and the sandals and the hat of darkness, that I may give them back to their owners, but the Gorgon's head you shall keep awhile, for you will need it in your land of Greece. Then you shall lay it up in my temple at Seriphos, that I may wear it on my shield for ever, a terror to the Titans and the monsters and the foes of gods and men. And as for this land, I have appeased the sea and the fire, and there shall be no more floods nor earthquakes. But let the people build altars to Father Zeus and to me, and worship the Immortals, the lords of heaven and earth.'

And Perseus rose to give her the sword and the cap and the sandals, but he woke, and his dream vanished away. And yet it was not altogether a dream, for the goatskin with the head was in its place, but the sword and the cap and the sandals were gone, and Perseus never saw them more.

Then a great awe fell on Perseus. And he went out in the morning to the people and told his dream and bade them build altars to Zeus, the father of gods and men, and to Athené, who gives wisdom to heroes, and fear no more the earthquakes and the floods, but sow and build in peace. And they did so for a while, and prospered. But after Perseus was gone they forgot Zeus and Athené, and worshipped again Atergatis the queen, and the undying fish of the sacred lake, where Deucalion's deluge was swallowed up; and they burnt their children before the Fire King, till Zeus was angry with that foolish people and brought a strange nation against them out of Egypt, who fought against them and wasted them utterly, and dwelt in their cities for many a hundred years.

And when a year was ended Perseus hired Phoenicians from Tyre and cut down cedars, and built himself a noble galley, and painted its cheeks with vermilion and pitched its sides with pitch. And in it he put Andromeda and all her dowry of jewels and rich shawls and spices from the East, and great was the weeping when they rowed away. But the remembrance of his brave deed was left behind; and Andromeda's rock was shown at Iopa in Palestine till more than a thousand years were past.

So Perseus and the Phoenicians rowed to the westward across the sea of Crete, till they came to the blue Aegean and the pleasant Isles of Hellas and Seriphos, his ancient home.

Then he left his galley on the beach, and went up as of old, and he embraced his mother and Dictys his good foster-father, and they wept over each other a long while, for it was seven years and more since they had met.

Then Perseus went out, and up to the hall of Polydectes; and underneath the goatskin he bore the Gorgon's head.

And when he came into the hall, Polydectes sat at the table-head, and all his nobles and landowners on either side, each according to his rank, feasting on the fish and the goat's flesh, and drinking the blood-red wine. The harpers harped and the revellers shouted, and the wine-cups rang merrily as they passed from hand to hand, and great was the noise in the hall of Polydectes.

Then Perseus stood upon the threshold and called to the king by name. But none of the guests knew Perseus, for he was changed by his long journey. He had gone out a boy, and he was come home a hero; his eye shone like an eagle's and his beard was like a lion's beard, and he stood up like a wild bull in his pride.

But Polydectes the wicked knew him, and hardened his heart still more; and scornfully he called:

'Ah, foundling! Have you found it more easy to promise than to fulfil?'

'Those whom the gods help fulfil their promises; and those who despise them, reap as they have sown. Behold the Gorgon's head!'

Then Perseus drew back the goatskin, and held aloft the Gorgon's head.

Pale grew Polydectes and his guests as they looked upon that dreadful face. They tried to rise up from their seats: but from their seats they never rose, but stiffened, each man where he sat, into a ring of cold grey stones.

Then Perseus turned and left them, and went down to his galley in the bay. And he gave the kingdom to good Dictys, and sailed away with his mother and his bride.

THE CHIMAERA

Nathaniel Hawthorne

There was once a fountain which gushed out of a hill-side in the marvellous land of Greece. And for aught I know, after so many thousand years, it is still gushing out of the very selfsame spot. At any rate, there was the pleasant fountain, welling freshly forth and sparkling down the hill-side in the golden sunset, when a handsome young man named Bellerophon drew near its margin. In his hand he held a bridle, studded with brilliant gems, and adorned with a golden bit. Seeing an old man, and another of middle age, and a little boy, near the fountain, and likewise a maiden, who was dipping up some of the water in a pitcher, he paused, and begged that he might refresh himself with a draught.

'This is very delicious water,' he said to the maiden, as he rinsed and filled her pitcher, after drinking out of it. 'Will you be kind enough to tell me whether the fountain has any name?'

'Yes; it is called the Fountain of Pirene,' answered the maiden; and then she added, 'My grandmother has told me that this clear fountain was once a beautiful woman; and when her son was killed by the arrows of the huntress Diana, she melted all away into tears. And so the water, which you find so cool and sweet, is the sorrow of that poor mother's heart!'

'I should not have dreamed,' observed the young stranger, 'that so clear a well-spring, with its gush and gurgle, and its cheery dance out of the shade into the sunlight, had so much as one tear-drop in its bosom! And this, then, is Pirene? I thank you, pretty maiden, for telling me its name. I have come from a far-away country to find this very spot.'

A middle-aged country fellow (he had driven his cow to drink out of the spring) stared hard at young Bellerophon, and at the handsome bridle which he carried in his hand.

'The water-courses must be getting low, friend, in your part of the world,' remarked he, 'if you come so far only to find the Fountain of Pirene. But, pray, have you lost a horse? I see you carry the bridle in your hand; and a very pretty one it is, with that double row of bright stones upon it. If the horse was as fine as the bridle, you are much to be pitied for losing him.'

'I have lost no horse,' said Bellerophon, with a smile. 'But I happen to be seeking a very famous one, which, as wise people have informed me, must be found hereabouts, if anywhere. Do you know whether the winged horse Pegasus still haunts the Fountain of Pirene, as he used to do in your forefathers' days?'

But then the country fellow laughed.

Pegasus was a snow-white steed, with beautiful silvery wings, who spent most of his time on the summit of Mount Helicon. He was as wild, and as swift, and as buoyant in his flight through the air, as any eagle that ever soared into the clouds. There was nothing else like him in the world. He had no mate; he had never been backed or bridled by a master; and for many a long year he led a solitary and a happy life.

Oh, how fine a thing it is to be a winged horse! Sleeping at night, as he did, on a lofty mountain-top, and passing the greater part of the day in the air, Pegasus seemed hardly to be a creature of the earth. Whenever he was seen up very high above people's heads, with the sunshine on his silvery wings, you would have thought that he belonged to the sky, and that, skimming a little too low, he had got astray among our mists and vapours, and was seeking his way back again. It was very pretty to behold him plunge into the fleecy bosom of a bright cloud, and be lost in it for a moment or two, and then break forth from the other side. Or, in a sullen rain-storm, when there was a grey pavement of clouds over the whole sky, it would sometimes happen that the winged horse descended right through it, and the glad light of the upper region would gleam after him. In another instant, it is true, both Pegasus and the pleasant light would be gone away together. But anyone that was fortunate enough to see this wondrous spectacle felt cheerful the whole day afterwards, and as much longer as the storm lasted.

In the summer time, and in the beautifullest of weather, Pegasus often alighted on the solid earth, and, closing his silvery wings, would gallop over hill and dale for pastime, as fleetly as the wind. Oftener than in any other place, he had been seen near the Fountain of Pirene, drinking the delicious water, or rolling himself upon the soft grass of the margin. Sometimes, too (but Pegasus was very dainty in his food), he would crop a few of the clover-blossoms that happened to be sweetest.

To the Fountain of Pirene, therefore, people's great-grandfathers had been in the habit of going (as long as they were youthful, and retained their faith in winged horses), in hopes of getting a glimpse at the beautiful Pegasus. But of late years he had been very seldom seen. Indeed, there were many of the country folk, dwelling within half an hour's walk of the fountain, who had never beheld Pegasus, and did not believe that there was any such creature in existence. The country fellow to whom Bellerophon was speaking chanced to be one of those incredulous persons.

And that was the reason why he laughed.

'Pegasus, indeed!' cried he, turning up his nose as high as such a flat nose could be turned up. 'Pegasus, indeed! A winged horse, truly! Why, friend, are you in your senses? Of what use would wings be to a horse? Could he drag the plough so well, think you? To be sure, there might be a little saving in the expense of shoes; but then, how would a man like to see his horse flying out of the stable window? – yes; or whisking him up above the clouds, when he only wanted to ride to mill? No, no! I don't believe in Pegasus. There never was such a ridiculous kind of a horse-fowl made!'

'I have some reason to think otherwise,' said Bellerophon quietly.

And then he turned to an old, grey man, who was leaning on a staff, and listening very attentively, with his head stretched forward, and one hand at his ear, because, for the last twenty years, he had been getting rather deaf.

'And what say you, venerable sir?' inquired he. 'In your younger days, I should imagine, you must frequently have seen the winged steed!'

'Ah, young stranger, my memory is very poor!' said the aged man. 'When I was a lad, if I remember rightly, I used to believe there was such a horse, and so did everybody else. But, nowadays, I hardly know what to think, and very seldom think about the winged horse at all. If I ever saw the creature, it was a long, long while ago; and, to tell you the truth, I doubt whether I ever did see him. One day, to be sure, when I was quite a youth, I remember seeing some hoof-tramps round about the brink of the fountain. Pegasus might have made those hoof-marks; and so might some other horse.'

'And have you never seen him, my fair maiden?' asked Bellerophon of the girl, who stood with the pitcher on her head, while this talk went on. 'You certainly could see Pegasus, if anybody can, for your eyes are very bright.'

'Once I thought I saw him,' replied the maiden, with a smile and a blush. 'It was either Pegasus or a large white bird, a very great way up in the air. And one other time, as I was coming to the fountain with my pitcher, I heard a neigh. Oh, such a brisk and melodious neigh as that was! My very heart leaped with delight at the sound. But it startled me, nevertheless; so that I ran home without filling my pitcher.'

'That was truly a pity!' said Bellerophon.

And he turned to the child who was gazing at him, as children are apt to gaze at strangers, with his rosy mouth wide open.

'Well, my little fellow,' cried Bellerophon, playfully pulling one of his curls, 'I suppose you have often seen the winged horse.'

'That I have,' answered the child, very readily. 'I saw him yesterday, and many times before.'

'You are a fine little man!' said Bellerophon, drawing the child closer to him. 'Come, tell me all about it.'

'Why,' replied the child, 'I often come here to sail little boats in the fountain, and to gather pretty pebbles out of its basin. And sometimes, when I look down into the water, I see the image of the winged horse in the picture of the sky that is there. I wish he would come down and take me on his back, and let me ride him up to the moon! But, if I so much as stir to look at him, he flies far away out of sight.'

And Bellerophon put his faith in the child, who had seen the image of Pegasus in the water, and in the maiden, who had heard him neigh so melodiously, rather than in the middle-aged clown, who believed only in cart-horses, or in the old man, who had forgotten the beautiful things of his youth.

Therefore, he hunted about the Fountain of Pirene for a great many days afterwards. He kept continually on the watch, looking upward at the sky, or else down into the water, hoping for ever that he should see either the reflected image of the winged horse, or the marvellous reality. He held the bridle, with its bright gems and golden bit, always ready in his hand. The rustic people, who dwelt in the neighbourhood, and drove their cattle to the fountain to drink, would often laugh at poor Bellerophon; and sometimes take him pretty severely to task. They told him that an able-bodied young man like himself ought to have better business than to be wasting his time in such an idle pursuit. They offered to sell him a horse, if he wanted one; and when Bellerophon declined the purchase, they tried to drive a bargain with him for his fine bridle.

Even the country boys thought him so very foolish that they used to have a great deal of sport about him, and were rude enough not to care a fig although Bellerophon saw and heard it. One little urchin, for example, would play Pegasus, and cut the oddest imaginable capers by way of flying, while one of his schoolfellows would scamper after him, holding forth a twist of bulrushes, which was intended to represent Bellerophon's ornamental bridle. But the gentle child, who had seen the picture of Pegasus in the water, comforted the young stranger more than all the naughty boys could torment him. The dear little fellow often sat down beside him, and, without speaking a word, would look down into the fountain and up towards the sky, with so innocent a faith that Bellerophon could not help feeling encouraged.

Now you will, perhaps, wish to be told why it was that Bellerophon had undertaken to catch the winged horse. And we shall find no better opportunity to speak about this matter than while he is waiting for Pegasus to appear.

If I were to relate the whole of Bellerophon's previous adventures, they might easily grow into a very long story. It will be quite enough to say that, in a certain country of Asia, a terrible monster, called a Chimaera, had made its appearance, and was doing more mischief than could be talked about between now and sunset. According to the best accounts which I have been able to obtain, this Chimaera was nearly, if not quite, the ugliest and most poisonous creature, and the strangest and unaccountablest, and the hardest to fight with, and the most difficult to run away from, that ever came out of the earth's inside. It had a tail like a boa-constrictor; its body was like I do not care what; and it had three separate heads, one of which was a lion's, the second a goat's, and the third an abominably great snake's. And a hot blast of fire came flaming out of each of its three mouths! Being an earthly monster, I doubt whether it had any wings; but, wings or no, it ran like a goat and a lion, and wriggled along like a serpent, and thus contrived to make about as much speed as all the three together.

Oh, the mischief, and mischief, and mischief, that this naughty creature did! With its flaming breath, it could set a forest on fire, or burn up a field of grain, or, for that matter, a village, with all its fences and houses. It laid waste the whole country round about, and used to eat up people and animals alive, and cook them afterwards in the burning oven of its stomach. Mercy on us, little children, I hope neither you nor I will ever happen to meet a Chimaera!

While the hateful beast (if a beast we can anywise call it) was doing all these horrible things, it so chanced that Bellerophon came to that part of the world on a visit to the king. The king's name was Iobates, and Lycia was the country which he ruled over. Bellerophon was one of the bravest youths in the world, and desired nothing so much as to do some valiant and beneficent deed, such as would make all mankind admire and love him. In those days, the only way for a young man to distinguish himself was by fighting battles, either with the enemies of his country or with wicked giants, or with troublesome dragons, or with wild beasts, when he could find nothing more dangerous to encounter. King Iobates, perceiving the courage of his youthful visitor, proposed to him to go and fight the Chimaera, which everybody else was afraid of, and which, unless it should be soon killed, was likely to convert Lycia into a desert. Bellerophon hesitated not a moment, but assured the king that he would either slay this dreaded Chimaera or perish in the attempt.

But in the first place, as the monster was so prodigiously swift, he bethought himself that he should never win the victory by fighting on foot. The wisest thing he could do, therefore, was to get the very best and fleetest horse that could anywhere be found. And what other horse in all the world was half so fleet as the marvellous horse Pegasus, who had wings as well as legs, and was even more active in the air than on the earth? To be sure, a great many people denied that there was any such horse with wings, and said that the stories about him were all poetry and nonsense. But, wonderful as it appeared, Bellerophon believed that Pegasus was a real steed, and hoped that he himself might be fortunate enough to find him; and, once fairly mounted on his back, he would be able to fight the Chimaera at better advantage.

And this was the purpose with which he had travelled from Lycia to Greece, and had brought the beautifully ornamented bridle in his hand. It was an enchanted bridle. If he could only succeed in putting the golden bit into the mouth of Pegasus, the winged horse would be submissive and own Bellerophon for his master, and fly whithersoever he might choose to turn the rein.

But, indeed, it was a weary and anxious time while Bellerophon waited and waited for Pegasus, in hopes that he would come and drink at the Fountain of Pirene. He was afraid lest King Iobates should imagine that he had fled from the Chimaera. It pained him, too, to think how much mischief the monster was doing, while he himself, instead of fighting with it, was compelled to sit idly poring over the bright waters of Pirene, as they gushed out of the sparkling sand. And as Pegasus came thither so seldom in these latter years, and scarcely alighted there more than once in a lifetime, Bellerophon feared that he might grow an old man, and have no strength left in his arms nor courage in his heart, before the winged horse would appear. O, how heavily passes the time while an adventurous youth is yearning to do his part in life, and to gather in the harvest of his renown! How hard a lesson it is to wait! Our life is brief, and how much of it is spent in teaching us only this!

Well was it for Bellerophon that the child had grown so fond of him, and was never weary of keeping him company. Every morning the child gave him a new hope to put in his bosom, instead of yesterday's withered one.

'Dear Bellerophon,' he would cry, looking up hopefully into his face, 'I think we shall see Pegasus today!'

And at length, if it had not been for the little boy's unwavering faith, Bellerophon would have given up all hope, and would have gone back to Lycia, and have done his best to slay the Chimaera without the help of the winged horse. And in that case poor Bellerophon would at least have been terribly scorched by the creature's breath, and would most probably have been killed and devoured. Nobody should ever try to fight an earth-born Chimaera, unless he can first get upon the back of an aerial steed.

One morning the child spoke to Bellerophon even more hopefully than usual.

'Dear, dear Bellerophon,' cried he, 'I know not why it is, but I feel as if we should certainly see Pegasus to-day!'

And all that day he would not stir a step from Bellerophon's side; so they ate a crust of bread together, and drank some of the water of the fountain. In the afternoon there they sat, and Bellerophon had thrown his arm around the child, who likewise had put one of his little hands into Bellerophon's. The latter was lost in his own thoughts, and was fixing his eyes vacantly on the trunks of the trees that overshadowed the fountain, and on the grape-vines that clambered up among their branches. But the gentle child was gazing down into the water; he was grieved, for Bellerophon's sake, that the hope of another day should be deceived, like so many before it; and two or three quiet tear-drops fell from his eyes, and mingled with what were said to be the many tears of Pirene, when she wept for her slain children.

But, when he least thought of it, Bellerophon felt the pressure of the child's little hand, and heard a soft, almost breathless whisper.

'See there, dear Bellerophon! There is an image in the water!'

The young man looked down into the dimpling mirror of the fountain, and saw what he took to be the reflection of a bird which seemed to be flying at a great height in the air, with a gleam of sunshine on its snowy or silvery wings.

'What a splendid bird it must be!' said he. 'And how very large it looks, though it must really be flying higher than the clouds!'

'It makes me tremble!' whispered the child. 'I am afraid to look up into the air! It is very beautiful, and yet I dare only look at its image in the water. Dear Bellerophon, do you not see that it is no bird? It is the winged horse Pegasus!'

Bellerophon's heart began to throb! He gazed keenly upward, but could not see the winged creature, whether bird or horse; because, just then, it had plunged into the fleecy depths of a summer cloud. It was but a moment, however, before the object reappeared, sinking lightly down out of the cloud, although still at a vast distance from the earth. Bellerophon caught the child in his arms, and shrank back with him, so that they were both hidden among the thick shrubbery which grew all around the fountain. Not that he was afraid of any harm, but he dreaded lest, if Pegasus caught a glimpse of them, he would fly far away, and alight in some inaccessible mountain-top. For it was really the winged horse. After they had expected him so long, he was coming to quench his thirst with the water of Pirene.

Nearer and nearer came the aerial wonder, flying in great circles, as you may have seen a dove when about to alight. Downward came Pegasus, in those wide, sweeping circles, which grew narrower and narrower still as he gradually approached the earth. The nigher the view of him, the more beautiful he was, and the more marvellous the sweep of his silvery wings. At last, with so slight a pressure as hardly to bend the grass about the fountain, or imprint a hoof-tramp in the sand of its margin, he alighted, and, stooping his wild head, began to drink. He drew in the water with long and pleasant sighs, and tranquil pauses of enjoyment; and then another draught, and another and another. For, nowhere in the world or up among the clouds, did Pegasus love any water as he loved this of Pirene. And when his thirst was slaked, he cropped a few of the honey-blossoms of the clover, delicately tasting them, but not caring to make a hearty meal, because the herbage just beneath the clouds on the lofty sides of Mount Helicon, suited his palate better than this ordinary grass.

After thus drinking to his heart's content, and, in his dainty fashion, condescending to take a little food, the winged horse began to caper to and fro and dance, as it were out of mere idleness and sport. There never was a more playful creature made than this very Pegasus. So there he frisked, in a way that it delights me to think about, fluttering his great wings as lightly as ever did a linnet, and running little races, half on earth and half in air, and which I know not whether to call a flight or a gallop. When a creature is perfectly able to fly, he sometimes chooses to run just for the pastime of the thing; and so did Pegasus, although it cost him some little trouble to keep his hoofs so near the ground. Bellerophon, meanwhile, holding the child's hand, peeped forth from the shrubbery, and thought that never was any sight so beautiful as this, nor ever a horse's eyes so wild and spirited as those of Pegasus. It seemed a sin to think of bridling him and riding on his back.

Once or twice Pegasus stopped and snuffed the air, pricking up his ears, tossing his head, and turning it on all sides, as if he partly suspected some mischief or other. Seeing nothing, however, and hearing no sound, he soon began his antics again.

At length – not that he was weary, but only idle and luxurious – Pegasus folded his wings, and lay down on the soft green turf. But, being too full of aerial life to remain quiet for many moments together, he soon rolled over on his back, with his four slender legs in the air. It was beautiful to see him, this one solitary creature, whose mate had never been created, but who needed no companion, and, living a great many hundred years, was as happy as the centuries were long. The more he did such things as mortal horses are accustomed to do, the less earthly and more wonderful he seemed. Bellerophon and the child almost held their breath, partly from a delightful awe, but still more because they dreaded lest the slightest stir or murmur should send him up, with the speed of an arrow-flight, into the farthest blue of the sky.

Finally, when he had had enough of rolling over and over, Pegasus turned himself about, and, indolently, like any other horse, put out his fore legs, in order to rise from the ground; and Bellerophon, who had guessed that he would do so, darted suddenly from the thicket, and leaped astride of his back.

Yes, there he sat, on the back of the winged horse!

But what a bound did Pegasus make, when, for the first time, he felt the weight of a mortal man upon his loins! A bound, indeed! Before he had time to draw a breath, Bellerophon found himself five hundred feet aloft, and still shooting upward, while the winged horse snorted and trembled with terror and anger. Upward he went, up, up, up, until he plunged into the cold misty bosom of a cloud, at which, only a little while before, Bellerophon had been gazing, and fancying it a very pleasant spot. Then again, out of the heart of the cloud, Pegasus shot down like a thunderbolt, as if he meant to dash both himself and his rider headlong against a rock. Then he went through about a thousand of the wildest caprioles that had ever been performed either by a bird or a horse.

I cannot tell you half that he did. He skimmed straight-forward, and sideways, and backward. He reared himself erect, with his fore legs on a wreath of mist, and his hind legs on nothing at all. He flung out his heels behind, and put down his head between his legs, with his wings pointing right upward. At about two miles' height above the earth, he turned a somersault, so that Bellerophon's heels were where his head should have been, and he seemed to look down into the sky, instead of up. He twisted his head about, and looking Bellerophon in the face, with fire flashing from his eyes, made a terrible attempt to bite him. He fluttered his pinions so wildly that one of the silver feathers was shaken out, and floating earthward, was picked up by the child, who kept it as long as he lived, in memory of Pegasus and Bellerophon.

But the latter (who, as you may judge, was as good a horse-man as ever galloped) had been watching his opportunity, and at last clapped the golden bit of the enchanted bridle between the winged steed's jaws. No sooner was this done, than Pegasus became as manageable as if he had taken food all his life out of Bellerophon's hand. To speak what I really feel, it was almost a sadness to see so wild a creature grow suddenly so tame. And Pegasus seemed to feel it so likewise. He looked round to Bellerophon, with the tears in his beautiful eyes, instead of the fire that so recently flashed from them. But when Bellerophon patted his head, and spoke a few authoritative, yet kind and soothing words, another look came into the eyes of Pegasus; for he was glad at heart, after so many lonely centuries, to have found a companion and a master.

Thus it always is with winged horses, and with all such wild and solitary creatures. If you can catch and overcome them, it is the surest way to win their love.

While Pegasus had been doing his utmost to shake Bellerophon off his back, he had flown a very long distance; and they had come within sight of a lofty mountain by the time the bit was in his mouth. Bellerophon had seen this mountain before, and knew it to be Helicon, on the summit of which was the winged horse's abode. Thither (after looking gently into his rider's face, as if to ask leave) Pegasus now flew, and, alighting, waited patiently until Bellerophon should please to dismount. The young man, accordingly, leaped from his steed's back, but still held him fast by the bridle. Meeting his eyes, however, he was so affected by the gentleness of his aspect, and by his beauty, and by the thought of the free life which Pegasus had heretofore lived, that he could not bear to keep him a prisoner if he really desired his liberty.

Obeying this generous impulse, he slipped the enchanted bridle off the head of Pegasus, and took the bit from his mouth.

'Leave me, Pegasus!' said he. 'Either leave me, or love me.'

In an instant, the winged horse shot almost out of sight, soaring straight upward from the summit of Mount Helicon. Being long after sunset, it was now twilight on the mountain-top, and dusky evening over all the country round about. But Pegasus flew so high that he overtook the departed day, and was bathed in the upper radiance of the sun. Ascending higher and higher, he looked like a bright speck, and at last could no longer be seen in the hollow waste of the sky. And Bellerophon was afraid that he should never behold him more. But, while he was lamenting his own folly, the bright speck reappeared, and drew nearer and nearer, until it descended lower than the sunshine; and behold, Pegasus had come back! After this trial, there was no more fear of the winged horse making his escape. He and Bellerophon were friends, and put loving faith in one another.

That night they lay down and slept together, with Bellerophon's arm about the neck of Pegasus, not as a caution, but for kindness. And they awoke at peep of day, and bade one another good-morning, each in his own language.

In this manner, Bellerophon and the wondrous steed spent several days, and grew better acquainted and fonder of each other all the time. They went on long aerial journeys, and sometimes ascended so high that the earth looked hardly bigger than the moon. They visited distant countries, and amazed the inhabitants, who thought that the beautiful young man, on the back of the winged horse, must have come down out of the sky. A thousand miles a day was no more than an easy space for the fleet Pegasus to pass over. Bellerophon was delighted with this kind of life, and would have liked nothing better than to live always in the same way, aloft in the clear atmosphere; for it was always sunny weather up there, however cheerless and rainy it might be in the lower region. But he could not forget the horrible Chimaera, which he had promised King Iobates to slay. So, at last, when he had become well accustomed to feats of horsemanship in the air, and could manage Pegasus with the least motion of his hand, and had taught him to obey his voice, he determined to attempt the performance of this perilous adventure.

At daybreak, therefore, as soon as he unclosed his eyes, he gently pinched the winged horse's ear, in order to arouse him. Pegasus immediately started from the ground and pranced about a quarter of a mile aloft, and made a grand sweep around the mountain-top, by way of showing that he was wide awake, and ready for any kind of an excursion. During the whole of this little flight, he uttered a loud, brisk and melodious neigh, and finally came down at Bellerophon's side, as lightly as ever you saw a sparrow hop upon a twig.

'Well done, dear Pegasus! well done, my sky-skimmer!' cried Bellerophon, fondly stroking the horse's neck. 'And now, my fleet and beautiful friend, we must break our fast. Today we are to fight the terrible Chimaera.'

As soon as they had eaten their morning meal, and drank some sparkling water from a spring called Hippocrene, Pegasus held out his head, of his own accord, so that his master might put on the bridle. Then, with a great many playful leaps and airy caperings, he showed his impatience to be gone; while Bellerophon was girding on his sword, and hanging his shield about his neck, and preparing himself for battle. When everything was ready, the rider mounted, and (as was his custom, when going a long distance) ascended five miles perpendicularly, so as the better to see whither he was directing his course. He then turned the head of Pegasus towards the east, and set out for Lycia. In their flight they overtook an eagle, and came so nigh him, before he could get out of their way, that Bellerophon might easily have caught him by the leg. Hastening onward at this rate, it was still early in the forenoon when they beheld the lofty mountains of Lycia, with their deep and shaggy valleys. If Bellerophon had been told truly, it was in one of those dismal valleys that the hideous Chimaera had taken up its abode.

Being now so near their journey's end, the winged horse gradually descended with his rider; and they took advantage of some clouds that were floating over the mountain tops, in order to conceal themselves. Hovering on the upper surface of a cloud, and peeping over its edge, Bellerophon had a pretty distinct view of the mountainous part of Lycia, and could look into all its shadowy vales at once. At first there appeared to be nothing remarkable. It was a wild, savage, and rocky tract of high and precipitous hills. In the more level part of the country there were ruins of houses that had been burnt, and here and there the carcasses of dead cattle strewn about the pastures where they had been feeding.

'The Chimaera must have done this mischief,' thought Bellerophon. 'But where can the monster be?'

As I have already said, there was nothing remarkable to be detected, at first sight, in any of the valleys and dells that lay among the precipitous heights of the mountains. Nothing at all; unless, indeed, it were three spires of black smoke, which issued from what seemed to be the mouth of a cavern, and clambered sullenly into the atmosphere. Before reaching the mountain-top, these three black smoke-wreaths mingled themselves into one. The cavern was almost directly beneath the winged horse and his rider, at the distance of about a thousand feet. The smoke, as it crept heavily upward, had an ugly, sulphurous, stifling scent, which caused Pegasus to snort and Bellerophon to sneeze. So disagreeable was it to the marvellous steed (who was accustomed to breathe only the purest air) that he waved his wings, and shot half a mile out of the range of this offensive vapour.

But, on looking behind him, Bellerophon saw something that induced him first to draw the bridle, and then to turn Pegasus about. He made a sign, which the winged horse understood, and sunk slowly through the air, until his hoofs were scarcely more than a man's height above the rocky bottom of the valley. In front, as far off as you could throw a stone, was the cavern's mouth, with the three smoke-wreaths oozing out of it. And what else did Bellerophon behold then?

There seemed to be a heap of strange and terrible creatures curled up within the cavern. Their bodies lay so close together that Bellerophon could not distinguish them apart; but, judging by their heads, one of these creatures was a huge snake, the second a fierce lion, and the third an ugly goat. The lion and the goat were asleep; the snake was broad awake, and kept staring about him with a great pair of fiery eyes. But – and this was the most wonderful part of the matter – the three spires of smoke evidently issued from the nostrils of these three heads! So strange was the spectacle, that, though Bellerophon had been all along expecting it, the truth did not immediately occur to him that here was the terrible three-headed Chimaera. He had found out the Chimaera's cavern. The snake, the lion, and the goat, as he supposed them to be, were not three separate creatures, but one monster.

The wicked, hateful thing! Slumbering, as two thirds of it was, it sti held, in its abominable claws, the remnant of an unfortunate lamb – or possibly (but I hate to think so) it was a dear little boy – which its three mouths had been gnawing before two of them fell asleep!

All at once Bellerophon started as from a dream, and knew it to be the Chimaera. Pegasus seemed to know it at the same instant, and sent forth a neigh that sounded like the call of a trumpet to battle. At this sound the three heads reared themselves erect, and belched out great flashes of flame. Before Bellerophon had time to consider what to do next, the monster flung itself out of the cavern and sprung straight towards him, with its immense claws extended, and its snaky tail twisting itself venomously behind. If Pegasus had not been as nimble as a bird, both he and his rider would have been overthrown by the Chimaera's headlong rush, and thus the battle have been ended before it was well begun. But the winged horse was not to be caught so. In the twinkling of an eye he was up aloft, half-way to the clouds, snorting with anger. He shuddered, too, not with affright, but with utter disgust at the loathsomeness of this poisonous thing with three heads.

The Chimaera, on the other hand, raised itself up so as to stand absolutely on the tip-end of its tail, with its talons pawing fiercely in the air, and its three heads spluttering fire at Pegasus and his rider. My stars, how it roared, and hissed, and bellowed! Bellerophon, meanwhile, was fitting his shield on his arm, and drawing his sword.

'Now, my beloved Pegasus,' he whispered in the winged horse's ear, 'thou must help me to slay this insufferable monster; or else thou shalt fly back to thy solitary mountain-peak without thy friend Bellerophon. For either the Chimaera dies, or its three mouths shall gnaw this head of mine, which has slumbered upon thy neck!'

Pegasus whinnied, and, turning back his head, rubbed his nose tenderly against his rider's cheek. It was his way of telling him that, though he had wings and was an immortal horse, yet he would perish, if it was possible for immortality to perish, rather than leave Bellerophon behind.

'I thank you, Pegasus,' answered Bellerophon. 'Now, then, let us make a dash at the monster!'

Uttering these words, he shook the bridle; and Pegasus darted down aslant, as swift as the flight of an arrow, right towards the Chimaera's three-fold head, which all this time was poking itself as high as it could into the air. As he came within arm's-length, Bellerophon made a cut at the monster, but was carried onward by his steed before he could see whether the blow had been successful. Pegasus continued his course, but soon wheeled round, at about the same distance from the Chimaera as before. Bellerophon then perceived that he had cut the goat's head of the monster almost off, so that it dangled downward by the skin, and seemed quite dead.

But, to make amends the snake's head and the lion's head had taken all the fierceness of the dead one into themselves, and spit flame, and hissed, and roared, with a vast deal more fury than before.

'Never mind, my brave Pegasus!' cried Bellerophon. 'With another stroke like that, we will stop either its hissing or its roaring.'

And again he shook the bridle. Dashing aslantwise as before, the winged horse made another arrow-flight towards the Chimaera, and Bellerophon aimed another downright stroke at one of the two remaining heads as he shot by. But this time neither he nor Pegasus escaped so well as at first. With one of its claws the Chimaera had given the young man a deep scratch on his shoulder, and had slightly damaged the left wing of the flying steed with the other. On his part Bellerophon had mortally wounded the lion's head of the monster, insomuch that it now hung downward, with its fire almost extinguished, and sending out gasps of thick black smoke. The snake's head, however (which was the only one now left), was twice as fierce and venomous as ever before. It belched forth shoots of fire five hundred yards long, and emitted hisses so loud, so harsh, and so ear-piercing, that King Iobates heard them fifty miles off, and trembled till the throne shook under him.

'Well-a-day!' thought the poor king; 'the Chimaera is certainly coming to devour me!'

Meanwhile Pegasus had again paused in the air, and neighed angrily, while sparkles of a pure crystal flame darted out of his eyes. How unlike the lurid fire of the Chimaera! The aerial steed's spirit was all aroused, and so was that of Bellerophon.

'Dost thou bleed, my immortal horse?' cried the young man, caring less for his own hurt than for the anguish of this glorious creature, that ought never to have tasted pain. 'The execrable Chimaera shall pay for this mischief with his last head!'

Then he shook the bridle, shouted loudly, and guided Pegasus, not aslantwise as before, but straight at the monster's hideous front. So rapid was the onset, that it seemed but a dazzle and a flash before Bellerophon was at close grips with his enemy.

The Chimaera, by this time, after losing its second head, had got into a red-hot passion of pain and rampant rage. It so flounced about, half on earth and partly in the air, that it was impossible to say which element it rested upon. It opened its snake-jaws to such an abominable width that Pegasus might almost, I was going to say, have flown right down its throat, wings outspread, rider and all! At their approach it shot out a tremendous blast of its fiery breath, and enveloped Bellerophon and his steed in a perfect atmosphere of flame, singeing the wings of Pegasus, scorching off one whole side of the young man's golden ringlets, and making them both far hotter than was comfortable from head to foot.

But this was nothing to what followed.

When the airy rush of the winged horse had brought him within the distance of a hundred yards, the Chimaera gave a spring, and flung its huge, awkward, venomous, and utterly detestable carcass right upon poor Pegasus, clung round him with might and main, and tied up its snaky tail into a knot! Up flew the aerial steed, higher, higher, higher, above the mountain peaks, above the clouds, and almost out of sight of the solid earth. But still the earth-born monster kept its hold, and was borne upward, along with the creature of light and air. Bellerophon, meanwhile, turning about, found himself face to face with the ugly grimness of the Chimaera's visage, and could only avoid being scorched to death, or bitten right in twain, by holding up his shield. Over the upper edge of the shield he looked sternly into the savage eyes of the monster.

But the Chimaera was so mad and wild with pain, that it did not guard itself so well as might else have been the case. Perhaps, after all, the best way to fight a Chimaera is by getting as close to it as you can. In its efforts to stick its horrible iron claws into its enemy, the creature left its own breast quite exposed; and perceiving this, Bellerophon thrust his sword up to the hilt into its cruel heart. Immediately the snaky tail untied its knot. The monster let go its hold of Pegasus, and fell from that vast height, downward: while the fire within its bosom, instead of being put out, burned fiercer than ever, and quickly began to consume the dead carcass. Thus it fell out of the sky, all aflame, and (it being nightfall before it reached the earth) was mistaken for a shooting star or a comet. But, at early sunrise, some cottagers were going to their day's labour, and saw, to their astonishment, that several acres of ground were strewn with black ashes. In the middle of a field there was a heap of whitened bones a great deal higher than a haystack. Nothing else was ever seen of the dreadful Chimaera!

And when Bellerophon had won the victory, he bent forward and kissed Pegasus, while the tears stood in his eyes.

'Back now, my beloved steed!' said he. 'Back to the Fountain of Pirene!'

Pegasus skimmed through the air, quicker than ever he did

before, and reached the fountain in a very short time. And there he found the old man leaning on his staff, and the country fellow watering his cow, and the pretty maiden filling her pitcher.

'I remember now,' quoth the old man, 'I saw this winged horse once before, when I was quite a lad. But he was ten times handsomer in those days.'

'I own a cart-horse worth three of him!' said the country fellow. 'If this pony were mine, the first thing I should do would be to clip his wings!'

But the poor maiden said nothing, for she had always the luck to be afraid at the wrong time. So she ran away, and let her pitcher tumble down and broke it.

'Where is the gentle child,' asked Bellerophon, 'who used to keep me company, and never lost his faith, and never was weary of gazing into the fountain?'

'Here am I, dear Bellerophon!' said the child, softly.

For the little boy had spent day after day, on the margin of Pirene, waiting for his friend to come back; but when he perceived Bellerophon descending through the clouds, mounted on the winged horse, he had shrunk back into the shrubbery. He was a delicate and tender child, and dreaded lest the old man and the country fellow should see the tears gushing from his eyes.

'Thou hast won the victory,' said he, joyfully, running to the knee of Bellerophon, who still sat on the back of Pegasus. 'I knew thou wouldst.'

'Yes, dear child!' replied Bellerophon, alighting from the winged horse. 'But if thy faith had not helped me, I should never have waited for Pegasus, and never have gone up above the clouds, and never have conquered the terrible Chimaera. Thou, my beloved little friend, hast done it all. And now let us give Pegasus his liberty.'

So he slipped off the enchanted bridle from the head of the marvellous steed.

'Be free for evermore, my Pegasus!' cried he, with a shade of sadness in his tone. 'Be as free as thou art fleet!'

But Pegasus rested his head on Bellerophon's shoulder and would not be persuaded to take flight.

'Well, then,' said Bellerophon, caressing the airy horse, 'thou shalt be with me as long as thou wilt; and we will go together, forthwith, and tell King Iobates that the Chimaera is destroyed.'

Then Bellerophon embraced the gentle child, and promised to come to him again, and departed. But, in after years, that child took higher flights upon the aerial steed than ever did Bellerophon, and achieved more honourable deeds than his friend's victory over the Chimaera. For, gentle and tender as he was, he grew to be a mighty poet!

HERCULES IN HELL

Mike Ashley

EURYSTHEUS, KING of Tiryns, sighed as he looked upon the undaunted countenance of Hercules. There stood the man-mountain, proud and defiant.

'Twelve tasks I have agreed to complete,' Hercules was saying. 'Eleven are accomplished. What is your final test?'

Eurystheus winced. How he hated Hercules. The man might be a blood relative, but his supporters were legion, and his claim to the throne of the sons of Perseus which Eurystheus held had only been thwarted by his delayed birth. There had to be some way to be rid of him, yet although he had set him eleven impossible tasks, every time he had triumphed. Was there no way Eurystheus would see this man in Hell?

And with that thought the idea of the final task came to mind and for the first time in many years, Eurystheus smiled.

'Cousin, as you say, one task remains. I want you to fetch Cerberus from the Underworld.'

Eurystheus expected to see even Hercules hesitate. This task surely was impossible. Even if Hercules could survive the journey into the realms of darkness, Cerberus itself would be unconquerable and the Dark Lord Pluto would not agree to Cerberus being taken.

Yet Hercules bowed, and walked from Eurystheus' chamber seemingly without concern. 'Clearly he's mad,' Eurystheus spoke to the air, 'just as we all knew.' Eurystheus was referring to the reason Hercules was under his control in the first place. Some years before Hercules had been seized with a fit of madness and had murdered his own sons and nephews. For atonement the oracle at Delphi had ordered Hercules to serve Eurystheus and to undertake twelve tasks. Although Hercules' madness had passed, Eurystheus was convinced the man could never be totally sane. He was mad with his own strength, the power that he drew from Zeus, his father, which no mortal could contain. But perhaps set against the Lord of the Underworld, Hercules might at last meet his match.

Hercules, armed as ever with his poisoned arrows and his massive club, left Tiryns and headed for the city of Eleusis, on the coast beyond Athens. To venture into the depths of Hell, Hercules knew he must be purified of all sin, and only the Lords of the Mysteries at Eleusis could cleanse him of his past. But for the first time in his labours, Hercules met the opposition of his fellow man. The initiation ceremonies at Eleusis were reserved for Athenians alone and Hercules was no Athenian. Regardless of his power, Hercules could not be admitted.

A younger Hercules would have torn the temple apart, but now more mature and trying to control his power Hercules sought to reason. He had learned on previous adventures that sometimes the mind was more powerful than muscle. On his quest to obtain the Golden Apples of the Hesperides, Hercules had asked Atlas to help him. Atlas was only too welcome and, for a while, Hercules took the burden of the Heavens upon his shoulders while Atlas sought out the Apples. But when he returned Atlas decided he did not want to take back the Heavens and prepared to take the Apples to Eurystheus himself. Hercules outwitted Atlas, though, by asking him to place a pad upon Hercules' neck to help spread the load. As Atlas did so, Hercules slipped out leaving Atlas bearing the full weight of the Heavens again.

Perhaps reason could work again here. Supposing Hercules became an Athenian? Would they accept an adopted son of Athens? Hercules appealed to the king of Athens, his friend Theseus, and Theseus agreed, suggesting that one of the senior citizens be an adoptive father. This threw the Eleusinians into a quandary, but not wishing to argue with Theseus or Hercules, they consented.

The studies and rites were extensive and arduous, testing Hercules' mind in ways far harder than ever his muscles. But he applied himself and after almost a year the Eleusinians agreed that Hercules was ready for his initiation. This led to further debate because the ceremony at Eleusis was only for

Athenians. As a result they agreed to hold a special ceremony outside Eleusis. Thus in the earliest days of spring, Hercules bathed and cleansed himself in the river Ilissus and was purified by the priest.

Now Hercules, his mind and body both spiritually strong, was ready to enter the darkest depths of Hell.

It was a new Hercules who set out. Gone was the lion skin that he had worn since, as a youth, he had killed the lion that ravaged the cattle at Cithaeron, the first of his mighty deeds. Instead he wore a simple linen tunic, white and pure.

Hercules prayed to Zeus for guidance. To help him Zeus sent Hermes who led Hercules south across the Peloponnese to the southernmost point of the Greek mainland to the rich marble quarries of Taenarum. There Hermes bade Hercules to search for the entrance.

Hercules first went to pay homage to Poseidon, whose Temple was at Taenarum. Poseidon had always admired Hercules' strength, though he had never supported him because Hercules was always fighting and killing Poseidon's own offspring. But he saw no reason why he should not help Hercules on his way, particularly as the trip into Hell might be the best way to be rid of him.

As Hercules prayed at the Temple, Poseidon caused a spring to burst forth from the ground. Hercules, hearing the trickling water, followed the sound and found where the water bubbled from the rocks. The trickle formed a small stream which Hercules followed, and the stream led to a dark cave. There at the mouth stood Hermes.

'Beware Hercules,' Hermes warned. 'The waters of Acheron are poisonous. Do not drink therefrom or bathe in it.'

Hercules now followed Hermes into the dark mouth of the cave. His descent into the Underworld had begun.

The moment they were out of the sun a chillness settled about them. Hercules, dressed only in his linen tunic, found the cold more numbing than anything he had previously experienced. This would test his strength past endurance.

Led by light from Hermes' staff, the two followed the stream down through the dark caverns. Gradually, as Hercules' eyes became accustomed to the darkness, he became aware of other shapes moving along the walls. Shapes that vanished when he turned to look at them fully, but which returned when he looked ahead. A few at first they began to increase in number, some coming close to whisper his name, but vanishing as soon as he turned his head.

'What visions are these?' Hercules grunted, as he unleashed his club from around his waist. But Hermes stayed his hand.

'What do you expect to find in the Underworld, son of Zeus, but wraiths of the dead? You cannot harm them, and they can harm you no more.'

But though the shades could not injure Hercules physically, they could taunt his mind and threaten his madness. He needed to draw upon all that he had learned at Eleusis to control his fear.

The dark waters of Acheron led them further into gloom and at length the passageway opened onto a vast cavern whose ceiling was lost in the heights. The cavern glowed with a dim twilight, lit by the fires of the river Phlegethon. Here the Acheron flowed into another river, the Styx.

Through the twilight of the cavern Hercules perceived a short way off a boat, and in the boat waited Charon, the ancient boatman who ferried the souls of the dead across to Hades. Charon was a strong old man with a hideous countenance and a long white beard. His garment was ragged and dirty and his forehead covered with wrinkles. He looked on Hercules with piercing eyes.

'You are living,' said he. 'Get thee hence. My boat is for the dead.'

'You shall ferry me across,' Hercules affirmed. 'By the will of Zeus I go to bring Cerberus to the light of day.'

'Where is thy money to pay me?' asked Charon. 'Without it you cannot pass, but must wander by these shores a hundred years.'

'I have no money, but that will not stop me.'

So saying Hercules leaped into the boat. Despite his fearsomeness, Charon was terrified of the might and will of Hercules. He gave way and ferried him over, all the while grumbling, 'Pluto will have me in prison for this; no one can pass without payment.'

All the while they crossed Hercules was aware of the wailing of souls about him as spirits awaited their fate. The waters of the Styx were oily black and silent as death. As Hercules peered into them he was aware he could see no reflection. Instead the water seemed to draw him toward it. He felt as if it were sucking his very soul from his body. Again he had to draw upon the strength of his initiation to fight back. Only a pure mind could combat the agonies of Hell.

Eventually Charon reached the far shore where all the new spirits were gathered. At the sight of Hercules most fled, but two stood their ground. Hercules found it hard at first to see either as they seemed to fade as he looked directly and were always at the side of his vision. But gradually one face came to him which did not fade. This face had hair that seethed and writhed, and an expression of total hatred. It was a face that no one could look upon and live, the face of the gorgon, Medusa.

'Hercules,' it whispered, 'do you know me?'

Hercules put up his arm to shield his face.

'I know you, daughter of Phorcys, but you do not trouble me.'

Hercules reached for his club, but Hermes stayed his hand.

'Pass her by, Hercules. The dead cannot harm you.'

But still the monster taunted. 'Once I had life, Hercules, until your forebear, Perseus, struck me dead. I shall have revenge upon his seed.'

As she spoke the hissing of the snakes about her head increased, their sibillance luring Hercules to sleep. Slowly he lowered his arm. Deep down his soul cried for help.

There was a flash of brilliance within the cave which caused Hercules to again shield his eyes. In that moment the goddess Athene appeared and held her shield in front of Medusa's head. The serpents were forced to obey their goddess and the writhing and hissing ceased.

Athene spoke through the blinding light.

'Pass on, Hercules. Your mission awaits you.'

But now the other spirit called to Hercules. Again as his vision cleared Hercules recognised his old friend Meleager, the mighty hero whom Hercules had accompanied on the hunt for the Calydonian Boar, and who had been one of the Argonauts in Jason's quest for the Golden Fleece. Fate had struck Meleager a savage blow. His life had been safe so long as a certain log had remained unburnt. But Meleager, like

Hercules, suffered bouts of madness and in one such fit had killed his brothers. In anger his mother, who had kept the log safe, threw it on the fire, and as it burned so Meleager died.

'Hercules, my old friend,' Meleager whispered. 'My sister Deianeira believes you dead and weeps for you.'

Hercules remembered Deianeira with much love and tenderness. He vowed to Meleager that once he had finished this final labour he would seek out Deianeira and look after her. Little did Hercules know at that moment that he was sealing his fate, though it would be many years and many adventures before that day came.

Hercules now passed Meleager by, following the river Styx toward the Gates of Hell itself. At this point Hermes stopped Hercules and spoke to him.

'You are now on the Plains of Hell, Hercules, and ahead lie the Gates of Hades. This is where I agreed to take you, and is where I leave you. Fare well, son of Zeus, until we meet again.' And so saying Hermes rose on his winged feet and vanished into the darkness above.

Alone on the Plains of Hell, Hercules detected a sound of chains ahead of him. Were these the tormented souls of Hell?

As Hercules drew near he saw two men chained to a rock as black as pitch. Suddenly Hercules recognised them. They were his past comrades in adventures, Theseus, king of Athens, and Pirithous, king of the Lapithae. Hercules could not help but laugh at seeing these two heroes in their plight.

Theseus explained what had transpired in the year while Hercules studied at Eleusis. Hercules learned of the battle between the Lapithae and their half-brothers the Centaurs. This had happened after the centaur Eurution, far the worse for drink, had abducted Pirithous' bride Hippodameia. In the subsequent battle Hippodameia had died. Theseus, who had helped in the fight, agreed that each would aid the other find a new bride. Theseus had abducted the young Helen of Troy, which had led to further adventures, though not the famous Trojan War. But Pirithous would settle for no one less than Persephone, the wife of Pluto.

Now Persephone was under an agreement to spend part of her life in the upper world, but rather than wait for her to appear, Pirithous insisted on seeking her in the Underworld.

Against his better judgement Theseus agreed to help. But even before they had reached the gates of Hades, Pluto thwarted their presumption and had them chained to a rock to live forever amongst the dead.

Now Pirithous pleaded with Hercules to set them free. Hercules agreed provided they return to the upper world and forget their quest. Theseus agreed. With one tug from his mighty wrists, Hercules broke the chain that bound Theseus and set him free.

But Pirithous argued and was determined to claim Persephone. This angered Pluto who began to shake the rocks around Pirithous until he sank into a crack.

'You deserve your fate, Pirithous,' Hercules shouted into the chasm. 'There you shall remain until you mend your ways. But do you, dear Theseus, return to the world of light. I must continue on my quest.'

Hercules was now nearing the Gates of Hell. Around him gathered the souls of the dead, and the magnitude of these ghosts daunted even the spirit of Hercules. He decided to appease them with a gift of blood.

Nearby on the Plain of Hell were the cattle of Pluto. Hercules slaughtered one of them, pouring the blood over the Earth on which the ghosts feasted as their one last taste of life.

But the herdsman Monoetius challenged Hercules. 'You have no right to slaughter Pluto's cattle,' he cried, shaking his fist.

'I have no argument with you, Monoetius. Let me pass.'

But Monoetius would not and challenged Hercules to a wrestling match. Hercules first prayed to Zeus for his blessing, and then rose to meet Monoetius. The herdsman was a mighty man, but pale of skin and with long white hair. The two grappled and Hercules soon gripped Monoetius by the waist crushing his ribs. Had Hercules continued he would have broken the herdsman's back and killed him. But a voice from the darkness cried stop.

Hercules dropped Monoetius and looked ahead into the gloom. From out of the darkness came Persephone, the wife of Pluto. She was beautiful and fair, but her countenance was sad and pale. She always longed for the flowery valleys of earth, the light of the sun and the laughter of the living.

'Welcome, Hercules my brother, but stay your hand.

Monoetius is proud and loyal, but does not deserve to die. Spare him and I will grant you audience with Pluto.'

Hercules bowed his head to Persephone, the Queen of the Night, and agreed to follow her.

Persephone led Hercules along the banks of the Styx. Shortly, on either side of the river rose monstrous silver columns that stretched and vanished into the twilight, and there at the Gates of Hell waited Cerberus.

Though dog-shaped, Cerberus had three heads, a neck of hissing serpents and the tail of a scorpion. As Hercules approached the dog rose, baring its poisonous teeth and growled deeply in each of its three throats, but as Persephone raised her hand the dog ceased its growling and allowed them to pass.

Hercules now entered the Palace of Hell. There sat Pluto, high on a throne of sulphur set over the point where all the rivers of Hell met. He was a hard-hearted and inexorable god of a grim and dismal countenance.

'Hail, Pluto,' said Hercules. 'I am commanded by Eurystheus to bring Cerberus from your kingdom and into the eye of day.'

'Thou may be Hercules,' said Pluto, his voice darker than dread, 'but neither you nor Eurystheus have authority over me. Thou art a madman to make such a request. Who then would guard the gates of my kingdom?'

Hercules tensed at the reference to being mad, and called upon the Mysteries to contain his ire.

'Pluto, you have many servants to do thy work. But as for me, I am alone to do the work which Zeus has laid upon me. Eleven labours have I performed. I have been to the ends of the earth, and felt the weight of the heavens on my back; and now this last labour will I perform, if I have to pull down the walls of Hades and perish in the undertaking.'

'I believe you would, Hercules. Very well. If you think you are so powerful, then take Cerberus, but you must capture him first. And if you succeed, you must return him to me within the month. But do not believe that you have conquered Hades. That thou never will. A place awaits you here after your adventures and wanderings. And the next time you shall never leave.'

Hercules thanked Pluto and bowed deeply to the Dark Lord

and his wife. He then returned to the Gates of Hell where Cerberus waited as he had for eternity stopping any souls from leaving.

The monster's eyes glowed red and its three jaws opened revealing huge teeth dripping with venom. It moved out toward the centre of the Gates and crouched low, ready to spring.

But Hercules sprang first taking the beast by surprise. With one hand Hercules gripped the hellhound by the throat and with the other he grasped its poisonous tail and held the monster over his head. No matter how it writhed and struggled it could not escape Hercules' mighty grip. Hercules now tightened his grip around the creature's throat where all three necks joined. Although huge and as strong as iron the throat began to yield to Hercules' almighty strength and the beast found itself choking. Knowing it could not beat Hercules it ceased its struggling and relaxed. Gradually Hercules placed the beast on the ground where it lay in submission. Hercules gathered the chains that had previously bound Theseus to the rock and bound Cerberus.

Persephone had followed Hercules and watched the battle.

'You have achieved your quest, Hercules. Go, take Cerberus back to the land of life, but return him hence or my Lord Pluto will take his revenge.'

Hercules agreed and bowing to Persephone hefted Cerberus onto his mighty shoulders.

As he left he took one final glance back at Persephone. 'Remember me to the world,' she said, and then she turned and went back to Darkness.

Hercules seized Cerberus and carried him aloft out of the Halls of Hell. Charon readily ferried him back across the Styx. He had already received his punishment from Pluto for allowing Hercules in and was commanded to take Cerberus' place until Hercules returned.

As Hercules began to approach the upper world Cerberus began to struggle. The monster had never seen the sun and daylight and was afraid. With a blow of his fist Hercules knocked him unconscious, but as they emerged into the daylight, the dog's venomous spittle spattered the ground, and thereabout the plant aconite grew thereafter.

At last, after an absence of almost two years, Hercules returned to Tiryns. He cast the fearful monster at the feet of

Eurystheus. Cerberus held him in his baleful glare, his teeth dripping venom.

Eurystheus quailed and implored Hercules to keep hold of the monster. 'Very well, Hercules. You have performed the tasks I placed upon you. You are free to go. But first you must join me in a sacrifice of thanks to the gods.'

Hercules had no trust in Eurystheus but could not taunt the gods. At the celebrations Eurystheus handed Hercules a small portion of meat, whilst granting much larger portions to his sons. Hercules' temper could hold no longer.

'Eurystheus, I am no longer bound to you and you have no hold over me. From this day forth live in fear for the day shall come when not I, but my children, shall avenge me.'

As Hercules stormed from the Palace, three of Eurystheus' sons jumped upon him with their swords, but with one swing of his club he dashed out their brains. Eurystheus looked on in horror and wept. He watched his doom go forth.

Hercules now had to complete his promise to Pluto. Shouldering again the burden of Cerberus, which continued to whimper against the sunlight, Hercules returned to the Halls of Hell. The beast was much pleased to behold the fearful gates and the thousand thousand gliding shadows of the dead and the dim uncertain light of his own land.

But Hercules did not pass through the Gates of Hell this time. He turned back to light and life. He was now free from the yoke of Eurystheus and the world was his. There was still much for Hercules to achieve, but first he had his promise to Meleager to fulfil and the next step along the road to fate was about to begin.

SIEGFRIED AND THE DRAGON FAFNIR

James Baldwin

REGIN THE BARD took up his harp, and his fingers smote the strings; and the music which came forth sounded like the wail of the winter's wind through the dead tree tops of the forest. And the song which he sang was full of grief and wild hopeless yearning for the things which were not to be. When he had ceased, Siegfried said, 'That was indeed a sorrowful song for one to sing who sees his hopes so nearly realized. Why are you so sad? Is it because you fear the curse which you have taken upon yourself? or is it because you know not what you will do with so vast a treasure, and its possession begins already to trouble you?'

'Oh, many are the things I will do with that treasure!' answered Regin; and his eyes flashed wildly, and his face grew red and pale. 'I will turn winter into summer; I will make the desert-places glad; I will bring back the golden age; I will make myself a god: for mine shall be the wisdom and the gathered wealth of the world. And yet I fear –'

'What do you fear?'

'The ring, the ring – it is accursed! The Norns, too, have spoken, and my doom is known. I cannot escape it.'

'The Norns have woven the woof of every man's life,' answered Siegfried. 'Tomorrow we fare to the Glittering Heath, and the end shall be as the Norns have spoken.'

And so, early the next morning, Siegfried mounted Greyfell, and rode out towards the desert-land that lay beyond the forest and the barren mountain-range; and Regin, his eyes flashing with desire, and his feet never tiring, trudged by his side. For seven days they wended their way through the thick greenwood, sleeping at night on the bare ground beneath the trees, while the wolves and other wild beasts of the forest filled the air with their hideous howlings. But no evil creature dared come near them, for fear of the shining beams of light which fell from Greyfell's gleaming mane. On the eighth day they came to the open country and to the hills, where the land was covered with black boulders and broken by yawning chasms. And no living thing was seen there, not even an insect, nor a blade of grass; and the silence of the grave was over all. And the earth was dry and parched, and the sun hung above them like a painted shield in a blue-black sky, and there was neither shade nor water anywhere. But Siegfried rode onwards in the way which Regin pointed out, and faltered not, although he grew faint with thirst and with the overpowering heat. Towards the evening of the next day they came to a dark mountain-wall which stretched far out on either hand, and rose high above them, so steep that it seemed to close up the way, and to forbid them going farther.

'This is the wall!' cried Regin. 'Beyond this mountain is the Glittering Heath, and the goal of all my hopes.'

And the little old man ran forwards, and scaled the rough side of the mountain, and reached its summit, while Siegfried and Greyfell were yet toiling among the rocks at its foot. Slowly and painfully they climbed the steep ascent, sometimes following a narrow path which wound along the edge of a precipice, sometimes leaping from rock to rock, or over some deep gorge, and sometimes picking their way among the crags and cliffs. The sun at last went down, and one by one the stars came out; and the moon was rising, round and red, when Siegfried stood by Regin's side, and gazed from the mountain-top down upon the Glittering Heath which lay beyond. And a strange, weird scene it was that met his sight. At the foot of the mountain was a river, white and cold and still; and beyond it was a smooth and barren plain, lying silent and lonely in the pale moonlight. But in the distance was seen a circle of flickering flames, ever changing – now growing brighter, now fading away, and now shining with a dull, cold light, like the glimmer of the glow-worm or the fox-fire. And as Siegfried gazed upon the scene, he saw the dim outline of some hideous monster moving hither and thither, and seeming all the more terrible in the uncertain light.

'It is he!' whispered Regin, and his lips were ashy pale, and his knees trembled beneath him. 'It is Fafnir, and he wears the Helmet of Terror! Shall we not go back to the smithy by the great forest, and to the life of ease and safety that may be ours there? Or will you rather dare to go forwards, and meet the Terror in its abode?'

'None but cowards give up an undertaking once begun,' answered Siegfried. 'Go back to Rhineland yourself, if you are afraid; but you must go alone. You have brought me thus far to meet the dragon of the heath, to win the hoard of the swarthy elves, and to rid the world of a terrible evil. Before the setting of another sun, the deed which you have urged me to do will be done.'

Then he dashed down the eastern slope of the mountain, leaving Greyfell and the trembling Regin behind him. Soon he stood on the banks of the white river, which lay between the mountain and the heath; but the stream was deep and sluggish, and the channel was very wide. He paused a moment, wondering how he should cross; and the air seemed heavy with deadly vapors, and the water was thick and cold. While he thus stood in thought, a boat came silently out of the mists, and drew near; and the boatman stood up and called to him, and said, 'What man are you who dares come into this land of loneliness and fear?'

'I am Siegfried,' answered the lad; 'and I have come to slay Fafnir, the Terror.'

'Sit in my boat,' said the boatman, 'and I will carry you across the river.'

And Siegfried sat by the boatman's side; and without the use of an oar, and without a breath of air to drive it forwards, the little vessel turned, and moved silently towards the farther shore.

'In what way will you fight the dragon?' asked the boatman.

'With my trusty sword Balmung I shall slay him,' answered Siegfried.

'But he wears the Helmet of Terror, and he breathes deathly poisons, and his eyes dart forth lightning, and no man can withstand his strength,' said the boatman.

'I will find some way by which to overcome him.'

'Then be wise, and listen to me,' said the boatman. 'As you go up from the river you will find a road, worn deep and smooth, starting from the water's edge, and winding over the moor. It is the trail of Fafnir, adown which he comes at dawn of every day to slake his thirst at the river. Do you dig a pit in this roadway – a pit narrow and deep – and hide yourself within it. In the morning, when Fafnir passes over it, let him feel the edge of Balmung.'

As the man ceased speaking, the boat touched the shore, and Siegfried leaped out. He looked back to thank his unknown friend, but neither boat nor boatman was to be seen. Only a thin white mist rose slowly from the cold surface of the stream, and floated upwards and away towards the mountain-tops. Then the lad remembered that the strange boatman had worn a blue hood bespangled with golden stars, and that a gray kirtle was thrown over his shoulders, and that his one eye glistened and sparkled with a light that was more than human. And he knew that he had again talked with Odin. Then, with a braver heart than before, he went forwards, along the river-bank, until he came to Fafnir's trail – a deep, wide furrow in the earth, beginning at the river's bank, and winding far away over the heath, until it was lost to sight in the darkness. The bottom of the trail was soft and slimy, and its sides had been worn smooth by Fafnir's frequent travel through it.

In this road, at a point not far from the river, Siegfried, with his trusty sword Balmung, scooped out a deep and narrow pit, as Odin had directed. And when the gray dawn began to appear in the east he hid himself within this trench, and waited for the coming of the monster. He had not long to wait; for no sooner had the sky begun to redden in the light of the coming sun than the dragon was heard bestirring himself. Siegfried peeped warily from his hiding-place, and saw him coming far down the road, hurrying with all speed, that he might quench his thirst at the sluggish river, and hasten back to his gold; and the sound which he made was like the trampling of many feet and the jingling of many chains. With bloodshot eyes, and gaping mouth, and flaming nostrils, the hideous creature came rushing onwards. His sharp, curved claws dug deep into the soft earth; and his bat-like wings, half trailing on the ground, half flapping in the air, made a sound like that which is heard when Thor rides in his goat-drawn chariot over the dark thunder-clouds. It was a terrible moment for Siegfried, but still he was not afraid. He crouched low down in his hiding-place, and the bare blade of the trusty Balmung glittered in the morning light. On came the hastening feet and the flapping wings: the red gleam from the monster's flaming nostrils lighted up the trench where Siegfried lay. He heard a roaring and a rushing like the sound of a whirlwind in the forest; then a black, inky mass rolled above him, and all was dark. Now was Siegfried's opportunity. The bright edge of Balmung gleamed in the darkness one moment, and then it smote the heart of Fafnir as he passed. Some men say that Odin sat in the pit with Siegfried, and strengthened his arm and directed his sword, or else he could not thus have slain the Terror. But, be this as it may, the victory was soon won. The monster stopped short, while but half of his long body had glided over the pit; for sudden death had overtaken him. His horrid head fell lifeless upon the ground; his cold wings flapped once, and then lay, quivering and helpless, spread out on either side; and streams of thick black blood flowed from his heart, through the wound beneath, and filled the trench in which Siegfried was hidden, and ran like a mountain-torrent down the road towards the river. Siegfried was covered from head to foot with the slimy liquid, and, had he not quickly leaped from his hiding-place, he would have been drowned in the swift-rushing stream.

The bright sun rose in the east, and gilded the mountain-tops, and fell upon the still waters of the river, and lighted up the treeless plains around. The south wind played gently against Siegfried's cheeks and in his long hair, as he stood gazing on his fallen foe. And the sound of singing birds, and rippling waters, and gay insects – such as had not broken the silence of the Glittering Heath for ages – came to his ears. The Terror was dead, and Nature had awakened from her sleep of dread. And as the lad leaned upon his sword, and thought of the deed he had done, behold! the shining Greyfell, with the beaming, hopeful mane, having crossed the now bright river, stood by his side. And Regin, his face grown wondrous cold, came trudging over the meadows; and his heart was full of guile. Then the mountain vultures came wheeling downwards to look upon the dead dragon; and with them were two ravens, black as midnight.

And when Siegfried saw these ravens he knew them to be Odin's birds – Hugin, thought, and Munin, memory. And they alighted on the ground near by; and the lad listened to hear what they would say. Then Hugin flapped his wings, and said, 'The deed is done. Why tarries the hero?'

And Munin said, 'The world is wide. Fame waits for the hero.'

And Hugin answered, 'What if he win the Hoard of the Elves? That is not honor. Let him seek fame by nobler deeds.'

Then Munin flew past his ear, and whispered, 'Beware of Regin, the master! His heart is poisoned. He would be thy bane.'

And the two birds flew away to carry the news to Odin in the happy halls of Gladsheim.

When Regin drew near to look upon the dragon, Siegfried kindly accosted him: but he seemed not to hear; and a snaky glitter lurked in his eyes, and his mouth was set and dry, and he seemed as one walking in a dream.

'It is mine now,' he murmured: 'it is all mine, now – the Hoard of the swarthy elf-folk, the garnered wisdom of ages. The strength of the world is mine. I will keep, I will save, I will heap up; and none shall have part or parcel of the treasure which is mine alone.'

Then his eyes fell upon Siegfried; and his cheeks grew dark with wrath, and he cried out, 'Why are you here in my way? I am the lord of the Glittering Heath: I am the master of the Hoard. I am the master, and you are my thrall.'

Siegfried wondered at the change which had taken place in his old master; but he only smiled at his strange words, and made no answer.

'You have slain my brother!' Regin cried; and his face grew fearfully black, and his mouth foamed with rage.

'It was my deed and yours,' calmly answered Siegfried. 'I have rid the world of a Terror: I have righted a grievous wrong.'

'You have slain my brother,' said Regin; 'and a murderer's ransom you shall pay!'

'Take the Hoard for your ransom, and let us each wend his way,' said the lad.

'The Hoard is mine by rights,' answered Regin still more

wrathfully. 'I am the master, and you are my thrall. Why stand you in my way?'

Then, blinded with madness, he rushed at Siegfried as if to strike him down; but his foot slipped in a puddle of gore, and he pitched headlong against the sharp edge of Balmung. So sudden was this movement, and so unlooked for, that the sword was twitched out of Siegfried's hand, and fell with a dull splash into the blood-filled pit before him; while Regin, slain by his own rashness, sank dead upon the ground. Full of horror, Siegfried turned away, and mounted Greyfell.

'This is a place of blood,' said he, 'and the way to glory leads not through it. Let the Hoard still lie on the Glittering Heath; I will go my way from hence; and the world shall know me for better deeds than this.'

And he turned his back on the fearful scene, and rode away; and so swiftly did Greyfell carry him over the desert land and the mountain waste, that, when night came, they stood on the shore of the great North Sea, and the white waves broke at their feet. And the lad sat for a long time silent upon the warm white sand of the beach, and Greyfell waited at his side. And he watched the stars as they came out one by one, and the moon, as it rose round and pale, and moved like a queen across the sky. And the night wore away, and the stars grew pale, and the moon sank to rest in the wilderness of waters. And at day-dawn Siegfried looked towards the west, and midway between sky and sea he thought he saw dark mountain tops hanging above a land of mists that seemed to float upon the edge of the sea.

While he looked, a white ship, with sails all set, came speeding over the waters towards him. It came nearer and nearer, and the sailors rested upon their oars as it glided into the quiet harbor. A minstrel, with long white beard floating in the wind, sat at the prow; and the sweet music from his harp was wafted like incense to the shore. The vessel touched the sands: its white sails were reefed as if by magic, and the crew leaped out upon the beach.

'Hail, Siegfried the Golden!' cried the harper. 'Whither do you fare this summer day?'

'I have come from a land of horror and dread,' answered the lad; 'and I would fain fare to a brighter.'

'Then go with me to awaken the earth from its slumber, and

to robe the fields in their garbs of beauty,' said the harper. And he touched the strings of his harp, and strains of the softest music arose in the still morning air. And Siegfried stood entranced, for never before had he heard such music.

'Tell me who you are!' he cried, when the sounds died away. 'Tell me who you are, and I will go to the ends of the earth with you.'

'I am Bragi,' answered the harper, smiling. And Siegfried noticed then that the ship was laden with flowers of every hue, and that thousands of singing birds circled around and above it, filling the air with the sound of their glad twitterings.

Now, Bragi was the sweetest musician in all the world. It was said by some that his home was with the song-birds, and that he had learned his skill from them. But this was only part of the truth: for wherever there was loveliness or beauty, or things noble and pure, there was Bragi; and his wondrous power in music and song was but the outward sign of a blameless soul. When he touched the strings of his golden harp, all Nature was charmed with the sweet harmony: the savage beasts of the wood crept near to listen; the birds paused in their flight; the waves of the sea were becalmed, and the winds were hushed; the leaping waterfall was still, and the rushing torrent tarried in its bed; the elves forgot their hidden treasures, and joined in silent dance around him; and the ström-karls and the musicians of the wood vainly tried to imitate him. And he was as fair of speech as he was skilful in song. His words were so persuasive that he had been known to call the fishes from the sea, to move great lifeless rocks, and, what is harder, the hearts of kings. He understood the voice of the birds, and the whispering of the breeze, the murmur of the waves, and the roar of the waterfalls. He knew the length and breadth of the earth, and the secrets of the sea, and the language of the stars. And every day he talked with Odin the All-Father, and with the wise and good in the sunlit halls of Gladsheim. And once every year he went to the North-lands, and woke the earth from its long winter's sleep, and scattered music and smiles and beauty everywhere.

Right gladly did Siegfried agree to sail with Bragi over the sea; for he wot that the bright Asa-god would be a very different guide from the cunning, evil-eyed Regin. So he went on board with Bragi, and the gleaming Greyfell followed them, and the sailors sat at their oars. And Bragi stood in the prow, and touched the strings of his harp. And, as the music arose, the white sails leaped up the masts, and a warm south breeze began to blow; and the little vessel, wafted by sweet sounds and the incense of spring, sped gladly away over the sea.

[illegible]
[illegible]
[illegible]
[illegible]
[illegible]

THE SLAYING OF GRENDEL

Alfred J. Church

IN THE DAYS of old the House of the Scyldings ruled in Denmark. The first of the line was Scyld, whom men called 'Son of the Sheaf' because he came no man knew whence, being a little child in a boat with a sheaf of corn. He grew to be a mighty man of valour, subduing the robber tribes that sailed over the seas seeking for plunder, and compelling the nations round about to pay him tribute. A good and great King was he and God gave him a son for the comfort of his people, for He knew in what evil case that nation stands that lacks a king to rule over it.

Now the time came that King Scyld must die, for he had grown old and feeble. So he said to his warriors, 'Carry me, comrades, to the shore, for as I came by the sea, so by the sea must I go.' So they carried him to the shore; there stood his ship, newly adorned, and with sails set as for a voyage. There in the middle of the ship, hard by the mast, did the comrades of Scyld the King lay down their dead lord. And they laid with him many precious things, ornaments gathered from many far countries. Never have I heard of ship that was adorned in more comely fashion with warriors' gear and weapons of war, battle-axes and coats of mail. Rich in truth was the store that they put in his keeping that he might carry them with him far away into the land of waters. Not less, then, was the wealth that he took than that which he brought. With empty hands he came, but he departed with a king's treasure. And over his head they set up a banner wrought in gold. And the helm they left free that the sea might take him whithersoever it would. But who received that burden not the wisest man that is under heaven knows to this day.

King Scyld having thus gone to his place, Beowulf his son reigned in his stead for many years even unto old age; and after Beowulf, Healfdene, a hero famous in war; and after Healfdene, Hrothgar, who excelled all that had gone before him in valiant deeds.

It came into the mind of this Hrothgar that he would build a banqueting-hall, greater than man had ever before heard tell of. And as he purposed so he did. Quickly was the hall set up, and when it was finished it was the stateliest hall in all the earth, a home of peace, towering high into the air. Nor did any that beheld it dream that there should ever be strife within it, or that its splendour should be devoured by flames.

And when the great hall was built, the King's warriors resorted to it with much joy and gladness, till there came within its doors an evil guest that worked desolation and woe. Grendel was his name, and he dwelt among the moors and fens. He was of an accursed race, the race of Cain the murderer, whom the Lord separated from the children of men. For, indeed, of this first father come all strange broods, giants, and elves, and ogres.

On a certain night, when the darkness had fallen, this Grendel set forth to search out this lofty hall, and to see how the Danes had bestowed themselves in it. A princely troop he found sleeping after the feast. Thirty of them did the monster seize, and hied him back to his den, rejoicing with loud cries over his prey. But when the day broke all men might see what desolation he had wrought, and great was the grief of the King. Again, on the very next night, the monster came, and seized a fresh prey. And so it happened for the space of twelve winters. No man dared abide in the hall for fear of Grendel; nor did they escape him in the chambers of the castle. Whether a man was a tried warrior, or a youth, it mattered not; all were his prey. And over the moors he wandered, seizing such as found access there. Only to the throne itself he could not approach, for God would not suffer him so to do. Oft did the nobles take counsel together how they might abate this plague; often did they offer sacrifices to their gods if haply they might win help from them; but neither sacrifice nor counsel availed.

Now in the land of the Goths there was a certain King, Hygelac by name, and this King had a nephew, whose name was Beowulf, a youth that had in him the strength of thirty men. To him came the report of King Hrothgar's trouble, and he conceived in his mind the purpose to help him. So he set sail to the land of the Danes, having fourteen comrades with him, the bravest that he could find in all the land of the Goths. All that day and all that night they sailed, and on the morrow, at the very hour of their setting out, they saw land, a land of great cliffs and of headlands jutting far out into the sea. So they drove the ship to the beach, and sprang ashore in their warriors' gear, and made fast their craft.

When the warden of the coast espied them, he rode down to the shore, with a great spear in his hand. 'Who are ye,' he said, 'who come so boldly to this land? Many years have I been warden in this place, having been set to watch the sea-robbers, lest they should work mischief to the land of the Danes, but never have I seen men land in more open guise. Nor do ye know, I take it, any password or token such as kinsmen have between them. Say then who ye are, for, indeed, I see among you one whose peer may not easily be found, so stalwart and strong is he to look upon. No common man is he that has decked himself out with splendid armour. But say, strangers, who ye are before ye go further into the land of the Danes.'

Then Beowulf made answer: 'We are of the race of the Goths, and we are come with friendly purpose to thy lord, King Hrothgar; nor is there any need to hide it. We have heard – and whether it be true or no thou knowest – that some monster comes by night to devour the King's warriors in his hall. For this evil we bring a remedy.'

The warden said: 'Yea, I know it well; a faithful squire must needs know the troubles of his lord. But ye, for ye seem to be a friendly company, pass on with your weapons of war, and I will bid my comrades keep watch and ward over your ship till ye return, that it may carry you safely back to the land of your birth.'

So Beowulf and his company marched on, with the warden for guide of their way; and as they went, the sun shone on the golden boars' heads that they carried on their helmets. Eager for battle they went on till they could see before them the hall of the King where it stood in its splendour. Then the warden pointed with his hand and said: 'Now I must depart; for I must needs return to the shore to keep it against the approach of the enemy. And may the Almighty Father keep you in your way!'

So they marched along the path of stone till they came to the hall; there they set up their shields against the wall, and stacked their spears together, and sat down upon a bench, for they were weary with their journey.

To them came forth an officer of the King, and questioned them of their kindred and country: 'Whence do ye bring,' he said, 'your warriors' gear, your shields and spears? Know that I am squire and herald to King Hrothgar. Never yet have I seen so fair a company of strangers. 'Tis, I trow, on some bold errand that ye are come.'

The chief made reply: 'We sit at the table of Hygelac, King of the Goths. As for me, I am Beowulf; my errand I will set forth to the King, if he will grant us of his good grace that we may see him.'

Then said Wulfgar the herald: 'I will ask the King his pleasure, and bring thee back his answer without delay.'

So the herald went to where King Hrothgar sat, an old man among his warriors, and spake: 'Certain men are newly come, my lord, to this place far across the sea from the land of the Goths, and the name of their chief is Beowulf. They make petition that they may see thee, and I would counsel that thou refuse not their request, for their gear is that of worthy men, and their chief is a noble prince.'

The King made answer: 'I knew him well when he was yet a boy. His father was Egthean, to whom Hethel the Goth gave his only daughter in marriage. And now he has grown to man's estate, and is come to visit us. And indeed it is well, for they who carried our gifts over the seas to the Goths say that he has in his grip the strength of thirty men. Haply God has sent him of His grace to help us against the monster Grendel. Go, therefore, and say to him and his company that they are welcome to the land of the Danes.'

So Wulfgar the herald returned and said: 'The King bids you welcome to the land of the Danes, for he knows of what race ye are. Leave, therefore, your shields and spears till ye have spoken with him.'

So Beowulf and some of his company went in to speak to

the King, and the others tarried behind to keep watch over the war gear.

And when they stood before the King, Beowulf stood forth and said: 'Hail to thee, King Hrothgar! I am Beowulf, kinsman to King Hygelac. Many deeds of note have I done in my youth, and now the report of the doings of Grendel the monster has brought me to this land. For strangers from over the sea have told us how that this fair hall stands empty of guests so soon as the evening falls. 'Twas my comrades that put the thought in my heart, for they had seen my valorous deeds, how I had conquered the foes of my country, and brought the race of the giants low, and slain monsters both on sea and on land. So now I am come, my lord King, to fight single-handed against this Grendel. Now, therefore, I make my petition to thee, O Prince, first that I may undertake this enterprise alone, and next, seeing that this monster despises weapons, that I may also forego all use of the same, and carry neither sword, nor shield, nor coat of mail to this battle. With the grip of my hands only will I deal with this enemy, struggling with him, life for life. But who shall live and who shall die, let it be as God shall will. I doubt not, O King, that if he have his way he will devour the champions of the Goths, even as he has devoured the champions of the Danes. And as for me, thou wilt not need to lay my body in the earth and raise a mound over it, for he will carry it off to the moors where he dwells and devour it there. Only I would pray thee to send back to King Hygelac the armour that I wear; for it came to me by inheritance, and Weland, the smith of the gods, wrought in the old time. But that which Fate has ordered shall come to pass.'

To him King Hrothgar made answer: ''Tis well, O Beowulf, that thou art come to help me in this my need, for I knew thy father in the old time; he was a mighty man of valour, and there was a bond of friendship between him and me. But as for this Grendel, it is a shame to tell what desolation he has wrought in my hall. He has swept away the whole company of my warriors. Who can stay him in his ill-deeds? God doubtless can do so, but I know of none besides. Often have my warriors boasted, when they were merry with their drink, that they would stand up, sword in hand, against the monster. But when morning came, lo! the hall was bespattered with gore, and the benches reeked with blood, and I was the poorer by many brave warriors. But now, I pray thee, sit down to the feast, thou and thy brave comrades with thee.'

So a table was cleared, and the warriors of the Goths sat down together in the pride of their strength. And one of the King's thanes waited on them, bearing the ale-can in his hands, and, once and again, a minstrel sang with clear voice of the deeds of the men of old, and there was mirth in the hall.

But while they feasted envy stirred in the heart of Unferth, son of Ecglaf. He was the King's orator, and he took it ill that Beowulf should have come to the land of the Danes on this great enterprise, for he was one who could not endure that any man under heaven should do greater deeds than himself. Therefore he stood up in the hall and spake: 'Art thou that Beowulf who contended with Breca in swimming on the open sea? 'Twas, indeed, a foolhardy thing so to put your lives in jeopardy, yet no man could turn you from your adventure. Seven days and nights ye toiled, one against the other, but he in the end prevailed, for he had the greater strength. And on the eighth morning the waves cast him ashore on the land of the Heathoram, whence he journeyed back to the city of the Bronding, of which he was lord. So did Breca, son of Beanstan, make good his boast against thee. And thou, I trow, wilt have worse luck than this, though doubtless thou art a sturdy warrior in the shock of battle, if thou shalt dare to abide for the space of a night the strength of the monster Grendel.'

Then said Beowulf: 'Surely the ale-can has wrought with thee, friend Unferth, that thou hast said such things about Breca, the son of Beanstan, and how he strove with me in swimming. But I say to thee that in buffeting the waves of the sea I have more strength than any other man under heaven. Now hear the truth. This Breca and I, in our boyhood, when we were pages at the King's court, were wont to talk of this, how we would put our lives in jeopardy on the sea, and we made agreement to contend the one against the other. So we swam, each of us holding in one hand a sword wherewith to defend ourselves against the whale-fishes of the sea. Not one whit further than I could he swim, nor I one whit further than he. So for the space of five days and five nights we twain swam together; but on the sixth day the floods parted us, for the wind blew mightily against us from the north, and the waves were rough. So was I left alone, and then the rage of the sea-monsters was roused against me; but my coat of mail stood me in good stead against their attacks. Yet did one great beast – spotted he was with spots – seize me in his grip and drag me to the bottom of the sea. Yet strength was given me to pierce the monster with my sword, and then I slew him. Nor yet in truth was I quit of my enemies; for they pressed against me in my rage, and I dealt them blows with my sword and stinted not. They counted to devour me, foul robbers of the sea that they were, to devour me for their supper. But they fared far otherwise. Verily they lay the next morning high and dry upon the shore, having met their fate by the sword. And truly it was a good deed to slay them, for never more would they hinder in their course such as fare across the sea. And when I had finished my task, lo! it was morning, and I saw the headlands. So does fortune rescue the warrior if he be not doomed of Fate, and if he be bold of heart. Verily it came of my good luck that I was able to slay with my sword nine monsters of the deep and to escape with my life. Never was a man more hardly pressed by the waves of the sea or come into greater peril of death. After this the sea cast me up on the land of the Finns. I have heard of no such deeds as done by thee, Unferth, son of Ecglaf; no, nor hath Breca achieved the like. And this I say to thee, that Grendel had never wrought such woe and desolation for thy King hadst thou in truth possessed the courage of which thou makest boast. But he, methinks, takes but small heed of the spearmen of the Danes, nor fears lest they requite him, slaughter for slaughter. Rather he takes toll from them at his will; he slaughters and he feasts, but he has no thought of fight. But now there has come one who shall show him what a Goth can do in battle, and shall make King Hrothgar's hall a fit abiding-place again for men.'

So Beowulf spake, and the old King heard him with great joy, seeing that he was steadily purposed in his heart to contend and to prevail. So there was mirth in the hall, and much laughter of heroes, and music, and songs of rejoicing.

Then came Elfrida, Queen of King Hrothgar, into the hall, clad in cloth of gold, and she bore a great beaker in her hand, for she was careful to observe all ancient customs. To the King of the East Danes first she handed the great cup, wishing him joy and the love of his lords. And after him she went the round to all the warriors where they sat in their places, the old by themselves and the young by themselves; last of all she brought the cup to Beowulf, and greeted him right courteously, and gave thanks to God that He had given them such an answer to their prayers. 'For now,' she said, 'I believe that we have a warrior who will rid us of our troubles.' Beowulf made answer to the Queen: 'Lady, when I embarked on this voyage with my fellows, I promised that I would either do this deed, or perish by the hands of this monster. And to this I am bound; either I will fulfil this promise, or I will meet my death in this hall.' Well pleased was the Queen with this saying, and she went in her gold attire to sit by the side of her lord, King Hrothgar.

So all the company of Danes and Goths sat in the hall, and made good cheer, till the King rose from his place to go to his chamber. Well he knew that the time was come when the monster issued forth to his cruel deeds, for Grendel was of the creatures of darkness that come forth when the sun has set. And when he rose, all the company stood up. Then said the King to Beowulf, the while he wished him all good fortune, 'Never since I first laid my right hand to the sword and bare the shield on my left have I given this hall of the Danes to any man to keep. And now I give it in trust to thee. Do thou keep it as befits its grace. Be of good hope; be valiant; watch. And verily, if thou comest with thy life out of this conflict, there is no wish in thy heart which thou shalt not see fulfilled.' So King Hrothgar went to his chamber, and his chiefs followed him. But Beowulf abode still in the hall, resolved in his heart to do the service which he had promised. And first he took from off his body his stout coat of mail and doffed his helmet, and then he gave to his squire his good sword. 'Keep thou,' he said, 'all my warrior's gear.' But before he climbed up on his bed he spake aloud saying, 'Now indeed I reckon myself to be not one whit behind this Grendel in deeds of war. Therefore I am resolved not to make an end of him with the sword, as well I might, for he knows nought, I trow, of the noble art of arms, how to strike with the sword and parry, though he be expert in deeds of darkness. So it shall be that when we come to trial of our strength this night we will have no weapon in our hands. And may He who knows all things give the victory as it shall please Him.'

So saying, the warrior laid him down on a bed and round

him lay many valiant lovers of the sea, his comrades in this enterprise. Without fear they lay, though there was not one who thought that he should ever see again land, and kindred, and the home of his youth, for they knew what havoc the monster Grendel had wrought in that same hall among the Danish folk. But they fared better than they had thought, for God gave them deliverance by the hand of a single champion. It pleased Him so to do, and verily He is the ruler of the world.

Meanwhile the destroyer came on his way, bent on his errand of mischief. And they who should have guarded the hall slept all of them: Beowulf only kept watch and ward, awaiting the trial of battle. In haste the monster approached, hoping to catch some man for his prey. Many a time before had he visited King Hrothgar's hall, and never had he gone away empty. But, of a truth, he had not found it before in the keeping of so stout a warrior.

And now he was come to the hall, and straightway, at the first touch of his hands, the door, fastened though it was with bars of iron wrought by a cunning smith, flew open. Thereafter he looked about him, with ravening eyes, whose light was like to burning fire. And as he looked he saw, fast bound in sleep, a troop of warriors, kinsmen all of them. And as he saw he laughed, thinking to himself that ere the day should dawn he would slay them all, for he deemed that fortune had favoured him again. But it was not so decreed of fate, but rather that he should not after that night make his meal again of the flesh of man.

Great was the rage in the heart of Beowulf when he saw the monster, but he held it back, waiting to see what the creature would do. Nor indeed did Grendel long delay. Speedily he seized a sleeping warrior and tore him in twain, crunching the bones with his teeth, and drinking the blood from his veins. In a trice he had devoured the body to the very feet and hands. This done, he came near to the bed of Beowulf, and stretched out to lay hold on him. But the champion seized the monster's arm with such a grip as he had never felt before. Nowhere had he found such strength in mortal man. Great was his fear and eager his desire to depart. Such grim entertainment he had not met before in King Hrothgar's hall. But Beowulf remembered what boast he had made that night, how he would carry this work to its full accomplishment. Therefore he stood up in his place, and grappled with the monster, holding him fast, though it seemed as if his fingers would burst. And when Grendel turned to flee, then the Earl followed him. Fain would the ogre have fled to his dwelling in the moors, for he knew that the grip of a deadly foe was on him. That was in truth a rash journey that he had made to King Hrothgar's hall.

Loud were the cries of the two as they fought together, and great the terror of all that were in the hall, Danes and Goths alike. The very bravest could not hear it with an untroubled heart. Verily it was a wonder that the house itself endured such conflict; nor had it stood but that it was cunningly set up within and without with stanchions of iron. And still Beowulf held the monster fast, with all his strength – nor, indeed, was there in any man such strength as his – for he was not minded to let so evil a thing escape. And then, for all their fear, the Earl's comrades unsheathed their swords, thinking to help their lord, and rescue him, if it might be, from his great peril. So they thought, but they knew not that not the keenest sword on earth, no, nor the stoutest battle-axe, could avail to touch that evil thing, for he had guarded himself by enchantments against all edge of steel. Nevertheless there was now come upon him a woeful end, fit recompense for one that had wrought such woe to men. He could not by any means free himself from the strong hand-grip of the Earl. And as he strove, there came in his shoulder a great crack, and the sinews sprang apart and the joints of the bones burst asunder. Then at last he fled to his hiding-place in the moors; but he had suffered a deadly loss, for his arm he left behind him in the champion's grip.

So did Beowulf accomplish that which he had promised, delivering the hall of the Danes from the terror which had made it desolate. In token thereof he hung up high on the gable of the roof hand and arm and shoulder.

The tidings of what had befallen were soon noised abroad, and the chiefs of the Danes came from far and near to see the place and the signs of the battle. Glad of heart were they as they tracked the monster's course, seeing it red with blood, till they came to the place where he had hidden himself in his terror, knowing that his end was come, even the lake of the pixies. And when they looked on the face of the lake, they saw that it was dark with blood, the blood of Grendel. Then they rode back again in great glee, and many sang of Beowulf's mighty deed. 'There is not on earth,' so said they all, 'among warriors that bear the shield, a champion mightier or more worthy to bear rule than he!' So they sang, yet did not fail in due honour to King Hrothgar. Verily he was a worthy king! Then the bard, the maker of lays, after telling of the dreadful deeds of Grendel and of how Beowulf had vanquished him, sang thus:

How shall we praise him? to whom compare?
To Sigemund, Waelson, the dragon-slayer.
Never, I trow, did braver lord
In the battle-press bear shield and sword;
And ever, where fiercest ran the tide
Of the great war-torrent, by his side
Stout Fitela stood, his sister's son,
A stalwart comrade and true; but one,
And the dourest deed of all, alone
King Sigemund wrought, by the Dragon-stone,
Where the dreadful Worm from days of yore
Kept watch and ward o'er the treasure-store,
A fearsome beast, but the Waelsing Lord,
Nothing afraid, with his noble sword
Shore him through with so stout a blow
That the good steel sank in the earth below,
And the treasure-store of gems and gold
He stored away in his swift ship's hold.

So the company returned with great gladness to the town, and King Hrothgar himself came forth from his chamber, and the Queen with him, and a bevy of fair ladies in gay apparel. And when the King saw the gable of the hall, and the hand and arm of Grendel fixed upon it, he brake forth in speech, saying:

'Now let us thank Almighty God for giving us to see this sight with our eyes! Many things have I suffered from this Grendel, and now the Lord hath wrought a wonderful deliverance. I never thought to see a remedy, for this hall evermore ran with blood, and my warriors and counsellors availed nothing to abate this woe. Yet now hath this warrior achieved our deliverance, God helping him. Happy the mother, and favoured of the Almighty, who bare such a son! And now hearken, Beowulf. I love thee as though thou wert my son; and indeed from this day forth thou shalt be as a son to me. Nothing that thou shalt desire shalt thou lack, so far as I have power to give it. And indeed I have given noble gifts and great honours to many a one who was not thy match in courage or great deeds.'

Beowulf made answer to the King: 'We did our work with a good heart. Only I would that thou hadst the creature himself. I thought, indeed, to have held him down in the place where I grappled him till he died. But I could not; I did not hold him fast enough. Nevertheless he left his hand, aye and his arm and shoulder also, behind him. Nor will he live one hour the longer for that he has escaped. From the deadly wound that he has suffered there is no flight.'

So spake Beowulf, and there was mirth in the hall. But one man sat and spake nothing, and he was Unferth, the son of Ecglaf. For had he not spoken scornfully of the hero? – and lo! there before his eyes and the eyes of all the nobles of the land, high up on the gable of the roof, was the hand of the monster! Like to spurs of steel were all the fingers, spurs or spikes, so keen were they and so hard. Not the most famous sword that the great smiths of old had wrought by their craft had availed to sever such a hand as the hand of Grendel.

Then King Hrothgar commanded that they should adorn the hall anew. So they adorned it with willing hands, both men and women. Grievously desolated had it been by the monster Grendel; not a part of it had escaped save the roof only, but now it was decked out with tapestries woven with threaded gold and with pictures. And when the work of adorning was finished, King Hrothgar came into the hall and sat down to the feast, and a fair company of guests, kinsmen, and nobles sat down with him. From end to end it was filled with friends, friends true at heart, for in those days no man of the Danish race cherished a thought of treachery in his heart.

Then King Hrothgar gave to Beowulf an ensign of gold on a staff richly dight, and a helmet, and a coat of mail, and a great sword from the royal treasury. Eight horses also, each with cheek-plates of gold, did the King give him, and one of these was saddled with a saddle adorned with silver. 'Twas the

King's own warhorse, on which he was wont to ride in the days when he entered into the battle. These were the gifts that King Hrothgar in true kingly wise gave to the champion Beowulf. Also he gave gifts, precious things that had come down to him as an inheritance from the kings of old, to each one of the comrades of Beowulf. And he gave also a blood-price, many pieces of gold, for him whom Grendel slew cruelly in the hall. So they sat in the hall and feasted, the King with his nobles and his guests about him, and a minstrel sang to the harp the lay of the Sons of Finn:

> To the Frisian land,
> With a chosen band,
> Brave sons of the Dane,
> O'er the ocean plain
> Did Hnaef of the race of the Scyldings go:
> In the stress of battle Fate laid him low.

And when the lay of the Sons of Finn was ended, the drawers filled up the cups and the revellers drank again. And as they drank came Elfrida the Queen, with the crown of gold upon her head. To the King she came, and said to him: 'Take this beaker, my lord King, and drink, and speak comfortable words to our guests from Gothland. Dear they are to thee, and their chief Beowulf thou wouldst gladly count for a son of thine own. And indeed thou doest well to love them, for thy hall is purged of its troubles by their means, and the years that are coming shall be years of peace. And when the time shall be for thee to depart hence, thou wilt leave thy people and thy realm to thy children after thee. And if thy sons be over young for government, then shall Hrothulf thy neighbour counsel them dutifully, remembering how we two gave him nurture in time past when he was yet but an infant.' So saying, she turned to the bench where sat the two lords her sons, Hrethin and Hrothmund, and the sons of the nobles sat by them, all the youths together.

And the Queen bade Beowulf drink of the cup, and she gave into his hand chains of twisted gold, and armlets, and a mantle and rings. Never were seen jewels so precious since Hama carried away the necklace of the Brisings, which Freia the goddess wore. And when the Queen gave him these gifts, she said: 'Wear this collar, dear youth, with good fortune, and put this mantle about thy shoulders, and prosper. Make thyself fame by thy valour, and be happy as long as thou shalt live. And, I pray thee, help these my sons with counsel wise and kind. Verily thou shalt have thy reward.'

So spake the Queen, and went back to her chair. And with great joy did the company revel in the hall. And when they had enough of feasting, then they cleared away the tables and spread out the beds. So the warriors lay down to their rest, each man setting up his shield at his head, and over it his helmet, and his coat of mail, and his spear. But for one of them that lay down it was decreed of fate that he should not rise up again. But no man knows his doom, whether it shall come soon or late.

* * *

In peace and confidence the warriors laid them down to sleep, but there was one among them that was doomed to pay dearly for his rest. And this was the way in which the matter came to pass. Grendel, indeed, was dead, but an avenger lived, even his mother, a troll-wife that dwelt in the moorland streams. Of savage temper was she, neither did ruth dwell in her heart, and now she was wrought to fury by the death of her son. Therefore she came to King Hrothgar's hall, and burst in upon the warriors as they slept. Great was the fear among them – not so great, of a truth, as it was when Grendel himself had come among them, for the might of a woman is not as the might of a man, but the thing troubled them much.

Now the troll-wife was in great haste, for though she was bent on avenging her son, yet she desired to escape with her life. Therefore she was content to seize but one of the sleepers in the hall. Him she grappled with her hands, crushing him to death as he slept, and then she returned with all speed to her dwelling among the trees; but she did not forget to take away with her the hand and arm of her son. From the gable she took it down and carried it off with her.

Great was King Hrothgar's trouble when he heard of this cruel deed; for the man that had perished in this way was dearer to him than all his thanes. So he sent a messenger to Beowulf, bidding him come with all speed, for Beowulf had not slept in the hall, but a chamber had been prepared for him elsewhere, in which he might take his rest and also bestow the precious gifts which had been given him. And when he had heard from the messenger the King's desire he went, and his comrades with him. And first he said: 'Hast thou slept well, O King?'

King Hrothgar made answer: 'Talk not of welfare to me. Aescher is dead, Aescher who was my scribe and counsellor, aye, and the squire of my body in the old time when we stood together in the battle. And now he is dead. The destroyer has slain him in my hall, and whither the creature is gone, carrying with her the prey, I know not. Grendel thou didst slay yesterday, grappling him right manfully in thy hands, and now this creature has avenged his death, and the bravest and best of my lords lies dead, slain by her hands.

'Now hear how I come to know that it is she that has done this deed. Often have the dwellers in the moorland seen these two. One was in the semblance of a man, only more huge than any man has been seen: this was Grendel, the same that was slain by thee; and the other was in woman's shape. These two were wont to dwell in secret places in the wilderness. If thou wouldst know more closely the place, hearken to my words. There is a certain lake, not many miles from this hall. All about it are woods, whose great roots go down to the water. Night by night on its waters may be seen a flame, and as for its depth, no man knows what it is. A fearful place is this lake; the stag, however sorely the hounds may have pressed him in the hunt, would sooner die than plunge his head in the water. And now it is to thee, O Beowulf, that we look for help and counsel. The place thou hast not seen, but yet, if thou darest to track this monster to her lair, go and prosper. Verily, if thou returnest again victorious, I will recompense thee with great store of treasure.'

Then said Beowulf: 'Be of good comfort my lord King. 'Tis better for a man to avenge his friend than that he should sit down and spend his time in useless lamenting. Verily for every one of us there is ordained a certain end of life; let us therefore take such occasion as God may give us of winning renown while life still remains to us, for there is nothing better for a man than renown. Come, then, my lord King, let us go and track the path of this foul creature that is of Grendel's kindred. And this I vow. She shall not escape, nor hide herself from me; no, neither in the bowels of the earth, nor in the secret places of the wood, nor in the depths of the sea. Have patience, then, in thy troubles, for I am assured that all will go well with thee.'

Then King Hrothgar gave thanks to God for Beowulf's comfortable words, and commanded that his horse should be saddled. In stately guise he rode, and his warriors round about him. Nor was it a hard matter to follow the track of the monster. That was indeed easy to see across the moor, the evil path by which it had carried off King Hrothgar's best beloved comrade. So Beowulf and a few of his warriors with him, the stoutest and bravest of all his company, followed the track with light steps, over rocky heights, and through narrow glades, where the pixies dwelt. And of a sudden they came upon a wood. Gloomy of aspect it was, and dark the rocks on which it grew, and dreary the water that lay beneath in its shade. A gloomy place it was, and terrible the sight, for there on the rock by the water's edge was the head of the brave man Aescher, King Hrothgar's chosen counsellor, and the lake itself seethed and bubbled with blood. Then he that bore the horn sounded, once and again, a cheering blast, and Beowulf and his company sat down and looked. Strange was the sight; great serpents and monstrous snakes of the sea at their gambols, and dragons, and many another monstrous thing. But when they heard the bugle-blast they were fain, one and all, to depart. Only Beowulf set an arrow to the string, and drew the bow and let fly the shaft. It pierced one of the monsters in a mortal part, and stayed him from his swimming for ever. Then Beowulf's comrades, with boat-poles, armed with harpoons, dragged the monster to the shore, marvelling much, so huge was he and so terrible to behold.

Then Beowulf donned his war-gear. Light of heart he was, though great was the danger. And first he put upon him his coat of mail. Well it knew how to protect the champion's body from the grip of the enemy, but now for the first time it was to make trial of the water. And so was it with the helmet that guarded his head. It also must be plunged into the deep, with its ornaments of silver, and the boar-figures, wrought of old by the hand of some cunning smith, that were set about it, keeping it safe from all the sword-strokes of the enemy.

But of all the things that helped his valour the best was the good sword which the orator of King Hrothgar sent to him. A precious heirloom it was, and its edge was tempered with the blood of men. Never in the stress of battle had it failed the man who wielded it with undoubted hands. Nor was it now the first time that it was called to do a hero's work. Unferth, son of Ecglaf, it was who lent it to Beowulf, for he remembered no longer how he had scoffed at the champion, and indeed he knew that he lacked courage in his heart to plunge into the sea on such errand as that to which Beowulf now addressed himself.

And when the champion was now altogether ready for the fight, he said: 'Remember now, my lord King, what we two have talked together. Thou hast promised that if the doom of death should overtake me in thy service, thou wouldst be in the place of a father to me. Protect, therefore, I pray thee, my kinsmen and comrades, and cause the gifts which thou hast given me to be sent to King Hygelac. So will he understand, when he sees so great a store of gold and jewels, that I had good luck while fortune favoured me. And let Unferth the orator have the sword Hardedge, with its damasked blade, that has come down to me from my fathers, and I with the sword Hrunting will either achieve high renown, or perish.'

So spake the lord of the Goths, nor did he await reply, but plunged headlong into the lake. It was morning when he leapt, but the day was far spent when he reached the land that lay at the bottom of the mere. Not long was the monster in perceiving that one of the sons of men was visiting her dwelling-place for the first time in a hundred years. Swiftly she flew at him, and caught him in her talons; but for all their strength and sharpness she could not break through the coat of mail with which his body was girt about. But though she could not reach his flesh to tear it with her claws, she carried him away to the hall in which she dwelt at the bottom of the mere, nor could he, for all his strength, resist her, or wield his weapons against her. In her grip she carried him, and as he went the great water-beasts butted at him with their tusks.

The dwelling of the monster was indeed a marvellous place.

Under the water it was, but the water troubled not them that were in it, for it was kept from them by the roof. Also there was a strange light in it, a light as of fire. And by this light Beowulf saw of what shape was the creature that had assailed, that it was the monster which men had sometime seen upon the moor in the form of a woman. Straightway he dealt a great blow at her with his sword, even the mighty sword Hrunting that Unferth, the King's orator, had lent him. Mighty was the blow, but the edge of the sword could not bite. For the first time since its forging it failed its master. Oft had it dealt death in the press of battle, cleaving buckler and corslet and helmet, but now it availed nothing. In great wrath Beowulf threw away the blade. He would trust to the grip of his hands only. Thus had he vanquished Grendel, thus would he vanquish Grendel's dam.

So should a man bear himself, to work his work as best he may and have no thought of life.

Then, heedless of peril, Beowulf sprang upon Grendel's dam, and seized her by the shoulder. Full of rage he was, and he grappled the dreadful creature so mightily that she sank down upon the ground. But she was not yet overcome. No, indeed, for in her turn she grappled with him, closing in upon him, and flinging him, strongest among men though he was, upon the pavement of the floor; for his breath failed him, and his strength was spent. Then the hag sat upon him and drew her knife, broad of blade it was and brown; willingly would she have slain him, for she was minded to take vengeance for the death of her son. Then of a truth had Beowulf perished, but for the coat of mail that was about his body. This the hag could not pierce; neither with blade nor with point could she drive her knife through it. So did the Almighty Father help the champion in his need.

Then again Beowulf, with a great struggle, threw the hag from off him, and stood upright on his feet. And as he looked about the hall, he saw among the armour that was hanging about it a great sword, a weapon of giants, keen of edge, a very king among swords; only it was so huge that no other man upon earth could wield it in the press of battle save only Beowulf the Goth. He seized it with his hands, thinking to himself, 'If this avails me not, I die,' and smote the beldam so fiercely on the neck that the steel shore her body right through, and she fell dead upon the pavement of the hall. And even as she fell, the light that he had seen at the first, blazed up again and showed him all the place. By the wall side he went, still holding the sword of the giants in his hand. And as he went he saw Grendel lying dead upon the floor. With his sword he cut the monster's head from his body and so turned him to depart.

Meanwhile King Hrothgar and the Danish lords sat by the side of the mere and watched the water. And when they saw how it grew troubled, and how the surf was red with blood, they said among themselves, 'The champion will not come back, bringing victory with him. Without doubt we shall not see him any more. The she-wolf has torn him in pieces.' So thinking, the King and his nobles departed. But the Goths sat still by the mere side and waited, though they were sick at heart. Greatly did they long to look upon their captain again, but there was no hope in their hearts.

But now, beyond all expectation, he came back. Nought did he take from the hall under the mere, though there were many precious things in it, and he saw them with his eyes. Only the head of Grendel he brought with him in one hand, and in the other the hilt of the giant's sword. There was nothing left of it save the hilt only, for in the blood of Grendel and of Grendel's dam there was so deadly a fire that it devoured all the blade. Glad of heart were the Goths when they saw the chief returning, and they thanked the merciful God who had delivered them from the hand of the enemy.

After this they set out to return to King Hrothgar's hall by the same way by which they had come. And in the midst of the company four stout warriors bare upon a pole the head of Grendel. And when they came to the hall, Beowulf took the head from the pole and carried it within, holding it by the hair. Truly a marvellous thing it was for the King and his nobles and Queen Veleda to behold. Never had any man looked on so terrible a face.

Then said Beowulf to King Hrothgar: 'Hail, O King. Gladly do we bring to thee from the mere the spoils that thou seest before thee, in token that the work is done. Hardly, indeed, did I win through it with life; in the battle beneath the water I had failed, but that the Almighty shielded me. As for the sword Hrunting I could do nothing with it, though it be a good weapon; but by the grace of God I saw hanging upon the wall an old sword exceeding large and heavy, and He who helps men when of other help there is none, put it in my heart that I should lay hold of that weapon. And this I did, and dealt therewith to the monster a mighty and effectual blow. See now the hilt of this sword, for the blade has melted away into nothing with the blood of the monster. Now, therefore, O King, I bid thee sleep in peace, nor fear, as heretofore, any danger in the night.'

So saying, he gave the hilt into the hands of the King. And when the King looked upon it he saw that there was written upon it the story of how the Flood swept away the herd of the Giants who had hardened themselves against the Ruler of the world. This was written upon it, and also for whom the Smiths of old had wrought this marvellous work.

And when King Hrothgar had perused the hilt, he said to Beowulf: 'Friend, thy fame is spread abroad throughout the world, but thou bearest it modestly and discreetly. Behave thyself so, and thou shalt be a comfort to thy people and their lords. Not so did Herenod that was King of Denmark before the days of Scyld. For did he not slay the chiefs, his comrades, at the feast? and did he not wander away alone from all companionship of man? God had given him strength and power beyond all other men, but he used them so ill that there was not one that loved him. Take thou, therefore, warning by him, O Beowulf. Sometimes God gives a man a wide dominion and great power and much prosperity. Sickness comes not near him, nor does old age bow him down, nor care trouble his heart. All his neighbours are at peace with him, and everything falls out to his mind. Then there grow up within his heart pride and arrogancy; and conscience, that should keep watch in his soul against evil, falls into a deep sleep, and wicked thoughts take possession of his heart. Then he thinks to himself that his abundance is not sufficient for him; he grows covetous for himself, and grudges others their due. The end of that man is that he is overthrown and that another takes the wealth which he has gathered. Take thou, therefore, good heed, O Beowulf, against pride and arrogancy. Now, indeed, thou art in the pride of thy strength and the power of thy age, but there will come of a surety, sooner or later, either sickness or the sword; the fire shall consume thee, or the floods swallow thee up. Be it in one fashion or another, death will subdue thee who hast so mightily subdued others. So I myself reigned for fifty years over the Danes, and had the mastery over all my enemies, so that I feared no rival from the one end of heaven to the other. Then there befell me great trouble, and I had heaviness in the place of mirth, for this Grendel came an evil guest to my hall. From this thou hast delivered me and my people, for do I not see with mine eyes the head of the enemy? And now let us come to the feast; tomorrow I have other gifts to give thee.'

So they sat down to the feast, King Hrothgar and his lords, and Beowulf and his comrades. And in a while they went to their beds; right glad was Beowulf, after all his toils, to lay him down to sleep.

And now the time was come for the champion to depart. First he gave back the good sword Hrunting to Unferth the orator. ''Tis a right good sword,' he said, 'and will serve thee well in war, though it availed not against the evil hag, the mother of Grendel.'

To the King he said: 'We now must needs return to our own land and to Hygelac our King. Thou hast used great hospitality to us and hast given us many and great gifts. If, then, there is aught else in which I can do thee service, willingly will I do it. If thy neighbours press thee hard, then will I come again, and a thousand warriors with me. And if Prince Hrethin, thy son, is minded to come as a guest to our court, verily he will find there many friends.'

King Hrothgar made answer to him: 'God puts into thy mouth words of wisdom, O Beowulf. Never have I heard from man so young speech so weighty. Good service hast thou done to me; and this also thou hast achieved that there shall be henceforth mutual friendship between thy heart and mine.'

Then the King gave him twelve jewels from his store; and after this he threw his arms about the young man's neck, weeping the while, for he knew in his heart that he should see his face no more, and indeed he loved him no less than a father loves his son.

So Beowulf and his comrades rode down to the shore. And when the warden of the shore saw them from the peak whereon he kept his watch, he made haste to meet them, not as heretofore with suspicion, but with greeting of welcome. 'Glad am I to see you safe returning;' and he led them down to their ship where it lay on the beach. Then Beowulf gave to the warden of the boat a sword bound with gold; high place did the man hold thenceforth among his fellows by reason of this gift.

Then the Goths embarked upon their ship, and set sail; and the wind blew fair behind, stretching the canvas to the full, and the prow divided the sea-waves, throwing the foam on either side, till the men beheld the cliffs of Gothland, headlands well known to their eyes. High up on the beach was the ship driven, and the shore-warden was ready to receive it, glad to welcome his countrymen. He bade some fasten the ship with anchor-cables on either side, lest haply it should be broken by the violence of the waves; and others he commanded to bear the precious gifts, gold and jewels, to the hall of King Hygelac, for the hall was night at hand, where the King dwelt with Hygda his Queen, a gracious dame, young and fair. And one ran and told the King, saying: 'Beowulf is come again, safe and sound from the battle.'

So the King said, 'Bring him hither to me.' And they brought him, and he sat down by the King's side, and Hygda, the gracious lady, went about the hall carrying in her hands the meadbowl to the men of war.

Said King Hygelac: 'How hast thou fared, my kinsman? Hast thou rid King Hrothgar of his troubles? I entreated thee, as thou knowest, to let the Danes settle their own quarrel with Grendel. But now I give thanks to God that I see thee again safe and sound.'

Thereupon Beowulf told the tale of how he had grappled with Grendel in the hall, and how the monster had wrenched himself away, but with an hand and arm the less, wounded to the death; and how he had sought for Grendel's dam in the mere among the hills and found her, and done fierce battle with her, and vanquished her, but hardly and after long struggle, and with grievous peril of his life.

And when he had ended the tale of his doings he said: 'Now for these things King Hrothgar gave me many gifts and precious. To me he gave them, but I give them to thee, O King; for indeed it was for thee I won them, and if thou art satisfied, then am I well pleased.'

Then he bade his comrades bring into the hall a helmet with a crest that towered in the press of battle, and a coat of mail, and a mighty sword. 'This,' he said, 'King Hrothgar gave me, having had it from his fathers before him.' Also he gave to the King four noble steeds, so like that none could tell the one from the other. And to Hygda he gave a jewel marvellously wrought that Queen Veleda had bestowed upon him, and three palfreys, gaily caparisoned.

After this King Hygelac bade them bring the great sword, mounted in gold, that had belonged to King Hrethet, his father. In all Gothland there was not a treasure of greater account than the sword of King Hrethet. And he gave him also a great revenue in money, and a stately dwelling, and a high place among his lords.

Now it came to pass as time went on that King Hygelac made war against the men of Friesland, and he took with him a great host and many famous chiefs, of whom Beowulf was the greatest. But the men of Friesland had made alliance with the Chatti and with others of the nations round about; and the battle went against King Hygelac and the Goths, and the King was slain and all his nobles with him, save Beowulf only. He, indeed, when the enemy pressed him hard, leapt into the sea. Thirty sets of war-harness had he on his arm when he leapt. Small cause had the Chatti to rejoice that day, seeing that few only of their host escaped from the sword of Beowulf to go back to their home. So the champion escaped by swimming, and came back to Gothland lonely and sad of heart. Then Queen Hygda would have had him take the throne to himself, for her son was but of tender years and she feared that he would not have strength to guard the realm against the assaults of the enemy. But she did not prevail with Beowulf, no, nor did the nobles of the land, when they joined with her in her prayers. 'Nay,' said Beowulf, 'but I will keep the kingdom for the boy till he become of years to keep it for himself.' So he kept it faithfully and with a prudent soul. But after a while there came to the court of King Heardred – he was Hygelac's son – two outlawed men, sons of Ohthere the Swede, who had rebelled against their lord the King of Sweden. Heardred showed them hospitality, but they for recompense slew him with the sword. Lo, and when he was dead, the nobles took counsel together, and came to Beowulf saying, 'There is now none who can be King over the Goths save thou only.' So Beowulf consented to their desire, and took the kingdom upon himself, ruling the people prudently for fifty years. Well did he avenge the death of Hygelac and his son. But the tale of how he also came to his end yet remains to be told.

THE LAMBTON WORM

Jessie Adelaide Middleton

For nine generations direct in their line,
No one in his bed shall die;
In red war and in surgy sea,
And some by their own hand lie.

(OLD BALLAD)

LONG AGO, in the days when the Lambtons were so brave and powerful that they feared neither God nor man, the young heir of Lambton went a-fishing in the river Wear on a Sunday, according to his profane custom, and, meeting with no success, he vented his ill-luck in curses loud and deep, to the horror of the pious folk who passed him on their way to Mass.

At last he felt a sharp tug at his line, and joyfully began to draw the expected fish to land; but, to his surprise and disappointment, he found he had hooked a worm of disgusting appearance, which he hastily tore off his hook, and threw into a neighbouring well.

He continued to fish, and presently a stranger of venerable appearance drew near.

'What sport?' quoth he.

'Why, I think I've catched the devil,' was young Lambton's reply; 'go and look in yonder well.'

The stranger looked at the Worm long and silently. 'I never saw the like of it before,' he said gravely. 'It betokens no good. Why, it has nine holes on each side of its mouth.'

Lambton laughed and went on with his fishing, and presently the stranger passed on his way.

Left in the well, the Worm throve apace. It grew and grew until the well became too small to hold it, and then it crawled forth to seek a new resting place. As the old chap-book version of the story says:

> It betook itself to Wear's cool stream,
> Nurs'd by the flood, so fast
> It grew till, within nine circling folds,
> A neighbouring hill it grasp'd.

It soon found a stone crag in the river Wear, round which it lay coiled during the daytime, and in the evening it wrapped itself nine times round the foot of a neighbouring hillock, which is called to this day the Worm Hill. It now became the terror of the whole countryside, laying waste the land, injuring the cattle, frightening the villagers, devouring lambs, and sucking the milk from the cows.

Meanwhile young Lambton had repented him of his evil life, and, having bathed himself in holy water and made the sign of the Cross, he joined the Crusaders and went off to distant lands. He was, therefore, quite in ignorance of the fact that the worm he had caught was devastating the country round his home, and laying waste the lands of his forefathers. His father, the old lord, bowed down by grief and sorrow, lived still at Lambton Hall, and on its hill the Worm held sway.

The household met in council, and an old retainer, far advanced in years, suggested that the large trough belonging to the courtyard should be filled with milk to propitiate the Worm. This was accordingly done. The Worm approached, drank the milk, and retired to the hill with its appetite appeased, and from that day forth it demanded a daily supply of milk of 'nine kye', and if refused it would plunder and slay without mercy, and tear up the trees in the park with violent lashing of its tail.

Of course, such a state of things could not be borne, and many a gallant knight set out to slay the Worm, but each one as he came was vanquished, with loss of life or limb, for no sooner was the Worm cut asunder than it immediately joined itself together again and renewed the attack.

So, after a time, it was left in undisputed possession of its hill.

Years passed by, and Lambton returned from the holy wars. He had fought the Saracen foe, trodden on Calvary's Hill, and imprinted a kiss on his Saviour's grave. Full of horror, he listened to the story of the Worm's depredations, and with eyes full of tears beheld the broad lands of his ancestors now made barren as a wilderness. After tenderly greeting his father (who had long thought him dead and was overjoyed at his return), he crossed the river to see for himself the monster who had wrought such devastation, and which the boldest knight had failed to kill:

> By the struggling light of early morn
> It lies in its resting-place,
> Its argus head on the waters clear,
> The rock in its embrace.

Next morning he consulted a sibyl, or wise woman, who consented to help him to overcome the Worm, but before giving him advice, the knight, she added, must take a solemn vow that, if successful, he would offer as a sacrifice the first living thing he met after the combat. Should he fail to do this, his race would be accursed, and *the lords of Lambton for nine generations would never die in their beds*.

Lambton agreed to the conditions, and the sibyl then bade him put on his coat of mail, well studded with spear-blades, take his trustiest sword in his hand, and boldly attack the Worm on the water before it hied from the Wear to the Hall to partake of its morning meal.

Lambton instructed his aged father that if he vanquished the Worm he was to blow three blasts on his horn. This would be the signal to let loose his favourite greyhound, which would immediately fly to the sound of the horn, and would thus be the first thing to meet him and be slain, according to the sibyl's condition. The father promised to carry out these instructions, and the knight, having made the solemn vow in Brigford Chapel, armed himself cap-à-pie, and started out to the fray.

He took his stand on the rock with his sword in his hand, and when the Worm saw him it left the hill round which it was coiled, and went down to the river to attack him.

Then began a fearful combat between the Knight and the Worm. The Knight struck at it again and again with all his might as it closed on him with its deadly embrace, coiling round him and trying to strangle him in its folds. But now the spear blades upon his coat did their work, for the closer the Worm pressed the more frightfully was it cut through and through by their sharp edges. Even so, the several pieces quickly united again, and the fierce combat went on till the Wear ran red with blood. Then Lambton, calling upon the Saints to help him, stepped to the river, raised his sword, and with a mighty stroke cut the Worm in two. This time the pieces were carried away by the stream, and the vanquished monster was unable to reunite himself:

Thrice does he kiss the cross round his neck,
Thrice to the saints he prays,
Then draws his sword so sharp and long,
Nor to the combat he delays.

For anon unto Wear's strong stream he goes,
His sword direct he wields,
The monster's gore thick crimsons the Wear,
And nor wound nor cut now heals.

For the Wear's strong stream fast floods away
The parts that are cut in twain
By the razored coat that the Worm enfolds,
Or the sword strokes made amain.

The victorious knight blew three loud blasts on his horn as a signal for the greyhound to be released, but his aged father was so filled with rapture at hearing the tidings of his son's victory, that, in his impatience to embrace him, he forgot everything else, and in the excitement of the moment ran forward to meet him.

Now was Lambton face to face with a dreadful alternative. Either he must become a parricide, or bring the curse upon his descendants. He again blew his horn, and the greyhound bounded forward, and was sacrificed with the still reeking sword; but it was killed in vain, for the vow had stipulated that the *first* creature he met should die, and so the curse fell upon the Lambtons, and the sybil's prediction was fulfilled.

But no Christian might his father slay,
No penance the deed atone;
And no Lambton for nine ages past
To die in his bed was known.

Afterword

Popular tradition traces the curse back to Robert Lambton, who died in 1442, leaving by his will 100 marks to his brother, John Lambton, Knight of Rhodes. A curious old manuscript, lately owned by the Middletons of Offerton, has the following entry: 'John Lambton that slew ye worm was Knight of Rhodes and Lord of Lambeton and Wod Spilton after the dethe of four brother, sans esshew malle.' Nine succeeding generations brought the curse down to Henry Lambton, whose death in 1761 broke the spell. During his lifetime there was great curiosity to know whether the curse would hold good to the end; but to the relief of the superstitious he died in his coach while crossing a bridge within a mile of Lambton Hall. His brother, General Lambton, it is said, was so afraid that his servants would forcibly fulfil the ancient prophecy in him as well, that, during his last illness, he kept a horsewhip by his bedside.

The Lambtons, on whom the curse fell, died various deaths, both valorous and untimely. Sir William Lambton was slain at Marston Moor, while serving under Charles I and his son William received his death-wound at the battle of Wakefield. Robert, the son of John Lambton, who slew the Worm, was drowned in Newbig, and others died 'in red war and in surgy sea.'

The ruins of the Chapel of Brigford, where Lambton vowed his rash vow, were still to be seen in 1820, and so is the Worm Hill today, near Fatfield, about a mile and a half from old Lambton Hall. The Worm Well lies between the hill and the river Wear; it once had a reputation as a wishing well, and midsummer eve revels were carried on round it.

At Lambton Hall, the seat of the present Earl of Durham, two stone figures are preserved, the exact date of which is not known. One represents a knight, armed cap-à-pie, *his visor raised, and part of his coat of mail inlaid with spear blades. Coiled round his legs is the Worm, which is not represented as a reptile, but as a creature bearing a strong family likeness to the dragon – 'full of fyre and also of venyme,' so dear to the hearts of the ballad-monger of the fourteenth century. The other is a female figure supposed to represent the sibyl.*

PART V:
BATTLES AND CONQUESTS

THE SHADOWY ONE

Peter Tremayne

'A YOUNG BOY is approaching the gate, Scáthach,' announced Cochar Croibhe, the gatekeeper of Dún Scaith, whose great fortifications rose on the Island of Shadows in Alba, an island which today is still called the Island of Scáthach or Skye.

'A boy?' Scáthach was a tall woman, of pleasing figure and long fiery red hair. A closer look at her form would show the well-toned muscles. The easiness of her gait belied a body so well trained that in a moment the great sword, which hung from her slender waist, would be in her hand and that sword was not for ornament. Indeed, Scáthach was acclaimed one of the greatest warriors in all the world. No one had ever bested her in combat which was why all the warriors, who had ambition to be champions, were sent to her academy where she taught them the martial arts. Her school was famous in every land.

Cochar Croibhe, the gatekeeper, was himself a warrior of no mean abilities, for such he had to be in order to guard the gates of Dún Scaith. He shrugged.

'A boy,' he confirmed, 'but accoutred as a warrior.'

'Does he come alone?'

'He is quite alone, Scáthach.'

'A talented boy, then,' mused Scáthach, 'for such he would have to be to reach this place by himself.'

Cochar Croibhe conceded the fact after some thought. After all, Scáthach's military academy lay on the Island of Shadows and to reach it one had to pass through black forests and desert plains. There was the Plain of Ill-Luck, for example, which could not be crossed without sinking into bottomless bogs for it was one great quagmire. There was the Perilous Glen which was filled with countless ravening beasts.

It was with curiosity that Scáthach mounted the battlements of her fortress to view the approach of the boy. She decided that Cochar Croibhe did not lie but the youth was more than a mere boy. He was short, muscular and handsome, and he carried his weapons as a veteran used to arms.

'He may have crossed the Plain of Ill-Luck and the Perilous Glen,' sneered Cochar Croibhe, at her side, 'but he still has to cross the Bridge of Leaps.'

Now Scáthach's island, the Island of Shadows, was separated from the mainland by a deep gorge through which tempestuous, boiling seas, flooded. And the sea was filled with ravening creatures of the sea. The only way across was by a high bridge which led to the gate of her fortress. The point of this bridge was that it had been constructed by a god in a time before time. When one man stepped upon one end of this bridge, the middle would rise up and throw him off, and if he leapt into the centre then it would do likewise so that he might be flung into the gorge to the waiting creatures of the deep. Only Scáthach knew the secret of the safe crossing and only when her pupils had graduated from her academy and sworn a sacred oath of friendship, did she reveal to them the secret.

As Scáthach watched, the youth trotted up to the end of the bridge. She smiled and turned to Cochar Croibhe.

'We will wait to see if he can overcome this obstacle to assess his worthiness.'

They waited. The youth came and examined the bridge and then, to their surprise, he sat down on the far shore and built a fire where he rested.

'He cannot cross,' chuckled Cochar Croibhe. 'He waits for us to go out and show him the way.'

Scáthach shook her head.

'Not so. I think he does but rest from his long journey here and when his strength is recovered he will attempt the crossing.'

Sure enough, when the grey mists of evening were approaching, the youth suddenly stood up. He walked back a distance and made a run at the bridge. As soon as his foot touched the end of it, it rose up and flung him backwards. He landed without dignity on his back on the ground. Cochar Croibhe laughed sourly.

'He is not finished yet,' smiled Scáthach. 'Look.'

The youth tried once more, and again he was flung off the bridge but thankfully not into the foaming waters below. A third time he tried and with the same result. Then the youth stood for a while in thought. They saw him walk back a distance and run for the bridge.

'My best sword as a wager that he will be thrown into the sea this time,' cried Cochar Croibhe eagerly.

'Done! My best shield will answer your wager,' cried Scáthach in reply.

With the fourth leap, the youth landed on the centre of the bridge. In a fraction of a second, it started to rise but the youth had made a further leap and was safely across and at the gates of Dún Scaith, demanding entrance.

'Let us go down and admit this young man for his courage and vigour has won him a place in this academy whatever his name and station.'

Grumbling at the loss of his best sword, Cochar Croibhe went and brought the youth in and escorted him into the presence of Scáthach.

'What is your name?' she asked.

'I am named Setanta and I am from the kingdom of Ulaidh.'

Scáthach's eyes widened as she gazed on the handsome, muscular youth.

'I have heard that a youth named Setanta, coming late to a feast at the fortress of Cullan, was confronted by a ferocious hound, which Cullan, thinking his guests were all in the fortress, had loosed to guard the place. This hound was so strong that Cullan had no fear of attack save only if an entire army marched on his fortress. The story I heard was that this youth was named Setanta. When attacked by the hound, he killed it. And while the warriors of Ulaidh were amazed by the feat, Cullan was sorrowful that his faithful hound had died for the safety of his house. The youth Setanta then offered to guard Cullan's house until such time as a hound whelp had been trained to take its sire's place. So Setanta became Cullan's hound – Cúchullain.'

'I am that Setanta, the hound of Cullan,' replied the youth solemnly.

'Then you are thrice welcome, Cúchullain.'

Cochar Croibhe glowered in the background for jealousy was in his soul.

It happened that Scáthach had a beautiful daughter and her name was Uathach, which means 'spectre'. It was Uathach's duty to serve at the table when the students of her mother's academy were having their evening meal. One evening, therefore, when Uathach was serving meat, she came to the young man Setanta. She held out the dish of meat to him and he took it.

Their eyes met and through their eyes their souls found attraction.

In this moment, Setanta forgot his strength and, in taking the dish of meat from the girl's hands, his hand closed upon hers and her finger broke in his grasp.

Uathach let out a scream of anguish.

Setanta dropped to his knees before her and asked for her forgiveness. This the girl, in spite of her pain, willingly gave.

But Cochar Croibhe, the jealous doorkeeper, who already had cause to dislike the young man, came running into the feasting hall in answer to the girl's cry. Now it was known that Cochar Croibhe coveted Uathach and his amorous suit had twice been rejected by her in spite of the fact that he was acclaimed the bravest champion at Dún Scaith . . . with the exception of Scáthach, of course.

Straightaway he challenged Setanta to single combat as reparation for the injury.

Uathach protested that she had already forgiven the young man but Cochar Croibhe grew insulting and spoke of a boy hiding behind the apron of a girl.

Setanta stood quietly, for he was not one to lose his temper without just cause.

Osmiach, the physician, having heard Uathach's scream, came into the feasting hall and set the girl's finger and applied pain-killing poultices.

All the while Cochar Croibhe, in spite of Uathach's protests, taunted young Setanta. Finally, he pointed out that everyone knew that Setanta had no father for was it not common knowledge that his mother, Dectera, had vanished one day from the court of Conchobhar Mac Nessa and then reappeared with the boy child which she named Setanta?

Now this was true, for Dectera had been beloved of none

other than the great god Lugh Lámhfada, and the child was Lugh's gift to Ulaidh. But Setanta could not bear to hear his mother so insulted.

'Choose your weapons,' he finally snapped at Cochar Croibhe, who was a master of all weapons, but was incomparable with the spear or javelin.

'Javelin and buckler!'

And with that the two went out into the courtyard of Dún Scaith.

Scáthach had the power to stop the fight but she did not.

'We shall see,' mused Scáthach to herself, watching from a window. 'If Setanta bests Cochar Croibhe in combat than it will mean that I am right to have accepted him for he will become the greatest champion of Ulaidh.'

And the combat commenced.

Cochar Croibhe came running forward, buckler before him, javelin held high.

Setanta merely stood there, watching his advance with a frown. He did not even raise his buckler to defend himself. Yet his muscles tightened on his javelin and moved it back into position. Then Cochar Croibhe halted in his run, halted a split second, dropped his buckler and held back his arm for the throw. At that point, Setanta loosed his own javelin. So fast and so swiftly did it cleave the air that it transfixed Cochar Croibhe before he had time to cast his own spear. Spear and buckler dropped from his grasp and he sank on his knees, staring in horrified surprise. Then he collapsed on his side.

'Dead,' exclaimed Osmiach the physician dispassionately.

Setanta's gaze met that of Uathach but she was not distressed. Admiration shone from her eyes.

Scáthach appeared, standing frowning at the young man.

'You have slain my gatekeeper,' she said without emotion.

'Then as I fulfilled the duties of Cullan's hound, and guarded Cullan's fortress, let me now be your gatekeeper for as long as I stay here.'

So it was, that for a year and a day, Setanta stayed at the martial arts academy of Scáthach and each night Uathach warmed his bed. And Scáthach herself taught Setanta all he needed to know to become the greatest warrior in all Éireann and the fame of Cúchullain, or Cullan's hound, for as such he was better known than as Setanta, spread far and wide.

At the end of a year and a day, Scáthach drew Setanta to her and led the way down to a large underground cavern where none but they were allowed to enter. Inside, lit by brand torches, was a great pool of bubbling sulphur, warm and liquid grey.

'Here we will make the final test,' Scáthach announced. 'We will wrestle and it shall be the winner of three throws shall be the greater.'

'I cannot wrestle you!' protested Setanta, for as much as he realised that she was the greatest female champion of Alba, it was against his sense of honour to wrestle a woman.

'You will wrestle as I direct or it shall be known that you feared a challenge from me,' she said simply.

So the two of them stripped off, there and then, and took their places on either side of the sulphur pool. At the first clash, Scáthach threw Setanta. The next time they touched, Setanta, no longer fearful to harm her, threw her. And then the third time they came together in the centre of the sulphur pool. They held each other so tightly in an embrace that neither could throw the other. And after an hour Scáthach released her hold and said:

'The pupil has become the master.'

Setanta then made love with her for it is written that the apprentice must show his willingness to marry his vocation.

In return, Scáthach gave Setanta a special spear which was called the Gae-Bolg, or belly spear. This spear was thrown by the foot. It made one small wound when it entered a man's body but then thirty terrible barbs opened so that it filled every limb and crevice with mortal wounds. Scáthach gave this to Setanta and taught him how to cast it.

And both Scáthach and Uathach knew that the time was now approaching when Setanta would leave Dún Scaith.

It happened about this time that Scáthach received a challenge to combat from her own sister Aoife, whose name means 'radiantly beautiful'. Now she was Scáthach's twin sister and they had both been born of the goddess of war, the Mórrígán. Each was as proficient as the other in arms but each claimed to be the superior of the other. Sibling rivalry warped their relationship.

Aoife had sent Scáthach a message saying: 'I hear that you have a new champion at Dún Scaith. Let us test his mettle. My champions and your champions will contest together.'

When she read this, Scáthach was fearful for the safety of Setanta for she knew, deep in her heart, that her sister was the greater of the two; that she was the fiercest and strongest champion in the world. But the challenge could not be rejected and so Scáthach prepared her warriors to go out and meet her sister Aoife.

The night before they were to set forth, Scáthach called Osmiach, the physician, to her and told him to prepare a potion which would send a man to sleep for four and twenty hours. And Osmiach prepared the sleeping draught and it was administered in secret to Setanta.

The warriors of Scáthach set out to meet the warriors of Aoife.

What Scáthach overlooked was that the potion which might have served to cause an ordinary man to sleep for four and twenty hours, only held Setanta in sleep for one hour.

As the armies gathered, great was Scáthach's astonishment when Setanta's chariot came careering up and he joined her lines, for he had followed Scáthach's army by the tracks of the chariots.

The champions met in combat and great deeds were wrought that day. Setanta and two sons of Scáthach fought with six of Aoife's mightiest warriors and slew them. Several of Scáthach's pupils were cut down but they did not fall alone. As the day grew dark, both armies were still evenly matched.

Then Aoife challenged Scáthach directly to combat to resolve matters.

Setanta intervened and claimed the champion's right to meet Aoife in place of Scáthach and such was the ethics of the situation that Scáthach could not refuse him.

'Before I go,' Setanta said, 'tell me what your sister Aoife loves and values most in the world.'

Scáthach frowned.

'Why, she loves her two horses, her chariot and her charioteer, in that order.'

So Setanta drove out into the battlefield to meet Aoife.

At first he was amazed that Aoife was so like Scáthach, but her beauty seemed more radiant than Scáthach's and she handled her weapons with greater dexterity. It was truly said that she was the greater warrior of the two. They clashed together, Setanta and Aoife. They fought in single combat and tried every champion's feat they knew. Blow to blow, shield to shield, eye to eye. Then skill was with Aoife. She aimed such a blow that the sword of Setanta shattered at the hilt. She raised her sword for the final strike.

Setanta cried out: 'Look! Your horses and chariot have fallen from the cliff into the gorge!'

Aoife hesitated and glanced round fearfully.

At once Setanta rushed forward, seized her around the waist and flung her to the ground. Before she could recover, there was a knife at her throat and Setanta was demanding her surrender. Angrily, she realised that she had no option but to plead for her life and Setanta granted it on condition that she made a lasting peace with her sister Scáthach and gave Scáthach hostages for the fulfilment of the pledge.

'You are the first person who has bested me in combat,' Aoife ruefully admitted, staring at the handsome youth. 'Albeit, it was by a trick.'

'Victory is victory however it was achieved,' replied Setanta calmly.

'There is wisdom on your tongue,' agreed Aoife. 'Come and join me at my fortress that we may get better acquainted.'

To this invitation, Setanta agreed.

Scáthach and her daughter Uathach watched his departure with Aoife in sadness but in resignation of his Destiny. He would become Aoife's lover and she would bear his son, Connla, whom the gods would force him to kill. In sadness, he would stride forth to become the defender of Ulaidh, his name praised in the mouths of all men; charioteers and warriors, kings and sages would recount his deeds and he would win the love of many. He would be – Cúchullain. And whenever the name of Cúchullain was spoken, the name of his famous tutor would also drop from the tongue – Scáthach, the Shadowy One, ruler of Dún Scaith on the Isle of Skye.

BRAN AND BRANWEN

Peter Tremayne

THERE WAS GREAT rejoicing throughout the Isle of the Mighty when Bran, son of Llyr, announced that his beautiful sister Branwen, 'the Fair Blossom', would be married to Matholwch, king of Éireann. It was a union that everyone rejoiced in, for it meant peace between the two kingdoms. Others rejoiced that Branwen should find a husband in the handsome warrior-king and a king so rich that he had sent no less than thirteen great ships to Aber Alaw, which is now called Aberffraw, filled with rich gifts. It was at Aber Alaw that the wedding feast was to be held.

Great pavilion tents were pitched around the sea port and for nine days and nine nights there was feasting and entertainment.

Branwen and Matholwch gazed upon one another and neither could find fault in the choice.

Bran, the king of the Isle of the Mighty, was much pleased with the match for, above all things, he desired peace for his people. But there were some in the kingdom, and within his own family, who did not. Some were ready for mischief and war. Penardun, the daughter of Dôn, who, by Llyr was the mother of Bran and Branwen, had married again to a champion called Eurosswyd. To him she bore twins. One was called Nisien and the other was Efnisien. The first grew to be a youth of gentle nature and a lover of peace, while the second was one who loved nothing better than strife and conflict.

Because this was known, Bran the king decided that Efnisien should not be invited to Branwen's wedding feast. So enraged did Efnisien become that he came to the celebrations anyway, although he did not make his presence known. He slunk into the camp of Matholwch in disguise and proceeded to cut off the tails, ears, eyebrows and lips of all the king of Ireland's horses.

Matholwch stormed into Bran's tent the next morning and demanded an explanation for the great insult that had been paid him. Bran explained that the deed had been done without his knowledge and, as token of his good faith, Bran would replace every horse that had been mutilated. In addition he gave Matholwch a plate of purest gold as big as his face and a staff of silver as tall as Matholwch himself. To this Bran also added a special gift. It was a magical cauldron that had been brought from Éireann.

Matholwch was mollified by these gifts. In fact, he was more than delighted with the cauldron. Matholwch knew of this magical cauldron and knew where it had once been kept, at a spot called the Lake of the Cauldron in the heart of his kingdom. Walking by that lake many years before, Matholwch had met a tall, ugly man, with a wife larger and uglier than himself. The man, who was called Llassar Llaesgyfnewis, had the cauldron strapped to his back. Every six weeks his wife, called Cymideu Cymeinfoll, gave birth to a fully armed warrior. And if any one warrior was killed, Llassar would put the corpse in the cauldron and the warrior would emerge as alive as ever but lacking the power of speech.

At first they had taken service with Matholwch but the continual growth of the warrior family, who could never be killed, and their incessant bickering caused the king of Éireann many a heartache. Finally he could stand no more and knew that the only thing to do was to destroy Llassar and Cymideu and all their children together.

He had enticed them all into a house made of iron and had coals heaped on it hoping that it would roast the whole family to death. As soon as the iron walls grew white hot, Cymideu and Llassar had burst through them, but their bickering children had remained behind and were roasted to death. Cymideu and Llassar, together with their magic cauldron, had crossed to the Isle of the Mighty where Bran had allowed them to settle and, in return for this kindness, they had given Bran the magic cauldron.

So Matholwch was well pleased at receiving the cauldron but

without the fierce pair who had previously owned it and all the warriors to which they gave birth.

So the wedding feast continued and, at the end of the nine days and nights, Matholwch and his beautiful bride, Branwen, set sail for his court at Tara in Éireann. And before the year was out Branwen bore Matholwch a son who was called Gwern and because he was the heir to the five kingdoms of Éireann he was sent to be fostered among the greatest families of the land.

In the second year of their marriage, tales of the insult Matholwch had suffered at his wedding feast were made known to the people of Éireann. Stories were spread that Matholwch was weak, having accepted a token compensation from Bran. The people of Éireann, prompted by these stories, grew indignant. They demanded that Matholwch should seek vengeance. Now Matholwch was rather worried at this for he knew that behind the stories were his foster brothers who were envious of his throne. They were stirring up this trouble in order to oust him as king and claim the throne for themselves.

So Matholwch decided to appease his people by publicly degrading Branwen. He had her removed to the kitchens of the palace and forced her to cook and clean and ordered the chief cook to give her a blow on the ears every day so that she would know her place. All traffic of ships between Éireann and the Isle of the Mighty was forbidden so that no news of how Branwen was being punished should reach her brother.

For three years Branwen bore the punishment, working from sunrise to sunset in the kitchens and being sent to sleep in a draughty attic at night. It was in the attic, in the brief period before dawn, that she found a young starling with a broken wing. She mended the wing and taught the starling how to fly. Then she wrote a letter to her brother Bran, telling him what was taking place. The starling took the message under its wing and flew up into the sky.

Away eastward from Éireann it flew until it alighted at Caer Seiont in Arfon. Indeed, not only did it alight in Caer Seiont but it set down on the very shoulder of Bran, the king himself.

Bran's rage grew as he read the letter from his sister and he called his son Caradawc to him and told him to send out to all the chieftains of the Isle of the Mighty to prepare a great army to invade Éireann. No less than one hundred and forty-four kings came to his aid. Leaving Caradawc to rule the Isle of the Mighty in his absence, Bran set sail with his great armada.

Messengers soon came to Matholwch telling him that a great forest was growing on the sea and this vast wood was moving towards the shores of Éireann.

Branwen heard the news and cried in joy. 'It is the masts and yards of the fleet of Britain.'

The chief cook reported this outburst to Matholwch who immediately sought the advice of his council. They decided that the army of Bran was so vast that it could not be met in battle where advantage was with it. Matholwch, however, ordered a great palace to be constructed for Bran to placate him. A great feasting would be held and all homage done to the king of the Isle of the Mighty. Branwen would be released and her son Gwern brought to the court.

However, this was an outward subterfuge. The plan was that Bran and all his sub-kings and chieftains would be invited into the new palace feasting hall. Of course, according to ancient law, no one could enter a feasting hall with arms. So the Britons would be defenceless. Matholwch secretly arranged that at each of the pillars behind the seats at the feasting tables were to be hung two leather bags. And in each bag would be an armed warrior of Éireann. A signal would be given and the warriors would then fall on the guests and slaughter them.

Now it chanced that Efnisien had come with Bran's army and while Matholwch was greeting Bran and inviting him to the banquet, Efnisien entered the feasting hall. Efnisien saw the bags and asked one of Matholwch's attendants: 'What is in this bag?' 'Meal, good soul,' replied the servant. So Efnisien put his hand in the bag and felt the head of the warrior inside. He squeezed the head until his fingers met together in the brain as the bone cracked. He went to the next bag and asked the same question. The attendant tried to brazen it out. But Efnisien went through the entire hall and crushed all two hundred warriors' heads while they were hiding in the bags, even the head of one warrior who was wearing an iron helmet.

When the feasting began, Matholwch made a great play of preaching peace and concord. Branwen, suitably clothed once more as a princess, was told to enter the feast and pretend to her brother Bran that her letter of despair was all a mistake.

Matholwch had brought her son – the boy Gwern – to the feasting hall and threatened to kill him if Branwen disobeyed. And when the boy was led in Bran and his followers embraced their young nephew in whom the kingship of Éireann rested. But when the boy came to Efnisien, the boy's half-uncle, Efnisien seized him and flung him into the blazing fire in the hearth saying: 'No son of Matholwch can be trusted, for treachery runs deep in his blood!' Branwen with a cry of despair would have leapt after him but Bran seized her and held her back.

Matholwch called his warriors to strike but they lay dead in their sacks.

Realising now that he had been betrayed by Matholwch, Bran ordered his men to arms while Matholwch and his nobles beat a hurried retreat from the feasting hall. Thereafter, the men of the Isle of the Mighty and the men of Éireann closed in battle and the combat continued far into that first night.

During the night the men of Éireann told Matholwch that they were losing too many warriors. And so Matholwch ordered that the magic cauldron be readied and the bodies of the dead were thrown inside. Come the next morning, the dead warriors emerged alive but without the power of speech. The fresh army of Matholwch renewed the attack on the exhausted army of Bran and there was great slaughter.

Now Efnisien, who had inherited a little of the purity of spirit of his mother Penardun, for he was still half-brother to Bran and Branwen, was filled with remorse for what he had done. He realised that he was responsible for everything that had come to pass since the wedding of Branwen. 'It is up to me to find a way of delivering my people safely from this catastrophe,' he said. And so he hid himself that evening among the dead warriors of Éireann. He was taken up with their corpses and transferred to the hidden place of the cauldron during the night. Then he was flung inside with the others and once inside he rent the cauldron into four pieces so that it could not be used again. Such was the effort of his deed that his own heart burst asunder.

The men of Éireann and the men of the Isle of the Mighty continued to wage war but, finally, all the men of Éireann were slain and only five pregnant women of Éireann were left to repopulate that ravaged land. And among the warriors from the Isle of the Mighty only seven remained. Bran himself was wounded in the foot by an arrow bearing poison and he knew that the poison was spreading through his body. So he called the remaining warriors of Britain to him.

They were Bran's brother Manawyddan ap Llyr; Pryderi, son of Pwyll and Rhiannon; the great bard Taliesin; Gluneu son of Taran; Ynnawc; Grudye son of Muryel; and Heilyn son of Gwynn Hen.

Bran gazed at them sadly.

'I am dying. Before the poison reaches my head and destroys my soul, cut off my head. Take it with you to the fortress of Llyr and bury it on the White Hill. There shall my head be placed so that it faces east and then no foreigner will invade Britain while it is there. Once you have cut off my head, I shall remain and talk to you through my head, and be pleasant company on your sad journey back to the Isle of the Mighty. I shall remain with you until you have completed your task.'

Then the seven cut off Bran's head and, together with a sorrowing Branwen, those survivors left the ravaged shores of Éireann where so many had perished. And although the Head of Bran talked and was as joyful as it had been in life, the more Branwen grew mournful and depressed. And when the party reached the shores of the Isle of the Mighty and came to Aber Alaw, where she had once been so happy at her marriage feast, Branwen sat down in grief.

'Grief is on me that I was ever born. Two island kingdoms have been destroyed because of me. Though yesterday my grief was unbearable, today it is twice so.'

Without another word, the beautiful Branwen groaned and her heart broke.

Softened were the voices in the brakes
Of the wondering birds
On seeing the fair body of Branwen.
Will there not be a relating again
Of that sadness that befell the Fair Blossom
At the stream of Alaw?

The seven survivors gathered round and they built her a four-sided grave on the banks of the Alaw which spot they called Ynys Branwen.

As they journeyed eastward, the seven found that Caswallon son of Beli had overthrown Caradawc, Bran's son, and destruction had settled upon the Isle of the Mighty. Caradawc had died of grief and only Pryderi's foster father, Pendaran had escaped the destruction. And while Manawyddan should have been king of the Isle of the Mighty, Caswallon ruled instead for the destiny had been laid on the seven that they should first accompany the head of their beloved leader to its final resting place.

They journeyed onward, eating, drinking and feasting with the noble head of Bran.

Finally, they came to the fortress of Llyr, Llyr's dun, which is now called London, and they took the head to a hill overlooking the place, called the White Hill, where in later years the Tower of London was raised. Here they buried the head with its face to the east. And it came to pass for many centuries no conquerors truly conquered the Isle of the Mighty and Britain remained under the rule of the descendants of the Children of Dôn.

It is said that ages afterwards, Arthur, in his Christian pride, thought it beneath his dignity to rely on the prophecy wrought by Bran, and he had the fabulous head dug up and thrown into the sea. Within a short time, Arthur was slain at Camlann and the godless hosts of Angles and Saxons were swarming into Britain across the Northern Sea.

[illegible] the [illegible] Cadwallon [illegible] upon the isle of the Mighty. [illegible] Pryderi [illegible] the destruction of [illegible] Manawyddan [illegible] of the Isle of the Mighty. Caswallon [illegible] after the [illegible] the seven that they should [illegible] the head of their beloved leader to its final resting place.

They pursued [illegible] eating, drinking, and feasting with the [illegible] head of Bran.

Finally they came to the fortress of [illegible], which is now called London, and they took the head to a small [illegible] a place called the White Hill, where [illegible] they buried the head [illegible] the [illegible] of the Mighty [illegible] under the [illegible] of 1066.

[illegible] they said [illegible] into the sea. Within a short time [illegible] Saxon [illegible]

KING LAURIN'S ROSE-GARDEN

Wilhelm Wägner

I

King Dietrich was one day about to mount his horse, and set out to visit his brother monarch, the Emperor Ermenrich, when a warrior rode into the court. The king at once knew him to be Heime. He was not much pleased to see him back at Bern, but when Heime told him that he had been victorious in many battles against giants and robbers, he consented to receive him once more into the ranks of his comrades, and desired him to accompany him and certain of his followers to Romaburg.

At Fritilaburg, where they rested, Dietrich accepted the offered service of a man who called himself Ilmenrik, son of a Danish yeoman Soti; and enrolled him amongst his servants.

When they came to Romaburg, they were received with all honour by the emperor, who gave them both board and lodging. But the emperor forgot one thing in his plans, and that was, to provide food for the servants. Ilmenrik fed them the first night. On the second, his private resources being exhausted, he pawned Heime's armour and horse for ten gold pieces; on the third, he pawned Wittich's goods for twenty; and on the fourth, he got thirty for the weapons and horse of the king. On the fifth day, when the king gave orders for their return home, Ilmenrik asked for money to free the articles he had pawned. Dietrich was astonished and angry when he heard how extravagant his servant's ideas had been. He took him before

Ermenrich, who at once said he would pay the sum required, and asked how much it was. The emperor and all his court made merry at Ilmenrik's expense, especially Walter of Wasgenstein (Vosges), who asked him if he was a were-wolf, and well up in strange knowledge of all kinds. Ilmenrik modestly answered that he had learnt to perform many feats of strength and skill from his father, such as putting the stone and throwing the hammer; and that he would wager his head against the lord of Wasgenstein's that he could beat him in this. Walter accepted his challenge, and the trial began.

Such skill as Ilmenrik displayed had never been seen before. The heroes all feared for the life of the brave warrior of Wasgenstein. The emperor then called the young victor to him.

'Hearken to me, young sir,' he said; 'I will buy the head of my vassal from you at whatever price you list. Gold for blood is the old law.'

'Fear not, sire,' answered Ilmenrik, 'the head of the brave hero is in no danger from me. I do not want it. But if you wish to do me a kindness, lend me so much money as I have expended for the keep of the servants, that I may redeem the weapons, garments, and horses that I pawned.'

'Treasurer,' said the emperor, turning to one of his ministers, 'weigh out sixty marks of red gold, that the fellow may redeem his pledges, and another sixty marks to fill his purse.'

'Thank you, my lord,' returned the young man, 'I do not need your gift, for I am a servant of the rich king of Bern, who will see that I lack nothing; but if you will keep us another day here, I will, with this sixty marks, treat the servants to a better feast than before, and also my master, all his warriors, and you yourself, should you desire to join the party, even if I have to pawn horses and coats of mail again.'

The warriors all laughed at the merry youth, but Heime frowned, and said that if ever he pawned his horse again it should cost him his life.

The feast which the servant prepared them was of royal magnificence. All were pleased except Heime, who secretly feared that his property was again in pawn. The young fellow seated himself at his side, and asked him in a low voice if he knew who had given him that scar on his forehead. Heime answered that it was Dietleib, son of Yarl Biterolf, adding that he would know him again in a moment, and that the scar should be avenged in blood.

Ilmenrik replied:

'Methinks, bold warrior, your memory has gone a-wool-gathering. If you look me in the face, you will see that I am that Dietleib whom you and your robbers attacked as he was riding through a forest with his father. We slew the robber Ingram and his companions, but you escaped with that wound, thanks to the speed of your good horse. If you don't believe me, I have a witness here that will prove my words in the open field. But if you will trust me, the matter may remain a secret between us.'

Towards the end of the feast, Dietrich told the youth that he should no longer be a servant, but should be received into the ranks of his comrades; and he, thanking him, answered that he was really Dietleib, son of Yarl Biterolf, whose glorious deeds were known far and wide.

All the king's followers, except Heime, received the young hero into their ranks with pleasure. He returned to Bern with the king, and proved himself his trusty comrade in many an adventure. But he was of a restless mind, and wished to see more of the world; so after a time he took service under Etzel, king of the Huns, at whose court he found his father settled. Father and son together were the doers of many a daring deed. King Etzel, wishing to keep them in his service, offered them the land of Steiermark (Styria) as a fief. Biterolf gave up his share to his son, who was therefore surnamed the Styrian.

II

DIETLEIB ONCE CAME unexpectedly on a visit to Master Hildebrand at his castle of Garden. He looked sadder than of old, and returned the master's greeting without an answering smile. Hildebrand inquired the cause of his sadness, and he replied that he had a sweet and wise sister named Künhild, who had kept house for him in Styria. One day, when she was dancing with other maidens in a green meadow, and he looking on, she suddenly vanished from the circle, and no one knew what had become of her.

'Since then,' he continued, 'I have learnt from a magician that it was the dwarf king Laurin that hid her under a cap of darkness, and carried her off to his hollow mountain. This mountain is in Tyrol, where the dwarf has also a wonderful Rose-garden. Now, good master, I have come to you for advice. How can I free my sister from the power of the goblin?'

'It is a ticklish matter,' said Hildebrand, 'and may cost many a good life. I will go with you to Bern, to see Dietrich and our other comrades, and then we can agree in council what is the best plan to pursue. For the dwarf is powerful, not only because of the extent of his empire, but from his knowledge of magic.'

When the heroes heard what had brought Hildebrand and Dietleib to Bern, Wolfhart spoke first, and said that he would adventure himself alone upon the quest, fetch home the maiden safe and sound, and bring the royal mannikin to Bern bound to his saddle-bow. Dietleib then asked Hildebrand if he knew the way to the Rose-garden. He replied that he did, but that Laurin watched over the garden himself, and exacted the left foot and right hand of any one who was bold enough to venture within its bounds, and spoil the roses.

'He cannot exact this tribute,' said Wittich, 'unless he gets the better of the warrior in fair fight.'

'Well then,' added the king, 'we will not touch the lovely flowers. All we want is to save our friend's sister from the hands of the dwarf, and that is a labour beseeming a warrior.'

The heroes all swore to do no hurt to the garden, and then Hildebrand consented to be their guide. The adventurers were Hildebrand, Dietrich, Dietleib, Wittich, and Wolfhart.

Their road led them northward among the wild mountains, and over crevasses, ice, and snow. It was a perilous way they trod, but they recked nothing of fatigue or danger, for their hearts beat high with hope. At length they reached the garden: a lovely place, where spring reigned eternally, making it a flowery oasis in a wintry desert. The heroes feasted their eyes on the beautiful sight, and felt as though they had reached the gates of paradise.

Wolfhart was the first to break the spell: setting spurs to his horse, he called to his comrades to follow, and galloped towards the garden. His mad career was soon checked by an iron door with golden letters inscribed on it. He tried to break open the door, but in vain; his comrades came to his aid, and the door was at last beaten in by the four strong men. The garden was still defended by a golden thread, such as used to surround the palaces of the Ases in the olden time. The warriors trod down the thread, and then, in spite of Hildebrand's warnings, began to pluck the roses and trample the garden. Dietrich did not join in the work of destruction, but stood apart under a linden tree.

Suddenly Hildebrand called out, 'Draw your swords! Here comes the master of the garden.'

They all looked up, and saw something bright advancing rapidly towards them. Soon they were able to distinguish the form of a horseman riding a steed that was swift as the wind. He was small of stature, and habited in a complete suit of armour. His helmet was of specially beautiful workmanship, and was further adorned with a diadem of jewels, in the midst of which a carbuncle blazed like a sun. On beholding the damage that had just been done, he drew rein, and exclaimed angrily:

'What harm have I ever done you, robbers as you are, that you should thus destroy my roses? If you had aught against me, why did you not send me a challenge like honourable men? You must now expiate your crime by each giving me his right hand and left foot.'

'If you are King Laurin,' answered Dietrich, 'we do indeed owe you reparation, and will pay you a fine in gold; but we cannot afford to lose our right hands, for we require them to wield our swords; and as to our left feet, we could not well ride were we deprived of them.'

'He would be a coward who talked of paying any fine except in blows,' cried Wolfhart; 'and I am determined to dash that hop-o'-my-thumb, together with the cat he is riding, against the cliffs over yonder, and then his bones will break into such tiny pieces that even his grasshopper subjects can never collect them.'

Upon this Laurin answered in words of defiance, and the combat with Wolfhart began, only to end in the latter's overthrow the moment he felt the touch of the dwarf's spear. Wittich was not more fortunate than his friend, for he also was thrown from his saddle at the first encounter.

Laurin sprang from his horse, drew out a large knife, and

approached the hero, who lay senseless on the ground. Dietrich sprang forward to rescue his comrade.

'Do not venture the spear thrust, but close with him,' said Hildebrand in a low voice. 'Laurin has three magic charms of which you must deprive him; and these are, a ring with the stone of victory on his finger, a belt that gives him the strength of twelve men round his waist, and in his pocket a cap of darkness, which makes him invisible when he puts it on.'

After a long and fierce wrestle, Dietrich managed to get possession of the ring, which he at once gave into the master's charge. Again the combat raged, neither side gaining any advantage. At last Dietrich begged for a short truce, which Laurin granted.

The truce over, the two kings renewed the fight. Dietrich caught Laurin by the belt, and at the same moment the latter clasped him round the knees so tight that he fell backwards. The violence of his fall broke the belt he was holding, and it slipped from his hand. Hildebrand then rushed forward and caught it before the dwarf could pick it up. No sooner was this done than Laurin went out of sight. Dietrich still felt the blows he gave, but could not see him. Filled with a berserkir rage at his own powerlessness, he forgot the pain of his wounds; he flung away both sword and spear, sprang like a tiger in the direction in which he heard the whistling of the invisible sword, and seized his adversary for the third time. He tore away the cap of darkness, and Laurin stood before him praying for peace.

'I shall first cut off your right hand and left foot, and then your head, and after that you may have peace,' cried the angered hero, setting off in pursuit of the dwarf, who now took to his heels.

'Save me, Dietleib, my dear brother-in-law,' cried Laurin, running up to that warrior; 'your sister is my queen.'

Dietleib swung the little creature on horseback before him, and galloped away into the wood. There he set him down, and told him to hide himself until the king's anger was abated.

Coming back to the place of combat, the warrior found Dietrich on horseback, and as furious as before.

'I must have either the dwarf's head or yours,' cried Dietrich.

In another moment their swords were flashing; a second fight would have begun had not Hildebrand held back the king by main force, while Wittich did the same to Dietleib. After a little they succeeded in making peace between the angry men, and also in gaining grace for the dwarf. Later still the warriors might have been seen in friendly converse with each other and with Laurin, who was then and there admitted as one of Dietrich's comrades.

This point settled, the dwarf proposed to show them the wonders of his hollow mountain, saying that Dietleib should then give his sister to him as wife, with the usual ceremonies.

'It is the old law,' answered the hero of Steierland, 'that when a maiden has been carried away from her home and is recovered by her friends, she should have free choice given her either to remain with her husband, or return to her people. Are you willing that it should be so in this case?'

'By all means,' said the dwarf. 'Now let us go. Do you see that snow-capped mountain? My palace is there – so to horse, that my eyes may no longer be pained by seeing the wreck you have wrought in my garden. The roses will bloom again in May.'

The journey to the snow-capped mountain was much longer than the warriors had imagined. It lasted till noon of the following day. Below the snow, they came to a meadow that was as beautiful as the rose-garden. The air was filled with the perfume of flowers. Birds were singing in the branches, and little dwarfs were to be seen hurrying to and fro. They followed Laurin into the dark entrance of his underground kingdom. The only one of their number who felt the least distrust was Wittich, who had not forgotten the thrust of the dwarf king's spear.

III

A SOFT TWILIGHT reigned in the vast hall of the palace to which they now came. The walls were of polished marble, inlaid with gold and silver. The floor was formed of a single agate, the ceiling of a sapphire, and from it there hung shining carbuncles like stars in the blue sky of night. All at once it became light as day. The queen came in surrounded by her maidens. Her girdle and necklace were jewelled, and in her coronet was a diamond that shone like the sun, bringing the brightness of day wherever it came. But the lady herself was more beautiful than aught else. None could take their eyes off her face. She seated herself beside Laurin, and signed to her brother Dietleib to sit down at the other side of her. She embraced him and asked him many questions about her old home and friends. By this time supper was ready. Laurin was a perfect host, and his guests were soon quite at their ease. Even Wittich forgot to be suspicious. When the meal was over, the dwarf king left the hall, and Dietleib seized the opportunity to ask his sister whether she was willing to remain in that underground paradise as its queen. She answered with tears that she could not forget her home and friends; that she would rather be a peasant girl in the upper world than a queen among the dwarfs, and that though she must admit that Laurin was very good and kind, yet he was not as other men. Dietleib then promised to save her, or lose his life in the attempt.

Laurin now returned, and asked the hero if he would like to retire to his bedchamber. He took him there, and remained talking with him for some time. At last he told him that his comrades were all condemned to death, and that he had only spared him because he was his brother-in-law.

'Traitor, false dwarf!' cried Dietleib. 'I live and die with my comrades, but you are in my power!'

He started forward, but the dwarf was gone, and the door was shut and locked on the outside.

Laurin then returned to the hall, filled the goblets of the warriors from a particular jar, and entreated them to drink the wine, which would insure them a good night's rest. They did so, and immediately their heads sank upon their breasts, and a heavy drugged sleep fell upon them. Then turning to the queen, Laurin desired her to go to her room, for these men must die in punishment for the wreck they had made of his rose-garden; adding that her brother was safely locked up in a distant room, that he might escape the fate of his comrades. Künhild wept aloud, and said that she would die if he carried out his cruel purpose. He gave her no distinct answer, but reiterated his command.

As soon as the queen had retired, he sounded his horn, and immediately five giants and a number of dwarfs hurried into the room. He commanded them to bind the warriors so tight with cords that they could not move when they awoke. After that he had them dragged to a dungeon, where they might remain until he should decide their fate next morning. Having seen his orders carried out, he went to bed, and began to think whether it would be better to let the men off to please the queen, or to punish them for their evil deed. The last seemed to him the wiser plan, and he fell asleep, gloating over the intended slaughter of his helpless victims.

Dietrich awoke soon after midnight; he felt that he was bound hand and foot, and called to his comrades for aid; but they were as powerless as he. Then Dietrich's wrath was roused to such a pitch, that his fiery breath burnt the cords that bound one hand, and left it free. After that, it was a matter of little difficulty to untie the knots at his wrist and feet, and then to set his comrades at liberty. What was to be done now? They could not break open their dungeon door. They had neither weapon nor coat of mail. They were helpless victims. At this very moment, while they were looking at each other in despair, they were startled by hearing a woman's voice asking in a low whisper if they were yet alive.

'We thank you, noble queen,' answered Hildebrand, 'we are alive and well, but totally unarmed.'

So Künhild opened the door, and appeared on the threshold with her brother. She placed her finger on her lips to enforce silence, and led the way to where the heroes' armour was piled. As soon as they were ready, the queen gave each of them a ring, by means of which he could see the dwarfs, even when they wore their caps of darkness.

'Hurrah!' cried Wolfhart. 'We can make as much noise as we like, now that we have our armour on, and our weapons in our hands.'

Laurin, wakened by Wolfhart's loud tones, knew that the prisoners were free, and at once summoned his dwarfish army to his assistance. The battle began, and raged for a long time without any advantage being gained by either side. Laurin was pleased in his heart of hearts that matters had turned out as they had, for he was a bold little fellow, and liked open war better than trickery. At length the underground forces were routed with great loss, and Laurin himself was taken prisoner.

Dietrich spared the life of the dwarf king at fair Künhild's request, but deposed him from royal power, and gave the mountain to Sintram, another dwarf of high rank, for a yearly tribute. When everything was ordered to their liking, the heroes returned to Bern, taking Laurin with them as a prisoner.

There was great joy in Bern at the return of the heroes, who were much praised for their valiant deeds, while the unfortunate Laurin was laughed at by all. There was only one person who showed him any sympathy, and that was Künhild. One day she met him when he was wandering about alone and melancholy, She spoke to him kindly, tried to comfort him, and told him he would soon gain the king's friendship if he proved himself to be faithful and true.

'Ah,' he laughed bitterly; 'they think that they have kicked a dog who will lick their hands; but a trodden snake bites! You may know what I intend to do. I have sent to inform Walberan, my uncle, who rules over the dwarfs and giants from the Caucasus to Sinai, of what has happened, and he is coming at the head of his forces to be my avenger. He cannot fail to win the day, slay strong Dietrich and his comrades, and lay the whole land waste. When that is done, I will take you back to my kingdom, and replant my Rose Garden, that it may be lovelier in May than it ever was before.'

'Laurin,' she answered, 'you carried me away from home by trickery and magic spells; but I have not been blind to your love, and feel myself honoured by its greatness. I cannot live in your underground kingdom, but I will love you and be your queen in the Rose Garden, if you will think of love and faithfulness, and not of revenge.'

She left him, and he sat pondering the matter for a long time.

A few days afterwards, Dietrich came to the Dwarf King, and, taking him by the hand, said, that he had been his prisoner long enough, that he must now sit with his comrades, or return to his own home, whichever he liked best.

'And then,' continued the king, 'I will go with you to your Rose Garden next spring, and see it in its beauty.'

The dwarf silently followed the king into the hall. He sat at Dietrich's side at the feast, and thought over the vengeance he would take when his uncle came.

But lovely Künhild appeared and filled his goblet, saying a few kind words the while, and immediately love conquered hatred, and he cried, emptying the goblet to the last drop –

'Henceforward I am your faithful comrade in life and death.'

Whilst the warriors were still at the feast, a messenger from King Walberan came in, and declared war on Dietrich in the name of his master, unless Laurin were at once restored to his kingdom, and unless the hero of Bern sent Walberan all the money and all the weapons in the country, as well as the right hand and left foot of every warrior who had taken part in the destruction of the Rose Garden.

Dietrich answered proudly, that he intended to keep his money, arms, hands, and feet, and those of his subjects also.

'And tell him,' added Laurin, 'that I send him my thanks and greeting for coming to my assistance, but that I am now free, and have entered into a bond of love and friendship with the King of Bern.'

Both sides prepared for battle, but before a blow was struck, Laurin rode into his uncle's camp, and tried to make peace between Walberan and Dietrich. His uncle told him he was no better than a broken-spirited serf, and refused to listen to his words. So the fight began, and raged furiously for many hours. At length, late in the afternoon, Dietrich and Walberan met, and challenged each other to single combat. It was a terrible struggle – both kings were severely wounded, and it seemed to the onlookers as if both must die. Suddenly Laurin threw himself unarmed between their swords, flung his arms round King Walberan, and entreated him to make peace. Almost at the same moment Hildebrand did the same by the angry Dietrich, and after much expenditure of words, the peacemakers had their way.

So the fighting was changed to feasting, and the kings entered into a friendly alliance at the banquet that evening. The hero of Bern made a long speech in praise of Laurin, who had endangered his life in endeavouring to make peace, and to whom he therefore restored the free and independent rule over his kingdom and Rose Garden. When he had finished, Queen Virginal came forward, leading fair Künhild, and laid the hand of the maiden in that of Laurin, saying that she knew he would regard her reward of his faithfulness as the greatest he had that day received; for Künhild had promised to be his wife if her brother did not object. As no dissentient voice was heard, the marriage was celebrated there and then.

In the May-month of the following year, when the roses were again in bloom, the dwarfs put the finishing touches to a beautiful palace, which they had built in the Rose Garden. Many a herdsman and Alpine hunter has seen it; but to those who go in search of it from mere curiosity, it remains ever invisible.

To this day, Laurin and Künhild show themselves at odd times in the valleys of Tyrol, and there are people yet alive who are reported to have had a distant glimpse of the wonderful Rose Garden.

IV

DIETRICH WAS NOW a man in the prime of life – a perfect hero, and man of valour. The number of his comrades had much increased, and many doughty deeds had been done.

Once when the king was feasting with many of his comrades, he looked round the table with pride, and said he believed that no ruler on earth had such heroes about him, that no other had prospered so well as he with the help of his chosen comrades, and that none might be compared with them. The warriors shouted their approbation. One alone was silent. The king turned to him, and asked whether in all his journeys he had seen bolder warriors.

'That I have,' cried Herbrand. 'I have seen some that have not their match upon earth. It was at the good town of Worms, near the River Rhine, in the land of Burgundy. It is there that the great Rose Garden lies – five miles long by two-and-a-half broad. The queen and her ladies tend it themselves, and twelve great warriors keep watch and ward lest any one enter the garden without the queen's permission. Whoever does so must fight with the guard, and no one yet, whether giant or warrior, has been able to withstand them.'

'Let us go and pluck the roses that have been watered with the blood of heroes,' cried Dietrich. 'I think that my comrades and I will get the better of the guard.'

'If you mean to try your luck,' said Herbrand, 'you must

know that the victor will receive a kiss and a wreath of roses from lovely women.'

'Ah, well,' said the old master, 'for the sake of a rose and a woman's kiss I would not risk a single hair of my head or beard. He who wishes to pluck roses or kiss women will find enough at Bern; he need not go to the Rhine to find them.'

Trusty Eckehart and a few more of the comrades agreed with him, for well they knew what the Burgundian warriors were like. But Dietrich loudly declared that he was not going to fight for the sake of roses and kisses, but for honour and fame; and that if his comrades did not wish to go with him, he could go alone. Of course, they would not hear of that, and all who were present agreed to go. The names of those who thus adventured their lives were: Dietrich himself, Master Hildebrand, strong Wittich, Henne called the Grim, Wolfhart, the young heroes Siegestab and Amelung (or Omlung), Trusty Eckehart, and Hertnit, Prince of the Reussen; but they only numbered nine in all, and twelve were needed to meet the twelve watchmen of the garden. Hildebrand knew what was to be done. He said –

'Good Rüdiger of Bechelaren will not refuse to be the tenth; the eleventh must be brave Dietleib of Styria, and the twelfth my pious brother, the monk Ilsan.'

They started forth at once to induce the chosen three to join them. They went first to Bechelaren, in the land of the Danube. Rüdiger received them hospitably, and at once consented to go with them, but said that he must first get leave of absence from Etzel, whose margrave he was. The heroes then went on to Styria to visit Dietleib. They did not find him at home, but his father Biterolf, who was there, earnestly entreated them to give up the journey to the Rhine, because, he said, only a fool would undertake a conflict for life or death with the world's bravest warriors, for the sake of a rose and a kiss. But when they met the young hero a short time after, they found him ready to go with them. This settled, they went on to Münchenzell, the monastery to which Hildebrand's brother belonged. As soon as Ilsan heard the object of their journey, he went straight to the abbot, and asked leave to accompany the hero of Bern to the Rose Garden. The abbot told him that such was scarcely a monkish quest, but Ilsan grew so angry, and so loudly affirmed that valiant deeds were in his eyes as seemly for a monk as for any other man, that the abbot quailed before him, and gave him leave to go. So Ilsan donned his armour under his monkish dress, and started with his friends. His heart beat high with joy that he was again bound on one of Dietrich's adventures, while his brother monks stood by and shook their heads, saying they feared it would not end well, seeing it was no saintly quest, but a worldly.

The heroes went first to Bern, which was to be the general meeting-place. Margrave Rüdiger was the last to arrive, for he had been detained by his visit to Etzel. Rüdiger was now sent on before the others as ambassador to King Gibich at Worms, to inform him of their intended invasion of the Rose Garden. The Margrave was well known in the Rhineland, and was received as an old friend by the king, who rejoiced to hear of his leader's enterprise.

The garden was entered on the appointed day, and the warriors stood opposite each other ready for battle; twelve against twelve, and yet always one against one. It was a terrible sight, for many a hero fell dying amongst the roses, and watered them with his heart's blood. When proud Wolfhart had slain his adversary, he contemptuously refused the kiss offered him by a lovely maiden, and contented himself with the garland of roses. The monk, Ilsan, walked into the lists on foot, clad in his grey robes. He jumped about among the roses with such strange agility that his opponent thought he had a madman to deal with. But he soon found that his reverend foe was made of sterner metal than he supposed, for he lay vanquished, a wiser man, though wounded almost to the death. The victor received the wreath of roses on his tonsured head, but when he kissed the lovely maid who gave it him, she shrieked aloud, for his bristly beard had stung her rosy lips. Seeing this, he said with comical disgust –

> 'The maidens of Rhineland are fair to see,
> But far too tender to pleasure me.'

Many other heroes received the prize of victory, while others were severely wounded. Peace was not concluded until sunset. The brave hero of Bern soon afterwards returned home, pleased with the result of his quest.

THE CHILDREN OF LOKI

Annie & Eliza Keary

I

Now, in the city of Asgard dwelt one called Loki, who, though amongst the Aesir, was not of the Aesir, but utterly unlike to them; for to do the wrong, and leave the right undone, was, night and day, this wicked Loki's one unwearied aim. How he came amongst the Aesir no one knew, nor even whence he came. Once, when Odin questioned him on the subject, Loki stoutly declared that there had been a time when he was innocent and noble-purposed like the Aesir themselves; but that, after many wanderings up and down the earth, it had been his misfortune, Loki said, to discover the half-burnt heart of a woman; 'since when,' continued he, 'I became what you now see me, Odin.' As this was too fearful a story for anyone to wish to hear twice over Odin never questioned him again.

Whilst the Aesir were building their city, Loki, instead of helping them, had been continually running over to Jötunheim to make friends amongst the giants and wicked witches of the place. Now, amongst the witches there was one so fearful to behold in her sin and her cruelty, that one would have thought it impossible even for such a one as Loki to find any pleasure in her companionship: nevertheless, so it was that he married her, and they lived together a long time, making each other worse and worse out of the abundance of their own wicked hearts, and bringing up their three children to be the plague, dread, and misery of mankind. These three children were just what they might have been expected to be from their parentage and education. The eldest was Jörmungand, a monstrous serpent; the second Fenrir, most ferocious of wolves; the third was Hela, half corpse, half queen. When Loki and his witch-wife looked at their fearful progeny they thought within themselves, 'What would the Aesir say if they could see?' 'But they cannot see,' said Loki; 'and, lest they should suspect Witch-wife, I will go back to Asgard for a little while, and salute old Father Odin bravely, as if I had no secret here.' So saying, Loki wished his wife good-morning, bade her hide the children securely indoors, and set forth on the road to Asgard.

But all the time he was travelling Loki's children went on growing, and long before he had reached the lofty city Jörmungand had become so large, that his mother was obliged to open the door to let his tail out. At first it hung only a little way across the road; but he grew, Oh, how fearfully Jörmungand grew! Whether it was from sudden exposure to the air, I do not know; but, in a single day he grew from one end of Jötunheim to the other, and early next morning began to shoot out in the direction of Asgard. Luckily, however, just at that moment Odin caught sight of him, when, from the top of Air Throne, the eyes of this vigilant ruler were taking their morning walk. 'Now,' said Odin, 'it is quite clear, Frigga, that I must remain in idleness no longer at Asgard, for monsters are bred up in Jötunheim, and the earth has need of me.' So saying, descending instantly from Air Throne, Odin went forth of Asgard's golden gates to tread the earth of common men, fighting to pierce through Jötunheim, and slay its monstrous sins.

In his journeyings Odin mixed freely with the people of the countries through which he passed; shared with them toil and pleasure, war and grief; taught them out of his own large experience, inspired them with his noble thoughts, and exalted them by his example. Even to the oldest he could teach much; and in the evening, when the labours of the day were ended, and the sun cast slanting rays upon the village green, it was pleasant to see the sturdy village youths grouped round that noble chief, hanging open-mouthed upon his words, as he told them of his great fight with the giant of long ago, and then pointing towards Jötunheim, explained to them how that fight was not yet over, for that giants and monsters grew round them on every side, and they, too, might do battle bravely, and be heroes and Aesir of the earth.

One evening, after thus drinking in his burning words they all trooped together to the village smithy, and Odin forged for them all night arms and armour, instructing them, at the same time, in their use. In the morning he said, 'Farewell, children; I have further to go than you can come; but do not forget me when I am gone, nor how to fight as I have taught you. Never cease to be true and brave; never turn your arms against one another; and never turn them away from the giant and the oppressor.'

Then the villagers returned to their homes and their field-labour, and Odin pressed on, through trackless uninhabited woods, up silent mountains, over the lonely ocean, until he reached that strange, mysterious meeting-place of sea and sky. There, brooding over the waters like a grey sea fog, sat Mimer, guardian of the well where wit and wisdom lie hidden.

'Mimer,' said Odin, going up to him boldly, 'let me drink of the waters of wisdom.'

'Truly, Odin,' answered Mimer, 'it is a great treasure that you seek, and one which many have sought before, but who, when they knew the price of it, turned back.'

Then replied Odin, 'I would give my right hand for wisdom willingly.'

'Nay,' rejoined the remorseless Mimer, 'it is not your right hand, but your right eye you must give.'

Odin was very sorry when he heard the words of Mimer, and yet he did not deem the price too great; for plucking out his right eye, and casting it from him, he received in return a draught of the fathomless deep. As Odin gave back the horn into Mimer's hand he felt as if there were a fountain of wisdom springing up within him – an inward light; for which you may be sure he never grudged having given his perishable eye. Now, also, he knew what it was necessary for him to do in order to become a really noble Asa,* and that was to push on to the extreme edge of the earth itself, and peep over into Niflheim. Odin knew it was precisely that he must do; and precisely that he did. Onward and northward he went over ice-bound seas, through twilight, fog, and snow, right onward in the face of winds that were like

* Asa – the singular of Aesir.

swords until he came into the unknown land, where sobs, and sighs, and sad, unfinished shapes were drifting up and down. 'Then,' said Odin, thoughtfully, 'I have come to the end of all creation, and a little further on Niflheim must lie.'

Accordingly he pushed on further and further until he reached the earth's extremest edge, where, lying down and leaning over from its last cold peak, he looked into the gulf below. It was Niflheim. At first Odin imagined that it was only empty darkness; but, after hanging there three nights and days, his eye fell on one of Yggdrasil's mighty stems. Yggdrasil was the old earth-tree, whose roots sprang far and wide, from Jötunheim, from above, and this, the oldest of the three, out of Niflheim. Odin looked long upon its time-worn, knotted fibres, and watched how they were for ever gnawed by Nidhögg the envious serpent, and his brood of poisonous diseases. Then he wondered what he should see next; and one by one spectres arose from Naströnd, the Shore of Corpses – arose and wandered pale, naked, nameless, and without a home. Then Odin looked down deeper into the abyss of abysses, and saw all its shapeless, nameless ills; whilst far below him, deeper than Naströnd, Yggdrasil, and Nidhögg, roared Hvergelmir, the boiling cauldron of evil. Nine nights and days this brave wise Asa hung over Niflheim pondering. More brave and more wise he turned away from it than when he came. It is true that he sighed often on his road thence to Jötunheim; but is it not always thus that wisdom and strength come to us weeping.

II

WHEN, AT LENGTH, Odin found himself in the land of giants – frost giants, mountain giants, three-headed and wolf-headed giants, monsters and iron witches of every kind – he walked straight on, without stopping to fight with any one of them, until he came to the middle of Jörmungand's body. Then he seized the monster, growing fearfully as he was all the time, and threw him headlong into the deep ocean. There Jörmungand still grew, until, encircling the whole earth, he found that his tail was growing down his throat, after which he lay quite still, binding himself together; and neither Odin nor anyone else has been able to move him thence. When Odin had thus disposed of

Jörmungand, henceforth called the Midgard Serpent, he went on to the house of Loki's wife. The door was thrown open, and the wicked Witch-mother sat in the entrance, whilst on one side crouched Fenrir, her ferocious wolf-son, and on the other stood Hela, most terrible of monsters and women. A crowd of giants strode after Odin, curious to obtain a glance of Loki's strange children before they should be sent away. At Fenrir and the Witch-mother they stared with great eyes, joyfully and savagely glittering; but when he looked at Hela each giant became as pale as new snow, and cold with terror as a mountain of ice. Pale, cold, frozen, they never moved again; but a rugged chain of rocks stood behind Odin, and he looked on fearless and unchilled.

'Strange daughter of Loki,' he said, speaking to Hela, 'you have the head of a queen, proud forehead, and large, imperial eyes; but your heart is pulseless, and your cruel arms kill what they embrace. Without doubt you have somewhere a kingdom; not where the sun shines, and men breathe the free air, but down below in infinite depths, where bodiless spirits wander, and the cast-off corpses are cold.'

Then Odin pointed downwards towards Niflheim, and Hela sank right through the earth, downward, downward, to that abyss of abysses, where she ruled over spectres, and made for herself a home called Helheim, nine lengthy kingdoms wide and deep.

After this, Odin desired Fenrir to follow him, promising that if he became tractable and obedient, and exchanged his ferocity for courage, he should not be banished as his brother and sister had been. So Fenrir followed, and Odin led the way out of Jötunheim, across the ocean, over the earth, until he came to the heavenly hills, which held up the southern sky tenderly in their glittering arms. There, half on the mountain-top and half in air, sat Heimdall, guardian of the tremulous bridge Bifröst, that arches from earth to heaven.

Heimdall was a tall, white Van, with golden teeth, and a wonderful horn, called the Giallar Horn, which he generally kept hidden under the tree Yggdrasil; but when he blew it the sound went out into all worlds.

Now, Odin had never been introduced to Heimdall – had never even seen him before; but he did not pass him by without speaking on that account. On the contrary, being altogether much struck by his appearance, he could not refrain from asking him a few questions. First, he requested to know whom he had the pleasure of addressing; secondly, who his parents were, and what his education had been; and thirdly, how he explained his present circumstances and occupation.

'My name is Heimdall,' answered the guardian of Bifröst, 'and the son of nine sisters am I. Born in the beginning of time, at the boundaries of the earth, I was fed on the strength of the earth and the cold sea. My training, moreover, was so perfect, that I now need no more sleep than a bird. I can see for a hundred miles around me as well by night as by day; I can hear the grass growing and the wool on the backs of sheep. I can blow mightily my horn Giallar, and I for ever guard the tremulous bridge-head against monsters, giants, iron witches, and dwarfs.'

Then asked Odin, gravely, 'Is it also forbidden to the Aesir to pass this way, Heimdall? Must you guard Bifröst, also, against them?'

'Assuredly not,' answered Heimdall. 'All Aesir and heroes are free to tread its trembling, many-coloured pavement, and they will do well to tread it, for above the arch's summit I know that the Urda fountain springs; rises, and falls, in a perpetual glitter, and by its sacred waters the Nornir dwell – those three mysterious, mighty maidens, through whose cold fingers run the golden threads of Time.'

'Enough, Heimdall,' answered Odin. 'Tomorrow we will come.'

III

ODIN DEPARTED FROM Heimdall, and went on his way, Fenrir obediently following, though not now much noticed by his captor, who pondered over the new wonders of which he had heard. 'Bifröst, Urda, and the Norns – what can they mean?'

Thus pondering and wondering he went, ascended Asgard's Hill, walked through the golden gates of the City into the palace of Gladsheim, and into the hall Valhalla, where, just then, the Aesir and Asyniur were assembled at their evening meal. Odin sat down to the table without speaking, and, still absent and meditative, proceeded to carve the great boar, Saehrimnir, which every evening eaten, was every morning whole again. No one thought of disturbing him by asking any questions, for they saw that something was on his mind, and the Aesir were well-bred. It is probable, therefore, that the supper would have been concluded in perfect silence if Fenrir had not poked his nose in at the doorway, just opposite to the seat of the lovely Freyja. She, genius of beauty as she was, and who had never in her whole life seen even the shadow of a wolf, covered her face with her hands, and screamed a little, which caused all the Aesir to start and turn round, in order to see what was the matter. But Odin directed a reproving glance at the ill-mannered Fenrir, and then gave orders that the wolf should be fed; 'after which,' concluded he, 'I will relate my adventures to the assembled Aesir.'

'That is all very well, Asa Odin,' answered Frey; 'but who, let me ask, is to undertake the office of feeding yon hideous and unmannerly animal?'

'That will I, joyfully,' cried Tyr, who liked nothing better than an adventure; and then, seizing a plate of meat from the table, he ran out of the hall, followed by Fenrir, who howled, and sniffed, and jumped up at him in a most impatient, un-Aesir-like manner.

After the wolf was gone Freyja looked up again, and when Tyr was seated once more, Odin began. He told them of everything that he had seen, and done, and suffered; and, at last, of Heimdall, that strange white Van, who sat upon the heavenly hills, and spoke of Bifröst, and Urda, and the Norns. The Aesir were very silent whilst Odin spoke to them, and were deeply and strangely moved by this conclusion to his discourse.

'The Norns,' repeated Frigga, 'the Fountain of Urd, the golden threads of time! Let us go, my children,' she said, rising from the table, 'let us go and look at these things.'

But Odin advised that they should wait until the next day, as the journey to Bifröst and back again could easily be accomplished in a single morning.

Accordingly, the next day the Aesir and Asyniur all rose with the sun, and prepared to set forth. Niörd came from Noatun, the mild sea-coast, which he had made his home, and with continual gentle puffings out of his wide, breezy mouth, he made their journey to Bifröst so easy and pleasant, that they all felt a little sorry when they caught the first glitter of Heimdall's golden teeth. But Heimdall was glad to see them; glad, at least, for their sakes. He thought it would be so good for them to go and see the Norns. As far as he himself was concerned he never felt dull alone. On the top of those bright hills how many meditations he had! Looking far and wide over the earth how much he saw and heard!

'Come already!' said Heimdall to the Aesir, stretching out his long, white hands to welcome them; 'come already! Ah! this is Niörd's doing. How do you do, cousin,' said he; for Niörd and Heimdall were related.

'How sweet and fresh it is up here!' remarked Frigga, looking all round, and feeling that it would be polite to say something. 'You are very happy, Sir,' continued she, 'in having always such fine scenery about you, and in being the guardian of such a bridge.'

And in truth Frigga might well say 'such a bridge,' for the like of it was never seen on the ground. Trembling and glittering it swung across the sky, up from the top of the mountain to the clouds, and down again into the distant sea.

'Bifröst! Bifröst!' exclaimed the Aesir, wonderingly; and Heimdall was pleased at their surprise.

'At the arch's highest point,' said he, pointing upward, 'rises that fountain of which I spoke. Do you wish to see it today?'

'That do we, indeed,' cried all the Aesir in a breath. 'Quick, Heimdall, and unlock the bridge's golden gate.'

Then Heimdall took all his keys out, and fitted them into the diamond lock till he found the right one, and the gate flew open with a sound at the same time sad and cheerful, like the dripping of leaves after a thunder-shower.

The Aesir pressed in; but, as they passed him, Heimdall laid his hand upon Thor's shoulder, and said 'I am very sorry, Thor; but it cannot be helped. You must go to the fountain alone by another way; for you are so strong and heavy, that if you were to put your foot on Bifröst, either it would tremble in pieces beneath your weight, or take fire from the friction of your iron heels. Yonder, however, are two river-clouds, called Körmt and Ermt, through which you can wade to the Sacred Urd, and you will assuredly reach it in time, though the waters of the clouds are strong and deep.'

At the words of Heimdall Thor fell back from the bridge's head, vexed and sorrowful. 'Am I to be sent away, then, and have to do disagreeable things,' said he, 'just because I am so strong? After all, what are Urda and the Norns to me, and Körmt and Ermt? I will go back to Asgard again.'

'Nay, Thor,' said Odin, 'I pray you, do not anything so foolish. Think again, I beseech you, what it is that we are going to see and hear. Körmt and Ermt lie before you, as Bifröst before us. It is yonder, above both, that we go. Neither can it much matter, Thor, whether we reach the Fountain of Urd over Bifröst or through the cloud.'

Then Thor blushed with shame at his own weakness, which had made him regret his strength; and, without any more grumbling or hanging back, he plunged into the dreadful river-clouds, whose dark vapours closed around him and covered him. He was hidden from sight, and the Aesir went on their way over the glittering bridge.

Daintily and airily they trod over it; they swung themselves up the swinging arch; they reached its summit on a pale, bright cloud. Thor was there already waiting for them, drenched and weary, but cheerful and bold. Then, all together, they knocked at the door of the pale, bright cloud; it blew open, and they passed in. Oh! then what did they see! Looking up to an infinite height through the purple air, they saw towering above them Yggdrasil's fairest branches, leafy and of a tender green, which also stretched far and wide; but, though they looked long, the Aesir could distinguish no topmost bough, and it almost seemed to them that, from somewhere up above, this mighty earth-tree must draw another root, so firmly and so tall it grew. On one side stood the Palace of the Norns, which was so bright that it almost blinded them to look at it, and on the other the Urda fountain plashed its cool waters – rising, falling, glittering, as nothing ever glitters on this side the clouds. Two ancient swans swam under the fount, and around it sat Three. Ah! how shall I describe them – Urd, Verdandi, Skuld. They were mighty, they were wilful, and one was veiled. Sitting upon the Doomstead, they watched the water as it rose and fell, and passed golden threads from one to another. Verdandi plucked them with busy fingers from Skuld's reluctant hand, and wove them in and out quickly, almost carelessly; for some she tore and blemished, and some she cruelly spoiled. Then Urd took the woof away from her, smoothed its rough places, and covered up some of the torn, gaping holes; but she hid away many of the bright parts, too, and then rolled it all round her great roller, Oblivion, which grew thicker and heavier every moment. And so they went on, Verdandi drawing from Skuld, and Urd from Verdandi; but whence Skuld drew her separate bright threads no one could see. She never seemed to reach the end of them, and neither of the sisters ever stopped or grew weary of her work.

The Aesir stood apart watching, and it was a great sight. They looked in the face of Urd, and fed on wisdom; they studied the countenance of Verdandi, and drank bitter strength; they glanced through the veil of Skuld, and tasted hope. At length, with full hearts, they stole away silently, one by one, out by the pale, open door, re-crossed the bridge, and stood once more by the side of Heimdall on the heavenly hills; then they went home again. Nobody spoke as they went; but ever afterwards it was an understood thing that the Aesir should fare to the Doomstead of the Nornir once in every day.

IV

YEARS PASSED AFTER Odin had brought Fenrir home with him to Asgard. All this time Odin entertained some hope that the wholesome, bright air of Gladsheim, the sight of the fair faces of the Asyniur and the hearing of the brave words which day by day fell from the lips of heroes, would, perhaps, have power to change the cruel nature Fenrir had inherited from his father, and make him worthy of his place as a dweller in the City of Lords.

To Tyr, the brave and strong-handed, Odin assigned the task of feeding Fenrir, and watching him, lest, in his cruel strength, he should injure any who were unable to defend themselves. And truly it was a grand sight, and one that Asa Odin loved, to see the two together, when, in the evening after the feast was over in Valhalla, Fenrir came prowling to Tyr's feet to receive his food from the one hand strong enough to quell him.

Tyr stood up in his calm strength like a tall, sheltering rock in which the timid sea-birds find a home; and Fenrir roared and howled round him like the bitter, destroying wave that slowly undermines its base.

Time passed on. Tyr had reached the prime of his strength; but Fenrir went on growing, not so rapidly as to awaken fear, as his brother Jörmungand had done, but slowly, surely, continually – a little stronger and a little fiercer every day.

The Aesir and the Asyniur had become accustomed to his presence; the gentlest lady in Asgard no longer turned away from the sight of his fierce mouth and fiery eye; they talked to each other about the smallest things, and every daily event was commented on and wondered about; but no one said anything of Fenrir, or noticed how gradually he grew, or how the glad air and the strong food, which gave valour and strength to an Asa, could only develop with greater rapidity fierceness and cruelty in a wolf. And they would have gone on living securely together while the monster grew and grew, if it had not been that Asa Odin's one eye, enlightened as it was by the upspringing well of wisdom within, saw more clearly than the eyes of his brothers and children.

One evening, as he stood in the court of Valhalla watching Tyr as he gave Fenrir his evening meal, a sudden cloud of care fell on the placid face of All-Father, and when the wolf, having satisfied his hunger, crouched back to his lair, he called together a council of the heads of the Aesir – Thor, Tyr, Bragi, Hoenir, Frey, and Niörd; and, after pointing out to them the evil which they had allowed to grow up among them unnoticed, he asked their counsel as to the best way of overcoming it before it became too strong to withstand.

Thor, always ready, was the first to answer. 'One would think,' he said, 'to hear the grave way in which you speak, Father Odin, that there was no such thing as a smithy near Asgard, or that I, Asa Thor, had no power to forge mighty weapons, and had never made my name known in Jötunheim as the conqueror and binder of monsters. Set your mind at rest. Before tomorrow evening at this time I will have forged a chain with which you shall bind Fenrir; and, once bound in a chain of my workmanship, there will be nothing further to fear from him.'

The assembled Aesir applauded Thor's speech; but the cloud did not pass away from Odin's brow.

'You have done many mighty deeds, Son Thor,' he said; 'but, if I mistake not, this binding of Fenrir will prove a task too difficult even for you.'

Thor made no answer; but he seized Miölnir, and, with sounding steps, strode to the smithy. All night long the mighty blows of Miölnir rang on the anvil, and the roaring bellows breathed a hot blast over all the hill of Asgard. None of the Aesir slept that night; but every now and then one or other of them came to cheer Thor at his work. Sometimes Frey brought his bright face into the dusky smithy; sometimes Tyr entreated permission to strike a stout blow; sometimes Bragi seated himself among the workers, and, with his eyes fixed on the glowing iron, poured forth a hero song, to which the ringing blows kept time.

There was also another guest, who, at intervals, made his presence known. By the light of the fire the evil form of Fenrir was seen prowling round in the darkness, and every now and then a fiendish, mocking laugh filled the pauses of the song, and the wind, and the ringing hammer.

All that night and the next day Thor laboured and Fenrir watched, and, at the time of the evening meal, Thor strode triumphantly into Father Odin's presence, and laid before him Laeding, the strongest chain that had ever yet been forged on earth. The Aesir passed it from one to another, and wondered at its immense length, and at the ponderous moulding of its twisted links.

'It is impossible for Fenrir to break through this,' they said; and they were loud in their thanks to Thor and praises of his prowess; only Father Odin kept a grave, sad silence.

When Fenrir came into the court to receive his food from Tyr, it was agreed that Thor and Tyr were to seize and bind him. They held their weapons in readiness, for they expected a fierce struggle; but, to their surprise, Fenrir quietly allowed the chain to be wound round him, and lay down at his ease, while Thor, with two strokes of Miölnir, riveted the last link into one of the strongest stones on which the court rested. Then, when the Aesir were about to congratulate each other on their victory, he slowly raised his ponderous form, which seemed to dilate in the rising, with one bound forward snapped the chain like a silken thread, and walked leisurely to his lair, as if no unusual thing had befallen him.

The Aesir, with downcast faces, stood looking at each other. Once more Thor was the first to speak. 'He who breaks through Laeding,' he said, 'only brings upon himself the still harder bondage of Dromi.' And having uttered these words, he again lifted Miölnir from the ground, and, weary as he was, returned to the smithy and resumed his place at the anvil.

For three days and nights Thor worked, and, when he once more appeared before Father Odin, he carried in his hand Dromi – the 'Strong Binding'. This chain exceeded Laeding in strength by one half, and was so heavy that Asa Thor himself staggered under its weight; and yet Fenrir showed no fear of allowing himself to be bound by it, and it cost him very little more effort than on the first evening to free himself from its fetters.

After this second failure Odin again called a council of Aesir in Gladsheim, and Thor stood among the others, silent and shamefaced.

It was now Frey who ventured first to offer an opinion. 'Thor, Tyr, and other brave sons of the Aesir,' he said, 'have passed their lives valiantly in fighting against giants and monsters, and, doubtless, much wise lore has come to them through these adventures. I, for the most part, have spent my time peacefully in woods and fields, watching how the seasons follow each other, and how the silent, dewy night ever leads up the brightly-smiling day; and, in this watching, many things have been made plain to me which have not, perhaps, been thought worthy of regard by my brother Lords. One thing that I have learned is, the wondrous strength that lies in little things, and that the labour carried on in darkness and silence ever brings forth the grandest birth. Thor and Miölnir have failed to forge a chain strong enough to bind Fenrir; but, since we cannot be helped by the mighty and renowned, let us turn to the unknown and weak.

'In the caverns and dim places of the earth live a tiny race of people, who are always working with unwearied, noiseless fingers. With Asa Odin's permission, I will send my messenger, Skirnir, and entreat aid of them; and we shall, perhaps, find that what passes the might of Asgard may be accomplished in the secret places of Svartheim.'

The face of Asa Odin brightened as Frey spoke, and, rising

immediately from his seat, he broke up the council, and entreated Frey to lose no time in returning to Alfheim and despatching Skirnir on his mission. In spite of the cloud that hung over Asgard all was fair and peaceful in Alfheim. Gerda, the radiant Alf Queen, made there perpetual sunshine with her bright face. The little elves loved her, and fluttered round her, keeping up a continual merry chatter, which sounded through the land like the sharp ripple of a brook over stony places; and Gerda answered them in low, sweet tones, as the answering wind sounds among the trees.

These must have been pleasant sounds to hear after the ringing of Miölnir and the howling of Fenrir; but Frey hardly gave himself time to greet Gerd and his elves before he summoned Skirnir into his presence, and acquainted him with the danger that hung over Asgard, and the important mission which the Aesir had determined to trust to his sagacity. Skirnir listened, playing with the knot of his wondrous sword, as he was wont to do, in order to make known to everyone that he possessed it; for, to confess the truth, it was somewhat too heavy for him to wield.

'This is a far different mission,' he said, 'from that on which you once sent me – to woo fairest Gerd; but, as the welfare of Asgard requires it, I will depart at once, though I have little liking for the dark caves and cunning people.'

Frey thanked him, and, putting a small key into his hand, which was, indeed, the key to the gate of Svartheim, he bade him farewell, and Skirnir set out on his journey.

The road from Alfheim to Svartheim is not as long as you would be apt to imagine. Indeed, it is possible for a careless person to wander from one region to another without being at once aware of it. Skirnir, having the key in his hand, took the direct way. The entrance-gate stands at the opening of a dim mountain-cave. Skirnir left his horse without, and entered; the air was heavy, moist, and warm, and it required the keenest glances of Skirnir's keen eyes to see his way. Innumerable narrow, winding paths, all leading downwards, opened themselves before him. As he followed the widest, a faint clinking sound of hammers met his ear, and, looking round, he saw groups of little men at work on every side. Some were wheeling small wheelbarrows full of lumps of shining metal along the ledges of the rock: some, with elfin pickaxes and spades, were digging ore from the mountain-side; some, herded together in little caves, were busy kindling fires, or working with tiny hammers on small anvils. As he continued his downward path the last remnant of daylight faded away; but he was not in total darkness, for now he perceived that each worker carried on his head a lantern, in which burned a pale, dancing light. Skirnir knew that each light was a Will-o'-the-wisp, which the dwarf who carried it had caught and imprisoned to light him in his work during the day, and which he must restore to the earth at night.

For many miles Skirnir wandered on lower and lower. On every side of him lay countless heaps of treasure – gold, silver, diamonds, rubies, emeralds – which the cunning workers stowed away silently in their dark hiding-places. At length he came to the very middle of the mountain, where the rocky roof rose to an immense height, and where he found himself in a brilliantly-lighted palace. Here, in truth, were hung all the lights in the world, which, on dark, moonless nights, are carried out by dwarfs to deceive the eyes of men. Corpse-lights, Will-o'-the-wisps, the sparks from glow-worms' tails, the light in fire-flies' wings – these, carefully hung up in tiers round and round the hall, illuminated the palace with a cold blue light, and revealed to Skirnir's eyes the grotesque and hideous shapes of the tiny beings around him. Hump-backed, cunning-eyed, open-mouthed, they stood round, laughing, and whispering, and pointing with shrivelled fingers. One among them, a little taller than the rest, who sat on a golden seat thickly set with diamonds, appeared to be a kind of chief among them, and to him Skirnir addressed his message.

Cunning and wicked as these dwarfs were, they entertained a wholesome fear of Odin, having never forgotten their one interview with him in Gladsheim; and, therefore, when they heard from whom Skirnir came, with many uncouth gesticulations they bowed low before him, and declared themselves willing to obey All-Father's commands. They asked for two days and two nights in which to complete their task, and during that time Skirnir remained their guest in Svartheim.

He wandered about, and saw strange sights. He saw the great earth central fire, and the swarthy, withered race, whose task it is ceaselessly to feed it with fuel; he saw the diamond-makers, who change the ashes of the great fire into brilliants; and the dwarfs, whose business it is to fill the cracks in the mountain-sides with pure veins of silver and gold, and lead them up to places where they will one day meet the eyes of men. Nearer the surface he visited the workers in iron and the makers of salt-mines; he drank of their strange-tasting mineral waters, and admired the splendour of their silver-roofed temples and dwellings of solid gold.

At the end of two days Skirnir re-entered the audience-hall, and then the chief of the dwarfs put into his hand a slender chain. You can imagine what size it was when I tell you that the dwarf chief held it lightly balanced on his forefinger; and when it rested on Skirnir's hand it felt to him no heavier than a piece of thistledown.

The Svart King laughed loud when he saw the disappointment on Skirnir's face. 'It seems to you a little thing,' he said; 'and yet I assure you that in making it we have used up all the materials in the whole world fit for the purpose. No such chain can ever be made again, neither will the least atom of the substances of which it is made be found more. It is fashioned out of six things. The noise made by the footfall of cats; the beards of women; the roots of stones; the sinews of bears; the breath of fish; and the spittle of birds. Fear not with this to bind Fenrir; for no stronger chain will ever be made till the end of the world.'

Skirnir now looked with wonder at his chain, and, after having thanked the dwarfs, and promised to bring them a reward from Odin, he set forth on his road home, and, by the time of the evening meal, reached Valhalla, and gladdened the hearts of the Aesir by the tidings of his success.

V

Far away to the north of Asgard, surrounded by frowning mountains, the dark lake, Amsvartnir, lies, and, above the level of its troubled waters, burns Lyngvi, the island of sweet broom, flaming like a jewel on the dark brow of Hela. In this lonely isle, to which no ship but Skidbladnir could sail, the Aesir, with Fenrir in the midst, assembled to try the strength of the dwarfs' chain.

Fenrir prowled round his old master, Tyr, with a look of

savage triumph in his cruel eyes, now licking the hand that had so long fed him, and now shaking his great head, and howling defiantly. The Aesir stood at the foot of Giöll, the sounding rock, and passed Gleipnir, the chain, from one to another, talking about it, while Fenrir listened. 'It was much stronger than it looked,' they said; and Thor and Tyr vied with each other in their efforts to break it; while Bragi declared his belief that there was no one among Aesir or giants capable of performing so great a feat, 'unless,' he added, 'it should be you, Fenrir.'

This speech roused the pride of Fenrir; and, after looking long at the slender chain and the faces of the Aesir, he answered, 'Loath am I to be bound by this chain; but, lest you should doubt my courage, I will consent that you should bind me, provided one of you put his hand into my mouth as a pledge that no deceit is intended.'

There was a moment's silence among the Aesir when they heard this, and they looked at one another. Odin looked at Thor, and Thor looked at Bragi, and Frey fell behind, and put his hand to his side, where the all-conquering sword, which he alone could wield, no longer rested.

At length Tyr stepped forward valiantly, and put his strong right hand, with which he had so often fed him, into the wolf's cruel jaws.

At this signal the other Aesir threw the chain round the monster's neck, bound him securely with one end, and fastened the other to the great rock Giöll. When he was bound Fenrir rose, and shook himself, as he had done before; but in vain he raised himself up, and bounded forward – the more he struggled the more firmly the slender chain bound him.

At this sight the Aesir set up a loud shout of joy; for they saw their enemy conquered, and the danger that threatened Asgard averted. Only Tyr was silent, for in the struggle he had lost his hand.

Then Thor thrust his sword into the mouth of Fenrir, and a foaming dark flood burst forth, roared down the rock and under the lake, and began its course through the country a turbid river. So it will roll on till Ragnarök be come.

The sails of Skidbladnir now spread themselves out to the wind; and the Aesir, seated in the magic ship, floated over the lake silently in the silent moonlight; while, from the top of Bifröst, over the Urda fount and the dwelling of the Norns, a song floated down. 'Who,' asked one voice, 'of all the Aesir has won the highest honour?' and, singing, another voice made answer, 'Tyr has won the highest honour; for, of all the Aesir, he has the most worthily employed his gift.'

'Frey gave his sword for fairest Gerd.'

'Odin bought for himself wisdom at the price of his right eye.'

'Tyr, not for himself, but for others, has sacrificed his strong right hand.'

WHEN THE WOMAN CHIEF WAS YOUNG

Jessica Amanda Salmonson

THE CHIEF OF the Klamath nation was wise and valiant. As he grew older, he became a man of considerable wealth. One day he looked about and saw that he had achieved all his life's goals but one. He had no son to be his heir. With heavy heart he asked, 'To whom will I teach the ways of justice?' In his distress, he sought the counsel of three prophets who knew the ways of divine beings as intimately as the chief knew the ways of mortals. These wise men put their heads together and spoke with great spirits of sun, earth, wind, and water. They perceived that come autumn, at the time of the wapato root harvest, the chief's wife would bear a child worthy to be his heir.

The following autumn, a child was born. To the chief's chagrin, his wife bore a baby girl.

As she grew, her father the chief, remembering the prophesies of his wise men, saw to the instruction of his daughter. She learned to hunt; she rode in battle; she learned the ways of wisdom in mediating disputes and rendering fair judgments. Her name was Chao, the Antelope, though many years later she was called Wolkotska the Cougar.

She was as lovely as the dawn, and the Klamaths loved her for her courage and kindness. That she went clad in the garments of a hunter only heightened the effect of her beauty. One day she was hunting in the mountains and was seen by Llao, ruler of the demons of Crater Lake and of the world below. From his lofty throne at the lake's western edge, he observed the boyish maiden for a long while, admiring her tracking skills. Everything about her appealed to him, her quill-worked shirt of fawn skin, her mantle of cougar fur, her high beaded moccasins, the colorfully fletched arrows in her quiver. The demon king came down from his rocky throne and said to Chao, 'Live with me at the center of the world. You will be wealthy beyond dreams as queen of powerful armies.' Chao laughed and refused him. He dared not take her by force, as she gleamed with a personal magic, and she was armed with a bow, sharp arrows, and a knife.

The following day the demon-king was seen coming across a meadow toward the Klamath village. The people saw his big grey face, his horned ears, his tough sinewy arms and taloned claws, and the people were greatly alarmed. When he smiled, his teeth were not reassuring, and when he hailed the chief with friendly words, the harshness of his voice was disheartening.

Llao entered into a bargaining with Chao's father and mother. Because he was a god, he was able to offer good hunting and fishing, fair weather, and large harvests in exchange for Chao as his wife. In addition he would provide personal wealth in the form of dentalia shells, obsidian for making spear and arrow heads, copper beads from under the earth, and a great many furs of black otters and white foxes.

The chief said, 'As you can see, my daughter is not like other maidens; she is also my son and will rule the Klamaths when I have gone to the land of the spirits. I do not wish to anger you, yet must ask that you turn your heart to another.'

Llao glowered silently for some while before he replied, 'You will regret this' and strode away across the meadow.

* * *

The following autumn there was a poor wapato harvest, and other roots were just as hard to find. Then came a terrifyingly cold winter. The game fled to warmer climes and the salmon could not be expected until late in spring, by which time many Klamaths would starve to death. The chief called together the three prophets. They said, 'What mortal can oppose the dark god Llao, ruler of the underworld? We must seek a champion, and who better than Skell, king of the skyworld?'

Skell's lodge was beyond the Yamsay River. As it happened, he had one day seen Chao running in pursuit of a deer. She had hunted far and wide to assist her hungry people, and so wandered into Skell's country seeking meat. He fell in love with the huntress at once and followed her secretly to her village.

The deer which Chao carried to her people was insufficient to feed everyone. Skell saw his chance to win his way into her heart. He commanded his eagles to fetch a large number of hares and bring them to the hungry village at once. When golden eagles appeared from every part of the forest with their offerings, the Klamaths were astonished and delighted. Then Skell came forth and said to the chief, 'My heart aches for your daughter. You did wisely to refuse her hand to Llao, for as his queen she would have lived miserably in the darkness of the world-cavern, worshipped by slavering monsters. At my side, she will become queen of sun and sky. Flowers will arise in the places of her footsteps. She will rule the children of the fox, the deer, and all that dwells in the forest; it shall be as though she were their only mother, before whom all life bows.'

The chief felt despair welling inside him. He had hoped to seek out Skell as a champion for his people against the malignant Llao, but now he must risk angering even the good god, saying, 'Great Skell, once I was without an heir, and I made sacrifices and supplications to the spirits of sky and earth, wind and water, and you were yourself among the divinities whose intercession I requested. Through my wise men I was promised an heir, and Chao was sent to me. I asked, "Is it possible the gods have made an error?" and I answered, "Indeed not; this girl will be my heir." This being so, how can I send her to live in the sky? I am old and will soon rest forever. Chao must remain with her people, who have already accepted her as my son. As chief of the Klamaths, she will choose her spouse, and not be chosen.'

Skell said, 'Well do I remember your prayers and sacrifices, but even gods may err, for each of us has his own design. Little did I know what giving you Chao would mean for me, or for my rival Llao. Know this, Chief of the Klamaths, that for the sake of your daughter, the huntress Chao, there will be war between the upper world and the lower world. When gods do battle, mortals invariably feel the tragic repercussions of divine severity.'

* * *

Thereafter Skell took it upon himself to protect the Klamaths from Llao's hostilities. When Llao called forth clouds of icy storms, Skell called forth warm sunlight to soften the stormy blows. When Llao's forces tried to frighten away all the game of the region, Skell sent troops of game from his own country to sacrifice themselves before the arrows of Klamath hunters. When Llao's underground fiends blighted essential roots and berries, Skell secretly arranged sunlit meadows with plenitude, revealing these sites to Chao.

The Klamaths moved their village to Klamath Lake near which Skell's meadows were discovered. Here Llao's evil influences were weakest, due to Skell's handiwork. Llao discovered that the fish in this lake were beyond his command. He became increasingly annoyed with Skell for negating his efforts to starve and punish the Klamaths.

One night when Llao's frustrations had reached a peak, the demon king called forth a large number of his shadowy, monstrous soldiers. They gathered with the demon-king upon Llao's rock, and he said to them, 'For so long as Skell lives as the protector of the Klamaths, I will not be able to slay the old chief and steal away Chao for my underworld bride.'

For five days they chanted dirge-like war songs and beat huge base drums made from the skins of tattooed men. Demons arrived in increasing numbers from the bottom of the lake and from the black depths of caves, bearing clubs and knives and savage faces, waving their knotted fists, eager for a fight. All this while Llao breathed forth a fetid smokiness that spread across the land.

At the end of the five days, the world was as dark by day as by night, as choking as a cedar lodge with its smoke-holes closed tight. Then Llao sent his legions into Skell's country to wreak havoc.

As Skell was a divinity of sunlight, the smoky darkness bewildered him. He called upon his legions of foxes, eagles, mountain goats, elk, bear, antelope and cougars, but all these were made sleepy and befuddled by the incessant night. They feared the smoke as a harbinger of fire, and knew not which way to run. Meanwhile the shades which Llao brought from the underworld roved about the land unchecked. When they came to the lodge of Skell they dragged him out into the blinding smoke. They bludgeoned him with their clubs, laughing hideously as they rent him piece from piece with their dreadful knives. Finally they carved out Skell's immortal beating heart and ran howling and hooting back to Crater Lake in Llao's land.

The conjured smoke dispersed from the countryside. A natural night descended, filled with stars and a fat bright moon reflecting on the cold waters of Llao's perfectly round lake. He and his legions gathered on the throne-rock, screeching their victory chants. Then Llao threw the beating heart of Skell into the lake, where numerous giant, brilliantly red crawfishes caught it and threw it from one clawed monster to another. They played with the heart of Skell as though it were a ball at a festival game. Llao and his army sat along the cliffs cheering and encouraging the moonlit sport of the giant crawfishes.

The game went on all night long. At dawn, the huntress Chao appeared unexpectedly at the eastern edge of the lake, the opposite side from Llao's Rock. She called across the waters in a chiding manner, 'How weak you are! Can't you throw Skell's heart any higher than that? The smallest child in my village could throw it higher!'

The crawfishes were insulted. Llao's legion chanted to the players, 'Throw it higher! Throw it higher!' Skell's heart was given a mighty toss from a crawfish's claw. When another crawfish caught it, Chao laughed mockingly, and said, 'Is that so high? Oh, such weaklings!' Each time Chao chided them, the crawfishes threw the heart still higher. Then an eagle streaked across the sky, caught Skell's heart in its talons, sped over the lake's surface pursued by crawfishes, and dropped the heart into Chao's upstretched hands.

The huntress immediately fled with the prize. Llao shouted, 'After her! After her!' and all the legions chased her through the wilderness toward the land of the River Yamsay.

The huntress was as swift as the antelope for which she was named. The rising sun burned the eyes of her pursuers. Wolves and bears leapt at the demons with claws and teeth, while foxes and deer led them astray. With this assistance, Chao left her pursuers far behind, and came alone to the lodge of Skell. Outside the lodge, Skell's pale lifeless limbs lay strewn about in pieces. His head was upside-down by a stump. His torso lay before the door of the lodge. Chao carefully put his body back together, then inserted the heart in his chest, so that the god sprang back to life.

* * *

For the span of half a moon, Chao nursed the sky-god, during which time Llao continued to terrorize the band of Klamaths. The tribe moved from Klamath Lake to Little Klamath Lake in their efforts to avoid the demon-king's minions. Throughout this time the Klamaths had no news of their princess and grieved that both she and Skell had been slain in the war against Llao.

One night the demons of Llao surrounded the harried village at Little Klamath Lake and began to take the people prisoner. They bound everyone with hazel rope and marched them away. The old chief and his wife they whipped with a cord. All through the night they tramped toward Crater Lake; men and women, old and young, all were so dispirited by events and weakened by weeks of poor nourishment that they could do nothing in their own behalf.

When the lake was reached, the people saw against the moonlight the terrible shadow of Llao atop his great rock. In a bellowing, thunderous voice he demanded, 'Where have you hidden Chao the Beautiful One, my chosen bride? Reveal her at once, or you shall all be fed to my crawfishes!'

Hearing their name called, the crawfish-monsters raised their beady-eyed faces above the water and created a froth in the starlit waters about them, stirring with their clacking claws. Yet the terror of this vision was not as effective as it might otherwise have been, for the Klamaths realized for the first time, by Llao's own demand, that he had failed to capture or slay their princess! The old chief stepped forth, his back bleeding from the whipping the devils had given him. He said, 'We have not seen Chao for half a moon. Perhaps she is licking her wounds in some secret place, we don't know. When she is able, she will return, and wage an avenging battle against you, like a good son.'

The Klamaths laughed and hollered in agreement and began to sing the name of Chao. The devils backed away, disliking the sound of human laughter. It was then that the spirit-canoe appeared in the east of the lake, and in it stood the huntress Chao and the sky-god Skell. Skell flew out of the canoe and over the lake, landing alongside Llao on the throne-rock. They were shadows against the moon, locked arm in arm in mortal combat. They fell to their sides still embracing, and no one could tell whose knife it was that glinted on the left, and whose knife glinted on the right.

Chao stepped out of the spirit-canoe and confronted five devils. She unleashed two arrows before the devils ran away, two of them severely wounded. She hurried to her mother and father and untied their hands, and soon everyone was untying someone else. Just as everyone's spirits were highest, they were stunned to hear the thunderous voice of Llao cry out, 'Feast, my crawfishes, upon the arms of Skell!'

The shadowy king threw two severed body parts into the lake, which the crawfish rent into small pieces as the waters grew black with the god's blood.

The dark figure atop the rock bent down to again hack at the corpse. Then he stood and cried out, 'Feast, my crawfishes, upon the legs of Skell!'

The monsters caught the falling limbs and began to devour them with rapacious delight.

A third time the Klamaths heard the horrible bellowing, 'Feast, my beauties, upon the heart and torso of Skell!' as he threw the greater part of his foe into the roiling waters.

The hearts of the Klamath people were dashed low. The devils, no longer cowed, came forth from the places where Chao had sent them hiding. However, in the next moment, the Klamaths were cheering excitedly, for it was Skell upon the rock! Skell laughed in his own handsome voice, crying out, 'Last of all I give to you the head of your master Llao!'

As Llao's head struck the surface of the water, it was transformed into Wizard Island. His gaping mouth became the island's burning crater. The crawfishes in a horror of having eaten their king sank away into the unnatural depths of the lake, never to be seen again. The devilish warriors along the lakeshore ran forth planning to avenge their ruler by battling the Klamaths, who were all unarmed save Chao. But as they ran forward, they began to dissipate in the rising dawn. Their shadowy forms faded into morning's mist which clung a while to the surface of the lake, then was gone.

* * *

It was not long after these events that the father of Chao died peacefully in the fulfillment of his life. His wife's spirit followed after him in due course. For many years thereafter, in the long past age that is today but an echo of a dream, the Maklak clan of Klamaths dwelt among their lakes and the vales, ruled by a noble and wise woman chief whose footfalls in the forest were as light as Wolkotska the Cougar, who was as gracefully fleet-footed as Chao the Antelope, and who was beloved of all her people.

TEWDRIG, TYRANT OF TREHEYL

Peter Tremayne

'TEWDRIG! A STRANGE ship has appeared in the estuary,' cried Wron the Druid, bursting into the great feasting hall of Tewdrig, king of Treheyl and emperor of all Kernow, that south-western peninsula of the Isle of the Mighty that is today called Cornwall.

Tewdrig glanced up in agitated surprise.

'What guards do I have that I am not warned of the sight of a strange sail until a ship sails into the estuary?' he demanded vehemently. 'I should be informed as soon as a sail appears on the distant horizon.'

Wron made a dismissive gesture.

'Better to learn late than learn never, my king.'

'Does it come in war or does it come in peace?' demanded Tewdrig, buckling on his great sword, and taking up his rounded buckler.

Tewdrig was a strong man, as tall as a spear and as straight, with long black hair and a face that was saturnine and cruel. Skill with his weapons had brought Tewdrig power and his domains spread through the land of Kernow as far east as the great River Tamar, the quietly flowing river that marked the border with the kingdom of Dumnonia.

It was not strength alone, however, by which Tewdrig had kept his kingdom secure. He believed in the gods and the old ways in a world that was rapidly changing. In the east, whole kingdoms were falling before the hordes of Saxons with their mighty gods of war. Countless tribes had fled north, west and south to escape massacre by the children of Woden.

So far, the kingdom of Kernow had been kept safe. But Tewdrig was ever vigilant. Only a battle hardened king could keep harm from his people.

Now he hurried to the battlements of his fortress at the place of the estuary, Treheyl, and looked out across its waters. The estuary of the river, which was also called Heyl, formed a wide sac stretching two miles which, at low tide, was a stretch of mud banks on which numerous seabirds nested. The ramparts of Tewdrig's fortress rose dominantly above them.

Wron had obviously alerted the guards for they were gathered ready, their weapons in their hands.

Tewdrig came to the battlements and halted.

Indeed, there was a ship sailing into the estuary, its sails filled before the wind. It was heading towards the quay below Treheyl.

The king's eyes narrowed.

'It bears a strange emblem on the sail, Wron. Can you identify it?'

The Druid peered forward and shook his head.

'I cannot identify it, my king. It is not a symbol that is familiar in this land. Though from the cut of the vessel I would say that it is from the western island of Ywerdhon.'

Ywerdhon was the name by which the people of Kernow called the land of the goddess Éire.

Tewdrig bit in irritation at his lip, a habit he had often tried to control since childhood.

'Well, if they are foreign and mean us harm, they can harm us little. There is not room enough on that little craft for many warriors and their approach is open enough.'

Wron nodded: 'Nevertheless, my king, it would be best to have the men stand ready.'

Tewdrig turned to Dinan, chieftain of Pendinas, who was the captain of his guard, and told him to take a company of warriors to the quay to greet the strangers. Dinan was, in fact, Tewdrig's own brother and as fair as Tewdrig was dark yet they were both born at the same hour of the same mother and father. Dinan was Tewdrig's right hand and his shield at every battle. Firm in battle and as shrewd in war was Dinan. Some said that without Dinan, Tewdrig could not have maintained his kingdom. Though this was never said before either Tewdrig or Dinan. Further, many said that Tewdrig was as evilly tempered to those nearest to him as Dinan was amiable and obliging. Indeed, at Tewdrig's sharp commands, Dinan smiled but a gentle acknowledgement of his brother's order and went down in obedience to it.

Tewdrig turned back to examine the sail and its strange emblem again. It consisted of two curving lines which crossed each other so that the emblem appeared as if it was meant to be the outline of a fish.

Tewdrig was seated in the great hall of his palace when Dinan escorted the visitors to him. Wron the Druid stood at his right elbow for Wron was his chief counsellor.

There were five people who came before him; three men and two women. And while they were all clad in simple attire they stood tall and had the look of nobility on their faces. Around the neck of each one of them there hung a silver cross on a leather thong. Tewdrig's eyes narrowed for the cross seemed to be a badge of their fellowship.

'These, my brother, are travellers from Ywerdhon,' Dinan announced.

Their leader stepped forward. He was a tall, elderly man with a regal countenance.

'The Blessing of the Living God on you, Tewdrig of Treheyl,' he greeted.

Tewdrig frowned before he replied.

'The prosperity of each of the gods of my ancestors on you, stranger. Who are you and what do you seek in this land?'

'I was a king in my own country but have given up earthly pomp to follow a more glorious life. My name is Germoe.'

'Welcome then, Germoe. And what is more glorious in your eyes than temporal splendour?' smiled Tewdrig indulgently, wondering if the man was mad.

'To follow the ways of the Son of God and teach His truth and peace to your people.'

Wron drew his brows together.

'The Son of God? The Father of the Gods had many sons, each of them gods in their own right. Of which do you speak?'

'The one and indivisible God,' replied Germoe. 'Him we shall speak of anon if you allow me and my band to stay in your kingdom.'

'And who are these others?'

'I am Coan,' said one of the two young men.

'I am Elwyn,' announced the other.

'My name is Breage,' one of the young women added.

'I am Crowan,' said the last.

'We are all servants of the Living God,' Germoe said. 'We seek your permission to settle in peace and preach the new faith of our God.'

Wron glanced at the king.

'To settle in peace?' he sneered. 'Yet you would preach against our faith, destroy our beliefs and our laws. Do you call this peace?'

'Once you have opened your ears to the word of our Lord in heaven, it will be peace,' replied Germoe confidently. 'Our God is not a God of war, strife or dissension.'

'I would hear them, brother,' Dinan suddenly said. 'Let them go where they will in our land. For what can five people do to shake the faith of a nation?'

Wron flashed an angry glance at Dinan.

'I like it not. If they must stay let them go south away from this place so that they may not contaminate our good government.'

Tewdrig chuckled suddenly in humour.

'We will give in to our brother's urgings,' he said. 'For I agree – what harm can five strangers do in our midst? But Wron is my counsellor. Go southward, strangers, and preach as you wish.'

They all left Treheyl and journeyed south. But Crowan was the first to break away and took an eastern road until she came to a spot where she built a round enclosure and she prospered. They call this place Crowan to this day.

The others continued southwards. Then Coan also turned east and found a river called the Fal. On its eastern bank he started to preach the word of the Son of the Living God. But it is said that this land owed allegiance to Wron the Druid who stirred up the people against Coan and in their anger they stoned him to death. So the place where this happened was afterwards called Merther, which stands between Tresillian and St Michael Penkevil. The word *merther*, in the Cornish tongue, means 'martyr'.

The others continued southwards. And first Germoe halted

at the southern coast of Kernow and established a house where he taught and the spot became named after him. The others continued to the south-east following the coast. Then Breage stopped and under the shadow of a fortress called Pencaire, between the hills of Tregonning and Godolphin, she built her house and began to teach and so the place was called Breage after her. Finally, the young man named Elwyn came to the sea's edge and to a small port where he established himself and taught. The place was thereafter called Porth Elwyn, or Elwyn's port which is now Porthleven.

Now Tewdrig watched the progress of the strangers, with their strange stories of the Son of God, with anxiety on his brow. His people, who had followed the wise Druids of old, had begun to fall away from the rituals at the stone circles and the worship of the old gods. In spite of the martyrdom of Coan, the other members of Germoe's party were gaining converts throughout the southern lands of Kernow.

What Tewdrig did not realise was that his own brother had listened to the word and accepted the truth of the new faith.

It happened that a year and a day after the coming of Germoe and his followers, Wron came running to Tewdrig who was seated in his feasting hall.

'Tewdrig! A strange ship has appeared in the estuary,' cried Wron.

Tewdrig glanced up from his wine in agitated surprise.

'What guards do I have that I am not warned of the sight of a sail until a ship sails into the estuary?' he demanded vehemently. 'I should be informed as soon as a sail appears on the distant horizon.'

Wron made a dismissive gesture.

'Better to learn late than learn never, my king.'

'Does it come in war or does it come in peace?' demanded Tewdrig, buckling on his great sword, and taking up his rounded buckler.

'Perhaps it does not matter,' said Wron slyly, 'for the last strange ship that came here was supposed to come in peace and its honey-tongued crew have sewn dissension through the land.'

They climbed to the battlements and Tewdrig's eyes narrowed. Indeed, there was a ship sailing in the broad estuary before Treheyl, a ship with its sails filled before the wind.

Tewdrig gasped and pointed.

'See, Wron, look at its sail. It carries the same design as the ship of Germoe.' And, indeed, he was right for the sail carried two curving lines which crossed each other forming the outline of a great fish.

Wron drew in a deep breath.

'Then this ship is of the same nation as Germoe and his tribe. We would do well to slaughter them before they come ashore.'

Even so, Tewdrig hesitated and by the time he had made up his mind, his brother Dinan had gone down to the quay to welcome the strangers to Treheyl.

So Tewdrig hurried to the hall of his palace and slumped upon his throne while Wron stood moodily at his side.

Five strangers entered with Dinan.

'These, my brother, are travellers from Ywerdhon,' he said.

Tewdrig was filled with apprehension for though this time there were three men and two women, like the five that had come before them, they each carried a silver cross hung around their necks, and while the clothes they wore were simple, they all carried themselves with noble bearing.

'The Blessing of the Living God on you, Tewdrig of Treheyl,' greeted their leader.

He was a tall, handsome man.

'The prosperity of the gods of my ancestors greet you,' replied Tewdrig, frowning.

'I am called Gwinear, I was a prince in my own land but I have given up all temporal pomp to serve the true God.'

'All the gods are true,' snapped Wron, irritably.

'There is but one God,' replied the woman at Gwinear's side.

Tewdrig's eyes bulged a little as he beheld her, for never had he seen a maiden so comely as this.

Gwinear smiled, not noticing the look in the king's eyes: 'This is my sister, Piala.'

'My name is Ia,' the second maiden said. She was as fair as Piala was dark but just as beautiful, or so Dinan thought for he had not taken his eyes from the girl since she had set foot on the quay of Treheyl.

'I am called Erth, and I am brother to Ia,' announced one of the young men.

'While I am Uny,' added the third man, 'brother of Ia and Erth.'

'And I suppose you want to stay in my kingdom and live in peace?' queried Tewdrig, a hint of sarcasm in his voice. But the derision was taken from his voice when his eyes dwelt on the beauty of Piala.

'That is our earnest request,' Gwinear responded.

'But in doing so you would want freedom to preach your religion?' Wron prompted.

'That is what we desire,' Piala smiled sweetly in innocence at Tewdrig.

The heart of the king gave a lurch and a passion began to throb within him.

'My king, we cannot grant this,' Wron leant forward and whispered into the ear of the king of Treheyl.

Tewdrig glanced up startled.

'Why so?'

Wron closed his eyes in anguish.

'Have you forgotten so soon how Germoe and his followers are disrupting the kingdom in the south?'

Tewdrig bit his lip and then stared across at Piala.

'Then we will allow these good people to stay with us, provided they stay within sight of Treheyl that we may know what they are doing.'

Now this idea had occurred to Tewdrig not because of the reason he implied to his Druid but because he wanted to be near the beautiful Piala. Further, he rose and went down to Piala, smiling, and said: 'And in good faith, and to keep you safe, I will grant you land at the gate of my fortress and there you may preach to those of Treheyl who would hear you.'

Thus did the spot where Piala set up her dwelling become known as Phillack, in her honour, yet it was under the shadow of the king's gloomy fortress at Treheyl.

Piala's brother, Gwinear, wandered a mile or so further to the east and established himself at a spot which is still named after him. And Erth also stayed within a short distance from Treheyl and the spot where he taught also took the name of St Erth. And Uny crossed the estuary opposite to Tewdrig's fortress and the place he taught was called the enclosure of the church – Lelant.

Now Ia tarried a while with Dinan, for in those days the sons and daughters of the church could marry and did so. Love and marriage between men and women, even though they be of the church was not then forbidden as it was in later centuries. Ia was as attracted to Dinan as he was to her. Dinan promised her that he would hand over to her a tiny island at the end of a small bay to the west on which he had a fortress. That fortress was called Pendinas. Ia established her church on this island and there lived with Dinan.

Wron the Druid was angered by these happenings and began to wonder whether the land of Kernow was in need of a new king to govern. The preachers of the new religion were gaining converts from the old and in teaching love and forgiveness were allowing their enemies to rage and pillage unchecked along the eastern border of the kingdom where ran the mighty River Tamar. Within the kingdom, there was also rumblings and dissent, and many came to call Tewdrig a tyrant and godless king.

To the south-east, Geraint, chieftain of Gerrans, was openly preaching insurrection for he had been converted to the new religions. In spite of Wron's pleas, Tewdrig would not stir against him.

'Plenty of time to teach him a lesson,' Tewdrig assured Wron. 'Let him have his say. The howling of a dog at the moon will not change its course.'

Tewdrig was too infatuated with Piala to notice the danger. In fact, desire still burned deep within him. Piala was polite and greeted him in friendship, not being of the world to read the depth of the craving in his eyes. Indeed, there was a fearful emotion which smouldered restlessly there. Like a dog, Tewdrig followed her about, pretending interest in her teachings in order to sit in her company for hours on end.

Wron realised that the veil of desire must be lifted from his king's eyes or else Kernow would be doomed. It would be wracked by internal dissension and then it would be attacked from without. So Wron sat and pondered the problem and a crafty plan began to form in his mind. He would create bloodshed between Tewdrig and the Ywerdhon; if the Ywerdhon died then well and good, if Tewdrig died, then he would be able to rouse all Kernow against all the Ywerdhon preachers there. Then Wron arose with a great smile on his thin features and, saddling his horse, he rode for the church of Gwinear.

'Greetings, Ywerdhon,' he said.

'Blessings of God on you, Wron of Treheyl.'

'I will come straight to the point,' Wron said, as he dismounted and sat before Gwinear's fire.

'A good place to start,' acknowledged Gwinear.

'My king is besotted with your sister Piala.'

Gwinear at once looked troubled for he had seen the carnal fire in the eyes of the tyrant of Treheyl.

'My sister has sworn to celibacy, for she will serve no other than the Son of God.'

Wron hid his contempt and simply nodded.

'Very laudable,' he exclaimed. 'But Tewdrig has sworn to have no other woman seated by his throne.'

'This is grave news. Perhaps I should speak to the king and explain our ways?'

'An excellent idea. I know that this evening, Tewdrig goes to plight his troth to Piala. Be there at the ninth hour. Tewdrig is a reasonable man and will listen to argument.'

So saying, Wron mounted his horse and rode back to Treheyl. There he sought out the sulking Tewdrig.

'What ails you, my king?' Wron asked.

'I am as restive and fretful as a young man in the first vapours of love. I send Piala tokens and she dispenses them as charity to the poor. What am I to do?'

Wron's thin lips twitched but he controlled his cunning smile.

'If that is all that ails you, fret no more.'

'What do you mean?' demanded Tewdrig.

'I have just come from the lady. She does return your love. This she has told me. But she says she must act with decorum before her brother, for these Ywerdhon have strange beliefs and ways. Though under that faint cloak they are as passionate as we. However, it is clearly fear of her brother's anger which bids her hold you at arm's length. He is the problem here.'

'Speak further,' Tewdrig invited, much intrigued.

'She tells me that she shares your passions. Her cloak of indifference shall be discarded if you come to her just before the ninth hour and, because of her customs, you must not heed her protest but take her like the great man and mighty king she knows you to be.'

A smile of lascivious joy spread over Tewdrig's face.

Wron went off to his meal well pleased with his day's work.

So it happened, as dusk was falling before the ninth hour, Tewdrig went to the place where Piala had set up her church, which is called Phillack. Those the beautiful maiden was instructing in the ways of the new religion had departed to their houses and Piala was kneeling praying before the image of a young man hanging on a cross. Two candles were lit before it.

Tewdrig entered the church, his body tingling with desire as his lustful eyes fell on the maiden.

Piala started at the noise of his entry and turned round, her eyes widening as she beheld the tyrant of Treheyl.

'Why, King Tewdrig,' she said, scrambling from her knees, 'what brings you here at this hour of the night?'

'That you know well,' smiled Tewdrig, confidently.

Piala bit her lip in agitation for she now recognised the meaning of the many presents Tewdrig had bestowed on her during the last months.

'I must tell you the ways of those who follow the Son of God, Tewdrig!'

Tewdrig let forth an oath.

'You may tell me later, for my body aches for our union.'

Piala went pale as she discerned his purpose.

'This must not be!' she gasped. 'I am sworn to celibacy in the service of . . .'

But Tewdrig moved forward and seized her, delighting in her struggles because he believed it to be, as Wron had told him, her way of greeting his love-making.

An angry exclamation halted Tewdrig. He turned in annoyance as a figure burst into the church.

It was Gwinear, his face working in anger.

'Lecherous dog! You dare the sacrilege of this place by attacking a daughter of the church?'

Tewdrig pushed Piala to one side and drew for his sword.

'Begone, little man! Preach not to me for I am not of your faith.'

Now it has been said that Gwinear was a king in his own land before he followed the path of the Son of God. The blood of champions still flowed in his veins and a battle rage came upon him. He moved forward with only his wooden staff for courage. Tewdrig, whatever else he was, was a great warrior but he lacked the warrior's will to self-control. He saw Gwinear's approach and made only three strokes of his sword. The first stroke cut the staff into two useless pieces; the second stroke pierced Gwinear's heart while the third stroke decapitated his head.

Piala let forth a tremendous shriek. She rushed to her brother's side and picked up his head and kissed it fervently. The eyes of Gwinear flicked open, for the ancients rightly believed that the soul resided in the head, and his voice spoke: 'I have sinned. Do not you do likewise, my sister. Unto him that smiteth thee on the one cheek offer also the other. Remember.'

With that Gwinear's soul departed.

Piala, too, was born of the blood of champions and it burnt with a fierce fire. It is one thing to hear a philosophy with the mind but blood is strong.

In blind vengeance she seized the dagger which Gwinear wore in his belt, for each man must carry a means to cut his meat. She seized it and lunged forward.

It can be said for Tewdrig that he acted only out of instinct. The point of his sword met Piala's onward rush at breast level and entered it. The blood spurted from her heart and she fell to the ground.

Tewdrig stood in a daze at the swiftness of what had happened.

Then Wron entered, for the sly Druid had been watching all the time, and while he was pleased at what had befallen he pretended horror at the scene.

'Now the remaining Ywerdhon will preach rebellion against you, Tewdrig, and join with Geraint of Gerrans. You must act to stop this rebellion before it has time to flower and bear fruit.'

Tewdrig moved in a stupor and Wron had to shout to snap him out of it.

'Take the head of Gwinear and wash it in the well, then place it on a spike and have it carried before you so all Kernow may know your serious intent to rid the land of the Ywerdhon.'

Now the reason for this was not so much to put fear in people but because of the religious symbolism of the head wherein the

Druids believed the soul dwelt. To carry the head of your enemy endowed you with the strength and valour and intellect of that enemy.

Soon, Tewdrig came to his old self and realised that Wron was right. Before the next dawn, Tewdrig and his men had ridden to the churches of Erth and Uny and the brothers were slain before they had time to raise an alarm.

'Where is Ia, the last of this breed?' Tewdrig commanded as he stood by the bloody remains of Uny.

His warriors looked uncomfortably at each other.

'Why she is with your brother Dinan at Pendinas,' they said.

Anger was on Tewdrig's face now.

'Then we will go to Pendinas and finish this job. And woe to any, brother or no, who tries to defend this Ywerdhon from my wrath!'

His army arrived at Pendinas the next day and were surprised when they found Geraint of Gerrans with an army there before them. Geraint had gathered the rebellious men of Kernow from the four corners of the kingdom. Before this great hosting stood Breage, Crowan and Elwyn as well as Ia. By Ia's side, on his warhorse, sat Tewdrig's own brother Dinan. And before all of them was Geraint, a handsome young man of princely countenance. At his side was the venerable Germoe and Germoe carried a great cross of silver to act as their standard.

Tewdrig rode forward and by his side rode Wron, who carried the pole on which the head of Gwinear was set. And Geraint came forward with Germoe riding by his side bearing the silver cross.

'You are in rebellion against your just king,' cried Tewdrig in anger.

Geraint smiled gently.

'Is it not written in our ancient law – what makes a king weaker than a servant on the poorest farm? It is because the people ordain the king, the king does not ordain the people. While you sat in justice, promoting our commonweal, Tewdrig, we followed you. But a bad deed you have done and we will now have done with you.'

'Then, by the gods, I challenge you to the right of single combat!' cried Tewdrig.

Both men drew their swords.

Now as Tewdrig was about to spur forward, the head of Gwinear, set atop the great pole held by Wron, suddenly fell. It fell straight and true and struck Tewdrig on the head with such impact that his iron helm was shattered and he was knocked to the ground.

Wron dismounted and examined his king and when he looked up there was fear in his eyes.

'His skull has been crushed by the head of Gwinear,' he whispered.

'The true God has spoken,' cried Germoe. 'Vengeance is mine, says the Lord. Geraint is king.'

And they departed, each to his own place. The head of Gwinear was buried at the town named after him. Ia continued to preach at Pendinas with support of the prince Dinan, rejecting all worldly treasures, and eventually the spot was named after her and is known today as St Ives. Geraint became a good and just king whose name is still spoken of today and Gerrans, named after him, still exists. He, it was, who encouraged many saints to come to Kernow and soon all the land was following the faith of the Son of God.

As for Wron, he departed the field unseen and was never punished. They say he went to hide in a cold, dark granite cave, within the sound of the blustery billows of the sea, and is there waiting for his time for he was sure that that time, which was, must be and will come again.

RED WOLF'S DAUGHTER AND BLOODY CHIEF'S SON

Jessica Amanda Salmonson

A FIERCE BATTLE was engaged in the snowy forest of pine and tamaracks above Wallowa Lake. Red Wolf's Chute-pa-lu band whirled ravenously in the midst of the ambushed Blackfoot scouting party.

For long moons, Blackfeet had been striving to displace Red Wolf's Chute-pa-lu Nez Perce from their ancient fishing and hunting grounds. With a thousand streams, and rivers, and lakes, it was good country, worth a fight. When the interlopers first began troubling the established tribe, it seemed they could not hope to succeed and would soon return to their lands defeated.

All the early battles fell to the valor of Red Wolf and his courageous followers, familiar as they were with the region. But by degrees, Blackfeet had increasingly mastered the forest, it became more and more difficult to surprise the foe. A great leader had arisen among them. That man was Bloody Chief, a clever tactician who drew more Blackfeet from beyond Shining Mountain to join him. Increasingly it was Red Wolf's men who were surprised by ambushes.

Today, however, the Nez Perce met with good luck. A band of enemy scouts came running up the forest slope away from the lake, shouting among themselves about something hideous they had seen. They made so much ridiculous noise they gave themselves away while still at some distance. Then they stopped short, shocked to discover they had fled straight into the arms of Red Wolf and his warriors.

The cluster of eight Blackfoot scouts spun about as though

intending to run back the way they came. Yet they were seemingly even more afraid of retreating in that direction than they were of facing impossible odds against the Nez Perce. In that moment of indecision, the Nez Perce were upon them. Red Wolf swung his long warclub of polished hardwood beveled along an edge and inlaid with the teeth of wolves. His opponent tried ineffectually to deflect a blow. In the next moment, blood and brain spattered freshly tramped snow. He fell backward and lay with tongue and one eye hanging out.

After a few hard breaths, it was done. All the birds had flown away. The forest was silent save for the harsh breathing of the victors. The Blackfeet lay dead at the feet of their enemies, whereas Red Wolf had but one man down. Red Wolf stalked amidst the Blackfoot corpses, saw one man not yet fully dead, and bashed his skull. Then he knelt beside the injured Nez Perce. He looked at the gaping wound, took the warrior's arm and said, 'Press your hand here, so.' Then he motioned four men to carry the one, and they started down the hill. When they reached the snowline, they knew their village was near.

One of Red Wolf's warriors said, 'I wonder what those scouts were running from?'

'Strong spirits guard this place,' said Red Wolf. 'They are Chute-pa-lu spirits, angered by the presence of Blackfeet.'

His men did not contradict this, for they hoped Red Wolf's opinion was inspired by the spirit-power that was in him. They would not like to see him proven wrong.

* * *

At a bonfire in the center of the village, the people gathered for a communal feast. They ate trout, crawfish and fernbrake. It was a good meal, but nothing compared to what in better times was expected from the rich forest. With the present war, there had been little opportunity to hunt elk or bear.

As the warriors told expansive versions of that day's successful battle, the tribe became cheerful. Each man in turn was encouraged to tell of the battle from his point of view. With every retelling, the story was embellished and improved. The part about the Blackfeet petrified in their tracks, too frightened either to attack or run away, won screeches of laughter.

But underlying the momentary cheerfulness of women, old men and children there was a continuous thrum of fear. Reflected on the waters of icy Wallowa Lake was the greater bonfire of Blackfeet on the further shore. They were dancing and hollering and pounding drums. Perhaps as yet they did not know eight of their men were killed. When they learned of it, they would seek swift vengeance. The sound of the Blackfoot celebration reached the Chute-pa-lu, muted but clear, and Chute-pa-lu laughter was insufficient to shut out the noise of the big gathering of their foe.

The sorry fact was, the Nez Perce village had lost the majority of its young warriors during a year of raids back and forth, whereas the Blackfeet seemed to spring in ever increasing numbers, as though descending from out of the sky.

Red Wolf declined to tell his version of the victory. He was not able to eat. He accepted a carved juniper trough with a fat portion of trout, but could only look at it as though it were something he disliked. He stood from the circle of his men and walked away without a word, carrying the trough with him. All knew by his moodiness and demeanor that they must not call after him. He faded into the darkness outside the circle of firelight.

* * *

In a tipi near an old spruce, the injured man lay upon a bearskin robe, his lower body covered with a blanket of marmot skins. He was not young, though he was famous for the many adventures of his youth. He was proud to be called Old Strength. Often Red Wolf had tried to convince him to remain in the village as its guard. Always he replied, 'What! Like an old man? Let's go kill Blackfeet!' Now, if he recovered, the muscle of his arm was so deeply cut he would never again be strong enough to fight.

His bare chest glistened with sweat, though the early autumn evening was chill. A small fire burned in the center of the floor. A trail of smoke rose in a thin line and escaped where the tipi's braces joined. He was attended by Red Wolf's daughter Wahluna, a shamanic healer. She was singing a magic song that went, 'Healing spirits, healing spirits, see this man, see him.' It was like a lullaby.

From a medicine bag she drew forth herbs which she pounded in a mortar, adding pure lakewater until she had a green paste. This she smeared on Old Strength's broad, ragged wounds. There were two wounds, made with a single thrust of a spear that bared a rib at his side and parted the flesh of the inner muscle of his right arm. Wahluna pressed boiled moss into the paste upon the wounds. Over the curative concoction she bound muskrat hides. Through all her endeavors, Old Strength scarcely winced, though his jaw quivered with the pain.

When Red Wolf entered the tipi, his daughter Wahluna ceased her soft chant. The wounded man tried to sit up, as it was improper to lay in the presence of Red Wolf. Wahluna put her hand on his chest to hold him down. She said, 'If you move, you will not live long.' Red Wolf sat on the ground near the sad-looking warrior. He broke a piece of the tender trout and held it to Old Strength's mouth. At first Old Strength turned his head away, but he turned back with moist eyes and let himself be fed. Wahluna took up her healing lullaby while Old Strength was fed like a baby.

'You are Red Wolf, and should not serve me so,' said Old Strength.

Red Wolf said, 'You served my father, and you have served me. You were like an uncle when I was small. Haven't the Blackfeet killed all your sons? Didn't your wife die of grief? Who are your relatives now? A chief must be every man's father. Wahluna must be every man's mother.'

At this, Old Strength smiled in earnest. Not only was he deeply touched, but he was amused to think of the young princess as an aging warrior's mother. She helped prop him against a rolled fur so he could sit up. She pulled the marmot blanket to his shoulders. Old Strength grew extremely serious. He asked, 'How long, Red Wolf, can we go on? We are slowly being picked off, while more Blackfeet come from their nation into ours. Today we were fortunate. But what will happen tomorrow?'

'Tomorrow?' Red Wolf echoed, and his gaze rose along the little column of smoke until he spotted one star through the opening where the poles joined. 'Today, the warriors are filled with boasts and hold their hands above their heads. Tomorrow, it may be their shoulders will sag with weight of sorrows. You were my father's counselor. Should I pretend in your presence that things are well? Tomorrow? There is only today, Old Strength. And today we are victorious.'

Having said so much, Red Wolf left the tipi of Old Strength. He stood alone by Wallowa Lake, listening dejectedly to chants and drums of Blackfeet on the far shore.

* * *

Wahluna covered Old Strength with the blanket, then looked about until she found a well-worn buffalo robe and laid that on him too. Then she asked the warrior, 'Old Strength, why do the Blackfeet fight us? Why do we fight the Blackfeet?'

Old Strength replied, 'You are too young to understand.'

'I am old enough to be your mother,' she teased.

'Ha! Well then, little mother, you are not a child after all. So I will tell you that not one of us can know the reason why men kill men. Your grandfather, who died when you were little, of the same sickness that carried away your mother, was called Red Wolf like your father. He was a great buffalo hunter. Today we lake people do not go to the place of the buffalo, but when I was young, we went every summer. There were many Blackfeet that came from their place beyond the buffalo grounds. We watched each other killing buffalo, and when they made a mistake, we laughed. When we failed, they made light of us and hooted. Then they stole some of our horses, thinking themselves clever. We stole them back, and some of theirs as well.

'Somehow it came about that every year when we went to hunt buffalo, we went to kill Blackfeet as well. They had the best horses, so we had to be smarter. We found out what route they took to reach the buffalo grounds. One year we went early. From a high point, overlooking a narrow canyon, we were able to kill very many Blackfeet. Among the Chute-pa-lu, however, not one man fell! It is my thought, little mother, that if some of us had died on that day, the Blackfeet would not hate us so much. They have avenged themselves many times since, but they remember that first humiliation, when your grandfather led us home to the mountain country, bringing Blackfoot horses! We built great fires and danced for days and nights. Oh! Those were good days, little mother. I miss those days so much.'

Then Wahluna let Old Strength sleep. She went out to see if she could find her father. But Red Wolf had vanished into the forest to commune with his own heart. Under the starry sky, Wahluna felt alone on the earth. She could hear her people laughing and telling stories. So too she could hear the whooping Blackfeet across the lake. They did not seem entirely real to her. They were ghosts from a bad, bad dream.

She went among the thickly draping willows at the lake's edge. From the willow roots a stream leapt forth into the lake, the rippling music erasing all the other sounds of night. Hidden as she was amidst draping leaves, Wahluna's sad loneliness became a boon of solitude while she watched the moon reflected on the water.

Against the moon she saw a nighthawk dipping and flitting. She thought to herself, 'My soul is with the nighthawk. I am up there dipping and flitting. What is my soul seeking? It seeks happiness and peace. Can you hear me, spirit of Wallowa? Does not the bloodshed hurt you, as it hurts me? I call to you, spirit of the lake! I call to the mother-spirit and the father-spirit. I call to the tree-spirits and the wind-spirits. I pray to all of you, give me strength, give me wisdom. Show me by what means I may stop the killing. No price is too great for me to pay! I would be a slave to the Blackfeet if that would bring peace. I will give my life!'

As she spoke, she saw the waters stirring in the light of moon and stars. Then she spotted an empty skin-canoe at the lake's edge. As she had not seen it a moment before, it seemed to her a thing materialized from a vision. She took the appearance of the canoe to be an invitation to go upon the lake.

Wahluna paddled silently through the darkness. She crossed the lake to the enemy village. She left with such stillness the Nez Perce did not hear her go, nor did the Blackfeet detect her arrival until she was within the circle of a bonfire. At the sight of this beautiful maiden appearing as though from nowhere, celebrant drummers ceased beating their tomtoms. Singers stilled their voices. The only sound was the crackling of the fire as Wahluna approached Bloody Chief who sat crosslegged on a blanket alongside Tlesca, his son, each wearing beautifully woven robes of feathers, quills and fibers, the insignias of their rank.

'I am Wahluna, princess of my tribe, come to speak to a great chief,' she began. 'Many of the young men of my tribe have been slain. I despair for the survival of my people. Today the remnant of our fighters met Blackfoot scouts lurking in our forest. All those scouts were slain. It has made my people joyous, but such joy cannot be sustained, for our women have long sung songs of mourning.

'I hear your followers gasp with anger to learn of our luck in today's battle, though I speak of these things not to boast. Tomorrow, you may seek revenge for eight lives. Perhaps my family and all my people, with all that I have known in this life, will be exterminated once and for all. Yet I have come to you to say, 'Have pity!' for there can be no greatness in slaying old men, women and small children, for this is nearly all that is left of us now. If you will allow me to take to my father your offer of peace, it may be that we can learn to share the bounty of the forest and the lake without so great an enmity.'

Bloody Chief barely considered her words before he answered, 'What cowardly people send a girl to beg? Such a tribe merits death!'

But Tlesca was impressed with the maiden. Though a great warrior of necessity, his spirit was inclined to gentleness. He said, 'Father, open your heart to her words. This maiden bravely loves her people. As for me, I am moved beyond my capacity for speech. Never again will I kill one of her people.'

Having made such a bold statement, he stood from the blanket on which he had been sitting. He removed his cloak of authority as he stepped to Wahluna's side.

Bloody Chief made a growling sound in his throat, for he had often wished for a harsher son. Even so, he greatly loved Tlesca, and could not dismiss his son's words. He said, 'My son, one day you must become a great chief. You cannot rely on kindheartedness to rule. Her people are mere dogs. Come! Put on your robe, for this girl must die.'

Tlesca was insistent. 'We have battled Red Wolf's bravest warriors. Remember how Red Wolf fought, days on end, to save his people? I recall how impressed you were! For many weeks we gave him no opportunity to capture game; we harried him until he was weak from hunger. We even saw him stagger! Even then, when he was at his weakest, who was brave enough to fight him face to face? I alone answered his challenge. He fought like a cougar. With his warclub, he broke my shoulder, which was long in healing.

'How often I think of that day! Many of our warriors fell before Red Wolf as they rushed forth to draw me away when you, my father, commanded me not to try to fight one-handed. Do you say we were routed by a dog, my father? Did my shoulder hurt because I was weaker than a dog?

'No, my father, Red Wolf is a noble warrior, and this maiden who has come before us is noble too. Look! I have taken off my robe of authority to place it about the shoulders of this maiden! See? It suits her well. She looks as powerful as a warrior!'

Bloody Chief closed his eyes and thought. The people gathered near were motionless. Then Bloody Chief raised his eyes and addressed the crowd. 'My son speaks well. I have heard his words. Therefore will I rise and place my robe upon his.'

Wahluna stood straight and tall as Bloody Chief wrapped his robe about her. The two robes were tokens of a promise of peace, to be worn before her father Red Wolf so that he would know for whom she spoke of truce.

As she turned to leave the circle of firelight, no one followed. Prince Tlesca strode away into woods above the lake. Yet when Wahluna arrived at her canoe by the lakeside, there stood Tlesca, who had hurried to skirt the edge of the village, to reach the lake in secret. He wished to see Wahluna off without detection. He said, 'Wahluna, truly my heart is made lighter in your presence.'

She replied, 'I, too, was moved by your manly beauty and the fairness of your speech. But you must not hope the two of us will become as one. If my father suspected my love for a Blackfoot prince, he would rise up and fight to the death. If your father thought you loved a Chute-pa-lu princess, he would exterminate my people rather than give his blessing to such a union. You must turn your heart toward a Blackfoot maiden. As for me, I have sworn my life to the spirit of Wallowa Lake in exchange for a prosperous peace for our peoples.'

'Blackfoot girls are beautiful and many have expressed their love for Tlesca,' he admitted. 'Even so, my heart seeks none but Wahluna.'

She said, 'What you desire cannot be.'

'It may be that we must keep our feelings to ourselves,' he said, taking her by the arm for fear that she would leave too soon. 'But Wahluna, listen. We can meet secretly in our canoes on dark nights in the middle of the lake. No one will suspect. When I wish to see you, you will hear me make the sound of a coyote. When you wish to see me, call to me in the voice of the owl. By these signals we will come together and speak.'

'I cannot promise such a thing,' she said, though already she knew she would lay awake nights listening for the coyote call. Then, warm in the cloaks of chief and prince, she knelt into her canoe and paddled to her village.

* * *

The successful peace-talks which ensued were greatly facilitated by Wahluna's previously unsuspected skill as a mediator. Many meetings were required. Many bad feelings were mollified. For six moons, as the truce held, Red Wolf and Bloody Chief met in neutral places in the mountains, bringing with them none but Wahluna and Tlesca, whose natures were more giving than their hardened fathers.

Many times she despaired, fearing these two men would never acknowledge how each saw greatness in the other. Many nights she lay awake thinking she was failing at mediation, and the soothing speeches of Tlesca were failing also. So too it was painful to see the youth she secretly loved, under conditions which demanded that neither give evidence of the affection which intensified daily.

One evening as she lay worrying in her tipi, she heard a coyote singing. At first she did not heed the call, for it sounded like a true coyote. When it called again, she thought it sounded as though it were in the middle of the lake. Only then did she rise swiftly to slip to the lakeside where she called out like an owl. She knelt in her canoe which lay hidden in shallows amidst overhanging willows.

She paddled toward the center of the lake and stopped alongside Tlesca. They reached their hands to one another to pull the canoes closer, and Tlesca said, 'I am in an agony of lonely sorrow. I see you only in the presence of our fathers. When can we tell our peoples of our love?'

Wahluna, too, was steeped in melancholy. She said, 'I have sworn myself to the spirit of the lake. I offered everything to this spirit, even my life, in exchange for peace between our tribes. For six moons there has been no arrow exchanged by Blackfeet and Nez Perce. By this I know the spirit has heeded my prayer. Were I to accept all that is in your heart, the lake would only take it from me, for all that I receive belongs to the spirit of the Wallowa.'

'If it is so,' said Tlesca, 'then what good is my life? My heart is yours even now. I will fight this spirit!'

'You must not say so!' exclaimed Wahluna.

The water had become agitated. As they gazed at the dark surface, a slowly funneling maelstrom encircled them and caused their canoes to turn around and around. Tlesca gaped in amazement. Wahluna said, not to Tlesca but to the spirit of the lake, 'Do not grow angry, O Spirit of Wallowa!'

At her plea, the water grew still, and Tlesca said softly, 'If the power of this lake possesses all that is yours, then this power possesses me. I will not fight it, but will share in your destiny.'

* * *

When the most difficult matters of the truce were settled, joy at last arose among the Nez Perce. One morning a great many children, women and men old and young arrived from the Blackfoot village singing songs of friendship. The men brought fresh-killed dear and bear hunted in the mountains. The women bore fish trapped in streams.

Throughout the festivities, Wahluna and Tlesca exchanged meaningful glances whenever they thought no one could see them flirting. Wahluna and other Nez Perce women assisted the Blackfoot wives and daughters in preparing the great feast. It seemed to her that a real affection had developed between the tribes. She began to allow herself to hope her fondness for the Blackfoot prince might after all be revealed without reawakening anger.

As the afternoon progressed into evening, Wahluna became bolder when casting glances at Tlesca, thus several Nez Perce girls noticed. They began to whisper, 'There is something going on between Wahluna and that beautiful young Blackfoot.'

The gossip spread throughout the village. Soon all the Nez Perce women were considering the possibilities. Some were joyful at the thought; a few were jealous, for they had been trying to catch a glance from the prince without success. Not everyone agreed such a match would be a good idea, for the friendship between the two peoples was as yet very new and untested. There remained many suspicions and ill-healed wounds of grief because of sons lost in battles.

Divided opinions fueled the rumors, which soon spread to the Blackfoot women as well.

In evening's dusk, when half the people were done feasting, several women began gambling with engraved beaver teeth, tossing like dice. A Blackfoot woman, tall and handsome, won a Nez Perce woman's woven conical hat. Sorry to have wagered the hat, the stout Nez Perce woman said, 'Take these moccasins instead, for I love that hat.'

The tall woman answered, 'Your moccasins are worn thin; I'll keep this.'

They argued back and forth until the Nez Perce woman leapt at the Blackfoot and knocked her to the ground. They rolled in the dust while the other gambling women broke into opposing camps to cheer and encourage their champion. Blackfeet cheered the tall woman; Nez Perce cheered the woman who was stout.

Into this fracas Tlesca strode in order to separate the women. The hat was damaged during their wrestling match. The woman who had won the hat spat on the ground and said, 'You think your princess is worthy of our prince? They will never marry!'

The Nez Perce woman shot back, 'Who says she wants to marry him? As our young men have become bones for wolves to gnaw, so should this haughty chief's son be killed and left to rot in the forest!'

They tried to get at each other again, but Tlesca held them apart, alarmed though he was by what they were saying.

Bloody Chief and Red Wolf had all this while been smoking the pipe together. The women's quarrel was on everyone's tongue except for these two chiefs, who knew not what to say.

After a long silence between them, Bloody Chief finally spoke. 'My son's heart reaches for your daughter. He is a great warrior and will rule after me. Your Wahluna has proven herself a great mediator. Who else is their equal? Perhaps we should not stand in their way.'

Red Wolf and his people had suffered so long at the hands of the Blackfoot warriors, it was painful to accept such a marriage. Yet Red Wolf was a wise man and came to a sensible conclusion. He said, 'Yes, I too have heard of their secret meetings. I confess I turned my face and hoped it was not so. Yet now, if in truth Wahluna's heart reaches out to Tlesca, she may go with him to his lodge.'

* * *

In days that followed, Red Wolf sent runners to announce the wedding to friends among the Cayuse, Wenatchees and Yakamas. A three-day wedding feast was planned. People came into the Nez Perce village from far and near, for the joining of two famous families who were formerly rivals was a great thing and deserved to be attended by many.

The Blackfoot village was empty of all but a few dogs and ponies, for all had left to participate in the extravagant affair with the Nez Perce. At sunset on the first day of the feast, the newly joined couple set out in a canoe to head for Tlesca's lodge across the lake, where they could be alone. People stood on the shore and the hillside watching the beautiful couple paddling across Wallowa Lake, with the high mountains forming a dark backdrop against a fading sky of red dusk.

Halfway across the lake, the lake's calm was disrupted. At first there were only mild ripples upon the water, which caused their boat to wobble. But the ripples rose into a roil so that the canoe was greatly endangered. Tlesca dropped the paddle and clung to Wahluna. They spoke to one another earnestly and did not look frightened. The tumultuous waters rose in waves, spinning the little skin canoe around and around.

Old Strength, the aged warrior, shoved one of the largest canoes into the lake, intending to assist the couple who were caught in the inexplicable maelstrom. Red Wolf leapt into the big canoe with Old Strength. Others followed close behind, Nez Perce and Blackfeet, including Bloody Chief. All were eager to save Wahluna and Tlesca before their vessel was swamped and carried under.

As the would-be helpers neared, Wahluna cried out, 'Old Strength! Father! Come no nearer!'

Tlesca called, 'Father, hold back!'

The tiny fleet of canoes halted. The little skin canoe continued to turn around and around as Wahluna called out in calm resignation, 'This is what I promised the spirit of the lake in exchange for peace between our tribes!'

Tlesca added, 'With open eyes, I have sworn to share Wahluna's fate! Live in peace, my father and my father-in-law! Do not fight again! Do not grieve too long for us!'

The waters abruptly parted, revealing a monstrous creature. Its furred neck rose higher and higher. Its head was like the head of a gigantic pony, with the down-turned horns of a buffalo. It swept its gaze from side to side, watching the fleet of canoes as hollering Nez Perce and Blackfeet paddled madly for their respective shores. Then the creature raised its long, heavy tail from out of the water and thrashed it downwards, hard upon the tiny canoe, cutting it in half.

Wahluna and Tlesca continued to cling tightly to one another as they were thrown into the water. Even now they conveyed no fear of dying; they offered no useless struggle. They closed their eyes, placed their faces each upon the shoulder of the other, and the quickening maelstrom sucked them down and down forever.

The dragon dove after them into the funnel of water. Afterward, all grew still beneath night's canopy of stars. Only a few small bubbles broke the surface of the lake, to mark the passing of beast and lovers.

* * *

At dawn, when it was certain the lovers were truly lost, there arose among Nez Perce women a continuous lamentation lasting many days. Their grief inspired many new songs of sorrow. Some sang that Wahluna had been taken from them because she had wrongly loved the enemy, while others sang in guilty sadness how all were punished for feeling critical of the marriage as their small hearts continued to despise Blackfeet.

Bloody Chief believed he had lost his son because his people tried to conquer the Nez Perce in order to take possession of their lake and forest. The monster had come to punish the Blackfeet for their greed. Feeling nothing beyond self-blame and sorrow, Bloody Chief led his people away from the accursed lake which had stolen his son.

The Blackfeet left Wallowa afoot and on horseback. Their heads hung low; they moaned with grievous sorrow. Along the way, they stopped but once, at a crossroad where Red Wolf and Old Strength stood waiting to bid last farewells.

Although neither chief could find words, they spoke deeply through the tragedy reflected in their eyes. Red Wolf stepped forth to the side of Bloody Chief's pony and tried to return to him the pair of robes that had been given to Wahluna by Tlesca and Bloody Chief. But the Blackfoot chief would not take them. Red Wolf had thought this might occur and so handed the robes to Old Strength. Then he removed from the strap at his side the famous warclub inlaid with wolf teeth. This he gave to Bloody Chief as a parting gift. Only then did the long line of Blackfeet continue on their way to their country beyond the Shining Mountain, returning nevermore to the Land of Many Waters.

PART VI:

LOVE, REVENGE AND SELF-SACRIFICE

EAST OF THE SUN AND WEST OF THE MOON

William Morris

East of the sun, west of the moon!

All day long Gregory's fishing boat had been flitting hither and thither upon the broad Norwegian firth, so belike it was the memory of that long day's cruise that led him at night-time to dream of a country whose direction was so quaint and puzzling. And as the dream lingered in his mind next morning, and pleased him, idle though it was, he took pains to turn it into verses, which many a generation has listened to within the halls and cottages of Norway.

Here is the story which came to him in his dreams.

A well-to-do husbandman in a certain part of Norway farmed his own land with the help of his two elder sons. He had a third son, but this John, although a tall, strong lad, was of little use upon the farm. Many an hour he trifled away at the fireside in winter, and still more in the woods and orchard when summer came round. Whatever he might make of his handsome face, his dreamy wits, the store of old rhymes and such other scraps of learning as were his, he would never prove a good farmer, said his father. 'Let John go his own ways,' the goodman would exclaim; 'he is not worth training on my fields!'

One summer morning the farmer went to look at a meadow where he expected his rich crop of hay would soon be ready for the scythe, but, alas! a melancholy sight met his eyes when he looked across the wattled fence – a great patch of the meadow grass was trampled down, so that no mower could possibly pass his scythe through the tangle.

The farmer came home with a frown on his brow. 'Thorolf,'

he cried to his eldest son, 'tonight you must take your crossbow, and lie in watch amongst the hawthorns that skirt the south meadow. Someone has come by night and beaten down the ripening grass; whether it be an enemy of ours – who would have thought we had any! – or a mischievous vagrant, he shall be well punished if he plant foot within the meadow a second time!'

So Thorolf went out after supper to keep watch over the meadow, but what with his hard day's work, and a very comfortable meal at the close of it, he was not long in falling into a doze, and from that he passed into a deep sleep that lasted well into the morning. When he arose from his bed of wood-sorrel he found that the long grass was trodden down in fresh places, and he was obliged to go home and own, to his father's chagrin, that matters were now worse than ever.

The next evening Thord, the second son, was sent in place of Thorolf, but when he returned to confess with downcast face that he had done no better than his elder brother, and that by this time there was only one corner of the meadow left untrodden, the farmer altogether lost his temper, and rated them both soundly, calling them good-for-nothing, slothful young fellows.

Hearing his brothers called names that were generally bestowed upon him alone, John, who was strolling past the group, stopped, and stretching himself lazily: 'I am truly sorry you have not done your work better, my brothers,' he said, with a pretence at reproach in his voice, 'for now our good father will insist upon sending me out to take a turn at night watching. Well, well, father, you need vex no more; by this time tomorrow I shall have found out where the mischief comes from.'

'You!' cried his father indignantly. 'Do you think you can succeed where Thorolf and Thord have both failed? If you find out the offender it will be the first time in your life, my boy, that you have shown yourself worth your keep. Go and try the post tonight, by all means, but I cannot say that I expect to learn more from you than from my other brave watchers.'

Quite unmoved by his father's scoff, John went calmly on his way. He spent the day in sleep – a wise enough preparation for night work – and when the time came for him to go on watch, he went down to the meadow without bow or knife in his hand. 'If I have to deal with a rough set of men, they would soon make an end of me should I draw bow upon them,' thought he, 'and still less use have I for weapons, if the trespassers prove, as methinks they will, to be gentle fairy-folk.'

Amongst the hawthorn bushes he found a hiding-place close to the untrodden part of the hayfield. Hour after hour passed, and yet no visitant, either of earth or fairy-land, set foot upon the meadow. The dawn broke, a light breeze stirred the long grass, and one by one the birds in the wood began to twitter shyly. Up to this time John had kept wide awake, but now drowsiness would have overpowered him had he not heard a strange, rushing sound of wings overhead, and, parting the boughs that screened his face, he watched breathlessly to see what manner of bird might alight. Slowly seven white swans came circling towards the meadow, and dropped on the dewy grass only a stone's cast from where he lay crouching beneath the hawthorn. He was ready to raise a shout, and frighten them from the place, if need be; but so long as they did no harm to his father's crops, he took pleasure in watching them close beside him, bridling, and preening their snow-white feathers.

Satisfied that they were moving about on the edge of the field where there was nothing to spoil, he closed his eyes for a few moments. A sudden hush made him start, and he glanced round to see if the stately birds were still before him. No, they were not; but on the grass stood seven maidens, as fresh and lovely as the white feathers that they had cast down at their feet! One of them was standing with her face turned away from the hawthorn brake, so that John saw but the ripples of her golden hair, over which the morning breeze was playing lightly; yet as he hearkened to the sweet notes of her voice, his heart beat wildly, and he cried to himself that she was the fairest of the fays, and the queen of his heart now and for ever! And when at length she turned, and he eagerly scanned her features, one glance told him that he had judged aright by her voice, for indeed the sweetness of her face passed all imagining.

A while the seven sisters stood murmuring softly to one another, glad, it seemed, to indulge in talk when they regained their voices along with their human form; then, as if to enjoy all that they might, before they again put on their feathery dress, they danced lightly and merrily over the long, dewy grass, and laughed for joy as they frolicked carelessly in the farmer's dearly prized meadow. Not for worlds would the watcher amongst the hawthorns have disturbed them. Every smile, every word, and every movement of the swan-maiden whom he had singled out for his love, made his heart thrill with happiness. But ah! what would he do when she flew away with her sisters, and he was left to mourn, perchance never to see her again? The swan-skin which she had cast aside, lay within his reach. If he hid it from her, at least she would have to speak a word to him before she could recover it and soar away, thought he, and, yielding to the impulse, he stretched out his hand stealthily, and drew the skin into his nest beneath the thorn-trees.

The sun, that had shot its first level beams across the meadow when the maidens started upon their dance, now rising high in the heavens, warned them that it was no longer safe to linger where men might soon be passing to their day's work. In a long line they tripped back, one after another, and slipped on their snow-white swan-skins; but when she upon whom John's eyes were bent, came to look for hers, a sharp cry of distress rang from her lips – the downy wrap was not to be found! In vain she searched for it, in vain her sisters flitted through the tangled grass, looking for what lay hidden securely in John's keeping beneath the hawthorn boughs. Every minute the sun beat more strongly upon wood and field, a stern reminder to the swan-maidens that fate forbade them to remain longer upon earth. The six fair white birds clustered around their poor sister, striving without avail to comfort her, and she, softly stroking their plumes with one hand in silent farewell, hid her tearful eyes with the other as they unwillingly prepared to take their flight. So long as they were with her, she tried to conceal her anguish, but when she heard them rise on the wing and soar away far above the meadow, her grief broke out wildly; her whole body was shaken with sobs, and the tears splashed down on the grass through the slim fingers that hid her face.

A sound of footsteps amongst rustling twigs startled her even in the midst of her distress, and in fear of being seen by mortal eyes, she fled across the trampled ground, and cowered low down in the beaten grass, like a wounded bird that lies in terror of its destroyer. The eyes that met hers, however, were not such as could inspire fear; they were almost as startled and timid as her own. Moved by her grief, John had come to own, in shame, that he had stolen the swan-skin; and though at first the maiden had trembled at his coming, she saw now that he was looking tenderly upon her, and she divined that it was love for her, and a longing to keep her beside him, that had prompted his theft. 'Ah! do you think,' she cried passionately, 'that because you have been cruel enough to hide my swan-skin, and keep me bound to earth, I can love you and live happily amongst mortal men?' Wisely she worked upon his feelings, begging him, since he did not wish to do her harm, to win her grateful thanks by letting her fly away safely. 'You make it too hard for me to set you free, maiden,' he answered; 'every word from your lips, every glance from your bright eyes so enthralls me that I cannot bear to let you go.'

'Alas!' she sobbed, 'what can I do? I would fain listen to your love, but I must not dwell with mortals upon earth; it would be death alike to you and to me if you kept me beside you any longer. Will you not come with me, and share our life in our far-distant country? Nay, nay; it would be too much to ask you to leave your home and your kinsfolk for my sake. Let me bid you farewell, then; be wise, and yield to fate; let me soar away in my swan-skin, and do you turn back and dwell contentedly in your own land, knowing that you have won my heart by your gentleness, your pity, and your love.'

'Nay,' said he eagerly; 'I will not let you go alone. Take me with you, I pray, and let me live for ever in your far country, for worthless would I count my life on earth if I should never look again on your dear face.'

So the swan-maiden, though she doubted the wisdom of his choice, suffered him to lead her to the shade of a neighbouring beech-wood, where, taking from him her white swan-skin, she made ready for their strange journey. First, she set a gold ring with a dark green stone upon his finger as a seal to their love; then, bidding him lie down on the withered leaves beneath a beech-tree, she laid a spell upon him, and immediately his eyes grew dim, and sleep stole over his senses.

A long, long time passed until at length his eyes opened upon a new world. His love stood beside him in a beautiful land, whose sunshine and flowers were as unmatched by what he had hitherto known, as was the girlish beauty of her upon whom the pink blossoms were now falling from the trees. 'My land and yours!' she cried, following his bewildered gaze with a smile.

'You look too grave, sweetheart; does it not please you well?' But the only reason why the earth-born stranger looked so grave was that he was striving to recall something of the gloom and trouble that overshadowed mortal life, so that he might the better gauge the joy of his new home, where all was unclouded peacefulness and bliss.

Three harvests had been gathered in his father's fields when John began to think wistfully of the life that had once been his in Norway. It was not that he was dissatisfied with the fairyland in which he dwelt, or that his love was growing cold towards the lady of his heart, but more and more he yearned to share again his brothers' lot and to see how things sped with them. He fancied that he showed no sign of uneasiness, however, so the swan-maiden's question surprised him when one morning she asked: 'What burden lies heavy upon your spirit? Do you fear that I have hid from you the knowledge of coming trouble, and that our careless, happy years are soon to have an end? Yes; you are right. I have said nothing of what I foresaw, because so long as we could close our eyes to it, there was no call to disturb our peaceful days, but now, alas! our parting is at hand.'

John turned to her anxiously. 'Parting?' said he. 'Why should we part?'

Then the swan-maiden told him that fate willed he should return to his own country for a time, and that their future happiness depended solely upon whether he could keep the commands that must be laid upon him whilst he revisited his old home. 'Let not a sigh for me escape your lips,' she warned him solemnly, 'for were you to call on me, I would have to appear beside you upon earth, and ill would it be for both of us if I were seen of mortals. Yet though you must not ask me to join you, I have power to call you back, should I need you sorely. Every evening you shall go to the meadow where you first saw me, wait there an hour, and if I would recall you, I will send a sign. Rest contented, nor strive to return until you are bidden of me, and above all, sweetheart, let no one know the story of our love.' Then, telling him that he must not delay his departure, she led him to the spot where he had first awakened in her fairyland, and, bending over him with sad and tender farewell, she soon sang him to sleep beneath a mystic spell. He knew that he was being wafted farther and farther away from her, for her sweet voice, half choked with sobs, grew fainter each moment, and before his eyes there flitted a countless number of forms, unlike what he had ever seen either on earth or in fairyland – birds of gorgeous plumage, giant trees that seemed like overgrown ferns, dim-eyed beasts, and unthought-of creatures that aped mankind. By and by he became unconscious, as on his former journey, and when he awakened he was lying in a thick wood, where he had spent many an hour bird-nesting in his boyhood. He was again in Norway!

How well he remembered every step that he took towards his father's house! When he reached open ground he saw the farm-roofs, studded with bright house-leeks, rising above a distant clump of trees, and at the same time he heard the horn summoning the field workers to dinner – a summons which they were not slow to answer, for every one was at table when John, a few minutes later, came up to the porch, his footsteps unnoticed amid the general clatter of tongues and dishes. He listened anxiously until he caught the sound of his father's voice, for he had feared that by this time the old man might be dead; but now, reassured by the cheerfulness that reigned in the homestead, he stepped forward briskly, took the horn from its peg beside the door, and wound it, as a stranger might, to announce his arrival.

The honest farm-folk stared in amazement when they saw upon the threshold a stranger whose dress was a mass of gold from head to foot. No one recognised John; even his father thought he was a nobleman, and, rising up, he courteously invited him to rest in the hall and share their simple meal, if he were so inclined.

John thanked him, and, feeling that it was not a fit time at which to declare himself, he answered that he would be glad to rest with them a while, for he was a stranger in those parts, and, having had the mishap to lose his horse that morning, he had been forced to walk till he was footsore. Satisfied with the explanation, the goodman gave him a place at the head of the table, and treated him with the utmost honour; but his mother, on the other hand, was less convinced by his story, and watched him narrowly, wondering why he should so strongly remind her of her youngest boy, whom, in spite of his waywardness, she had loved most tenderly, and whose sudden disappearance had caused her untold suffering.

Meanwhile John had been taking note of all who were at table. Father and mother, his two brothers Thorolf and Thord, and most of the old servants were still there. A few new faces there were, one of which he looked at with interest – by his younger brother's side sat a handsome woman, whom he rightly guessed to be Thord's bride. For one glance that John gave this Thorgerd, she shyly returned two, for she was much charmed by the good looks and the pleasant manners of the stranger.

When dinner was over the men returned to their work in the fields; but before they left, the master of the house begged his guest to rest in the farmhouse as long as he pleased, and John answered that he would be glad to stay a while. The women were sent to their tasks by their mistress, who gave her orders to her young daughter-in-law, Thorgerd, amongst the others. Unwillingly Thorgerd rose from the table, and, throwing a last glance towards John, left him and his mother alone in the hall. But not yet did the goodwife dare to ask this handsomely dressed stranger the question that was trembling on her lips. If he really were her son he would soon show it, she believed; and instead of leading him to talk, she slipped out of the hall, and prepared to test him by a simple little device. She sent a maid to throw down an armful of clothes on the settle close to which the stranger was resting, and the maid having done so, John was again left alone in the hall. His eyes fell upon the bundle of clothes beside him, and he immediately recognised them to be a masquerader's quaint cloak and hood which he had worn four years ago at a Yule-tide gathering.

The whole scene came back to him: the snowy ground, the figures around him, and the song that they sang that evening:

> News of a fair and a marvellous thing,
> *The snow in the street and the wind on the door.*
> Nowell, nowell, nowell we sing!
> *Minstrels and maids, stand forth on the floor.*

He rose dreamily, threw off his gold-embroidered coat, and, wrapping himself in the spangled finery, he paced the floor singing verse after verse of the old carol. His mother stole back to the hall, and saw what she had expected – her own boy, recalled by the memories of a past night, breaking into songs of the countryside, and hugging the quaint cloak about him as he wandered up and down the room in his dreamy fashion as of old.

He ran towards her as he caught sight of her loving eyes fixed upon him. 'Mother,' he cried, looking into the wistful face, and kissing her fondly, as he had done when he was but a boy, 'mother, your ne'er-do-well has come back, and glad am I that I may yet be a joy to you. I have come to see you but for a time, for my new home is far distant, and ere long I must return to it. But if I give you news of how I have fared these three years, tell me in return all that has come to pass amongst you in that time.'

So mother and son sat and talked hand-in-hand until the others came in at nightfall, when John rose, and told them that he was indeed the lad who had disappeared three summers ago. Mindful of the warning given him by the swan-maiden, he told no one, not even his old mother, the true story of his fairy love, but spoke of how he had met people from a far country the morning that he had been on watch beside the south meadow, and how they had taken him with them, and, settling in their midst, he had fared surpassingly well, and was now wedded to a lovely princess.

There was great rejoicing amongst the simple folk when they learned that the handsome stranger was the idle young dreamer whose chances of fortune had seemed so slender in the past. His elder brothers welcomed him without the least touch of jealousy; while the goodman, for the first time in his life, felt proud of his youngest son, and his only regret was that John would have to quit Norway again, when the seamen who had brought him on this visit should return to take him back to his new home.

And now John had got his desire. He was free to enjoy life on his father's farm as of old; but just as he had wearied for the pleasure of that rough life when he was shut off from it in the swan-maiden's country, so now that he was again upon earth, what would he not have given to see his love at his side? He began to grieve sadly, and the people in the homestead noticed that he came home more unhappy each evening from his solitary walk to the south meadow. They would fain have discovered why he took his nightly walk alone; but he did not encourage them to talk about his affairs, and, saving Thorgerd, no one ventured to question him. His sister-in-law, however, had fallen hopelessly in love with him, and she did everything in her power to win his heart and learn the secrets that lay buried there. She would slip out to join him on his way back from the meadow at nights, when he, love-lorn and despairing, sometimes wondered if he might not tell the story of his woe to this soft-eyed friend who was so anxious to listen to his talk and try to comfort him.

It was only by remembering how earnestly the swan-maiden had entreated him to keep the secret of her love from mortal ears, that he withstood his longing to unburden himself to Thorgerd. And yet, although he never willingly revealed the reason of his sadness, there came at length a night when rash words escaped him, and brought grievous trouble upon him and his beloved.

On Christmas Eve the snow lay thick upon the ground, and heavy grey clouds were resting on the hillsides, to be ever and again swept along by a bitingly cold wind that howled around the old farmhouse as John set out on his customary evening walk to the meadow. The chill and dreary look of the country was in keeping with his sense of misery, and in a sudden fit of despair he cried aloud when he reached the spot where he had first seen the swan-maiden: 'Come to me, sweetheart! I cannot live without you. Come to me now!'

Would a fair white swan float down towards him from that cold, wind-swept mass of clouds? No; no answer came either by sight or sound. A long time he waited breathlessly, trembling at his rashness in having called his beloved; but the sky grew darker and darker, night closed in, and at last he realised that it was useless to wait longer. Bitterly reproaching his love for having deceived him in saying that she would come at a sigh from him, he turned, and strode homeward. A slender woman wrapped in a grey cloak stood waiting him as he entered the courtyard; here, surely, was his swan-maiden! Not a word could he cry, for joy and surprise overmastered him. He saw her glide up to him, and felt her soft, warm hand slipped into his. Then he stammered,

'Oh, sweetheart, I have done no wrong, have I? I called on you because I could no longer endure life without you.'

A gentle voice answered that in her eyes he could do no wrong, and that to know he loved her was the one desire of her heart. But when he recognised the speaker, John dropped her hand quickly, for it was not his swan-maiden, but Thorgerd, who had come to meet him. Forgetting that there was a listener beside him, he cried recklessly 'O my beloved, do you care for me no longer? Have I been indeed deceived? Yet think not that my love can fail like yours; while life lasts, never shall I cease to mourn for you!'

Thorgerd did not interrupt him. Silently she walked beside him across the snowy courtyard to the hall-door, then, stopping abruptly, she asked him in a smothered voice who it was that he had hoped to see that night – was it not she herself? She had loosened her grey cloak, and the light from the open door sparkled upon her golden hair and on the rich, embroidered robe which she wore in honour of the Christmas feast. A more beautiful woman could hardly have been found in all Norway; but John had not a thought to give her, and cared not though his words pained her deeply. He answered that the lady-love whom he longed to see was afar off. 'Ah, if she would but cross this threshold tonight!' he sighed despairingly; and as Thorgerd heard him, she turned away sullenly, knowing that there would never be a place for her in his heart, and wild with shame and anger that she had vainly betrayed to him the secret of her love.

The great Yule-tide feast was being celebrated in the hall, and everyone belonging to the homestead was there, John and Thorgerd among the rest; she, trying to bury her chagrin in forced merriment, he, weary at heart, still thinking of his lost love. It was late in the evening before he could rouse himself to join in the revelry around the table; but at length he made the effort to bear his part, and, rising to his feet, he was about to call some well-known toast, when a horn rang out clear, though far away across the fields, and at the sound of the blast the words died upon his lips. Again the horn was wound, this time louder than before, and John grew pale and trembled at the thought of what it might betoken. When for the third time the blast was heard, now close at hand, he could neither speak nor move, and the other men snatched up their weapons, not knowing what enemy might be upon them at that late hour; another minute, and the arms were dropped, for the door opened, and upon the threshold stood a gentle lady in robes white as the snow that lay about her feet – John's true love had come to him!

'Joy and peace to the house,' she said in her pretty, birdlike voice, looking round the smoky hall with a bright inquiring glance. 'I have come to join my loved one. Will you give me your welcome, John?'

How timidly, and yet with what rapture, did John come forward to whisper his joy at seeing her; how proudly he led her before his father and the others, telling them that for his sake his bride had come a far journey to his home! If anyone had been inclined to doubt the story of John's fortunes, there was none now but believed it every whit, when they saw his mate, whom no princess in their country could equal in sweetness and beauty. The evening that had begun so gloomily for John, had now become a season of bewildering joy, and he watched with delight how his beloved won the hearts of all at table. She spoke gently and lovingly to the goodman and his wife, wishing them many long years of happiness together; she joined in the mirth around her, and when a shade of doubt and anxiety crossed John's face, she smiled upon him gaily, as if to assure him that he must not regret the rash words which brought her to his world.

'Let us be glad together for at least one night,' she whispered; and so, in spite of secret misgivings, he smiled back to her, and gave himself up to the enjoyment of her sweet presence.

Hours after, when the banquet was over and the house wrapped in slumber, a poor, heart-broken little swan-maiden arose, and bent tearfully over John, who was lying fast asleep. 'Farewell, dearest,' she sobbed as she drew the gold ring off his finger. 'Alas that we should have to part! Yet so it must be, because in your impatience you called me to appear amongst mortals. How mournful henceforth will your life be, and oh! how desolate mine, when I go to dwell in that land far beyond the world's end, *east of the sun and west of the moon*! Ah! love, would that these words might reach you in your sleep, and sink deep into your memory, so that you might afterwards arise and seek me in that home of hapless lovers, whither no one has yet journeyed of his own will!'

Then she turned, and stole softly downstairs to the deserted hall, and out into the white world of snow on which the moon was pouring its silver light. But where her path led, no one might ever know, for when John discovered his loss in the morning, and ran out, wild with grief, to try and trace her steps, he found that the snow had fallen afresh, and not a print remained to tell of her passing.

In speechless anguish, he fled from his old home before any of the household was astir, and all day he wandered aimlessly through the countryside until at nightfall he reached a small seaport. He had but one thought, and that was to roam the wide world, so long as life lasted, in search of his beloved. But where was he to turn his steps? He was haunted by the memory of a phrase – part of a forgotten dream, he fancied – which told of a dreary land where the love-lorn dwell, far removed from earth's joys; but, try as he might, he could not recall the exact words which might help him upon his well-nigh hopeless quest.

Having determined to seek his lost one overseas, he had to wait many weeks at the little seaport until the wintry weather gave place to a mild springtide, when the sailing boats could safely leave the harbour. At length, one fair March evening, he went on board the first ship that was southward bound that season, and although he had nothing to guide him in his wanderings, he felt it a comfort at least to be moving onward to a new country. His dreams that night were of travels, untried and perilous, yet full of promise, and when he awakened in time to see the sun rise while the moon was still shining faintly, the words that had haunted his memory since that sad Christmas night suddenly flashed upon him, and he cried; '*East of the sun and west of the moon!* That is the land where I shall find my swan-maiden. But oh! my sweetheart, how am I to reach you there?'

He looked up gratefully at sun and moon, which together had reached the phrase that henceforth was go guide his steps, and little else he thought of, for the rest of his voyage; but how he could journey to that unknown abode of the love-lorn. When his ship reached the shores of England he disembarked at the easterly port of Dunwich, and since he could expect no news of foreign lands in the quiet country villages around, he turned his steps towards London, where he might hear talk amongst the seamen on the wharfs about strange journeys – perchance of what lay beyond the world's end.

Sometimes when he stopped for the night at a hostle or abbey, he would relate this own sad love-story (always pretending, however, that it was the tale of another man), in the hope that some listener might rise to tell something more about that land of exiled lovers. But though his audience heard him with deep interest, and told him that no minstrel could have given them a merrier tale, yet never a man had a word to add about the country of which the poor wanderer was fain to hear. In time he reached London, and went down to the riverside, where he mixed with all sorts of travellers and heard indeed of many a curious voyage; but to that land east of the sun and west of the moon no one seemed ever to have journeyed, or at least no one had ever returned from its shores. Then he resolved that he would begin travelling himself, and form that time onward he sailed from one quarter of the globe to another, till many years had been spent in fruitless search that brought him no nearer to his heart's desire.

Once he returned to his father's house in Norway, but when he learned that his mother was dead, the ties which bound him to his kinsmen were severed; and after he had seen his father and brothers, strong and hearty as ever, and Thorgerd no less beautiful, he bade them farewell hastily, for the place reminded him too sadly of his swan-maiden, and scarcely could he restrain himself from falling down in a passion of tears to kiss the threshold on which her slender white feet had rested that fateful Christmas night.

Reckless of dangers, he continued to roam through many countries until he found himself in an Eastern land in the company of certain traders who were preparing for a cruise to far-distant shores, where they expected to find great abundance of gold and precious stones. At his request they took him aboard, and presently they set out upon their voyage with every prospect of success.

Time passed, however, and the land which the sailors expected to have sighted was nowhere visible; day after day they sailed on, and still nothing but sea and sky met their gaze; then seamen and merchants grew alike disquieted, while, strange to say, John felt calmer and more hopeful than his wont.

Standing one evening by the prow, he gazed at the setting sun with hopes so bright that he was almost afraid to harbour them in his heart. While the sun dropped upon the western horizon he saw the sickle of the new moon shining aloft; and at the sight of sun and moon he pondered on the course he wished to keep – east of the sun, west of the moon, and something seemed to whisper to him that this evening he was approaching his long journey's end. He cared not that the sailors were anxiously watching a heavy bank of grey clouds that lay upon the water's edge in the east; the threatening storm had no terrors for him, and at night-time he lay down and slept, while the others, open-eyed, and shuddering at the great waves that rose like mountains above the ship's side, crouched together in fear of instant death. The night grew darker and darker, and the sea tossed the frail timber-built vessel, as though it were made of paper, now to the crest of a huge billow and again down into a trough at the very roots of the waves. And still John slept, until a great wave swept over the deck and hurled him against the mast, around which he had the presence of mind to fling both arms, so that he escaped being washed overboard. Whether others, like himself, were still clinging to the wreck, he could not see, but it was soon plain that all were alike doomed, for the ship was rapidly filling with water. On and on he was swept through the billows, while through his mind rushed crowded memories of his loved swan-maiden; and horror of the shipwreck and the raging black sea was lost in strangely peaceful dreams of her for whose sake he was even then drifting to an untimely end. Then the wrecked vessel reeled beneath a last, violent shock, the waves met with a roar above his head, and John sank down quietly into depths where he felt and knew no more.

But all was not over. The swan-maiden's lover awoke to find himself on a sunny stretch of sand where the green sea rippled gently at his feet, without a trace of the storm that had raged the night before. A strange contentment filled his heart as he thought of all the toils and perils he had safely passed through;

surely, said he, his life would not have been preserved, had he not been destined to see his beloved once again. For a little while he lay at ease, basking in the warm sunshine, and wondering vaguely what country this might be, which had all the charm of earth's fairest places and was yet unlike any land that he had ever visited.

At length he rose, and with a last gaze upon the ocean, which he was dimly conscious he would not cross again, he passed inland over daisied slopes, where never a building of any kind nor a human being was to be seen.

From the sea-level the ground rose first to grassy hills and then to an unbroken line of lofty, rugged mountains, which, having no passes, would have to be scaled by the stranger who wished to make his way to the valley beyond. John stopped to take his first refreshment in this lonely outland, from an apple-tree on whose boughs blossoms and delicious ripe fruit hung side by side, and then he pressed uphill until the sun set, and he was forced to wait till dawn before he gained the heights from which he hoped to look down into the heart of the country. So early indeed was he afoot next day that the sun had but risen when he reached the summit. Looking eagerly inland, he saw beneath him a wonderfully beautiful vale, in which the hand of man had been at work, cultivating fruits and raising pleasant homesteads by the side of the stream that flowed between the low meadows. On the slopes immediately beneath the bare rocky brow of the hill, lay terraced vineyards and rich wheat fields; lower down, there were patches of orchards which skirted the fertile meadows on the level ground. Cottages and trim farmhouses were there in plenty, and as John gazed down upon the valley, which the sun was now flooding with a golden haze, he fancied that the happy folk who dwelt there must be sheltered from all the woes that afflict mortals whose lot is cast in less pleasant places.

From this restful scene his eyes turned to the wan ghost of the moon, which hung low above the hills facing him, and then, feeling the sun waxing warm upon his shoulders, he gave a sudden shout of joy. '*East of the sun and west of the moon*! At last, at last I have reached the land where my loved one is to be found!'

He looked to find a path from the rocky ridge down to the hollow, and, seeing that it was impossible to descend the steep cliffs at the point where he stood, he made his way along the crest of the hill for some little distance, until the valley beneath him, which had at first been but narrow, widened out to a great expanse of sheltered lowland, through which the river swept in a wide bend. Far away upon the curve of the river, gleamed the golden roofs of a castle, and at the sight of it John's heart beat fast, for there, surely, was the abode of the love-lorn! Presently the hillside became less precipitous, and, climbing down the rocks, he reached the grassy slopes, where men were afoot, making ready for their day's work in field and orchard. They were a well-thriven race, comely for the most part, and of honest appearance, but never had John seen such grave faces as they wore. They showed no interest in the stranger; if their sad eyes happened to meet his, they gave him no second glance, and none answered his greeting. On his way to the palace he hailed in turn a woodman, an elderly dame, riding upon a mule, and a young boy, who was walking by her side, but for all the notice that they took of his questions, they might have been dead folk. Indeed, so much did he doubt whether they were living men and women, that when he passed a group of girls filling their jars with water at the palace fountain, he laid his fingers lightly upon the soft hand of a maid to feel if there were any warmth in it. Yes; the blood coursed freely in her veins, but his touch could not rouse her from the indifference in which she, like the others in this enchanted land, seemed to be irretrievably lost.

Through groups of servants, men-at-arms, and gentlefolk, he passed from the court to the hall, where all were streaming in to their early meal without a summons from either bell or horn. He stood aside and watched the dumb figures take their places until only one seat remained empty, and that was the throne in the centre of the dais. Then in his sea-stained, tattered clothes, he strode barefooted, past the handsomely dressed knights and ladies, and seated himself in the chair of honour. Just as no one had questioned his right to enter the palace, so no one showed either displeasure or surprise at his taking his seat upon the throne. The meal was taken in unbroken silence; unasked, the servants brought John all that he could wish; and then, smiling at the absurdity of a poor wanderer like himself having been entertained so royally, he wandered out of the hall before the others, and turned his steps along a cool cloister.

A maid brushed closely past him, walked to the end of the paved way, and disappeared through a door in the wall. The disappointment which John had felt when he saw that his swan-maiden was not amongst the people in the hall, gave place suddenly to overwhelming excitement. The door in front of him led, without doubt, to the women's courts, and there, if anywhere in this enchanted castle, he would find his lost one. With bated breath he hastened to raise the latch, and stepped into a court which was shaded by pink-blossomed trees and cooled by the playing of a fountain in the midst. There in the centre of a busy group of girls, bending silent-tongued over their spinning, sat his dearly loved swan-maiden!

Her face was as joyless as those around her; she had no smile upon her lips, and her eyes were heavy and downcast, but except for her sadly changed expression, her beauty was as exquisite as ever. John's joy unnerved him, and, too faint to move, he stood for a time and feasted his eyes upon that sweet form which for many a long year he had seen only in dreams. When would she raise her face, he wondered; and would her eyes brighten when they fell upon him? With trembling limbs he crossed to where she sat listlessly working at a piece of embroidery. Like all others banished to this land of hopeless love, she was deaf to any sound, and even when his glad, faltering words of greeting were uttered, she did not notice the man who stood before her; only, as if she were troubled by a dream, she gave a little start and clenched her white hands.

'Sweetheart,' he sobbed, 'surely your love has not grown cold? Ah! look into my eyes, I pray you, and behold your true lover, who all these years has found no rest nor happiness without you.' Then he poured into her unheeding ears the story of his love, from the morning when she won his heart in the meadow by his old Norwegian home, on to the late sad years when he had roamed the whole world in his distress. 'Have not we both been sorely punished for my folly and impatience in calling you to join me amongst mortal men?' he pleaded. 'Through all those bitter years I have never ceased to believe that our punishment would one day come to an end, and that I would find you in that country of which you must have whispered when you left me in my sleep that Christmas night. Did you not tell me, sweetheart, that

I must seek you in this strange land, *east of the sun and west of the moon*?'

The potent words had no sooner crossed his lips than his loved one awakened from her languor. She rose to her feet, raised her eyes, and, seeing her devoted lover, with the sweetest of glad cries she sprang forward to welcome him fondly. Words came again to her lips, joy took possession of her soul, and she became, as of old, a light-hearted swan-maiden, radiant with love and happiness.

But it was not to his beloved alone that John brought deliverance. The spell that bound all the dwellers in that country of lost loves was broken, once for all, when the name of the land, *east of the sun and west of the moon*, was uttered by one whose devotion had led him, through countless toils and perils, to win back his sweetheart from that silent, gloomy life. One and all awoke now to enjoy renewed speech and laughter, and to praise the constancy of the Norwegian, who had rested not until he had accomplished the journey, which no other mortal ever undertook of his own free will.

THE BARNACLE MAID

Jessica Amanda Salmonson

OUT IN DECEPTION PASS, with the ebb and flow of the tide, the hair of a sea maiden can be seen drifting back and forth, back and forth, like a bed of kelp. Many people claim to see her even to this day. In her mortal life, this maiden had been the tribal princess Ko-Kwalawut, famed far and wide for her beauty and wisdom.

She lived before the coming of white settlers. In those days, the Samish people were famous fishermen. The coastline was dense with ancient forests and the many streams and rivers were pure and clear. It was a paradise given to the Indians to oversee and defend. The men were commonly out in their canoes, either upon the rivers or on Puget Sound. The women were more apt to be gatherers of clams, oysters, and crabs along the shoreline.

One day Princess Ko was filling her basket with shellfish. She had struggled to dig up an especially large clam, but when she grasped it in her hand, it seemed to come to life and sprang into the shallows. She waded out to get the shellfish, but when she picked it up, it leapt into a deeper part of the water, as though upon invisible feet! She waded farther, and the same thing happened once more, so that she was standing waist deep in the cold, swift water.

When she started back toward the beach, a long nubbly arm covered with sand and seaweed reached upward from the sand at her feet. It caught hold of her wrist and held her fast. She struggled to get free, but could not shake the chill and powerful grip. Then a voice from the water said to her, 'Do not fear me. I, a prince of the sea, have greatly admired your beauty. I have fallen in love with you, and now that I have gotten hold of you, I will never let go.'

'But you must let me go,' said Princess Ko, a brave calmness in her voice. 'Do you not know that I will drown if you drag me into your world.'

'How can I let you leave me after I have planned so long to capture you?' the prince asked.

She moved her foot back and forth to see if she could uncover his face in the sandy sea bottom, but all she detected was the upraised arm. Still, when he spoke, she heard him clearly. He said, 'If you will promise to visit me in this cove from time to time, I will let you go.'

She agreed, and during each of their meetings, the sea spirit held her hand for longer and longer periods of time. He spoke loving words to her, and finally asked her to marry him. Princess Ko said, 'Only the chief, my father, can give me into marriage. You must ask his permission, and I must abide by his decision.'

The spirit rose out of the sea and followed the princess to the village. Princess Ko was unafraid, but the people were frightened of his appearance, for he was encrusted with barnacles. Seaweed hung all about him. He had eyes like a fish, perfectly round and with no eyelids.

Everyone dreaded the prospect of their beautiful princess marrying such a monster. His presence caused a coldness throughout the village. When he asked the chief for Princess Ko's hand, her father was incensed. He said, 'No! If my daughter entered the sea, she would die!'

'She shall not die,' said the sea's prince. 'She shall become one among my people, and live forever. I have such love for her, believe me, she would not be harmed.'

'No! She is the pride of our people, and I will not permit her to go into the sea. Go away at once!'

An icy wind exuded from the sea spirit. His chest swelled and he seemed to inhale all the luck of the tribe. His eyes narrowed with anger and his massive, encrusted fingers coiled into a fist. In a low, threatening voice he said, 'If you refuse me, the water in all the streams will be undrinkable. The fish will depart. Your people will die of thirst and famine.'

'Go! Go!' shouted the chief, angered by such threats.

* * *

So it was that the streams turned dark with foul scum and mud, or were made salty by the invasion of the sea, or dried up altogether. There were no fish to be caught, no clams or oysters or crabs to be found. Night and day, a coldness filled the longhouses, and bonfires burned without heat. The people grew thin and ill. The children cried out constantly for food and water.

Princess Ko went to the cove where she had often met with the spirit, and chastised him for his cruelty to her people. 'How can I return your affection when you perform evil deeds?' she scolded. She demanded he restrain himself from his heartless acts. If he would take away the curse, she would beg her father to permit her marriage. Having heard her words, the sea spirit relented a little, and there was almost enough to eat, although it was still a hard time for the Samish.

Princess Ko went every day to talk to her father, and at last he was convinced of her desire to marry the sea-spirit. He said he would give his blessing to the marriage under one condition. Once each year, his daughter must be allowed to return to the Samish village, so that everyone could judge her happiness for themselves, and because otherwise they would miss her too much. The spirit arose from the sea until he stood atop the waters of Deception Pass. At the spirit's feet, water roiled furiously. The chief shivered at the coldness.

Then Princess Ko in her beautifully beaded and feathered wedding garments walked out on the surface of the water. She took her husband's hand, and slowly they sank downward together, until all that was visible was the beautiful dark hair of Princess Ko waving to and fro with the tide.

* * *

From that day on, the rivers ran crystal clear. Salmon hurried up the streams, coming from the sea, and the nets of the Samish people were filled. The beaches were dense with shellfish and all the women's baskets were filled with razor clams and butter clams and oysters. There was greater prosperity than ever before, because the sea had married a Samish princess.

A year later, the princess came to visit. The salmon catch had been excellent the day before her arrival, which had been a sign of her coming, and everyone greeted her with reverence and awe. In spite of her friendliness, her relatives were uncomfortable around her, because Princess Ko exuded the terrible coldness of creatures of the sea, and this affected the atmosphere wherever she passed.

There was a great feast, and everyone danced and sang. Yet for all the joy of the reunion, a degree of superstitious dreadfulness underlay the festivities, for Ko's people felt strange about her new life. Her coloring had become ever so slightly mottled and greenish, and the chilliness her body generated made people want to sit or stand apart from her.

The following year there was another extraordinarily fine catch, followed by the arrival of the princess. But during the feast, everyone thought Princess Ko looked uncomfortable and agitated, as though she hated to be so long out of the sea. They feared her a little more than they had on her first visit, since strange things so often frightened people. Their fear made the princess melancholy in their presence.

The year after that, it was even more difficult for the people to get into a festive mood, despite so much food and singing. For by now, their beloved princess had undergone dramatic changes. Her beautiful eyes had become like the eyes of a fish, flat and round and unblinking. Upon her arms and on her neck, barnacles had taken hold. As she stood among her people, a cold wind whipped about her, and even her loving father could not stand close to her without shaking with a chill.

On the fourth year, she came again. The people were horrified. That face that had once been so beautiful was now entirely sheathed in barnacles. Her arms were like barnacle-encrusted driftwood. Seaweed clung to her everywhere. Only her raven hair was still the same, assuring the people that she was indeed their beloved princess.

* * *

Sad though it made her father the chief, he released his daughter from her vow to return once each year, for she was not happy out of the sea, and the people had become afraid of her coldness and appearance.

The Samish chanted this tale to the beat of drums. The old

songs and the old ways are rarer now than they once were. But the people remember Princess Ko, and to this day her hair can be seen flowing to and fro with the tides. They say she is still protecting the Samish people.

BATTLE ON THE BRIDGE OF THE GODS

Jessica Amanda Salmonson

THE GIANTESS LOOWIT had lived to great old age. She could hardly believe it, but after thousands of years, she had become a terrible looking crone. Her cheeks sagged; her chin sagged too. Her hair that once was a splendid midnight waterfall had become white and wild like a tormented frothing river. Underneath her tired old eyes were large red cups full of melancholy which at times spilled forth to wet the earth in sundry sorrows. Her hands, that once were so delicate and slender, were like the claws of eagles, with long sharp dark nails.

Even so, in her heart, she had never aged. When she went to the river with a bucket, she betimes chanced to see her own reflection. She was startled by her appearance, her crinkled complexion, her eagle's nest of wild white hair.

Where, she wondered, was the beautiful maiden she once had been? That maiden was still present, inside an old woman.

* * *

Loowit was a very great shaman in the days when humanity was newly made. All people were giants then and often mingled with gods. Loowit was the inventor of a firemaking device. For a long time she kept this device a secret, hidden as it was in her cavernous home in the heart of a certain mountain today called Mount St. Helens. This mountain's hollow was well-lit on account of her ingenious invention. The mountain was like a tipi to Loowit, with the smoke of her miraculous fire rising through the smoke-hole at the top.

Then as now, the means and methods of certain arts were protected as secrets among artisans. Those who did not know the secrets of an art imagined such things were done solely by magic. Having told no one of her invention, various valley peoples and peoples near the sea believed Loowit manufactured fire by a supernatural method. Such peoples came to the door of Loowit's cavern and paid homage to her. She would then deposit a single coal inside a clamshell which each visitor brought along for the purpose. By this means, these individuals were able to deliver fire to their various villages.

But if in a village the fire went out, they knew not how to make another. In the winter, travel was difficult, and they might not be able to reach Loowit's mountain. They must therefore live in misery until the journey could be made. Then again, since Loowit was an ascetic, she was not always available with a new coal, for she was deep in the labyrinth of her cavern, lost in meditations. Thereby many made the terrible journey only to find their efforts fruitless, since Loowit did not invariably come forth proffering the burning coals. No one expected Loowit to be at the instant beck and call of people foolish enough to let their fires die. Therefore none complained to her about how often they went without fire.

Yet when Loowit went into the world in the guise of an elderly beggar, she saw that people suffered cold misery during many a winter. Rain, wind, flood, or some error of neglect, was apt to douse a fire, after which there befell terrible woe. People lived in blind fear of the night, wherein ghosts cried out with the voices of owls. So, too, having no fire to cook their venison and salmon, they ate raw flesh, their white teeth gnawing.

Loowit became heartsick to see the peoples wet and cold. She said to herself, 'If I show them my ingenious device, each will be able to make a fire without need of my services. Their lot will be improved. But once I have revealed my secret, what will I be but an old woman of no importance to anyone?'

Even so, her heart could not deny the world. Children had frozen to death, and Loowit could not allow such tragedies to continue. She went to her cavern and prayed to Tyhee Saghalie, Chief of the Gods. He heard her in his heavenly place and came striding down the Milky Way from the north and trod along the Cascade peaks. As he was visible from a long way off, two of his earthly sons saw him, and they arose from their places to join their father. These sons were called Pahtoe and Wyeast, who dwelt in the mountains later known as Adams and Hood. The Great Chief together with his powerful sons sat in counsel with Loowit, who was indeed a great Shaman to speak with such gods as these.

She showed Tyhee Saghalie her invention, which was a drill that made fire when it was whirled with correct dexterity. For his own needs, Tyhee Saghalie always made fire with great explosions of lightning. This was not entirely practical for just anyone. So he was very impressed by Loowit's cleverness.

Loowit said, 'Tyhee Saghalie, I am too old to travel about the nations of all the peoples of the valleys and the shores in order to teach this great secret. So I am giving my drill to you. As you can see, it is easily duplicated. Will you and your sons deliver my gift to the peoples, so that they may easily achieve their needs whenever fire is required?'

'I and my sons will do as you have asked,' said Tyhee Saghalie. He held the drill in his hand, and parted it by a miraculous means, so that there were two drills. He gave one to his right-hand son, and the other to his left-hand son, instructing them, 'Tell the peoples this is the gift of the mountain witch Loowit.' And the two princes sat in awe of the soul of Loowit, which was a very great and giving soul.

Then to the old Shaman woman, Tyhee Saghalie said, 'But what of your own future? Do you think I did not see you had horded your invention? Do you think I knew not why you kept the secret for so long? Now that you have given away the only thing you possessed, you will have nothing.'

'Will I not have the affection of the people?'

'You will have the affection of the people,' said Tyhee Saghalie, 'and in honor of your selflessness, potlatches will be held each year, and the richest of every tribe will give their wealth to others. Never will such selflessness go unrewarded by Tyhee Saghalie. To you, Loowit, I will grant whatever is the one thing you have most in your life desired. What is there you would have from me?'

'I am forlorn of my youth,' said Loowit, 'and would live in

happiness to be once more that which in my heart I have always remained.'

Therefore the Chief of the Gods restored Loowit to her former maidenliness. And because she was a priestess, but no longer sole guardian of fire, he made her, instead, the guardian of the Bridge of the Gods. This was the bridge which in former times joined the Washington Cascades to the Oregon Cascades, spanning the Columbia River, a river known to Chinookan peoples as Wauna.

The bridge over the Wauna was made in days before there were people, when Coyote was digging in the ground as coyotes do even now. Coyote dug through under the mountain range so that the Wauna flowed to the sea, and salmon swam to villages on the upper Wauna. Beneath the bridge there arose a lonesome island, invisible in the darkness, upon which dead fish, broken canoes, rotting bits of lodges and human corpses were strewn as flotsam. There was good magic above the bridge so that mystagogues were able to pass from it onto the Milky Way, and visit the country of Tyhee Saghalie.

'By this bridge,' said the Chief of Gods, 'I am visited by the giants of the earth. You, Loowit, will be the guide who opens and shuts the spirit-bridge that exists in tandem with the physical bridge. Those who are giants of body but not of soul must never have the spirit bridge opened to them, but you will advise them on the Road of Mountains. Those who are giants in spirit, whatever their physical proportions, for these you may reveal the spirit-bridge, that I may see them.'

Having been greatly honored with a signal duty, Loowit left the cavern of her mountain. She went to live in a small stone house in the middle of the bridge high above the Columbia.

Loowit was thereafter very beautiful. Many people came to the Bridge of the Gods to worship her as a Goddess. The sons of all the chiefs in every tribe desired her in marriage, but she rebuffed them in a kindly way. She remained an ascetic and a guide to many, belonging to no one man.

The princes Pahtoe and Wyeast had been impressed by the greatness of her soul even when she had the appearance of a crone. Now, whenever they gazed upon her, they each knew there was no other wife for them. They boasted each in turn that he and he alone would marry her. When they were rebuffed as swiftly as were her common beaus, the two mountainous princes declared to one another their intent to induce her by any means to choose between them.

After they had given to the peoples the gift of fire, in accordance with the directions of their father and Loowit, each returned to the Bridge of the Gods in order to woo the maiden. She said, 'I am flattered by your sincere attentions, but must ask that you desist, as I am an ascetic and devoted to the well-being of the whole of the world. I cannot be restricted to the needs of a single man or a single house. Simply put, I do not wish to marry, and will remain pure in my duties as a priestess.'

The princes said to one another, 'If she will not decide between us, we will do battle with one another. Who wins will take Loowit by main force, whether or not she agrees.' Having said this, they threw off their white robes, and rushed at one another.

They had many of the powers of their father the Great Chief. For this reason, their battle was terrible to see. Their feet gouged new rivers in the land, and heaped up new mountains, changing the direction of the Wauna River and causing whole forests to become submerged. Where the princes fell down wrestling, a vast wilderness was wasted. They rolled about clinging body to body so that prairies were ironed out. They dashed at one another, Wyeast with hurricanes, Pahtoe with fiery bolts of lightning. They were not yet worn out when they began to shove one another back and forth along the Bridge of the Gods until that mighty span collapsed into the Wauna River.

Now they sat in the rushing river of the gorge, alarmed by the destruction they had wrought. At the sound of the bridge crashing down, Tyhee Saghalie came striding down the Milky Way and stood atop the Cascades with his arms folded, his eyes flashing with anger. He snatched Wyeast and fixed him in the heart of Mount Hood, from whence he never could escape to cause mischief. He grabbed Pahtoe from the river as well, and fixed him in the heart of Mount Adams.

Loowit sat on the edge of the river, looking at the ruins of the bridge. She said, 'Now I am guardian neither of fire nor of the wonderful bridge. Was it my vanity that brought about this ruin? O Tyhee Saghalie, I will retire anew to the furnaces of my cavern, and never go forth among people, lest the beauty you have bestowed upon me inspire further harm.'

Taking pity on her, Tyhee Saghalie said, 'The Spirit of the Bridge of Gods exists within you, Loowit. Only the material bridge is ruined. I have reduced the size of humanity, so that no two may commit such harm as my sons have committed; but the hearts of people I have not changed. Some have great hearts, some have little. At my command, Loowit, you will unfold the spirit-bridge for those of the earth who are giant of heart. But if my will, and my laws, and my creation are hampered and harmed in future generations, then know that I have bestowed upon you a very grave power of destruction, so that even my spirit-bridge may fall, if ever I command thee.'

STORY OF THE THREE STRONG MEN

Charles G. Leland

THERE WAS A chieftain in the days of yore. He had a great desire for a poor girl who was a servant, and who worked for him. To win this girl he first must lose his wife. He took his wife afar into the woods to gather spruce-gum, and then left her there.

She soon found out that she had lost her way, and, wandering, she lost it more and more for many days, until she came at last to a bear's den, where, going in, she found the Chief of all the bears, who welcomed her, provided for her wants, and furnished her with pleasant food; but as the meat was raw he went into a neighboring town for fire. And as she lived with him she was to him in all things as he wished, and as a wife.

So that it came to pass, as time went on, that a new-comer was expected, and she bade the Bear provide the baby's clothes. And when the long-expected infant came it was a boy, large, beautiful, and strong; he was in everything beyond all other boys.

And as the child was born in a strange way, he very soon displayed a magic power. No baby ever grew so rapidly: when four months old he wrestled with the Bear and threw him easily upon the floor. And so the mother saw that he would be a warrior, and the chief of other men.

She loathed the life she led, and wished to leave, and live as she had done in days of old. To this the Bear would in no wise consent, and as her son was human, like herself, he loved his mother best, and thought with her.

One day he said, 'Now I can wrestle well and throw the Bear

as often as I choose. When I next time cast him upon the ground, catch up a club; the rest remains for you!'

They waited yet a while till he had grown so strong that the Bear was nothing in his grasp. One day they wrestled as they ever did, and then the woman, with a vigorous blow, strengthened by hate and famishing desire of freedom and a better human life, laid him in death upon the mossy floor.

They went their way back to the chieftain's town, and found him married to the servant-girl. The mother only spoke, and the wild boy tore down the wigwam of the Indian chief just with a blow, and then he called aloud unto the Lightning in the sky above, 'Come down to me and help me in my need! Build a grand wigwam such as man ne'er saw! Build it, I say, and for my mother here!'

The Lightning came, and with a single flash built such a home as man had never seen.

And then he said, 'Mother, I mean to go and travel everywhere, until I find another man who is as strong as I. When he is found I will return to thee.'

So on he went afar until he saw a man who lifted up a vast canoe with many people in it. This he did, raising it in the water; but the boy bore it ashore, and lifted it on land.

And so the two agreed that they would go on together until they found a third equal to them in strength, if such a man were living anywhere in all the world.

So traveling by hill and lake, they went, until one day, far in a lonely land, they saw a man rolling a mighty rock, large as the largest wigwam, up a hill. But the Bear's son, lifting the stone with ease, threw it afar over the mountain-top – threw it afar beyond the rocky range; they heard it thunder down the depths below.

Then the three strong men went to hunt the moose. He who had tossed the ship remained in camp to do the cooking, while the others went with bow and spear afar to find their game.

Now when the sun was at the edge of noon, just balancing to fall, there came a boy, a little wretched, elfish-looking child, as sad and sickly as a boy could be, who asked the man for food. He answered him, 'Poor little fellow! there, the pot is full of venison, so go and eat your fill.'

He ate, indeed, the dinner for the three. When he had done he did not leave a scrap; then walked into the stony mountain-side, as any man might walk into the fog, and in a second he was seen no more.

Now when the two returned and heard the tale they were right angry, being hungry men. The man who rolled the stone stayed next in turn, but when the little fellow came to him he seemed so famished and he shed such tears that this one also gave him leave to eat. Then, in a single swallow, as it seemed, he bolted all the food, and yelled aloud with an insulting laugh. The man, enraged, grappled him by the throat, but the strange boy flung him away as one would throw a nut, and vanished in the mountain as before.

On the third day the mighty man himself remained at home, and soon the starveling child came and began to beg, with tears, for food. 'Eat,' said the chief, 'as other people eat, and no more tricks, or I will deal with you.' But as it was with him the day before, so it went now; he swallowed all the meat with the same jeering yell. Then the strong man closed with the boy. It was an awful strife; they fought together from the early morn until the sun went down, and then the elf – for elf he was – cried out, 'I now give in!' So both his arms were tightly bound behind, and with a long, tough cord of plaited hide the strong man kept his prey, the lariat fast noosed about his neck. The child went on, the strong man ever following behind, holding the cord well twisted round his hand.

And so they went into the mountain-side, and ever on, a long and winding way, down a deep cavern, on for many a mile, – the light of sorcery shining from the elf made it all clear – until at last the guide stopped in his course, and said:

'Now list to me. I am the servant of a frightful fiend, a seven-headed devil, whom I deemed no man could ever conquer, he and I being of equal strength; but I believe that thou mayst conquer him, since I have found, by bitter proof, that thou canst conquer me. Here is a staff, the only thing on earth that man may smite him with and give him pain. Now, do your best; it is all one to me which of you gains, so one of you be slain, for well I wot 't will be a roaring fight.'

In came the evil being with a scream, and clutched the Indian with teeth and claws. There, in the magic cavern, many a mile from the sun's rays, they fought for seven days, the stubborn devil and the stubborn man, whose savage temper gave him fresher strength with every fresh wound; the more his blood ran from his body all the more his heart grew harder with the love of fight, until he beat away the monster's seven heads. And so he slew him, and the watching elf burst into laughter at the victory.

'Now,' said the elf, 'I have a gift for thee. I have three sisters: all are beautiful, and all shall be thine own if thou wilt but unbind my hands.' The strong man set him free. And so he led the man to another cave, and there he saw three girls so strangely fair they seemed to be a dream. The first, indeed, was very beautiful, and yet as plump as she was lovely; then the second maid was tall, superb, and most magnificent, in rarest furs, with richest wampum bands, the very picture of a perfect bride; but fairer than them both, as much more fair as swans outrival ducks, the youngest smiled. And the young chieftain chose her for his own.

With the three girls he went into the day. Far on the rocks above him he could see his two companions, and a sudden thought came to his mind, for he was quick to think; and so he called, 'I say, let down a rope; I have three girls here, and they cannot climb.' And so the two strong men let down a cord: then the first fairy-maid went up by it, and then the second. Now the chief cried out, 'It is my turn; now you must pull on me!' And saying this, he tied a heavy stone, just his own weight, unto the long rope's end, then bid them haul. It rose, but as it came just to the top the traitors let it fall, as he supposed they would, to murder him.

And then the chieftain said unto the elf, 'You know the mountain and its winding ways: bear me upon thy back, and that in haste, to where those fellows are!' The goblin flew, and in an instant he was by their side.

He found the villains in a deadly fight, quarreling for the maids; but seeing him they ceased to wrestle, upon which he said, 'I risked my life to bring away these girls; I would have given each of you a wife: for doing this you would have murdered me. Now I could kill you, and you both deserve death at the stake, vile serpents that you are; but take your lives – you are too low for me, – and with them take these women, if they wish to wed with such incarnate brutes as you!'

They went their way; the women followed them along the forest paths, and ever on. Into this story they return no more.

And then the strong man said to his young bride, 'I must return unto my village; then I'll come again to you; await me here.' But she, as one to elfin magic born, replied, 'I warn you of a single thing. When you again are at your wigwam door a small black dog will leap to lick your hand. Beware, I say; if he succeed in it, you surely will forget me utterly.' As she predicted so it came to pass.

And so she waited in the lonely wood beside the mountain till a month was gone, and then arose and went to seek her love. All in the early dawn she reached the town, and found the wigwam of the sagamore. She sought a neighboring hiding-place, where she might watch unseen, and found a tree, a broad old ash, which spread its stooping boughs over the surface of a silent pool.

An old black Indian had a hut hard by. His daughter, coming, looked into the spring, and saw a lovely face. The simple girl thought it was hers, her own grown beautiful by sorcery which hung about the place. She flung away her pail, and said, 'Aha! I'll work no more; some chief shall marry me!' and so she went to smile among the men.

Then came the mother, who beheld the same sweet, smiling, also girlish face. She said, 'Now I am young and beautiful again; I'll seek another husband, and at once.' She threw her pail afar and went away, losing no time to smile among the men.

And then in turn the old black Indian came, and looking in the spring beheld the face. He knew right well that it was not his own, for in his youth he never had been fair. So looking up above he saw the bride, and bade her come to him; and then he said, 'My wife has gone away; my daughter, too. You were the cause of it; it is but right that you should take the place my wife has left. Therefore remain with me and be my own.'

He fares but ill who weds unwilling witch. When night came on they laid them down to sleep, and then the bride murmured a magic prayer, begging the awful Spirit of the Wind, the giant Eagle of the wilderness, to do his worst. A fearful tempest blew, and all night long the old black Indian was out-of-doors, working with all his power to keep the lodge from being blown away. As soon as he had pinned one sheet of bark into its place another blew away, and then a tent pole rattling in the rain bounded afar. It was weary work, but all night long the young bride slept in peace, until the morning came, and then he slept.

Then she arose, and, walking to the wood, sat down beside a stream and sang a song:

> There are many men in the world,
> But only one is dear to me.
> He is good and brave and strong.
> He swore to love none but me;
> He has forgotten me.
> It was a bad spirit that changed him,
> But I will love none but him.

And as she sat and sang, the sagamore her husband, paddling by in his canoe, heard the sweet song intoned in magic style, and all at once recalled what had been lost – the two strong giants, the cavern and the elf, the seven-headed monster and the fight, the sisters and the evil-minded men, and the black dog who leaped to lick his hand: it flashed upon him like some early dream brought out by sorcery. He saw her sit beside the stream, and still he heard her song, soft as a magic flute. He went to her, and in a minute he was won again.

And then she said, 'This world is ever false. I know another, let us go to it.' So then again she sang a magic spell, and as she sang they saw the great Culloo, the giant bird, broad as a thunder cloud, winging his way towards them. Then he came; they stepped upon him, and he soared away. But to this earth they never came again.

THE LAY NUN WHO GAVE OF HERSELF

Jessica Amanda Salmonson

When Guatama Buddha came to Benares, he stayed in a deer park called Isipatana. Near the park there was a devout lay nun, Suppiya, who devoted herself to the faith. She went to the Arama and, going from cell to cell, asked the mendicant monks, 'Who here is ill that I can nurse?'

There was a mendicant who had overreached himself in ascetic practices and lay as one dying in his cell. 'Sister,' he said, 'it is my belief that I can recover if I can obtain a bit of meat broth.'

Suppiya said, 'I will procure it for you at once, reverend sir.' She hurried to her house and gave orders to a servant, 'Quickly, go and see if there is any meat to be had.'

The servant sought throughout Benares for meat, but could find none. Suppiya was informed, 'The killing of animals is prohibited on this day, and there is presently no meat anywhere in the town that is ready.'

Suppiya said to herself, 'That monk will increase his sickness if he has no broth. He may well die. How can I fail in my promise to help him? There must be some manner by which I can procure meat for him.'

So saying, she drew forth a knife and cut a piece of flesh from her own thigh. She gave it to a maid and said, 'Hurry and prepare a broth from this meat, carefully so that all the strength will be got from it. Then take it to the Arama for the sick mendicant. If anyone should ask after me, tell them I have fallen ill.'

Then she bandaged her thigh, went into the inner chamber of the house, and took to her bed.

Suppiya's husband, who was also a lay devotee, returned that evening from a trip he had taken, only to find his wife abed. He asked, 'Are you ill, Suppiya?'

'I am ill.'

'But what is the matter?'

Then Suppiya told her husband what had transpired.

'How marvelous you are!' he said. 'How pious to give even of your flesh to an indigent! If you would give even this, surely you would deny nothing to your faith!'

Thus speaking elatedly of his wife's excellence, he left her, and hurried to the deer park Isipatana where all the lay devotees were gathering to hear Guatama speak.

Guatama turned to where Suppiya's husband was sitting and asked, 'Why is our splendid sister not among us?'

'She is sick.'

'Well, have her come to me in any case.'

'She is unable to walk, Lord.'

'Well then, go and bring her to me, carrying her in your arms.'

Thus Suppiya's husband hurried home, and, lifting her into his arms, carried her to the deer park and into the presence of the Buddha. In the very moment that the blessed one set eyes upon her, her terrible wound was healed. There was good skin there, with tiny hairs growing from it, soft and fine. Suppiya showed her gratitude with many words of praise and by prostrating herself before the blessed one whose gaze was miraculous.

Later that day, Guatama went into the Arama and asked, 'Who among the mendicants asked that meat be brought to him?'

He was led to the cell of the pale mendicant who was recovering from his illness.

Guatama asked, 'O Monk, has broth been brought to you?'

'It was brought, Lord.'

'Have you eaten it, O Monk?'

'It was very tasty, Lord.'

'Did you inquire, O Monk, how the meat was taken?'

'I did not inquire, Lord.'

'Oh foolish one, you have eaten human flesh. It will not do that mendicants take advantage of the faithful. Listen! Once a mendicant ate the flesh of an elephant, and it was his fate to be trampled by an elephant later in his life. Once some hunters killed a lion, and when a mendicant came begging alms, they gave him meat of the lion, which he devoured. The next day he was passing through the forest, when a lion leapt out and devoured him. During a famine, another mendicant was so hungry that he ate a serpent. He was soon after bitten by an adder, and so died. So as you can see, such meals are forbidden with good cause! But you have eaten human flesh. Do you not fear that men will descend upon the faith?'

'I fear it, Lord.'

'Then this once I will alleviate you of worry, for you have inadvertently upraised our sister Suppiya, whose act of goodness cleanses you of guilt. Her name will be sung in Heaven, and she will have rewards even in this life, not only in the next. Now up with you, and go into the world, rebuked and foolish one! Go about your mendicant business with repentance in you, and think never again to take advantage of the faithful.'

THE ONE-HANDED GIRL

Edward Steere

AN OLD COUPLE once lived in a hut under a grove of palm trees, and they had one son and one daughter. They were all very happy together for many years, and then the father became very ill, and felt he was going to die. He called his children to the place where he lay on the floor – for no one had any beds in that country – and said to his son, 'I have no herds of cattle to leave you – only the few things there are in the house – for I am a poor man, as you know. But choose: will you have my blessing or my property?'

'Your property, certainly,' answered the son, and his father nodded.

'And you?' asked the old man of the girl, who stood by her brother.

'I will have blessing,' she answered, and her father gave her much blessing.

That night he died, and his wife and son and daughter mourned for him seven days, and gave him a burial according to the custom of his people. But hardly was the time of mourning over, than the mother was attacked by a disease which was common in that country.

'I am going away from you,' she said to her children, in a faint voice; 'but first, my son, choose which you will have: blessing or property.'

'Property, certainly,' answered the son.

'And you, my daughter?'

'I will have blessing,' said the girl; and her mother gave her much blessing, and that night she died.

When the days of mourning were ended, the brother bade his sister put outside the hut all that belonged to his father and his mother. So the girl put them out, and he took them away, save only a small pot and a vessel in which she could clean her corn. But she had no corn to clean.

She sat at home, sad and hungry, when a neighbour knocked at the door.

'My pot has cracked in the fire, lend me yours to cook my supper in, and I will give you a handful of corn in return.'

And the girl was glad, and that night she was able to have supper herself, and next day another woman borrowed her pot, and then another and another, for never were known so many accidents as befell the village pots at that time. She soon grew quite fat with all the corn she earned with the help of her pot, and then one evening she picked up a pumpkin seed in a corner, and planted it near her well, and it sprang up, and gave her many pumpkins.

At last it happened that a youth from her village passed through the place where the girl's brother was, and the two met and talked.

'What news is there of my sister?' asked the young man, with whom things had gone badly, for he was idle.

'She is fat and well-liking,' replied the youth, 'for the women borrow her mortar to clean their corn, and borrow her pot to cook it in, and for all this they give her more food than she can eat.' And he went his way.

Now the brother was filled with envy at the words of the man, and he set out at once, and before dawn he had reached the hut, and saw the pot and the mortar were standing outside. He slung them over his shoulders and departed, pleased with his own cleverness; but when his sister awoke and sought for the pot to cook her corn for breakfast, she could find it nowhere. At length she said to herself,

'Well, some thief must have stolen them while I slept. I will go and see if any of my pumpkins are ripe.' And indeed they were, and so many that the tree was almost broken by the weight of them. So she ate what she wanted and took the others to the village, and gave them in exchange for corn, and the women said that no pumpkins were as sweet as these, and that she was to bring every day all that she had. In this way she earned more than she needed for herself, and soon was able to get another mortar and cooking pot in exchange for her corn. Then she thought she was quite rich.

Unluckily someone else thought so too, and this was her brother's wife, who had heard all about the pumpkin tree, and sent her slave with a handful of grain to buy her a pumpkin. At first the girl told him that so few were left that she could not spare any; but when she found that he belonged to her brother, she changed her mind, and went out to the tree and gathered the largest and the ripest that was there.

'Take this one,' she said to the slave, 'and carry it back to your mistress, but tell her to keep the corn, as the pumpkin is a gift.'

The brother's wife was overjoyed at the sight of the fruit, and when she tasted it, she declared it was the nicest she had ever eaten. Indeed, all night she thought of nothing else, and early in the morning she called another slave (for she was a rich woman) and bade him go and ask for another pumpkin. But the girl, who had just been out to look at her tree, told him that they were all eaten, so he went back empty-handed to his mistress.

In the evening her husband returned from hunting a long way off, and found his wife in tears.

'What is the matter?' asked he.

'I sent a slave with some grain to your sister to buy some pumpkins, but she would not sell me any, and told me there were none, though I know she lets other people buy them.'

'Well, never mind now – go to sleep,' said he, 'and tomorrow I will go and pull up the pumpkin tree, and that will punish her for treating you so badly.'

So before sunrise he got up and set out for his sister's house, and found her cleaning some corn.

'Why did you refuse to sell my wife a pumpkin yesterday when she wanted one?' he asked.

'The old ones are finished, and the new ones are not yet come,' answered the girl. 'When her slave arrived two days ago, there were only four left; but I gave him one, and would take no corn for it.'

'I do not believe you: you have sold them all to other people. I shall go and cut down the pumpkin,' cried her brother in a rage.

'If you cut down the pumpkin you shall cut off my hand with it,' exclaimed the girl, running up to her tree and catching hold of it. But her brother followed, and with one blow cut off the pumpkin and her hand too.

Then he went into the house and took away everything he could find, and sold the house to a friend of his who had long wished to have it, and his sister had no home to go to.

Meanwhile she had bathed her arm carefully, and bound on it some healing leaves that grew near by, and wrapped a cloth round the leaves, and went to hide in the forest, that her brother might not find her again.

For seven days she wandered about, eating only the fruit that hung from the trees above her, and every night she climbed up and tucked herself safely among the creepers which bound together the big branches, so that neither lions nor tigers nor panthers might get at her.

When she woke up on the seventh morning she saw from her perch smoke coming up from a little town on the edge of the forest. The sight of the huts made her feel more lonely and helpless than before. She longed desperately for a draught of milk from a gourd, for there were no streams in that part, and she was very thirsty, but how was she to earn anything with only one hand? And at this thought her courage failed, and she began to cry bitterly.

It happened that the king's son had come out from the town very early to shoot birds, and when the sun grew hot he felt tired.

'I will lie here and rest under this tree,' he said to his attendants. 'You can go and shoot instead, and I will just have this slave to stay with me!' Away they went, and the young man fell asleep, and slept long. Suddenly he was awakened by something wet and salty falling on his face.

'What is that? Is it raining?' he said to his slave. 'Go and look.'

'No, master, it is not raining,' answered the slave.

'Then climb up the tree and see what it is,' and the slave climbed up, and came back and told his master that a beautiful girl was sitting up there, and that it must have been her tears which had fallen on the face of the king's son.

'Why was she crying?' inquired the prince.

'I cannot tell – I did not dare to ask her; but perhaps she would tell you.' And the master, greatly wondering, climbed up the tree.

'What is the matter with you?' said he gently, and, as she only sobbed louder, he continued:

'Are you a woman, or a spirit of the woods?'

'I am a woman,' she answered slowly, wiping her eyes with a leaf of the creeper that hung about her.

'Then why do you cry?' he persisted.

'I have many things to cry for,' she replied, 'more than you could ever guess.'

'Come home with me,' said the prince; 'it is not very far. Come home to my father and mother. I am a king's son.'

'Then why are you here?' she said, opening her eyes and staring at him.

'Once every month I and my friends shoot birds in the forest,' he answered, 'but I was tired and bade them leave me to rest. And you – what are you doing up in this tree?'

At that she began to cry again, and told the king's son all that had befallen her since the death of her mother.

'I cannot come down with you, for I do not like anyone to see me,' she ended with a sob.

'Oh! I will manage all that,' said the king's son, and swinging himself to a lower branch, he bade his slave go quickly into the town, and bring back with him four strong men and a curtained litter. When the man was gone, the girl climbed down, and hid herself on the ground in some bushes. Very soon the slave returned with the litter, which was placed on the ground close to the bushes where the girl lay.

'Now go, all of you, and call my attendants, for I do not wish to stay here any longer,' he said to the men, and as soon as they were out of sight he bade the girl get into the litter, and fasten the curtains tightly. Then he got in on the other side, and waited till his attendants came up.

'What is the matter, O son of a king?' asked they, breathless with running.

'I think I am ill; I am cold,' he said, and signing to the bearers, he drew the curtains, and was carried through the forest right inside his own house.

'Tell my father and mother that I have a fever, and

want some gruel,' said he, 'and bid them send it quickly.'

So the slave hastened to the king's palace and gave his message, which troubled both the king and the queen greatly. A pot of hot gruel was instantly prepared, and carried over to the sick man, and as soon as the council which was sitting was over, the king and his ministers went to pay him a visit, bearing a message from the queen that she would follow a little later.

Now the prince had pretended to be ill in order to soften his parents' hearts, and the next day he declared he felt better, and, getting into his litter, was carried to the palace in state, drums being beaten all along the road.

He dismounted at the foot of the steps and walked up, a great parasol being held over his head by a slave. Then he entered the cool, dark room where his father and mother were sitting, and said to them:

'I saw a girl yesterday in the forest whom I wish to marry, and, unknown to my attendants, I brought her back to my house in a litter. Give me your consent, I beg, for no other woman pleases me as well, even though she has but one hand!'

Of course the king and queen would have preferred a daughter-in-law with two hands, and one who could have brought riches with her, but they could not bear to say 'No' to their son, so they told him it should be as he chose, and that the wedding feast should be prepared immediately.

The girl could scarcely believe her good fortune, and, in gratitude for all the kindness shown her, was so useful and pleasant to her husband's parents that they soon loved her.

By and by a baby was born to her, and soon after that the prince was sent on a journey by his father to visit some of the distant towns of the kingdom, and to set right things that had gone wrong.

No sooner had he started than the girl's brother, who had wasted all the riches his wife had brought him in recklessness and folly, and was now very poor, chanced to come into the town, and as he passed he heard a man say, 'Do you know that the king's son has married a woman who has lost one of her hands?' On hearing these words the brother stopped and asked, 'Where did he find such a woman?'

'In the forest,' answered the man, and the cruel brother guessed at once it must be his sister.

A great rage took possession of his soul as he thought of the girl whom he had tried to ruin being after all so much better off than himself, and he vowed that he would work her ill. Therefore that very afternoon he made his way to the palace and asked to see the king.

When he was admitted to his presence, he knelt down and touched the ground with his forehead, and the king bade him stand up and tell wherefore he had come.

'By the kindness of your heart have you been deceived, O king,' said he. 'Your son has married a girl who has lost a hand. Do you know why she has lost it? She was a witch, and has wedded three husbands, and each husband she has put to death with her arts. Then the people of the town cut off her hand, and turned her into the forest. And what I say is true, for her town is my town also.'

The king listened, and his face grew dark. Unluckily he had a hasty temper, and did not stop to reason, and, instead of sending to the town, and discovering people who knew his daughter-in-law and could have told him how hard she had worked and how poor she had been, he believed all the brother's lying words, and made the queen believe them too. Together they took counsel what they should do, and in the end they decided that they also would put her out of the town. But this did not content the brother.

'Kill her,' he said. 'It is no more than she deserves for daring to marry the king's son. Then she can do no more hurt to anyone.'

'We cannot kill her,' answered they; 'if we did, our son would assuredly kill us. Let us do as the others did, and put her out of the town.' And with this the envious brother was forced to be content.

The poor girl loved her husband very much, but just then the baby was more to her than all else in the world, and as long as she had him with her, she did not very much mind anything. So, taking her son on her arm, and hanging a little earthen pot for cooking round her neck, she left her house with its great peacock fans and slaves and seats of ivory, and plunged into the forest.

* * *

For a while she walked, not knowing whither she went, then by and by she grew tired, and sat under a tree to rest and to hush her baby to sleep. Suddenly she raised her eyes, and saw a snake wriggling from under the bushes towards her.

'I am a dead woman,' she said to herself, and stayed quite still, for indeed she was too frightened to move. In another minute the snake had reached her side, and to her surprise he spoke.

'Open your earthen pot, and let me go in. Save me from sun, and I will save you from rain,' and she opened the pot, and when the snake had slipped in, she put on the cover. Soon she beheld another snake coming after the other one, and when it had reached her it stopped and said, 'Did you see a small grey snake pass this way just now?'

'Yes,' she answered, 'it was going very quickly.'

'Ah, I must hurry and catch it up,' replied the second snake, and it hastened on.

When it was out of sight, a voice from the pot said:

'Uncover me,' and she lifted the lid, and the little grey snake slid rapidly to the ground.

'I am safe now,' he said. 'But tell me, where are you going?'

'I cannot tell you, for I do not know,' she answered. 'I am just wandering in the wood.'

'Follow me, and let us go home together,' said the snake, and the girl followed him through the forest and along the green paths, till they came to a great lake, where they stopped to rest.

'The sun is hot,' said the snake, 'and you have walked far. Take your baby and bathe in that cool place where the boughs of the tree stretch far over the water.'

'Yes, I will,' answered she, and they went in. The baby splashed and crowed with delight, and then he gave a spring and fell right in, down, down, down, and his mother could not find him, though she searched all among the reeds.

Full of terror, she made her way back to the bank, and called to the snake, 'My baby is gone! – he is drowned, and never shall I see him again.'

'Go in once more,' said the snake, 'and feel everywhere, even among the trees that have their roots in the water, lest perhaps he may be held fast there.'

Swiftly she went back and felt everywhere with her whole hand, even putting her fingers into the tiniest crannies, where a crab could hardly have taken shelter.

'No, he is not here,' she cried. 'How am I to live without him?' But the snake took no notice, and only answered, 'Put in your other arm too.'

'What is the use of that?' she asked, 'when it has no hand to feel with?' but all the same she did as she was bid, and in an instant the wounded arm touched something round and soft, lying between two stones in a clump of reeds.

'My baby, my baby!' she shouted, and lifted him up, merry and laughing, and not a bit hurt or frightened.

'Have you found him this time?' asked the snake.

'Yes, oh, yes!' she answered, 'and, why – why – I have got my hand back again!' and from sheer joy she burst into tears.

The snake let her weep for a little while, and then he said –

'Now we will journey on to my family, and we will all repay you for the kindness you showed to me.'

'You have done more than enough in giving me back my hand,' replied the girl; but the snake only smiled.

'Be quick, lest the sun should set,' he answered, and began to wriggle along so fast that the girl could hardly follow him.

By and by they arrived at the house in a tree where the snake lived, when he was not travelling with his father and mother. And he told them all his adventures, and how he had escaped from his enemy. The father and mother snake could not do enough to show their gratitude. They made their guest lie down on a hammock woven of the strong creepers which hung from bough to bough, till she was quite rested after her wanderings, while they watched the baby and gave him milk to drink from the cocoa-nuts which they persuaded their friends the monkeys to crack for them. They even managed to carry small fruit tied up in their tails for the baby's mother, who felt at last that she was safe and at peace. Not that she forgot her husband, for she often thought of him and longed to show him her son, and in the night she would sometimes lie awake and wonder where he was.

* * *

In this manner many weeks passed by.

And what was the prince doing?

Well, he had fallen very ill when he was on the furthest border of the kingdom, and he was nursed by some kind people who did not know who he was, so that the king and queen heard nothing about him. When he was better he made his way slowly home again, and into his father's palace, where he found a strange man standing behind the throne with the peacock's feathers. This was his wife's brother, whom the king had taken into high favour, though, of course, the prince was quite ignorant of what had happened.

For a moment the king and queen stared at their son, as if he had been unknown to them; he had grown so thin and weak during his illness that his shoulders were bowed like those of an old man.

'Have you forgotten me so soon?' he asked.

At the sound of his voice they gave a cry and ran towards him, and poured out questions as to what had happened, and why he looked like that. But the prince did not answer any of them.

'How is my wife?' he said. There was a pause.

Then the queen replied:

'She is dead.'

'*Dead!*' he repeated, stepping a little backwards. 'And my child?'

'He is dead too.'

The young man stood silent. Then he said, 'Show me their graves.'

At these words the king, who had been feeling rather uncomfortable, took heart again, for had he not prepared two beautiful tombs for his son to see, so that he might never, never guess what had been done to his wife? All these months the king and queen had been telling each other how good and merciful they had been not to take her brother's advice and to put her to death. But now, this somehow did not seem so certain.

Then the king led the way to the courtyard just behind the palace, and through the gate into a beautiful garden where stood two splendid tombs in a green space under the trees. The prince advanced alone, and, resting his head against the stone, he burst into tears. His father and mother stood silently behind with a curious pang in their souls which they did not quite understand. Could it be that they were ashamed of themselves?

But after a while the prince turned round, and walking past them into the palace he bade the slaves bring him mourning. For seven days no one saw him, but at the end of them he went out hunting, and helped his father rule his people as before. Only no one dared to speak to him of his wife and son.

At last one morning, after the girl had been lying awake all night thinking of her husband, she said to her friend the snake:

'You have all shown me much kindness, but now I am well again, and want to go home and hear some news of my husband, and if he still mourns for me!' Now the heart of the snake was sad at her words, but he only said:

'Yes, thus it must be; go and bid farewell to my father and mother, but if they offer you a present, see that you take nothing but my father's ring and my mother's casket.'

So she went to the parent snakes, who wept bitterly at the thought of losing her, and offered her gold and jewels as much as she could carry in remembrance of them. But the girl shook her head and pushed the shining heap away from her.

'I shall never forget you, never,' she said in a broken voice, 'but the only tokens I will accept from you are that little ring and this old casket.'

The two snakes looked at each other in dismay. The ring and the casket were the only things they did not want her to have. Then after a short pause they spoke.

'Why do you want the ring and casket so much? Who has told you of them?'

'Oh, nobody; it is just my fancy,' answered she. But the old snakes shook their heads and replied:

'Not so; it is our son who told you, and, as he said, so it must be. If you need food, or clothes, or a house, tell the ring and it will find them for you. And if you are unhappy or in danger, tell the casket and it will set things right.' Then they both gave her their blessing, and she picked up her baby and went her way.

She walked for a long time, till at length she came near the town where her husband and his father dwelt. Here she stopped under a grove of palm trees, and told the ring that she wanted a house.

'It is ready, mistress,' whispered a queer little voice which made her jump, and, looking behind her, she saw a lovely palace made of the finest woods, and a row of slaves with tall fans bowing before the door. Glad indeed was she to enter, for she was very tired, and, after eating a good supper of fruit and milk which she found in one of the rooms, she flung herself down on a pile of cushions and went to sleep with her baby beside her.

Here she stayed quietly, and every day the baby grew taller and stronger, and very soon he could run about and even talk. Of course the neighbours had a great deal to say about the house which had been built so quickly – so very quickly – on the outskirts of the town, and invented all kinds of stories about the rich lady who lived in it. And by and by, when the king returned with his son from the wars, some of these tales reached his ears.

'It is really very odd about that house under the palms,' he said to the queen; 'I must find out something of the lady whom no one ever sees. I dare say it is not a lady at all, but a gang of conspirators who want to get possession of my throne. Tomorrow I shall take my son and my chief ministers and insist on getting inside.'

Soon after sunrise next day the prince's wife was standing on a little hill behind the house, when she saw a cloud of dust coming through the town. A moment afterwards she heard faintly the roll of the drums that announced the king's presence, and saw a crowd of people approaching the grove of palms. Her heart beat fast. Could her husband be among them? In any case they must not discover her there; so just bidding the ring prepare some food for them, she ran inside, and bound a veil of golden gauze round her head and face. Then, taking the child's hand, she went to the door and waited.

In a few minutes the whole procession came up, and she stepped forward and begged them to come in and rest.

'Willingly,' answered the king; 'go first, and we will follow you.'

They followed her into a long dark room, in which was a

table covered with gold cups and baskets filled with dates and cocoa-nuts and all kinds of ripe yellow fruits, and the king and the prince sat upon cushions and were served by slaves, while the ministers, among whom she recognised her own brother, stood behind.

'Ah, I owe all my misery to him,' she said to herself. 'From the first he has hated me,' but outwardly she showed nothing. And when the king asked her what news there was in the town she only answered:

'You have ridden far; eat first, and drink, for you must be hungry and thirsty, and then I will tell you my news.'

'You speak sense,' answered the king, and silence prevailed for some time longer. Then he said:

'Now, lady, I have finished, and am refreshed, therefore tell me, I pray you, who you are, and whence you come? But, first, be seated.'

She bowed her head and sat down on a big scarlet cushion, drawing her little boy, who was asleep in a corner, on to her knee, and began to tell the story of her life. As her brother listened, he would fain have left the house and hidden himself in the forest, but it was his duty to wave the fan of peacock's feathers over the king's head to keep off the flies, and he knew he would be seized by the royal guards if he tried to desert his post. He must stay where he was, there was no help for it, and luckily for him the king was too much interested in the tale to notice that the fan had ceased moving, and that flies were dancing right on the top of his thick curly hair.

The story went on, but the story-teller never once looked at the prince, even through her veil, though he on his side never moved his eyes from her. When she reached the part where she had sat weeping in the tree, the king's son could restrain himself no longer.

'It is my wife,' he cried, springing to where she sat with the sleeping child in her lap. 'They have lied to me, and you are not dead after all, nor the boy either! But what has happened? Why did they lie to me? and why did you leave my house where you were safe?' And he turned and looked fiercely at his father.

'Let me finish my tale first, and then you will know,' answered she, throwing back her veil, and she told how her brother had come to the palace and accused her of being a witch, and had tried to persuade the king to slay her. 'But he would not do that,' she continued softly, 'and after all, if I had stayed on in your house, I should never have met the snake, nor have got my hand back again. So let us forget all about it, and be happy once more, for see! our son is growing quite a big boy.'

'And what shall be done to your brother?' asked the king, who was glad to think that someone had acted in this matter worse than himself.

'Put him out of the town,' answered she.

RAYAMATI, THE SAVIORESS

Jessica Amanda Salmonson

Arishtameni was the son of Queen Siva and King Samudravigaya, who ruled one part of the twin-city of Sauryapura. Arishtameni was gifted with an excellent voice. His body was well proportioned and strong as a bull, and his skin was black.

Across the river were another king and queen. They had a daughter named Rayamati. Her beauty was greatly pronounced and she shone like the Lightning-goddess Rodasi. She was an aggressive girl, just like Rodasi. She could drive a chariot swiftly and was expert at throwing spears. In the game yards she rode horses along with the boys of the palace, holding the reigns in her teeth and wielding swords in both hands. However, on official occasions and in privacy, she loved to wear jewelry and silk and was exceedingly vain of her perfect, slender body.

Many said the prince and the princess were two parts of the same divinity, a blue lotus prince and white lotus princess. Almost from birth, their marriage was assumed, though there had never been an official betrothal. In the twin-city, on both sides of the river, romantic tales were invented about them, these becoming favorites in the dens of the storytellers and in small, pictorial booklets sold near the shrines of erotic deities.

They had been kept from one another, and had only seen each other's portraits. Even so, they believed in the truth of the tales woven about themselves. Each was in love with the portrait of the other. Neither had ever seen such unsurpassed beauty except in mirrors. They knew indeed their spirits were as one. For this and future lives, they would be together.

When both came of age, King Samudravigaya sent a messenger to King Ugrasena asking if Princess Rayamati would be willing to marry Prince Arishtameni.

King Ugrasena replied, 'Have the prince come to our palace, and I will present him to my daughter.'

Prince Arishtameni was so excited by the news, he could hardly speak to anyone. His smile was a beacon in his dark face and his eyes gleamed like precious stones, lit by the celestial happiness of his spirit. He bathed in herbal essences and performed other essential ceremonies. He wore a splendid blue robe and was greatly ornamented with sapphires. Carrying a vajra in his left hand and a mace sceptor in his right, he mounted a well-appointed elephant and looked like a splendid jewel on the elephant's head.

The prince rode under a raised umbrella. He was fanned with fans made from peacock feathers, held by two languid youths who sat behind him on the elephant's massive back. He passed through the shallow fording-place of the river and entered the city of the princess.

How his heart was beating! Everything was going so well. An army of footsoldiers went beside the elephant, their swords like polished golden moons, their spears ornate and jewel-encrusted, sweeping to and fro in a rhythmic sword-dance. Musicians followed in their wake, playing heavenly songs, and all these many fine attendants chanted sweet divine hymns of love and glory.

Along the way to the palace, the prince spied many things his sensitized heart had not been opened to before that day. There were animals kept in cages and tethered to trees, all of them miserable and frightened. Some were domestic beasts, others were wild and beautiful, and none of them were happy. All were destined to be sacrificed to sundry divinities, or slaughtered for celebratory meals; for the marriage of a prince and princess required huge feasts and numerous holy offerings.

'It is for the sake of my marriage all these beasts are suffering,' thought Prince Arishtemeni. Unexpectedly, his heart was burdened with unhappiness. As uplifted as he had felt the moment before, that was how low his emotions plunged. The low-caste people who crowded the sides of the street to catch a glimpse of him, how thin they were! How pitiful the rags that served as clothing! How could they gaze upon him with admiration when they themselves were always left to suffer?

Seeing these things, his heart felt constricted. He could barely breathe. He stopped the procession and climbed down from his elephant, embracing an old, decrepit kandala woman, to her great joy. She opened wide her toothless mouth and laughed, and the prince heard a musical echo of her lost youth that rent his heart further.

Then he removed his many jewels, passing them among the poor people by the road, whose misery had never previously affected him so much. How selfish he had always been in the palace of his father and mother! Now that his eyes were opened, he felt only shame and horror.

He tore off his silken garments and traded them to those who in their whole lives had worn only ragged pieces of cloth. Then he fled to Mount Raivataka.

When Rayamati heard that the beautiful prince had taken vows as a Jain ascetic, gaiety forsook her shimmering brow. She lamented, 'From the time I was small, everyone said it was preordained that he and I should marry. We were acclaimed in the temples as made for one another. Songs were written for us though we had never met, and storybooks were passed among the children who learned to recite fables of our former lives together. Now my life has come to a shameful impasse. He would rather live as a beggar than succumb to this marriage. Why should I do otherwise? I will be a nun!'

Having made her decision, she brought her maids to her, and had them pluck all the hairs from her head, until her pate was red and bald. The lovely tresses became a sheaf of sinister black hay, taken away to be enshrined.

Many of her maids lamented their mistress's decision, wailing in the palace as though Rayamati were dead. Others remained sombre, plucking out their hairs so as to join her.

The princess founded an order of mendicant nuns who travelled about the countryside struggling by means of their simplicity to achieve perfection and influence others to seek salvation by the ascetic path. The fame of the order spread throughout the country, and the place of Rayamati's enshrined hair was forever after a center for virgin pilgrimage.

In time, even the companionship of her fellow nuns came to

represent a luxury to Rayamati. 'Luxury is against my vow,' she told her beloved sisters, and, kissing the tears from their cheeks, said farewell. She started barefoot toward the sacred Himalayas, thinking of far places where her royalty would be unknown and she could live untethered by family, pride, prestige, or ambition.

On her way to Mount Raivataka, she thirsted, and begged at a wayside inn. The innkeeper was struck by her beautiful holiness, and gave her a sweet beverage in a golden cup, insisting she keep even the cup, which was an heirloom, telling her to sell it to finance her journey. After quenching her thirst, she put the golden cup inside her beggar's pouch, then strolled onward.

An unexpected storm burst from heaven. She knew at once that heaven was angry that she had kept the golden cup. However, she offered no apologies, for she meant to abandon it at a poor shrine where it might finance a roof, and gain nothing by it herself.

The rain fell on her in torrents. Her ragged garment became drenched. Her feet were covered with mud. She took refuge in a cavern. In the darkness, she removed her dripping garment.

Farther back in the cavern sat Rathanemi, the brother of the prince who had renounced the world and his marriage. Rathanemi had been travelling home from a farther place and, like Rayamati, found it expedient to take refuge from the rain. He realized the mendicant nun, undressing in the entry, could not see him in the depths of the cavern. He was laughing in his heart to see her naked. Because she gleamed like the Lightning-goddess, and was as beautiful as Sri Laksmi the Goddess of Fortune, the young prince could not help but fall in love with her at once.

Rayamati's peace of mind became disturbed. She gazed about, then detected Prince Rathanemi. She grew fretful upon realizing she was naked and alone with a young man. Folding one arm over her breasts, she squatted down and reached for her wet garment.

The prince put one foot on her garment so that she could not reclaim it. 'Dear, beautiful lady! I am Prince Rathanemi. Accept me for your lover and you will never have cause for regret. Come, let us enjoy pleasures together! After we have enjoyed one another, O slender one, you may reclaim the ascetic path at your leisure. Please, do not resist, for I love you greatly.'

Rayamati perceived that she must defend herself. As the Lightning-goddess was called the Spear of the Storm Clouds, so was Rayamati strong and able if violence was inescapable. She took a defensive posture, ready to maintain her honor and her vows. She said, 'If you were as beautiful as a god, I should have no desire for you. Remove your foot from my garment. Let us not be rude to one another while we await the passing of the storm.'

But Rathanemi gazed at her with doting eyes, and kept his foot upon her garment. As he moved neither to relieve her discomfort, nor to impose himself further, she relaxed somewhat. She took from her beggar's pouch the golden cup she had received as an offering from the wayside inn. Into the cup she vomited the sweet beverage. This she handed to the prince, saying, 'Drink! It was excellent this afternoon, sweet and refreshing.'

The prince drew away from her, disgusted. Rayamati said, 'Your elder brother vomited me out of his life to become an ascetic, as I have vomited the sweet brew into this golden cup. As for you, a strong and famous knight, fie! You wanted to quaff the vomited Rayamati, yet you reject Rayamati's vomited beverage! Rather than lower yourself so much, renounce your life at once!'

Having heard the beautiful and chastising words of the well-spoken and virtuous nun, Rathanemi was driven to repent his life, though until that moment he had imagined no flaw in his pursuits. He took vows and thereafter practiced austerities. When he achieved enlightenment late in life, he was welcomed into heaven by a company of divinities. He said, 'I am as you see me because of one who was wise and virtuous and turned me from the path of pleasure. Tell me, has she come to this place before me?'

'Alas,' said the company of divinities, 'it will be long before we have the pleasure of her presence. She has elected to remain upon the earth and save others. Rayamati is above us and below us. She is within us and without us.

She is in our past, our present, and our future. She is everywhere, and nowhere, and can neither be seen, nor forgotten.'

Thus said the divinities.

ECHO AND NARCISSUS

A. R. Hope-Moncrieff

TO THE RIVER-GOD Cephissus was born a son named Narcissus, who seemed to his fond mother the most beautiful of children, and anxiously she sought from the blind prophet Tiresias to know his fate.

'Will he live to old age?' she asked; to which the dark-seeing prophet made answer – 'If he shall not have known himself!'

What these mystic words meant, time only would show. The boy grew up rarely beautiful, not only in his mother's eyes but in all that were not blind. There was no maiden but cast loving looks upon him; and less favoured youths must envy the charms that, alas! made Narcissus vain above all sons of earth. Blushes, sighs, and sparkling eyes were heeded by him but as tributes to his loveliness; and when he had bloomed to the flower of manhood, he was in love with himself alone.

Shunning all who would fain have been his companions, it was his wont to walk apart in solitary places, lost in admiration of the graceful form which he thought no eye worthy to behold but his own. One day, as he wandered through a wood, unawares he was spied by the wood-nymph Echo, who loved him at first sight, but was dumb to open her heart till he should ask its secret. For on her a strange fate had been laid: Hera, displeased by her chattering tongue, took away from her the power of speech unless in answer to some other voice. So now, when Echo slunk lightly among the thickets, shadowing the steps of that beautiful youth, eager as she was to accost him, she must wait for him to speak first, nor durst she show herself but at his desire. But he, given up to his sweet thoughts of self, strolled on silently, and the maiden followed him lovingly, unseen, till at last, as he halted to drink from a cool spring, his ear was caught by a rustle in the branches.

'Who is there?' he exclaimed, raising his eyes to peer into the green shade.

'*There!*' came echoed back; but he saw not who spoke.

'What do you fear?' he asked; and the invisible voice answered –

'*Fear!*'

'Come forth here!' he cried in amazement, when thus his words were given mockingly back to him; and still the voice took no shape.

'*Here!*' was the reply; and now glided forth the blushing Echo, to make as if she would have thrown her arms round his neck.

But in the crystal pool the youth had caught another form that better pleased his eyes; and he roughly brushed away the enamoured nymph, with a harsh word.

'What brings you?'

'*You!*' she faltered, shrinking back from his frown.

'Begone!' he bid her angrily. 'There can be nothing between such as you and the fair Narcissus.'

'*Narcissus!*' sighed Echo, scarcely heard, and stole away on tiptoe to hide her shameful looks in the deep shade, breathing a silent prayer that this proud youth might learn for himself what it was to love in vain.

When left alone, Narcissus turned eagerly back to that spring in which he believed to have seen a fairer face. Like a silver mirror it lay, shining in sunlight, framed by a ring of flowery plants, as if to guard it from the plashing tread of cattle. On his knees at the edge, he stretched himself over the bright well, and there looked down upon a face and form so entrancingly beautiful, that he was ready to leap into the water beside it. A priceless statue it seemed, of one at his own blooming age, every limb chiselled like life, with features as of breathing marble, and curling locks that hung above ivory shoulders.

'Who art thou that hast been made so fair?' cried Narcissus; and the lips of the image moved, yet now came no answer.

He smiled, and was smiled back to. He flushed for delight, then the face in the water was overspread with rosy blood, its eyes sparkling like his own. He stretched out his hands towards it, and so the beautiful form beckoned to him; but as soon as his touch broke the clear surface, it vanished like a dream, to return in all its enchantment while he was content to gaze motionless, then again growing dim beneath the tears of vexation he shed into the water.

'I am not one to be despised,' he pleaded with his coy charmer, 'but such a one as mortal maidens and nymphs, too, have loved in vain.'

'*Vain!*' resounded the sad voice of Echo from the woods.

Again and again he leaned down to clasp that lovely shadow in his arms, but always it eluded him; and when he spoke entreating it to his embrace, it but simulated his gestures in unfeeling silence. Maddened by so strong allurement of his own likeness, he could not tear himself away from the mirror in which it ever mocked his yearning fancy. 'Alas!' was his constant cry, that always came sighing back from the retreats of the woeful nymph. Hour after hour, day after day, he hung over the pool's brink, nor cared to let food pass his lips, crying all in vain for that imaginary object of adoration, till at last his heart ceased to throb with despair, and he lay still among the water lilies that made his shroud. The gods themselves could not but be touched with pity for so fair a corse; and thus was Narcissus transformed into the flower that bears his name.

As for poor Echo, who had invoked such punishment on his cold heart, she gained nothing but grief that her prayer was heard. Out of sight, she pined away for despised love, till all left of her was an idle voice. And that still haunts the rocks where never since can she be seen by startled eyes; but always she must be allowed the last word.

VASAVADATTA THE COURTESAN

Jessica Amanda Salmonson

THERE WAS A courtesan of noble bearing and extraordinary beauty. Her name was Vasavadatta. In the same city was a youth named Upagupta who, though only a perfumer's son, was perpetually rooting about in the regions of divine knowledge, and excelled at occult learning. Everyone who saw him thought that he was splendidly beautiful, therefore Vasavadatta became curious to meet him. She sent her serving girl with a message for Upagupta. When her maid returned, Vasavadatta said, 'Dear child! Have you robbed that simple perfumer's son? You bring back so many perfumes!'

'Dear mistress,' said the girl, 'Upagupta is surely the handsomest man in the world! He is clever and charming. He asked me to bring these perfumes to you as gifts, and to apologize in his behalf, but he is certain the time is not yet right for you to meet him.'

Vasavadatta's interest was piqued, and she developed a firm longing for Upagupta. Indeed, she felt herself truly to be in love with a youth as yet unmet. She sent her maid again, to announce that Vasavadatta would be coming on such-and-such a night to make love to Upagupta. Once more the maid returned with starry eyes, and handed over to the courtesan twenty pieces of gold, and Upagupta's message, 'It is not yet the time that we should meet.'

'Dear child,' said Vasavadatta to her maid. 'Upagupta must have heard somehow that I am the nation's most costly courtesan, and as an honest man, he lacks the five hundred pieces of gold. Hurry, go tell him never to worry about this amount, for

I seek only to pursue pleasure with him.' But when the maid returned, Upagupta had reasserted his feeling that the time was not right for them to meet.

Some while later, a caravaneer came up from the north country to sell five hundred horses, all of them strong and swift. Having gained a trunk of gold from his sales, he then asked, 'Who is the best courtesan of your city?' He was told at once that Vasavadatta was the finest courtesan not only of the city, but of the nation. He gathered together five hundred pieces of gold, but more than that, he selected an array of excellent presents and set out for the house of Vasavadatta.

Messengers arrived to tell the courtesan of the caravaneer who would soon arrive with gifts and gold. Vasavadatta informed her client of the moment that he must leave immediately. He was a rowdy, unpleasant young man, but as the son of a guildmaster, he was spoiled, rich, full of himself, and accustomed to having his way. He refused to be dismissed. So Vasavadatta gave a shrill whistle which called into her house the seven armed maidens who people called 'the heavenly demonesses.' They beat the guildmaster's son black and blue and threw him in a cess pool. He lay in it a long time unable to climb out, all the while forming plans of vengeance.

When the relatives of the guildmaster's son learned of his mistreatment by a courtesan, they pressured the governor on the youth's behalf. In response, the governor sent soldiers to Vasavadatta's house. They cut off her hands, feet, nose, and ears, then threw her into the cremation grounds. She lay there in her blood, attended by her weeping serving maid. The news spread swiftly, and Upagupta heard of it. He said to himself, 'She sought me for sensual purposes, but now her hands, feet, nose and ears have been cut off. She has lost pride, passion, and joy. Now is the moment to discover her true nature.'

When Vasavadatta's maid saw the handsome youth coming toward the cremation grounds, she told her suffering mistress, 'Upagupta, to whom you sent me time and again, is drawing near.'

'Quickly,' said Vasavadatta, 'gather up my hands, feet, nose, and ears and place them where they belong about my body. Then cover me with a gown.'

Upagupta came and sat down beside her in the smoky

cemetery. Vasavadatta asked him, 'Have you come at last out of passion and desire? But here I am on the ground, laying in my blood, afflicted and suffering. Many times I sent for you, and you sent word back, telling me, "Sister, it is not yet time for us to meet." Today I am not so well disposed to sensual pleasures. Why have you waited until my lustre is gone?'

Upagupta said, 'How could I, seeking the road away from the cycle of rebirths, come to you for pleasure? Now sharp swords have cut from you all vanity and pleasure. I come not with desire, but with compassion. I wish to know your intrinsic nature.'

Vasavadatta said, 'I would like for you to have seen this body of mine when it was still a shining lotus, bedecked in silks and jewelry. How ashamed I am that you should see me, instead, plastered with blood and funereal ashes. Am I not a fearful thing, that once gave only joy and play and wonder?'

'I see nothing fearful in you,' said Upagupta. 'When you were covered in ornaments and excelled in all arts conducive to pleasure, none could see who you were. Now, free from trappings, your true form may be seen, and I think you are beautiful. I cannot understand that people love gross flesh, for it is but a living carcass. Why are people so attached to sinew, blood, and skin? When we observe those things that are beautiful on the outside, we know nothing of the inner being. They may well be corrupt and horrible. But a corpse that is obviously vile, what false sentiment need we suppress? Therefore we can see that part which was always good. Truly, in my father's trade, I have learned that a rich perfume can hide a foul odor. When tears of sorrow wash away falsity, what remains is the truth of our lives, a putrescent body that once we cherished to no end but death. Having given up desire, we lose also weariness, sadness, and suffering. We come to the tranquil center of the cosmic yoni, the pure light of nirvana.'

Hearing these words, and many others in their night-long discourse, Vasavadatta also came to be disgusted by the realm of desire. She gained a pure understanding of Truth, receiving the fruits of a non-returner's wisdom. An hour before dawn, she said, 'You have shown me the hidden road away from the heavily travelled path to the lower states of being. Until now, the light has been kept from me, yoked as I have been to pleasures and to sorrows. The meritorious realm is opening up to me! I can see the center of the cosmic yoni! Momentarily, blessed enlightened saint, I will leave your company. Glad I am to know that you will not weep for me, knowing as you do that my refuge is dazzling as a freshly opened lotus.'

Soon thereafter Vasavadatta arrived among the deities. The whole of the country saw the heavens open up to receive her splendid spirit. Upagupta came among them with the pieces of her body, to which the people paid homage. She was canonized as the Courtesan of the Noble Truth, whereas her persecutors were forgotten, and few knew even of the splendid deed of the Seven Heavenly Demonesses who had served Vasavadatta.

A few days after their mistress's escape to heaven, the seven demonesses broke into the house of the guildmaster by night, clubbing the whole family to death, sparing only the guildmaster's son, who lived many years without his ears, nose, feet, or hands, then was reborn to the lower realm, experiencing further torments.

PART VII:
WONDERS AND MYSTERIES

THE COURTESAN WHO WORKED A MIRACLE

Jessica Amanda Salmonson

A SAGE STOOD BY the Ganges River. He had gathered about him a great crowd of admirers. All the citizens of the city of Pataliputta were there, as were many travellers from afar. Even the king of Pataliputta was in attendance.

'Only by good deeds and noble thoughts,' said the sage, 'are great things possible. By means of an Act of Truth, a king may ride in a chariot of fire drawn by lions. What is truth without action? A dam can be built to hold back a river, but can Truth do this without action?'

'Impossible!' the populace agreed. 'Truth requires action!'

But one voice was heard in the moment after the crowd had spoken together. That one voice came from Bindumati, a certain courtesan. She said, 'Truth requires nothing but itself to prove its power.'

All eyes fell upon her, as though she had blasphemed. She stepped forth from the crowd and stood at the river's edge. As even the sage challenged her with his eyes, she explained herself.

'Here I am, a lowly harlot in the city of Pataliputta. By the sale of my body do I make a livelihood. It keeps me from poverty, but it does not raise me to a noble status. Am I steeped in noble deeds? Could I, even aided by a million strong hands, turn back this river by means of a concerted action?'

They agreed she could not perform such a deed even with a million hands, but insisted also that it was because she lacked the purity required for action to be equated with truth.

'Observe, then,' said Bindumati, 'what faith in the Truth, rather than in truthful action, can achieve!'

Bindumati began to recite sacred hymns. At her back the mighty Ganges began to roil and rage. In a din of waves and whirlpools, it rolled itself backward, and flowed toward the Himalayas.

The king cried out, 'How is it possible the mighty Ganges is flowing backward?'

Filled with profound emotion, he hurried forth to the courtesan and asked her, 'Is it true that by faith you have used Truth to force back these waters?'

'It is true, sire.'

The king asked, 'How is it you have power of this magnitude, but live as a harlot? I have taken the Word to heart, and carried it forward by my actions. Yet beside you, my authority is insignificant, for never could I have turned back the mighty river.'

'It is not my power,' said Bindumati. 'It is the power of Truth.'

The king asked, 'How can that power be in a woman who lives without restraint, who plunders fools, who is full of transgressions?'

'That is just the kind of creature I am,' said Bindumati, as though she were proud of it. 'Therefore even my doubtful nature embodies Truth, which by itself can turn the worlds of divinity and humanity upside down. I live by Great Truth, so the waters turned back at my request.'

'What is this Great Truth that requires no further action?'

'O King, whosoever comes to me for pleasure, and carrying gold, whether he is a brahman, a tradesman, a prince, or a servant, I regard them as one. I make no distinctions. If I am told he is a slave, or an outcast, or an imbecile, I do not despise him. I neither fawn on him, nor dislike him; I do service to whoever buys me. This, O King, is the Truth by which I have turned back the Ganges.'

Then by raising her hands, she let the Ganges return to its normal path.

THE KING'S SON AND THE WHITE-BEARDED SCOLOG

Jeremiah Curtin

Not in our time, nor the time of our fathers, but long ago, there lived an old king in Erin. This king had but the one son, and the son had risen up to be a fine strong hero; no man in the kingdom could stand before him in combat.

The queen was dead, and the king was gloomy and bitter in himself because old age was on him. The strength had gone from his limbs, and gladness from his heart. No matter what people said, they could not drive sorrow from him.

One day the king called up his son, and this is what he said to him, 'You are of age to marry. We cannot tell how long I'll be here, and it would cheer and delight me to see your wife; she might be a daughter to me in my last days.'

'I am willing to obey you,' said the son; 'but I know no woman that I care for. I have never seen any one that I would marry.'

With that, the old king sent for a druid, and said, 'You must tell where my son can find the right bride for himself. You must tell us what woman he should marry.'

'There is but one woman,' said the druid, 'who can be the right wife for your son, and she is the youngest daughter of the white-bearded scolog; she is the wisest young woman in the world, and has the most power.'

'Where does her father live, and how are we to settle it?' asked the king of the druid.

'I have no knowledge of the place where that scolog lives,' said the druid, 'and there is no one here who knows. Your son must go himself, and walk the world till he finds the young woman.

If he finds her and gets her, he'll have the best bride that ever came to a king's son.'

'I am willing to go in search of the scolog's daughter,' said the young man, 'and I'll never stop till I find her.'

With that, he left his father and the druid, and never stopped till he went to his foster-mother and told her the whole story – told her the wish of his father, and the advice the old druid had given him.

'My three brothers live on the road you must travel,' said the foster-mother; 'and the eldest one knows how to find that scolog, but without the friendship of all of them, you'll not be able to make the journey. I'll give you something that will gain their good-will for you.'

With that, she went to an inner room, and made three cakes of flour and baked them. When the three were ready, she brought them out, and gave them to the young man.

'When you come to my youngest brother's castle,' said she, 'he will rush at you to kill you, but do you strike him on the breast with one of the cakes; that minute he'll be friendly, and give you good entertainment. The second brother and the eldest will meet you like the youngest.'

On the following morning, the king's son left a blessing with his foster-mother, took one for the road from her, and went away carrying the three cakes with him. He travelled that day with great swiftness over hills and through valleys, past great towns and small villages, and never stopped nor stayed till he came in the evening to a very large castle. In he went, and inside was a woman before him.

'God save you!' said he to the woman.

'God save yourself!' said she; 'and will you tell me what brought you the way, and where are you going?'

'I came here,' said the king's son, 'to see the giant of this castle, and to speak with him.'

'Be said by me,' replied the woman, 'and go away out of this without waiting for the giant.'

'I will not go without seeing him,' said the king's son. 'I have never set eyes on a giant, and I'll see this one.'

'I pity you,' said the woman; 'your time is short in this life. You'll not be long without seeing the giant, and it's not much you'll see in this world after setting eyes on him; and it would be better for you to take a drink of wine to give you strength before he comes.'

The king's son had barely swallowed the wine when he heard a great noise beyond the castle.

'Fee, faw, foh!' roared someone, in a thundering voice.

The king's son looked out; and what should he see but the giant with a shaggy goat going out in front of him and another coming on behind, a dead hag above on his shoulder, a great hog of a wild boar under his left arm, and a yellow flea on the club which he held in his right hand before him.

'I don't know will I blow you into the air or put my foot on you,' said the giant, when he set eyes on the king's son. With that, he threw his load to the ground, and was making at his visitor to kill him when the young man struck the giant on the breast with one of the three cakes which he had from the foster-mother.

That minute the giant knew who was before him, and called out, 'Isn't it the fine welcome I was giving my sister's son from Erin?'

With that, he changed entirely, and was so glad to see the king's son that he didn't know what to do for him or where to put him. He made a great feast that evening; the two ate and drank with contentment and delight. The giant was so pleased with the king's son that he took him to his own bed. He wasn't three minutes in the bed when he was sound asleep and snoring. With every breath that the giant took in, he drew the king's son into his mouth and as far as the butt of his tongue; with every breath that he sent out, he drove him to the rafters of the castle, and the king's son was that way going up and down between the bed and the roof until daybreak, when the giant let a breath out of him, and closed his mouth; next moment the king's son was down on his lips.

'What are you doing to me?' cried the giant.

'Nothing,' said the king's son; 'but you didn't let me close an eye all the night. With every breath you let out of you, you drove me up to the rafters; and with every breath you took in, you drew me into your mouth and as far as the butt of your tongue.'

'Why didn't you wake me?'

'How could I wake you when time failed me to do it?'

'Oh, then, sister's son from Erin,' said the giant, 'it's the poor night's rest I gave you; but if you had a bad bed, you must have a good breakfast.'

With that, the giant rose, and the two ate the best breakfast that could be had out of Erin.

After breakfast, the king's son took the giant's blessing with him, and left his own behind. He travelled all that day with great speed and without halt or rest, till he came in the evening to the castle of the second giant. In front of the door was a pavement of sharp razors, edges upward, a pavement which no man could walk on. Long, poisonous needles, set as thickly as bristles in a brush, were fixed, points downward, under the lintel of the door, and the door was low.

The king's son went in with one start over the razors and under the needles, without grazing his head or cutting his feet. When inside, he saw a woman before him.

'God save you!' said the king's son.

'God save yourself!' said the woman.

The same conversation passed between them then as passed between himself and the woman in the first castle.

'God help you!' said the woman, when she heard his story. ' 'Tis not long you'll be alive after the giant comes. Here's a drink of wine to strengthen you.'

Barely had he the wine swallowed when there was a great noise behind the castle, and the next moment the giant came in with a thundering and rattling.

'Who is this that I see?' asked he, and with that, he sprang at the stranger to put the life out of him; but the king's son struck him on the breast with the second cake which he got from his foster-mother. That moment the giant knew him, and called out, 'A strange welcome I had for you, sister's son from Erin, but you'll get good treatment from me now.'

The giant and the king's son made three parts of that night. One part they spent in telling tales, the second in eating and drinking, and the third in sound, sweet slumber.

Next morning the young man went away after breakfast, and never stopped till he came to the castle of the third giant; and a beautiful castle it was, thatched with the down of cotton grass, the roof was as white as milk, beautiful to look at from afar or near by. The third giant was as angry at meeting him as the other two; but when he was struck in the breast with the third cake, he was as kind as the best man could be.

When they had taken supper together, the giant said to his sister's son, 'Will you tell me what journey you are on?'

'I will, indeed,' said the king's son; and he told his whole story from beginning to end.

'It is well that you told me,' said the giant, 'for I can help you; and if you do what I tell, you'll finish your journey in safety. At midday tomorrow you'll come to a lake; hide in the rushes that are growing at one side of the water. You'll not be long there when twelve swans will alight near the rushes and take the crests from their heads; with that, the swan skins will fall from them, and they will rise up the most beautiful women that you have ever set eyes on. When they go in to bathe, take the crest of the youngest, put it in your bosom next the skin, take the eleven others and hold them in your hand. When the young women come out, give the eleven crests to their owners; but when the twelfth comes, you'll not give her the crest unless she carries you to her father's castle in Ardilawn Dreeachta (High Island of Enchantment). She will refuse, and say that strength fails her to carry you, and she will beg for the crest. Be firm, and keep it in your bosom; never give it up till she promises to take you. She will do that when she sees there is no help for it.'

Next morning the king's son set out after breakfast, and at midday he was hidden in the rushes. He was barely there when the swans came. Everything happened as the giant had said, and the king's son followed his counsels.

When the twelve swans came out of the lake, he gave the eleven crests to the older ones, but kept the twelfth, the crest of the youngest, and gave it only when she promised to carry him to her father's. The moment she put the crest on her head, she was in love with the king's son. When she came in sight of the island, however much she loved him when they started from the lakeside, she loved him twice as much now. She came to the ground at some distance from the castle, and said to the young man at parting –

'Thousands of kings' sons and champions have come to give greeting to my father at the door of his castle, but every man of them perished. You will be saved if you obey me. Stand with your right foot inside the threshold and your left foot outside;

put your head under the lintel. If your head is inside, my father will cut it from your shoulders; if it is outside, he will cut it off also. If it is under the lintel when you cry "God save you!" he'll let you go in safety.'

They parted there; she went to her own place and he went to the scolog's castle, put his right foot inside the threshold, his left foot outside, and his head under the lintel. 'God save you!' called he to the scolog.

'A blessing on you!' cried the scolog, 'but my curse on your teacher. I'll give you lodgings tonight, and I'll come to you myself in the morning'; and with that he sent a servant with the king's son to a building outside. The servant took a bundle of straw with some turf and potatoes, and, putting these down inside the door, said, 'Here are bed, supper, and fire for you.'

The king's son made no use of food or bed, and he had no need of them, for the scolog's daughter came soon after, spread a cloth, took a small bundle from her pocket, and opened it. That moment the finest food and drink were there before them.

The king's son ate and drank with relish, and good reason he had after the long journey. When supper was over, the young woman whittled a small shaving from a staff which she brought with her; and that moment the finest bed that any man could have was there in the room.

'I will leave you now,' said she; 'my father will come early in the morning to give you a task. Before he comes, turn the bed over; 'twill be a shaving again, and then you can throw it into the fire. I will make you a new bed tomorrow.'

With that, she went away, and the young man slept till daybreak. Up he sprang, then turned the bed over, made a shaving of it, and burned it. It was not long till the scolog came, and this is what he said to the king's son, 'I have a task for you today, and I hope you will be able to do it. There is a lake on my land not far from this, and a swamp at one side of it. You are to drain that lake and dry the swamp for me, and have the work finished this evening; if not, I will take the head from you at sunset. To drain the lake, you are to dig through a neck of land two miles in width; here is a good spade, and I'll show you the place where you're to use it.'

The king's son went with the scolog, who showed the ground, and then left him.

'What am I to do?' said the king's son. 'Sure, a thousand men couldn't dig that land out in ten years, and they working night and day; how am I to do it between this and sunset?'

However it was, he began to dig; but if he did, for every sod he threw out, seven sods came in, and soon he saw that, in place of mending his trouble, 'twas making it worse he was. He cast aside the spade then, sat down on the sod heap, and began to lament. He wasn't long there when the scolog's daughter came with a cloth in her hand and the small bundle in her pocket.

'Why are you lamenting there like a child?' asked she of the king's son.

'Why shouldn't I lament when the head will be taken from me at sunset?'

' 'Tis a long time from this to sunset. Eat your breakfast first of all; see what will happen then,' said she. Taking out the little bundle, she put down before him the best breakfast a man could have. While he was eating, she took the spade, cut out one sod, and threw it away. When she did that, every spadeful of earth in the neck of land followed the first spadeful; the whole neck of land was gone, and before midday there wasn't a spoonful of water in the lake or the swamp – the whole place was dry.

'You have your head saved today, whatever you'll do tomorrow,' said she, and she left him.

Toward evening the scolog came, and, meeting the king's son, cried out, 'You are the best man that ever came the way, or that ever I expected to look at.'

The king's son went to his lodging. In the evening the scolog's daughter came with supper, and made a bed for him as good as the first one. Next morning the king's son rose at daybreak, destroyed his bed, and waited to see what would happen.

The scolog came early, and said, 'I have a field outside, a mile long and a mile wide, with a very tall tree in the middle of it. Here are two wedges, a sharp axe, and a fine new drawing knife. You are to cut down the tree, and make from it barrels to cover the whole field. You are to make the barrels and fill them with water before sunset, or the head will be taken from you.'

The king's son went to the field, faced the tree, and gave it a blow with his axe; but if he did, the axe bounded back from the trunk, struck him on the forehead, stretched him on the flat of his back, and raised a lump on the place where it hit him. He gave three blows, was served each time in the same way, and had three lumps on his forehead. He was rising from the third blow, the life almost gone from him, and he crying bitterly, when the scolog's daughter came with his breakfast. While he was eating the breakfast, she struck one little chip from the tree; that chip became a barrel, and then the whole tree turned into barrels, which took their places in rows, and covered the field. Between the rows there was just room for a man to walk. Not a barrel but was filled with water. From a chip she had in her hand, the young woman made a wooden dipper, from another chip she made a pail, and said to the king's son –

'You'll have these in your two hands, and be walking up and down between the rows of barrels, putting a little water into this and a little into that barrel. When my father comes, he will see you at the work and invite you to the castle tonight, but you are not to go with him. You will say that you are content to lodge tonight where you lodged the other nights.' With that, she went away, and the king's son was going around among the barrels pouring a little water into one and another of them, when the scolog came.

'You have the work done,' said he, 'and you must come to the castle for the night.'

'I am well satisfied to lodge where I am, and to sleep as I slept since I came here,' said the young man, and the scolog left him.

The young woman brought the supper, and gave a fresh bed. Next morning the scolog came the third time, and said, 'Come with me now; I have a third task for you.' With that, the two went to a quarry.

'Here are tools,' said the scolog, pointing to a crowbar, a pickaxe, a trowel, and every implement used in quarrying and building. 'You are to quarry stones today, and build between this and sunset the finest and largest castle in the world, with outhouses and stables, with cellars and kitchens. There must be cooks, with men and women to serve; there must be dishes and utensils of every kind and furniture of every description; not a thing is to be lacking, or the head will go from you this evening at sunset.'

The scolog went home; and the king's son began to quarry with crowbar and pickaxe, and though he worked hard, the morning was far gone when he had three small pieces of stone quarried.

He sat down to lament.

'Why are you lamenting this morning?' asked the scolog's daughter, who came now with his breakfast.

'Why shouldn't I lament when the head will be gone from me this evening? I am to quarry stones, and build the finest castle in the world before sunset. Ten thousand men couldn't do the work in ten years.'

'Take your breakfast,' said the young woman; 'you'll see what to do after that.'

While he was eating, she quarried one stone; and the next moment every stone in the quarry that was needed took its place in the finest and largest castle ever built, with outhouses and cellars and kitchens. A moment later, all the people were there, men and women, with utensils of all kinds. Everything was finished but a small spot at the principal fireplace.

'The castle is ready,' said the scolog's daughter; 'your head will stay with you today, and there are no more tasks before you at present. Here is a trowel and mortar; you will be finishing this small spot at the fire when my father comes. He will invite you to his castle tonight, and you are to go with him this time. After dinner, he will seat you at a table, and throw red wheat on it from his pocket. I have two sisters older than I am; they and I will fly in and alight on the table in the form of three pigeons, and we'll be eating the wheat; my father will tell you to choose one of his three daughters to marry. You'll know me by this: there will be a black quill in one of my wings. I'll show it; choose me.'

All happened as the scolog's daughter said; and when the king's son was told to make his choice in the evening, he chose the pigeon that he wanted. The three sprang from the table, and when they touched the floor, they were three beautiful women. A dish priest and a wooden clerk were brought to the castle, and the two were married that evening.

A month passed in peace and enjoyment; but the king's son wished to go back now to Erin to his father. He told the wife what he wanted; and this is what she said to him, 'My father will refuse you nothing. He will tell you to go, though he doesn't wish to part with you. He will give you his blessing; but this is all pretence, for he will follow us to kill us. You must have a horse for the journey, and the right horse. He will send a man with you to three fields. In the first field are the finest horses that you have ever laid eyes on; take none of them. In the second field are splendid horses, but not so fine as in the first field; take none of these either. In the third field, in the farthest corner, near the river, is a long-haired, shaggy, poor little old mare; take that one. The old mare is my mother. She has great power, but not so much as my father, who made her what she is, because she opposed him. I will meet you beyond the hill, and we shall not be seen from the castle.'

The king's son brought the mare; and when they mounted her, wings came from her sides, and she was the grandest steed ever seen. Away she flew over mountains, hills, and valleys, till they came to the seashore, and then they flew over the sea.

When the servant man went home, and the scolog knew what horse they had chosen, he turned himself and his two daughters into red fire, and shot after the couple. No matter how swiftly the mare moved, the scolog travelled faster, and was coming up. When the three reached the opposite shore of the sea, the daughter saw her father coming, and turned the mare into a small boat, the king's son into a fisherman, and made a fishing-rod of herself. Soon the scolog came, and his two daughters with him.

'Have you seen a man and a woman passing the way riding on a mare?' asked he of the fisherman.

'I have,' said the fisherman. 'You'll soon overtake them.'

On went the scolog; and he never stopped till he raced around the whole world, and came back to his own castle.

'Oh, then, we were the fools,' said the scolog to his daughters. 'Sure, they were the fisherman, the boat, and the rod.'

Off they went a second time in three balls of red fire; and they were coming near again when the scolog's youngest daughter made a spinning-wheel of her mother, a bundle of flax of herself, and an old woman of her husband. Up rushed the scolog, and spoke to the spinner, 'Have you seen a mare pass the way and two on her back?' asked he.

'I have, indeed,' said the old woman; 'and she is not far ahead of you.'

Away rushed the scolog; and he never stopped till he raced around the whole world, and came back to his own castle a second time.

'Oh, but we were the fools!' said the scolog. 'Sure, they were the old woman with the spinning-wheel and the flax, and they are gone from us now; for they are in Erin, and we cannot take our power over the border, nor work against them unless they are outside of Erin. There is no use in our following them; we might as well stay where we are.'

The scolog and his daughters remained in the castle at Ardilawn of Enchantment; but the king's son rode home on the winged mare, with his wife on a pillion behind him.

When near the castle of the old king in Erin, the couple dismounted, and the mare took her own form of a woman. She could do that in Erin. The three never stopped till they went to the old king. Great was the welcome before them; and if ever there was joy in a castle, there was joy then in that one.

THE ADVENTURE OF THE HOLY GRAIL

Alfred J. Church

IT FELL OUT on the Feast of Pentecost in a certain year when the King and his knights were come back from worshipping in the Minster they saw on the seats of the Round Table letters newly written in letters of gold, 'Here ought to sit this one,' and the name of a knight following, and on each seat a name. But on the Perilous Seat was written, 'When four hundred winters and fifty and four shall be accomplished then shall this seat be filled.' Then Sir Lancelot, making count of the years, cried out, 'Then ought this seat to be filled this same day, for this is the Feast of Pentecost in the four hundred and fifty-fourth year. But I would counsel that these letters be not seen, till the knight that is to fill it be come.' So, by consent, was made a cloth of silk to cover the seat. Then would the King have gone to his dinner. But Sir Kaye the Seneschal said, 'If you go now to meat, you break the old custom of the court, which is that you wait till you hear some adventure.' While he spake there came in a squire, who said, 'Sir, I bring to you marvellous tidings.' 'What be they?' said the King. 'There is floating on the river, as I have seen with mine own eyes,' said he, 'a great stone, and in the stone is a sword sticking.' Said the King, 'I will see this marvel.' So he went to the river, and all his knights went with him. And when they were come to the river, they saw the stone floating, and it was like to red marble, and in it was stuck a fair and rich sword on the handle of which was written in fine letters of gold, 'No man shall draw me hence, but he only by whose side I ought to hang, and he shall be the best knight in the world.' Said King Arthur, 'Lancelot, this sword is surely yours; you are the best knight in the world.' But Sir Lancelot answered soberly, 'Nay, sire, this sword is not mine, nor dare I put my hand to it, for it is not by my side that it ought to hang. And I know full well that whoso shall seek to take it and fail therein, it shall so wound him that he shall not easily be made whole.'

Then the King turned to Sir Gawaine, and said to him, 'Fair nephew, I bid you for the love of me, make trial of that sword.' Sir Gawaine said, 'I will obey your bidding,' and he took the sword by the handle, but could not move it. And the King thanked him for his endeavour, but Sir Lancelot said, 'Know that this sword shall so trouble you, that you will wish never to have set your hand thereto, no, not for the fairest castle in all the land.' 'Sir,' Sir Gawaine made answer, 'I could not disobey my uncle's commandment.' The King was troubled to hear this; nevertheless he bade Sir Percival try the sword. Then Sir Percival also set his hand to it, and drew at it strongly, but he could not move it at all. And when these three had failed, none others dared to put to their hands. 'Now, sir,' said Sir Kaye to the King, 'you may go to your meat, for you have seen a marvellous adventure.' So the King and his knights went to their meat, and all the seats were filled, save the Perilous Seat only.

While they thus sat at the meat, the squires serving them, there came to pass a marvellous thing. All the doors and windows of the palace shut themselves of their own accord, and yet the place was not darkened. Then spake the King, 'Fair knights, we have already seen many marvels this day; yet I doubt not that ere it be night we shall see yet greater.' And even as he spake there came into the hall an old man very venerable, clothed all in white, but no man knew whence he came. The old man brought with him a young knight, clad in red armour, without shield or sword, but with a scabbard only hanging by his side. The old man said to the King, 'Sir, I bring you this young knight who is of the lineage of Joseph of Arimathea; he shall accomplish marvellous things.' The King made answer, 'You are heartily welcome, sir, and this young knight also.' Then the old man bade the young knight doff his armour. And it was seen that he was clad in a coat of red satin, and a mantle furred with fine ermines on his shoulder. This done, the old man said to him, 'Follow me,' and so brought him to the Perilous Seat, whereby sat Sir Lancelot. Then the old man lifted up the cloth, and on the seat was written, 'This is the seat of Sir Galahad, the good knight.' The old man said, 'Be assured that this place is yours.' So the young knight sat him down in the seat with all boldness and said to the old man, 'Sir, you may now go your way, for you have done right well that which was commanded you. Commend me to my grandsire, King Pelleas, and say that I shall come to see him so soon as may be.' So the old man went his way, and there met him twenty noble squires who bare him company.

When the dinner was done, the King took Sir Galahad by the hand, and led him down to the place where the stone floated on the water, the Queen also, with many ladies, following. Said the King to Sir Galahad, 'Here is as great a marvel as ever I saw. Many knights have made trial of this sword to draw it from its place, but none have availed to do it.' 'Sir,' answered Sir Galahad, 'this is no marvel, for it is not their adventure but mine; so sure was I of this sword, that I brought none other with me, but only this scabbard that hangs by my side.' So saying, he laid his hand upon the sword, and drew it full easily out of the stone, and thrust it into the scabbard. Then he said to the King, 'This is the sword that belonged aforetime to Sir Balin, who was a passing good knight; therewith he slew his brother Sir Balan unawares, which thing was a grievous pity. This Balin also gave my grandfather, King Pelleas, a wound that has never been healed, no, nor shall be till I myself heal him.'

After this the King, willing to try Sir Galahad, of what mettle he was, bade all his knights joust together in a meadow that was by Camelot. So they jousted, and none bare himself more bravely than did Sir Galahad. Many knights of the Round Table he overthrew. But there were two whom he overthrew not, and these two were Sir Lancelot and Sir Percival. When the jousting was ended, then Sir Galahad unlaced his helmet before the King and the Queen and all the court, and they saw that he was so like unto Sir Lancelot, that never two knights in all the world were more alike than these two.

After this all the company repaired to the Minster, and from the Minster they repaired to the hall and sat down to meat. And as they sat they heard a great crack as of thunder, so loud that it seemed as if the hall were riven in twain. And in the midst of this thundering there entered a sunbeam, seven times brighter than was ever the light of the sun. And every knight, as he looked on his fellow, saw him fairer than he had ever seen him before. So they sat and gazed, none daring to speak a word, till there came into the hall the Holy Grail, a fair vessel of gold, covered all about with white samite, in which was the Holy Body. But how it was borne none saw, nor did any behold the Vessel itself, for it was closely covered about, but the hall was filled with a most heavenly odour. Then the Holy Grail departed out of the hall, and as none knew whence it came, so neither did any know whither it went.

When it was gone, the knights had breath to speak. First the King gave thanks to God who had suffered them to see the Holy Vessel at this Feast of Pentecost. After him Sir Gawaine spake out: 'We have been this day beguiled so that, though the Holy Grail came among us, yet we saw it not, so covered was it. Now, therefore, I make this vow that tomorrow I will set out seeking the Holy Grail, and that in this seeking I will continue for a twelvemonth and a day and will not return till I have seen it more plainly than it has been seen today.' And when the other knights of the Round Table heard Sir Gawaine so speak, they stood up, for the most part, and promised and vowed the same thing.

But the King was greatly troubled at this, and said to Sir Gawaine, knowing that it was he that stood up the first, and that the others took example by him, 'You have well-nigh slain me by this vow and promise, for you have bereft me of the fairest fellowship of knights that ever was in this world. For I am sure that they who shall depart on this quest shall never more meet together in this world.'

Now you shall hear how Sir Gawaine fared in the Quest. He rode many journeys forwards and backwards, seeking to join himself to Sir Galahad, and when he came to a certain abbey where Sir Galahad had been, he said to the monks, 'If I may meet Sir Galahad, I will not lightly depart from him, for all his strange adventures.' Then said one of the monks, 'He will not be of your fellowship.' 'Why so?' said Sir Gawaine. 'Because he is holy and you are sinful,' said he. The next day he rode to a certain hermitage where he asked a shelter of the hermit, which the good man willingly granted to him, asking him who he was and whence he came. 'I am of King Arthur's court,' said he, 'and my name is Gawaine, and I seek the Holy Grail.' 'I know you,' said the monk. Then Sir Gawaine told him how the monk at the abbey had called him a wicked knight. 'He might well say it,' said the hermit. 'You might have followed virtuous living when you were made a knight, but you would do otherwise. But Sir Galahad has chosen the better part. Therefore you shall fail and he shall prosper. Yet 'twere something should you do penance for your sins.' 'What penance shall I do?' 'said Sir Gawaine. 'What I shall set you,' answered the hermit. 'That may not be,' said Gawaine, 'we knights that seek adventure suffer pain enough.' Then the hermit said, 'God better you!' and held his peace.

Not many days after, Sir Gawaine met Sir Ector that was brother to Sir Lancelot. 'I am weary of this quest,' said he; and Sir Ector answered, 'I have met twenty knights, and they were all in the same case.' And riding on they came to a ruined chapel; and sitting down on the seats, fell asleep for weariness, and while they slept they dreamt, both of them, strange dreams. Afterwards they saw – for this was not a dream but a vision – a hand clothed in red samite, and in the hand was a candle burning very clear, and these two passed into the chapel, and so vanished out of their sight. And even as it vanished there came a voice to them saying, 'Ye knights that are evil of life and poor of faith, the adventure of the Holy Grail is not for you.'

When they had departed from the chapel, there met them a knight, who proffered to joust with them. 'Now,' said Sir Gawaine, 'since I left Camelot, there has no one proffered to joust with me.' 'Let me joust,' said Sir Ector. 'Nay,' answered Sir Gawaine, 'not so, but if I be beaten you shall come after me.' So the two jousted, and both fell to the ground. And when Sir Gawaine drew his sword, it was found that the other could not lift himself from the ground, for he was smitten through the body. 'Now you must yield you,' said Sir Gawaine. 'I am but a dead man,' answered the other, 'but take me to a house of religion where I may receive the Holy Sacrament.' 'I know of none such,' said Gawaine. But when the knight said that he would guide him, Gawaine set him on his horse, and sustained him till he came to the place. And when he had taken the Holy Sacrament, he prayed Sir Gawaine that he would draw the spear out of his body. 'I am a knight,' said he, 'of the Round Table, and we are sworn brethren, and I was in search of the Holy Grail, even as you, and now you have slain me. May God forgive you therefor.' And when the spear was drawn out from his body he died. Then Sir Gawaine and Sir Ector buried him, weeping the while, and so departed.

All this time they saw not Sir Galahad, but at the last they met with him and in this wise. At a certain castle they saw a party of knights that would enter by the gate, and another party that hindered them. They joined themselves to the knights without, and these got by far the better. Meanwhile Sir Galahad joined himself to the knights within and did great deeds of arms. And he came by chance to Sir Gawaine and smote him so hard that he brake through the helm and smote him to the ground and also carved in two the shoulder of his horse. This done he stole away secretly. Then said Gawaine, 'Now are the words of Lancelot come true that the sword in the stone would deal me such a buffet as I would not have for the best castle in the world. But now my quest is ended.'

Thus did Sir Gawaine fare in his Quest of the Holy Grail.

Now I will tell of Sir Lancelot.

After many adventures of which there is no need to tell, as he slept on a certain night there came a voice to him saying, 'Arise, Lancelot, and enter into the first ship that you shall find.' So he arose, and not long after came to a strand, and on the strand was a ship, into which he entered. In this he abode for a full month. And at the end of the month there came a knight riding. Him he saluted, saying, 'You are welcome.' And the knight saluted him again, saying, 'My heart is much inclined to you,' and asked his name. 'My name,' said he, 'is Lancelot du Lake.' 'No wonder,' said the other, 'that I love you, for you are my father,' 'Are you Sir Galahad?' said he; and when he knew that 'twas he, there was great joy between them, and they lived long time together in the ship.

After this there came one who said, 'Sir Galahad, you have been long time enough with your father; arise and go.' Said Sir Galahad to his father, 'I know that I shall not see you any more.' And Sir Lancelot said, 'Pray for me that God may keep me in His service.' While they talked, there came a voice, saying, 'Be careful to do well, for ye shall not see each other till the day of doom.' Then Sir Galahad mounted his horse and rode away.

Then a wind arose and drove the ship in which Sir Lancelot was for a whole month. At the end of the month he came to a castle, with two lions keeping the door, and heard a voice that said, 'Enter, Lancelot, and you shall have a part of your desire.' So he drew his sword for fear of the lions. But then came a dwarf that smote him on the arm so hard that the sword dropped out of his hand, and a voice said to him, 'Man of little faith, why trust you in your harness more than in your Maker?'

Then he made a cross on his forehead and passed by the lions, which harmed him not. So he went through many doors that opened before him, till he came to a door that was fast shut. And he knew that the Holy Grail was within. Then he prayed that God would show him something of that which he sought. But when the door opened, and he would have entered, there came a voice, saying, 'Enter not, Sir Lancelot; for it is not for you to do it.' Then he looked, and saw a table of silver and the Holy Grail on it, with red samite over it, and many angels round about, of whom one held a candle, and others divers other things. Then he entered the chamber and came near to the silver table. Whereupon there smote him on the face a fiery breath, and he fell to the ground, having lost all power over his body, and his hearing also and his speech. So he lay, well-nigh as one dead. But he was aware of many hands about him, which took him, and bare him out of the chamber, and cast him down without the door. And on the morrow, when it was day, the people of the place found him so lying, and wondered whether there was any life in him. And finding that there was life, they put him in a bed, where he lay without sense or speech for many days.

Thus did Sir Lancelot fare in the Quest.

* * *

After Sir Galahad left the King's court, he came to a castle where was King Bagdemagus. Said he to the King, 'What has brought you hither?' King Bagdemagus answered, 'In this castle there is a shield which if any man essay to wear about his neck, except he be worthy of it, he will either die within three days, or get some sore mischief. Now I am minded to essay it; and if I fail, then you shall essay it, for I know that you will not fail.' 'You please me well,' answered Sir Galahad, 'for I have as yet no shield.' On the morrow the King asked where this shield might be, and a monk showed it to him hanging behind the altar. It was white, with a red cross upon it. Then the King took it down from its place, and hung it about his neck, and so having put on his harness, went forth from the castle to seek adventures. But he took with him a squire, who should take news to Sir Galahad of how it fared with him. When they had ridden two miles, they came to a valley where there was a hermitage, and they saw a knight coming to meet them that was clad in white armour. And he had his spear in rest, and came on as fast as might be. The King also put his spear in rest and rode against the knight and brake his spear on him. But the knight smote the King on the shoulder, where the shield covered him not, and bore him from his horse. Then he lighted down from his horse, and took the shield from him, saying, 'This was great folly to bear a shield that may not be borne save by the best knight in the world.' And to the squire he said, 'Bear this shield to Sir Galahad, and greet him well from me.' The squire said, 'Tell me your name.' 'Take no heed of my name,' said the knight, 'for it is not for you to know. But be sure that this shield is for no man but Sir Galahad.' Then they carried the King to an abbey, where he was healed of his wound. But he scarce escaped with his life.

After this Sir Galahad rode away carrying the shield, and came to the hermitage. There the knight in white armour met him, and the two greeted each other right courteously, and when Sir Galahad would know the story of the shield, he told it to him, that it was borne in old time by a certain King Evelake against the Saracens, having been given to him by Joseph of Arimathea, and that when Joseph lay dying, he made a cross upon the shield with his blood, and that after this the shield was put away till the best knight in the world should come for it. After this the white knight vanished out of Sir Galahad's sight.

Then Sir Galahad, being now fully armed – for hitherto he had lacked a shield – rode on his way, and had many adventures. One while he met Sir Lancelot and Sir Percivale, that were the two strongest knights in the world, save, maybe, Sir Tristram of Lyonesse. And first he smote Sir Lancelot and his horse down to the ground, and afterward he served Sir Percivale in the same fashion, and this latter he had slain but that, by good chance, the sword swerved somewhat. But they knew not who he was till a recluse, that dwelt in a hermitage hard by, cried aloud, 'Hail, now, the best knight in the world.' This the two hearing, knew that it was Sir Galahad, and would fain have joined themselves to him, but he rode away as fast as he could.

Then he met with Sir Gawaine, and dealt him a very sore blow, and how he dwelt for a while with Sir Lancelot his father has been told already. Many other adventures he had, till there remained but one thing for him to do before the finding of the Grail, which thing was the healing of King Pelleas from the dolorous stroke which Sir Balin had dealt him, as has been told before.

When he came to the castle where King Pelleas dwelt, he and Sir Percivale and Sir Bors, for it was granted to them to be with him, they saw a man attired like to a bishop, with four angels about him. The angels set him in a chair before the table of silver whereon was the Holy Grail; then came in other angels, that bore candles of wax, and a towel, and a spear that dropped drops of blood in a marvellous fashion. And the man that was attired as a bishop said to the knights, 'This is the Holy Grail. Ye see it now, and shall see it yet more plainly in the place whither ye shall next go.' Then he gave them his blessing, and so vanished out of their sight.

Then went Sir Galahad to the spear, and touched the blood, and having touched it he anointed the King, who was straightway healed of his wound.

After this these three entered into a ship which carried them to a certain city of heathen folk, whose King put them in prison. But at the end of the year the king, having fallen sick, sent for them, and cried for mercy on what he had done. So they forgave him.

When he was dead the people of that city would not be content but they must have Sir Galahad to their king. And being King, he made for the table of silver a chest of gold to be a covering of the Holy Grail, and every day he and his companions said their prayers before it. At the year's end it was granted to Sir Galahad to see the Holy Grail full plainly, as no man ever saw it but he. When he had seen it, he went to Sir Percivale and kissed him, and also to Sir Bors and kissed him, and commended them both to God. This done, he bade them salute Sir Lancelot, and tell him, said he, 'that he remember how unstable is the world.' Having said this he died, and the angels carried his soul to heaven. And then came down a hand that took the Holy Grail and the spear, and carried them away.

Thus did Sir Galahad accomplish the adventure of the Holy Grail, because he was pure and without spot.

THE PRINCE WHO SOUGHT IMMORTALITY

Leonora Lang

ONCE IN THE very middle of the middle of a large kingdom, there was a town, and in the town a palace, and in the palace a king. This king had one son whom his father thought was wiser and cleverer than any son ever was before, and indeed his father had spared no pains to make him so. He had been very careful in choosing his tutors and governors when he was a boy, and when he became a youth he sent him to travel, so that he might see the ways of other people, and find that they were often as good as his own.

It was now a year since the prince had returned home, for his father felt that it was time that his son should learn how to rule the kingdom which would one day be his. But during his long absence the prince seemed to have changed his character altogether. From being a merry and light-hearted boy, he had grown into a gloomy and thoughtful man. The king knew of nothing that could have produced such an alteration. He vexed himself about it from morning till night, till at length an explanation occurred to him – the young man was in love!

Now the prince never talked about his feelings – for the matter of that he scarcely talked at all; and the father knew that if he was to come to the bottom of the prince's dismal face, he would have to begin. So one day, after dinner, he took his son by the arm and led him into another room, hung entirely with the pictures of beautiful maidens, each one more lovely than the other.

'My dear boy,' he said, 'you are very sad; perhaps after all your wanderings it is dull for you here all alone with me. It would be much better if you would marry, and I have collected here the portraits of the most beautiful women in the world of a rank equal to your own. Choose which among them you would like for a wife, and I will send an embassy to her father to ask for her hand.'

'Alas! your Majesty,' answered the prince, 'it is not love or marriage that makes me so gloomy; but the thought, which haunts me day and night, that all men, even kings, must die. Never shall I be happy again till I have found a kingdom where death is unknown. And I have determined to give myself no rest till I have discovered the Land of Immortality.'

The old king heard him with dismay; things were worse than he thought. He tried to reason with his son, and told him that during all these years he had been looking forward to his return, in order to resign his throne and its cares, which pressed so heavily upon him. But it was in vain that he talked; the prince would listen to nothing, and the following morning buckled on his sword and set forth on his journey.

He had been travelling for many days, and had left his fatherland behind him, when close to the road he came upon a huge tree, and on its topmost bough an eagle was sitting shaking the branches with all his might. This seemed so strange and so unlike an eagle, that the prince stood still with surprise, and the bird saw him and flew to the ground. The moment its feet touched the ground he changed into a king.

'Why do you look so astonished?' he asked.

'I was wondering why you shook the boughs so fiercely,' answered the prince.

'I am condemned to do this, for neither I nor any of my kindred can die till I have rooted up this great tree,' replied the king of the eagles. 'But it is now evening, and I need work no more today. Come to my house with me, and be my guest for the night.'

The prince accepted gratefully the eagle's invitation, for he was tired and hungry. They were received at the palace by the king's beautiful daughter, who gave orders that dinner should be laid for them at once. While they were eating, the eagle questioned his guest about his travels, and if he was wandering for pleasure's sake, or with any special aim. Then the prince told him everything, and how he could never turn back till he had discovered the Land of Immortality.

'Dear brother,' said the eagle, 'you have discovered it already, and it rejoices my heart to think that you will stay with us. Have you not just heard me say that death has no power either over myself or any of my kindred till that great tree is rooted up? It will take me six hundred years' hard work to do that; so marry my daughter and let us all live happily together here. After all, six hundred years is an eternity!'

'Ah, dear king,' replied the young man, 'your offer is very tempting! But at the end of six hundred years we should have to die, so we should be no better off! No, I must go on till I find the country where there is no death at all.'

Then the princess spoke, and tried to persuade the guest to change his mind, but he sorrowfully shook his head. At length, seeing that his resolution was firmly fixed, she took from a cabinet a little box which contained her picture, and gave it to him saying:

'As you will not stay with us, prince, accept this box, which will sometimes recall us to your memory. If you are tired of travelling before you come to the Land of Immortality, open this box and look at my picture, and you will be borne along either on earth or in the air, quick as thought, or swift as the whirlwind.'

The prince thanked her for her gift, which he placed in his tunic, and sorrowfully bade the eagle and his daughter farewell.

Never was any present in the world as useful as that little box, and many times did he bless the kind thought of the princess. One evening it had carried him to the top of a high mountain, where he saw a man with a bald head, busily engaged in digging up spadefuls of earth and throwing them in a basket. When the basket was full he took it away and returned with an empty one, which he likewise filled. The prince stood and watched him for a little, till the bald-headed man looked up and said to him: 'Dear brother, what surprises you so much?'

'I was wondering why you were filling the basket,' replied the prince.

'Oh!' replied the man, 'I am condemned to do this, for neither I nor any of my family can die till I have dug away the whole of this mountain and made it level with the plain. But, come, it is almost dark, and I shall work no longer.' And he plucked a leaf from a tree close by, and from a rough digger he was changed into a stately bald-headed king. 'Come home with me,' he added; 'you must be tired and hungry, and my daughter will have supper ready for us.' The prince accepted gladly, and they went back to the palace, where the bald-headed king's daughter, who was still more beautiful than the other princess, welcomed them at the door and led the way into a large hall and to a table covered with silver dishes. While they were eating, the bald-headed king asked the prince how he had happened to wander so far, and the young man told him all about it, and how he was seeking the Land of Immortality. 'You have found it already,' answered the king, 'for, as I said, neither I nor my family can die till I have levelled this great mountain; and that will take full eight hundred years longer. Stay here with us and marry my daughter. Eight hundred years is surely long enough to live.'

'Oh, certainly,' answered the prince; 'but, all the same, I would rather go and seek the land where there is no death at all.'

So next morning he bade them farewell, though the princess begged him to stay with all her might; and when she found that she could not persuade him she gave him as a remembrance a gold ring. This ring was still more useful than the box, because when one wished oneself at any place one was there directly, without even the trouble of flying to it through the air. The prince put it on his finger, and thanking her heartily, went his way.

He walked on for some distance, and then he recollected the ring and thought he would try if the princess had spoken truly as to its powers. 'I wish I was at the end of the world,' he said, shutting his eyes, and when he opened them he was standing in a street full of marble palaces. The men who passed him were tall and strong, and their clothes were magnificent. He stopped some of them and asked in all the twenty-seven languages he knew what was the name of the city, but no one answered him. Then his heart sank within him; what should he do in this strange place if nobody could understand anything? Suddenly his eyes fell upon a man dressed after the fashion of his native country, and he ran up to him and spoke to him in his own tongue. 'What city is this, my friend?' he inquired.

'It is the capital city of the Blue Kingdom,' replied the man, 'but the king himself is dead, and his daughter is now the ruler.'

With this news the prince was satisfied, and begged his countryman to show him the way to the young queen's palace. The man led him through several streets into a large square, one side of which was occupied by a splendid building that seemed borne up on slender pillars of soft green marble. In front was a flight of steps, and on these the queen was sitting wrapped in a veil of shining silver mist, listening to the complaints of her people and dealing out justice. When the prince came up she saw directly that he was no ordinary man, and telling her chamberlain to dismiss the rest of her petitioners for that day, she signed to the prince to follow her into the palace. Luckily she had been taught his language as a child, so they had no difficulty in talking together.

The prince told all his story and how he was journeying in search of the Land of Immortality. When he had finished, the princess, who had listened attentively, rose, and taking his arm, led him to the door of another room, the floor of which was made entirely of needles, stuck so close together that there was not room for a single needle more.

'Prince,' she said, turning to him, 'you see these needles? Well, know that neither I nor any of my family can die till I have worn out these needles in sewing. It will take at least a thousand years for that. Stay here, and share my throne; a thousand years is long enough to live!'

'Certainly,' answered he; 'still, at the end of the thousand years I should have to die! No, I must find the land where there is no death.'

The queen did all she could to persuade him to stay, but as her words proved useless, at length she gave it up. Then she said to him: 'As you will not stay, take this little golden rod as a remembrance of me. It has the power to become anything you wish it to be, when you are in need.'

So the prince thanked her, and putting the rod in his pocket, went his way.

Scarcely had he left the town behind him when he came to a broad river which no man might pass, for he was standing at the end of the world, and this was the river which flowed round it.

Not knowing what to do next, he walked a little distance up the bank, and there, over his head, a beautiful city was floating in the air. He longed to get to it, but how? neither road nor bridge was anywhere to be seen, yet the city drew him upwards, and he felt that here at last was the country which he sought. Suddenly he remembered the golden rod which the mist-veiled queen had given him. With a beating heart he flung it to the ground, wishing with all his might that it should turn into a bridge, and fearing that, after all, this might prove beyond its power. But no, instead of the rod, there stood a golden ladder, leading straight up to the city of the air. He was about to enter the golden gates, when there sprang at him a wondrous beast, whose like he had never seen. 'Out sword from the sheath,' cried the prince, springing back with a cry. And the sword leapt from the scabbard and cut off some of the monster's heads, but others grew again directly, so that the prince, pale with terror, stood where he was, calling for help, and put his sword back in the sheath again.

The queen of the city heard the noise and looked from her window to see what was happening. Summoning one of her servants, she bade him go and rescue the stranger, and bring him to her. The prince thankfully obeyed her orders, and entered her presence.

The moment she looked at him, the queen also felt that he was no ordinary man, and she welcomed him graciously, and asked him what had brought him to the city. In answer the prince told all his story, and how he had travelled long and far in search of the Land of Immortality.

'You have found it,' said she, 'for I am queen over life and over death. Here you can dwell among the immortals.'

A thousand years had passed since the prince first entered the city, but they had flown so fast that the time seemed no more than six months. There had not been one instant of the thousand years that the prince was not happy till one night when he dreamed of his father and mother. Then the longing for his home came upon him with a rush, and in the morning he told the Queen of the Immortals that he must go and see his father and mother once more. The queen stared at him with amazement, and cried: 'Why, prince, are you out of your senses? It is more than eight hundred years since your father and mother died! There will not even be their dust remaining.'

'I must go all the same,' said he.

'Well, do not be in a hurry,' continued the queen, understanding that he would not be prevented. 'Wait till I make some preparations for your journey.' So she unlocked her great treasure chest, and took out two beautiful flasks, one of gold and one of silver, which she hung round his neck. Then she showed him a little trap-door in one corner of the room, and said: 'Fill the silver flask with this water, which is below the trap-door. It is enchanted, and whoever you sprinkle with the water will become a dead man at once, even if he had lived a thousand years. The golden flask you must fill with the water here,' she added, pointing to a well in another corner. 'It springs from the rock of eternity; you have only to sprinkle a few drops on a body and it will come to life again, if it had been a thousand years dead.'

The prince thanked the queen for her gifts, and, bidding her farewell, went on his journey.

He soon arrived in the town where the mist-veiled queen reigned in her palace, but the whole city had changed, and he could scarcely find his way through the streets. In the palace itself all was still, and he wandered through the rooms without meeting anyone to stop him. At last he entered the queen's own chamber, and there she lay, with her embroidery still in her hands, fast asleep. He pulled at her dress, but she did not waken. Then a dreadful idea came over him, and he ran to the chamber where the needles had been kept, but it was quite empty. The queen had broken the last over the work she held in her hand, and with it the spell was broken too, and she lay dead.

Quick as thought the prince pulled out the golden flask, and sprinkled some drops of the water over the queen. In a moment she moved gently, and raising her head, opened her eyes.

'Oh, my dear friend, I am so glad you wakened me; I must have slept a long while!'

'You would have slept till eternity,' answered the prince, 'if I had not been here to waken you.'

At these words the queen remembered about the needles. She knew now that she had been dead, and that the prince had restored her to life. She gave him thanks from her heart for what he had done, and vowed she would repay him if she ever got a chance.

The prince took his leave, and set out for the country of the bald-headed king. As he drew near the place he saw that the whole mountain had been dug away, and that the king was lying dead on the ground, his spade and bucket beside him. But as soon as the water from the golden flask touched him he yawned and stretched himself, and slowly rose to his feet. 'Oh, my dear friend, I am so glad to see you,' cried he, 'I must have slept a long while!'

'You would have slept till eternity if I had not been here to waken you,' answered the prince. And the king remembered the mountain, and the spell, and vowed to repay the service if he ever had a chance.

Further along the road which led to his old home the prince found the great tree torn up by its roots, and the king of the eagles sitting dead on the ground, with his wings outspread as if for flight. A flutter ran through the feathers as the drops of water fell on them, and the eagle lifted his beak from the ground and said: 'Oh, how long I must have slept! How can I thank you for having awakened me, my dear, good friend!'

'You would have slept till eternity if I had not been here to waken you', answered the prince. Then the king remembered about the tree, and knew that he had been dead, and promised, if ever he had the chance, to repay what the prince had done for him.

At last he reached the capital of his father's kingdom, but on reaching the place where the royal palace had stood, instead of the marble galleries where he used to play, there lay a great sulphur lake, its blue flames darting into the air. How was he to find his father and mother, and bring them back to life, if they were lying at the bottom of that horrible water? He turned away sadly and wandered back into the streets, hardly knowing where he was going; when a voice behind him cried: 'Stop, prince, I have caught you at last! It is a thousand years since I first began to seek you.' And there beside him stood the old, white-bearded, figure of Death. Swiftly he drew the ring from his finger, and the king of the eagles, the bald-headed king, and the mist-veiled queen, hastened to his rescue. In an instant they had seized upon Death and held him tight, till the prince should have time to reach the Land of Immortality. But they did not know how quickly Death could fly, and the prince had only one foot across the border, when he felt the other grasped from behind, and the voice of Death calling: 'Halt! now you are mine.'

The Queen of the Immortals was watching from her window, and cried to Death that he had no power in her kingdom, and that he must seek his prey elsewhere.

'Quite true,' answered Death; 'but his foot is in *my* kingdom, and that belongs to me!'

'At any rate half of him is mine,' replied the Queen, 'and what good can the other half do you? Half a man is no use, either to you or to me! But this once I will allow you to cross into my kingdom, and we will decide by a wager whose he is.'

And so it was settled. Death stepped across the narrow line that surrounds the Land of Immortality, and the queen proposed the wager which was to decide the prince's fate. 'I will throw him up into the sky,' she said, 'right to the back of the morning star, and if he falls down into this city, then he is mine. But if he should fall outside the walls, he shall belong to you.'

In the middle of the city was a great open square, and here the queen wished the wager to take place. When all was ready, she put her foot under the foot of the prince and swung him into the air. Up, up, he went, high amongst the stars, and no man's eyes could follow him. Had she thrown him up straight? the queen wondered anxiously, for, if not, he would fall outside the walls, and she would lose him for ever. The moments seemed long while she and Death stood gazing up into the air, waiting to know whose prize the prince would be. Suddenly they both caught sight of a tiny speck no bigger than a wasp, right up in the blue. Was he coming straight? No! Yes! But as he was nearing the city, a light wind sprang up, and swayed him in the direction of the wall. Another second and he would have fallen half over it, when the queen sprang forward, seized him in her arms, and flung him into the castle. Then she commanded her servants to cast Death out of the city, which they did, with such hard blows that he never dared to show his face again in the Land of Immortality.

THE CHANGELINGS

Jessica Amanda Salmonson

A STRANGE CREATURE called the Huluk used to live in Lake Tualatin, now called Wapato Lake, a quiet shallow lake surrounded by gorgeous greenery. The Huluk is not there now, because it outgrew the lake, and went to live elsewhere. Today no one sees it; long ago, it was often seen. This story happened in bygone days when the Huluk still dwelt in that lake.

By nature sluggish, the Huluk waddled like a porcupine when it was out of the water. It dragged its big flat tail which was akin to that of a beaver, but spiked all about the rump with enormous quills. It had a long, slender, blunt-ended horn on the top of its head between its huge clamshell ears, above the eyes that were two protuberant half-globes, black and moist and never blinking.

The Huluk's horn was covered in red and white spots. The fur of the Huluk was slick and mottled.

Three children were out digging roots one day, a little girl, a little boy, and an older boy. The girl wore a sleeveless dress of seal fur interlaced with braids of mountain sheep wool. Upon her head she wore a bobcat-fur cap. The two boys wore striped coats of tanned deerskin decorated with red beads. When the creature came out of the water the little boy saw it first. At first he thought it was a beaver the size of a grizzly bear. He was a fearless boy, and the very idea of such a big beaver made him laugh.

'What are you laughing at?' asked his sister. 'What do you see?'

The little boy pointed and exclaimed, 'I like that creature's horn! I want it to belong to me!'

When his little sister saw it, she joined the laughter. The

horn was indeed very appealing. Together they ran toward the creature.

'Come back!' cried their older brother, understanding better the dangers of inexplicable beasts. He tried to run after his siblings, but his feet would not move, as though they were stuck in mud, or roots had grabbed him. The little ones did not listen to him, did not come back.

So the Huluk scooped up the little boy on its horn. Then it scooped up the little girl. They were taken into the water riding on the horn. From where the older child was standing knee-deep in muck, it looked as though they might have been impaled, but he wasn't sure, for they were obviously alive; he could still hear them laughing. As the creature slid into the lake, the older boy's legs were mysteriously freed from the muck, and he turned to flee.

He made it home and told his mother and father, 'Brother and sister have been carried away! The Tualatin lake-monster either drowned them or impaled them, I don't know which!'

Then the boy grew ill from his adventure. He lay down on a mat in the longhouse. He was sweating and moaning. His mother laid over him a cougar skin blanket, thoroughly tanned, and as she did so, she saw that he was covered with red and purple spots.

* * *

The father was called Wawinxpa, a chief. He took a carved box out from under a bench in the longhouse and opened it. He drew forth all his best clothes. He dressed himself in a shirt of tanned elkskin which his wife had decorated with beads and quills, tanned leggings and breechcloth, new moccasins of deerhide with the fur intact.

His marmot fur knife-belt was decorated with feathers from a white swan's back. His necklace consisted of bear claws, symbolic of warrior strength, plus the rare small shells of a shaman. He blacked his cheeks with pitch soot. Last of all he put on a headdress. It was made of white swan-feathers interspersed with red and black woodpecker-feathers. The circlet of feathers stuck straight up from his head.

Wawinxpa went to the place where his youngest children had

been taken away below the water. At the lake's edge he saw a big hole and followed the Huluk's tracks into a cave. When he came out the other side of the tunnel, the sky was made of shimmering earth, and trees were growing downward from the roof of the sky.

Off in the misty distance, he caught a glimpse of his children. They were clinging to the speckled horn of the monster, which trod slowly but steadily away. It moved awkwardly across pitted earth, dragging its tail and gouging the ground with its arrow-length quills, leaving a wide track that was easy to follow.

The father pursued them through the dismal world up and down deep gulleys. Time and again he caught sight of his children, but the monster was never closer or farther. It was always the same distance away. On the upper bank of the first gulley Wawinxpa motioned with his hands and cried out for his children to let go of the horn and come to him.

His children clung fast and called back, 'Father we are different, different, different!'

The next day, from the top of the second gulley, he called to them again. But they only replied, 'We are different, different!' as they held fast to the Huluk's horn. The monster waddled on and on, and though it never exerted itself, it managed somehow always to keep the same distance. The father grew increasingly despondent.

He made a camp each night in sheltered places low in one or another gulley. Five days he stayed in the strange land. Five times he ascended to a different gulley's ridge and called out, 'Come to me, my children, come!' He could never catch up to them, and their reply was always the same.

After the fifth try, the father saw his children no more. He looked everywhere, but the Huluk was no more to be seen. Its wide trail vanished on a lava bed. Wawinxpa came out of the cave, into the good world, but the world seemed less good without his children. He went home and told his wife, 'The Tualatin monster has taken our children to live under the mountain. All the trees in that place grow straight down out of the sky. I saw our children on the horn of the monster, but could not catch them.'

Then he sat down with his wife and together they cried.

The older son lay sick with fever, sleeping fitfully. His mother prepared strong medicinal teas of herbs, crab apple bark and spruce sap, but the boy could not keep liquids in him.

Through the night, Wawinxpa lay near his son and for a long time could not sleep for worrying that his last child would die.

Finally, Wawinxpa slept, and his night was filled with dreams. He drew dream-power into himself as he was sleeping. The next day his wife could not wake him. She waited patiently, watching her husband fretfully as she attended her sick son. Toward noon, Wawinxpa opened his eyes and said, 'I have seen them in my dream. I will try again to bring them home.'

Once more he made himself ready, wearing his many fine garments. He covered his forehead with black pitch. He made speckles on the rest of his face with red paint, white clay and coal. Then in the forest he twisted a long hazel rope and tied one end around his waist. The other end he tied to a tree beside Lake Tualatin. Then he swam out to the middle of the lake and peered down.

Deep in the clear, clear water he saw his children on the horn of the monster. He called down into the waters, 'Let go of the horn, my children, and swim up here to me!'

But they replied, 'Father, we are different, different, different.'

He swam about the middle of the lake until he was weary, with just the feathers of his headdress sticking up. The whole time he prayed and prayed for assistance from good spirits. He prayed to the clouds, to the lake, to the mountains, to the trees, to the birds and to the kindly spirit he had met in the forest when he came of age and which was always with him. Then he was so tired he couldn't even swim to shore. He sank from view, and would have drowned. His wife came wearing a cedar-bark dress and robe of interwoven seal, coon and bobcat furs. She pulled on the hazel rope, drawing her husband out of the water.

She raised him in her arms, wrapped him in a cougar hide blanket, and held him fast until he was warm.

The next morning, he went out into the lake again, with just his headdress of swan and woodpecker feathers showing in the distance. He called to his children, but their answer was the same as before. On the fifth day, he saw that his children had changed markedly. Their hair was gone. Their eyes were half-globes of darkness without lids. Their bodies had merged into one speckled body with two heads.

He called down to them, 'Children, swim up here to me!'

Both heads spoke at once, saying, 'Father, I am different, different, different.'

* * *

Wawinxpa's five days of prayers and ascetic acts had assisted in the recovery of his one remaining child. The boy had only white scars to show how the Huluk had seen him. On that last day of the father's prayer, fast, and swimming, the son came with his mother to the lakeshore. Together they pulled on the hazel cord.

For the last time Wawinxpa was drawn out of the water. He clung to his wife and son, and his feather headdress fell off to the ground. All he could say was, 'The children belong forever to the Huluk. Weep, my wife; weep, my only son; weep for they are different, different, different.'

THE STORY OF A GAZELLE

Edward Steere

THERE ONCE LIVED a man who wasted all his money, and grew so poor that his only food was a few grains of corn, which he scratched like a fowl from out of a dust-heap.

One day he was scratching as usual among a dust-heap in the street, hoping to find something for breakfast, when his eye fell upon a small silver coin, called an eighth, which he greedily snatched up. 'Now I can have a proper meal,' he thought, and after drinking some water at a well he lay down and slept so long that it was sunrise before he woke again. Then he jumped up and returned to the dust-heap. 'For who knows,' he said to himself, 'whether I may not have some good luck again.'

As he was walking down the road, he saw a man coming towards him, carrying a cage made of twigs. 'Hi! you fellow!' called he, 'what have you got inside there?'

'Gazelles,' replied the man.

'Bring them here, for I should like to see them.'

As he spoke, some men who were standing by began to laugh, saying to the man with the cage: 'You had better take care how you bargain with him, for he has nothing at all except what he picks up from a dust-heap, and if he can't feed himself, will he be able to feed a gazelle?'

But the man with the cage made answer: 'Since I started from my home in the country, fifty people at the least have called me to show them my gazelles, and was there one among them who cared to buy? It is the custom for a trader in merchandise to be summoned hither and thither, and who knows where one may find a buyer?' And he took up his cage and went towards the scratcher of dust-heaps, and the men went with him.

'What do you ask for your gazelles?' said the beggar. 'Will you let me have one for an eighth?'

And the man with the cage took out a gazelle, and held it out, saying, 'Take this one, master!'

And the beggar took it and carried it to the dust-heap, where he scratched carefully till he found a few grains of corn, which he divided with his gazelle. This he did night and morning, till five days went by.

Then, as he slept, the gazelle woke him, saying, 'Master.'

And the man answered, 'How is it that I see a wonder?'

'What wonder?' asked the gazelle.

'Why, that you, a gazelle, should be able to speak, for, from the beginning, my father and mother and all the people that are in the world have never told me of a talking gazelle.'

'Never mind that,' said the gazelle, 'but listen to what I say! First, I took you for my master. Second, you gave for me all you had in the world. I cannot run away from you, but give me, I pray you, leave to go every morning and seek food for myself, and every evening I will come back to you. What you find in the dust-heaps is not enough for both of us.'

'Go, then,' answered the master; and the gazelle went.

When the sun had set, the gazelle came back, and the poor man was very glad, and they lay down and slept side by side.

In the morning it said to him, 'I am going away to feed.'

And the man replied, 'Go, my son,' but he felt very lonely without his gazelle, and set out sooner than usual for the dust-heap where he generally found most corn. And glad he was when the evening came, and he could return home. He lay on the grass chewing tobacco, when the gazelle trotted up.

'Good evening, my master; how have you fared all day? I have been resting in the shade in a place where there is sweet grass when I am hungry, and fresh water when I am thirsty, and a soft breeze to fan me in the heat. It is far away in the forest, and no one knows of it but me, and tomorrow I shall go again.'

So for five days the gazelle set off at daybreak for this cool spot, but on the fifth day it came to a place where the grass was bitter, and it did not like it, and scratched, hoping to tear away the bad blades. But, instead, it saw something lying in the earth, which turned out to be a diamond, very large and bright. 'Oh, ho!' said the gazelle to itself, 'perhaps now I can do something for my master who bought me with all the money he had; but I must be careful or they will say he has stolen it. I had better take it myself to some great rich man, and see what it will do for me.'

Directly the gazelle had come to this conclusion, it picked up the diamond in its mouth, and went on and on and on through the forest, but found no place where a rich man was likely to dwell. For two more days it ran, from dawn to dark, till at last early one morning it caught sight of a large town, which gave it fresh courage.

The people were standing about the streets doing their marketing, when the gazelle bounded past, the diamond flashing as it ran. They called after it, but it took no notice till it reached the palace, where the sultan was sitting, enjoying the cool air. And the gazelle galloped up to him, and laid the diamond at his feet.

The sultan looked first at the diamond and next at the gazelle; then he ordered his attendants to bring cushions and a carpet, that the gazelle might rest itself after its long journey. And he likewise ordered milk to be brought, and rice, that it might eat and drink and be refreshed.

And when the gazelle was rested, the sultan said to it: 'Give me the news you have come with.'

And the gazelle answered: 'I am come with this diamond, which is a pledge from my master the Sultan Darai. He has heard you have a daughter, and sends you this small token, and begs you will give her to him to wife.'

And the sultan said: 'I am content. The wife is his wife, the family is his family, the slave is his slave. Let him come to me empty-handed, I am content.'

When the sultan had ended, the gazelle rose, and said: 'Master, farewell; I go back to our town, and in eight days, or it may be in eleven days, we shall arrive as your guests.'

And the sultan answered: 'So let it be.'

All this time the poor man far away had been mourning and weeping for his gazelle, which he thought had run away from him for ever. And when it came in at the door he rushed to embrace it with such joy that he would not allow it a chance to speak.

'Be still, master, and don't cry,' said the gazelle at last; 'let us sleep now, and in the morning, when I go, follow me.'

With the first ray of dawn they got up and went into the forest, and on the fifth day, as they were resting near a stream, the gazelle gave its master a sound beating, and then bade him stay where he was till it returned. And the gazelle ran off, and about ten o'clock it came near the sultan's palace, where the road was all lined with soldiers who were there to do honour to Sultan Darai. And directly they caught sight of the gazelle in the distance one of the soldiers ran on and said, 'Sultan Darai is coming: I have seen the gazelle.'

Then the sultan rose up, and called his whole court to follow him, and went out to meet the gazelle, who, bounding up to him, gave him greeting. The sultan answered politely, and inquired where it had left its master, whom it had promised to bring back.

'Alas!' replied the gazelle,' he is lying in the forest, for on our way here we were met by robbers, who, after beating and robbing him, took away all his clothes. And he is now hiding under a bush, lest a passing stranger might see him.'

The sultan, on hearing what had happened to his future son-in-law, turned his horse and rode to the palace, and bade a groom to harness the best horse in the stable and ordered a woman slave to bring a bag of clothes, such as a man might want, out of the chest; and he chose out a tunic and a turban and a sash for the waist, and fetched himself a gold-hilted sword, and a dagger and a pair of sandals, and a stick of sweet-smelling wood.

'Now,' said he to the gazelle, 'take these things with the soldiers to the sultan, that he may be able to come.'

And the gazelle answered: 'Can I take those soldiers to go and put my master to shame as he lies there naked? I am enough by myself, my lord.'

'How will you be enough,' asked the sultan, 'to manage this horse and all these clothes?'

'Oh, that is easily done,' replied the gazelle. 'Fasten the horse to my neck and tie the clothes to the back of the horse, and be sure they are fixed firmly, as I shall go faster than he does.'

Everything was carried out as the gazelle had ordered, and

when all was ready it said to the sultan: 'Farewell, my lord, I am going.'

'Farewell, gazelle,' answered the sultan; 'when shall we see you again?'

'Tomorrow about five,' replied the gazelle, and, giving a tug to the horse's rein, they set off at a gallop.

The sultan watched them till they were out of sight: then he said to his attendants, 'That gazelle comes from gentle hands, from the house of a sultan, and that is what makes it so different from other gazelles.' And in the eyes of the sultan the gazelle became a person of consequence.

Meanwhile the gazelle ran on till it came to the place where its master was seated, and his heart laughed when he saw the gazelle.

And the gazelle said to him, 'Get up, my master, and bathe in the stream!' and when the man had bathed it said again, 'Now rub yourself well with earth, and rub your teeth well with sand to make them bright and shining.' And when this was done it said, 'The sun has gone down behind the hills; it is time for us to go': so it went and brought the clothes from the back of the horse, and the man put them on and was well pleased.

'Master!' said the gazelle when the man was ready, 'be sure that where we are going you keep silence, except for giving greetings and asking for news. Leave all the talking to me. I have provided you with a wife, and have made her presents of clothes and turbans and rare and precious things, so it is needless for you to speak.'

'Very good, I will be silent,' replied the man as he mounted the horse. 'You have given all this; it is you who are the master, and I who am the slave, and I will obey you in all things.'

So they went their way, and they went and went till the gazelle saw in the distance the palace of the sultan. Then it said, 'Master, that is the house we are going to, and you are not a poor man any longer: even your name is new.'

'What *is* my name, eh, my father?' asked the man.

'Sultan Darai,' said the gazelle.

Very soon some soldiers came to meet them, while others ran off to tell the sultan of their approach. And the sultan set off at once, and the viziers and the emirs, and the judges, and the rich men of the city, all followed him. Directly the gazelle saw them coming, it said to its master: 'Your father-in-law is coming to meet you; that is he in the middle, wearing a mantle of sky-blue. Get off your horse and go to greet him.'

And Sultan Darai leapt from his horse, and so did the other sultan, and they gave their hands to one another and kissed each other, and went together into the palace.

The next morning the gazelle went to the rooms of the sultan, and said to him: 'My lord, we want you to marry us our wife, for the soul of Sultan Darai is eager.'

'The wife is ready, so call the priest,' answered he, and when the ceremony was over a cannon was fired and music was played, and within the palace there was feasting.

'Master,' said the gazelle the following morning, 'I am setting out on a journey, and I shall not be back for seven days, and perhaps not then. But be careful not to leave the house till I come.'

And the master answered, 'I will not leave the house.'

And it went to the sultan of the country and said to him: 'My lord, Sultan Darai has sent me to his town to get the house in order. It will take me seven days, and if I am not back in seven days he will not leave the palace till I return.'

'Very good,' said the sultan.

And it went and it went through the forest and wilderness, till it arrived at a town full of fine houses. At the end of the chief road was a great house, beautiful exceedingly, built of sapphire and turquoise and marbles. 'That,' thought the gazelle, 'is the house for my master, and I will call up my courage and go and look at the people who are in it, if any people there are. For in this town have I as yet seen no people. If I die, I die, and if I live, I live. Here can I think of no plan, so if anything is to kill me, it will kill me.'

Then it knocked twice at the door, and cried 'Open,' but no one answered. And it cried again, and a voice replied:

'Who are you that are crying "Open"?'

And the gazelle said, 'It is I, great mistress, your grandchild.'

'If you are my grandchild,' returned the voice, 'go back whence you came. Don't come and die here, and bring me to my death as well.'

'Open, mistress, I entreat, I have something to say to you.'

'Grandchild,' replied she, 'I fear to put your life in danger, and my own too.'

'Oh, mistress, my life will not be lost, nor yours either; open, I pray you.' So she opened the door.

'What is the news where you come from, my grandson,' asked she.

'Great lady, where I come from it is well, and with you it is well.'

'Ah, my son, here it is not well at all. If you seek a way to die, or if you have not yet seen death, then is today the day for you to know what dying is.'

'If I am to know it, I shall know it,' replied the gazelle; 'but tell me, who is the lord of this house?'

And she said: 'Ah, father! in this house is much wealth, and much people, and much food, and many horses. And the lord of it all is an exceeding great and wonderful snake.'

'Oh!' cried the gazelle when he heard this; 'tell me how I can get at the snake to kill him?'

'My son,' returned the old woman, 'do not say words like those; you risk both our lives. He has put me here all by myself, and I have to cook his food. When the great snake is coming there springs up a wind, and blows the dust about, and this goes on till the great snake glides into the courtyard and calls for his dinner, which must always be ready for him in those big pots. He eats till he has had enough, and then drinks a whole tankful of water. After that he goes away. Every second day he comes, when the sun is over the house. And he has seven heads. How then can you be a match for him, my son?'

'Mind your own business, mother,' answered the gazelle, 'and don't mind other people's! Has this snake a sword?'

'He has a sword, and a sharp one too. It cuts like a flash of lightning.'

'Give it to me, mother!' said the gazelle, and she unhooked the sword from the wall, as she was bidden. 'You must be quick,' she said, 'for he may be here at any moment. Hark! is not that the wind rising? He has come!'

They were silent, but the old woman peeped from behind a curtain, and saw the snake busy at the pots which she had placed ready for him in the courtyard. And after he had done eating and drinking he came to the door:

'You old body!' he cried; 'what smell is that I smell inside that is not the smell of every day?'

'Oh, master!' answered she, 'I am alone, as I always am! but today, after many days, I have sprinkled fresh scent all over me, and it is that which you smell. What else could it be, master?'

All this time the gazelle had been standing close to the door, holding the sword in one of its front paws. And as the snake put one of his heads through the hole that he had made so as to get in and out comfortably, it cut it off so clean that the snake really did not feel it. The second blow was not quite so straight, for the snake said to himself, 'Who is that who is trying to scratch me?' and stretched out his third head to see; but no sooner was the neck through the hole than the head went rolling to join the rest.

When six of his heads were gone the snake lashed his tail with such fury that the gazelle and the old woman could not see each other for the dust he made. And the gazelle said to him, 'You have climbed all sorts of trees, but this you can't climb,' and as the seventh head came darting through it went rolling to join the rest.

Then the sword fell rattling on the ground, for the gazelle had fainted.

The old woman shrieked with delight when she saw her enemy was dead, and ran to bring water to the gazelle, and fanned it, and put it where the wind could blow on it, till it grew better and gave a sneeze. And the heart of the old woman was glad, and she gave it more water, till by and by the gazelle got up.

'Show me this house,' it said, 'from beginning to end, from top to bottom, from inside to out.'

So she arose and showed the gazelle rooms full of gold and precious things, and other rooms full of slaves. 'They are all yours, goods and slaves,' said she.

But the gazelle answered, 'You must keep them safe till I call my master.'

For two days it lay and rested in the house, and fed on milk and rice, and on the third day it bade the old woman farewell and started back to its master.

And when he heard that the gazelle was at the door he felt like a man who has found the time when all prayers are granted, and he rose and kissed it, saying: 'My father, you have been a long time; you have left sorrow with me. I cannot eat, I cannot drink, I cannot laugh; my heart felt no smile at anything, because of thinking of you.'

And the gazelle answered: 'I am well, and where I come from it is well, and I wish that after four days you would take your wife and go home.'

And he said: 'It is for you to speak. Where you go, I will follow.'

'Then I shall go to your father-in-law and tell him this news.'

'Go, my son.'

So the gazelle went to the father-in-law and said: 'I am sent by my master to come and tell you that after four days he will go away with his wife to his own home.'

'Must he really go so quickly? We have not yet sat much together, I and Sultan Darai, nor have we yet talked much together, nor have we yet ridden out together, nor have we eaten together; yet it is fourteen days since he came.'

But the gazelle replied: 'My lord, you cannot help it, for he wishes to go home, and nothing will stop him.'

'Very good,' said the sultan, and he called all the people who were in the town, and commanded that the day his daughter left the palace ladies and guards were to attend her on her way.

And at the end of four days a great company of ladies and slaves and horses went forth to escort the wife of Sultan Darai to her new home. They rode all day, and when the sun sank behind the hills they rested, and ate of the food the gazelle gave them, and lay down to sleep. And they journeyed on for many days, and they all, nobles and slaves, loved the gazelle with a great love – more than they loved the Sultan Darai.

At last one day signs of houses appeared, far, far off. And those who saw cried out, 'Gazelle!'

And it answered, 'Ah, my mistresses, that is the house of Sultan Darai.'

At this news the women rejoiced much, and the slaves rejoiced much, and in the space of two hours they came to the gates, and the gazelle bade them all stay behind, and it went on to the house with Sultan Darai.

When the old woman saw them coming through the courtyard she jumped and shouted for joy, and as the gazelle drew near she seized it in her arms, and kissed it. The gazelle did not like this, and said to her: 'Old woman, leave me alone; the one to be carried is my master, and the one to be kissed is my master.'

And she answered, 'Forgive me, my son. I did not know this was our master,' and she threw open all the doors so that the master might see everything that the rooms and storehouses contained. Sultan Darai looked about him, and at length he said:

'Unfasten those horses that are tied up, and let loose those people that are bound. And let some sweep, and some spread the beds, and some cook, and some draw water, and some come out and receive the mistress.'

And when the sultana and her ladies and her slaves entered the house, and saw the rich stuffs it was hung with, and the beautiful rice that was prepared for them to eat, they cried: 'Ah, you gazelle, we have seen great houses, we have seen people, we have heard of things. But this house, and you, such as you are, we have never seen or heard of.'

After a few days, the ladies said they wished to go home again. The gazelle begged them hard to stay, but finding they would not, it brought many gifts, and gave some to the ladies and some to their slaves. And they all thought the gazelle greater a thousand times than its master, Sultan Darai.

The gazelle and its master remained in the house many weeks, and one day it said to the old woman, 'I came with my master to this place, and I have done many things for my master, good things, and till today he has never asked me: "Well, my gazelle, how did you get this house? Who is the owner of it? And this town, were there no people in it?" All good things I have done for the master, and he has not one day done me any good thing. But people say, "If you want to do anyone good, don't do him good only, do him evil also, and there will be peace between you." So, mother, I have done: I want to see the favours I have done to my master, that he may do me the like.'

'Good,' replied the old woman, and they went to bed.

In the morning, when light came, the gazelle was sick in its stomach and feverish, and its legs ached. And it said 'Mother!'

And she answered, 'Here, my son?'

And it said, 'Go and tell my master upstairs the gazelle is very ill.'

'Very good, my son; and if he should ask me what is the matter, what am I to say?'

'Tell him all my body aches badly; I have no single part without pain.'

The old woman went upstairs, and she found the mistress and master sitting on a couch of marble spread with soft cushions, and they asked her, 'Well, old woman, what do you want?'

'To tell the master the gazelle is ill,' said she.

'What is the matter?' asked the wife.

'All its body pains; there is no part without pain.'

'Well, what can I do? Make some gruel of red millet, and give to it.'

But his wife stared and said: 'Oh, master, do you tell her to make the gazelle gruel out of red millet, which a horse would not eat? Eh, master, that is not well.'

But he answered, 'Oh, you are mad! Rice is only kept for people.'

'Eh, master, this is not like a gazelle. It is the apple of your eye. If sand got into that, it would trouble you.'

'My wife, your tongue is long,' and he left the room.

The old woman saw she had spoken vainly, and went back weeping to the gazelle. And when the gazelle saw her it said, 'Mother, what is it, and why do you cry? If it be good, give me the answer; and if it be bad, give me the answer.'

But still the old woman would not speak, and the gazelle prayed her to let it know the words of the master. At last she said: 'I went upstairs and found the mistress and the master sitting on a couch, and he asked me what I wanted, and I told him that you, his slave, were ill. And his wife asked what was the matter, and I told her that there was not a part of your body without pain. And the master told me to take some red millet and make you gruel, but the mistress said, "Eh, master, the gazelle is the apple of your eye; you have no child, this gazelle is like your child; so this gazelle is not one to be done evil to. This is a gazelle in form, but not a gazelle in heart; he is in all things better than a gentleman, be he who he may."

'And he answered her, "Silly chatterer, your words are many. I know its price; I bought it for an eighth. What loss will it be to me?"'

The gazelle kept silence for a few moments. Then it said,

'The elders said, "One that does good like a mother," and I have done him good, and I have got this that the elders said. But go up again to the master, and tell him the gazelle is very ill, and it has not drunk the gruel of red millet.'

So the old woman returned, and found the master and the mistress drinking coffee. And when he heard what the gazelle had said, he cried: 'Hold your peace, old woman, and stay your feet and close your eyes, and stop your ears with wax; and if the gazelle bids you come to me, say your legs are bent, and you cannot walk; and if it begs you to listen, say your ears are stopped with wax; and if it wishes to talk, reply that your tongue has got a hook in it.'

The heart of the old woman wept as she heard such words, because she saw that when the gazelle first came to that town it was ready to sell its life to buy wealth for its master. Then it happened to get both life and wealth, but now it had no honour with its master.

And tears sprung likewise to the eyes of the sultan's wife, and she said, 'I am sorry for you, my husband, that you should deal so wickedly with that gazelle'; but he only answered, 'Old woman, pay no heed to the talk of the mistress: tell it to perish out of the way. I cannot sleep, I cannot eat, I cannot drink, for the worry of that gazelle. Shall a creature that I bought for an eighth trouble me from morning till night? Not so, old woman!'

The old woman went downstairs, and there lay the gazelle, blood flowing from its nostrils. And she took it in her arms and said, 'My son, the good you did is lost; there remains only patience.'

And it said, 'Mother, I shall die, for my soul is full of anger and bitterness. My face is ashamed, that I should have done good to my master, and that he should repay me with evil.' It paused for a moment, and then went on, 'Mother, of the goods that are in this house, what do I eat? I might have every day half a basinful, and would my master be any the poorer? But did not the elders say, "He that does good like a mother!"'

And it said, 'Go and tell my master that the gazelle is nearer death than life.'

So she went, and spoke as the gazelle had bidden her; but he answered, 'I have told you to trouble me no more.'

But his wife's heart was sore, and she said to him: 'Ah, master, what has the gazelle done to you? How has he failed you? The things you do to him are not good, and you will draw on yourself the hatred of the people. For this gazelle is loved by all, by small and great, by women and men. Ah, my husband! I thought you had great wisdom, and you have not even a little!'

But he answered, 'You are mad, my wife.'

The old woman stayed no longer, and went back to the gazelle, followed secretly by the mistress, who called a maid-servant and bade her take some milk and rice and cook it for the gazelle.

'Take also this cloth,' she said, 'to cover it with, and this pillow for its head. And if the gazelle wants more, let it ask me, and not its master. And if it will, I will send it in a litter to my father, and he will nurse it till it is well.'

And the maidservant did as her mistress bade her, and said what her mistress had told her to say, but the gazelle made no answer, but turned over on its side and died quietly.

When the news spread abroad, there was much weeping among the people, and Sultan Darai arose in wrath, and cried, 'You weep for that gazelle as if you wept for me! And, after all, what is it but a gazelle, that I bought for an eighth?'

But his wife answered, 'Master, we looked upon that gazelle as we looked upon you. It was the gazelle who came to ask me of my father, it was the gazelle who brought me from my father, and I was given in charge to the gazelle by my father.'

And when the people heard her they lifted up their voices and spoke:

'We never saw you, we saw the gazelle. It was the gazelle who met with trouble here, it was the gazelle who met with rest here. So, then, when such a one departs from this world we weep for ourselves, we do not weep for the gazelle.'

And they said furthermore:

'The gazelle did you much good, and if anyone says he could have done more for you he is a liar! Therefore, to us who have done you no good, what treatment will you give? The gazelle has died from bitterness of soul, and you ordered your slaves to throw it into the well. Ah! leave us alone that we may weep.'

But Sultan Darai would not heed their words, and the dead gazelle was thrown into the well.

When the mistress heard of it, she sent three slaves, mounted on donkeys, with a letter to her father the sultan, and when the sultan had read the letter he bowed his head and wept, like a man who had lost his mother. And he commanded horses to be saddled, and called the governor and the judges and all the rich men, and said:

'Come now with me; let us go and bury it.'

Night and day they travelled, till the sultan came to the well where the gazelle had been thrown. And it was a large well, built round a rock, with room for many people; and the sultan entered, and the judges and the rich men followed him. And when he saw the gazelle lying there he wept afresh, and took it in his arms and carried it away.

When the three slaves went and told their mistress what the sultan had done, and how all the people were weeping, she answered:

'I too have eaten no food, neither have I drunk water, since the day the gazelle died. I have not spoken, and I have not laughed.'

The sultan took the gazelle and buried it, and ordered the people to wear mourning for it, so there was great mourning throughout the city.

Now after the days of mourning were at an end, the wife was sleeping at her husband's side, and in her sleep she dreamed that she was once more in her father's house, and when she woke up it was no dream.

And the man dreamed that he was on the dust-heap, scratching. And when he woke, behold! that also was no dream, but the truth.

YUKI-ONNA

Lafcadio Hearn

IN A VILLAGE of Musashi Province, there lived two woodcutters: Mosaku and Minokichi. At the time of which I am speaking, Mosaku was an old man; and Minokichi, his apprentice, was a lad of eighteen years. Every day they went together to a forest situated about five miles from their village. On the way to that forest there is a wide river to cross; and there is a ferryboat. Several times a bridge was built where the ferry is; but the bridge was each time carried away by a flood. No common bridge can resist the current there when the river rises.

Mosaku and Minokichi were on their way home, one very cold evening, when a great snowstorm overtook them. They reached the ferry; and they found that the boatman had gone away, leaving his boat on the other side of the river. It was no day for swimming; and the woodcutters took shelter in the ferryman's hut – thinking themselves lucky to find any shelter at all. There was no brazier in the hut, nor any place in which to make a fire: it was only a two-mat hut, with a single door, but no window. Mosaku and Minokichi fastened the door, and lay down to rest, with their straw raincoats over them. At first they did not feel very cold; and they thought that the storm would soon be over.

The old man almost immediately fell asleep; but the boy, Minokichi, lay awake a long time, listening to the awful wind, and the continual slashing of the snow against the door. The river was roaring; and the hut swayed and creaked like a junk at sea. It was a terrible storm; and the air was every moment becoming colder; and Minokichi shivered under his raincoat. But at last, in spite of the cold, he too fell asleep.

He was awakened by a showering of snow in his face. The door of the hut had been forced open; and, by the snow-light (*yuki-akari*), he saw a woman in the room – a woman all in white. She was bending above Mosaku, and blowing her breath upon him – and her breath was like a bright white smoke. Almost in the same moment she turned to Minokichi, and stooped over him. He tried to cry out, but found that he could not utter any sound. The white woman bent down over him, lower and lower, until her face almost touched him; and he saw that she was very beautiful, – though her eyes made him afraid. For a little time she continued to look at him; then she smiled, and she whispered: 'I intended to treat you like the other man. But I cannot help feeling some pity for you, because you are so young . . . You are a pretty boy, Minokichi; and I will not hurt you now. But, if you ever tell anybody – even your own mother – about what you have seen this night, I shall know it; and then I will kill you . . . Remember what I say!'

With these words, she turned from him and passed through the doorway. Then he found himself able to move; and he sprang up, and looked out. But the woman was nowhere to be seen; and the snow was driving furiously into the hut. Minokichi closed the door, and secured it by fixing several billets of wood against it. He wondered if the wind had blown it open; he thought that he might have been only dreaming, and might have mistaken the gleam of the snow-light in the doorway for the figure of a white woman: but he could not be sure. He called to Mosaku, and was frightened because the old man did not answer. He put out his hand in the dark, and touched Mosaku's face, and found that it was ice! Mosaku was stark and dead . . .

By dawn the storm was over; and when the ferryman returned to his station, a little after sunrise, he found Minokichi lying senseless beside the frozen body of Mosaku. Minokichi was promptly cared for, and soon came to himself; but he remained a long time ill from the effects of the cold of that terrible night. He had been greatly frightened also by the old man's death; but he said nothing about the vision of the woman in white. As soon as he got well again, he returned to his calling – going alone every morning to the forest, and coming back at nightfall with his bundles of wood, which his mother helped him to sell.

One evening, in the winter of the following year, as he was on his way home, he overtook a girl who happened to be travelling by the same road. She was a tall, slim girl, very good-looking; and she answered Minokichi's greeting in a voice as pleasant to the ear as the voice of a song-bird. Then he walked beside her; and they began to talk. The girl said that her name was O-Yuki; that she had lately lost both of her parents; and that she was going to Yedo, where she happened to have some poor relations, who might help her to find a situation as servant. Minokichi soon felt charmed by this strange girl; and the more that he looked at her, the handsomer she appeared to be. He asked her whether she was yet betrothed; and she answered, laughingly, that she was free. Then, in her turn, she asked Minokichi whether he was married, or pledged to marry; and he told her that, although he had only a widowed mother to support, the question of an 'honorable daughter-in-law' had not yet been considered, as he was very young . . . After these confidences, they walked on for a long while without speaking; but, as the proverb declares, *Ki ga aréba, mé mo kuchi hodo ni mono wo iu*: 'When the wish is there, the eyes can say as much as the mouth.' By the time they reached the village, they had become very much pleased with each other; and then Minokichi asked O-Yuki to rest awhile at his house. After some shy hesitation, she went there with him; and his mother made her welcome, and prepared a warm meal for her. O-Yuki behaved so nicely that Minokichi's mother took a sudden fancy to her, and persuaded her to delay her journey to Yedo. And the natural end of the matter was that Yuki never went to Yedo at all. She remained in the house, as an 'honorable daughter-in-law'.

O-Yuki proved a very good daughter-in-law. When Minokichi's mother came to die – some five years later – her last words were words of affection and praise for the wife of her son. And O-Yuki bore Minokichi ten children, boys and girls – handsome children all of them, and very fair of skin.

The country-folk thought O-Yuki a wonderful person, by nature different from themselves. Most of the peasant-women age early; but O-Yuki, even after having become the mother of ten children, looked as young and fresh as on the day when she had first come to the village.

One night, after the children had gone to sleep, O-Yuki was sewing by the light of a paper lamp; and Minokichi, watching her, said:

'To see you sewing there, with the light on your face, makes me think of a strange thing that happened when I was a lad of eighteen. I then saw somebody as beautiful and white as you are now – indeed, she was very like you.'

Without lifting her eyes from her work, O-Yuki responded:

'Tell me about her . . . Where did you see her?'

Then Minokichi told her about the terrible night in the ferryman's hut – and about the White Woman that had stooped above him, smiling and whispering – and about the silent death of old Mosaku. And he said:

'Asleep or awake, that was the only time that I saw a being as beautiful as you. Of course, she was not a human being; and I was afraid of her – very much afraid – but she was so white! . . . Indeed, I have never been sure whether it was a dream that I saw, or the Woman of the Snow.'

O-Yuki flung down her sewing, and arose, and bowed above Minokichi where he sat, and shrieked into his face:

'It was I – I – I! Yuki it was! And I told you then that I would kill you if you ever said one word about it! . . . But for those children asleep there, I would kill you this moment! And now you had better take very, very good care of them; for if ever they have reason to complain of you, I will treat you as you deserve!'

Even as she screamed, her voice came thin, like a crying of wind; then she melted into a bright white mist that spired to the roof-beams, and shuddered away through the smoke-hole . . . Never again was she seen.

PART VIII:
FULFILMENT AND FATE

BHADRA AND THE MENDICANT

Jessica Amanda Salmonson

MANY PEOPLE HAVE heard the story of the demonic asuras who attacked a certain town and were carrying livestock and infants away through the air. They were rending warriors to pieces and causing much grief and bloodshed. At the height of the carnage, a fair princess ran forth, and, reciting an incantation, drew out of the forest a company of yaksas and yaksinis, who were like ghostly hunters and huntresses armed with bows and arrows and axes. These demi-gods and -goddesses fell upon the asuras mightily, and the town was saved.

Until this event, no one had known that Princess Bhadra had power over yaksas. Since that time, she has become famous for her abilities. But she was not born a great woman. It is hard to realize that previously she was hardly noticed by the divinities. And the first yaksini she ever met disliked her greatly. This is the story of how she angered a yaksini and learned by her fearful experience.

Bhadra had always lived an exemplary life for all outward appearances, performing such rituals and sacrifices as were expected of her, and causing no worry or concern to her father, King Kausalika, a widower. At no time had she known travail, or hunger, or suffering, and, while she meant no actual harm to anyone, she was selfish and vain without knowing she was these things, and caused grief to other people by her pride and careless indifference, scarcely knowing she was doing so.

She grew to be an exceedingly handsome young woman, taking for granted people's admiration. She was well versed in the Vedas, and was often reassured by the brahmans that as long as her family gave a percentage of their treasures to the priests, then King Kausalika's family, and especially his splendid daughter, would continue to prosper even into future lives.

It would have surprised her greatly to realize that in the Hall of the Offerings to Heaven, the divinities placed all her sacrifices in a room reserved to those called Stolid, Upright, and Insufferable. For all her earthly beauty, she was spiritually nondescript.

She was betrothed to Rudradeva, a good-looking brahman, and this was regarded by everyone, including Bhadra, as a superior match. She was quite pleased with the prospect of being Rudradeva's wife. She went about making her well-intended offerings at her family shrine in the deer park, and performing other rituals as were part of her preparations for the pending marriage. She burnt incense and presented rice cakes, flesh, prayers, and money to the Goddess of the shrine.

She liked to imagine the Heavenly Ones sitting in a neat row just like the brahmans, watching her pray, and smiling at her on account of her piety and her generally pleasing appearance. In actuality, the divinities were off somewhere else and, for that matter, didn't even know who she was.

A yaksini, or fairy-divinity, who was the guardian of the shrine, came as usual with a ho-hum and a who-cares, intending to gather up the smoke of Bhadra's incense, and the essence of the rice offering, and take these to the Room of the Upright and Insufferable. The meat and the money were of no concern to the yaksini, as such offerings were in actuality for the brahmans. As for Bhadra's prayers, the yaksini left those behind simply because there was no heavenly offering-room for banalities.

The yaksini was in a bad mood that day. For some while she had been bestowing good luck on visitors to the shrine, but yaksinis are somewhat unpredictable, and have to balance the good things they do with one or another offensive act. They tend to be just in their actions, however, even if human beings sometimes disagree with what a yaksa or yaksini considers justifiable.

The yaksini was invisible to mortals. Had she chosen to reveal herself, she might easily be mistaken for a beautiful young Goddess. She had firm round breasts and a flat stomach with a golden girdle. She had a lovely headdress and a third eye on her forehead. Although she usually had only two arms, she could sometimes reveal herself with four. She was a very elegant yaksini and delighted in punishing people who desecrated the shrine and rewarding those who were pious.

Unexpectedly, she felt something very pleasing in her vicinity. Despite her bad mood, an inexplicable feeling made her smile. She let loose of the essence of the rice and incense offered by Bhadra, and it dissipated into nothingness, not that it would be missed in heaven. She looked around for the source of the excellent emanations, and spied a Jain monk with filthy hands, praying in a gloomy corner of the shrine for the salvation of all the miserable and stupid people of the world.

This man, whose name was Bala, observed all rules in regard to walking, begging, speaking, vacuating, praying, restraining himself from idle pleasures, and being always attentive to duty. He protected his thoughts, speech, and body by subduing the senses. He was devoid of hatred and impurity. He never bathed, for Truth alone was his bathing pool, and his soul was among the cleanest of all mortals.

This mendicant was so humble in his heart, he did not even know he was a great sage, but thought himself nothing more than a small and undeserving monk whose simplicity and holiness might be noticed in heaven, but only if he was lucky, and his inarticulate prayers might sometimes be considered, but only because he was too pitiful to ignore.

'Ah, such a lovely monk,' said the yaksini. 'I shall take his prayers straightaway to the Room of the Saints of Truth!'

Princess Bhadra had had quite a different response to him. To be fair, it must be confessed that a yaksini cannot smell unbathed human skin, but is susceptible only to human spirit. Thus Bala made quite a different impression on Bhadra than on the yaksini. Even so, Bhadra was ungenerous. She was in the midst of a prayer she thought quite splendid. She had worked on it for a couple of days and was even thinking of having it published. Then an unexpected stench broke her concentration. She looked around and saw the mendicant, emaciated by austerities, with the most ragged clothing, and she shivered with disdain and dread of such a foul being.

Motioning to the row of brahman priests sitting by the altar, she indicated the presence of the vile beggar. The brahmans laughed at Bala, then went over to where he was sitting quietly.

They behaved like ruffians toward him. 'Look at this miserable swarthy monster with a boar hog's nose! What are you doing here, dirty little man with filthy clothes dangling from your soiled neck? Get out of here! Go away!'

The yaksini had often been annoyed by these brahmans, who were animal-killers and didn't know a good sacrifice from a bad one. They imagined themselves holy because of their high birth rather than their deeds, but they were, at best, insufferable prigs, and usually not even as good as that. She had given one of them a boil on the tip of his penis, and another, who was quite vain of his looks, was growing a wen on his cheek because the yaksini couldn't stand his pettiness and self-importance. She scowled at the brahmans, then looked to where Princess Bhadra sat quietly, wondering how to punish her. The princess was trying to look so innocent of the matter at hand, and was sitting in a very pretty lotus posture with her eyes averted. Yet she was all too eager to see the little monk gotten rid of.

The monk said to his persecutors, 'I am a chaste mendicant with no property. I eat neither meat nor cooked food. My mother was the chieftainess Gauri the Fair of a kandala tribe, the lowest caste, and my father was chief Harikesa the Yellow-haired. My tribe lives on the banks of the Ganges where it floods each spring. Life is difficult for them. I have become a Jain ascetic seeking always for the salvation of those who suffer. I have come here to pray and to beg for something to eat. Here at this shrine, much food is consumed, and much food is thrown away. Let a mendicant have what is thrown away.'

But the brahmans paid him no heed and dragged him out of the shrine and beat him at the edge of the grove. Then, to justify themselves and to feel magnanimous, they told him to go sit among the gardening rubble, where the leavings of each afternoon meal were composted. They promised to throw something edible to him later. He thanked them and went to sit atop the gardening rubble.

As Princess Bhadra was leaving the shrine grounds, the yaksini ran after her and leapt inside her body. By this means the yaksini came to the palace of King Kausalika. When a meal was served, Princess Bhadra was taken by the sudden impulse to throw food about. She snatched a fish from the plate of a young prince and threw it across the table, where it smote the king in the face, which considerably startled him. Bhadra laughed, then ran out of the room like a dart.

She went into the main greeting hall where stood her father's throne, and, climbing onto the dais, snatched his gold embroidered pillow and rent it all to pieces, laughing wildly the whole time. Servants and courtiers followed her about the palace as she caused damage here and there. When she began to break ancient vases and artifacts of incalculable value, she was finally restrained.

At her father's command, Bhadra was dragged kicking to her suite, where she was bound wrist and ankle to her bedposts. The whole while she was cursing her father and the memory of her mother and swearing all manner of vengeance on her maids who had helped tie her up. Everyone was weeping, as though she were dead and unreclaimable. Her betrothed, the brahman Rudradeva, was called to the palace for consultation. As he was versed in occult matters, he knew at once that she was possessed of a yaksini. He performed a severe exorcism, but the yaksini held fast to Bhadra's body, and caused her to say wicked things.

At last, Rudradeva thought to ask the yaksini what she wanted that caused her to hold onto the body of Bhadra. The yaksini spoke through Bhadra's mouth, saying, 'I am in love with Bala, the Jain monk who is staying in the holy grove, with no shelter and little to eat. If Bhadra will marry him, then I can experience his embrace for a full night. Only then will I leave the princess!'

Rudradeva was startled and unhappy, for Bhadra was to be his bride. Yet he went to the king and told him, 'Your daughter insulted an ascetic in the shrine today, and had the brahmans throw him out because of his odor. The yaksini of the shrine has possessed Bhadra in order to punish her rudeness. The fairy-spirit will not leave until Bhadra and the monk Bala have spent a wedding night together.'

As there was no other method, the king agreed to the marriage. The yaksini was informed she would soon have her wish. She then let Bhadra regain control of her senses. Repenting her aversion to the monk, Bhadra returned to the shrine and found the monk sitting on the compost heap. She said, 'Holy man! We must become married, for otherwise the yaksini of this shrine will not leave my body. You, in spite of your lowly kandala origins, can become a prince by wedding me! What greater reward can have come to you because of your austerities?'

Bala replied, 'I have vowed never to seek worldliness or pleasure. Think not ill of me if I reject your offer of marriage. As for the yaksini, I will speak to her in your behalf. Naughty yaksini! Do not trouble this young woman! You do me an injustice to punish anyone on my account. I suffer in this world so that others need not suffer!'

Thus chastised, the yaksini leapt out of Bhadra. She manifested herself as a pleasing young woman with three eyes and four arms. But feeling spurned and chastised, when she had sought only to act in his behalf, the mischievous part of her character rose again to the surface. She called forth ten yaksas from out of the trees, who looked like splendid young hunters. She told them, 'This ascetic wants to suffer! Beat him at once!' And the ten yaksas began to beat the monk at the yaksini's request.

Princess Bhadra threw herself upon the frail monk, pleading with an appeasing tone, 'Do not harm him! This chaste man, who would not accept me in marriage even when my father, King Kausalika, would have made him a prince, do you not know who he is? This is Saint Bala, a man of great piety and power, who could smite you easily if he were not so concerned even for your well-being! You might as well eat iron with your teeth as to treat this monk contemptuously! Come not against him with your willow sticks, lest he consume you in the fire of his virtue as moths are consumed when they dash toward an altar fire.'

When the yaksas heard these well-spoken words, they began to assist the sage, picking the thorns out of his ragged clothing, and bowing to him with admiration. The yaksini said, 'I have neglected my duties of late. I must take your excellent speech straightaway to the Hall of Offerings and the Room of Truth, where it will be enshrined as the first of your great offerings. From this day on, O Bhadra, you have power over yaksas and yaksinis. Because you are the protectress of a sage mighty in spirit, we bow to you.'

At that moment there fell a perfumed rain from heaven. The

yaksas produced drums and struck them, singing the praises of Bala and Bhadra. The Jain monk said, 'The power of penance has become visible. The Truth of the Law is that compassion is great, anger is a small thing.'

Bhadra said, 'My life until now has been nothing. This shrine that feeds brahmans, but which belongs to my father, I will petition be turned over as a waystation for traveling ascetics. Those priests who injure living things and slay pitiful animals grow fat on the spoils of people's fear of dying. Let them find another place! Birth and death are nothing, and compassion is all. O blessed day that the yaksini possessed me! I will devote my life to the care of wandering monks and nuns, and if my betrothed Rudradeva wishes to pursue the brahman path, I will never marry.'

THE REBORN DIVINITIES

Jessica Amanda Salmonson

Even divinities are subject to the cycle of birth and rebirth. Thus four of them came to the earth as mortals. They were born in a town called Ishukara, which was in the Kuru country long ago. In those days, the whole region was almost as beautiful as heaven.

They were born into noble families, two of the brahman caste, two within the royal house. They knew every pleasure.

One who was reborn was Yasa, whose beauty reflected her previous divinity. She married Bhrigu, a handsome youth who matched Yasa's sweet appearance.

The third to be reborn was Queen Kamalavati. Her husband was the famous King Ishukara. These two ruled in the country beautiful as heaven.

All four were born within days of one another. The children of the brahman grew up knowing the royal children, so all were fast friends, just as they had been in heaven. They retained a slight awareness of their heavenly origins, but rarely spoke of their suspicions. They hoped to escape the wheel of birth. They sampled all pleasures, abandoning them one after the other, no refinement being sufficient to fill the void within them. They grew fearful of birth, old age, and death.

Their aversion to both human and heavenly pleasures developed into a disgust for all the wickedness that was in the world. They desired liberation. They became filled with faith. One by one, they became Jain ascetics, first Bhrigu, then Yasa, then Kamalavati, and finally Ishukara.

Yasa's father was a famous brahman priest, well versed in the Vedas. He heard that his daughter and son-in-law were considering the ascetic path. He hurried to their house to dissuade them from rash decisions. He said, 'The Vedas tell us that there is no better world awaiting those who fail to procreate. My children, after you have studied the Vedas and have given offerings to priests; after you have had children to carry on the name of your house; and when you have lived a full life and grown old, that is the time to depart for the woods as praiseworthy ascetics.'

By his manner, they could see their father was consumed with grief. Yet he spoke importantly, as one who has grown used to giving sage advice, rarely hearing criticisms. They were sorry for him, seeing that he had been blown into terrible blazes of agony by the winds of delusion. He wept, cajoled, and bribed, but they were immovable, and more than a little surprised that he would demean himself so.

Yasa took her father's hands in hers. She said to him in a kindly way, 'The study of Vedas will not save us. The feeding of priests leads us from darkness to darkness. The birth of children binds others to the wheel of birth.'

Her husband added, 'Worldly pleasures bring momentary respite, but when we suffer, it goes on and on. Happiness is fleeting and anguish boundless, hence we cannot balance one with the other. The good things as well as the bad are obstacles holding us from our liberation. We must flee the pleasures if we are to flee the evils.'

Their father persisted. 'People who practice austerities do so in order to obtain wealth, position, and exquisite pleasures in another life. But you have these things for the asking. There is no reason for you to choose the austere path.'

Bhrigu replied, 'All who fail to abandon pleasure grieve day and night. Possessions cannot save us. We have this, but want that. We fret about robbers, so we hire guards, but the guards are themselves robbers. We have authority, but fear revolt. Wealth and power are no different from old age and death.'

Yasa said, 'What use are riches in the practice of religion? We shall live as mendicants, possessed of virtue rather than property, wandering from place to place.'

The sorrowful father lamented. 'Without you, I am bereft, as a bird without wings, as a merchant without goods, as a king standing amidst battle without followers. A snake sloughs its skin, just as you, my children, abandon grief and pleasure.

Perhaps you are admirable after all. Why should I live alone? Why should I not follow in the dusty prints of your naked feet? A fish breaks a weak net; a heron conquers gravity and flies away. So too will I escape all that I have lived to possess, and go with you!'

Therefore, without even closing up their houses, they set forth to seek perfection.

Now when Queen Kamalavati learned that Yasa and Bhrigu had taken vows of poverty, going so far as to convert their priestly father, she went quickly to speak with her husband, King Ishukara.

She was distraught with the world and with her own weakness in needing things. Thinking of her good friends striding barefoot from place to place, she was filled with admiration. For the first time she felt a strength well up inside her.

'Oh my husband,' said the queen. 'When in sickness someone vomits all that they have devoured, who would praise the man who hurried forth to feast upon that vomit? Yet you, my lord, have sent vassals to confiscate the property of the brahman family who has vomited everything to become ascetics. Remember this, my lord, that when we are dead, nothing in all we own can ever be salvation.'

'Why have you come to speak to me thus, O my Queen?' said the king, unused to such rebukes.

'My lord, as a bird hates its cage, so do I hate this world. I shall go forth to live as a nun, impoverished, without children or desire, without greed or hatred. Consider! When a forest is burning, the animals leap up and flee the forest. But what fools are we humans! The world is consumed with the fire of love and hate, yet we fail to escape what is blazing all about us. Those who have known pleasure, then renounce pleasure, are like the wind. They are birds unchecked in their flight.'

'Pray, O Queen, whose tongue is sweet and bitter to my ears, what would you have of me?'

'Consider the bird when it is held by its wings. It struggles, as we must struggle in our fetters. We must live as the wind, attached to no one place, affixed to no set objects. Pleasure is but a snare binding us to worldly existence, therefore we must put aside all that we have mistaken for treasure, then seek the greater destination. This, O great king Ishukara, is the wonderful truth that until this day has troubled me, but which now I am eager to embrace. O my husband, leave this kingdom and all the pleasures which have become dear to you! Abandon what pleases the senses! Give up idle amusements. Give up power. Become famed for severe penance and firm energy. By this means we shall both gradually obtain enlightenment.'

'O Queen, it is true that I have cluttered my existence with many things, fearful of birth and death, burying my fear in useless endeavors. You have won me over! In abandoning pleasure, we can at last seek an end to misery.'

All doubts were dispersed. The king descended from his throne, threw off his robes and crown, and together with his wife set out to seek perfection.

ISLAND OF THE OCEAN GOD

Peter Tremayne

MAC CUILL, which means 'son of the hazel', was, in fact, the son of the great god of eloquence and literacy, Ogma. He had so named his son for the hazel is a mystical tree and Ogma used it to signify the third letter of the alphabet which he had devised. And, indeed, Mac Cuill was the third son of Ogma for his brothers were Mac Gréine, 'son of the sun', and Mac Cécht, 'son of the plough'. The three brothers were married to three sisters: Mac Gréine was married to the goddess Éire, while Mac Cécht was married to her sister Fótla and Mac Cuill was married to the youngest sister named Banba.

There came a time when the gods themselves fell from grace, when the sons of Míl conquered them. And it was said that Mac Gréine was slain by the great Druid Amairgen; that Mac Cécht met his end from the sword of Eremon and that Mac Cuill was slain by the spear of Eber.

And when the gods were defeated by the sons of Míl, the wives of Mac Gréine, Mac Cécht and Mac Cuill – Éire, Fótla and Banba, went to greet the conquerors of the land of Inisfáil, the island of destiny.

'Welcome warriors,' cried Éire. 'To you who have come from afar this island shall henceforth belong, and from the setting to the rising sun there is no better land. And your race will be the most perfect the world has ever seen.'

Amairgen the Druid asked her what she wanted in reward for this blessing.

'That you name this country after me,' replied Éire. But her sisters chimed in that the country should be named after them. So Amairgen promised that Éire would be the principal name for the country while the poets of Míl would also hail the land by the names of Fótla and Banba. So it has been until this day.

Now as the sons of Ogma were gods, and therefore 'The Ever Living Ones', they could not die completely and so their souls were passed on through the aeons. And in the rebirths of Mac Cuill he began to lament the lost days of power, of the days he had been happy with Banba. He grew bitter and resentful with each rebirth until he was reborn as a petty thief in the kingdom of Ulaidh, which is one of the five provincial kingdoms of Éire. Each province was called *cúige* or a fifth and the five made up the whole and the whole, one and indivisible, governed by the Ard-Rígh, or High King.

There was no better thief in all Ulaidh than Mac Cuill and he became the terror of the land. His deeds came to the ears of the High King himself and he sent his personal Brehon, or judge, named Dubhtach, to the provincial king of Ulaidh, saying: 'Mac Cuill must be captured and punished.' Eventually, Mac Cuill the thief, was caught, and he was taken before the High King's Brehon. And there was a tall, white-haired man standing by the Brehon's side. They called him by the name of an ancient god of war, which is Sucat.

'Why should we not kill you for your evil life, Mac Cuill?' demanded Dubhtach the Brehon.

Now Mac Cuill was full of guile and he smiled.

'Kill me now, Brehon. I have reached my last rebirth on this earth. I cannot descend lower than a thief. I will have been wiped from the Brandubh board of this world.' Brandubh, which means 'black raven', was a wooden board game, which many compare to the eastern game of chess. 'Yet,' he added with evasive craft, 'Kill me now and there will be no hope of redemption, no hope of reparation for my sins. Spare me and perhaps there is still some goodness in my soul whereby I might change my life for the better.'

Now Mac Cuill spoke with irony, in mocking tones, but his words held some truth. The Brehon pondered and could reach no decision. Finally, it was Sucat who said: 'The decision is not for us to make, for man is often flawed in his perceptions of his fellows. What is justice for one is injustice for another. So let us leave it to the Creator to decide. You will have the judgment of the sea.'

Now the judgment of the sea can be a terrifying thing. But Mac Cuill, who had lived many lifetimes, was not afraid. And Sucat had the wrists of Mac Cuill bound in a chain of iron which he fastened by a padlock with his own hand. And he flung the key into the waves of the sea, saying to Mac Cuill: 'Loose not that chain until the key be found and brought to you.' The Brehon then had Mac Cuill taken to a boat which is called a curragh. The boat was without oars and without a sail and no food or drink was placed in it. This boat, containing Mac Cuill, was rowed several miles from the coast of Ulaidh and cast adrift. The fate of Mac Cuill was left to whichever way the winds and tides took him. Whoever found him could make a slave of him.

Now of all the ancient gods one of the last to live upon the Earth with their ancient powers was Manánnan Mac Lir, the tempestuous god of the oceans, who, with his angry breath, could raise large white-crested waves that could wreck entire fleets of ships. At the time of the fall of the gods, Manánnan Mac Lir had retired to his favourite island called Inis Falga which lay between Inisfáil and the Isle of the Mighty. Eventually that island became called after the great Manánnan and every Manxman is called, in his own tongue, Maninagh.

Now Manánnan, seeing the plight of Mac Cuill, reborn in a weak human body, was moved to compassion. He remembered the ancient times when he and Mac Cuill and the other Children of Danu had fought the evil Fomorii on the Plain of Towers to claim the Island of Destiny. So Manánnan breathed gently on the ship and sent a current which turned its bows towards his own mist-shrouded island of Inis Falga.

But even Manánnan's breath could not break the lock of the chain which bound Mac Cuill's wrists.

After several days the little boat, without oars or sails, and with Mac Cuill more dead than alive, bumped against a rocky shore.

Now on the island there were living two wise men named Conindri and Romuil. Both had heard the words of the Son of God and preached the new religion of love and forgiveness. They saw the half dead Mac Cuill and realised that his crimes must be great for him to have been cast into the sea in such a fashion. Yet they took him from the boat and laid him in their own beds and nursed him until he recovered his wit and strength.

As Mac Cuill was recovering, Conindri and Romuil spoke to him of the Creator and His Son and the new religion of love and brotherhood. And as they spoke, they did their best to unfasten the chain about Mac Cuill's wrists. But they could not do so, no matter how they tried.

Mac Cuill laughed. 'In a previous life I was a god. As I was once, so will your new God and His Son become – cast out and forgotten when they no longer serve the needs of the people.'

'You are proud, Mac Cuill. Our Lord taught: 'Blessed are the poor in spirit, for theirs is the kingdom of heaven.'

Mac Cuill laughed again. 'If poverty of spirit is a virtue than it does man little good. When men are poor in spirit, then the proud and haughty oppress them. When I was a god men were true and determined in spirit and resisted oppression.'

'But to him that smiteth thee on the one cheek offer also the other.'

Mac Cuill sneered.

'He who courts oppression shares the crime. If that is the teaching, then you are inviting further injury at the hand of the oppressor and thief.'

'Him that taketh away thy cloak, forbid not to take thy coat also. Give to every man that asketh of thee . . . Blessed be ye poor, for yours is the kingdom of heaven.'

Mac Cuill chuckled deeply, shaking his head.

'Now this new religion is ideal for a thief such as me. It tells people to accept with good grace when I rob them. The poor in spirit will not fight me. This is a good land and here I will prosper as a thief if all believe as you do. I will set forth to find a smithy to break my chains asunder.'

Mac Cuill set out and walked along the sea shore leaving the wise good men, Conindri and Romuil in sorrow behind him.

As he walked on the foreshore he heard a gentle singing and around a headland of rocks he came across a beautiful woman. The spot was called Langness in the parish of Kirk Malew. The girl sang sweetly.

Come to our rich and starry caves
Our home amid the ocean waves;

Our coral caves are walled around
With richest gems in ocean found.
And crystal mirrors, clear and bright.
Reflecting all in magic light.

Mac Cuill stopped and gazed upon the beautiful sad face. It reminded him of the one whom he had loved so long ago – the face of his wife in a former life – of Banba.

'Who are you, young maiden?' he demanded.

The young girl started and looked upon Mac Cuill and her eyes lit up in a smile of happiness.

'I am for you, son of the hazel,' she said.

'That cannot be. Nothing is for me unless I steal it. I am a thief and will take what I want.'

'I am Blaanid,' continued the girl, and reaching down beside the rock on which she sat, she drew forth a basket filled with coral and precious stones and other fabulous metals garnered from the ocean bed. 'You may have these, for we are all thieves now.'

'I will not accept that which is given when it is my place to take,' cried Mac Cuill in disgust. 'But if you can break the chains on my wrists, I will accept your gifts.'

Suddenly, Blaanid threw her arms around Mac Cuill and so surprised was he, and so great her strength, that she dragged him to the edge of the sea and plunged in. Though he struggled, she drew him downwards to the dwellings of the merfolk who lived beneath the waves. And Blaanid took Mac Cuill to a beautiful city under the sea. It was a place of many towers and gilded minarets and stood in all magnificence. It was deep down, beyond the region of the fishes where there was air which was strangely clear and the atmosphere serene. The streets were paved in coral and a shining kind of pebble which glittered like the sunbeams reflecting on glass. Streets and squares were on every side. Buildings were embossed with mother of pearl and shells of numerous colours and there were flashing crystals to decorate their walls.

But around the circle perimeter were countless wrecks of ships. Fearful wrecks, strewn on the slimy bottom, yet the city was protected from them. And among the wrecks, Mac Cuill saw the decomposing bodies of men, women and children.

There were countless eyeless skeletons, all scattered and on which the fishes gnawed. And from the dead peoples' skulls, which worms and fish inhabited, there arose a fearful wailing sound. The noise was so penetrating that Mac Cuill had to stop his ears.

'What manner of place is this?' he gasped.

Blaanid smiled and pointed. He could see people moving through the streets. He gasped, for he recognised his brothers and the other Children of Danu.

'This is our home now, and this could be your home. For you wish to exist by what you steal. The gods and goddesses are only left with theft in this new world. We have built our city from the ships that we entice to our mist-shrouded island and wreck upon the rocks above. Each ship comes tumbling through the seas to our city and we may take from them great heaps of pearls, wedges of gold, inestimable stones, unvalued jewels . . . thus our city prospers.'

Mac Cuill swallowed hard.

'And the souls of the dead sailors? Look at the bodies of the dead, of the drowned women and the children! Do you not hear their cries?'

'They are but poor in spirit,' Blaanid said. 'We grow accustomed to their wailing and take what we must.'

Mac Cuill grew sick in his soul. He stared into the face of Blaanid and he saw in it the face of Banba.

'Is this what we are reduced to?' he whispered.

Where once the Children of Danu had bestrode the earth in goodness and strength of spirit, Mac Cuill realised they had descended to thieves who preyed on the spiritual tragedy of others.

'This is but a shadow show of the choice you can make,' replied Blaanid.

'If there are choices still, then I shall choose to be released from my purgatory,' cried Mac Cuill. And he held out his chained wrists.

'Alas, wealth and prosperity can be yours but we cannot unchain your wrists,' replied Blaanid. 'You may remain in the realm of the Ocean God as you are or you may be reborn in the new religion and release your soul from its eternal bitterness. Here we have only illusions of the past.'

With that he found himself back on the headland of Langness in Kirk Malew.

He found himself staring at the grey seas and thought that he heard a whispering sound.

> Come to our rich and starry caves
> Our home amid the ocean waves . . .

Slowly he retraced his footsteps to where he had left Conindri and Romuil. They were standing as he had left them, for in earthly time he had not been long gone from their sight.

They smiled joyfully at his return.

'Tell me more about your God and his Son.'

And so they taught him. And he came to believe with a passion and they called him Maccaldus, for that was the form of his name in the language of the new religion. So Maccaldus, who had been the foremost thief of Ulaidh, felt repentance for his past lives and Conindri and Romuil took him to a stream and poured water over his head and confirmed him in the new religion.

That evening Conindri was cooking a fish that he had caught and he brought it to the table to divide between the three of them. As he cut open the fish they saw a key in its belly and Mac Cuill recognised it as the same one with which Sucat had locked the chains about his wrist. When he told Conindri and Romuil, they were astounded.

'Sucat Mac Calphurn is the foremost preacher of our faith which is why we call him Patricius – father of citizens.'

Conindri immediately unlocked the chains and they fell at Mac Cuill's feet.

The very next day Mac Cuill went out into the island of Inis Falga and began to preach the new religion. And he went up to the Lonan stone circle, near Baldrine, where he found the Druids, set in the ancient ways, about to sacrifice a human child. A stone altar had been heated by fire and it was proposed to throw the child upon it. As the child was being flung forward, Mac Cuill threw a phial of water that had been blessed by the saints and it landed on the stone before the child and split it asunder. And the child was not harmed.

Straightaway the Druids fled but Mac Cuill called them back

and he also called before him the King of Inis Falga and told them henceforth to worship in the new religion.

One chieftain refused and this was GilColumb whose name meant servant of the dove. But he was named with irony for he was no follower of the peaceful path. And this GilColumb and his three sons desired to kill Mac Cuill and one night they slunk stealthily to the church which Mac Cuill had built. Mac Cuill and his followers, hearing that his enemies were approaching, guided his people into the subterraneous caverns beneath his church.

With loud shrieks, GilColumb and his three sons, and his followers, burst into the church.

'Where are you departed?' yelled GilColumb in anger, finding no one there.

And Mac Cuill appeared before him with his pastoral staff. GilColumb's followers stepped back in awe.

'What have you against me, GilColumb? Why have I offended you that you should attack my sanctuary with slaughter in mind?'

'Are you Mac Cuill, the former thief?' sneered GilColumb, braver than his band of men.

'I am Maccaldus, the bishop of this land,' replied Mac Cuill solemnly. 'I am the servant of the Christ.'

GilColumb laughed and raised his sword to smite him.

Mac Cuill, however, leaned forward and tapped GilColumb over the heart with his pastoral staff. The impious chieftain uttered an horrendous shriek and then his tongue clove to his mouth. After six hours GilColumb died in agony and all those who lived on Inis Falga realised that Mac Cuill was the one chosen to bring them to the new religion.

Therefore, one evening, Manánnan Mac Lir himself appeared before Mac Cuill on the foreshore.

'So it has come to this,' the old god said. 'We who were young together on the Isle of Destiny are gods no longer. Bitterness and rebirth have brought you to the human state where now you preach a new philosophy. Our journeys through life no longer converge nor even go in parallel direction. The people no longer need the gods of their forefathers and mothers.'

Mac Cuill was sad.

'There is no returning. This is the destiny of the world. No footsteps back.'

Manánnan shook his head.

'Perhaps I could have prevented this had I not blown you to this island which was my last refuge.'

'But that was written in the book of destiny, Manánnan son of Lir. Even before Danu, the divine waters, first moistened this earth.'

'People no longer believe in me and so I am reduced to a shadow and like a shadow I will be extinguished in the light of the new learning.'

'Your spirit shall abide among the grey seas and the misty mountains of this island for so long as one person remembers you,' replied Mac Cuill.

'One person?' mused the ocean god. 'Where would I find that one?'

'I shall remember you,' replied Mac Cuill softly.

Henceforth, Inis Falga was known as Ellan Vannin, the Island of Manánnan Mac Lir, which today is still known by the shortened version of the Isle of Man. Mac Cuill himself was known first as Maccaldus and then as Maughold and it is as St Maughold that he is still venerated in the Island of the Ocean God.

THE ROVER OF THE PLAIN

Henri Junod

A LONG WAY OFF, near the sea coast of the east of Africa, there dwelt a man and his wife. They had two children, a son and a daughter, whom they loved very much, and, like parents in other countries, they often talked of the fine marriages the young people would make some day. Out there both boys and girls marry early, and very soon, it seemed to the mother, a message was sent by a rich man on the other side of the great hills offering a fat herd of oxen in exchange for the girl. Everyone in the house and in the village rejoiced, and the maiden was despatched to her new home. When all was quiet again the father said to his son:

'Now that we own such a splendid troop of oxen you had better hasten and get yourself a wife, lest some illness should overtake them. Already we have seen in the villages round about one or two damsels whose parents would gladly part with them for less than half the herd. Therefore tell us which you like best, and we will buy her for you.'

But the son answered:

'Not so; the maidens I have seen do not please me. If, indeed, I must marry, let me travel and find a wife for myself.'

'It shall be as you wish,' said his parents; 'but if by and by trouble should come of it, it will be your fault and not ours.'

The youth, however, would not listen; and bidding his father and mother farewell, set out on his search. Far, far away he wandered, over mountains and across rivers, till he reached a village where the people were quite different from those of his own race. He glanced about him and noticed that the girls were fair to look upon, as they pounded maize or stewed something that smelt very nice in earthen pots – especially if you were hot and tired; and when one of the maidens turned round and offered the stranger some dinner, he made up his mind that he would wed her and nobody else.

So he sent a message to her parents asking their leave to take her for his wife, and they came next day to bring their answer.

'We will give you our daughter,' said they, 'if you can pay a good price for her. Never was there so hard-working a girl; and how we shall do without her we cannot tell! Still – no doubt your father and mother will come themselves and bring the price?'

'No; I have the price with me,' replied the young man, laying down a handful of gold pieces. 'Here it is – take it.'

The old couple's eyes glittered greedily; but custom forbade them to touch the price before all was arranged.

'At least,' said they, after a moment's pause, 'we may expect them to fetch your wife to her new home?'

'No; they are not used to travelling,' answered the bridegroom. 'Let the ceremony be performed without delay, and we will set forth at once. It is a long journey.'

Then the parents called in the girl, who was lying in the sun outside the hut, and, in the presence of all the village, a goat was killed, the sacred dance took place, and a blessing was said over the heads of the young people. After that the bride was led aside by her father, whose duty it was to bestow on her some parting advice as to her conduct in her married life.

'Be good to your husband's parents,' added he, 'and always do the will of your husband.' And the girl nodded her head obediently. Next it was the mother's turn; and, as was the custom of the tribe, she spoke to her daughter:

'Will you choose which of your sisters shall go with you to cut your wood and carry your water?'

'I do not want any of them,' answered she; 'they are no use. They will drop the wood and spill the water.'

'Then will you have any of the other children? There are enough and to spare,' asked the mother again. But the bride said quickly:

'I will have none of them! You must give me our buffalo, the Rover of the Plain; he alone shall serve me.'

'What folly you talk!' cried the parents. 'Give you our buffalo, the Rover of the Plain? Why, you know that our life depends on him. Here he is well fed and lies on soft grass; but how can you tell what will befall him in another country? The food may be bad, he will die of hunger; and, if he dies we die also.'

'No, no,' said the bride; 'I can look after him as well as you. Get him ready, for the sun is sinking and it is time we set forth.'

So she went away and put together a small pot filled with healing herbs, a horn that she used in tending sick people, a little knife, and a calabash containing deer fat; and, hiding these about her, she took leave of her father and mother and started across the mountains by the side of her husband.

But the young man did not see the buffalo that followed them, which had left his home to be the servant of his wife.

No one ever knew how the news spread to the kraal that the young man was coming back, bringing a wife with him; but, somehow or other, when the two entered the village, every man and woman was standing in the road uttering shouts of welcome.

'Ah, you are not dead after all,' cried they; 'and have found a wife to your liking, though you would have none of our girls. Well, well, you have chosen your own path; and if ill comes of it beware lest you grumble.'

Next day the husband took his wife to the fields and showed her which were his, and which belonged to his mother. The girl listened carefully to all he told her, and walked with him back to the hut; but close to the door she stopped, and said:

'I have dropped my necklace of beads in the field, and I must go and look for it.' But in truth she had done nothing of the sort, and it was only an excuse to go and seek the buffalo.

The beast was crouching under a tree when she came up, and snorted with pleasure at the sight of her.

'You can roam about this field, and this, and this,' she said, 'for they belong to my husband; and that is his wood, where you may hide yourself. But the other fields are his mother's, so beware lest you touch them.'

'I will beware,' answered the buffalo; and, patting his head, the girl left him.

Oh, how much better a servant he was than any of the little girls the bride had refused to bring with her! If she wanted water, she had only to cross the patch of maize behind the hut and seek out the place where the buffalo lay hidden, and put down her pail beside him. Then she would sit at her ease while he went to the lake and brought the bucket back brimming over. If she wanted wood, he would break the branches off the trees and lay them at her feet. And the villagers watched her return laden, and said to each other:

'Surely the girls of her country are stronger than our girls, for none of *them* could cut so quickly or carry so much!' But then, nobody knew that she had a buffalo for a servant.

Only, all this time she never gave the poor buffalo anything to eat, because she had just one dish, out of which she and her husband ate; while in her old home there was a dish put aside expressly for the Rover of the Plain. The buffalo bore it as long as he could; but, one day, when his mistress bade him go to the lake and fetch water, his knees almost gave way from hunger. He kept silence, however, till the evening, when he said to his mistress:

'I am nearly starved; I have not touched food since I came here. I can work no more.'

'Alas!' answered she, 'what can I do? I have only one dish in the house. You will have to steal some beans from the fields. Take a few here and a few there; but be sure not to take too many from one place, or the owner may notice it.'

Now the buffalo had always lived an honest life, but if his mistress did not feed him, he must get food for himself. So that night, when all the village was asleep, he came out from the wood and ate a few beans here and a few there, as his mistress had bidden him. And when at last his hunger was satisfied, he crept back to his lair. But a buffalo is not a fairy, and the next morning, when the women arrived to work in the fields, they stood still with astonishment, and said to each other:

'Just look at this; a savage beast has been destroying our crops, and we can see the traces of his feet!' And they hurried to their homes to tell their tale.

In the evening the girl crept out to the buffalo's hiding-place, and said to him:

'They perceived what happened, of course; so tonight you had better seek your supper further off.' And the buffalo nodded his head and followed her counsel; but in the morning, when these women also went out to work, the traces of hoofs were plainly to be seen, and they hastened to tell their husbands, and begged them to bring their guns, and to watch for the robber.

It happened that the stranger girl's husband was the best marksman in all the village, and he hid himself behind the trunk of a tree and waited.

The buffalo, thinking that they would probably make a search for him in the fields he had laid waste the evening before, returned to the bean patch belonging to his mistress.

The young man saw him coming with amazement.

'Why, it is a buffalo!' cried he; 'I never have beheld one in this country before!' And raising his gun, he aimed just behind the ear.

The buffalo gave a leap into the air, and then fell dead.

'It was a good shot,' said the young man. And he ran to the village to tell them that the thief was punished.

When he entered his hut he found his wife, who had somehow heard the news, twisting herself to and fro and shedding tears.

'Are you ill?' asked he. And she answered: 'Yes; I have pains all over my body.' But she was not ill at all, only very unhappy at the death of the buffalo which had served her so well. Her husband felt anxious, and sent for the medicine man; but though she pretended to listen to him, she threw all his medicine out of the door directly he had gone away.

With the first rays of light the whole village was awake, and the women set forth armed with baskets and the men with knives in order to cut up the buffalo. Only the girl remained in her hut; and after a while she too went to join them, groaning and weeping as she walked along.

'What are you doing here?' asked her husband when he saw her. 'If you are ill you are better at home.'

'Oh! I could not stay alone in the village,' said she. And her mother-in-law left off her work to come and scold her, and to tell her that she would kill herself if she did such foolish things. But the girl would not listen and sat down and looked on.

When they had divided the buffalo's flesh, and each woman had the family portion in her basket, the stranger wife got up and said:

'Let me have the head.'

'You could never carry anything so heavy,' answered the men, 'and now you are ill besides.'

'You do not know how strong I am,' answered she. And at last they gave it her.

She did not walk to the village with the others, but lingered behind, and, instead of entering her hut, she slipped into the little shed where the pots for cooking and storing maize were kept. Then she laid down the buffalo's head and sat beside it. Her husband came to seek her, and begged her to leave the shed and go to bed, as she must be tired out; but the girl would not stir, neither would she attend to the words of her mother-in-law.

'I wish you would leave me alone!' she answered crossly. 'It is impossible to sleep if somebody is always coming in.' And she turned her back on them, and would not even eat the food they had brought. So they went away, and the young man soon stretched himself out on his mat; but his wife's odd conduct made him anxious, and he lay awake all night, listening.

When all was still the girl made a fire and boiled some water in a pot. As soon as it was quite hot she shook in the medicine that she had brought from home, and then, taking the buffalo's head, she made incisions with her little knife behind the ear, and close to the temple where the shot had struck him. Next she applied the horn to the spot and blew with all her force till, at length, the blood began to move. After that she spread some of the deer fat out of the calabash over the wound, which she held in the steam of the hot water. Last of all, she sang in a low voice a dirge over the Rover of the Plain.

As she chanted the final words the head moved, and the limbs came back. The buffalo began to feel alive again and shook his horns, and stood up and stretched himself. Unluckily it was just at this moment that the husband said to himself:

'I wonder if she is crying still, and what is the matter with her! Perhaps I had better go and see.' And he got up and, calling her by name, went out to the shed.

'Go away! I don't want you!' she cried angrily. But it was too late. The buffalo had fallen to the ground, dead, and with the wound in his head as before.

The young man who, unlike most of his tribe, was afraid of his wife, returned to his bed without having seen anything, but wondering very much what she could be doing all this time. After waiting a few minutes, she began her task over again, and at the end the buffalo stood on his feet as before. But just as the girl was rejoicing that her work was completed, in came the husband once more to see what his wife was doing; and this time he sat himself down in the hut, and said that he wished to watch whatever was going on. Then the girl took up the pitcher and all her other things and left the shed, trying for the third time to bring the buffalo back to life.

She was too late; the dawn was already breaking, and the head fell to the ground, dead and corrupt as it was before.

The girl entered the hut, where her husband and his mother were getting ready to go out.

'I want to go down to the lake, and bathe,' said she.

'But you could never walk so far,' answered they. 'You are so tired, as it is, that you can hardly stand!'

However, in spite of their warnings, the girl left the hut in the direction of the lake. Very soon she came back weeping, and sobbed out:

'I met someone in the village who lives in my country, and he told me that my mother is very, very ill, and if I do not go to her at once she will be dead before I arrive. I will return as soon as I can, and now farewell.' And she set forth in the direction of the mountains. But this story was not true; she knew nothing about her mother, only she wanted an excuse to go home and tell her family that their prophecies had come true, and that the buffalo was dead.

Balancing her basket on her head, she walked along, and directly she had left the village behind her she broke out into the song of the Rover of the Plain, and at last, at the end of the day, she came to the group of huts where her parents lived. Her friends all ran to meet her, and, weeping, she told them that the buffalo was dead.

This sad news spread like lightning through the country, and the people flocked from far and near to bewail the loss of the beast who had been their pride.

'If you had only listened to *us*,' they cried, 'he would be alive now. But you refused all the little girls we offered you, and would have nothing but the buffalo. And remember what the medicine-man said: "If the buffalo dies you die also!"'

So they bewailed their fate, one to the other, and for a while they did not perceive that the girl's husband was sitting in their midst, leaning his gun against a tree. Then one man, turning, beheld him, and bowed mockingly.

'Hail, murderer! hail! you have slain us all!'

The young man stared, not knowing what he meant, and answered, wonderingly.

'I shot a buffalo; is that why you call me a murderer?'

'A buffalo – yes; but the servant of your wife! It was he who carried the wood and drew the water. Did you not know it?'

'No; I did not know it,' replied the husband in surprise. 'Why did no one tell me? Of course I should not have shot him!'

'Well, he is dead,' answered they, 'and we must die too.'

At this the girl took a cup in which some poisonous herbs had been crushed, and holding it in her hands, she wailed: 'O my father, Rover of the Plain!' Then drinking a deep draught from it, fell back dead. One by one her parents, her brothers and her sisters, drank also and died, singing a dirge to the memory of the buffalo.

The girl's husband looked on with horror; and returned sadly home across the mountains, and, entering his hut, threw himself on the ground. At first he was too tired to speak; but at length he raised his head and told all the story to his father and mother, who sat watching him. When he had finished they shook their heads and said:

'Now you see that we spoke no idle words when we told you that ill would come of your marriage! We offered you a good and hard-working wife, and you would have none of her. And it is not only your wife you have lost, but your fortune also. For who will give you back your money if they are all dead?'

'It is true, O my father,' answered the young man. But in his heart he thought more of the loss of his wife than of the money he had given for her.

URASCHIMATARO AND THE TURTLE

David Brauns

THERE WAS ONCE a worthy old couple who lived on the coast, and supported themselves by fishing. They had only one child, a son, who was their pride and joy, and for his sake they were ready to work hard all day long, and never felt tired or discontented with their lot. This son's name was Uraschimataro, which means in Japanese, 'Son of the island', and he was a fine well-grown youth and a good fisherman, minding neither wind nor weather. Not the bravest sailor in the whole village dared venture so far out to sea as Uraschimataro, and many a time the neighbours used to shake their heads and say to his parents, 'If your son goes on being so rash, one day he will try his luck once too often, and the waves will end by swallowing him up.' But Uraschimataro paid no heed to these remarks, and as he was really very clever in managing a boat, the old people were very seldom anxious about him.

One beautiful bright morning, as he was hauling his well-filled nets into the boat, he saw lying among the fishes a tiny little turtle. He was delighted with his prize, and threw it into a wooden vessel to keep till he got home, when suddenly the turtle found its voice, and tremblingly begged for its life. 'After all,' it said, 'what good can I do you? I am so young and small, and I would so gladly live a little longer. Be merciful and set me free, and I shall know how to prove my gratitude.'

Now Uraschimataro was very good-natured, and besides, he could never bear to say no, so he picked up the turtle, and put it back into the sea.

Years flew by, and every morning Uraschimataro sailed his

boat into the deep sea. But one day as he was making for a little bay between some rocks, there arose a fierce whirlwind, which shattered his boat to pieces, and she was sucked under by the waves. Uraschimataro himself very nearly shared the same fate. But he was a powerful swimmer, and struggled hard to reach the shore. Then he saw a large turtle coming towards him, and above the howling of the storm he heard what it said: 'I am the turtle whose life you once saved. I will now pay my debt and show my gratitude. The land is still far distant, and without my help you would never get there. Climb on my back, and I will take you where you will.' Uraschimataro did not wait to be asked twice, and thankfully accepted his friend's help. But scarcely was he seated firmly on the shell, when the turtle proposed that they should not return to the shore at once, but go under the sea, and look at some of the wonders that lay hidden there.

Uraschimataro agreed willingly, and in another moment they were deep, deep down, with fathoms of blue water above their heads. Oh, how quickly they darted through the still, warm sea! The young man held tight, and marvelled where they were going and how long they were to travel, but for three days they rushed on, till at last the turtle stopped before a splendid palace, shining with gold and silver, crystal and precious stones, and decked here and there with branches of pale pink coral and glittering pearls. But if Uraschimataro was astonished at the beauty of the outside, he was struck dumb at the sight of the hall within, which was lighted by the blaze of fish scales.

'Where have you brought me?' he asked his guide in a low voice.

'To the palace of Ringu, the house of the sea god, whose subjects we all are,' answered the turtle. 'I am the first waiting maid of his daughter, the lovely princess Otohimé, whom you will shortly see.'

Uraschimataro was still so puzzled with the adventures that had befallen him, that he waited in a dazed condition for what would happen next. But the turtle, who had talked so much of him to the princess that she had expressed a wish to see him, went at once to make known his arrival. And directly the princess beheld him her heart was set on him, and she begged him to stay with her, and in return promised that he should never grow old, neither should his beauty fade. 'Is not that reward enough?' she asked, smiling, looking all the while as fair as the sun itself. And Uraschimataro said 'Yes,' and so he stayed there. For how long? That he only knew later.

His life passed by, and each hour seemed happier than the last, when one day there rushed over him a terrible longing to see his parents. He fought against it hard, knowing how it would grieve the princess, but it grew on him stronger and stronger, till at length he became so sad that the princess inquired what was wrong. Then he told her of the longing he had to visit his old home, and that he must see his parents once more. The princess was almost frozen with horror, and implored him to stay with her, or something dreadful would be sure to happen. 'You will never come back, and we shall meet again no more,' she moaned bitterly. But Uraschimataro stood firm and repeated, 'Only this once will I leave you, and then will I return to your side for ever.' Sadly the princess shook her head, but she answered slowly, 'One way there is to bring you safely back, but I fear you will never agree to the conditions of the bargain.'

'I will do anything that will bring me back to you,' exclaimed Uraschimataro, looking at her tenderly, but the princess was silent: she knew too well that when he left her she would see his face no more. Then she took from a shelf a tiny golden box, and gave it to Uraschimataro, praying him to keep it carefully, and above all things never to open it. 'If you can do this,' she said as she bade him farewell, 'your friend the turtle will meet you at the shore, and will carry you back to me.'

Uraschimataro thanked her from his heart, and swore solemnly to do her bidding. He hid the box safely in his garments, seated himself on the back of the turtle, and vanished in the ocean path, waving his hand to the princess. Three days and three nights they swam through the sea, and at length Uraschimataro arrived at the beach which lay before his old home. The turtle bade him farewell, and was gone in a moment.

Uraschimataro drew near to the village with quick and joyful steps. He saw the smoke curling through the roof, and the thatch where green plants had thickly sprouted. He heard the children shouting and calling, and from a window that he passed came the twang of the koto, and everything seemed to cry a welcome for his return. Yet suddenly he felt a pang at his heart as he wandered down the street. After all, everything was changed. Neither men nor houses were those he once knew. Quickly he saw his old home; yes, it was still there, but it had a strange look. Anxiously he knocked at the door, and asked the woman who opened it after his parents. But she did not know their names, and could give him no news of them.

Still more disturbed, he rushed to the burying ground, the only place that could tell him what he wished to know. Here at any rate he would find out what it all meant. And he was right. In a moment he stood before the grave of his parents, and the date written on the stone was almost exactly the date when they had lost their son, and he had forsaken them for the Daughter of the Sea. And so he found that since he had left his home, three hundred years had passed by.

Shuddering with horror at his discovery he turned back into the village street, hoping to meet someone who could tell him of the days of old. But when the man spoke, he knew he was not dreaming, though he felt as if he had lost his senses.

In despair he bethought him of the box which was the gift of the princess. Perhaps after all this dreadful thing was not true. He might be the victim of some enchanter's spell, and in his hand lay the counter-charm. Almost unconsciously he opened it, and a purple vapour came pouring out. He held the empty box in his hand, and as he looked he saw that the fresh hand of youth had grown suddenly shrivelled, like the hand of an old, old man. He ran to the brook, which flowed in a clear stream down from the mountain, and saw himself reflected as in a mirror. It was the face of a mummy which looked back at him. Wounded to death, he crept back through the village, and no man knew the old, old man to be the strong handsome youth who had run down the street an hour before. So he toiled wearily back, till he reached the shore, and here he sat sadly on a rock, and called loudly on the turtle. But she never came back any more, but instead, death came soon, and set him free. But before that happened, the people who saw him sitting lonely on the shore had heard his story, and when their children were restless they used to tell them of the good son who from love to his parents had given up for their sakes the splendour and wonders of the palace in the sea, and the most beautiful woman in the world besides.

HOW THE SERPENT-GODS WERE PROPITIATED

Rachel Harriette Busk

LONG AGES AGO there reigned over a flourishing province, a Khan named Kun-snang. He had a son named 'Sunshine' by his first wife who afterwards died. He also had a second son named 'Moonshine', by his second wife. Now the second wife thought within herself, 'If Sunshine is allowed to live, there is no chance of Moonshine ever coming to the throne. Some means must be found of putting Sunshine out of the way.'

With this object in view she threw herself down upon her couch and tossed to and fro as though in an agony of pain. All the night through also instead of sleeping, she tossed about and writhed with pain. Then the Khan spake to her, saying, 'My beautiful one! what is it that pains thee, and with what manner of ailment art thou stricken?' And she made answer –

'Even when I was at home I suffered oftwhiles after the same manner, but now is it much more violent; all remedies have I exhausted previous times, there remains only one when the pain is of this degree, and that means is not available.'

'Say not that it is not available,' answered the Khan, 'for all means are available to me. Speak but what it is that is required, and whatever it be shall be done, even to the renouncing of my kingdom. For there is nothing that I would not give in exchange for thy life.'

But for a long time she made as though she would not tell him, then finally yielding to his repeated inquiries, she said, 'If there were given me the heart of a Prince, stewed in sesame-oil, I should recover: it matters not whether the heart of Sunshine or of Moonshine, but that Moonshine being my own son, his heart would not pass through my throat. This means, O Khan, is manifestly not available, for how should it be done to take the life of Prince Sunshine? Therefore say no more, and let me die.'

But the Khan answered, 'Of a truth it would grieve me to take the life of Prince Sunshine. Nevertheless, if there be no other means of saving thy life, the thing must be done. I have not to consider "Shall the life of the Prince be spared or not?" but, "Which shall be spared, the life of the Prince, or the life of the Khanin?" And in this strait who could doubt, but that it is the life of the Khanin that must be spared by me? Therefore, be of good cheer, beautiful one, for that the heart of Prince Sunshine shall be given thee cooked in sesame-oil.'

This, he said, intending in his own mind to have the heart of a kid of the goats prepared for her in sesame-oil, saying, 'Behold, here is the heart of Prince Sunshine,' but to send away the Prince into a far country that she might not know he was not dead. Only when she was restored to health again, then he purposed to fetch back his son. But Moonshine being in his mother's apartments overheard this promise which the Khan had given, and he ran and told his brother all that the Khan, his father, had said, saying, 'When the Khan rises he will give the order to put thee to death; how shall this thing be averted?' and he wept sore, for he loved his brother Sunshine even as his own life.

Then Sunshine answered, saying, 'Seeing this is so, remain thou with our parents, loving and honouring them, and being loved by them. For me, it is clear the time is come that I must get me away to a far country. Farewell, my brother!'

But Moonshine answered, 'Nay, brother, for if thou goest, I also go with thee. How should I live alone here, without thee, my brother?' Therefore they rose quickly before the Khan could get up, and going privately to a priest in a temple hard by, that no one else might hear of their design and betray it to the Khan, they begged of him a good provision of baling-cakes, to support life by the way; and he gave them a good provision, even a bag-full, and they set out on their journey while it was yet night. It was the fifteenth of the month, while the moon shed abroad her light, and they journeyed towards the East, not knowing whither they went. But after they had journeyed many days over mountain and plain, and come to a land where was no water, but a muddy river the water whereof could not be drunk, and where was no habitation of man, Moonshine fell down fainting by the way. Sunshine therefore ran to the top of a high hill to see if he could discern any stream of water, but found none. When he came back Moonshine was dead! Then he fell down on the ground, and wept a long space upon his body, and at nightfall he buried it with solicitude under a heap of stones, crying, 'Ah! my brother, how shall I live without thee, my brother?' And he prayed that at Moonshine's next re-birth they might again live together.

Journeying farther on, he came to a pass between two steep rocks, and in one of them was a red door. Going up to the door, he found an ancient Hermit living in a cave within, who addressed him, saying, 'Whence art thou, O youth, who seemest oppressed with recent grief?' And Sunshine told him all that had befallen him. Without again speaking the Hermit put into the folds of his girdle a bottle containing a life-restoring cordial, and going to the spot where Moonshine lay buried, restored him to life. Then said he to the two princes, 'Live now with me, and be as my two sons.' So they lived with him, and were unto him as his two sons.

The desert where this Hermit lived belonged to the kingdom of a Khan dazzling in his glory and resistless in might. Now it was about the season when the Khan and his subjects went every year to direct the flowing of water over the country for fructifying the grain-seeds; but it was the custom every year at this season first, in order to make the Serpent-gods who lived at the water-head propitious, to sacrifice to them a youth of a certain age; and on this occasion it fell to the lot of a youth born in the Tiger-year. When the Khan had caused search to be made through all the people no youth was found among them all born in the Tiger-year. At last certain herdsmen came before him, saying, 'While we were out tending our cattle, behold we saw in a cave nigh to a pass between two steep rocks a Hermit who has with him two sons, and one of them born in the Tiger-year.'

When the Khan had listened to their words he immediately sent three envoys to fetch the Hermit's son for the sacrifice.

When the three envoys of the Khan had come and stood knocking before the red door of the Hermit's cave, the Hermit cried out to them, asking what they wanted of him. Then answered the chief of them, 'Because thou hast a son living with thee born in the Tiger-year, and the Khan hath need of him for the sacrifice; therefore are we come, even that we may bring him to the Khan.'

When the Hermit had heard their embassage, he answered them, 'How should a Hermit have a son with him out here in the desert?' But he took Sunshine, who was the youth born in the Tiger-year, and motioned him into a farther hole of the cave where was a great vessel of pottery; into this vessel he made him creep, then fastening the mouth of the vessel with earth, he made it to appear like to a jar of rice-brandy. Meantime, however, the Khan's envoys had broken down the door, and began searching through every recess of the cave. Finding nothing, they were filled with fury, and in their anger beat the Hermit on whose account they had come a bootless errand. But when Sunshine heard the men ill-treating the Hermit who had been to him as a father, he could not refrain himself, and called out from within the brandy-jar, 'Unhand my father!' Then the envoys immediately left off beating his father, but they turned and seized him and carried him off to the Khan, while the Hermit was left weeping with great grief at the loss of his adopted son, even as one like to die.

As the envoys dragged Sunshine along before the palace, the Khan's daughter was looking out of a window, and when she heard that the handsome youth was destined for the Serpent-sacrifice, she was filled with compassion. She went therefore to the men who had the charge to throw him into the water, saying, 'See how comely he is! He is worthy to be saved, throw him not into the water. Or else if you will throw him in, throw me in also with him.' Then the men went and showed the Khan her words; whereupon the king was wroth, and said, 'She is not worthy to be called the Khan's daughter; let them therefore be both sewn up into one bullock's skin, and so cast into the water.' The men therefore did according to the Khan's bidding, and sewing them both up in one bullock-hide together, cast them into the water to the Serpent-gods.

Then began Sunshine to say, 'That they should throw me to the Serpent-gods, because I was the only youth to be found who was born in the Tiger-year, was not so bad; but that this beautiful maiden, who hath deigned to lift her eyes on me, and to love me, should be so sacrificed also, this is unbearable!'

And the Khan's daughter in like manner cried, 'That I who am only a woman should be thrown to the Serpent-gods, is not so bad; but that this noble and beautiful youth should be so sacrificed also, this is unbearable!'

When the Serpent-gods heard these laments, and saw how the prince and the maiden vied with each other in generosity, they sent and fetched them both out of the water, and gave them freedom. Also as soon as they were set free, they let the water gently flow over the whole country, just as the people desired for their rice irrigation.

Meantime, Sunshine said to the Khan's daughter, 'Princess, let us each now return home. Go thou to thy father's palace, while I go back to the Hermitage, and visit my adopted father, who is like to die of grief for the loss of me. After I have fulfilled this filial duty, I will return to thee, and we will live for ever after for each other alone.'

The princess then praised his filial love, and bid him go console his father, only begging him to come to her right soon, for she should have no joy till he came back.

Sunshine went therefore to the Hermit, whom he found so worn with grief, that he was but just in time to save him from dying; so having first washed him with milk and water, he consoled him with many words of kindness.

The princess, too, went home to the palace, where all were so astonished at her deliverance that at first she could hardly obtain admission. When they had made sure it was herself in very truth, the people all came round her, and congratulated her with joy, for never had any one before been delivered from the sacrifice to the Serpent-gods.

Then said the Khan, 'That the Khan's daughter should be spared by the Serpent-gods was to be expected. They have the youth born in the Tiger-year for their sacrifice.'

But the princess answered, 'Neither has he fallen sacrifice. Him also they let free; and indeed was it in great part out of regard for his abnegation and distress over my suffering that we were both let free.'

Then answered the Khan, 'In that case is our debt great unto this youth. Let him be sought after, and besought that he come to visit us in our palace.'

So they went again to the cave in the rocky pass, and fetched Sunshine; and when he came near, the Khan went out to meet him, and caused costly seats to be brought, and made him sit down thereon beside him.

Then he said to him, 'That thou hast delivered this country from the fear of drought, is matter for which we owe thee our highest gratitude; but that thou and this my daughter also have escaped from death is a marvellous wonder. Tell me now, art thou in very truth the son of the Hermit?'

'No,' replied Sunshine, 'I am the son of a mighty Khan; but my step-mother, seeking to make a difference between me and this my brother standing beside me, who was her own born son, and to put me to death, we fled away both together; and thus fleeing we came to the Hermit, and were taken in by his hospitality.'

When the Khan had heard his words, he promised him his daughter in marriage, and her sister, to be wife to Moonshine. Moreover, he endowed them with immeasurable riches, and gave them an escort of four detachments of fighting-men to accompany them home. When they had arrived near the capital of the kingdom, they sent an embassage before them to the Khan saying, –

'We, thy two sons, Sunshine and Moonshine, are returned to thee.'

The Khan and the Khanin, who had for many years past quite lost their reason out of grief for the loss of their children, and held no more converse with men, were at once restored to sense and animation at this news, and sent out a large troop of horsemen to meet them, and conduct them to their palace. Thus the two princes returned in honour to their home.

When they came in, the Khan was full of joy and glory, sitting on his throne; but the Khanin, full of remorse and shame at the thought of the crime she had meditated, fell down dead before their face.

KOSHCHEI THE DEATHLESS

Alexander Afanasief

In a certain country there once lived a king, and he had three sons, all of them grown up. All of a sudden Koshchei the Deathless carried off their mother. Then the eldest son craved his father's blessing, that he might go and look for his mother. His father gave him his blessing, and he went off and disappeared, leaving no trace behind. The second son waited and waited, then he too obtained his father's blessing – and he also disappeared. Then the youngest son, Prince Ivan, said to his father: 'Father, give me your blessing, and let me go and look for my mother.'

But his father would not let him go, saying, 'Your brothers are no more; if you likewise go away, I shall die of grief.'

'Not so, father. But if you bless me I shall go; and if you do not bless me I shall go.'

So his father gave him his blessing.

Prince Ivan went to choose a steed, but every one that he laid his hand upon gave way under it. He could not find a steed to suit him, so he wandered with drooping brow along the road and about the town. Suddenly there appeared an old woman, who asked:

'Why hangs your brow so low, Prince Ivan?'

'Be off, old crone,' he replied. 'If I put you on one of my hands, and give it a slap with the other, there'll be a little wet left, that's all.'

The old woman ran down a by-street, came to meet him a second time, and said:

'Good day, Prince Ivan! why hangs your brow so low?'

Then he thought:

'Why does this old woman ask me? Mightn't she be of use to me?' – and he replied:

'Well, mother! because I cannot get myself a good steed.'

'Silly fellow!' she cried, 'to suffer, and not to ask the old woman's help! Come along with me.'

She took him to a hill, showed him a certain spot, and said:

'Dig up that piece of ground.'

Prince Ivan dug it up and saw an iron plate with twelve padlocks on it. He immediately broke off the padlocks, tore open a door, and followed a path leading underground. There, fastened with twelve chains, stood a heroic steed which evidently heard the approaching steps of a rider worthy to mount it, and so began to neigh and to struggle, until it broke all twelve of its chains. Then Prince Ivan put on armour fit for a hero, and bridled the horse, and saddled it with a Circassian saddle. And he gave the old woman money, and said to her:

'Forgive me, mother, and bless me!' then he mounted his steed and rode away.

Long time did he ride; at last he came to a mountain – a tremendously high mountain, and so steep that it was utterly impossible to get up it. Presently his brothers came that way. They all greeted each other, and rode on together, till they came to an iron rock a hundred and fifty poods in weight, and on it was this inscription, 'Whosoever will fling this rock against the mountain, to him will a way be opened.' The two elder brothers were unable to lift the rock, but Prince Ivan at the first try flung it against the mountain – and immediately there appeared a ladder leading up the mountain side.

Prince Ivan dismounted, let some drops of blood run from his little finger into a glass, gave it to his brothers, and said:

'If the blood in this glass turns black, tarry here no longer: that will mean that I am about to die.' Then he took leave of them and went his way.

He mounted the hill. What did not he see there? All sorts of trees were there, all sorts of fruits, all sorts of birds! Long did Prince Ivan walk on; at last he came to a house, a huge house! In it lived a king's daughter who had been carried off by Koshchei the Deathless. Prince Ivan walked round the enclosure, but could not see any doors. The king's daughter saw there was someone there, came on to the balcony, and called out to him,

'See, there is a chink in the enclosure; touch it with your little finger, and it will become a door.'

What she said turned out to be true. Prince Ivan went into the house, and the maiden received him kindly, gave him to eat and to drink, and then began to question him. He told her how he had come to rescue his mother from Koshchei the Deathless. Then the maiden said:

'It will be difficult for you to get at your mother, Prince Ivan. You see, Koshchei is not mortal: he will kill you. He often comes here to see me. There is his sword, fifty poods in weight. Can you lift it? If so, you may venture to go.'

Not only did Prince Ivan lift the sword, but he tossed it high in the air. So he went on his way again.

By and by he came to a second house. He knew now where to look for the door, and he entered in. There was his mother. With tears did they embrace each other.

Here also did he try his strength, heaving aloft a ball which weighed some fifteen hundred poods. The time came for Koshchei the Deathless to arrive. The mother hid away her son. Suddenly Koshchei the Deathless entered the house and cried out, 'Phou, Phou! A Russian bone one usen't to hear with one's ears, or see with one's eyes, but now a Russian bone has come to the house! Who has been with you? Wasn't it your son?'

'What are you talking about, God bless you! You've been flying through Russia, and got the Russian air up your nostrils, that's why you fancy it's here,' answered Prince Ivan's mother, and then she drew nigh to Koshchei, addressed him in terms of affection, asked him about one thing and another, and at last said:

'Whereabouts is your death, O Koshchei?'

'My death,' he replied, 'is in such and such a place. There stands an oak, and under the oak is a casket, and in the casket is a hare, and in the hare is a duck, and in the duck is an egg, and in the egg is my death.'

Having thus spoken, Koshchei the Deathless tarried there a little longer, and then flew away.

The time came – Prince Ivan received his mother's blessing, and went to look for Koshchei's death. He went on his way a long time without eating or drinking; at last he felt mortally hungry, and thought, 'If only something would come my way!' Suddenly there appeared a young wolf; he determined to kill it. But out from a hole sprang the she-wolf, and said, 'Don't hurt my little one; I'll do you a good turn.' Very good! Prince Ivan let the young wolf go. On he went and saw a crow. 'Stop a bit,' he thought, 'here I shall get a mouthful.' He loaded his gun and was going to shoot, but the crow exclaimed, 'Don't hurt me; I'll do you a good turn.'

Prince Ivan thought the matter over and spared the crow. Then he went farther, and came to a sea and stood still on the shore. At that moment a young pike suddenly jumped out of the water and fell on the strand. He caught hold of it, and thought – for he was half dead with hunger – 'Now I shall have something to eat.' All of a sudden appeared a pike and said, 'Don't hurt my little one, Prince Ivan; I'll do you a good turn.' And so he spared the little pike also.

But how was he to cross the sea? He sat down on the shore and meditated. But the pike knew quite well what he was thinking about, and laid herself right across the sea. Prince Ivan walked along her back, as if he were going over a bridge, and came to the oak where Koshchei's death was. There he found the casket and opened it – out jumped the hare and ran away. How was the hare to be stopped?

Prince Ivan was terribly frightened at having let the hare escape, and gave himself up to gloomy thoughts; but a wolf, the one he had refrained from killing, rushed after the hare, caught it, and brought it to Prince Ivan. With great delight he seized the hare, cut it open – and had such a fright! Out popped the duck and flew away. He fired after it, but shot all on one side, so again he gave himself up to his thoughts. Suddenly there appeared the crow with her little crows, and set off after the duck, and caught it, and brought it to Prince Ivan. The Prince was greatly pleased and got hold of the egg. Then he went on his way. But when he came to the sea, he began washing the egg, and let it drop into the water. However was he to get it out of the water? an immeasurable depth! Again the Prince gave himself up to dejection.

Suddenly the sea became violently agitated, and the pike brought him the egg. Moreover it stretched itself across the sea. Prince Ivan walked along it to the other side, and then he set out again for his mother's. When he got there, they greeted each other lovingly, and then she hid him again as before. Presently in flew Koshchei the Deathless and said:

'Phoo, Phoo! No Russian bone can the ear hear nor the eye see, but there's a smell of Russia here!'

'What are you talking about, Koshchei? There's no one with me,' replied Prince Ivan's mother.

A second time spake Koshchei and said, 'I feel rather unwell.'

Then Prince Ivan began squeezing the egg, and thereupon Koshchei the Deathless bent double. At last Prince Ivan came out from his hiding-place, held up the egg and said. 'There is your death, O Koshchei the Deathless!'

Then Koshchei fell on his knees before him, saying, 'Don't kill me, Prince Ivan! Let's be friends! All the world will lie at our feet.'

But these words had no weight with Prince Ivan. He smashed the egg, and Koshchei the Deathless died.

Ivan and his mother took all they wanted and started homewards. On their way they came to where the King's daughter was whom Ivan had seen on his way, and they took her with them too. They went further, and came to the hill where Ivan's brothers were still waiting for him. Then the maiden said, 'Prince Ivan! do go back to my house. I have forgotten a marriage robe, a diamond ring, and a pair of seamless shoes.'

He consented to do so, but in the meantime he let his mother go down the ladder, as well as the Princess – whom it had been settled he was to marry when they got home. They were received by his brothers, who then set to work and cut away the ladder, so that he himself would not be able to get down. And they used such threats to his mother and the Princess, that they made them promise not to tell about Prince Ivan when they got home. And after a time they reached their native country. Their father was delighted at seeing his wife and his two sons, but still he was grieved about the other one, Prince Ivan.

But Prince Ivan returned to the home of his betrothed, and got the wedding dress, and the ring, and the seamless shoes. Then he came back to the mountain and tossed the ring from one hand to the other. Immediately there appeared twelve strong youths, who said:

'What are your commands?'

'Carry me down from this hill.'

The youths immediately carried him down. Prince Ivan put the ring on his finger – they disappeared.

Then he went on to his own country, and arrived at the city in which his father and brothers lived.

There he took up his quarters in the house of an old woman, and asked her:

'What news is there, mother, in your country?'

'What news, lad? You see our queen was kept in prison by Koshchei the Deathless. Her three sons went to look for her, and two of them found her and came back, but the third, Prince Ivan, has disappeared, and no one knows where he is. The King is very unhappy about him. And those two Princes and their mother brought a certain Princess back with them; and the eldest son wants to marry her, but she declares he must fetch her her betrothal ring first, or get one made just as she wants it. But although they have made a public proclamation about it, no one has been found to do it yet.'

'Well, mother, go and tell the King that you will make one. I'll manage it for you,' said Prince Ivan.

So the old woman immediately dressed herself, and hastened to the King, and said:

'Please your Majesty, I will make the wedding ring.

'Make it, then, make it, mother! Such people as you are welcome,' said the king. 'But if you don't make it, off goes your head!'

The old woman was dreadfully frightened; she ran home, and told Prince Ivan to set to work at the ring. But Ivan lay down to sleep, troubling himself very little about it. The ring was there all the time. So he only laughed at the old woman, but she was trembling all over, and crying, and scolding him.

'As for you,' she said, 'you're out of the scrape; but you've done for me, fool that I was!'

The old woman cried and cried until she fell asleep. Early in the morning Prince Ivan got up and awakened her, saying:

'Get up, mother, and go out! take them the ring, and mind, don't accept more than one ducat for it. If anyone asks who made the ring, say you made it yourself; don't say a word about me.'

The old woman was overjoyed and carried off the ring. The bride was delighted with it.

'Just what I wanted,' she said. So they gave the old woman a dish full of gold, but she took only one ducat.

'Why do you take so little?' said the king.

'What good would a lot do me, your Majesty? if I want some more afterwards, you'll give it me.'

Having said this the old woman went away.

Time passed, and the news spread abroad that the bride had told her lover to fetch her her wedding-dress or else to get one made, just such a one as she wanted. Well, the old woman, thanks to Prince Ivan's aid, succeeded in this matter too, and took her the wedding-dress. And afterwards she took her the seamless shoes also, and would only accept one ducat each time. and always said that she had made the things herself.

Well, the people heard that there would be a wedding at the palace on such-and-such a day. And the day they all anxiously awaited came at last. Then Prince Ivan said to the old woman:

'Look here, mother! when the bride is just going to be married, let me know.'

The old woman didn't let the time go by unheeded.

Then Ivan immediately put on his princely raiment, and went out of the house.

'See, mother, this is what I'm really like!' says he.

The old woman fell at his feet.

'Pray forgive me for scolding you,' says she.

'God be with you,' says he.

So he went into the church and, finding his brothers had not yet arrived, he stood up alongside of the bride and got married to her. Then he and she were escorted back to the palace, and as they went along, the proper bridegroom, his eldest brother, met them. But when he saw that his bride and Prince Ivan were being escorted home together, he turned back again ignominiously.

As to the king, he was delighted to see Prince Ivan again, and when he had learnt all about the treachery of his brothers, after the wedding feast had been solemnised, he banished the two elder princes, but he made Ivan heir to the throne.

THE CIRCUMVENTION OF FATE

Jessica Amanda Salmonson

KING LAKSHIMINDRA TOSSED and turned on his covers, his brow sweating, his eyes wildly staring but seeing none of the women who worriedly surrounded him.

Queen Behula placed her maids on all sides of King Lakshimindra and assigned them the tasks of cooling his arms and brow with moistened scarves and holding him still when he raved. 'Watch over him in my absence,' she commanded. She then hurried from the palace, wrapped in a dark cloak, leaping upon a pony. She rode swiftly and met secretly with the sorcerous Dakini.

The Dakini's breasts sagged into her lap. Her old face was chestnut brown. Although there had been no herald of the queen's coming, and none outside the palace knew of the king's illness, the Dakini naytheless was prepared in advance for the royal one's arrival.

The Dakini's hut was warm and dimly lit by red coals. Incense was fuming. Four yoginis in tiger skins sat in the shadows of the four corners of the room. The yoginis were the maiden pupils of the aged Dakini. They wove mystic signs with their fingers, murmured spells, and struck ringing bowls with tiny mallets.

Without exchanging greetings, the queen sat across the coal-pit opposite the Dakini. The wise one did not ask even one question as to why the queen had come, but said, 'O sorrowful queen, the Serpent-goddess Manasa has sent fire into the brain of the king. This very night, he will be taken by a fever-demoness, and never again will you see him. This is his punishment for having spurned the Goddess many times, calling her venomous and cruel.'

'I have propitiated Manasa with prayers and offerings,' said

Queen Behula, 'and warned my husband to avoid insults. But he listened only to brahmans, and ignored my counsel. Even so, I seek to preserve him. Have you no herb, poultice, or amulet that will aid me? I will pay you anything you desire.'

The Dakini said, 'Long ago have I given up desire. I seek no grand reward. I would help you freely, were it in my power, but the king's destiny was written on his forehead by the Goddess Bidahata-Purasha when he was six days old. Even his folly was written there, so he cannot be fully blamed. There is no poultice or amulet that will change the outcome of his life. Resign yourself, O Queen, and praise Manasa even in your saddest hour! The ways of Manasa are glorious. She seems cruel, but slays only that which keeps us from purity and happiness. Her beautiful cobra-naginis liberate all of us from this sphere of illusion.'

The queen said, 'Much as I have honored Manasa, even so, I am not prepared for this. I would fight even She that is loved in order to aid my beloved king Lakshimindra'

'Your prowess is well known,' said the Dakini. 'Only, speak not blasphemously of Manasa, for your sake and the sake of the world.'

'Come what may, I must strive to save my husband,' said Behula. 'Tell me in truth, if I sit up with him through this night, mopping his brow, praying for his recovery, cooling his body with fans when he is hot, warming him with my body when he is chilled, is there even then no chance of his survival?'

'If you swab his brow, and cool him when he is burning, and warm him when he is chilled, your devotion to him may well restore his health. Even so, two days hence, he will go riding on his elephant, and fall from it, and be accidentally trampled.'

The queen considered this, then asked, 'But if I keep him from riding his elephant, and insist he take only a horse, will he not be spared such a fate?'

'Just so. But when he rides his horse under the city gate, a stone will fall from the arch and kill him.'

'Oh! But suppose laborers are sent to tear down the arch this very night? How will a stone fall and kill him if the arch has been dismantled?'

'By such an act you can save him from this fate. But while he is hunting the royal deer, an arrow will be unleashed by his closest friend. That arrow will fall wild, and pierce your husband in the neck, from which wound he will not recover.'

'Suppose someone insists that he and his retinue hunt only with spears?'

'Then surely he will escape that danger. But upon his return home, he will seek his bath, and slip upon a tile. His head will crack open, and after many days of anguish, he will die raving.'

'But suppose his meal is ready even as he enters the palace, and a petulant queen will not let him dally from the table long enough to take a bath?'

'In that case, he will never break his skull. But there will be fish at the meal. A part of it will lodge in his throat. His face will become livid, and he will die gagging.'

'What if someone sitting near him snatches the fish from his plate and insists he eat only fruit the rest of the day?'

'Yes, that will save him, but fresh dangers await. When the king is in his bed that night, Manasa's cobra will slither through the curtains and bite him.'

'Suppose someone who loves him with her life stands guard with a sword! At risk to herself, she may behead the cobra, and save her king.'

'Yes, yes, but if Manasa is angered by the death of her serpent, the king will turn into a block of yellow stone. O Queen, give up your bold plans. Be courageous in your heart, and accept the will of Manasa.'

'Never!' said the queen, pounding the earthen floor with an open hand. 'I have honored her greatly, but in this one thing she finds a foe! I know what must be done! I know how I can save him!'

So saying, Behula stood and swept out of the hut. The four yoginis were singing a macabre dirge. The Dakini shook her wizened, hoary head and frowned as the queen departed.

She rode swiftly on her pony, returning to the palace. She hurried to the inner chambers. Shoving aside the maids who stood over the suffering king, Behula exclaimed, 'My husband! I know how to save you!' And drawing forth a dagger from her garments, she slit his throat.

THE DESTRUCTION OF KER-YS

Peter Tremayne

At the hour of the birth of Gwezenneg, prince of Bro Érech, a holy man foretold that he would be king. But the holy man also issued a warning; that on the day Gwezenneg ate pork, drank watered wine and renounced his God then he would surely die. And his death would come about by poison, by burning and by drowning. Such was the nature of this prophecy that everyone at the court of Bro Érech laughed and sent the holy man away to his hermitage with patronising smiles but with gifts lest he be a man of true prophecy.

The years went by and Gwezenneg grew to be a tall, handsome prince. It came about, as the holy man foretold, that he was acclaimed king of Bro Érech, a kingdom in the southernmost part of Armorica, the land by the sea, which we now called 'Little Britain'. Gwezenneg married a princess of Kernascleden named Gwyar and she bore him two sons. And Gwezenneg grew in fame and sought to extend the borders of his kingdom and fought several wars with neighbouring princes to expand his kingdom.

All the while, however, he was aware of the prophecy made at his birth.

One day he was hunting in the great forests of Pont Calleck by the edge of the great lake there when he came upon a beautiful young woman. Never had he beheld such beauty before. She sat on a log by the shore of the lake combing her hair with a silver comb ornamented with gold. The sun was shining on her so that her two golden yellow tresses, each one braided in four plaits, with a bead at the end of each, glistened like liquid fire.

She was dressed in a skirt of green silk, with a tunic of red, all embroidered with designs of animals in gold and silver. She bore a round golden brooch with filigree work decorated with silver. From her slender shoulders there hung a cloak of purple.

Her upper arms were white as the snow of a single night and they were soft and shapely. Her cheeks had the tinge of the foxglove of the moor upon them. Her eyebrows were coloured black and her eyes were as blue as the bugloss. Her lips were vermilion. The blush of the moon was on her fair countenance and there was a lifting pride in her noble face.

'Maiden, tell me your name,' demanded Gwezenneg, alighting from his horse and going on his knees before her as a tribute to her beauty.

She smiled softly, a dimple of sport in both her cheeks, and she answered with a gentle womanly dignity in her voice.

'I am called "whirlwind", "tempest" and "storm".'

'Lady, I would give the kingdom of Bro Érech to know you.' His children and queen, Gwyar, were all forgotten. 'Lady of the rough winds, come as my mistress to my royal palace at Vannes. I will grant you anything that is in my power.'

'Think well, on this, O king,' replied the girl. 'I have warned you of the storm to come. Do you still desire me?'

'I do.'

'Then I will come to your palace on the condition that no Christian cleric shall ever set foot there and that you must submit to my will in all things.'

Without even thinking, Gwezenneg, mesmerised by the deep blue of her eyes, agreed.

So the girl, who said her name was Aveldro, the whirlwind, came to the king's palace at Vannes.

Horrified, Gwyar, Gwezenneg's queen, took her children and went straightaway to Guénolé, the bishop, and, sobbing, asked him to intervene and cure her husband's infatuation. And when Guénolé came to Gwezenneg, the king would not listen to him. The bishop then turned to Aveldro, who was sitting unconcerned by the side of her lover. He demanded whether she felt guilt. Aveldro turned to him with a smile.

'Guilt is for the followers of your god, Gunwalloe,' she said, using the ancient form of his name so that he would know his pagan past. 'Guilt is not for those who follow the old ways.'

And Guénolé was enraged.

'Do you not follow the Christ?' he demanded.

'I cleave not to the cleric of your church,' she replied. 'They chant nothing save unreason and their tune is unmelodious in the universe.'

Then Guénolé cursed King Gwezenneg and reminded him that his doom had already been foretold.

Gwezenneg grew afraid at this but Aveldro caused a great wind to blow through the palace which swept the cursing cleric from its halls. Now Aveldro had done this feat of magic in order to put heart into Gwezenneg. But he was awed by her great power and realised that she was a *dryades*, that is to say, a female Druid. And he feared Guénolé's curse and the prophecy of his birth. So he waited until Aveldro had retired before he summoned a messenger and told him to go after Guénolé telling the bishop that Gwezenneg would come to him as soon as he could and confess all his sins, do penance, and with his blessing would eject Aveldro from his court.

The next evening Aveldro summoned him for the evening meal and a dish of meat was placed before the king.

'What meat is this?' he demanded of his cook, after he had chewed and swallowed a large piece. His cook looked uncomfortable.

'Why, we had no slaughtered beef nor mutton in the kitchen and so your lady,' he glanced awkwardly at Aveldro, 'told us to serve the pig we had slaughtered for the servants. She said that you would approve.'

And Gwezenneg went white for he knew the significance of eating pig. He reached for his wine glass to swallow the wine in order to wash out the unclean meat from his mouth. He took one swallow before spitting out the rest of the wine in disgust.

'What weak wine is this?' he demanded of the chamberlain, who had served the wine.

His chamberlain looked awkwardly at Aveldro.

'Why, sire, we had only one flagon of good wine left in the palace and so your lady told us to add a little water to it, so that it would go that much further. She said that you would approve.'

'God be damned!' swore Gwezenneg, rising up in anger from his place. Then, realising the nature of his unthinking curse, he sat down abruptly. Gwezenneg sat white-faced and stared at Aveldro who smiled a knowing smile.

Aveldro was a skilful Druidess for she could read the thoughts of the king of Bro Érech just as surely as if he had spoken them aloud. She knew that he planned to go to Guénolé and betray her. So that same night she evoked a vision which mesmerised him. And once more he pleaded for Aveldro to come to bed with him and make love and, in the vision, she consented.

Then Gwezenneg awoke from his love-making with a dry mouth and a great thirst which lay heavily on him.

'I thirst,' he moaned, 'but can find no water.'

Aveldro smiled beside him.

'I will go to the kitchen, my lover, and bring you some crystal, cold water to assuage your thirst.'

When she returned, she handed him a glass of water. He drained the glass and returned to sleep.

She watched his sleep and was satisfied for she had placed poison in the glass.

At dawn she was abruptly wakened by distant shouting. She smelt smoke and burning. It had happened that Gwyar, driven to distraction with her anger, had come upon the palace that night and set a fire under her husband's sleeping chamber.

Aveldro, taking a last look at her poisoned lover, decided to flee the palace. She had wanted to be there when Gwezenneg's body was discovered so that no blame would attach itself to her. But with the flames licking at the walls, she decided that her journey westward to her home must be precipitate. She escaped from the burning fortress and disappeared into the dawn light.

Now Gwezenneg, drugged with the poison, was not yet dead. For he was a strong and healthy man and it took a time for the poison to work through his system. The noise of shouting awoke him and he saw great flames engulfing his chamber. In discomfort from the poison, he staggered from his bed and, standing swaying, he gazed about him, finding himself amidst the smoke and crackling fires. He sought for a means of escape. The heat was intense but he managed to flee from the bedchamber as the blazing ridge poles of the roof came crashing down.

He made his way down the stone stairs, with the stones so hot that they burnt and blistered his bare feet, and found himself in the kitchens of the palace. There he was trapped by a great sheet of flame and in desperation he saw the tall water vats. In an effort to escape the flame, he clambered into the first vat which was filled with water. He plunged into its icy depth, intending to wait there until the flames had passed.

But the poison had so weakened him that he could not swim and after a minute or two he sank into the cold water of the vat and was drowned.

The next day, when Guénolé came to the smouldering ruins of the palace, the attendants of King Gwezenneg told him what had happened, for they had found the body of the king in the debris. Guénolé knew then that the prophecy had been fulfilled. But he knew also that the cause of it was the mysterious woman named Aveldro, the whirlwind. He vowed that Aveldro, who had denied the Living God, would have to pay reparation for this deed if ever she was found.

The time came when Guénolé left the sad kingdom of Bro Érech and set about a journey westward to the kingdom of Kernev, which is Cornouaille, which stretched south from the Monts d'Arrée and east to the River Ellé, beyond the great realm of Domnonia. Guénolé had heard that this kingdom of Kernev was still fiercely pagan. So he set out to convert it and he built a great monastery, which is called Landévennec, and slowly the people of Kernev turned to him and accepted his teachings.

However, Kernev was ruled by an eminent king called Gradlon. Gradlon ruled from a great city called Ker-Ys, which is 'the beloved place'. Ker-Ys was situated in what is now the Baie des Trépassés, that is the Bay of the Dead, just off the Pointe du Raz, for at the time the land of Kernev stretched over this area of the sea.

Ker-Ys was a mighty place and spoken of in awe by those merchants who had travelled to its massive walls.

Guénolé was put in a mind to see the city and to bring the word of the Living God to its king Gradlon.

One day, seated in his cell at Landévennec, he sent for his disciple, Gwion, who had been a fisherman from Kerazan and had often sailed the western coast around Kernev.

'Tell me of this Gradlon and Ker-Ys for tomorrow I mean to make a journey to see them.'

Gwion looked slightly worried.

'They hold steadfast to the old gods,' he warned his master.

'So did many of us until we heard the truth,' Guénolé replied complacently.

'Gradlon is certainly a fair king,' Gwion said. 'A sad king, though. Once, many years ago, Gwezenneg of Bro Érech tried to extend the borders of his kingdom to the west and into the territory of Kernev. He brought an army with him and crossed the River Scorv at Hennebont, which is the old bridge.

'It happened on that day Gradlon's wife and queen, Dieub, was visiting her kinfolk at Belon. And with her was her son Youlek the Determined. Gwezenneg and his warriors came down like a plague of locusts, slaughtering all before them and leaving behind the blackened earth stained red with blood. And the blood of Gradlon's wife, Dieub, was among that which had mingled with the sorry clay. And the blood of Gradlon's son, Youlek, also drenched the earth for Youlek had tried to protect his mother with his sword. And all the generations of Dieub's family were slaughtered.'

Guénolé was troubled when he heard this for Gwezenneg had been a Christian king and unworthy to have committed such a slaughter.

'Did Gradlon seek vengeance for the deed?'

Gwion shook his head.

'No; he sent his ambassadors to Gwezenneg asking for reparation and was refused. Each year, at the festival of Imbolc, he sent his ambassadors and they came back from Vannes empty handed. His daughter, Dahud-Ahes, whose beauty is renowned in the west, and who, it is said, is a mighty Druidess, demanded that her father take his army and seize that which Gwezenneg refused to give. Gradlon is a wise and worthy king and refused to lower himself to the actions of Gwezenneg.'

Guénolé was pleased then for he knew that Gradlon was such a king as he could convert to the true faith. But he was worried when he heard about Dahud-Ahes.

The next morning he set out for the west and Ker-Ys. The farther west he went the more forbidding the country became, with bare heathland and no trees but scrubland and little stone walls here and there as a means of enclosing the scanty crops which grew. There came a long, narrow spur of land, torn by waves on either side, overlooking the sea from a height of two hundred feet, and this was prolonged seaward into a chain of reefs. Then to the north was a low green plain, protected from the sea by a long, high dyke, which stretched between the Pointe du Raz and the Pointe du Van, for as we have said, this area was once land. The great dyke had built into it two massive gates which acted in the manner of a lock, and no one could open these gates, for they would flood the city. The gates were secured by a massive padlock to which there was but one golden key which Gradlon carried on a chain around his neck.

Guénolé rode up to the gates of Ker-Ys and demanded entrance and access to Gradlon. Gradlon readily admitted the man and listened to all he had to say.

'There is much that is true in what you say,' Gradlon conceded, after a while. 'I would learn more.'

'I would not!' rang out a voice.

A most beautiful woman entered the hall and from the way the attendants bowed low, Guénolé knew he was in the presence of Dahud-Ahes, daughter of Gradlon. As his disciple, Gwion, had said, she was a mighty Druidess.

Then Guénolé peered closer.

'Are you not known as Whirlwind?' he demanded.

Dahud-Ahes smiled condescendingly.

'What do you think?' she parried.

Guénolé gasped.

'Yes, by the Living God. You are Aveldro, who caused the death of Gwezenneg!'

Dahud-Ahes stood without shame.

'It was my right to take vengeance. Did not this Gwezenneg take the life of my mother, Dieub, and my brother Youlek? And did he not slaughter all my mother's family?'

'Yet you took his life by sorcery,' breathed Guénolé genuflecting.

'I took his life as he took the lives of my kin,' affirmed Dahud-Ahes.

Gradlon hung his head in shame.

'What you have done is not justice, daughter. Vengeance is not reparation.'

'Vengeance satisfies the soul,' replied Dahud-Ahes. 'My soul is at peace.'

'We are born bound to the great wheel of life, Dahud-Ahes,'

warned Guénolé. 'There is no action without a consequence. Just as Gwezenneg has paid for his action, so must you pay for your action.' He turned to Gradlon. 'King, I feel that you wish to reach out for the truth of the Living God. When the time comes you will find me at the city of Kemper.'

So he left the court of Gradlon.

That evening Dahud-Ahes was in her bed-chamber when, without warning, a young man of surpassing handsomeness entered. He was so handsome that Dahud-Ahes found herself trembling from her desire of him.

'You are no mortal man,' she murmured.

'I am Maponos, the god of love,' he replied with a smile. 'And of all the women on the earth, I have heard that you were the most beautiful. Now I have seen the truth of it with my own eyes. And I desire you. Come away with me and dwell with me in the palace of love, which is far to the west of this place.'

Dahud-Ahes lost all her rationality. Indeed, as Gwezenneg had fallen under her spell, she fell under the spell of this young man.

'I will,' she replied with vehemence.

Then the handsome Maponos hesitated.

'I have admitted my love for you. But before we go to my eternal palace, you must prove that you love me. The entrance to my palace is known only to myself and if you share this secret I need a token of your love.'

'I will do anything,' she replied simply.

'Then fetch the golden key of the gate in the dyke which hangs around your father's neck. Fetch it and unlock the gates.'

'But the whole city will drown,' protested Dahud-Ahes.

'Not so. If you believe in me I will not let it drown. Am I not a god and cannot I stop such floods? If you desire to live with me in all eternity then you must do this thing to prove your worthiness.'

For Dahud-Ahes there was never any doubt of her desire and she ran straightaway to her father's bedchamber and finding him asleep, she took the golden key and chain from around his neck. Then she hurried to the great gate where the handsome young god stood.

'Open the gate,' instructed Maponos, 'if you trust and desire me. Prove to me that you believe in me.'

She put the key in the lock, turned it and flung open the gate. The vast green frothy sea rushed in. Dahud-Ahes turned eagerly to the young man.

'Now save the city, for I have proved my love for you,' she cried.

The young man started to laugh. He laughed and as he did so his body was transformed into a twisted, ageing devil with the evil, sneering face of Gwezenneg. Then, with the laughter still echoing, the figure disappeared.

In terror and despair, Dahud-Ahes ran through the city of Ker-Ys raising the alarm. The sea rushed down, its waves like hungry mouths swallowing all in their path.

'Mount up, behind, my daughter!'

Gradlon rode up beside her on his fastest charger, and Dahud–Ahes was swung up behind. The king rode as hard as he could before the mighty, oncoming tide, the powerful sinews of his horse bursting with the effort. But the sea began to overtake them, to swallow them. Gradlon began to despair when he heard the voice of Guénolé.

'If you would save yourself and your people, Gradlon, throw your unworthy and shameful daughter off into the sea. She has betrayed you for her own desires.'

With aching heart, Gradlon did as he was bid. He pushed his pleading daughter back into the hungry waves. The seas began to recede although Ker-Ys remained submerged. But all the people of Ker-Ys managed to reach the safety of dry land except for Dahud-Ahes who was swept under the mighty waves. But because Dahud-Ahes was bound to the wheel of fate, because she was not the beginning nor the ending of its cycle, Guénolé took pity on her.

'You will live your time as one of the merfolk, living in the sunken palaces of Ker-Ys for all eternity!'

And so it is, throughout time, Dahud-Ahes, in the form of a mermaid, still lures unwary sailors, drawn on by her unsurpassed beauty, to the bottom of the sea. Thus, in the language of the Bretons, the place is called *Boé an Anaon* or the Bay of Suffering Souls.

Gradlon, meanwhile, went on in sorrow to Kemper, which is still called Quimper to this day. And he became a convert of Guénolé. When that venerable man returned to his monastery at Landévennec, Gradlon chose, as the bishop of his city, Corentin, and ended his days in the odour of sanctity, guided and sustained by Corentin who became patron of the town. And if you climb the cathedral that is in the Place St Corentin today you will find that a statue of Gradlon on horse-back stands between its two spires.

But beware of standing on the Pointe du Raz, listening to the whispering of the sea amongst the rocks; beware lest you hear the seductive calling of Dahud-Ahes.

STORY NOTES AND ACKNOWLEDGEMENTS

The Ever-Living Ones

Peter Tremayne is the fiction-writing pseudonym of the Celtic scholar Peter Berresford Ellis (b. 1943) who has published many works on Celtic history and culture including *A Dictionary of Irish Mythology* (1987) and *A Dictionary of Celtic Mythology* (1992). The *Irish Democrat* said that he 'has done for Irish mythology what Robert Graves has done for Greek mythology.' As Peter Tremayne he has utilised his expert knowledge to write many fantasy novels and stories based on Celtic mythological themes.

The Celtic languages contain one of Europe's oldest and most vibrant mythologies. In fact the Irish language contains Europe's third oldest literature, for the oldest texts in Irish are predated only by Greek and Latin. Some 2,500 years ago the Celtic peoples spread through Europe from Ireland in the west to the central plain of Turkey in the east, and from Belgium in the north to as far south as Cadiz in southern Spain, and to Ancona, just north of the Apennines in Italy. They were the first non-Mediterranean civilisation to emerge into recorded history. Today, the Celts survive only on the north-west fringe of Europe and are divided into six modern cultures: the Irish, Manx and Scots, identified by their language as Goidelic Celts, and the Welsh, Cornish and Bretons, identified as Brythonic Celts. 'The Ever-Living Ones' contains not only Tremayne's reconstruction of the original Celtic Creation Myth but also the story of the fight between the Good and Evil gods and goddesses symbolised by the Battle of Magh Tuireadh (The Plain of Towers). This story is adapted mainly from the Irish *Leabhar Gabhála* (*Book of*

Invasions) whose earliest complete survival is in the *Leabhar na Nuachonghbhala* (popularly known as the *Book of Leinster*) compiled in AD 1150 by Fionn mac Gormain of Glendalough. The story is © 1995 by Peter Berresford Ellis. First printing original to this anthology. Used by permission of the author and the author's agent, A. M. Heath & Co.

The Star Maids and the Flea Man and The Star Maidens' Laughter

Although the author of over a hundred short stories, Jessica Salmonson (b. 1950) is probably best known for her heroic fantasy novels, such as the Tomoe Gozen trilogy, which recounts the adventures of a female Samurai in the world of Japanese myth. The sequence runs *Tomoe Gozen* (1981), *The Golden Naginata* (1982) and *Thousand Shrine Warrior* (1984). Another entrancing oriental fantasy is *Ou Lou Khen and the Beautiful Madwoman* (1985). Her short fiction often draws upon mystical legends. Relevant collections include *A Silver Thread of Madness* (1989), *Mystic Women* (1991), *The Mysterious Doom* (1993) and *Phantom Waters* (1995). These two stories are founded upon myths of the Tachi, Cahuilla and Maidu Indians of California as recorded by Edward W. Gifford and Gwendoline Harris Black in *California Indian Nights Entertainment* (1930). Both are © 1995 by Jessica Amanda Salmonson. First printing original to this anthology. Printed by permission of the author.

Bearskin Woman and Grizzly Woman

This is one of the creation myths of the Blackfoot Indians of North America. According to legend their tribe was founded by Napi, their folk hero, who saved the tribe from disaster at the time of the Great Catastrophe when they sought refuge in the great cave of Nina Stahu. The stars gave inspiration to the Blackfoot peoples as much as it did to many early cultures, and Jessica Salmonson has used one such myth here. The story is © 1994 by Jessica Amanda Salmonson. First published in *Daughters of Nyx 2* edited by Kim Antieau, 1994. Reprinted by permission of the author.

The Quest for Discovery

The legend of Theseus and the Minotaur is one of the best known of the Greek legends. For that reason I have avoided it here and instead selected a story about the youth of Theseus, the illegitimate son of Aegeus, King of Athens, who had to discover and prove his own identity. The story has been used by many writers, and I have selected here the interpretation by Andrew Lang. Lang (1844–1912) was a great Victorian folklorist and antiquarian. He is best remembered as the editor of twelve volumes of fairy stories which ran from *The Blue Fairy Book* (1889) to *The Lilac Fairy Book* (1910), but in his day he was a highly regarded authority on literature and the occult, contributing articles to many magazines as well as the *Encyclopedia Britannica*. Lang long held a fascination for the Greek myths. He collaborated with H. Rider Haggard on *The World's Desire* (1890), about the further adventures of Odysseus, and produced two volumes of his own retelling the key legends: *The Story of the Golden Fleece* (1903) and *Tales of Troy and Greece* (1907). It is from this last volume that 'The Quest for Discovery' is taken.

The Strange Tale of Caribou and Moose

Years ago I stumbled across a little book called *Canadian Wonder Tales* (1918) by Cyrus Macmillan. It was this book that first opened my eyes to the magical legends of the North American Indians. Macmillan (1882–1953) had followed in the footsteps of the Brothers Grimm and sought to capture the folk tales of North America. In his preface Macmillan passed his deepest thanks 'to the nameless Indians and habitants, the fishermen and sailors, the spinners and the knitters in the sun' from whose lips he heard these stories, adding that the stories were not of his own invention but were 'the common possession of the folk'. This research was the product of Macmillan's youth. It is interesting to note that the final proofs were corrected by him in the midst of the First World War while, as Major Macmillan, he was in the thick of the offensive at Vimy Ridge. One can easily imagine how the magic of North American myth would allow him to escape, if only for a moment, from the most horrendous carnage about him. Macmillan later became the head of the English Department at McGill University and a Member of the Canadian Parliament.

The Hero Makóma

This story comes from the Sena tribe in eastern Africa, from what is now the borders of Mozambique and Zimbabwe. It was drawn from oral tradition by the explorer and pioneer Kingsley Fairbridge (1885–1924). Fairbridge's family settled in Rhodesia in 1896. His father was a surveyor and explorer. Kingsley spent his teens exploring the wilds of Africa and learning the legends of the natives. He captured some of these memories in his Autobiography which became regarded as a classic of Rhodesian literature.

Prince Yamato Take

It was at the request of Andrew Lang that Yei Theodora Ozaki translated and edited a collection called *Japanese Fairy Tales* (1903), based upon a volume of Japanese myths and folktales compiled by Sadanami Sanjin. The insignia of the Empire consists of three treasures which have long been considered sacred. These are the Mirror of Yata, the Jewel of Yasakami and most precious of all, the Sword of Murakumo. The sword is the symbol of strength and talisman of invincibility of the Emperor. Nearly two thousand years ago this sword was kept at the shrines of Ite, the temples dedicated to the worship of Amaterasu, the powerful goddess of the Sun, from whom the Japanese emperors claim descent. 'The Story of Prince Yamato Take' reveals the background of the Sword and explains why its name was changed from Murakumo to Kasanagi, the grass-cleaver.

The Lad With One Sandal

My favourite of the Greek myths is the story of Jason and the Argonauts. It has everything. A fabulous quest, all the famous heroes, and travels into foreign lands facing many monsters and mysteries. It has fascinated many writers and is the subject of at least two excellent novels by Henry Treece and Robert Graves, as well as one of the better muscle-men dramas of the cinema, the 1963 film *Jason and the Argonauts* with excellent animation by Ray Harryhausen. It was also one of the favourite tales of the Greek poet Pindar, who lived in the sixth century BC and travelled throughout the Greek world reciting his famous narrative *Odes*. These *Odes* served as inspiration to Winifred Hutchinson who retold this story in her book, *The Golden Porch* (1907).

The Sons of Tuirenn

The adventures of the sons of Tuirenn have been likened to the tale of Jason and the Argonauts. It is a story about actions and consequences and represents Irish mythology at its best with warriors and gods facing an inescapable fate. This story is again based on an episode in the *Book of Invasions*. It is

My Lord Bag of Rice

Another story from *Japanese Fairy Tales* (1903) based on the stories by Sadanami Sanjin.

Prince Seyf el Mulouk

No book of legends would be complete without something from the Arabian Nights, which are amongst the best known legends in the world. I have, though, gone for something slightly different. The standard volumes of the Arabian Nights are based on the French translations by Antoine Galland under the familiar title of *The Thousand and One Nights*, but there was also a series called *The Thousand and One Days*, which, though well known in France, is almost unknown in the English-speaking world. *The Thousand and One Days* was the work of the French orientalist François Pétis de la Croix under the title *Persian Tales* (1710–12). He claimed his source as a Persian text called *Hazar Yek Ruz* which he acquired from a Dervish called Mocles whom he knew in Isfahan in 1675. These were tales that Mocles had collected from a variety of Arab, Indian and Turkish sources. Though English translations of de la Croix's work were made in 1714 and 1738, they then lay forgotten until the Victorian writer and scholar Justin Huntly McCarthy (1861–1936) made his own translation as *The Thousand and One Days* in 1892.

The Journey to Constantinople

Myths don't have to be from the dawn of time. Every generation and culture develops its own, and this was particularly true in the years after the reign of Charlemagne, or Charles the Great (AD 742–814), king of the Franks and Holy Roman Emperor. Such was the stature and power of Charles that he began to take on the legendary status of King Arthur. The number of legends are legion, many drawing not only upon his conquests but upon his deeply religious views and his penetrating wisdom, and two are presented here. The first, 'The Journey to Constantinople', whilst having its origins in France, travelled throughout Europe by way of balladeers and troubadours, eventually finding itself in Sweden. It is this Swedish version, collected by the Swedish ethnographer, Hans Shück, that is presented here. It was translated by William F. Harvey (not the same as the author of 'The Beast With Five Fingers') in a volume of Shück's works called *Mediaeval Stories* (1902).

Huon's Quest

The second of our Frankish legends deals with one of the most popular of the French *chanson de geste*, the story of 'Huon of Bordeaux'. It is believed this tale was first composed in the thirteenth century. Its popularity was such that it was amongst the earliest stories to be printed as a book. This was the English translation by Lord Berners which was printed by Wynkyn de Worde, Caxton's successor, in 1534. It was this version that was certainly known to Shakespeare who used the character of Oberon, the king of the fairies who helps Huon on his quest, in *A Midsummer Night's Dream* (1596).

Ascott Hope-Moncrieff (1846–1927) was a Scottish schoolmaster who found a more profitable career writing boys' adventure stories to which he turned full-time from 1865. In a career of over sixty years he produced more than a hundred books. Many drew upon old tales and legends, and increasingly these became of a scholarly nature. 'Huon's Quest' is taken from his volume *Romance and Legend of Chivalry* (1913).

Perseus and the Gorgon

Frequently in ancient myths we find kings fearful of their throne being usurped, usually by a son. The best known of these legends is that of Oedipus. His father was Laius, king of Thebes, who was told by an oracle that he would be killed by his son Oedipus. As a result Oedipus was exposed on a rock, but was found and reared and ultimately, fulfilling fate, killed his father and married his mother (both unwittingly). A similar fear haunted Acrisius, king of Argos, who was warned that his daughter, Danaë, would bear a son who would kill him. As a consequence he walled up his daughter in a stone tomb, but through the divine intervention of Zeus, she gave birth to Perseus. The story of Perseus, and his quest to fetch the head of the Gorgon Medusa fascinated the Victorian clergyman Charles Kingsley. Kingsley (1819–1875) is best known for his children's book *The Water Babies* (1863) but he had earlier written a volume of Greek legends, *The Heroes* (1856) which told not only of the adventures of Perseus, but also of Hercules, Theseus and Jason.

The Chimaera

Although Kingsley did not relate this version, one legend states that when Perseus beheaded Medusa, Pegasus, the winged horse, sprung from the blood. It was Pegasus who bore Perseus to the rescue of Andromeda. But Pegasus was a creature of the wild and not under the control of any mortal. Nevertheless Pegasus was tamed by another Greek hero, one who is less known than Perseus or Jason, but whose adventures are no less exciting. This was Bellerophon, one of the doomed Greek heroes, fated even more than Hercules. It was Bellerophon who tamed Pegasus and together they set off against the Chimaera, a fire-breathing dragon. This story is retold by Nathaniel Hawthorne (1804–1864) who included it in *A Wonder Book* (1852).

Hercules in Hell

Hercules, or more properly in Greek, Herakles, was the great-grandson of Perseus, and was dispossessed of his kingdom when the goddess Hera intervened and delayed his birth, thus making his cousin, Eurystheus, king of Tiryns. Nevertheless, Hercules was the favourite of Zeus, king of the gods, from whom he drew his great strength. This strength was present from his birth when Hera sent two snakes to kill him but the infant strangled them. Hercules however was to suffer bouts of madness and at one such time he killed not only his own children but those of his brother Iphicles. It was to atone for this that Hercules was bound to serve his cousin Eurystheus and that was how the twelve labours of Hercules began. The last and most difficult of these was his descent into the Underworld. In bringing together the story represented here I have blended elements from Charles Kingsley's version in *The Heroes* with those retold by Hope-Moncrieff in *Classical Mythology*, as well as drawing upon the extensive research of Robert Graves in *The Greek Myths*. This version is © 1995 by Mike Ashley.

Siegfried and the Dragon Fafnir

Siegfried is the archetypal hero of Teutonic and Scandinavian myth. His adventures are told in the *Nibelungenlied*, a series of connected narrative poems first laid down in German in the late twelfth century, but drawing on earlier tales in the Icelandic and Nordic eddas or sagas, most especially the *Volsunga Saga*. Siegfried can be alikened to the Greek Achilles, a hero made invulnerable as a child by bathing in the blood of a dragon, but having one vulnerable spot between his shoulder blades where a leaf had lain. The Nibelungs was the name given to those who guarded a vast treasure hoard which at length came into the possession of Siegfried. Siegfried's adventures have been immortalised over the last century thanks to the Ring Cycle of operas by Richard Wagner, but the legends had enthralled generations for centuries before. The extract used here comes from *The Story of Siegfried* (1882) by James Baldwin (1841–1925), an American historian and writer.

The Slaying of Grendel

When the Saxons and other Germanic tribes as well as the Vikings invaded the British Isles in the years from the fifth century on, they brought with them their own myths and sagas which rapidly passed into our native culture. The most famous of these legends is that of Beowulf, a Danish warrior of the fifth or sixth century. The adventures of Beowulf, particularly against the monster Grendel, would have been recounted endlessly to Danes settled in England, thinking of their homeland. The poem, which was written down around the year AD 1000, was probably extant for at least two centuries before that, and is the oldest surviving poem in Old English. The prose adaptation presented here is by Alfred Church (1829–1912), a classical scholar noted for his translation of Tacitus, and comes from his *Heroes of Chivalry and Romance* (1898).

The Lambton Worm

Many families have their own legends, especially amongst the nobility, and one of the most famous is that of the Lambton curse, which haunted the Earls of Durham for nine generations. Tradition came to link it with an earlier legend of the Lambton dragon which dates from at least the time of the Crusades in the twelfth century, and probably has links back to earlier legends like Beowulf and Grendel. The version presented here is from *The Grey Ghost Book* (1912) by Jessie Middleton who, at the turn of the century, wrote several books assembling stories of ghosts, superstition and family legends.

The Shadowy One

From Scotland comes a tale of the mysterious female warrior Scáthach, the Shadowy One. She ran a martial arts academy on the Isle of Skye, which takes its name from her – Sgitheanach, Isle of Shadows – where all the famous heroes of Éireann and Alba (Scotland) went for their military training. Scáthach appears infrequently in the 'Red Branch Cycle' of Irish myths, sometimes known as the 'Ulster Cycle'. More lengthy references appear in *Compert Scáthach Buanand (The Begetting of Scáthach the Victorious)* and *Tochmarc Emer (The Wooing of Emer)* whose fragmentary texts date to the tenth century. This is not only a story of warriors but of intense passion and jealousy. The story is © 1995 by Peter Berresford Ellis. First printing original to this anthology. Used by permission of the author and the author's agent, A. M. Heath & Co.

Bran and Branwen

This is one of the more famous stories from the *Mabinogi* (the Four Branches of the Mabinogion), the collective title for a group of tales which are the central surviving texts of Welsh mythology. The stories originate from different periods ranging from pre-Norman conquest through to the twelfth century. Elements of them appear in *The White Book of Rhydderch* (compiled *c.* 1300–1325) but the more complete text is in *The Red Book of Hergest* (compiled *c.* 1375–1425). The texts were not translated into English until Charlotte Guest began in 1838. Since then the tales have inspired many authors, especially Evangeline Walton and Alan Garner. The story included is © 1995 by Peter Berresford Ellis. First printing original to this anthology. Used by permission of the author and the author's agent, A. M. Heath & Co.

King Laurin's Rose-Garden

One of the principal characters in the German *Book of Heroes* is Dietrich von Bern. Dietrich is based on the historical character of Theodoric the Great, who established the great Eastern Gothic Empire in AD 493. Etzel, whom you also meet in this story, is Attila, the king of the Huns, although the lives of these two great conquerors did not historically overlap. Dietrich undergoes many fantastic adventures, not least when he encounters the dwarf-king Laurin (another name for Alberich) who has kidnapped his sister Künhild. That is where 'King Laurin's Rose-Garden' begins. The version here comes from *Epics and Romances of the Middle Ages* (1883) by Dr Wilhelm Wägner.

The Children of Loki

This is one of the many episodes from the heart of Nordic mythology. Loki, although classed as one of the Aesir – the chosen ones of Odin – was really something of a fallen angel. He was a mischief maker who fathers a family of evil creatures. The day comes when Odin sets out to face this evil once and for all. The story here has been extracted from *The Heroes of Asgard* (1857) by the Victorian novelist Annie Keary (1825–1879) and her sister Eliza. Annie Keary's best known work was *Castle Daly* (1875), set during the Irish famine.

When the Woman Chief was Young

This is based on a myth of the Klamath Indians in south central Oregon. The Klamath lived on the shores of Upper Klamath Lake and the Klamath Marsh and their culture is based heavily on the lakeside environment. This story is © 1995 by Jessica Amanda Salmonson. First published in *Phantom Waters* (Seattle: Sasquatch Press, 1995). Reprinted by permission of the author.

Tewdrig, Tyrant of Treheyl

This story derives from Cornish legend and is referred to in medieval hagiographies of Cornish saints, such as Gwinear, written in the twelfth century. Tewdrig also appears as a tyrant in *Bewnans Meryasek* (*Life of St Meryadoc*, a sixth-century bishop of Cornwall) which takes its place in literary importance as the only surviving full-length play about the life of a Cornish saint written in the Cornish language. The text of the surviving manuscript is dated AD 1504. This story is © 1995 by Peter Berresford Ellis. First printing original to this anthology. Used by permission of the author and the author's agent, A. M. Heath & Co.

Red Wolf's Daughter and Bloody Chief's Son

The Nez Perce Indians were so named by the French for their habit of having pierced noses. They live in Idaho and nearby Washington and Oregon. After the introduction of horses they became renowned horse breeders, but this legend goes back far earlier to the times of the battles with the Blackfoot tribe. This story is © 1995 by Jessica Amanda Salmonson. First published in *Phantom Waters* (Seattle: Sasquatch Press, 1995). Reprinted by permission of the author.

East of the Sun and West of the Moon

The title of this story has always been one of my favourites because it so evocatively captures the mystical enticement of other worlds. The story was originally collected by Peter Asbjörnsen (1813–1885) who with Jörgen Moe (1813–1882) had become encouraged to collect Norwegian folktales after discovering the works of the Brothers Grimm. The story was first collected in their *Norske Folkeeventyr* in the 1840s and translated into English in *Fairy Tales of All Nations* in 1849. The story became a favourite of William Morris (1834–1896) who included it in his long group of narrative poems *The Earthly Paradise*, a kind of Nordic Canterbury Tales, which Morris wrote between 1868 and 1870. These stories were later adapted into prose form by Madalen Edgar, in *Stories from the Earthly Paradise* (1919) and it is that version I have reprinted here.

The Barnacle Maid

Although this tale comes from the myths of the Salish Indians on the north-west coast of America, in Washington State and British Columbia it is reminiscent of so many legends of women who sacrifice themselves for their love. In most legends, as in Fouqué's retelling of *Undine* (1811), it is the sprite or nymph who falls in love with a human, but here the plot is twisted most effectively. The story is © 1992 by Jessica Amanda Salmonson and was first published in *The Mysterious Doom and Other Ghostly Tales of the Pacific Northwest* (Seattle: Sasquatch Press, 1992). Reprinted by permission of the author.

Battle on the Bridge of the Gods

The Columbia River has its birth in the Canadian Rockies. It meanders through the Northwest capturing other rivers such as the Snake and the Spokane, until it breaks mightily through the Cascade range between Mount Adams and Mount Hood, forming the Oregon–Washington border. After the river turns, there is a long, deep canyon, the Columbia River Gorge. The geographical, geological and meteorological oddities of this area have intrigued modern scientists, no less than they inspired aboriginal myths that still ring in our hearts with great authority.

Oregon's first historical novel was Frederic Homer Balch's *The Bridge of the Gods: a Romance of Indian Oregon* (1890), a national bestseller with many reprintings making the Bridge familiar to households in all quarters of America. A synopsis of a Klickitat telling of the myth is given as 'An Indian Legend' in Michael S. Spranger's compilation *The Columbia Gorge, A Unique American Treasure* (1984), and similar paraphrases in scores of popular books akin to Katharine B. Judson's *Myths and Legends of the Pacific Northwest* (1910) or Eleanor Marion Gridley's *Indian Legends of American Scenes* (1939). Clarence Orvel Bunnell's *Legends of the Klickitats* (1933) offers a series of interconnected tales associated with the Bridge, with a good deal of coloration derived as much from pioneer sentimentality as from the Klickitats. An overview of the myth can be found in Ella E. Clark's 'The Bridge of the Gods in Fact and Fancy' in *The Oregon Historical Quarterly*, March 1952.

Whether in enthographic or popular versions, there are contradictory variations of sequence and event. A variant supposes mounts Hood and St Helens were husband and wife; it was they who had the great fire-fight, with Hood getting the worst of it, since Loowit does seem to be a recollection of an all-powerful Earth-mother whose husband or husbands are her subordinates. In the majority of cases the antagonistic male mountains are Hood and Adams, who formed the pillars that upheld the sky-bridge. The St Helens Goddess who guards this bridge is sometimes a pure and noble virgin burdened by male possessiveness; elsetimes she is a coquette who intentionally arouses jealousy. The hag form lived either on the Bridge sharing fire with peoples who visited her from both sides, or she lived in her mountain attended by bats, seen by few.

Not every version identifies Loowit as fire-bringer, though many do. Her association with the region's most active volcano is invariable, indicating that she was indeed a Fire-goddess whether or not this was always recalled. Her name means 'Fire Top' and though no text suggests it, her hair may have been red, as was that of the nymphs or 'beaver women' who haunt rivers. There was among Salishan and Chinookan peoples a tradition that the oldest member of a family remained near the firepit at all times so the fire would never go out. This allowed the most enfeebled member of a family or tribe to continue to serve a necessary function. This appointment led to sundry legends of old women who hoard fire improperly without sharing it. In still other legends, it is the youngest of five brothers who guards the fire. A fifth of five brothers is roughly equivalent to the European idea of 'the seventh of seven sons' who possesses sorcery and wisdom. It may well be that in prehistory, the firepit guardian was a young priest or elderly priestess serving an Earth-mother not unlike the Hearth-goddesses of Europe served by Vestals. Loowit is, then, akin to the Greek Hestia or Roman Vesta, who was commonly identified with the Phrygian Mountain-goddess Cybele or Magna Mater, and whose youthful associate was Attis.

Loowit's wooers were Pahtoe the Fire Spirit of Mount Adams, grandfather of the Klickitat people who lived north over the semi-arid plains; and Wyeast the Wind Spirit of Mount Hood, grandfather of the Multnomahs who lived along the Willamette River. This supposes Loowit an ancestral divinity who had two husbands, even aside from their group role as geological personifications. Fire and Wind were certainly rational designations for the husband spirits, considering the actual weather patterns of the area. The Gorge, where dry and moist atmospheric conditions collide, is seasonally notoriously stormy. Winds from the west reach 100 miles per hour. The first time the American government put a weather station near the Gorge, the very next storm carried away all the instruments, as photographer Chuck Williams – himself a descendant of Cascade Indians – rather gleefully notes in his lovely volume *Bridge of the Gods, Mountains of Fire: A Return to the Columbia Gorge* (1980). So we can see how native mythmakers were actually teaching of natural phenomena, explaining how the hot breath of Pahtoe and the moist breath of Wyeast clash in the form of great battles at the Gorge.

Donald and Elizabeth Lawrence in 'Bridge of the Gods Legend: Its Origin, History and Dating,' in the mountaineer magazine *Mazama*, December 1958, speculate how the more expansive versions originated with Indian storytellers who were testing the limitations of white gullibility. Others suppose the legend was elaborated by whites themselves, with Indians re-adapting whatever parts they liked. Certainly the ethnographic texts, recorded directly from Indians, do not give such elaborate versions as found in the plethora of later popular books. It appears that prior to 1840, the Bridge was discussed in geologically feasible terms as a huge landslide-dam, and not as a supernatural epic. Early explorers were simply informed, 'We used to walk across without getting our moccasins wet.' Around seven hundred years ago, much of Greenleaf Peak and Table Mountain broke away in an earthquake, probably accompanied by nearby volcanic activity. A five square mile landslide was dumped into the river, and this was the actual Bridge of the Gods. Behind that bridge-dam, a great lake rose to five hundred feet and extended east to Umatilla. Many upstream villages were eradicated by inundation and loss of salmon runs. But the lake's overflow gradually weakened the landslide-dam, with attendant flooding catastrophes down river when the lake was finally unleashed. This story is © 1995 by Jessica Amanda Salmonson. Printed by permission of the author.

Story of The Three Strong Men

Charles Godfrey Leland (1824–1903) was a widely travelled authority on folklore throughout America and Europe. Although trained as a lawyer, which he practised between 1849 and 1853, he became a journalist and after the American Civil War travelled throughout Europe, settling for some years in London and Florence. He was the founder of the Hungarian Folklore Society and a President of the Gypsy-Lore Society. In his later years he travelled throughout New England collecting local stories which were published as *Algonquin Legends of New England* (1884).

The Lay Nun Who Gave of Herself

Some of the greatest tales come from Indian myth. This story is a Buddhist legend told in the *Milinda* (*Questions of Faith*) written in Sanskrit near the beginning of the Christian era. The story is © 1991 by Jessica Amanda Salmonson. First published in *Mystic Women: Their Ancient Tales and Legends* (Seattle: Street of Crocodiles, 1991). Reprinted by permission of the author.

The One-Handed Girl

This is one of the folk tales collected by Edward Steere in his travels around south-eastern Africa, especially the old colony of Zanzibar, and assembled in his book *Swahili Tales* (1870).

Rayamati, the Savioress

This legend of Jain asceticism is adapted from the *Uttarâdhyayana*. It is © 1991 by Jessica Amanda Salmonson. First published in *Mystic Women: Their Ancient Tales and Legends* (Seattle: Street of Crocodiles, 1991). Reprinted by permission of the author.

Echo and Narcissus

A simple tale from the later Greek myths captured by Ovid in his *Metamorphoses*, written at the very dawn of the Christian era. The version here is retold by Hope-Moncrieff from *Classical Mythology* (1913).

Vasavadatta the Courtesan

This is founded upon an episode from *Asokavadana (The Legend of King Asoka)* written in the second century AD but set several hundred years earlier. Asoka, who ruled in the third century BC, was the first to organise Buddhism as the state religion of India. This story is © 1991 by Jessica Amanda Salmonson. First published in *Mystic Women: Their Ancient Tales and Legends* (Seattle: Street of Crocodiles, 1991). Reprinted by permission of the author.

The Courtesan who Worked a Miracle

Another episode from the *Milinda*. © 1991 by Jessica Amanda Salmonson. First published in *Mystic Women: Their Ancient Tales and Legends* (Seattle: Street of Crocodiles, 1991). Reprinted by permission of the author.

The King's Son and the White-Bearded Scolog

One of the most refreshing volumes of legends I have read is *Hero-Tales of Ireland* by Jeremiah Curtin (1835–1906) which was first published in 1894, but is as lively today as ever.

The Adventure of the Holy Grail

It was impossible to compile a volume of legends without including at least one Arthurian story and there is none that has captivated the imagination of writers more than the quest for the Holy Grail. The Grail was the cup from which Christ drank the wine at the Last Supper and which later caught his drops of blood from the cross. It was brought by Joseph of Arimathea to Britain and supposedly hidden at Glastonbury, although research by Norma Lorre Goodrich suggests that the Grail Castle was on the Isle of Man. The significance of the Grail legend was first established in story form by the French romancist Chrétien de Troyes in *Le Conte del Graal* composed around 1190. It was further developed by the German poet Wolfram von Eschenbach in *Parzival* written a decade or two later, and was soon being embellished by the troubadours of the day. The version presented here recounts the legend in its simplest and purest form. It is from *Heroes of Chivalry and Romance* (1898).

The Prince Who Sought Immortality

I first encountered this story in a volume of Hungarian folktales selected by Gyula Ortutay (1910–1978), a noted Hungarian folklorist, but I was unable to secure the rights to the story. Fortunately I found an earlier and equally effective version by Leonora Alleyne, the wife of Andrew Lang. Mrs Lang has never received the full credit she deserves because it is she who translated, adapted and retold the bulk of the tales in Lang's long and popular series of *Fairy Books* for which he usually receives the credit.

The Changelings

This is a Wapato Lake legend from the Indians of Northwestern Oregon. It not only introduces us to the strange lake monster the Huluk, but like 'The Barnacle Maid' makes us aware of the transition from one state of existence to another, which is a common feature of the legends of the North American Indians. The story is © 1995 by Jessica Amanda Salmonson. First published in *Phantom Waters* (Seattle: Sasquatch Press, 1995). Reprinted by permission of the author.

The Story of a Gazelle

Another of the folk tales collected by Edward Steere in his travels around south-eastern Africa and assembled in his book *Swahili Tales* (1870). This one considers in particular the relationship between man and animals and their relative intelligence.

Yuki-Onna

I wanted to include at least one ghost story in this anthology, and the choice of one by Lafcadio Hearn was almost automatic. Hearn (1850–1904) was born in Greece, educated in France and England, emigrated to the United States in 1869 where he became a reporter, and then in 1891 settled in Japan as a writer and lecturer, becoming a Japanese citizen. His fascination with Japanese legends resulted in a number of books. This story comes from *Kwaidan* (1904).

Bhadra and the Mendicant

This is another Jaina tale based on characters and incidents from the *Uttarâdhyayana* along with alternative accounts of the legend. It is © 1991 by Jessica Amanda Salmonson. First published in *Mystic Women: Their Ancient Tales and Legends* (Seattle: Street of Crocodiles, 1991). Reprinted by permission of the author.

The Reborn Divinities

Another Jaina legend adapted from the *Uttarâdhyayana*. It is © 1991 by Jessica Amanda Salmonson. First published in *Mystic Women: Their Ancient Tales and Legends* (Seattle: Street of Crocodiles, 1991). Reprinted by permission of the author.

"Island of the Ocean God"

This story of Mac Cuill is based on a Manx legend from the Isle of Man. It is a curious one which seems to dwell on the death of the old gods, the naming of the Island and its conversion to Christianity. It also includes a description of an active watery-grave. The earliest source of the story is to be found in the *Liber Ardmachanus* (*Book of Armagh*), compiled by Feardomhnach in AD 807. This version is © 1995 by Peter Berresford Ellis. First printing original to this anthology. Used by permission of the author and the author's agent, A. M. Heath & Co.

The Rover of the Plain

This is a legend of the Thonga, or Tsonga, a Bantu-speaking people who live in southern Mozambique. The story was collected by the French ethnographer Henri Junod for his monograph *L'Etude Ethnographique sur les Baronga* and translated and adapted by Leonora Lang for *The Orange Fairy Book* (1906).

Uraschimataro and the Turtle

A Japanese folk legend collected by the German antiquarian David Brauns and published in *Japanische Märchen und Sagen* in 1885. This version was translated and adapted by Leonora Lang for *The Pink Fairy Book* (1897).

How the Serpent-Gods were Propitiated

This story is taken from the Saga of the Well-and-Wise-Walking Khan, a cycle of stories told by the Kalmouk nomads of eastern Tibet. The story-cycle is about two brothers, sons of a Khan, one of whom learns magic from seven magicians, and the other doesn't. The brother magician, seeking to impress the other, converts himself into a horse whom the other rides to the seven magicians. When they see a magic horse they try to kill it. A shape-changing battle ensues resulting in the brother killing the seven magicians. He knows he has done ill and his Master tells him to go to a distant grove where resides the Siddhî-kür (a dead body with magical powers) and bring it back. He must not talk to the Siddhîor it will return to its grove. Each time he tries he is tricked by a tale. This is the fifth tale. The stories were collected by the folklorist Rachel Busk (1818–1907) in *Sagas from the Far East* (1873).

Koshchei the Deathless

Koshchei is one of several evil spirits that haunt Russian legends and folktales. The cycle of stories in which he features comes to a climax in this tale where the hero confronts the spirit. The tale was collected by the Russian folklorist Alexander Afanasief (1826–1871) in *Russian Popular Legends* (1871). This version was translated by William S. Ralston in *Russian Folk-Tales* (1873).

The Circumvention of Fate

This story is founded upon a Bengali folk myth. It is © 1991 by Jessica Amanda Salmonson. First published in *Mystic Women: Their Ancient Tales and Legends* (Seattle: Street of Crocodiles, 1991). Reprinted by permission of the author.

The Destruction of Ker-Ys

We end where we started, with a Celtic legend, this one from Brittany. It features the popular motif of a city sinking beneath the sea, noted in Atlantis, Lyonesse and other legends, but this one introduces a Christian element. The earliest reference to it is in the eleventh-century *Cartulary of Redon*. This version is © 1995 by Peter Berresford Ellis. First printing original to this anthology. Used by permission of the author and the author's agent, A. M. Heath & Co.